I0589475

# 臥龍

## CROUCHING DRAGON
### ~ THE JOURNEY OF ZHUGE LIANG ~

**BY T. P. M. THORNE**

**COVER ART BY T. P. M. THORNE**

Published by PaMat Publishing

Copyright © 2012 T. P. M. Thorne

All rights reserved. Apart from any fair dealing for the purpose of private study, research, criticism or review, as permitted under the Copyright, Designs and Patents Act 1988, no part of this work may be reproduced, stored in a retrieval system, or transmitted in any form or by any means – electronic, electrical, chemical, mechanical, optical, photocopying, recording or otherwise – without the express written permission of the copyright owner. Enquiries should be directed to the author of this work.

The author, T. P. M. Thorne, has asserted the right under the Copyright, Designs and Patents Act 1988 to be identified as the author of this work.


Cover art: *artistic depiction of the disputed areas of China as they were when Zhuge Liang began his career: the north (Han-court-controlled, with Han Prime Minister Cao Cao controlling the court), the southwest (Yi and Hanzhong, semi-independent, semi-allied), the southeast (Eastern Wu, governed by the Sun family), and the central region (Jing, governed by Liu Biao and several independent local prefects).*

# TABLE OF CONTENTS

# FOREWORD

I first discovered the era of the Three Kingdoms (approx. 184AD – 280AD) roughly four years before I started writing this book. I was immediately fascinated by the layers of depth that could be found; as with all history, there is intrigue, deception, bloodshed, and all the other things that make us human, but the amount of folklore associated with this volatile time – and the mixing of that folklore with what little 'fact' is on offer from official state records – gives the era a sense of mysticism, humour and tragedy that can be revisited time and again, each time discovering new things that you did not see before.

There are many other characters in this turbulent period that can be explored in great depth – Cao Cao, Sima Yi, Liu Bei and Sun Quan, to name four – but none appealed to me more than a man associated with all of the things that embodied the time: political intrigue, military strategy, technical innovation, and seemingly divine fate. In some tales, Zhuge Liang - referred to in the narrative sections by his style name, *Kongming* - is a peerless mind, while in others, he is a magician; he is always shown as a standout figure, and his name still resonates today.

With hundreds of scholars, officials and generals taking part in proceedings, there are many ways to depict such a man's life. There are several attempts to choose from – mostly works that tell the tale of the era as a whole or in part – and they all have their own appeal. I have tried to present as original a presentation as possible, partly by looking at figures and events that are usually ignored or downplayed, and mainly by drawing on history more than folktales, although there is still some artistic license for the sake of telling a balanced story. All I can hope is that this book inspires or entertains someone out there as much as I have enjoyed writing it.

T. P. M. Thorne, the author

# PROLOGUE: A VISION AT MIANZHU

The vast lands of China were once ravaged by a war that lasted for almost a century: it began with the disaffection of the people with corrupt officials, and at its end, the imperial line was once again the dominant force in the land, though things would never be the same again.

In the west of the country, a few years before the end of that long conflict, a small contingent of soldiers from the northern state of Wei completed a tiring march across the humid, uneven terrain, having just completed a stealth infiltration through the near-unsurpassable mountains. They had already scored minor victories against the unprepared forces of the western state of Shu: now another city lay ahead.

The leader of those brave and tenacious soldiers was a man whose family name was Deng, and whose given name was Ai: he was a highly talented and highly respected figure in the state of Wei, and he was now, potentially, a few days away from becoming the man that would subjugate the Shu Emperor and leave nothing but the Empire of Eastern Wu as an obstacle to a reunified China. Deng Ai had brought his eldest son Chong with him on the expedition, so that he might share the glory of his famous father, who would soon be spoken of as a man whose talent equalled the likes of the man that had once been a pillar – and founding father – of the state of Shu: the strategist, politician, philosopher and inventor, Zhuge Liang.

The state of Shu had been founded by men who claimed either lineage or unflagging loyalty to the collapsed Empire of the Han: many called the state Shu Han, or even Han, as acknowledgement of this. The Han had – after many years of being weakened by internal power struggles and widespread corruption - been supplanted by Wei almost 40 years ago, and the north of China had accepted this: only the rulers of the independent states in the south and west refused to accept this for reasons of their own. The state of Shu had maintained a stubborn defence and launched relentless attacks against Wei for more than those 40 years, and the rulers of Wei – and in particular, its Prime Minister – knew that the fall of Shu and the final removal of any chance of a revival of the Han was essential if the Wei Empire was to be accepted by all.

"Commander Deng, defences in the capital city of Mianzhu are unreadable," a captain of the army of Wei reported.
Deng Ai surveyed the Mianzhu terrain and frowned thoughtfully. Mianzhu County had once been a part of an independent province that had resisted the future Shu rulers, and even claimed the life of one of Shu's greatest minds: but now, in a twist of fate, it was to be a last great bastion that protected Shu from ruin.
"Well," Deng Ai replied, "advance anyway... Shu has no more capable men."
The captain saluted Deng Ai and retreated to issue the orders.
"Father," Ai's son, General Deng Zhong, said nervously, "isn't Mianzhu defended by Zhuge Zhan, son of the legendary strategist Zhuge Liang...?"

"Why should that matter…?" Deng Ai replied. "Zhuge Liang is gone. Their main forces are trapped in the north, and nobody expected that anyone could get into their heartland through those mountains, so they didn't even bother to defend them: a mistake that great strategist – or any that had truly learned from him – would not have made."

"If Zhuge Zhan knows even half of his father's tricks," Deng Zhong protested, "we might have walked into a trap."

Before Deng Ai could answer, a messenger urged his presence at the newly developing battlefront.

What met Deng Ai was an uncomfortable sight: a massive array of Shu soldiers, arranged in a flawless military formation. The thousands of men shifted and swayed like a human barricade, forming walls of shields and swords, while cavalrymen darted in and out, anxious to lure an unprepared foe to certain death.

"…Eight Trigrams formation," Deng Zhong murmured fearfully.

"F-flag deployment… is unconventional," Deng Ai noted.

"**GENERAL DENG AI OF WEI!**" a voice boomed confidently: it was the voice of Zhuge Shang, the eldest son of Zhuge Zhan. He rode back and forth across the front line of the Shu forces on his well-groomed battle horse, and bellowed, "**DARE YOU ADVANCE, AND FACE THE PRIME MINISTER OF THE HAN?**"

"Impossible…!" Deng Ai whispered as, at the centre of the Shu army's front line, the soldiers parted to allow a familiar horseless carriage to be pushed into view: seated upon it was a frail elderly man in lilac robes, who had a long, grey beard, and carried a white feather fan.

"**ZHUGE LIANG!**" the Wei soldiers exclaimed; fear gripped the invaders that they had, indeed, fallen into a trap.

"*Impossible*…!" Deng Ai said again: he looked at the man in the carriage with respectful fear, for if it was the man that it appeared to be, there would be no victory for Deng Ai that day, or ever. "Zhuge Liang… *alive*…? …That's *absurd*!"

The famed strategist might not have been seen for almost 30 years to that date, but for the legend that was Zhuge Liang, no feat was deemed impossible.

✻✻✻✻✻✻✻✻✻✻✻✻

# ACT I: SEEKING A WISE LORD

## 1

"The Han have ruled China for four hundred years... but because of a few ambitious warlords, that will come to an end...?...That's absurd."

Three men sat cross-legged on small cloth mats, facing each other, surrounded by lush green. Each man was young, bright, and ambitious, but each in his own way. In the seat that overlooked the town, a grinning, confident youth in his late teens fanned himself majestically with a strategist's fan made of white feathers. He wore white robes, and his long hair was tied and covered by a small, white silk turban. To his left, a youth with rough, unappealing features and a dark, rough complexion grinned tauntingly, exposing his disordered teeth. He wore a wide-brimmed straw hat to shield his eyes from the sun, and he wore dark green robes patterned with images of the legendary phoenix. The last, blue-robed youth – whose demeanour was less confident, but still determined – was sat forward, his gaze fixed on the youth in white robes, awaiting an answer.

"...My dear Xu Yuanzhi," the white-robed youth chuckled as he continued to fan himself, "all the signs point to it: without able men to guide the honest ones, the 'Fire of the Han' will dim, and die out."
"...Nonsense!" the blue-robed youth scoffed irritably.
"Maybe not, I think...!" the green-robed youth suggested teasingly.
"...You both...!" the blue-robed youth retorted with anger.
"One must *look* in order to *see*," the white-robed youth declared. "And when you *look*, Pang Tong, Xu Shu... what do you *see*...? ...Here, in the countryside, we see false calm. ...But elsewhere... all you'll see is war and chaos."
"Too true, Kongming, too true," the green-robed youth sighed sadly.

The three were sat on the outskirts of a hill forest near the city of Longzhong, in China, discussing the events of the day. It was a time of war and chaos everywhere in the world; under the rule of Septimus Severus, the Roman Empire was sweeping across Europe, Africa and the Middle East, having defeated the Parthian Empire and raided their capital only two years previous. But in China, the warlords were duelling over an Empire in a state of flux; only a decade or so earlier, the Yellow Turbans – a Taoist-cult-inspired revolution against the imperial court – had been brutally stamped out, but stability had not returned.

"The Yellow Turban Rebellion was just the beginning," the white-robed youth continued with a knowledgeable air that exceeded his years. "If the court had returned to normal after their defeat, I'd say that things would remain as they are."
"...*Should* they remain as they are...?" the green-robed youth suggested.

"You...!" the blue-robed youth scolded; "How can you say things like that??? ...You... you're both letting your reputations go to your heads!"
"...*Are we*, Kongming...?" the green-robed youth asked as he turned his white-robed friend, who simply smiled in response.

The man in white robes, Zhuge Liang – known respectfully by his style name, *Kongming*, by friends – was also known by the Taoist name 'Crouching Dragon', and was considered a budding talent of the age. His green-robed friend, Pang Tong, was likewise known not only by his style name 'Shiyuan' to his friends, but by his Taoist name, 'Young Phoenix', in acknowledgement of his brilliance and his understanding of the affairs of the day. The last of the three, Xu Shu – whose style name was Yuanzhi – had no well-known Taoist name, and knew all too well that he was not held in the same high regard.

"...You're both becoming arrogant," Xu Shu suggested irritably.
"No... rather, you allow your devotion to the cause of Han to blind you to the threats that may destroy it," Kongming retorted as he fanned himself casually. "Now, as I was saying... if things had returned to normal... and yes, Shiyuan, there *are* those that believe that change is needed regardless..."
Pang Tong smiled silently.
"...Then I would say that 'normality' would remain," Kongming continued. "...But almost immediately, fingers of blame pointed at the 'Ten Eunuchs' that surrounded and controlled the Emperor, in order to prevent further rebellions. And when they easily abducted the Emperor and his brother to solicit their escape, who couldn't see that the Emperor was weak...?"
Xu Shu nodded reluctantly.
"...And then, of course, came *Dong Zhuo*," Kongming noted ominously; both Pang Tong and Xu Shu shuddered at the name. "To be saved from the eunuchs by such a man... is to be rescued from a pack of wild dogs by a wolf."
"Truly evil," Xu Shu recalled with disgust.
"Guarded by Lü Bu, he held all of the most powerful and prominent warlords in the land at bay, and did as he pleased, deposing the Emperor, and putting his brother, our present Emperor, in his place," Kongming continued. "Dong Zhuo tortured, raped, murdered whoever he pleased... until his contempt for his own subordinates cost him his life. But even *then*, was it over...? ...No, his former minions took the palace, and from them, it was won back by forces led by Cao Cao... whose own motives are less than clear. He is said to control the Imperial court, to come and go as he pleases..."
"And none strong enough to oppose him," Pang Tong sighed dramatically.
"Eh...?" Xu Shu chortled.
"...It may be so," Pang Tong added with a glint of mischief in his eye.
"If Dong Zhuo was defeated, why not Cao Cao...?" Xu Shu scoffed.
"One need only look at the landscape," Kongming retorted.

"When Dong Zhuo first usurped the court, there were numerous governors and warlords; Yuan Shao and Yuan Shu, the brother-cousins whose wealth and power was immense and terrifying, but whose personal differences were their undoing. Gongsun Zan, a man who can be considered as relatively righteous, and had many a strong general. Cao Cao himself, whose power was more in his ability to win over the able with his charisma... much like Liu Bei, who is his only true peer."

"...Mm," Pang Tong hummed with amusement.

"Then there was Sun Jian, the mighty 'Tiger of Jiangdong', who defeated Hua Xiong, Dong Zhuo's strongest general next to Lü Bu, and even sent Lü Bu himself to flight on more than one occasion, despite his invincible reputation," Kongming continued. "And Liu Biao, governor of Jing province, one of the few places where an intelligent man can live carefree... the honest Ding Yuan... Liu Yan, the ruler of Yi; Ma Teng; Liu Bei; and a number of other lesser figures, of course."

"*Of course*," Pang Tong said with mischief as he pulled his wide-rimmed hat over his eyes to shield them from the sudden glare of the sun.

"...Now things are different," Kongming sighed. "Lü Bu killed his foster father, Ding Yuan, and joined Dong Zhuo. Yuan Shao and Yuan Shu repeatedly turned on each other. Sun Jian was contented to serve Yuan Shu, and died a miserable death fighting Liu Biao... now his son and heir is more concerned with conquering the lands below the Great River than rescuing the Emperor. Ma Teng has fled northward, happy to accept a government post and rely on petty intrigue to seize an opportunity that will never come. ...And Lü Bu...? ...He redeemed himself by killing Dong Zhuo, but followed that by joining Yuan Shao on a purge of lesser warlords... and we all know *why*."

"...It became a game, didn't it, amongst us all... guessing who Lü Bu would side with or betray next," Pang Tong chuckled.

"Yes, it did," Kongming recalled with amusement. "Back and forth he went, until the warlords became collectively sick of him... he won't be missed."

"And then there was Yuan Shu declaring himself Emperor," Xu Shu sighed.

"Who *wasn't* angered by that...?" Kongming noted, aiming his fan at Xu Shu. "...And like Lü Bu before him, the other warlords rebuked him or fought him, and he died destitute and alone. Tell me, who foresaw *that* of Yuan Shu...?"

Xu Shu nodded agreeably.

"So many 'heroes' gone... but were any of them really as great and magnificent as they proclaimed to be...?" Kongming continued. "They were mostly the *descendants* of great men; 'son of this man', 'nephew of that man'... that means *nothing*. Whatever the Yuans did to earn their wealth and power, Shao and Shu lost it due to incompetence, and..."

"...*What*...?" Xu Shu exclaimed.

"...Kongming... have you been on the wine...?" Pang Tong teased.

"Exactly what I was thinking," Xu Shu chuckled. "Kongming, are you serious???"

"Completely," Kongming insisted as he continued to fan himself rhythmically.

"...*Drunk*," Pang Tong teased again. "Yuan Shao's still going, isn't he...?"

"...A slip of the tongue," Kongming snickered. "Yuan Shao is yet to lose his power... but he *will*, I guarantee it. He's made a lot of logistical errors that are the talk of scholars in Jing province. I tell you, he's doomed."

"*Yuan Shao*...?" Xu Shu chortled. "Who's going to defeat him...?"

"Technically, he'll defeat himself," Kongming replied. "But in actuality, Cao Cao."

"The two are sworn friends," Xu Shu countered, waving his hand dismissively.

"...Since when did that mean anything to men of ambition...?" Kongming chuckled.

"Even there's any truth in that, Yuan Shao commands over a hundred-thousand men!" Xu Shu protested. "Who is Cao Cao, compared to that???"

"...The best of them all," Kongming insisted. "He'll defeat Yuan Shao within a year or less, and in less than ten years, Liu Biao will follow. Yuan Shao and Liu Biao are senile idiots, and if Shao had a *million men*, Cao would still beat him. Liu Biao can't act against Cao Cao because he would need to divert troops from his eastern borders... which he can't do, since Sun Jian's son would seize Jing Province as revenge for his father's murder."

Xu Shu's expression softened, and his gaze wandered, to Pang Tong's amusement.

"...Liu Bei, Cao Cao and Sun Ce are the champions of the age," Kongming continued. "Liu Bei, while weak now, is a man who has the aura of a hero... Cao Cao is once said to have told Bei, 'Of all the warlords in China, there are but two heroes: you, and I'. Liu Bei is the only one Cao Cao truly fears, despite his having no land and nearly no troops... because fate is on his side, and his hardships are merely tests before his true purpose can be fulfilled."

"...But can Liu Bei do anything without land...?" Pang Tong taunted. "He has but the hair on his head and a horse these days, since losing Xu Province... he's hiding behind Yuan Shao, and his best general now serves *Cao Cao* loyally... does that sound like a man with a bright future to you...?"

"Quite right," Xu Shu suggested; Kongming fanned himself slowly, pondered how best to answer, and cleared his throat.

"...In war, one's fortunes are not consistent," Kongming countered. "Today's great giant is tomorrow's forgotten fool, and an ambitious vassal, tomorrow's titan. Take Yuan Shu as an example of the former, and Sun Ce as the latter."

Pang Tong and Xu Shu nodded agreeably.

"When Sun Jian died, Sun Ce was inheriting nothing more than the role of 'mercenary for hire'. But with a few good allies, charisma, drive, ambition... he now controls much of the south. Eighty-odd townships below the Great River are either his to rule or they soon will be," Kongming declared. "Tell me now, who could foresee that of the son of a vassal of Yuan Shu...?"

"I...!" Xu Shu began; Kongming gestured with his fan that he should let him say his piece to the end.

"Cao Cao had little but a handful of retainers and some connections," Kongming continued. "...Now, he *is* the Imperial court: he has his own fief, and great warriors and generals flock to his side, sensing his greatness."
Xu Shu concurred silently.
"A storm is brewing," Kongming concluded. "Cao Cao, Liu Biao, Sun Ce, Liu Bei, Yuan Shao... they will fight relentlessly until at least two of them fall. That fighting will leave no place in the land untouched... there will be nowhere to hide for the pacifist scholar, not even Jing Province... in fact, *especially* not Jing province."
"*Great*," Xu Shu sighed miserably.
"...I see great promise in Sun Ce," Pang Tong mused. "I... I wonder that I might end up going that way... see if I can get myself a post."
"Not a bad idea," Kongming said with a smile. "My brother recently entered his service, and is being treated very well... so I can hardly criticize."
"...And what will *you* do, Kongming...?" Xu Shu asked pointedly.
"I won't be going to Sun Ce," Kongming chuckled. "No... I intend to find a wife, settle here, and till the fields... the world's problems don't concern me."
"...Liar," Xu Shu chortled. "You know more about the affairs of the day than most scholars in the Imperial court do. Nobody knows as much as that, and makes a statement like 'there will be nowhere to hide', and then intends to do nothing."
"...Perhaps I just like to know the politics of the day," Kongming suggested with a wry grin. "And soldiers need grain... so a farmer's life is a stable one."
"...We should head back into town," Pang Tong proposed as he got to his feet and dusted his robes off nonchalantly.

"...Cao Cao massacred a hundred-thousand civilians in Xu Province when he wanted to avenge his father," Pang Tong whispered to Xu Shu as the two walked down the hill toward Longzhong. Kongming was walking ahead of them, and he was still fanning himself and grinning ambiguously.
"I know," Xu Shu retorted audibly. "You know that I know... what, you think that is why he is so fearful of Cao Cao...?"
Kongming stopped, turned to the other two men, and chuckled, "I don't fear Cao Cao... you should both know that. I don't necessarily hate him, either... war is war, and war has casualties. I simply see before me a man who will go far."
That said, Kongming turned and continued on his way; as he walked, he laughed, and suddenly recited a poem he had composed:

"Oh, Heaven and Earth, so displaced!
The fire of Han burns dim!
The lords' allegiances, so misplaced!
The hope for redemption grows slim!
And lo, in the cities and valleys,
Worthy men idle and sigh,
For when heroes come seeking their service,
Will they see them, or ride blindly by...?"

Pang Tong laughed softly at the words.

"...*He sees a man that will go far...*" Xu Shu pondered.

Pang Tong continued to watch Kongming walking confidently ahead of him, and whispered to himself,

"...*So do I.*"

************

# 2

Kongming's home was located within the forest near Longzhong, alongside a stream. The secluded nature of the place was perfect for him; he could pursue his texts by night, after the hard work in the fields, and nothing would disturb him. As the three men reached the fork in the road that lead to Kongming's home, Xu Shu and Pang Tong turned to their friend and nodded politely.

"...I'm going into town," Kongming announced.

"Oh...?" Xu Shu exclaimed.

"I heard that Mister Huang wanted to see you," Pang Tong noted pointedly.

"Uh... yes," Kongming replied with a little embarrassment.

"I wonder why," Pang Tong teased.

"...Mm... yes, so do I," Kongming said with an awkward smile.

The three men started to walk toward the town.

"...You're nearly twenty, Kongming," Xu Shu said suddenly. "Does that mean you shall be seeking a wife quite soon...?"

Pang Tong smiled mischievously.

"Laugh all you want, Shiyuan," Kongming scoffed. "To seek a wife whose mind is formidable... is not stupidity."

"And what about *you*, Yuanzhi...?" Pang Tong prompted as he turned to Xu Shu. "What great steps are you taking next in your promising life...?"

"I don't know," Xu Shu lamented. "I'm not considered a 'prodigy of the age', as you two are; what do I do...?"

"Honestly, I meant no harm," Pang Tong insisted. "You've a great future ahead of you, just like Liu Bei, Cao Cao, Kongming, and me."

Kongming laughed boisterously.

"...You don't think I'm right...?" Pang Tong challenged.

"I'm just wondering what 'great' means," Kongming replied. "I don't doubt we'll have great futures... I'm just not sure whether that's a good thing or not."

"...Should I go to Sun Ce, with you, Shiyuan...?" Xu Shu asked of Pang Tong.

"...If you feel that's what you should do," Pang Tong replied. "I'll make no choices for you, friend. You'd only hate me later, instead of yourself."

"Then... then perhaps, Kongming, I should remain in Longzhong...?" Xu Shu prompted awkwardly.

"...Oh, I see, so *I* can be the one to blame for your downfall, instead," Kongming chuckled. "No, Xu Yuanzhi... you should do what your own heart tells you to do."

"...Xiangyang is a big place... it's easy for a man to be noticed there," Xu Shu decided after a long and ponderous pause. "A lot of our friends are there."

"I almost forgot that Shi Tao is in town," Kongming replied. "He could help you find a place to stay... don't rule it out."

"I agree," Pang Tong said kindly. "I shall soon be off myself, though... to places further than Xiangyang."

"I'll miss you," Kongming said with a smile.

"...I doubt that," Pang Tong retorted mischievously. "You'll be the closest thing to a clever man in these parts when I'm gone."

Kongming laughed softly, and started to fan himself again.
"Him and that fan," Pang Tong teased. "He's already practicing to be the Chief Strategist for Liu Bei."
"Liu Bei...?" Xu Shu wondered.
"Enough, Shiyuan," Kongming insisted. "Say no more."
"...Very well," Pang Tong promised with a smirk.

The three men parted company with slight, solemn bows once they reached Longzhong. Kongming made his way through the busy, bustling streets toward the home of Huang Chengyan, dodging peddlers and traders selling everything from fish and meat to sandals and mats. When Kongming reached the Huang household, he asked for an audience with the master of the house, and awaited a response.
"Ah...! Young Master Zhuge!" Mister Huang Chengyan hailed, from the street behind Kongming; the young scholar was taken aback, which amused the old man greatly.
"Mister Huang," Kongming hailed in response. "You wanted to see me...?"
"I did!" Mister Huang replied. "I consider you to be one of the geniuses of our time, you know; perhaps you can find me a servant that knows when I'm in."
"...I'm flattered, Mister Huang," Kongming replied politely.
"I shall be direct," Mister Huang declared. "I know you are seeking a wife... I wonder, have you heard about my daughter, Yueying...?"
"I have," Kongming replied calmly.
"So you're aware she's a bit of an ugly one, then...?" Mister Huang sighed woefully. "That's a pity... you see, she's every bit a match for your talent, Kongming, and I would like to see you paired... but if you know about her dark, rough complexion, reddish hair, and general poor features, then..."
"I don't care," Kongming interrupted. "I should like to meet her."
"...You... you *would*...?" Mister Huang exclaimed.
"Yes," Kongming replied sincerely. "For me, all that will do is a kindred spirit, a woman with whom I can converse, debate, laugh and cry, argue as equals..."
"*Argue*...?" Mister Huang chuckled. "Well, my goodness... she probably wouldn't mind that, but... but yes, yes! You should meet her soon!"
"What about *now*...?" Kongming prompted. "Here we are, Mister Huang, right in front of your house..."
"...Yes... yes, I suppose... yes, yes!" Mister Huang chuckled heartily. "Come, come! After you...!"
"No, after you, please," Kongming insisted; Mister Huang entered his home, and Kongming followed, fanning himself slowly.

Kongming exchanged pleasantries with Mister Huang's wife, who was very pleased with the young man's demeanour. After an hour, a servant entered the living area and asked that Kongming might like to step out into the garden, where Huang Yueying was waiting.
Mister Huang sighed, and declared, "As I said, she's really quite unappealing, so she'll-"

"And as *I* said, I don't care," Kongming retorted; he bowed once again to Mrs Huang, and walked through to the garden at the back of the house. Yueying was sat on a low wall; she wore a beautiful pink silk robe adorned with an image of a crane, and a wide-brimmed hat and veil to cover her face.

"Zhuge Liang," Yueying hailed calmly. "...The 'Crouching Dragon' of Longzhong."

"Please, call me Kongming," Kongming insisted as he bowed with respect.

"Such a thing is acceptable only between friends," Yueying replied.

"And can we not be friends...?" Kongming countered.

"Alas, no," Yueying retorted. "We can only be strangers, or family."

"...Well put," Kongming chuckled as he sat on a short stool in front of Yueying, and tried to steal a glimpse of her face under the veil.

"...You should not sit below me," Yueying sighed as she lowered herself to sit on another stool facing Kongming.

"...So," Kongming prompted, "I understand that you are an avid reader."

"I enjoy reading very much," Yueying replied. "I have read the odes and many of the great works of poetry... I have also read books on warfare and military strategy."

"...*Warfare*...?" Kongming exclaimed.

"Does that genuinely surprise you...?" Yueying chuckled softly. "I'm dismayed... perhaps you are not so insightful a man after all."

"...Because I greeted your interest in warfare with surprise...?" Kongming chortled defensively. "I assure you, my lady, that I've met many a pedant scholar that turns his nose up at books on warfare and strategy... ignorant of the needs of the age. So any surprise is not out of contempt... but genuine pleasure."

"...Good," Yueying said after a pause. "Shall we have some tea...?"

"Why not...?" Kongming said with a smile.

"I think she likes him," Mister Huang whispered to his wife as they watched the scene from within the house.

"He is every bit the man you said he was," Mrs Huang replied. "A good choice, husband: a good choice."

Kongming would meet with Yueying many more times, and every time, Yueying would match wits with Kongming, forcing him to become more and more challenging in his responses. A strong friendship grew between the two – much to the disdain of Kongming's scholar friends – but one day, they decided to be married, and that was the beginning of one of the most important friendships in Kongming's eventful life.

∗∗∗∗∗∗∗∗∗∗∗∗

## 3

"...My, how things change."
Yueying smiled as her husband returned from a busy day of work and made his weary proclamation; much time had passed, and the statement was true.
"Such is life," Yueying replied. "But I take it you refer to something specific."
"I'm getting a bit of praise for 'accurately predicting' Yuan Shao's defeat at Boma," Kongming chuckled wearily as he sat, cross-legged, in front of his reading table, and swept aside one of the many bamboo scrolls that were scattered about for casual reference. "I *guessed*... such a man can only bring defeat upon himself."
"And what do you think of Liu Biao, and Sun Ce...?" Yueying prompted. "Do you still rate them poorly...?"
"...Perhaps," Kongming replied cautiously. "Why do you ask...?"
"Stability is a serious concern for raising a family," Yueying said. "I know from hearing you and Jun talking that..."
"Where is my brother, now that you mention him...?" Kongming interrupted, in an effort to change the subject.
"...That you are less than flattering regarding Liu Biao or Sun Ce, seeing both as 'walking corpses'," Yueying continued unabated. "And we both know that if the situation in Jing province ignites, the fact that I am the niece of the governor's wife might mean that you are forced to serve as an adviser, or we could have vital supplies confiscated, or the invading army could target us. ...I want to know if we will be together, *safely* together. Fate has a way of breaking families up. I do not want us to be separated, if it can be helped."
"...Sadly, you're right," Kongming sighed. "My two sisters, I barely see them... I remember them, scurrying about, when I was young... now, they are wives to busy men, mothers to children, housekeepers, and I don't see or hear from them."
"And your elder brother is hardly quick to write, he is so embroiled in the events in Jiangdong," Yueying suggested further. "I worry what will happen to us, I worry whether your children will see you, whether you will be a being of flesh to them, or a few ink characters on some pieces of paper."
"But my poor estimation of Liu Biao does not trouble you...?" Kongming asked.
"My aunt is self-serving; we are family in name only, and strangers in actual fact," Yueying replied honestly. "Liu Biao married her for her looks, not her charming personality."
"...A truly remarkable woman, you are," Kongming chuckled. "Yes, I'm worried too. I haven't sought out a lord and master because I want to avoid the fighting... but that will be impossible, and I know that. ...Your mother must sigh, sometimes, at your marrying a man who knows what he has to do but lives in denial."

"Like me, Mother married for something more than power," Yueying sighed sadly. "Father is good, kind, honest, outspoken, knowledgeable, funny... that's why she chose him. Sometimes he seems oblivious to the world around him... an act. He isn't looking for a high position with a warlord, but Mother doesn't care, he has enough to keep them both. ...No, Mother is very glad of our marriage."

"...Do you worry that I am a 'man of no promise'...?" Kongming fretted.

"Of course not," Yueying giggled. "I'm happy here, if that's what you want... but if you do end up in some capital, serving a powerful lord, or you are summoned to fight on the front line... then I will remain at your side, no matter what."

"My thanks," Kongming said quietly.

"We have been married for over a year now," Yueying said as she prepared tea. "And soon, I shall be giving you a child, I hope. The world is changing, as you said... one day, war will come here to visit us... what will you do...?"

"...Greet it," Kongming replied, "as with all guests, welcome and unwelcome... and decide how best to entertain it."

"...Sun Ce worries Cao Cao, I hear," Yueying prompted.

"He'll die for it," Kongming supposed. "For now, Cao will try alliances-by-marriage... but eventually, he'll deal with Sun Ce, when he has the freedom."

"And where is your own favourite, Liu Bei...?" Yueying asked knowingly.

Kongming grimaced as he replied, "It is widely believed that with the defeat at Boma, Liu Bei will not remain with Yuan Shao; he has reunited with his generals from the Yellow Turban days and..."

"...And...?" Yueying prompted after a short silence.

"...And is said to be retreating in this direction," Kongming admitted at last. "He is most likely intending to seek refuge with Liu Biao in Jing province. So yes, once Yuan Shao is gone, this region may then be set upon by Cao Cao."

"...An opportunity beckons," Yueying supposed encouragingly.

"...Perhaps," Kongming admitted reluctantly. "But who knows what Liu Biao will do... an edict has been discovered, written by the Emperor himself, declaring Cao Cao to be a seditious traitor, and that he should be executed ... with Liu Bei as one of the named conspirators, Liu Biao must risk going up against Cao Cao directly by taking him in. Such a thing may take strength that Liu Biao just doesn't have anymore."

"Jing Province is threatened," Yueying mused. "War will come... Cao will win."

"...Either way, Liu Biao cannot move closer to Cao, and with Sun Ce commanding so much of the land... interesting," Kongming pondered. "So... three distinct rival powers already begin to emerge from the chaos... interesting."

"It sits well with the 'tripod of power' theory," Yueying mused.

"...It does," Kongming replied. "Liu Bei in the west, Sun Ce in the south, and Cao Cao in the north... but as for Jing..."

"Liu *Biao*," Yueying corrected. "...Liu *Biao* in the west."

"...Liu *Bei*," Kongming insisted. "Liu Bei has ambition... he'll be one of those three powers, I know it. Liu Zhang is nothing like the warlord his father was... he is a craven weakling that will lose the support of his followers. His subordinate Zhang Lu is already breaking away from him; he's doomed. And Liu Biao is old, his children weak, so neither he nor his progeny will ever govern in the west, that much is certain."
Yueying continued to potter about the room silently, moving things needlessly and deliberately refusing to remain still for a moment.
"I'm going into Xiangyang in a few days," Kongming announced. "Hopefully, I should bump into Xu Shu and Shi Tao... see what they're up to."
"Yes, Xu Shu hasn't been by for a while," Yueying replied thoughtlessly. "If you see Ma Liang, and young Ma Su of course, you should say hello for me."
"I'll see if I can get them to come back with me," Kongming replied. "Sometimes I am ashamed at how little two men sworn to brotherhood see of each other!"
Yueying smiled warmly, and continued her work as Kongming picked up a text and started to read quietly.

As he had promised, Kongming travelled southward and over the River Han to Xiangyang a few days later, and travelled to what he knew were Xu Shu's current dwellings.

"...Kongming," Xu Shu hailed as he greeted his friend. "How are you...?"
"You seem thoughtful," Kongming suggested.
"...I am," Xu Shu admitted. "Liu Bei... his advance scouts have been going through this city and others, and I think that he will be here soon."
"A pity he brings war with him," Kongming sighed sadly.
"...He will also bring opportunity," Xu Shu retorted. "I have something of a good reputation here... I have decided that I will try to approach him."
"To render what service...?" Kongming enquired further.
"...A strategist," Xu Shu replied.
Kongming smirked silently.
"I can prove myself," Xu Shu insisted as he gestured for Kongming to follow him to his room.
"...It is unlikely," Kongming chuckled. "Remember that he has two intolerant generals in his service... some say they are like brothers, and would die for each other.

"Guan Yu... is a legend among men. He personally killed Yan Liang, one of Yuan Shao's best generals, in a surprise attack, while in the service of Cao Cao... and he knows a network of mercenaries that constantly harass Cao Cao in the north... though well-read, Guan dislikes scholars, believing himself to be an expert in the art of war and any who specialise solely in the written word to be worthless.

"Zhang Fei is a wealthy butcher, who was a junior financier to Liu Bei's entire operation in the beginning, as well as a formidable warrior... though an honest sort, he despises 'pedants' like us as soft, weak, and cowardly.

"It is hard enough to reach a man when someone else has his ear that doesn't respect you... these men have an ear each, so a man would have to shout quite loudly to be heard by Liu Bei."

Xu Shu laughed, saying, "In the same way that Jiang Ziya used odd behaviour in order to be noticed by King Wen, so will I, and that will..."

"Why not just get Mister Sima to put a good word in for you...?" Kongming sighed wearily. "You're not Jiang Ziya."

"How do you know that Liu Bei will consult Mister Sima?" Xu Shu countered.

"He's just been defeated by Cao Cao, fled from Yuan Shao's service, and been chased halfway across the country," Kongming chuckled. "He'll want to know of any worthy men in the area to join his cause... who else would you go to but a man like Mister Sima, a noted scholar that knows anyone worth knowing...?"

"True," Xu Shu conceded. "Oh, wait... is that why you're in Xiangyang?"

"I'm too young to be taken seriously by Liu Bei," Kongming lamented. "A farmer, twenty years of age, newly married, no children, never seen a battle first hand, trying to get the attention of a man that has already seen over a decade of active service, a man related to the Emperor, a man in his forties with two grown daughters...?"

"...Now I'm depressed," Xu Shu sighed miserably; he slouched into a seated position, and hung his head low. "How the hell can I get his attention either...?"

"You're older, and you have more hair," Kongming chuckled as he stroked his own soft beard. "You look older, you sound older... I really think you needn't worry. Me, on the other hand..."

"I'd put in a good word for you, so would your father-in-law, and so would Mister Sima," Xu Shu insisted. "You'll be as much of a welcome addition as I will."

"...My thanks," Kongming replied, "but what you say is years down the line."

"Any word from Shiyuan...?" Xu Shu wondered.

"He's in Nan Prefecture in southern Jing," Kongming sighed; "Mister Sima speaks highly of him... he's done very well."

"He's not in Jiangdong, then...?" Xu Shu asked pointedly. "What's he doing...?"

"...Officer of Merit, in Jiangling," Kongming replied awkwardly.

"...A professional brownnoser," Xu Shu surmised with amusement. "Pang Tong, a man who enjoys mischief and winding people up needlessly, has got himself a job appraising other people. ...How ironic."

"I hear," Kongming snickered, "that he is renowned for his glowing appraisals."

Xu Shu sat in dumbfounded silence for a moment; and then, as it hit him fully, he joined Kongming in laughing loudly.

"...That's cheered me up," Xu Shu panted as he tried to catch his breath after a long period of laughter. "...'Pang Tong, giver of encouraging words'...!"

"He *overpraises*, apparently," Kongming chuckled. "He... he 'feels it is only right, in this tumultuous age when people need encouraging words to spur them on to give their all in life'...!"

Xu Shu started to laugh again; after a few minutes, he exhaled, and chortled, "*He really is a comedian*."

"He'll go far," Kongming suggested.

"*Everyone* loves a kiss-arse," Xu Shu sighed. "Of course he will. I just never expected that of *Pang Tong*."

"...Yes... *what a world*," Kongming sighed as he started to fan himself slowly.

"...Indeed," Xu Shu agreed with a more sombre tone.

"...In only a few years, my friend, the entire landscape is new, a place I barely recognise," Kongming mused. "When you and Shi Tao came to this region, we were all carefree, all of us, and we passed the days by guessing the ways in which the times would change... now, Shi Tao is too busy to meet us even once a year... Pang Tong is gone... we've changed too."

"...Yes," Xu Shu whispered.

"None of it unexpected," Kongming continued, "but, all the same, a lot to digest, a lot to comprehend."

"...Yes," Xu Shu whispered again.

Kongming continued to fan himself as he said, with no real clear intent,

"...My, how things change."


************

**4**

The city of Xiangyang was alive with anxious whispering as two significant pieces of news started to circulate amongst the people some months later.

"...Sun Ce has been assassinated."
Xu Shu greeted the news from Kongming with a little shock as the two sat in a tavern, drinking heated wine.
"Assassinated...?" Xu Shu exclaimed. "But... but by *whom*...?"
"There are two theories," Kongming said with a soft laugh. "The more plausible story is that he was attacked by former followers of a prefect that he had killed for plotting against him. Others say he was cursed by a Taoist saint that he had killed for spreading heresy. My money's not on the curse, to be honest."
"...Oh, that Taoist...!" Xu Shu recalled. "I wonder if he really was a saint...?"
"Sainthood did not save his life, if he was," Kongming retorted. "Anyhow, Sun Quan, Ce's younger brother, has taken control."
"...Come to think of it, you said this would happen," Xu Shu murmured.
"I *guessed*," Kongming insisted. "I *guessed* that it *might* happen."
"Good *guess*...!" Xu Shu retorted with an ironic laugh. "You seem to be able to anticipate everything. ...So the Suns of Jiangdong are finished, then."
"Zhou Yu, Sun Ce's sworn brother and his chief military strategist, is a true genius of the age," Kongming said with respect. "Sun Quan also has the 'Two Zhangs' for domestic advice... a host of soldiers, sailors, pirates and generals under his command... six districts under his control. Unfortunately, though, Quan is not interested in going after Cao Cao, like his brother was. He's made peace with Cao Cao, and strengthened the forces along the Great River... which means that they're finally going to attack Jing, starting with Governor Huang Zu of Jiangxia."
"...Which doesn't bode well for Liu Bei, either," Xu Shu mused.
"No, it doesn't," Kongming lamented. "He has only just started to settle here, and already, bad luck follows him. If Liu Biao is caught in a pincer between Sun and Cao, then that will be the end of the 'Tripod of Power' theory."
"And Cao is bound and determined to attack Liu Biao," Xu Shu reported. "I was lucky enough to be noticed, and I have been asked for local advice..."
"...Congratulations," Kongming said with sincerity. "I knew that he would see the great talent you had."
"...I'm really not speaking to him, I'm speaking to his low-ranking advisers," Xu Shu insisted. "But Cao Cao is definitely coming... for now, there is word that he's sending Xiahou Dun, Li Dian, and Yu Jin, three of-"
"His best generals," Kongming interrupted worriedly. "Sending *three*... Cao Cao is really serious about this."
"I'm volunteering topographical advice, mainly," Xu Shu explained. "After all, like you're always telling me, you need to know the topography."
"...Fine," Kongming murmured.

"You've thought of something...?" Xu Shu supposed.

"Mm...?" Kongming said absent-mindedly. "Oh, uh... it's nothing. ...Nothing that nobody else will think of, leastways."

"...I have an idea," Xu Shu declared. "I'm going to scout, look at the topography... it'll be weeks before they get here, and weeks again before they'll make a decisive strike. Why don't you go back home, see your family, get some belongings, and follow me on my scouting missions...? Lord Liu will be sending troops with me, and he may even personally review our findings."

"That's very kind of you," Kongming said gratefully. "I'll go home... my wife will need to be told of my movements."

"...Why...?" Xu Shu asked bluntly.

"Because it's only fair," Kongming retorted. "I already told you, she's very talented in many ways..."

"Yes," Xu Shu teased. "At the least, she isn't really that ugly, despite the rumours."

"...No, that's right, she isn't," Kongming replied wearily.

"So go on... how did you know...?" Xu Shu asked at last.

"...I didn't," Kongming insisted calmly. "I really didn't care."

"...Really...?" Xu Shu prompted.

"No," Kongming replied immediately.

"...Your children..." Xu Shu began.

"...Will have exemplary intelligence, between the two of us," Kongming insisted emotionlessly. "Surely that is all that truly matters to a scholar's progeny...?"

"But she isn't ugly," Xu Shu chuckled. "Seriously, how did you...?"

"I didn't care," Kongming insisted again. "She is a very intelligent woman... she even got me thinking about things that I was sure I fully understood. She may even have some insight for the upcoming battle, since she studies maps."

"...Fine, well, let me know if she finds anything interesting," Xu Shu joked.

"I shall," Kongming replied in all seriousness.

"...And... does your marriage... have political benefit...?" Xu Shu prompted.

"Nothing that I've exploited," Kongming replied calmly. "Any job I get will be earned, not bought or granted."

Xu Shu nodded silently, and was inwardly ashamed that he had so blatantly raised the subject.


Kongming returned to his forest-based cottage, and was greeted at the door by his younger brother Jun.

"...Any interesting news, big brother...?" Jun prompted.

"Sun Ce's dead, Liu Bei's meeting Liu Biao to discuss fighting Cao Cao and Sun Quan," Kongming replied calmly as he fanned himself, and peered into the house.

"Sun Ce's *dead*...?" Jun whispered.

Ignoring Jun's pondering of the military news, Kongming asked, "How is she...?"

"Fine," Jun insisted. "You seem glad to be home."

"...I am," Kongming admitted with a smile.

"So why are you loitering...?" Jun wondered. "Are you going on another long journey, big brother...?"

"… … …I am an open book," Kongming chuckled as he made his way into the house at last, leaving his brother to carry on with his chores.

"…Welcome home, husband," Yueying hailed as she spotted Kongming. "…So how long before you go again…?"

"…Transparent, completely transparent…!" Kongming joked as he sat down, and Yueying prepared tea for him.

"Surely one of the hired hands can get me tea…?" Kongming protested.

"They have important work," Yueying replied. "Besides, I don't mind."

"…Xu Shu has got work with Liu Bei," Kongming reported.

"Good for him," Yueying replied.

"…He's proffering local topography advice for an upcoming confrontation between Liu Bei and Xiahou Dun," Kongming continued.

"…*Xiahou Dun*," Yueying mused. "…'Blind Xiahou'."

"The very same," Kongming applauded.

"The one-eyed general… Cao Cao's right-hand man," Yueying noted further.

"Cao Cao is intent on killing Liu Bei," Kongming sighed. "Yu Jin, another of his great generals, is with Xiahou Dun. They will be backed up by veteran troops, possibly thousands…"

"…Only an ambush would suffice," Yueying guessed as she passed tea to an impressed Kongming. "Is there anywhere that such a large ambush could be carried out…? Somewhere with flammable vegetation…?"

"…Great minds think alike," Kongming chuckled as he received his tea gratefully. "Yes, Xu Shu and I agreed that a fire attack is best… brutal, but necessary. There are a few good locations that spring to mind… to be honest, the best place is Bowang, and Liu Bei's men seem to be aware of the place already. But we're going to scout and see if there are any other good places."

"If Liu Bei's men know of it, so will Xiahou Dun's," Yueying suggested.

"*Yes*, but they have to be prepared to believe there is a credible threat," Kongming noted. "Xiahou Dun is a generous, caring man by all accounts, but ruthless and pitiless to his enemies… paradoxical, but there you go. He is hot-headed, violent… he can be angered, tricked into ignoring danger. …Yu Jin and Li Dian, however, are more cautious… that's why Cao Cao has partnered them, obviously."

"…You will be joining Liu Bei's army, then…?" Yueying asked plainly.

"No… not yet," Kongming sighed as he examined his fan. "I expect that Xu Shu will try and get me noticed, but… such things are a long time coming. …But that's a good thing! I shall see my family grow before I am called to service; so, in fact, I cannot and should not complain."

Yueying smiled gratefully.

"I will be setting out in the next couple of days," Kongming explained. "I'll be gone a while… in fact, I might stay on if I can, and watch the battle from a safe distance, get an idea about how you command troops from afar."

"It's all done with advance orders and signals, like flags," Yueying supposed.

"…Easier said than done, though," Kongming snickered as he sipped his tea.

Yueying continued to potter about silently, while Kongming pondered the future.

"…Any interesting news…?" Yueying prompted.

"Oh, right, yes… Sun Ce, the 'Little Conqueror' of the south, has been assassinated," Kongming said thoughtlessly.

Yueying stopped and turned to Kongming with surprise, exclaiming, "*Sun Ce…?*"

"Yes, it has that effect on everyone," Kongming chuckled casually as he started to fan himself and make sense of events. "…Sun Quan will do nothing for a while, so Liu Biao is safe from his wrath… for now. Sun Quan has to earn the respect of Sun Ce's officers, and maybe even Zhou Yu."

"He's only young, I expect," Yueying sighed.

"Very," Kongming said with a sad smile. "Less than twenty by my reckoning… how can such a youth command respect from veteran warriors and scholars…?"

Yueying hummed thoughtfully, aware that her husband intended the question not just with respect to Sun Quan, but to himself.

"As Xu Shu inadvertently pointed out, Sun Ce's death threatens to make a mockery of the tripod theory," Kongming sighed. "It is only with two states in opposition to Cao Cao that the Han can be fully restored… one can only hope Sun Quan is a hero at heart, or his territory will fall to Cao Cao within a decade."

"…One can only wonder what will happen next," Yueying said wearily.

"…Whatever happens next, Cao Cao will be at the heart of it," Kongming replied ominously as he stared at the draft of a map he was drawing. One day, he hoped to present that map as a sign of his hopes for things to come.

************

**5**

Months passed, and things continued to change at a relentless pace. Yuan Shao had an epic battle with Cao Cao at and around the strategically important region of Guandu, where the incompetent, outclassed Yuan Shao was definitively defeated. With Yuan Shao and his sons temporarily in disarray and the other warlords showing no signs of reacting to events, Cao Cao now turned his attentions to his old friend and enemy Liu Bei, and the ruler of Jing Province, Liu Biao.

Kongming and Xu Shu watched from the relative safety of a high hill as a battalion of well-ordered troops filed along the narrow paths of Bowang.
"…So that is Lord Liu," Kongming whispered.
"Did you have to bring that fan?" Xu Shu scolded. "…You look like you're in charge. You'll get us shot by archers if we're spotted."
Kongming was not listening: he was watching the leaders of the soldiers that marched along the paths. At the head of them were two men of obvious stature: one was middle-aged and not in the best of condition, but he rode his horse expertly, and was obviously a well-trained veteran cavalryman of some sort. From the distance at which he stood, Kongming could not make out any particular features, but the flag-bearer told him who this man was: Liu Bei, former governor of Xu Province. The other man rode under a slightly smaller standard, but was taller and more intimidating than Liu Bei. He was younger, and wore armour that shone brilliantly, as though it were made of stars from the sky. He carried a long spear, and wore a long sword at his waist; he was Zhao Yun, known to his familiars as Zilong, and he was one of Liu Bei's most trusted generals.
"Zhao Zilong," Kongming whispered.
"I actually got to speak to him," Xu Shu said with pride. "He's a genuinely honourable and courteous man. He used to serve under Gongsun Zan."
"Yes, I know," Kongming replied absent-mindedly as he scanned the troops, studying their marching arrangements. "…Far from perfect… but very good, nonetheless…"
"*What*…?" Xu Shu asked bluntly, as he was surprised at Kongming's apparent arrogance.
"The order of the troops, I mean… not Zilong," Kongming replied softly and thoughtfully. "…Such an array will provoke caution in his enemies… it's my understanding that you don't want that when you want them to pursue you into an ambush."
"Oh," Xu Shu said quietly. "I don't know the plan."
"I thought you were a strategist for him," Kongming retorted quietly as he continued to watch the troops disappear into the distance.
"…I mostly provided topographical information," Xu Shu replied. "He has Jian Yong, Mi Zhu, and Mister Sun, who help to form a lot of his plans… Guan Yu also makes suggestions based on his own…"

"Mm," Kongming interrupted. "That'll never do, not in the long run. Three of them are mere advisers, courtiers, and Guan Yu is a warrior. Against a man like Cao Cao, you need more than that. ...Who is the man bringing up the extra troops now...?"

"Chen Dao," Xu Shu replied. "I'm surprised that he isn't at Lord Liu's side... he's the leader of the Lord's most trusted vassals, his bodyguards, and he is a good man, like Zilong."

General Chen Dao was not as elaborately armoured as Zhao Yun, and did not leave much of a lasting impression on Kongming, who returned his gaze to the train of troops following Liu Bei.

"I see dust in the distance," Xu Shu reported. "They're coming."

Kongming raised his fan to his forehead in order to shield his eyes from the glare of the sun as he turned his gaze to the horizon; there was now a cloud of yellow dust as thousands of infantry and cavalrymen slowly descended on Bowang.

"Xiahou Dun..." Kongming murmured. "I wish I had a better view."

"Well, it isn't too late for you to strap on some armour and do your bit, Zhuge," Xu Shu chided. "I'll go and ask the supply captains."

"...Don't be like that," Kongming retorted. "It's just that you hear a lot about these generals and sometimes you want to see them for yourself."

"Well when you're the Director General, you can ride to the front with Lord Liu, can't you," Xu Shu teased. "Seriously, every soldier down there wishes he was somewhere else. Let's just watch."

Kongming and Xu Shu watched as, in the distance, the soldiers of Xiahou Dun formed neat, orderly lines facing Bowang. Flags were arranged, carrying the names of Cao Cao and the general who commanded the battalion. The rows of soldiers – each wearing rough sandals, black tunics with peach-coloured scarves, and cheap iron helmets – awaited the commands of their generals, who wore suits of mail and rode horses with resplendent saddles. The vanguard generals and overall commanders, Xiahou Dun and Li Dian, were wearing polished mail that sparkled in the afternoon sun; Kongming could only imagine the fierce, intimidating expression of Xiahou Dun, whose left eye had been lost during a battle with the forces of Lü Bu some years earlier.

The forces of Liu Bei filed onto the plains; they wore orange tunics that were of a poorer quality than those worn by Cao Cao's forces, and most had leather helmets rather than iron ones. The standard-bearers raised the yellow flags of Liu Bei, which received jeers of derision from the confident front lines of Xiahou Dun.

"...That's a little more like it," Kongming praised as Liu Bei's soldiers formed poor, disorganised lines, giving the impression of poor training. "Now let us hope that they fall for it."

Xiahou Dun rode forward, pointed his spear, and in a deafening voice he cried out, "**Where is Liu Bei???**"

Liu Bei rode forward. Zhao Yun and Chen Dao remained at his sides, and the rest of his elite cavalry bodyguards followed as closely as they could.

"...**Runt!**" Xiahou Dun taunted. "**Sandal-weaving maggot!**"

Liu Bei did not respond; instead, he ordered Zhao Yun out to battle while he retreated slightly with his bodyguards.

"...Are duels like this still typical...?" Kongming asked as Xiahou Dun and Zhao Yun took the centre of the battle field, and started to make dashing passes on horseback, trying to unseat the other with thrusts of their spears while drummers beat a steady pace on either side, and the soldiers roused their champions on.

"Yes," Xu Shu replied numbly. "Rarely, it decides the whole outcome."

"...Pity this can't be all they do," Kongming sighed. "...Xiahou is not the better man of the two. I expect he's adjusting to only having one eye."

Zhao Yun almost ran Xiahou Dun through on the ninth pass: Xiahou retreated to his own line, shouted in frustration, and turned to make a tenth pass, his temper now getting the better of him. At this point, a flag conspicuously dropped on the far right of Liu Bei's disordered battle lines, and Zhao Yun seemingly reeled from the attack, beating a hasty retreat to his own lines.

"The deception begins," Kongming noted.

As Zhao Yun retreated, Liu Bei's battle lines started to disintegrate: Xiahou Dun bellowed in triumph, and ordered a pursuit as Liu Bei and his followers disappeared into the dense forest of Bowang.

"Come on...!" Xu Shu said expectantly.

Xiahou Dun charged, and the front line of his infantry followed: Li Dian was conspicuously hesitant, and only rode forward after a minute or so, gesturing wildly for Xiahou Dun to stop as the battle gongs sounded.

"Damn it," Xu Shu lamented. "They're not going for it."

"...Be patient," Kongming suggested.

Xiahou Dun and Li Dian were visibly bickering, while their troops wavered, unsure of who to obey. Suddenly, Liu Bei's infantry reappeared and launched a rushed, disorganised attack on the Wei vanguard.

"No, no, don't do that...!" Xu Shu exclaimed as Xiahou's troops countered, and dozens of Liu Bei's men fell to spears and swords, with few reciprocal kills.

"Collateral damage," Kongming sighed. "Cruel, but necessary to lure the enemy: Xiahou's arrogance is at its peak... so they will retreat... *now*."

Liu Bei's battered forces broke up and retreated into the forest; Xiahou Dun shrugged off the despondent Li Dian and took the bulk of his forces into the forest.

"...It worked," Xu Shu whispered with relief.

Li Dian threw his spear to the ground and screamed in frustration as three quarters of the army pursued Xiahou Dun. Li Dian rode toward those that remained and rallied them for unknown purposes.

"Will he pursue, I wonder...?" Kongming mused.

Below the hill, Liu Bei was visible as he brought his troops deep into Bowang and beyond the line of the ambush; cries of the victorious soldiers serving Cao Cao got louder and louder as they reached the centre of the forest.

"...*Fool*," Kongming muttered as Li Dian led his own battalions into the forest after Xiahou Dun, anxious to catch up and assist his co-commander.

"Almost... *almost*...!" Xu Shu urged as Liu Bei and his soldiers left the danger zone, and their enemies reached a point of no return.

"...*Now*...!" Xu Shu whispered; from all about Xiahou's soldiers, flaming arrows whistled, igniting undergrowth and deliberately placed piles of disguised timber, and setting Bowang ablaze. The screams of thousands of terrified, pain-wracked men filled the air as the intense fires encircled the soldiers and burned many of them alive. Kongming waved his fan casually and watched the carnage unfold.

"...*Horrible*... and *yet*..." Kongming whispered as he watched soldiers flailing about maniacally, trying to put out the flames that were enveloping their bodies. Others were already dead, and lay in heaps, slowly turning to charcoal.

"No! They escaped!" Xu Shu exclaimed; Kongming followed Xu Shu's gaze, and saw a wildly meandering group of singed, battered soldiers staggering out of the forest and back onto the open plain, with several horseback generals – Xiahou Dun and Li Dian amongst them – retreating ahead of them, carrying scorched standards. From the outskirts of the forest – where hilly regions could hide an elephant – two small contingents of Liu Bei's soldiers appeared, and set about the desperate Cao forces with their spears and swords. At the head of one group was a tall, muscular man who wore a long green robe, had a ruddy complexion, and had a long, well-kept beard; he rode into the enemy forces on a magnificent brown steed, hacking at the soldiers with his pole-sword. The other – a stockier, fierce-faced man with tanned skin and short, wiry whiskers and beard, who wore a collection of scruffy, peach-coloured robes – screamed with triumph as he rode alongside some terrified stragglers and tore into them with his snake-tongued pike.

"Yunchang and Yide," Xu Shu reported.

"So that's them," Kongming mused; the green-robed man was Guan Yu – known familiarly as Yunchang – and the other was Zhang Fei, known as Yide to his friends and close colleagues. "So they're the 'limbs' Liu Bei relied on in his early days: they live up to their reputations," Kongming praised.

Soon, it was over; Guan Yu looked on coldly as Zhang Fei let out a cry of victory that was echoed by his soldiers. Only a dozen or so of the enemy were allowed to escape; Liu Bei rode onto the plain from a side road with Zhao Yun at his side and his bodyguards behind them, and gave a solemn nod of approval at the result.

"...So Xiahou Dun lives to fight another day," Kongming surmised. "Li Dian alone was not enough to control his impetuous nature... a sad day for Li Dian that Yu Jin remained at their camp. ...Now, they will be harassed until they withdraw in shame... such a pity for them."

"The smell in the air is awful," Xu Shu complained.

"Burnt bodies were never going to smell very good," Kongming replied casually as he used his fan to repel the stench. "But... strangely... I'm ready for this."

"We should probably retreat from here, that fire is out of control," Xu Shu suggested as he started down the hill.
Kongming nodded agreeably, and after one last look at the smoke that was billowing from what was now a funeral pyre for thousands of the soldiers of Cao Cao, Kongming smiled ambiguously, and followed his friend.

************

## 6

"**YEAH! Let Cao Cao chew on THAT!**"
Zhang Fei's proclamation encouraged cheers from the generals present at Liu Bei's victory banquet: Guan Yu, Liu Bei, Zhao Yun and the scholar-adviser groups remained silent.
"...**Come on, Elder Brother, a toast!**" Zhang Fei boomed: Liu Bei seemed almost embarrassed as Zhang Fei raised his wine dish and grinned unintelligently.
"...Brother Yide, *please*," Liu Bei protested. "We have to remain composed."
"*Sod that*!" Zhang Fei retorted with amusement; he drank the dish of wine in a single gulp, and bellowed in triumph.
Kongming hummed thoughtfully as he sat at the lesser end of the tent, watching the men that surrounded Liu Bei.
"Yide is always like this," Xu Shu chuckled awkwardly. "He is not a bad drinker, but... he likes to revel when there is something to revel about."
Liu Bei urged a silence, and got his wish within a few seconds.
"...My friends," Liu Bei began, "today we have won a small victory against Cao Cao's forces here at Bowang."
"Small...?" Zhang Fei chuckled as he messily devoured a piece of chicken; "...We **thrashed them!**"
"...*Yide*," Liu Bei scolded.
Zhang Fei lowered his eyes guiltily.
"It was only a small victory," Liu Bei insisted. "It was a great boon to us that Xiahou Dun was so easily drawn into that trap, but we must remember that the forces of Cao Cao are very great in number now, especially since Guandu."
Murmurs of concern erupted amongst the scholars and advisers.
"...**Pedants!**" Zhang Fei jeered. "...**Pedants an' pissy-arse cowards, the lot of you! Why don't you all go running to Cao Cao now, since you can't stand a little bit of...!**"
"...Yide, I won't warn you again," Liu Bei scolded for a second time: Zhang Fei lowered his eyes again, and munched on a piece of barbecued pork with a sulking expression on his face.
"We're going to find things more difficult without Yuan Shao as a buffer to distract Cao Cao from us," Liu Bei continued, "but we can win. Now we are here in Jing, a place where talented men are like sand, we can find the people we need to win us the greater battles that are to come."
Kongming hummed thoughtfully once again, and fanned himself slowly.
"Lord Liu Biao has agreed that we can remain stationed in Fan and Xinye for as long as we need to be... I have accepted his kind offer," Liu Bei added cautiously. "We will not lose this foothold in the way we lost Xu Province... we will be more diligent, and learn to spot the dangers before they can harm us."
"...This is all very formal after such a victory, my lord," a dignified young man in scholar's robes suggested from amongst a group of administrative staff.
"...Mi Zhu is right," Guan Yu concurred. "Another toast!"
"...That is Mi Zhu...?" Kongming said to Xu Shu as the uproar of celebration started again.

"Yes," Xu Shu confirmed. "His brother Mi Fang is the young man in green sitting opposite him."

"...So they are Liu Bei's sponsors," Kongming mused aloud.

"If you could *refrain* from saying such things...?" Xu Shu whispered irritably. "Mi Zhu and Mi Fang are very influential in Liu Bei's army... suggesting they bought that influence is ill-advised."

"...I said nothing of the sort," Kongming insisted as he looked at some of the other men that were present. "Mister Sun Qian is the old gentleman sat near Lord Liu...?"

"Yes," Xu Shu replied.

"...**Who's this...?**" a voice barked; Xu Shu shuddered reflexively as Zhang Fei loomed over Kongming, who grinned broadly and looked up at the general without fear.

"...Zhuge Liang," Xu Shu replied nervously. "K-Kongming... Zhuge Kongming."

"...Fancy yourself, don't you...?" Zhang Fei suggested as he prodded Kongming's feather fan with the half-eaten chicken wing he was holding.

"...You must be Zhang Yide," Kongming replied calmly.

"Zhang *Fei*," Zhang Fei barked in response. "Don't get familiar with me, I don't know you from a dog in Jiangdong."

"...My apologies," Kongming said with amusement.

"Why are you here...?" Zhang Fei asked bluntly.

"I invited him, so that he might meet Lord Liu," Xu Shu answered.

"...Why would Xuande want to meet this idiot...?" Zhang Fei growled as he eyed Kongming contemptuously. "He's a baby! Look at that fluffy beard! And the robes! And that stupid fan!"

"...General Zhang," a nearby general interrupted, "I think Lord Liu is urging you to return to your seat."

"...You'll speak to 'Lord Liu' the day my arse falls off," Zhang Fei growled at the cheerfully smiling Kongming. "...*Bastard pedant*."

With that, Zhang Fei returned to his seat, harrumphing angrily.

"...That went very well," Kongming said through a false, pride-saving grin.

"...Sorry," Xu Shu sighed. "Maybe you should leave."

"No, I'm here now," Kongming chuckled miserably. "Maybe, if I'm lucky, I'll get insulted again later."

The festivities continued. Many of the scholars left early, and eventually, many generals – including Zhao Yun, Guan Yu and Zhang Fei – left to pursue other things. Those that remained moved closer to Liu Bei so that he could talk to them: Kongming silently noted Liu Bei's charismatic air as he took a new seat.

"...Master Xu," Liu Bei hailed with a slight bow: Xu Shu smiled, and returned the gesture appropriately with a lower bow. "...Your knowledge of the topography and your agreed suggestion that we use fire was what won the day," Liu Bei praised.

"As you say," Xu Shu replied awkwardly, "the suggestion was shared by wiser men than I, and the topography was not entirely of my design either."

"Oh...?" a middle-aged man in adviser's robes chuckled: Liu Bei struggled to hide a smile as the man – his old friend Jian Yong – added, "It was my understanding that you planted every tree in Bowang yourself only last week."

"Master Jian," Xu Shu giggled nervously, "I meant that...!"

"Please," Liu Bei snickered, "leave the man be. Master Xu, your talent is obvious... might I ask, good sir, who the young man in Taoist robes is that sits with you...?"
All eyes turned to Kongming, who fanned himself calmly, and nodded slightly in small respect of Liu Bei.
"....*Bow*," Xu Shu urged desperately.
Kongming grinned, and bowed a little.
"You... you are twenty, if that," Jian Yong suggested. "Tell me, son, who let you in here, and what fool scholar let you play with his fan...?"
Many of those present smiled as Kongming failed to answer.
"...His age should not be an issue," Liu Bei said after an overly long period of awkward silence. "...After all, how old were *we*, when we set out of our village together to vanquish the rebels...?"
"...True," Jian Yong admitted. "...But this one has an air of the self-important about him; sorry, but you still haven't provided your name, friend."
"...My family name is Zhuge, given name, Liang," Kongming replied politely. "My style name is Kongming... my Taoist name, Crouching Dragon. I am twenty-two, and I tend farmland in Longzhong by day."
"...My, haven't you a lot of names," Jian Yong cooed sarcastically.
"...'Crouching Dragon'...?" Liu Bei noted.
"The local literati talk a lot about you," Mister Sun said as he rubbed his chin. "They say you're a gifted mind... tell me, what reputed works have you read...?"
"...I have perused the odes, and I am aware of other literary works," Kongming replied. "I consider the pursuit of knowledge to be about what one learns, rather than what one can recall."
"*Do you now...?*" Jian Yong chuckled as Mister Sun huffed irritably.
"As for the local men speaking well of me... well, I am fond of reciting poetry, but pretty words do not win wars," Kongming continued calmly as he made eye contact with Liu Bei.
"...Strategies, like those laid-down by the great Zhang Liang, Jiang Ziya, or perhaps, more relevantly, Yue Yi and Guan Zhong, are what win the day."
"...So you see yourself as *Guan Zhong*," Jian Yong scoffed. "And *Yue Yi*...! ...My friend, go home. This is not the place for an overinflated ego such as yours."
"Whatever my demeanour may suggest, I am no egotist," Kongming insisted. "I present myself as I do to maintain composure... which one must do to ensure victory in the face of defeat."
"...I have followed Lord Liu Xuande since he first set out," Jian Yong replied cuttingly. "I was there when he crushed the Yellow Turbans, defended Yu for Tao Qian, contested Lü Bu for Xu Province, and faced down Xiahou Dun this very day at Bowang. Where were *you*, farm boy...?"
"...That's a little harsh," Liu Bei said empathetically. "Remember, I have to endure remarks about being a sandal weaver, Xianhe... it does not sit well with me to judge the man on his origins, even if he does liken himself to men beyond his calibre."

"Who's doing that...?" Jian Yong retorted. "I merely point out that we have shared numerous battles... what do *you* know, 'Zhuge Kongming, Hidden Lizard', that you can preach to us about the dos and don'ts of warfare...?"

"...A man does not need to live a life to know of it," Kongming replied. "Know the topography; know your enemy; know your own limits; dictate your enemy's perception of you. The battle today was won by knowing and accepting you were outnumbered, knowing Xiahou Dun was easily provoked, knowing that Bowang was a good staging ground for a fire attack, and knowing that you needed to lure your enemy with a show of incompetence. Victory hinged on *what*...? ...That it didn't rain, that Li Dian didn't talk Xiahou Dun into exercising caution. Even with all the pieces in place, victory was based on luck and hope. And almost always, it is based on perception... an undefeatable man can win bloodlessly by showing his true strength in his actions... a composed man on the verge of defeat can win a victory by sowing doubt in his enemies' minds... a strong man can lure his foe to defeat with a show of weakness. Is this not all true...?"

Liu Bei studied Kongming uneasily, and he was visibly unsure if the young man was truly as intelligent as he seemed to be, or whether the words outweighed his true potential.

"...Well met," Jian Yong conceded, bowing to Kongming slightly. "Whatever your true worth, your debating skills are sound enough; tell me, do you intend to one day hold an official post...?"

Xu Shu – who had remained quiet throughout the debate – waited for what he felt was an obvious response from Kongming.

"...No," Kongming replied: Xu Shu was taken aback. "...My wife and I plan a family, and my land needs to be worked... there are others that can serve the cause of the Han far better than I... as you say, I am no Guan Zhong or Yue Yi."

Mister Sun scoffed, got up, and left the group.

"Your devotion to your family is commendable," Jian Yong sighed. "Perhaps if you are not so strong of will as to commit yourself to a greater mission, it is better that you remain on your land."

"Exactly my thinking," Kongming replied, grinning cheerfully.

"...Uh...!" Xu Shu exclaimed.

The ensemble melted away awkwardly, until only Xu Shu, Jian Yong, Liu Bei and Kongming were left.

"...Your family is well connected, is it not...?" Jian Yong asked.

Kongming smiled.

"Zhuge Kongming has a brother in Jiangdong, in the service of Sun Quan," Xu Shu answered uncomfortably for his silent friend. "His sisters are married into the Pang and Kuai clans, and his wife is the niece of Lady Cai, wife of Liu Biao."

"*Oh*...?" Liu Bei said with interest.

"Ah... so you hope to serve Liu Biao, then...?" Jian Yong prompted. "Or do you plan to join your brother in Jiangdong...? ...Or perhaps follow your equal, 'Young Phoenix' Pang Tong, into service in Jing...?"

"...So you *are* aware of us, then," Kongming chuckled.

"Like Mister Sun, I have spoken with able minds, and your name arises often, Zhuge Kongming," Jian Yong replied. "...You didn't answer my question."

Kongming looked at Liu Bei as he replied, "I have no desire to leave my cottage."

Liu Bei hummed ambiguously; Jian Yong smiled sadly.

"...Mister Xu," Jian Yong hailed. "Your contribution to today's victory was appreciated. Today, I am glad that you got to meet Lord Liu. I hope that you will be remaining with us."

"...I shall," Xu Shu replied uneasily as he eyed the quiet, reserved Kongming, who continued to fan himself casually.

"...Thank you," Jian Yong said with a slight bow to Xu Shu. "And Zhuge Kongming... I hope that one day the 'Crouching Dragon' decides to rise... a farmer's life, though honest and vital, is not for you, I think."

"...Should the day arise when my interest in the exigencies of the age grows beyond a casual one," Kongming replied politely, "I should certainly be glad to share what little talent I have with you to benefit the cause of restoring the Han."

Liu Bei eyed Kongming and nodded slowly, as though some sudden realisation had come over him; Kongming grinned broadly, got up from his seat, bowed, and prepared to take his leave.

"...I... I don't believe what you just did," Xu Shu exclaimed as he walked through the dark streets of Xinye with Kongming an hour later.

"Neither do I," Kongming admitted with a strange laugh. "I think... I think it was the right decision, though."

"...The right...!" Xu Shu said with exasperation. "You...! ...That was the opportunity of a lifetime!"

"Was it...?" Kongming retorted with a slight tinge of humour in his tone.

"Yes!" Xu Shu insisted. "You... you just turned down a personal offer of work from Lord Liu, a man that you yourself said was one of the heroes of the age! I thought... I mean, I thought that you...!"

"Jian Yong was enquiring after my plans for the future," Kongming interrupted. "It was he, not Lord Liu, that drove the conversation. That was a test... I passed it."

"...A test...?" Xu Shu murmured.

"Yes, a test," Kongming replied. "I am twenty-two years of age, Yuanzhi... if I were to offer my services now, I would be a petty adviser, a clerk in Jian Yong's office, and be so for years to come. When a ravenous man begs for food, he gets scraps. When a nourished man is offered food... he eats well, and lives content."

"...Nonsense!" Xu Shu said with disdain. "...Nonsense! What, you think he's going to come back to you now that you've humiliated him, told him to his face that you're 'happy to stay in your cottage'...?"

"...I guarantee it," Kongming replied. "Not now... not straight away... but he will."


************

## 7

As soon as Kongming finished relaying his eventful trip to his stunned wife Yueying, his brother Jun, and his father-in-law Mister Huang, he sipped his tea and awaited the response.

"…You turned him down…?" Mister Huang chuckled. "You really are a cheeky one. I like you for it, but at the same time…"

"The battle sounded like a waking nightmare," Yueying noted quietly. "Perhaps it is for the best."

"But then you said you felt like you could do it, Elder Brother!" Jun exclaimed. "I don't understand… why did you turn it down…?"

"Firstly, I am not ready," Kongming replied. "To join Liu Bei's service is as easy as turning over one's hand. To be of *genuine* service… to stand at his side, conduct his battles, or preside over court… for that, I'm not ready. I'm not ready to handle those roles, and I'm not old enough to be accepted by the pillars of his cause, like old Mister Sun, Guan Yu, and Zhang Fei. I would be a minor clerk, and play a tiny, inconsequential role… no, no, brother, I know what I'm doing."

"…I don't doubt that, even if others do," Mister Huang said seriously. "But what if others come seeking your service, like Sun Quan, and Cao Cao…?"

"Cao Cao, *never*," Kongming scoffed. "Sun Quan… has too many men around him as it is. I would simply be another… he has Zhou Yu, and Lu Su, and Zhang Zhao… so what need has he for Zhuge Liang…?"

"Your friends are going to be annoyed," Mister Huang noted. "If I were you, I'd steer clear of them, even your new 'sworn brother'."

"On the contrary," Kongming replied, "I intend to have it out with them. I'm heading to the city tomorrow, and I shall meet them in a tavern for a debate… let them challenge me."

"…So explain," a young man in patterned robes prompted as Kongming sat within a six-strong group that was seen as some of the brightest young stars in Jing Province.

"…Explain what…?" Kongming chuckled as he fanned himself. "I was offered a minor role in a petty office, and I refused it, brother Meng."

"…Lord Liu Xuande's forces… 'petty'…?" Meng Jian exclaimed. The two young men that sat either side of him – Shi Tao, and Cui Zhouping – shook their heads.

"Perhaps there is sense in his actions," another young man – whose eyebrows were characteristically dashed with white hairs – suggested hesitantly. "Do we know…"

"…Jichang," Meng Jian retorted, "even for men of lesser intellect than yours, there to be no excuse for not knowing who Lord Liu Xuande is!"

"Of course I know who he is!" Ma Liang protested. "Let me finish! I am saying that I think Brother Kongming is very sensible… there is perhaps some good reason in refusing to serve Lord Liu at this moment in time… like ascertaining his motivations, and considering our worth to him at this point…?"

"...I agree," another, slightly older man – Yi Ji – declared. "Lord Liu is in a precarious situation at the moment, and it would do well to let him establish himself properly before we go offering our energies to his cause. We might end up with low-ranking jobs, and never advance beyond them."

"How so...?" Cui Zhouping challenged. "Pang Tong is an Officer of Merit in Jing Province! Xu Shu is an adviser to Lord Liu! They are not petty roles, so why should any of us do any worse...?"

"Xu Shu has already offered to put in a good word for us," Shi Tao said in agreement. "You're going against your reputation, taking a big risk by..."

"...Not at all," Kongming replied calmly. "Lord Liu has in his service some very stalwart, stubborn types that I need to impress. You all know that."

"Zhang Fei," Shi Tao snickered. "Didn't he lose Xu Province for Lord Liu...?"

"Hearsay," Kongming insisted.

"...Wasn't he drunk when you met him...?" Cui Zhouping challenged.

"Yes, but most of them were... they'd just won a battle that, had it gone the other way, could have meant annihilation," Kongming countered. "Zhang Yide is a good man at heart... he dislikes pedants, and I can't blame him, to be honest... Mister Sun was pompous, arrogant, and cares only for what texts a man has read."

"...You did tell him that you're versed in every text worth reading...?" Shi Tao supposed.

Kongming shook his head slowly and grinned.

"...Why not...?" Meng Jian wondered.

"As I told Lord Liu, it is stratagems, not pretty words, that win wars," Kongming replied. "I saw the Battle of Bowang. I stood on the hill, and watched. I watched Lord Liu ride out to what could have been certain death... I watched the legions of Cao Cao descend on the place... I watched, heard, and smelled them burning alive in the ambush."

Cui Zhouping, Shi Tao, and Meng Jian balked at the idea.

"...To *see* such a thing... is sobering," Kongming admitted. "I *heard* about Cao Cao's attacks on Xu Province, but I'd never *seen* such a thing, so it was a fearful vision, not to be relied upon. To smell burning flesh, hear the screams of the dying... and then, only moments later, watch men shout in triumph at the 'victory'... and then, after the momentary horror of witnessing a celebration of death, to realise that it was a celebration of *life*... they had survived, and were glad to be alive. The deaths... they were necessary to sustain their own lives. To have to think in such a way, I thought, was barbaric... until I mused it further, and then I thought of every animal I have killed to feed a family, clothe a man... and once I saw the parallels, I saw that there is no difference... I ascertained that, cruel though it is, it is Heaven's design... and who am I to question it...?"

"...But then, if you 'understand' this thing, why turn down the offer...?" Meng Jian protested despairingly.

"Because I must have answers ready for Lord Liu's questions," Kongming replied casually. "I had none, I realised… I thought I had, but… I didn't, not really. Now, I know, I truly know… and I must put into words and figures all that I have come to understand, so that when we speak again, I…"

"Uh," Shi Tao interrupted, as Cui Zhouping and Meng Jian both tried to refrain from bursting into laughter, "you don't really think *he'll* come to *you*…?"

"…I will present him with my own interpretation of the tripod theorem," Kongming continued amid groans from the three doubters.

"That theorem is too easily questioned!" Cui Zhouping suggested. "I know that men like Lu Su are bandying it about… but please, Kongming, a smart man like you…? You know, as one of your oldest friends, that I speak frankly because I care about your reputation. …What *tripod*…? There are currently what, seven notable warlords…?"

"Six," Kongming replied as he started to fan himself slowly. "Yuan Shao is dead: else Cao Cao would not be so confident in confronting Liu Biao."

"Six," Cui Zhouping conceded. "Liu Biao, Sun Quan, Cao Cao, Liu Bei, Liu Zhang, Zhang Lu; six. ….**Six**. …So how do you envision a tripod…?"

"…The latter two you mention are doomed," Kongming insisted. "Lui Bei will come to power in Jing eventually, and then he will come to occupy Yi…"

"Really…?" Meng Jian said plainly. "I think, Kongming, that… that maybe you need to rethink yourself."

Kongming stared at Cui Zhouping, Shi Tao and Meng Jian with irritation: Cui Zhouping smiled, and said, "Come now… where is our usual jovial banter? …Kongming, let us consider the debate a draw, and say no more of it. It isn't worth ruining our friendship over, is it…? How about you recite for us a poem…?"

"…Very well," Kongming sighed. He began to recite a favourite poem of his, one about mourning the lost: originally, he had recited it in memory of his father, but now, as he closed his eyes to recall it, he saw the burning soldiers at Bowang, the cheering Zhang Fei, and the charismatic face of Liu Bei, whose strong eyes betrayed an indescribable desire to be a force of change.

Later, Cui Zhouping, Shi Tao and Meng Jian decided to join another noted figure in a lively debate about the meanings of ancient texts: Ma Liang and Yi Ji decided to remain with the sober, ponderous Kongming.

"…Go and join the others," Kongming urged as the other two men sat staring at him with wonder and concern. On the other side of the tavern, the now tipsy Cui Zhouping was reciting a well-known folk tale, to everyone's amusement.

"…What you were saying," Ma Liang prompted, "about the tripod theorem… there are those that say it is unworkable… I am wondering, why do you see it can work…? I have my own ideas, but… I should like to hear yours."

"…So would I," Yi Ji sighed, "but… I should go. Stay well, Kongming, Jichang… I'll see you both around sometime soon, I hope."

With that, Yi Ji left the tavern.

"...The tripod theorem is not completely sound, I admit," Kongming sighed, "but it is workable, provided one is creative. If Liu Bei were to somehow claim Yi, and inherit Jing from Liu Biao..."

"...Perhaps," Ma Liang said quietly. "My only surety is that Liu Biao is unfit to rule Jing Province."

"Oh, that is certainly true," Kongming chuckled. "Having met him... yes, Liu Bei is definitely the man who will torment Cao Cao in the years to come, not Liu Biao."

"...Brother," Ma Liang said hesitantly, "I should be grateful if you could explain to me all that you have come to understand; I hope one day to advance myself, and..."

"...Jichang," Kongming interrupted with a laugh, "I'd say that you are far from a fool, and my equal, so don't be so humble. In fact, I expect you to be in Lord Liu's service before I am. ...Oh, I forgot to ask, I really am slipping; how is your brother's studying going...?"

"...He's bright," Ma Liang replied. "I think Su will do very well one day."

"...Then today, I feel glad," Kongming said with cheer. "I have a wonderful wife... worthy brothers, blood and sworn... marvellous friends... and one day, we'll help to shape the fate of the land. What more could anyone want...?"

Ma Liang smiled, as he was sure that Kongming spoke rightly. But it would be some time before all would be clear.

************

## 8

Over the next few years, Kongming's life was very quiet. Cao Cao turned his attentions to other concerns, and Jing Province enjoyed a brief respite from war. After three years of silence, the southern warlord Sun Quan finally began his campaign of revenge by launching – as expected – an attack on Huang Zu, the prefect of Jiangxia in eastern Jing, and the man considered responsible for the death of Sun Quan's father. This new conflict made for an uneasy time in Xinye City, where Liu Bei's army was mostly based, and where he was cultivating popularity amongst the people while he waited for orders from his landlord, Liu Biao.

Kongming returned home from a day of hard work, and noted that a familiar coat had been placed, neatly folded, by the door.
"...Elder Brother...?" Kongming mused: he entered the he pondered the possible meaning of the visit as he entered the living quarters.
"Liang...!" Zhuge Jin hailed.
Kongming took a moment to observe the scene.
Zhuge Jin was dressed in casual robes, not those of an official. His face was weathered with age, but he was still the kindly, familiar man that Kongming remembered. Yueying was sat quietly, her head hung low, as though something was upsetting her; Jun, Kongming's younger brother, was also sat uncomfortably.
"...Elder Brother Jin," Kongming said with a smile: he bowed slightly, and then the two brothers embraced.
"...I have been speaking with your lady wife," Jin explained. "Lady Huang is an extraordinary woman... very insightful, and worldly. You've chosen your lifetime companion well."
"My thanks for your accolades," Kongming replied numbly: he could now guess why his wife was so quietly distressed.
"...How is your family...?" Kongming asked plainly.
"Very well," Jin replied. "Our oldest son is now more than two, and still healthy... our second son, born only so very recently, is also doing well. The air in Jiangdong is good, the likelihood of stability and peace increasing day by day... you and your family should visit us someday, and see it for yourself."
"...I expect that business will take me in that direction sooner or later," Kongming replied as he took up his fan and started waving it slowly to calm himself.
"I hope so," Jin said warmly.
"...So in general, you are prosperous," Kongming supposed.
"Sun Quan is a good, wise ruler," Jin suggested as the youngest brother, Jun, left the room. "He treats all of his vassals with courtesy... he avoids needless conflict, pursuing only noble endeavours, and is magnanimous."
"...Forgive my directness, Elder Brother, but to say that he avoids needless conflict is entirely the opposite of the truth," Kongming said with an irritated laugh.
"You...!" Jin exclaimed: Kongming walked past him slowly, and sat next to Yueying, who was grateful for his presence.

"By continuing to ignore the situation north of the Great River, here in the real world, your master continues to forsake the true for the false," Kongming suggested. "He disregards the usurpation of Han by seditious traitors, instead looking only at expanding the territory he governs, and continuing his feud with Liu Biao. How is petty revenge a noble endeavour, and saving the royal house from Cao Cao a needless conflict...?"

"...You understand nothing, being here in this thatched cottage," Jin retorted cuttingly. "You labour on fields, and pontificate with little groups of friends, ignorant of the true state of the world!"

"On the contrary," Kongming chuckled, "I am renowned for my understanding of the age we live in."

"By who...?" Jin challenged. "By pedantic scholars and elder statesmen of Jing Province, whose allegiances are to Liu Biao...? ...Their opinions are biased, Younger Brother. Remember that I, too, hail from this region, but I have had my eyes opened... everyone knows that the Sun family have always treated their vassals well, earning their loyalty for generations: look at the men around Lord Sun, and you can see that their loyalty to him is as strong as his sincere faith and gratitude for their service... your friend, Pang Tong, is now seeking a future in Jiangdong... Kongming, it is *you* that should not forsake the true for the false. Sun Quan is of noble heritage..."

"...An unsubstantiated claim that he is descended from Sun Tzu," Kongming countered. "What is certainly true is what is certainly known: in recent times, the Sun family have been lapdogs for the other warlords... tell me, Jin, what nobility there was in his father serving *Yuan Shu*...?"

"...You know nothing," Jin retorted angrily. "Sun Quan's brother was..."

"...Likened to a barbarian king, hailed as 'The Little Conqueror'," Kongming interrupted sternly. "Like his father before him, he was assassinated after instigating a petty feud that had nothing to do with the true matters of the day. One wonders what pathetic end Sun Quan will suffer, since his line is obviously doomed to it."

"*You*...!" Jin exclaimed again.

"You bring this on yourself," Kongming suggested. "You enter our home unannounced, and begin courting me for a role in some clerk's office in Jiangdong."

"I had no such intention!" Jin insisted. "I was just visiting my home!"

"Nonsense," Kongming scoffed. "You have not visited home until now... content with letters and gifts to placate us... no, Elder Brother, you came here to 'pluck me from obscurity'."

"...Kongming," Jin protested, "I confess, since you press the matter, that I intended to broach the matter of your joining me in Jiangdong... and I fail to understand your attitude. I hear that *Liu Bei* is sounding you out, and I *despair*! Why would you want to even consider entering the service of such a man...?"

"...What is his crime, that you call him 'such a man'...?" Kongming challenged.

"He has no promise," Jin suggested. "My lord wants to know about all of those who would be his enemies and rivals... he knows of Liu Bei. Since his founding days as a weaver of sandals, Bei has been aware of his tenuous connection to the imperial house, and has expressed a desire to be emperor, to the amusement of his peers."

"A child's whimsies," Kongming countered. "You wanted to rule Jing Province."

"...That aside," Jin – though flustered – continued, "he finally embarked on a mission to face a small contingent of Yellow Turbans, financed by horse merchants and butchers... his success won him a prefecture, which he then lost due to administrative incompetence."

"Conjecture," Kongming suggested, "but carry on."

"...He's wavered and meandered, this way and that, serving pretty much every lord in the region... and turning on them, one by one," Jin heckled. "He's ended up here, broken and disgraced, hiding in Liu Biao's shadow. Who in their right mind would want to serve such an incompetent, treacherous nomad, a man *without a home*...?"

"Sun Jian was a willing hired vassal of a would-be emperor, who himself had designs on the throne," Kongming retorted. "He met his end under rocks and arrows, a mere underling... his son's territory was acquired by force, not benevolence, using troops borrowed or stolen from his father's master. Who in their right mind would want to serve such an unscrupulous, devious autocrat, a man whose home was *stolen*...?"

"...It is true that you are strong in debate," Jin conceded. "We could do this all day... but I know that I would not win you over. You have made up your mind... I shall press the matter no further."

"...Perhaps you might also want to apologise to my wife for your insinuation that she has been unable to provide me with a child," Kongming said ominously.

Yueying looked at her husband with swollen, teary eyes.

"...I meant no offence," Jin insisted. "If any was taken by my poorly chosen words, then I beg forgiveness from you both."

"What then, was your intention...?" Kongming asked.

"I simply said that, since I now have two sons, there was always the possibility of your adopting one of them," Jin explained. "It is not meant as offence... the Liu Bei you hold so dear has an adopted son because he has yet to father a son of his own... and that child is not even a Liu by blood. *Surely* what is good enough for *Liu Bei* is good enough for *you*, Kongming...?"

"Again, your tone drifts towards contempt," Kongming seethed. "Why do you bear me such hostility...?"

"I am frustrated with you!" Jin admitted. "I *love you*, brother! We grew up in this house together, you and I, and we were solid as a rock! Now we are a land apart, opposite sides of the Great River, serving different masters, and *enemies*, no less! How can this not be distressing to me???"

"If your master were to follow the example he expects his generals to abide, then Sun and Liu would be allies this very day," Kongming replied calmly.

Jin knew and understood what the cutting remark referred to, and exhaled wearily.

"...Forgive me," Jin sighed. "You are as knowledgeable as they say... I cannot argue with you. ...Once again, I apologise... but my offer still stands, Kongming. If you and your graceful lady wife would condescend to adopting my youngest son, I should be most humbly grateful. And I meant no offence... after all, I am seven years your senior, and have only just started a family myself."

Before Kongming could answer, Yueying broke the etiquette of the day and said, "Even we are blessed with children born of our love, we would be honoured."

"...Lady Huang, you are peerless among women in your wisdom," Jin declared. "I envy you Kongming, for having such a wife by your side."

"...I suggest we refrain from further political debate," Kongming sighed wearily; he stopped fanning himself, and lowered his arm. "...Let us be brothers, and not ministers: let us be friends."

Jin smiled gratefully. For the rest of the day, the atmosphere was relaxed and warm, as Zhuge Jin fondly recalled his own time in the forest cottage.

Later that night – once Zhuge Jin was settled into the family guest room – Kongming and Yueying sat together silently in the living quarters, facing each other. Kongming was fanning himself once again.

"I hope you do not hold it against me that we have been unable to hold a child in our arms," Yueying said suddenly. "Perhaps it is not just my looks that are poor."

"...*Nonsense*...!" Kongming chuckled softly: he put the fan down, and embraced Yueying warmly. "We are busy, we are stressed... and as my brother said, even a mighty warlord like Liu Xuande, a man with two wives and concubines, has yet to father a son between them all. It is not a sign of weakness... it is, perhaps, a sign that we are to be doubly blessed. After all, do not people say, 'Great things come to those who wait'...?"

"You always know what to say," Yueying whispered miserably.

"...Not always," Kongming sighed. "Today, my brother challenged me on the reputation of Lord Liu... I must wonder if there is any truth in his interpretation, and decide whether that will affect my decision to assist him. I must heed my own words as well, and not ally myself with Sun Quan simply because it will reunite us in Jiangdong."

"You have much to ponder," Yueying murmured.

"Yes... and you have *nothing* to ponder, with regards to our happy home," Kongming insisted. "We have each other, and when Heaven blesses us, it will be when the time is right. Neither of us are at fault... it is Heaven's will. ...And to me, you are beautiful within and without... let no man say otherwise."

Yueying tightened her embrace slightly, and the two sat quietly, wrapped in their own thoughts about the future that lay ahead of them.

************

## 9

Zhuge Jin returned to Jiangdong after staying in his old home for a few days. Kongming pondered the encounter, but it was not long before he would be left pondering another.

"...Someone walking over the bridge," Zhuge Jun said as he approached his brother Kongming, who was sat reading an old text that was etched into a bamboo scroll.

"...Ma Liang...?" Kongming supposed without looking up: he had been expecting a visit from his sworn brother for a few days.

"No... 'Mister Yes'," Jun chuckled as he disappeared again.

"...Master Sima Hui...!" Kongming realised: he got up and rushed to greet the noted gentleman, who had travelled from the southern region of Jing province.

"...Ah, Kongming!" Mister Sima hailed. "All is well...?"

"Very," Kongming replied as he bowed in respect to the old gentleman. "My wife is currently visiting her father... we are both well, and..."

"Very good, yes! Very good!" Mister Sima replied cheerfully.

"And Jun is well, as you know," Kongming continued. "Ma Liang visits a lot... I still haven't been back to Xinye in any..."

"Very good, yes!" Mister Sima interrupted. "Yes, yes... very good!"

"...What brings you to my humble thatched cottage, Master...?" Kongming prompted, as he was aware that the pleasantries could become monotonous.

"I received a visit," Mister Sima proclaimed. "I spoke to Lord Liu Xiande!"

"...Really...?" Kongming replied: it had been three years since his own meeting with Liu Bei, and there had still been no attempt from Liu Bei's camp to contact Kongming at all.

"Yes," Mister Sima said cheerfully. "Very good man, very good indeed."

"...And... did anything eventful transpire...?" Kongming prompted: he was used to Mister Sima, who was very eccentric, and he knew that he needed to find the correct approach to continuing the conversation, else he would be locked in a repetitive stream of "Yes!" and "Very Good!" for the rest of the afternoon.

"Lord Liu asked if there were any capable men that I could name," Mister Sima reported, "his having heard that I was well informed of the talents of the day."

"...So Lord Liu is finally starting to realise his dependency on good advice," Kongming chuckled. "Master, I presume you guided him in the direction of such notables as Ma Liang, Cui Zhouping, Pang Degong, and Shi Tao...?"

"...**Very good, very good!**" Mister Sima said with a hearty laugh. "In fact, although they are, as you say, men of merit, I in fact said only two Taoist names: Crouching Dragon, and Young Phoenix!"

"...And, Master, his response was...?" Kongming asked with trepidation.

"I added further," Mister Sima continued, "that such men are not to be summoned... such men are to be *sought out*!"

"...You did...?" Kongming exclaimed with desperation. "And... what did he say to that, Master...?"

"Very good! ...Very good!" Mister Sima chuckled.

"No, really, Master, what did he say...?" Kongming prompted.

"He may visit you: that is all that he said," Mister Sima replied.

"...I see," Kongming sighed, since there was no absolute in the statement.

"He also said," Mister Sima added: Kongming ignored his frustration at the elder's way of doing things, and awaited the rest of the statement. "He also said that he may like to visit you soon. He has been meaning to do so... he said that as well."

Kongming hid his gratitude that his gut instinct had been right, and said, "My thanks, Master, for telling me of this... I am ready now, for whatever day he should choose to visit me."

"Don't be too eager," Mister Sima warned suddenly. "Remember..."

"...A ravenous beggar only gets scraps," Kongming chuckled. "I know... Lord Liu is a shrewd man... a man that does not care for those that will be of no use to him. If he now intends to visit me sincerely... then we are both ready."

"Very good, very good!" Mister Sima said with cheer: he clapped his hands together and laughed boisterously. "Yes, yes, very, *very* good indeed!"

"...Will you now be staying...?" Kongming asked. "I can have one of the lads prepare tea."

"Very good, very good!" Mister Sima chuckled. "...But I must be going. You take care, you and your family... there will be exciting times ahead."

Kongming bowed low: Mister Sima gestured for him to rise, bowed slightly, and departed, leaving Kongming to wonder how he should prepare for the upcoming visit by Liu Bei.

Days passed: it was springtime, and the days were cool and breezy. One evening, Kongming sat quietly, Yueying at his side, as the two read over some texts that Kongming had been writing.

"I think that he will be impressed," Yueying suggested kindly.

"No, no, not like this," Kongming fretted. "I must commit it all to mind."

"...You know it backwards," Yueying giggled. "You could probably draw the map from memory as well."

"...Yes... the map," Kongming sighed uncomfortably. "I know this is going to sound... bizarre... but..."

"You are not going to present the map," Yueying guessed.

"...You know me well," Kongming said softly. "...I suppose you know why, too."

"Because you do not fully trust Liu Bei," Yueying replied calmly. "Wang Mang of old times promised to defend the Han, and ended up usurping it and ruling by fear."

"Precisely," Kongming said with a congratulatory tone. "We have already had Dong Zhuo, Yuan Shu, Li Jue, Guo Si... and Cao Cao, all coveting the throne. What if Lord Liu is no better than them at heart...? ...I must speak with him, learn his innermost thoughts, learn his true motives... it is only by refusing to impart my knowledge that I will see him for who he truly is. If he grows impatient, and starts to bully me for the things that he wants to know, or leaves and does not return... then he not the man he claims to be."

50

"…I agree," Yueying said hesitantly. "If he is what you believe him to be… then you present him with the map…?"

"…More than that," Kongming admitted. "I will pledge allegiance to him, and promise to do all I can to make that map's vision a reality. If he really is that forthright… then it will be a wonderful thing to follow a just cause."

"…If we had a son," Yueying said suddenly, "What do you think he would grow up to do…?"

"…Whatever he dreamed of," Kongming replied. "I'd let him choose, as I did."

Kongming and Yueying embraced, and said no more.

The next day, a youth wearing the battle tunic of Liu Bei's army was spotted loitering near the bridge that led to Kongming's forest home.

"…Brother…!" Jun exclaimed.

"I know, I know… I saw him," Kongming replied uneasily.

"This is exciting…!" Jun said with glee.

"Why…?" Kongming asked calmly.

"…Because… be… because…" Jun said with sudden discomfort. "…B-but… he's… he's a Lord Liu… soldier."

"**Lad!**" Kongming bellowed: one of the servant boys that was employed at the Zhuge household ran into the living quarters and awaited instructions.

"…Find out… why he's here," Kongming ordered sternly: the boy left the house and crossed the bridge to speak to the soldier.

"…What's wrong…?" Yueying asked as she entered the living quarters, dressed as if to receive guests.

"…I'd rather you weren't seen," Kongming said with reflexive concern and warmth. "Just in case he… *isn't friendly.*"

Yueying disappeared into the sleeping quarters without another word, and Kongming started to fan himself slowly.

"There're more soldiers," Jun noted. He was correct, as a whole battalion of Liu Bei's infantrymen were now advancing on the land on the far side of the bridge. "…Brother… why's he brought so many soldiers…? I thought he wanted to talk to you."

"…I won't lie, this offends me," Kongming said angrily. "You do not bring a legion to chat with a scholar… the man is unschooled in good etiquette."

"Wait… who's that lot coming now…?" Jun wondered aloud.

Kongming looked to the distance: another group of soldiers, this time on horseback, was approaching.

"…This is starting to get a little intimidating," Kongming admitted.

Liu Bei, Guan Yu and Zhang Fei were leading the new group of cavalry: Kongming watched as Liu Bei appeared to berate Zhang Fei before seemingly dismissing the infantrymen with a harsh gesture.

"…Ah, I see," Kongming chuckled softly. "It's okay, brother… it seems that Lord Liu's subordinates have different ideas about 'paying me a visit'."

"Oh… does that mean we're okay then?" Jun asked warily.

"Yes, I just said so, didn't I…?" Kongming said with a laugh. "Go on, find something to do… this is a man I need to speak to alone."

Liu Bei was now approaching the cottage alone, having left his generals, bodyguard force and soldiers on the land past the bridge. Kongming's servant lad greeted Liu Bei, and guided him toward the cottage slowly and cautiously. Liu Bei had discarded his cloak and hooded travelling coat, but he was still an intimidating sight: he wore a green robe emblazoned with dragons, and an elaborate golden hairpiece over his long, wound hair. He carried a sword at his side, and wore light mail under the robe: the servant boy noted all of this worriedly.

"...Master!" the lad called as he reached the door: Kongming walked to the entrance, waving his fan casually and smiling cheerfully.

"Master Crouching Dragon," Liu Bei hailed. "It is a pleasure to see you again."

"The pleasure is all mine," Kongming replied with a low bow that conveyed deep respect: Liu Bei returned the gesture fully, and Kongming felt at ease at last.

"Please, follow me," Kongming said as he gestured with his fan for Liu Bei to join him in his living quarters: within a short space of time, the two were sat on mats, facing each other, with a pot of tea boiling on a fire in the kitchen.

"...I have been a fool," Liu Bei began frankly. "When Xu Yuanzhi introduced you to me at the banquet, after the battle at Bowang... I was not yet fully tempered, and failed to see your sagely presence."

"I think you overpraise me," Kongming said with a laugh. "When I attended that banquet, I can hardly say that I was on an equal footing with Mister Jian Yong."

"Nonsense," Liu Bei insisted, waving his hand dismissively. "You spoke very well, conducted yourself with dignity... Mister Jian's teasing, Mister Sun's loftiness and Zhang Fei's aggressive attitude were enough to dissuade anyone from placing faith in me, and for that, I apologise."

"No need," Kongming retorted. "I hope that you and your followers are well...?"

"Very well," Liu Bei replied. "Cao Cao has done little more than test us, since he has been busy fighting barbarian hordes to the north... I hear that his chief strategist, Guo Jia, is sickly, and – though I regret saying it – he will not live a long life, which will be a relief to us all, since his schemes have caused us many problems."

"Such a man can be troublesome," Kongming joked as he fanned himself slowly.

"...Indeed, were I in possession of such a man, I could rest easy," Liu Bei said with a nervous laugh. "Cao Cao and I are equals in many ways: he has his Xu Chu, I have Chen Dao. He has Zhang He, I have Zilong. He has Xiahou Dun and Xiahou Yuan as his limbs, and I have Guan Yunchang and Zhang Yide as mine. ...It is his adeptness as finding other talents that separates us."

"...True," Kongming replied frankly. "He has, in addition to those brave generals you mentioned, many more: Li Dian, Yue Jin, Yu Jin, Zhang Liao. Furthermore, he has reliable advisers, Xun Yu and Xun You, Jia Xu... even with the death of Guo Jia. You... do have Jian Yong, yes... but sadly, little else besides. Mister Sun, Mi Zhu, Mi Fang and the others, they are courtiers, not strategists..."

"...What you say is true," Liu Bei sighed.

"It is a pity," Kongming said with exaggerated sadness. "A terrible pity, indeed."

"I wonder," Liu Bei began cautiously, "if... if I might call on you, from time to time, Master, and speak with you about matters that concern me."

"I wonder what I could possibly help a man of your stature with," Kongming said with a laugh. "I'm a scholar, a pedant, a farmer... that's all."

"Not so," Liu Bei retorted. "Mister Sima speaks of you as one of the most envisioned men of the age... he said that you and 'Young Phoenix' were the two most capable minds in the country."

"I doubt that," Kongming countered.

"I believe it," Liu Bei insisted. "Xu Yuanzhi also spoke highly of you... both men agreed that to truly be worthy of your sagely counsel, I should visit you... that is why I am here. I remember what you said before... about not having a desire to leave this cottage... that is why I shall always come to visit you whenever I have a matter that I wish to discuss. If there is ever a day when I visit you and it is not convenient, then I shall leave, and return another day: tell me, Master, is that agreeable to you...?"

"...I... I am genuinely touched by your patronage, Lord," Kongming replied sincerely: he had hardly expected such humility from Liu Bei, especially when no advice had been given thus far. "I agree to your terms, of course... I can see nothing fairer, in all honesty."

"Good!" Liu Bei beamed. "Now, I understand that you saw my battle array at Bowang."

"I did," Kongming replied.

"Our intention was to feign incompetence," Liu Bei continued, "but... it has to be said that we are not fully prepared for a full-scale battle should Cao Cao employ a classic entrapment formation. Xu Yuanzhi... tells me that you are an avid student of the formations... I wonder, might I learn from you a few formations, and perhaps some advice to use in battle that pertains to weather, topography, and such...?"

Kongming got up and walked to the array of bamboo scrolls and rolled-up cloth diagram sheets that he kept on permanent display. As he searched for the appropriate place to begin, Liu Bei stared in wonderment at the diagrams and mantras that adorned the walls of the room.

"Truly," Liu Bei said with awe, "you are a man of learning. You are surrounded at all times with the profundities of the universe... truly marvellous."

"If you say so, Lord Liu," Kongming chuckled as he finally found the text that he had been looking for amongst the scrolls. "Now... let us look at formations first..."


✲✲✲✲✲✲✲✲✲✲✲✲

## 10

"Now Jichang, you must keep this to yourself for now," Kongming concluded.

Ma Liang was silently awestruck.

"...Are you alright, Jichang...?" Kongming asked with amusement as he gestured for a serving boy to fetch tea.

"You... you actually received a visit from *Lord Liu Xuande*...?" Ma Liang noted almost disbelievingly.

"I know, it seemed as though the day would never arrive," Kongming chuckled as he started to fan himself.

"Forgive me, Kongming, but... I never expected it to," Ma Liang admitted. "It isn't that I ever doubted you, brother... I doubted Lord Liu's ability to see your worth."

"He is not as selective as people would have you believe, no," Kongming said sadly. "Many around him are there because they are useful, like the Mi brothers and Mister Sun... but it must be said, there are just as many who are genuine. Before he left, he introduced me to his adopted son, Feng, who seemed to be a noble lad, well raised; I also saw Chen Dao, Guan Yu and Zhang Fei again... they are all of them upright in their own way. Let's put it this way... should I decide to leave this place... there are worse masters to serve than Liu Xuande."

"By 'selective'," Ma Liang prompted, "you mean...?"

"Guan Yu, as you know, has contacts in the 'underworld'... not evil spirits, but bandits," Kongming explained. "Some of Lord Liu's subordinates are also former Yellow Turbans... recruited after he fought alongside them for Yuan Shao. He has in his employ some criminals... but then, what warlord doesn't...?"

"...Sun Quan has whole brigades made up of pirates," Ma Liang noted. "Taishi Ci, one of his most trusted generals, is a wanted criminal, reasons for it aside."

"What's a 'criminal' these days...?" Kongming lamented. "Lord Liu is a criminal, and yet all he wants is to see the Han court restored to order... no, it is Cao Cao that's the criminal. ...If Lord Liu must utilise any resource to get the job done, then... well... so be it."

"I see your concern, though," Ma Liang said sadly. "How can former Yellow Turbans seek the restoration of the court...?"

"Because," Kongming replied, "Lord Liu has made them see that it was the people around the Emperor – the Ten Eunuchs, He Jin, and so on – that were the problem. The new Emperor is young, powerless, and therefore blameless... he is surrounded by evil men, and must be rescued from them before it is too late."

"You really, truly think that Cao Cao may usurp the throne one day...?" Ma Liang fretted.

"Of course he will," Kongming chuckled desperately. "Brother, Cao massacred thousands of a province's population just to avenge one man – his father – whom none of those he killed were responsible for. Such a man... cannot bask in the light of the Emperor for long without wanting to seize the throne, it is inevitable."

"You sound determined to help Lord Liu now," Ma Liang suggested plainly.

"...I do, don't I...?" Kongming realised. "Perhaps I need to regain my sense of objectivity: after all, the aim here is to see if he is truly worthy. I should be more critical... ... ...ah."
"What...?" Ma Liang wondered.
"Brother," Kongming said weakly, "I owe you an apology."
"...What for...?" Ma Liang wondered.
"I... Brother, I got carried away by the moment," Kongming began awkwardly. "As you know, Lord Liu seeks men of talent..."
"Have we gone back to the start of the conversation...?" Ma Liang joked.
"No, you see... before he left, Lord Liu asked indirectly if I knew any other men of talent besides myself and Young Phoenix... since Mister Sima had mentioned nobody else to him," Kongming rambled. "I... well... I mentioned *you*."
Ma Liang's gaze turned sideways as he absorbed the information.
"I told him that silly ditty," Kongming continued, "you know... 'Of the wise brothers Ma in Xiangyang, the best is white-browed Liang', and... well... I didn't expect him to do anything straight away, but..."
"...He wants to recruit me...?" Ma Liang realised with a sudden rush of adrenalin.
"...He wants to recruit *your entire family*," Kongming admitted. "I... I shouldn't have been so casual about it, I should have discussed it with you first, it's just that, well, the opportunity, and previously, you said..."
"Brother...!" Ma Liang exclaimed with tears in his eyes. "I... if we were not already sworn to brotherhood, I would not know what else to say...!"
Ma Liang got up, knelt down, and prostrated himself on the ground at Kongming's feet, pressing his forehead to the ground: this gesture – a kowtow – was the largest bow of respect that one could make. Distressed at the sudden show of overwhelming gratitude, Kongming reached down, took Ma Liang's hands, and pulled him to his feet.
"Please, please, brother Jichang...!" Kongming chuckled uncomfortably. "I..."
"You have done for me a great service, brother!" Ma Liang sobbed. "We... we will all of us be indebted to you for the rest of our days!"
"He'd have come looking for you eventually," Kongming insisted. "He'd heard of the Mas, he'd have..."
"I swear that I will repay you!" Ma Liang bleated as he kowtowed once again.
"Would you stop doing that...?" Kongming said with a nervous laugh. "We're sworn to brotherhood, you and I... no need for such ceremony. I did for you what I would do for any of my family... I'm just glad it's what you wanted."
"...Kongming," Ma Liang said as Kongming helped him back to his feet, "I... I know this is more of another request than reciprocation, but... my brother, Su, is-"
"Quite the burgeoning talent," Kongming interrupted. "I understand that he reads diligently, and is already versing himself in military stratagems: even at the tender age of fifteen, I hear his knowledge equals mine."

"Nonsense…!" Ma Liang chuckled dismissively. "He is really more a reader than a thinker: his words outshine his deeds, I think. He's a little arrogant… he tries to think, but he makes bad choices. I see him trying to understand things… Kongming, you could help him. If you would take him under your wing, tutor him…"

"Mm, well…" Kongming replied uneasily.

"Not now, not now!" Ma Liang insisted. "I know, you and Lady Huang have too much to do for now… when you are not so busy… or maybe when – or if – you yourself join Lord Liu, then we'll all be working together…"

"…So you intend to accept the offer…?" Kongming prompted.

"Of course…!" Ma Liang replied. "I know you have your doubts, Kongming… but you are a man whose talents extend beyond the ordinary. I'm no prodigy, nor are my kin, though we're well read. I… I can do no better."

"…I forget, you don't want to work for Liu Biao," Kongming sighed as he started to fan himself again.

"Liu Biao and Cao Cao… *never*," Ma Liang declared. "Sun Quan… I hear he has the aura of a man that will live long and rule well, but he is selfish: he will put his own interests before the Han. Lord Liu is magnanimous, and-"

"Uh-uh-uh…!" Kongming interrupted with amusement. "Remember, be impartial. You may one day need to question the man's motives openly… don't lose sight. He has ambition… sometimes that can steer a man onto a path he'd swore he'd never tread… even a man like Lord Liu has his faults. …But I'm happy for you."

"Kongming… you are a true and trusted man of good faith, and I will always remember this day," Ma Liang said with warm respect.

"…Fair enough," Kongming replied with a smile.

That evening, Kongming and Yueying sat together thoughtfully. Kongming played a favourite tune of theirs on his *qin*, which was a type of seven-stringed zither. His playing was precise, fluid, and yet tense and restless.

"I hope I have not embroiled Jichang in something terrible," Kongming said after a long, painful absence of words: he stopped strumming the qin, and relaxed.

"I heard your confusion in your playing," Yueying sighed. "You held the notes in a mournful way… don't blame yourself for any future calamity… you were doing something that was meant as a gesture of kindness."

"…I am struggling with my own soul," Kongming admitted. "I… I feel as though I was sending him to Lord Liu, so that I would be among friends *when*… not *if*… I joined him later on. Have I already decided…?"

"You have," Yueying replied.

"But *how*…?" Kongming asked with bewilderment. "I'm not normally so easily won over. I've seen what he's capable of… the burning at Bowang was bad enough, but the way his subordinates hacked the survivors to death… was that so different to the sins committed by Cao Cao…?"

"Cao Cao killed civilians," Yueying noted. "Liu Bei killed soldiers in self-defence."

"...That's what I keep telling myself," Kongming sighed as he pushed the qin away a little. "But... I'm still not clear."
"Of course," Yueying suggested. "You still do not fully trust him."
"But then, if that is so, how can I send my sworn brother – no, not just Jichang, but the *whole Ma family* – to Liu Bei?" Kongming despaired. "If I do not trust him, then I am guilty of sending them to him, and-"
"You *recommended* them," Yueying interrupted. "It is their choice to accept. Would you not need to blame Mister Sima if you are destroyed by Liu Bei...? After all, *he* recommended *you* to Liu Bei... didn't he...?"
Kongming pondered the point, exhaled, and nodded silently.
"Now come," Yueying said encouragingly, "play something more cheering... more optimistic. I should like that."
Kongming smiled warmly, nodded, and pulled the qin forward a little. This time, he played with vigour and strength: Yueying listened, and smiled.

************

## 11

Months went by, and Liu Bei did not return. Kongming continued to farm by day, and study by night; Ma Liang visited less and less as his work for Liu Bei increased, but since Ma Liang's descriptions of life in service were favourable, Kongming was generally warmed to Liu Bei more and more as time went by.

"...He's back again," Jun said as he looked out and saw horsemen at the bridge.
"...Who, Liu Bei...?" Yueying said with surprise.
"Yeah," Jun replied. "Where's Elder Brother...?"
"...I shall fetch him," Yueying said tensely.

"...My lord," Kongming hailed as the servants led Liu Bei to the living quarters.
"You look well, Master Zhuge Kongming," Liu Bei hailed in response.
Liu Bei was dressed in a plain green silk robe, and wore no armour; he wore an ornate hairpiece to keep his uncut hair in place, but was otherwise underdressed for his social position as an influential warlord. Kongming, by contrast, wore Taoist-style white robes, a white cloth turban over his uncut hair, and, as always, he carried his feather fan, which he was already using to fan himself casually.
"...All is very well, my lord," Kongming replied.
"I wish you were speaking of me as 'My Lord' in a more specific sense," Liu Bei said with sadness. "To not have such a great man as my adviser... but I promised that I would not pressure you, didn't I...!"
"...I am twenty-five," Kongming retorted. "What can you learn from me...?"
"Enough games!" Liu Bei chuckled as he gestured that they should both sit down.
"...Why have you once again graced my humble thatched cottage with your presence...?" Kongming asked pointedly as Liu Bei sat down.
"To once again talk with you about the age we live in," Liu Bei replied as Kongming sat down as well.
"...What would you discuss...?" Kongming asked.
"I just want to know your general viewpoint," Liu Bei replied cagily.
Kongming knew that Liu Bei was coaxing an opinion of all the heroes of the day, including Bei himself: he smiled toothily, but remained silent.

"The Han is in danger," Liu Bei continued. "Not since the treachery of Wang Mang of ancient times has the Han been so threatened. Wang Mang used his connections to the court to sow lies, to make his own name great, and those of his rivals meagre and untrustworthy... he manipulated the Empress Dowager, his own aunt, into deceiving the court, and eventually, he was a regent, and he ruled with a fist of evil. He poisoned the Emperor, he murdered his enemies, he taxed the people and starved them, and he brought the barbarians to the borders, lusting for his blood. Only hubris was his downfall... now, nearly two centuries later, we have had not only Dong Zhuo, but Cao Cao. ...I simply wish to know your thoughts."

"...What can I say beyond your own words...?" Kongming suggested. "Dong Zhuo was every bit the new Wang Mang; Cao Cao, the same. One can only hope, if Wang Mang is the model, that Cao will ruin himself, as Dong Zhuo did."

"...He won't," Liu Bei lamented. "Cao is too clever... his followers are many, as we have discussed before... his advisers, like grains of sand. He has the Emperor's army as his own, augmented now by the forces annexed from the four northern provinces won from Yuan Shao. ...He seems unstoppable."

"I'm sure Cao Cao felt much of the despair you do when he matched twenty-thousand troops to Yuan Shao's hundred-thousand," Kongming countered. "...However, Guandu speaks for itself... and Yuan Shao is no more."

Liu Bei nodded thoughtfully.

"...I suspect that it is not just Cao Cao that haunts you," Kongming prompted.

"No, you are quite right," Liu Bei replied immediately. "Sun Quan also concerns me, and... I wondered, Master, how you truly compare the men of the age."

This second prompt was more direct than the first: Kongming smiled silently.

"...I will abide by your appraisal of each man," Liu Bei prompted further.

"...I shall begin with Cao Cao," Kongming said calmly. "Cao Cao is your biggest threat. He has the respect of the court, since his father was adopted by the eunuch Cao Teng, and enjoyed high status. Even with his notorious mischief, and disregard for influence in court costing him a high post, Cao Cao has returned to court again and again, earning as many allies as enemies. His connection to the Xiahou family has given him solid, dependable retainers, and his good judge of character has given him many more besides. In addition to Xiahou Dun, Xiahou Yuan, Yu Jin, Yue Jin and Li Dian, he has earned mighty warriors like Zhang Liao, Lü Bu's former second; Zhang He, once one of Yuan Shao's vanguard generals and fearsome with it; Xu Chu, a man-mountain that serves as Cao's personal bodyguard; Xu Huang, a forthright hero that even Guan Yu has spoken highly of."

"That is true," Liu Bei noted sombrely.

"As for advisers, he has Xun Yu; Xun You; Jia Xu, Man Chong, and many more promising ones besides," Kongming continued. "But he is not always forthright and true: when his father was killed by bandits in Xu Province, his wrath was vented on its prefect, Tao Qian, and the penalty was a massacre of innocents... bodies stemmed the river, blood ran as water."

"I know," Liu Bei recalled with grief. "I was stationed there."

"It is only the bravery of your forces, and of Taishi Ci, that more did not die... but Cao won, stopped only by Lü Bu's treachery in Cao's own prefectures," Kongming continued. "I hear that Taishi Ci has died... a shame. But then, he condescended to serve the Sun family in Jiangdong... he aimed too low."

"Indeed," Liu Bei sighed tactlessly: Kongming hid a smirk.

"...And then there is Wan City, where Cao's seducing of the aunt of the recently surrendered governor led to reprisal, losing him his bodyguard Dian Wei, and one of his own sons... who sacrificed his own life to save his father," Kongming chuckled desperately. "But it was Dian Wei that Cao wept for... the pillar of strength that guarded him while he did as he pleased."

"Quite so," Liu Bei concurred.

"...And then there is his relationship with Yuan Shao," Kongming ventured further. "As childhood friends, the two were as brothers... now, Shao lies dead, Cao having betrayed his trust. And men that defected from Yuan Shao, also friends to Cao Cao, were randomly slaughtered to cover Cao's dependency on them to win the day. He kept Zhang He, I confess... but what about Cao's childhood friend Xu You, that helped him triumph over Yuan Shao at Guandu...? Are his head and body in the same place since he trusted Cao Cao...?"

"I agree," Liu Bei replied quietly.

"Now," Kongming continued, "Cao rules the Han court near uncontested, with – as you said – the Emperor's legions as his own, and any who oppose him are treated as rebels... sadly, my lord, I know that includes you."

"...It does," Liu Bei murmured.

"...To face Cao Cao alone would be folly, true folly, at your current strength, Lord Liu," Kongming insisted. "But then who would you face him with...?"

"I, too, wonder that," Liu Bei sighed theatrically.

"...There is Liu Zhang, governor of Yi Province, who I know is a distant relative of yours," Kongming suggested. "But... unlike his father, Li Yan, his grip on power is weak. The only reason he still has Yi under his control is due to the immense difficulty one might have in attacking it."

"That has been noted by some of my advisers," Liu Bei admitted.

"...But the enemy within is Zhang Lu," Kongming sighed. "Zhang Lu has started to take over much of the northern Yi region of Hanzhong, something that he would not have dared to do under Liu Yan. And Liu Zhang does nothing, nothing at all, while his border shrinks. ...Sadly, such a man – a man who has accepted titles from the court ruled by Cao Cao – will serve as no ally, kin of yours or not."

Liu Bei nodded slowly and silently.

"Zhang Lu is not interested in fighting Cao Cao either… nor is Ma Teng of Xiliang, and Cao knows that," Kongming continued. "That, of course, leaves only two warlords of any real strength: Liu Biao, and Sun Quan.

"Liu Biao was, in his day, a charismatic hero… but that day is long gone. Now, he is an old, sick man. He is, sadly, not long for this world… in a few years, his power will – like Liu Yan in Yi – need to be passed to another, and neither Liu Qi, his first son, nor Liu Cong, his second son, are fit to replace him. Liu Qi enjoys a life of indulgent pleasure, and has paid the price with disease. Liu Cong, though more disciplined, is too meek, and would capitulate to Cao Cao or Sun Quan if he were given a chance."

"…Sadly, your analysis is accurate," Liu Bei sighed. "Truly, it can be said that a man can know the situation of a place a thousand miles away… you, Master, could tell me of anything, I am sure."

"No, no!" Kongming insisted. "I am based within distance of the Jing court… I know of Liu Biao's affairs that way. …But my lord, Jing is, of course, a place of strategic importance: both Cao Cao and Sun Quan covet it, because it provides a gateway to conquering the other. …My lord, if there is ever an opportunity to receive this place yourself, it should not be ignored."

"…You are not alone in that thought," Liu Bei admitted. "But I refuse, on the grounds that it would be less than filial, and unpopular. He has already suggested my inheriting Jing, but I could never betray my honorary nephews, Qi and Cong, by stealing their father's territory from them."

"…Very well," Kongming said with a hint of disappointment. "…But of course I now come to Sun Quan.

"His father Sun Jian was a mercenary in his last days, a hired hand for Yuan Shu to send against his enemies. And had that not been the case, who knows…? Perhaps Sun Quan and Liu Biao would now be allies, not enemies. But the fates made Sun Jian attack Liu Biao, and Biao's men killed him. Since then, Sun Ce has waged continual war against Jing province, whilst simultaneously conquering the lands below the Great River… now, those lands… Jiangdong… are under the control of the Sun family. Poised to become a titan, Sun Ce then declared war on Cao Cao, possibly intending to join forces with Yuan Shao; and then, of course, he was assassinated.

"Sun Quan, his brother, inherited his officers, advisers, and his new empire: but instead of fulfilling the cause of Han, Sun Quan instead withdrew into his shell, consolidated his power, and refocused his energies on Liu Biao, leaving Yuan Shao to face Cao alone. Had Sun Quan allied with Yuan Shao, the two – aided by your army, and others – might have been victorious over Cao Cao. That is a legacy that Sun Quan must carry."

"…True enough," Liu Bei murmured ambiguously.

"Furthermore," Kongming added, "there are those that say the Sun family are guilty of exacerbating the crisis. When Dong Zhuo burned down the capital Luoyang, it's said that Sun Jian did not pursue the fleeing villain: instead, he combed the city for treasures, finding in the rubble an Imperial jade seal. He pocketed it, intending, no doubt, to declare himself Emperor one day… and then he was struck down.

"Sun Ce, it is said, inherited that seal, but he did not return it to the Han court: no, he kept it, and, it is said, was eventually forced to trade it to Yuan Shu in exchange for troops. If that story is true, could Yuan Shu have declared himself Emperor, and brought about his own downfall – as well as that of wandering warlord Lü Bu – without Sun Ce giving him that seal...? ...And for certain, this continual feud with Liu Biao... Sun Quan now has in his employ one Gan Ning, a former pirate."

"Wasn't Gan Ning once a vassal of Liu Biao's senior general, Huang Zu...?" Liu Bei noted.

"...Until three years ago, yes, he was," Kongming confirmed. "He defected after Huang Zu – himself a senile, incompetent fool, his best years gone – showed mistrust in him. ...But my point is this... before defecting he killed Ling Cao, a loyal vassal of Sun Quan. That man's son, Ling Tong, is said to hold a fatal grudge against Gan Ning... and yet is expected to serve alongside his father's killer. The argument for this is, I believe, that 'Gan Ning was merely doing his job whilst in another's employ'; but Sun Jian's own fate was due to his being in another's employ, and yet in that case, the matter cannot be dropped... is this not the greatest hypocrisy...? How can Sun Quan be considered 'reliable'...?"

"I agree fully," Liu Bei replied. "...You have estimated him most diligently."

"...I say only what I see," Kongming replied.

"And what do you see in *me*...?" Liu Bei asked. "I carry no sword... I will carry no malice if your estimation is not as I would like. I will see it as a chance to reform."

"...Very well," Kongming sighed. "You were born the descendant of a disinherited prince of the realm, wherein you worked as a weaver and seller of sandals and mats. When the call was made for men to rise up and crush the Yellow Turbans, you fought for the cause of Han, and recruited warrior Guan Yu, butcher Zhang Fei, and childhood friend Jian Yong to assist you, amongst others. With Zhang Fei's might, Guan Yu's heroism, and the donations of wealthy merchants, you formed an army, and played a significant part in defeating the rebels. You were made Governor of Anxi, but were forced to abandon the post when you were unwilling to submit bribes to a corrupt government inspector, so you went to Xu Province, where you became prefect of Gaotang for your work in supressing rebels there."

Kongming paused: Liu Bei was silent, his face unreadable.

"...When Dong Zhuo usurped the Imperial court, you again rose to the occasion, and your forces were again significant," Kongming continued. "But in the aftermath, you were forced to retreat northward and go into service for Gongsun Zan – who was then in an alliance with Yuan Shu and Tao Qian. You were defeated by Yuan Shao, and went to serve first Tian Kai, and then Tao Qian in Xu Province, where you successfully reduced the threat Cao Cao – who was then in alliance with Yuan Shao and Liu Biao – posed to the province."

"But, as you surreptitiously sidestepped there, Master... I was defeated again," Liu Bei sighed. "Lü Bu inadvertently saved me by invading Cao Cao's province while he was away, as you noted earlier."

"...But at least, my lord, your stay under Tao Qian was productive," Kongming suggested. "You earned the services of Mi Zhu, Mi Fang, Chen Deng and Chen Gui, married Lady Mi, and earned the trust and respect of the people of Xu Province. ...So much so, that you were eventually named its governor when Tao Qian died, and you made peace with Yuan Shao, shifting your allegiance to Yuan Shao, Cao Cao and Liu Biao to ensure stability."

"I did," Liu Bei confirmed tersely.

"...But then Lü Bu was defeated by Cao Cao and sought refuge with you... you were betrayed by him, and forced to go to Cao Cao for help," Kongming continued. "Eventually, Bu was dead, and you were forced to return to the capital with Cao Cao... but when Cao Cao and Yuan Shao parted ways, you fled the capital, joined forces with Yuan Shao-"

"And suffered defeat yet again," Liu Bei interrupted.

"...Your fortunes are due to the games that you are forced to play," Kongming insisted. "I am sure that you did not wish to switch your allegiance away from your friend Gongsun Zan, but... what choice did you have...? You did not dictate the sides you had to choose from."

"I am glad you see things that way," Liu Bei replied with a slight smile: Kongming noted a tear in his eye, and wondered if it was genuine.

"...But from that strategic move to join Yuan Shao, you then came to seek refuge with Liu Biao," Kongming concluded. "I... I do not know what else to say."

"You ended your synopsis of each of the other warlords with a brief opinion of their character, their moral fibre," Liu Bei prompted. "I wonder, Master Kongming, what you make of a privately financed sandal weaver that shifted allegiances so many times that he is in danger of giving Lü Bu a reputation for constancy...?"

Kongming's eyes darted about as he struggled, momentarily, for an answer: it came to him as a bolt of inspiration, and he smiled toothily.

"...Circumstance," Kongming replied, "is your master at the moment, my lord. A man's choices are his own, and yet at the same time are only as good as the options. And even then, there can sometimes be a right and a wrong."

"...Go on," Liu Bei urged.

"When the call for heroes was made, you could have won the love of weary, angry peasants by siding with the Yellow Turbans," Kongming suggested. "However, you chose the Han court, because the Yellow Turbans were a cult, no better than the seditious eunuchs that ruined the court... in fact, *worse*.

"You rescinded from your role as Anxi governor because you faced slander... you had no choice. You fled from one warlord to another because they were forcing you to make choices... and you had to make tactical decisions.

"You joined Gongsun Zan because he was righteous; but his ally, Yuan Shu, later declared himself Emperor. Lord Gongsun should also have distanced himself from such a man. You went to serve Tian Kai and Tao Qian to protect Xu Province from Cao Cao's genocides... but allied to Yuan Shao to save the province from invasion when Tao Qian died.

"You were then forced to take in Lü Bu because the man posed a threat if you immediately challenged him... his treachery was no fault of yours, and was inevitable. And it was that treachery that forced you to temporarily conceal your moral objections and join the villain Cao Cao, else Xu Province was at the mercy of Lü Bu. When Yuan Shao saw the light, you went to him, after finally eradicating Yuan Shu and Lü Bu. Yuan Shao forgave you for Yuan Shu's demise, and you fought Cao Cao together, only to be overwhelmed by stratagem. Yuan Shao was conceited, arrogant, and sadly doomed: to preserve your own chances of restoring the Han, you fled here... where the story ends, for now."

"...So you consider me to always have the best of motives...?" Liu Bei asked plainly. "I would not be offended if you said otherwise."

"I tell you only what I know," Kongming insisted.

"But what then, of your full opinion of me...?" Liu Bei asked.

"...I believe that, in a world of chaos, where men like Yuan Shu, Yuan Shao, Cao Cao and Sun Quan contend for purely selfish motives... that you sincerely wish to restore the Han dynasty, and that you try to do so by the most benevolent methods that are available," Kongming suggested cautiously. "Cao Cao once said you and he are the only true heroes of the day, I understand... if he did, I believe that too."

"...I see," Liu Bei noted. "...And, even believing that... you will not join me...?"

Kongming fanned himself slowly, and pondered how best to answer.


************

## 12

"And again, you said 'no'."
Mister Huang shook his head slowly as he pondered Kongming's latest revelation to his family: Jun had walked out of the room as soon as his brother had stopped talking minutes earlier.
"That's that, then," Mister Huang added soberly. "A farmer's life for you."
"*Father*," Yueying scolded. "My husband knows what he's doing."
"And besides, I didn't say 'No'," Kongming insisted.
"You said 'I am content to reside in this cottage'," Mister Huang retorted flatly. "Does that have another interpretation I'm not aware of...?"
"...You're angry," Kongming supposed.
"... ... ...No, no, I'm not angry," Mister Huang replied wearily. "I... I suppose that I am just surprised. I thought you wanted to be in Lord Liu Bei's service... I thought that it was your intention, since you had already recommended Ma Liang and his family... now, I do not understand you at all."
Kongming eyed Yueying, who smiled encouragingly.
"...I should take my leave of you," Mister Huang sighed. "Take care."
After an exchange of polite bows, Mister Huang left the cottage.
"...Are you angry too...?" Kongming asked of Yueying, who was still smiling.
"No," Yueying replied. "I know what you're doing."
"Oh...?" Kongming chuckled.
"You are testing him, as you said you would," Yueying explained. "I know that... he has tried asking for assistance, and then directly demanding appraisals... now, he will disappear for a while, ponder what you discussed... his next visit will tell you all that you need to know."
"Yes," Kongming snickered. "Will it be another polite, unarmed discussion... or Zhang Fei, two hundred guards and a length of rope to tie me up and drag me across the countryside...?"
"I doubt he'd let his men do that to you," Yueying giggled.
"...I'm scared," Kongming admitted. "The conversation we had was as much his testing me as the other way around. In fact, in addition to that, I am plagued with new doubts."
"...Like what...?" Yueying wondered.
"Until I relayed it in one stroke, single parts of our recent history made sense," Kongming sighed. "*Now... now*, I think about it, and it almost makes me want to weep. First, it was everyone against Dong Zhuo and Lü Bu... then it was Yuan Shu, Gongsun Zan and Tao Qian against Yuan Shao, Cao Cao and Liu Biao... then it was Yuan Shu and Lü Bu against Liu Bei, and then Lü Bu and Liu Bei against Yuan Shu, and then Liu Bei against Lü Bu, and then...!"
"I think I see what you are saying," Yueying giggled. "Although everyone chastises Lü Bu for inconstancy, they are *all* guilty of it."

"From where do you derive any *trust*...?" Kongming wondered. "Look at the current situation: Liu Biao and Liu Bei resist Sun Quan to the south and Cao Cao to the north, while Liu Zhang and Zhang Lu quibble over Yi, and serve no purpose whatsoever. So... so does that mean that Sun Quan – once a vassal of Yuan Shu, who was an enemy of Cao Cao – may now reconcile with Cao Cao to devour Liu Biao and Liu Bei, both of whom were once allies of Cao Cao...? ...It is enough to make someone ill."
"You *are* having serious doubts," Yueying noted.
"Yes," Kongming admitted. "What I am hoping is that Lord Liu will take what I said, realise that his best interests lie in seeking peace with *Sun Quan*, and do his best to avoid direct conflict with Sun Quan while remaining loyal to Liu Biao, and – I hate to say it – waiting for him to die, since the grudge might die with him."
"We can only hope," Yueying said quietly.
"Yes," Kongming chuckled. "But if he decides to let Liu Biao send him southward to fight Sun Quan..."
"...Ah," Yueying said numbly.
"It means that he will be fighting not just Sun Quan, but my brother as well," Kongming said desperately. "Who, then, do I side with...? Do I abandon Jing Province, and go to Jiangdong, and join a seditious rebel who will one day be defeated by Cao Cao...? ...Or do I join Lord Liu, and fight my own kin...?"
"You have family in the capital," Yueying noted. "When you fight Cao Cao, you fight them too."
"...I know," Kongming said wearily. "I know."
"So... what will you do...?" Yueying asked.
Kongming exhaled, and started to fan himself slowly.

It would be several months – almost a year, in fact – until Zhuge Liang , styled Kongming, and known as Crouching Dragon, would need to give the answer to the man that it mattered most to.


*************

## 13

"I... I don't believe it...! ...Brother... it's Liu Xuande again...!"
Kongming looked up from his reading and looked into his brother's eyes.
"...Seriously!" Jun insisted. "He's back!"
"...Really...?" Kongming chuckled. "...He really does pace his visits."

"...So you are here again, my lord," Kongming said calmly. Liu Bei was dressed humbly once again, this time opting for a plain cloth turban to keep his hair in order.
"...I have again been to see Master Sima Hui," Liu Bei said quietly. "Again, he named you and Young Phoenix as the men who truly understand the exigencies of the age. Again, Xu Shu has implored me to seek your counsel... so *yes*, Master Zhuge Kongming... I am here again, to most sincerely seek your guidance."
"...I am humbled," Kongming said hoarsely.
"When we last spoke, you gave me much to think about," Liu Bei declared. "Liu Biao has, twice, asked me to go to the front in Jiangxia, where his subordinate Huang Zu expects an attack by Sun Quan's navy at any moment. ...And twice, Master, I have refused."
"...I see," Kongming replied calmly, all the time fanning himself slowly.
"Although none of the men that are considered my contemporaries are of good character, Sun Quan looks to be the most durable, the most flexible, the most deep-thinking," Liu Bei continued. "Liu Biao is sickly, Liu Zhang indecisive, Zhang Lu unstable and Cao Cao irreconcilable. It can only be my hope that some accord can be struck with Sun Quan... though whether that is possible in Liu Biao's lifetime is sadly very doubtful."
Kongming hummed to acknowledge he was listening, and continued to fan himself slowly, taking note of Liu Bei's posture as he spoke.
"Although I am surrounded by many dependable men, you and I have twice discussed my lack of good advisers," Liu Bei said bluntly. "I am advancing in years... Heaven has denied me a son, so I have adopted a son born to another as my own. Heaven has denied me land, so here I am, adopting another's land as my own, until I can establish a proper base. Heaven has denied me the chance to adopt strong counsel... which is, perhaps, why I have had a string of defeats."
"...I beg to differ," Kongming interrupted, "on two counts. Firstly, you now have Ma Liang, and Xu Shu, both of whom will all serve you in that capacity along with Jian Yong, who has got you this far. ...I can recommend others: in fact-"
"Master Zhuge," Liu Bei said with a voice that almost broke into a sob, "I do not want to hear any more recommendations! I have come here today to... to beg of you your support."
With that, Liu Bei kowtowed, and said, "I humbly beg of you, before Heaven... Master Kongming, please provide me with your sagely counsel."
Kongming froze with surprise and fear, and the fan nearly fell from his hand.

"I have now visited you three times in your thatched cottage... and by Heaven I swear, I will visit a thousand times more if I must," Liu Bei continued as he lifted and lowered his head in repeated obeisance. "As things stand, I am on the verge of destruction: Liu Biao will not tolerate me forever, Cao Cao wants me dead, and Sun Quan will devour me if I run to him. Liu Zhang is incapable... Zhang Lu, dangerous... I have nowhere to go, yet everywhere to turn... please, Master! I need your help!"

Kongming finally unfroze, and hastily helped Liu Bei to his feet.

"...Please," Liu Bei sobbed: the tears in his eyes seemed to be genuine.

"A *warlord* cries thus...?" Kongming whispered. "My lord... do not do this to yourself. I... I, Liang, am only twenty-six... I do not know what I can do to help you, having never fought a battle, but only seen and read of them... I do not know how the age can be so desperate that a man of your stature should weep at my feet... but... please, Lord Liu, I have a gift for you."

"But...!" Liu Bei bleated: Kongming walked to his collection of materials and picked up a long, rolled piece of cloth.

"...This," Kongming said, "is what I think must be done."

Kongming walked to a mounting easel, and unfurled the map of the land that he had painstakingly prepared.

"...What is this...?" Liu Bei asked weakly as he walked to the map.

"My lord," Kongming began, "your current position is precarious, but recoverable. But you lack a plan for the future. There are several theories about how the land will be separated in times to come... this, I think, is a good estimation.

"Currently, Sun Quan holds all of the districts southeast of the Great River, and is formidable, if only the tiger bares its claws. His advisers, such as Zhang Zhao, are cowardly, and will suggest capitulation to Cao Cao... that is a problem we can work around with some diplomacy, and talking to the right people.

"Cao Cao now holds everything else except Yi and Jing. Both are critical... Yi, with its natural mountain defences and supplies abounding, would provide its ruler with wealth and resource enough to match Cao, and the barriers to keep him away at the same time. Jing is even more critical: from there, attacks can be launched against Cao in the north, and Sun in the south and east.

"Like it or not, the land will continue to be shared amongst fewer and fewer warlords... already, dozens has been whittled to only a handful, and that will continue to shrink. Cao Cao will soon commit himself to pressing southward... and his arrogance will compel him to seize first Jing, and then Sun's land beyond the Great River... I suspect that both Liu Biao and Sun Quan would rather surrender than face Cao's unbridled wrath, but we must change their minds... together, Liu and Sun can defeat Cao, and divide the land between them, until such time that one – Liu – can successfully force the subjugation of the other.

"Your first move should be to consolidate your foothold in Jing, gain greater influence. Next, you must seek either an alliance with, or the annexation of, the lands of Yi currently governed by Liu Zhang and Zhang Lu. With Jing and Yi as your domain to launch attacks on Cao Cao, and an alliance with Sun Quan to provide a decoy second pincer along the Great River front, the capital will be in your sights, and victory will be only footsteps away. But for the plan to succeed there can be no bisected land... only three partitions will work."

Liu Bei ran his finger along the impression of the Yangtze River, and lowered his gaze thoughtfully.

"...Jing Province will need to be secured," Kongming reiterated.

"It is said in warfare that two are easier to defeat than one, because they can be divided," Liu Bei suggested. "Is this plan not risky...?"

"In most cases, yes, but not this one," Kongming insisted. "The two difficult points are the governance of Jing, and maintaining peace with Sun Quan, whose power is too great for him to just disappear. The two interlock: Sun Quan covets Jing, and if you possessed it, it would become a bargaining tool in exchange for assistance. ...I reiterate that you will need to hold on to Jing while you endeavour to take Yi."

"You insinuate that I must be conqueror of my own kin," Liu Bei noted.

"...Jing can be 'held' by maintaining good relations with Liu Biao's heirs, if needs be," Kongming suggested. "Liu Zhang accepted rank from Cao Cao in exchange for his remaining neutral, thereby betraying any covenant you could ever have had with him to restore the Han... he has lost the confidence of his vassals, such as Zhang Lu, who now seeks to devour him. You only protect what has been in the possession of the Liu family for generations by replacing him as the prefect of that land."

Liu Bei nodded seriously, as if to agree.

"We must work with the situation as it is, and exploit advantages, rather than focus on the disadvantages. The advantage of three states – where yours is on good terms with one of the others – is that your ally will constantly serve as another enemy to your enemy, and keep their forces permanently divided," Kongming suggested. "With three, some external, grudge-bearing players that might not follow one ally might follow the other, rather than your enemy... were there to be only two, then it would be a bloody war of attrition that would end only after decades and decades of relentless war, and if there were more than three – as there are now – then there would be endless intrigue, with so many possible alliances and borders to watch... and the smaller the states are, the more likely that the barbarian tribes on our borders, like the Qiang and the Nan, will rise up as enemies to us all.

"Also, three partitions guarantees periods of nervous stalemate, and in fact, in this case, two are easier to defeat... two *halves* of a larger whole, split between its two enemies. The key to this will be maintaining good relations with Sun Quan *at all times*, however... if he were to be driven into serving as a vassal of Cao Cao by an act of aggression, that would be fatal. ...Of course, we can occasionally threaten to break faith and go to Cao Cao when they make unreasonable demands... that can be used to control them as well."

"...I understand your plan," Liu Bei said hesitantly.

"But you do not fully trust it," Kongming supposed.

"No... no, it is enlightening," Liu Bei said with a smile of gratitude. "I, Bei, have long sought guidance on matters such as this: here, all of this makes perfect sense! By using this plan, I, Bei, can *grow*... this plan is especially beneficial to one that must first have a base... yes, this is how I must proceed!"

"...I am glad you understand," Kongming said quietly.

"You have thought this through with me in mind," Liu Bei noted gratefully. "I, Bei, can never thank you enough for this guidance... it is like being without sight, and seeing for the first time!"

With that, Liu Bei began to prostrate himself in obeisance at Kongming's feet once again, prompting Kongming to say, "Please, my lord, do not be so humble..."

"You have shown me the way," Liu Bei sobbed as he got to his feet. "I, Bei... can never repay you."

Kongming was stunned: the humility that Liu Bei was showing was unheard of, especially to a man of limited rank, when Liu Bei was related to the Emperor. A rush of emotion swept over him: in a move that even surprised Kongming himself, he threw himself to the ground in prostration at Liu Bei's feet, saying, "To have come three times to visit me in my thatched cottage, my lord... to have shown me such respect... if you would so unpretentiously ask my service... then I am yours to command."

Liu Bei helped Kongming to his feet, and said, "It is fate that we stand here today, you and I... today, we are not only lord and vassal, but friends. Today you've shown me what I must do... together, let us defeat Cao Cao, and restore the fire of the house of Han!"

The two men locked gazes and smiled, sure that together, anything was possible.


"...Here he comes," Zhang Fei grumbled as Liu Bei and Kongming rode across the bridge to meet with Liu Bei's entourage.

"...Yunchang, Yide," Liu bei hailed; "I have good news! ...Master Zhuge has agreed, at long last, to assist us in our grand endeavour!"

"...*Whoopee*," Zhang Fei grunted as he eyed Kongming with contempt.

"I am honoured to be in your presence, both of you," Kongming said with a toothy grin: he bowed slightly to the two generals, who made slight and insincere bows in response.

"With Master Crouching Dragon in our midst, victory is within reach, at last...!" Liu Bei announced cheerfully.

"*Really*...? *Where*...?" Zhang Fei asked mockingly, as he looked about him.

"...**_Yide_**," Liu Bei scolded.

"It is fine," Kongming insisted as he looked at Zhang Fei and continued to smile. "I am sure that we will get along just fine."

Zhang Fei harrumphed and rode away, toward the city; Guan Yu eyed Kongming with sinister intent, and followed Zhang Fei; the soldiers – exempting Liu Bei's cavalry bodyguards – followed the two generals.

"I should like it very much if you would join us on our return to Fan," Liu Bei said with cheer. "You can meet my inner circle properly, and then, one day soon, we can travel to see Liu Biao..."

Yueying stood at the doorway of her cottage home and watched – with her husband's brother, Jun – as Kongming rode away with Liu Bei's army. The farewells had been brief, awkward and yet warm, and not at all sad.

"...I wonder when he'll come back," Jun said numbly.

Yueying walked away from the door and went to the living quarters, where she stared at one of the few writings that Kongming had left, and smiled silently. It read,

"As a wise bird picks a sturdy branch
On which to safely stand,

So a wise man picks a worthy lord
With whom he'll save the land."

Yueying walked to Kongming's qin, sat in front of it, closed her eyes, and strummed the strings with grace and skill. Jun watched with tears in his eyes as Yueying played a song that was mournful, reflective, and yet full of hope for the future.

"I didn't know you could play," Jun said weakly.

"...Neither does my husband," Yueying revealed. "...Sometimes, things are best left unsaid in troubled times. All that matters is what must be known."

"And what must be known...?" Jun asked.

"If a wise man has truly found his worthy lord," Yueying replied. "...Has he, I wonder...? ...I suppose only time will tell..."

************

# ACT II: THE CRISIS AT STEEP-SLOPE

## 14

"**So**," Zhang Fei barked as Liu Bei completed the welcome ceremony for his ministers and generals, "what can we hope for from this new 'strategist'…?"

Liu Bei eyed Zhang Fei angrily, as the eyes of the assembly fell on their latest addition, Zhuge Liang, styled Kongming, Taoist name 'Crouching Dragon'.

"…You can hope for my best," Kongming replied calmly.

"…I feel as though we have finally gained some ground," Liu Bei said with cheer.

The assembly murmured in agreement.

To Liu Bei's left, Kongming sat quietly, waving his fan slowly; the officials sat in a line to Kongming's left. Mi Zhu and Mi Fang – two of Liu Bei's senior ministers – smiled politely; Mister Sun Qian – Liu Bei's elder adviser, politician and diplomat – smiled condescendingly at Kongming. Jian Yong – who would be acting as Kongming's supervisor, as well as his peer – smirked, and kept his eyes lowered. Chen Zhen – a recent acquisition from former ally Yuan Shao – sat quietly, and volunteered nothing. Kongming's friends, Xu Shu and Ma Liang, were sat at the end of the row of officials, fretting quietly that Kongming was already subject to the wrath of Zhang Fei.

To Liu Bei's immediate right, Guan Yu sat silently, stroking his foot-long beard. To Guan Yu's immediate right, Zhang Fei sat and eyed Kongming with irritation. To Zhang Fei's right were the generals and warrior-officials that served in dual capacity: Zhao Yun – known to most as Zhao Zilong – was sat quietly, humbly observing Kongming and smiling politely.

"…So," Zhang Fei said, "is it me, or are the two rows unequal…?"

Guan Yu lowered his gaze and groaned with embarrassment.

"I'm trying to understand *why*," Zhang Fei said with mock confusion, despite irritated looks from Liu Bei. "I know… I know what it is, Elder Brother!"

Kongming grinned toothily, and continued to fan himself.

"I know what it is now!" Zhang Fei said with mock excitement. "It's because you **keep recruiting more BLOODY PEDANTS!**"

Mister Sun, Xu Shu and Ma Liang hung their heads; Jian Yong joined Kongming in grinning with amusement.

"**Obviously, this is some *marvellous scheme*!**" Zhang Fei barked sarcastically. "**You're just going to keep recruiting these men in robes to BORE Cao Cao witless until he surrenders; only I have a better one: get some more GENERALS to KILL HIM!**"

"…Yide," Guan Yu scolded.

"Yunchang," Zhang Fei retorted, "are you **BLIND???** …We have been to so many towns, met so many people… and all we keep recruiting is the likes of **them**!"

"…Watch your tongue," Liu Bei admonished.

"We're not offended," Mi Zhu insisted: Mi Fang nodded in reluctant agreement.

"Look, I'm not going to complain about you two, you're useful, you gave us money," Zhang Fei said reassuringly: Kongming covered his mouth with his fan to hide his laughter. "But what're the other lot doing for us...? ...Oh yes, I forget, the old man has fronted an army from time to time... even if he did always *lose*."
Mister Sun kept his gaze fixed on the floor and said nothing.
"That's a fair point, as it goes," Zhang Fei said suddenly. "How about everyone from that side of the room that has actually participated in a fight come over to this side of the room, and be honorary generals...? ...Oh wait, then it'll just be white-brows and 'Cringing Monkey' over there on their own, and that wouldn't be fair."
"**Yide!**" Liu Bei barked angrily. "Enough is enough!"
"...But really, you can't keep expecting me, Yunchang and Zilong to be your only decent field generals, Elder Brother," Zhang Fei protested.
"I don't," Liu Bei insisted. "I am recruiting generals as well... but it isn't all about fighting, Yide, I'm tired of telling you that. How do you intend to fight Cao Cao if he comes here with an army of two-hundred-thousand...? What good will a few extra generals be, mm...?"
Kongming started to fan himself as Zhang Fei locked eyes with him again.
"...So we're sending the boy with the fan to talk to him, then," Zhang Fei said with a sneer.
"... ... ...Not alone," Liu Bei replied after an angry pause. "Master Zhuge and I are going to meet Liu Biao, and discuss the next steps for repelling Cao Cao, and striking accord with Sun Quan."
"...*Good luck*," Zhang Fei said to Kongming with absolute insincerity.
"My thanks," Kongming replied with a toothy grin.
"Elder Brother," Guan Yu hailed, "it is not sufficient to keep recruiting these inexperienced young men in the hope that their knowledge of texts will somehow provide us with answers. We need capable fighters, brave-"
"...Forgive my intrusion," Kongming interrupted, "but you also need stratagems: that was the purpose behind recruiting Xu Yuanzhi, and me."
"Xu *who*...?" Zhang Fei grunted.
"...Me," Xu Shu hailed nervously.
"Oh, right... you help with topography, I don't mind you," Zhang Fei growled.
"I have read many military texts, and in particular, I have studied the trigrams formations," Kongming continued. "In our current, weak position, we must resort to tactics like those used at Bowang, but-"
"Right," Zhang Fei interrupted. "Lure 'em into a forest, burn 'em... we know that already, cowardly though it is, we've been doing that. So why do we need *you*...?"
"So if you were fighting on an open plain like Wuzhang, or by a river with no dense vegetation to lure them into, what would you do...?" Kongming enquired. "Ask Cao Cao to please relocate the battle to Bowang so you can burn him again...?"
Zhang Fei's grimaced and leant forward menacingly, saying, "Little runt, I'll shove that fan up your...!"

"**Yide!**" Liu Bei barked: he was half-laughing, but he could still see the danger in the situation. "Please, brother… no more! Master Zhuge has a valid point… we were lucky that we were able to fool Xiahou Dun into fighting us at Bowang. We may never get an opportunity like that again… to defeat large armies with small armies, you need to use formations as well as ambushes, and you need different types of ambushes. Master Zhuge is extensively read in this area, as is Ma Jichang."

"*Who…?*" Zhang Fei grunted.

"…Me," Ma Liang said feebly.

"Oh, right… *you*," Zhang Fei growled. "…Alright… okay. I suppose *we* were young once, weren't we."

"Yes, we were," Liu Bei chuckled. "Now come on, everyone… we're here to discuss next steps. Mister Jian, Master Zhuge, if you would."

"…You may begin," Jian Yong suggested to Kongming.

"My thanks," Kongming replied. "…Cao Cao is currently distracted… while Yuan Shao is dead, his three sons have been troublesome to eradicate. Cao Cao's chief strategist, Guo Jia, is truly terrifying… he has correctly anticipated many of their enemies' manoeuvres, and his sound counsel is the one thing we must truly fear."

"And *he*, Yide, is only thirty-five," Liu Bei noted. "Age is meaningless in strategic warfare: it is the man that counts."

"…Yeah, okay, I know," Zhang Fei begrudgingly conceded. "…Go on, Creeping Turtle, get on with it."

"…Guo Jia suggested, after Guandu, that Cao should ignore the Yuan brothers, instead focussing on building a force to march south against *us*," Kongming continued. "He insisted the Yuans would fight amongst each other: he was right. One brother, Yuan Shang, eventually escaped and sought refuge with Tadun, king of the Wuhuan tribes in the far north. Now, Cao Cao is threatened by Tadun and Yuan Shang… even Guo Jia is suggesting a march northward to supress them."

"…That's some distance to travel," Mi Zhu said with surprise. "Cao Cao would be drawn away from the capital for a long time if he pursued Yuan Shang."

"…And he'd be taking most of his army with him…!" Xu Shu noted.

"It would be a perfect opportunity to attack the capital and rescue the Emperor," Ma Liang supposed.

"…Perfect indeed…!" Guan Yu concurred.

"Then let's prepare!" Zhang Fei declared. "Let's get ready, and-"

"…Wait," Kongming interrupted: even Zhang Fei fell silent. "Guo Jia is no fool… he knows his enemies, including us, very well. He coordinated Guandu, and he gave Cao the advice to pursue you in Xu, and then at Bowang: had Guo Jia been in Bowang in person, none of you would have survived."

"Why do you give such high praise to this enemy of ours…?" Zhang Fei scolded.

"You must always respect your enemy," Kongming suggested. "To not do so is certain doom. Even they are your enemy… never dismiss them lightly, not even for the sake of morale. That is what killed Yuan Shao. I refuse to underestimate Guo Jia… sick and dying or not."

"I agree with Kongming," Jian Yong sighed. "He made fools of us in Xu Province."

"...He did," Mister Sun agreed.

"And Kongming is right about Yuan Shao," Chen Zhen sighed. "My former master's biggest faults were his arrogance and lack of foresight."

"But Guo Jia is ill, as you said," Mi Zhu noted. "Cao fears he will soon lose him."

"...Even sick, Guo Jia's dangerous," Kongming insisted. "*If* he's sick... that could be a ruse, to make his enemies think he's dying, like Sun Ce did to lure out Ze Rong. If he were left in the capital to 'recuperate' while Cao struck the Wuhuan... he's the dangerous one, remember...? Cao Cao would be following orders from afar, while Guo Jia could formulate plans to the occasion. We must not rush this."

"Okay," Zhang Fei sighed impatiently. "So *what then*...?"

"First, we make use of our contacts in the capital to gain up-to-date information on Cao's battle plans... where everyone is, what they're doing," Kongming continued. "It's true that if he attacks the Wuhuan, he'll need to take almost all of the main forces, which spares Jing from Cao Cao's wrath for quite some time... months, maybe even a year."

"Such a short time...?" Liu Bei fretted. "How can they attack the Wuhuan and return so quickly...?"

"...Guo Jia is well versed in the Art of War," Kongming suggested. "He will suggest marching double-time, maybe faster... by reducing baggage trains, he can reach the territories in half the expected time, and catch the unprepared Wuhuan unawares: such an attack would destroy them very quickly and decisively, as Cao's forces destroyed both Yuan Shang and Yuan Tan's own forces a short time ago. And remember, Cao has added Ji Province to his already massive domains by defeating the Yuans... and all the resources and troops that go with it."

"Nonetheless," Ma Liang noted, "it still leaves us with a small time to attack the capital... using the same double-time tactic, we could surprise them."

"I agree," Jian Yong said surely.

"As do I, in principle," Xu Shu sighed. "But there's one small problem..."

"...Numbers," Kongming said knowingly. "Liu Biao would have to help us."

"Why wouldn't he...?" Mister Sun asked bluntly. "He attacked Xuchang a few years ago... why not now...?"

"Aside from the obvious – a memory of defeat in that endeavour – there is one other factor that could terrify him into taking no action," Kongming suggested.

"...*Sun Quan*," Ma Liang supposed.

Kongming nodded slowly.

"**Nn**...!" Zhang Fei grunted angrily. "Why does the Mouse of Jiangdong have to ruin this for us???"

"He is preparing a second assault on Huang Zu as we speak," Kongming declared: Liu Bei, Mi Zhu, Mi Fang, Mister Sun and Chen Zhen murmured disconcertedly.

"...Which means we may be asked to go southward to assist Huang Zu," Guan Yu supposed.

Kongming nodded again.

"...Well, as long as we get to fight *someone*," Zhang Fei sighed wearily. "I'm getting sick of sitting around and *talking* about fighting!"

"...An attack on Jiangxia... that would be bad," Liu Bei noted.

"It would, my lord," Xu Shu said sadly. "As Kongming said, we need Liu Biao's help to take the capital... but we also need to maintain a neutral relationship with Sun Quan... we are in a precarious situation."

"Kongming," Liu Bei hailed; "you and I must speak with Liu Biao urgently."

Kongming nodded in agreement.

At that time, the Jing governor Liu Biao was based in Xiangyang City, which was south of the River Han in northern Jing; Liu Bei was based in Fan City, a heavily fortified settlement on the north side of the River Han that was in view of Xiangyang. Liu Bei and Kongming crossed the river to meet with Liu Biao in his palatial home.

"Xuande...!" Liu Biao hailed feebly. "Liu Xuande... and this must be the 'Master Crouching Dragon' that I have heard so much about."

Kongming finished his ritual bow of greeting and looked at the miserable wreck that was Liu Biao: he struggled with the urge to sigh.

Liu Biao had, in his day, been a handsome, charismatic figure that had inspired all those who met him: now, after decades of fighting, not only age but stress and the burden of conscience had caught up with the man, leaving him prematurely frail and weak. His face was wrinkled and heavy with jowls, and his hair and beard were white and grey. He moved awkwardly and painfully as he gestured for Liu Bei and Kongming to be seated: Liu Bei assisted Liu Biao in taking his own seat, before sitting next to Kongming.

"...Xuande... Master Zhuge," Liu Biao croaked. "What am I to do, what am I to do...? My sons... my sons are worthless...! ...Huang Zu, he is so old... and the Suns, they get ever younger, while I shrivel up and age! ...Why could this foolishness have not died with Sun Jian, or even his eldest son...? I did not kill Sun Ce... I had nothing to do with that fool boy's death. So with Yuan Shu dead, the man who sent Sun Jian to me to die, why am I still haunted by the Suns of Jiangdong...? When will their vendetta end...?"

"...I fear that Sun Quan has not just got revenge on his mind," Kongming sighed. "I am afraid, Lord Liu, that he covets the land of Jing, under the pretext of reparation."

"That can never be!" Liu Biao protested. "Xuande, please... I have offered you my lands before, do not refuse me again. Take Jing Province... it is yours."

"...No, esteemed honorary brother," Liu Bei insisted. "It would not be right, others would oppose it."

"...But I offer it to you!" Liu Biao bleated. "Nobody would dare oppose my will!"

"I think that you are wrong," Liu Bei chuckled. "Liu Qi, your eldest, is feisty enough, and Liu Cong would never allow an outsider, not even a kinsman, like me, to take that which is rightfully his and his brother's. I will not be a villain... I learned my lesson from Xu Province, when others persuaded me to disinherit Tao Qian's children on their father's request. While it was his will, many opposed it, and doubted my sincerity, and I was forced to submit to Yuan Shao and discredit myself in order to keep the province. Were I to repeat the mistake, it would be seen not as a mistake, but pattern occupation: I would be labelled as another Cao Cao, or worse, a Wang Mang or Dong Zhuo."

"...So you will not do as I ask," Liu Biao said quietly. "Hah... well, at least you disprove my wife's belief that I am harbouring a hungry tiger... if you will not even seize what is offered, what have I to fear from you...?"

"...Nothing," Liu Bei insisted. "We are distant relatives, but you are like my brother, so far as I'm concerned. ...Now, I fear we are here for pressing matters."

"...What can be more pressing than the situation in Jiangxia, Brother Xuande...?" Liu Biao said with an almost scolding tone.

"The fate of the empire," Liu Bei insisted. "The last of the Yuan brothers, Shang, has fled north, to join the Wuhuan."

"I am aware of that," Liu Biao scoffed. "Why should I be concerned by that...?"

"Cao Cao desperately wants to conquer your lands, as Sun Quan does," Liu Bei explained. "As soon as Yuan Shang is defeated, an army that may number as many as three-hundred-thousand will descend on Jing, and you will have no choices other than surrender, or a fight to the finish."

"I have around a hundred-thousand men, which is not enough to resist him," Liu Biao noted fretfully. "Alas, I am doomed whichever way I turn!"

"Not necessarily," Kongming proposed. "Cao Cao must destroy the Wuhuan before he can come after you, my lord... we will have a short time when Cao Cao will be marching north, and fighting, where the capital will be relatively undefended... a full-scale surprise attack would enable us to rescue Emperor Xian and regain control of the court from Cao Cao."

"...Are you mad...?" Liu Biao chortled hoarsely.

"Listen to him," Liu Bei pleaded. "If we were to strike the capital-"

"...Then I would be besieged by Sun Quan, who would take advantage of my army's absence to attack *my* capital while I was fighting Cao Cao!" Liu Biao said angrily. "Caught between the two, I would lose my home! I would be a nomad, a laughing stock! Cao Cao's three-hundred-thousand would return from destroying the Wuhuan and kick me out of the capital, and then where would I go???"

"Brother...!" Liu Bei pleaded.

"I will not take such a risky move, not for anything!" Liu Biao said furiously. "The discussion is over!"

Liu Biao started to cough violently: eventually, a serving girl approached with a cup of water for him. Kongming noted the signs of frailty and hummed thoughtfully.

"...Now," Liu Biao said after he recovered from the coughing fit, "have either of you spared time to consider the situation in Jiangxia???"

A short time later, Kongming said to Liu Bei as they left Liu Biao's presence, "Guo Jia predicted Liu Biao's hesitancy too... a fine mind indeed."
"So all we can do is wait, then, for Cao Cao's hordes to descend on us, and Sun Quan to divide Liu Biao's forces," Liu Bei sighed miserably. "All my plans, *ruined*... even before they were put into motion!"
"Do not fret, my lord," Kongming said encouragingly. "We can continue to grow your forces, and as long as we avoid conflict with Sun Quan, and cultivate a relationship with Liu Qi, we can recover from this setback."
"Yes... Liu Qi," Liu Bei murmured. "He will inherit Jing Province."
"That cough he had: Liu Biao has a year or two at the most, his vitals are fading," Kongming suggested. "Liu Qi, though himself a hedonist riddled with illness and not likely to last long, is our best bet for maintaining a presence in Jing. Liu Qi is also very aggressive and upfront... we can persuade him to fight a lot more readily than Liu Biao."
"...Well then, hopefully Liu Biao will die before Cao Cao gets here," Liu Bei scoffed quietly: the off-guard remark took Kongming by surprise, and left him with even more to ponder as they returned to Fan City.

************

## 15

Kongming finally left Liu Bei's presence after several days and met with Ma Liang and Xu Shu in a tavern in Fan City.

"So what did Liu Biao say…?" Ma Liang asked.

"…Exactly as Guo Jia predicted," Kongming sighed. "The memory of the previous defeat, illness, senility, his second wife's slanderous gossiping and the threat of Sun Quan's forces on Jiangxia… have all guaranteed that Liu Biao will not act."

"…Aiee!" Xu Shu exclaimed angrily. "Then we cannot march on Xuchang!"

"Worse than that," Kongming sighed. "…We are now helpless, awaiting the inevitable. We will hear of the defeat of the Wuhuan within a year or less… and a march on Jing Province within weeks of that. We must not just plan a sound defence, my friends…"

"…We have to plan a retreat," Ma Liang murmured.

"No!" Xu Shu protested with a contemptuous laugh. "Will Liu Biao, governor of Jing Province, so easily surrender this place to Cao Cao…?"

"…Will he even be *alive*…?" Kongming suggested.

"So he is very sick, then," Ma Liang sighed. "His sons are not of the substance to fight Sun Quan, never mind Cao Cao."

"B-but… but everything we know is in Jing Province," Xu Shu bleated. "Our friends… our families… our way of life."

"That is why we all joined Liu Xuande," Ma Liang noted. "We all knew, deep down, that this day would come. …Kongming, what shall we do…?"

Kongming was ponderously silent: he fanned himself slowly, and did not respond to Ma Liang's question.

"…Kongming!" Xu Shu barked. "Come on, snap out of the trance and tells us what you think we should do!"

"…We have to think of the morale of the army, and our own reputations," Kongming replied at last. "We could advise our families to flee…"

"Yes, but to *where*…?" Xu Shu implored.

"Precisely," Kongming sighed. "Xiakou would normally be the literal first port of call, but with Sun Quan threating to attack Jiangxia at any moment… he may target Xiakou again since he was successful there last time, so that would not be wise. Were we to send our families south of the river to a place outside of Liu Biao's domains, it would suggest that we were preparing to defect to Sun Quan. While we would not suffer more than a harsh rebuke from some of Liu Xuande's generals… Liu Biao would have us executed."

"Ah…" Xu Shu groaned. "I would have suggested that… you are right, and I would have been a fool."

"So what then…?" Ma Liang fretted. "We cannot just wait for Cao Cao's army to descend on us!"

"His merciless attitude to civilians scares me," Kongming admitted. "Myself, I do not fear for, for any calamity I suffer is self-inflicted, caused by the choices I've made… but the Zhuge family, the Ma family, and the Xu family are all tied to our decisions… sadly, the Yi family too."

"Yi Ji is now joining us…?" Ma Liang supposed.

"Yes, he has tendered his services, after my having foolishly mentioned him in a casual chat," Kongming sighed. "So the four of us are now in it up to our necks... I don't know for sure what to do."

"...All we can do is *wait*," Xu Shu said numbly.

"...Quite so," Kongming concurred. "Hopefully, Sun Quan will either retreat when he sees that Cao has a southward-bound army, and bolster his own defences... or attack Jiangxia while Cao Cao is busy, so that the troubles will be over by the time Cao attacks... then Xiakou will once again be a place we can send our families to."

"But if he wins and takes Jiangxia...?" Ma Liang suggested.

"Impossible," Kongming insisted. "Huang Zu isn't just the prefect of Jiangxia... his family *is* Jiangxia, its heart and soul. He has so much support that an occupation by Sun Quan would be incredibly unpopular, and his remaining there would be difficult... he would face continual unrest. No, he'll retreat once he has Huang Zu's head, I think, and plan for taking Xiangyang by another route another day."

"...But why does he *do this*???" Xu Shu said with upset. "This feud... it has gone on for so long now! Even it will destabilise not just the region south of the river, but the entire country, and hand Cao Cao easy victories... something that will ultimately lead to his own doom! ...*Why*???"

"...Human nature," Kongming sighed sadly. "If it were a mistake of one man, I would weep at the stupidity of it. But it is a mistake that was made by countless men before Liu Biao and Sun Quan, and it will be made by many more before the end of time. On such a grand scale, one can only assume it's a folly we're cursed with, a weakness to destroy us from within... and it is sad, indeed."

"...So what will you do now?" Ma Liang asked forlornly.

"Lord Liu is obsessed with my counsel at present," Kongming replied miserably. "I am asked to return to him as soon as possible, so that we may discuss our future accord with Liu Qi, Biao's eldest son."

"If I were our Lord Liu, I'd find peace with Liu Cong - his second son - first," Ma Liang suggested. "Liu Cong is married to the niece of Lady Cai, his father's own wife, his stepmother... forgive me, brother, since you are also married to..."

"It will lead to Liu Biao's ruin," Kongming grunted irritably. "I know."

"Cai Mao, Lady Cai's brother, commands the navy, and as Liu Cong's stepmother *and* aunt by marriage, she favours Liu Cong for the influence it will give her at court," Ma Liang continued. "People speak of Liu Cong as being so under the thumb of Lady Cai, it is as though she were his real mother. The Cai clan will hold sway after Liu Biao dies, not Liu Qi... we must court the Cais, and Liu Cong."

"I agree," Xu Shu said reluctantly. "Although they are a detestable family, we cannot afford to be isolated when Cao Cao comes... or the Cai clan will sacrifice Liu Xuande to save themselves."

"...Aiee," Kongming sighed angrily. "Why can this not just be a matter of course, a simple case of doing the right thing...? Why must we worry about pointless arguments over inheritance at a time like this...? ...Truly, we're cursed... cursed to be fools, and ruin ourselves. Why does the Great Progenitor permit the reincarnation of idiots???"

"So we're going to appease the Cais, then...?" Xu Shu supposed.

"At Liu Qi's expense...?" Kongming chuckled dismissively. "To favour the younger son over the older son is what doomed Yuan Shao. No, in inheritance matters, the eldest son always inherits the estate, property and titles. We must be honourable and adhere to law: besides, I've already discovered that Lady Cai is slandering Liu Xuande already... she and her brother already plot against him. Even my wife denounces Lady Cai, and she's a blood relation."

"...*Great*," Xu Shu sighed. "So we must align ourselves with the weaker side... join forces with an undisciplined, diseased belligerent that will not live more than five years from this day. ...A lost cause, indeed."

"I must return to Xuande," Kongming said with urgency. "Try and remain calm, and think of ways to quickly evacuate our families when the worst occurs. I'll try and meet with you again soon, but... I will also be requesting leave at some point to see my family. You should try and do the same."

Kongming left his friends in a hurry, paying minimal respects to save time: Xu Shu shook his head sadly.

"Kongming was right all along... this is ridiculous," Xu Shu murmured.

"We'd have it no easier as civilians, nor as the official of another warlord," Ma Liang countered. "Kongming also said it is human nature... true enough. We're trapped... let's just try and salvage what we can."

Xu Shu nodded quietly, keeping any further thoughts to himself.

Over the next few weeks, Liu Bei and Kongming planned their approach regarding the courting of Liu Qi, and finding ways to evade being sent to Jiangxia without losing the trust of Liu Biao. Meanwhile, Cao Cao marched north: as Kongming had suspected, Guo Jia had the Cao troops march at great speed, reducing their baggage train and forsaking normal rest periods. The attack took the Wuhuan by surprise: however, Cao Cao's strategist Guo Jia would not live to enjoy the rewards of success. He died of illness in the Imperial capital, aged just 35 years old.


************

## 16

"Brother, *no*...!"

Guan Yu's protests were to no avail: Zhang Fei shrugged him off, pushed Liu Bei's bodyguard Chen Dao aside, and barged into Liu Bei's private meeting room, where he sat in conference with Kongming.

"**Aha!**" Zhang Fei barked. "What a surprise: you and 'Dozy Donkey', talking nonsense again, and **wasting valuable time!**"

"...Yide," Liu Bei replied calmly, as Guan Yu averted his gaze in shame, and Kongming stifled laughter, "we are discussing important matters."

"You always have new favourites, Elder Brother, and discard the older, trusted allies," Zhang Fei accused. "When we started out, we were inseparable, you, me and Yunchang... then you got Chen Dao from Xu Province, and Zilong from your mate Gongsun Zan, and now we're yesterday's news!"

"...Yide," Liu Bei said again.

"**No, let me finish,**" Zhang Fei barked. "**You worshipped Mi Zhu and Mi Fang, marrying their sister... you worshipped Chen Gui and Chen Deng, and why...? ...Because they funded us! ...But now, even the Mi brothers are pushed to one side... even others that have served you well, like Jian Yong and Old Mister Sun, that you'd spend hours with... now, you spend all day and all night talking to *this*! What has he done to deserve so much of your attention???**"

"...Yide," Liu Bei said sternly, "we are as brothers, we always have been. In the early days, we were able to spend more time in counsel because matters were simpler. The Yellow Turbans knew no strategy: brute force was enough to scatter them to the winds.

"After that, we faced tougher, smarter opponents, like Cao Cao; deceitful ones, like Lü Bu... I used the stratagems and advice of Mister Sun, Jian Yong, Mi Zhu, Chen Deng... but in the end, I suffered defeat after defeat, because although their plans did me in good stead when all that was required was backroom intrigue, on the field of battle, even they will admit that they were next to useless in that endeavour, especially against the likes of Guo Jia."

"**Guo Jia is dead!**" Zhang Fei shouted angrily.

"...And he has no peers...?" Kongming chuckled softly.

"We're no longer fighting bandits and cultists," Liu Bei scolded. "We're fighting trained soldiers, marshalled by battle-hardened generals, men like Xiahou Dun, Zhang Liao, Zhang He! Cao's plotters know not only how to scheme, but also how to array troops! ...What use is an army that rides into an ambush, or tries to break a formation, or cannot form them for defence, and is annihilated???"

"...I...!" Zhang Fei seethed.

"Leave it, brother," Guan Yu insisted.

"…We are without a base," Liu Bei concluded. "We are without a large army, our funds and resources are limited, and we are surrounded by timid or unreliable allies, and bitter enemies. Before, I was lost, unsure how to deal with these matters, and my morale was slipping, day by day… I would weep at the thought of facing the world each morning. Now, with Kongming's sagely advice, I have found hope in our beleaguered situation… finding Kongming is, to me, as a fish finding water."

"…*What*…!" Zhang Fei spluttered with surprise and amusement: Guan Yu silenced him with a stern stare.

"Now I'll hear no more from either of you," Liu Bei commanded, "nor anyone else, for that matter: please, Yide, I have urgent matters to discuss. When we are masters of our own domains, the Han safely restored… *then* we will sit together, talk of old times, and drink until our hearts are content… but right *now*… I must speak with this wise young man, *alone*."

"…**AIEE!**" Zhang Fei exclaimed in desperate anger: he turned and stormed out of the room. Guan Yu did not follow him: instead, he stared at the smiling Kongming.

"…You have something to say, Yunchang…?" Kongming asked cheerfully.

"Yide is hot-headed… but he means well," Guan Yu said quietly. "I am well-read, and I know something of the Art of War, and the importance of grasping it… so if you are, as Xuande claims, a master of stratagems, then that is to our benefit."

"…And if I am *not*…?" Kongming prompted.

"If you are *not*," Guan Yu replied, "then I will take your ingratiating yourself with my lord without the skill to provide results to be a personal offence… if Xuande does not deal with you personally, and Yide does not overtake me, you will be mine to dispense with, Zhuge Liang… pray that day does not come."

"Yunchang," Liu Bei scolded, "please, do not threaten my new strategist! Go and make sure Yide is not upsetting anyone else!"

"…Yes, Elder Brother," Guan Yu replied obediently: after one last cutting stare at Kongming, he left the room, and General Chen Dao returned to his post in front of the doorway.

"…Forgive them," Liu Bei chuckled nervously.

"For what…?" Kongming replied with a laugh. "They mean well. Now, as we were saying… Liu Qi and Liu Cong will start to contend, now that Liu Biao's health is visibly fading. There are some that are saying that Liu Qi may go to Xiakou and take up the post of Inspector of Jiangxia, under Huang Zu."

"…That would take him out of Xiangyang, and that would give greater strength to the Cai clan and their own preferred heir," Liu Bei fretted. "Why would he do such a thing???"

"As usual, it is difficult to say whether it is his own choice, or his father has been manipulated into sending him there by the Cais," Kongming sighed wearily. "All we do know is that Sun Quan's forces are gathering near Jiangxia… they will attack soon, safe in the knowledge that Cao Cao is busy to the north."

"…So we cannot now attack Xuchang, that is for certain," Liu Bei lamented. "Our greatest chance… … …gone, right in front of our eyes!"

"We must plan ahead," Kongming urged.

84

"Retreat...?" Liu Bei chortled miserably. "...That, or a futile struggle with a massive force from the north. ...Why must we again retreat...?"

Kongming fanned himself slowly as he thought the matter through.

"...Let us... let us see the events as unavoidable, and try to gain what little we can," Kongming said suddenly. "Liu Qi's withdrawal to Jiangxia is to our advantage, in a way... there will then be no internal civil war between the Cais and Liu Qi, he will be too far away to contest the Cais, and Liu Cong will take over the province."

"How is that to our advantage...?" Liu Bei chuckled disbelievingly.

"Liu Qi will then be away from the front against Cao Cao, ready to assist us in our retreat," Kongming suggested, "and with a little diplomacy... ready to help us travel to Jiangdong, where we can seek an alliance with Sun Quan to resist Cao Cao."

"That I don't see," Liu Bei admitted, "but... if you think it will work..."

"You'd be surprised what an army of a quarter-of-a-million enemy soldiers advancing on your territory can do to your disposition," Kongming said with a soft laugh. "Sun Quan will want to talk."

Liu Bei nodded in reluctant agreement. The discussion then turned to resources, and continued for several hours.

As evening set in, Kongming walked through the streets of Fan City, shivering in the chilly air. He looked at the faces of Liu Bei's soldiers as they patrolled the city, and saw in their eyes an uncertainty and fear that had not been there before. Word was spreading about Liu Biao's health: fear was spreading about what would follow. Kongming sighed woefully, and continued walking, thinking all the time as he went.

"The waiting... is painful," Kongming whispered suddenly.

What the future held was now almost inevitable: now, it was a matter of when, not if, the forces of Sun Quan killed Huang Zu of Juangxia, Liu Biao died, Liu Cong seized the reins of power in Jing, and Cao Cao invaded with a near unstoppable army that was hell-bent on conquering the entire country.

"Part of me... almost wishes it would just happen *now*," Kongming chuckled as he stopped, and examined his strategist's fan, which had yet to be put to use in an actual battle. "Still," Kongming murmured with amusement, "I suppose I should be careful what I wish for..."

＊＊＊＊＊＊＊＊＊＊＊＊

## 17

Within weeks, Liu Bei was assembling his court to make a surprising announcement. All of the officials and generals – even those of lower rank – were in attendance. Liu Bei's adopted son Feng was noticeably subdued: Liu Bei, on the other hand, was noticeably jubilant. Kongming guessed the situation and fanned himself slowly, having also guessed what was to come.

"I have assembled you all here today to present some good news!" Liu Bei said with uncharacteristic relish. "...I have a son!"

"We know, he's sat there," Zhang Fei scoffed as he pointed at Liu Feng.

"...A new son, born by my fair Lady Gan... his name is A'Dou," Liu Bei continued: Mi Zhu and Mi Fang – the brothers of Liu Bei's other wife – now started to look as uncomfortable as Liu Feng.

Murmurs and gestures of congratulation greeted the news.

"...I know that this is not really a good reason to assemble the court," Liu Bei admitted, "but... well... it *is* good news, isn't it...?"

The ensemble gave a more enthusiastic congratulation.

"Now... if Master Zhuge would kindly remain behind," Liu Bei declared with noticeable disappointment, "the rest of you are graciously dismissed."

Once Liu Bei and Kongming were alone, Kongming bowed slightly, and said, "Congratulations again."

"... ... ...Master... no... *Kongming*, for I see us as friends," Liu Bei began, "I have a dilemma."

"I expect that you do," Kongming replied calmly as he fanned himself.

"...My dilemma is twofold," Liu Bei said plainly. "Firstly, Liu Biao has asked that – if I will not receive this province as my own – I will defend it, protect them – his sons, I mean – help, them, guide them, as their guardian."

Kongming hummed ambiguously.

"Secondly," Liu Bei said hesitantly, "my sons, Feng and A'Dou..."

"...What about them...?" Kongming asked calmly.

"We are neither of us fools," Liu Bei continued. "We have watched Yuan Shao's sons tear one-another apart over the matter of succession... Liu Biao's sons, Qi and Cong, are now at each other's throats..."

"Before you continue," Kongming said calmly, "your son A'Dou is only newly born... and Heaven can be as cruel as it can be kind. So..."

"...Very well, I shall drop the matter for now," Liu Bei sighed irritably.

"As for Liu Qi and Liu Cong," Kongming continued, "I would say that favouring Liu Qi is adhering to the way, while favouring Liu Cong adheres to adapting to circumstance... as you know, it is my advice that you wait and watch. If Liu Qi loses, let him go to Jiangxia for safety. If Liu Qi wins... which is unlikely... then there will be an attempted purge of the Cai family at court, and massive civil unrest that you should stay out of. If the successor to Jing surrenders to Cao Cao... take the province before it is ceded."

"I could not do that," Liu Bei protested.

"...Those are my thoughts," Kongming replied tersely.

"… … …You are tired," Liu Bei said with a smile. "Go and rest… we have nothing further to discuss for now. I shall return to Lady Gan, and A'Dou…"
Kongming bowed, and left Liu Bei.

"What did he want…?" Ma Liang asked as Kongming departed the court.
"It's private," Kongming retorted, "hence his speaking to me alone."
"…I see," Ma Liang sighed sadly.
"… … …Some things must remain private," Kongming insisted. "But… in this matter, I shall take you into confidence. The lord has doubts about his plans for the family succession."
"B-but… but the child is just born…!" Ma Liang exclaimed.
"That's exactly what *I* said," Kongming said disapprovingly. "The matter is dropped for now… but it will be raised again, and I shall have to choose well how I answer, Jichang, since the future of our endeavour depends on it."
Ma Liang nodded thoughtfully.

Within a few days, Kongming received an unexpected visitor. Kongming did not notice the official, since he was so immersed in his administrative duties: the visitor smiled toothily, and coughed.
"…What…?" Kongming asked irritably without looking up.
"You'll wear yourself out, Kongming," Pang Tong teased.
"…What…!" Kongming exclaimed: he looked up, and smiled as he saw his old friend, the 'Young Phoenix'. "By the heavens…! …What are you doing here, Shiyuan…? …Have you come to join us…?"
"*No*," Pang Tong scoffed unintentionally.
"…You value Lord Liu that little…?" Kongming asked with annoyance.
"Forgive me," Pang Tong said insistently. "Please, understand, I have no desire to serve a lord in military capacity as you do. I am happy as an Officer of Merit."
"Nonsense," Kongming snickered. "You want to be noticed by Cao or Sun… Lord Liu is not powerful enough to catch your gaze. But you're wrong."
"It's you that's wrong, about *me*," Pang Tong insisted. "I don't underestimate Liu Bei's potential… I just don't want to commit myself to such a thing."
"If that's true… then don't you consider it to be a failure on your part to render good service to the empire…?" Kongming asked.
"Not really," Pang Tong chuckled. "Why should I consider my current role to be anything but serving the empire…? Is not every job a necessary part of the smooth running of the administration of the land…?"
"Fanciful rhetoric," Kongming sighed. "You were always the more cynical and ruthless of the two of us, better suited for the tasks I take on now. Surely, Shiyuan, you do not intend to waste your life doing a pedant's work when you have the mind to do greater things…?"
"Don't judge me," Pang Tong admonished. "My choice is my own to make."
"…You're waiting to see who prevails, and you will tender your services to the winning side," Kongming accused.

"Why, now, do you think so badly of me?" Pang Tong said with hurt. "What a thing it is, Kongming, to hear you make cutting remarks questioning my character! ...Kongming, why do you now doubt me as a man of integrity...?"

"...I apologise," Kongming replied sincerely. "It's just... it's just that you are always so quiet, so reserved, so careful not to divulge your thoughts on matters of importance... so cautious and meticulous..."

"And you, Kongming, are not...?" Pang Tong chortled. "You really sadden me with this attitude. If you want to know a man of poor conviction, look instead to Xu Shu, who would gladly give his life to a cause, until it becomes a matter of difficult choices... see, then, what he does, and criticise me afterward."

Kongming was silent.

"I came here simply to visit you, since I had heard that you were in service at last, and congratulate you on winning a high office with a respected feudal lord," Pang Tong continued. "Now that I have done that, I shall return to Jiangling... but before I go, I'll offer you some advice. Firstly, don't be so judgemental; secondly, don't be so cynical; thirdly, don't be so trusting; fourthly, don't be so freely honest. Apply each as you know that they should be."

"...That was *advice*...?" Kongming scoffed wearily.

"...Lastly," Pang Tong said sincerely, "don't work so hard. You're tired, Kongming... get some rest."

"I wish people wouldn't keep telling me that I'm tired," Kongming complained.

"We'll probably not meet again for a while, since I am quite busy, and you are as well," Pang Tong said regrettably. "However, we will meet again... we're friends, Kongming, and regardless of whatever befalls your lord, I know you well enough to know that you'll survive... and we'll meet again."

"...I know," Kongming replied. "...Before you go..."

"No," Pang Tong insisted. "Your lord's woes are not my concern."

With that, Pang Tong left Kongming to his work.

"You came all this way just to *congratulate me*...?" Kongming chortled quietly once Pang Tong had gone. "...What did you *really* want...?"

*************

## 18

Months of preparation began, as news poured in about the distant events that would soon have an enormous impact on the people of Jing Province. For the majority of the recent conflicts to this point, Jing's involvement had been external, and the impact on the lives of its citizens slight in comparison to places like Xu Province: that situation was about to change.

Kongming met with Ma Liang, Xu Shu and Yi Ji – his colleagues and friends – and Jian Yong, Liu Bei's long-time adviser, to discuss a series of new events. They selected a tavern in the town as their meeting place.
"So Cao Cao is back in the capital," Ma Liang mused.
"He's been back for a short time now," Xu Shu sighed. "...By the way, have you seen the doctors in town...? They're all wearing white. Someone said they are in Xiangyang as well. Who are they mourning...? Liu Biao is okay, isn't he...?"
"...Cao Cao killed Hua Tuo," Kongming explained.
"*Hua Tuo*???" Jian Yong exclaimed. "You can't kill Hua Tuo! He is...!"
"Well, he *did*," Kongming sighed. "Hua Tuo is dead... and his work is gone forever. His famous book was burned, although there is conflicting information about where, when and who by."
"Hua Tuo was the finest physician of our age," Xu Shu lamented. "What a shame."
"Cao was having one of his episodes," Kongming continued. "He gets those headaches... starts to act strangely, become obsessed with conspiracies and the such... some say it's his conscience.
          "Hua Tuo was asked to treat him. He used his skills to cure the headaches, but they always recurred: Cao Cao asked for Hua Tuo to be his personal doctor, but Hua Tuo refused, stating a number of reasons, including not wanting to limit his work to a single subject.
          "It seems that the refusal angered Cao, and he had him incarcerated in order to terrify him into changing his mind," Kongming sighed in conclusion. "Obviously, it didn't work."
"...But killing him," Jian Yong exclaimed. "I knew about the imprisonment... but I never expected that. He was a genius, a one-of-a-kind..."
"I thought Cao Cao respected intelligent men," Xu Shu despaired.
"Obviously not 'disloyal' ones," Kongming chuckled ironically. "I think that everyone now shares my view, *hopefully*, that Jing will not be spared the fate that befell Xu Province just because there are lots of clever people here. Cao won't care... he'll tear this place to shreds and kill everyone, like he did in Xu."
"He didn't do that in Ji, and many other places he's conquered," Xu Shu protested.
"They weren't targets of his vengeance," Kongming retorted. "Liu Xuande was his friend, and is now his hated enemy, a man that conspired to kill him."
"...We shouldn't say that too loudly, Kongming," Yi Ji pleaded fretfully. "We do not need the people of Jing throwing him to Cao to save themselves... we'll be sacrificed too."

"...**MISTER ZHUGE LIANG!**" a voice bellowed: it took the advisers by surprise.

"...Who...?" Kongming wondered.

The group turned to face the source of the call: it was one of Liu Bei's messenger-soldiers.

"...You're wanted again," Jian Yong chuckled.

"...**MISTER JIAN YONG!**" the messenger shouted.

"We're not *deaf*," Jian Yong grumbled. "You're drawing attention to us."

"Sorry, Mister Jian," the messenger said humbly. "But I was told it was urgent, that you need to go to the court hall immediately."

"Cao Cao...?" Jian Yong wondered.

"We'll see when we get there," Kongming suggested. "Let's hurry."

Jian Yong nodded in agreement.


"Ah, my friends... please, enter," Liu Bei hailed as the five advisers arrived at court. Liu Bei's 'brothers', Guan Yu and Zhang Fei, were already present, as were Zhao Yun, the Mi brothers, and Mister Sun. There was also a guest: a man of unremarkable features and short stature, with a strange, discomforting expression. He wore plain brown robes and slouched gracelessly, which surprised the advisers all the more, given Liu Bei's distaste for vulgar people.

"This is...?" Jian Yong prompted as he nodded respectfully to the visitor, but took care not to bow until he knew who he was.

"...Family name Zhang, given name Song, styled Ziqiao," the man said tersely.

"...A pleasure," Kongming said with a bow, as he sensed great importance in or to the visitor.

Zhang Song bowed in response, and smiled: and then – sensing that Kongming's judgement was correct – the other advisers bowed as well. Zhang Song returned their gestures with respect, and started, almost immediately, to make more of an effort to be dignified.

"...Without ascertaining my purpose, you show me respect," Zhang Song said, reflexively rubbing his arm as he did so. "You are every bit as deserving of my visit as Fa Xiaozhi and Meng Ziqing thought you would be."

"...This is indeed splendid!" Liu Bei said with cheer.

"*What* is...?" Zhang Fei complained. "We've sat here for *half an hour* and we *still* don't know who this bloke is."

"Mm... would Fa Xiaozhi be Fa Zheng, by any chance...?" Jian Yong asked pointedly. "And Meng Ziqing, maybe, is Fa Zheng's acquaintance Meng Da...?"

"The very same!" the visitor, Zhang Song, said with gratitude. "Sir, you are...?"

The five advisers introduced themselves one by one to an increasingly delighted Zhang Song: Guan Yu, Zhang Fei and Zhao Yun then introduced themselves at last, and those that were not already seated soon were, smiling cheerfully at the relaxed atmosphere. Jian Yong continued to talk quietly with Zhang Song.

"I still don't see why we're all so happy," Zhang Fei whispered to Guan Yu and an amused Zhao Yun. "Is this man a magician...?"

"So Fa Zheng and Meng Da are vassals of Liu Zhang, the governor of Yi Province," Jian Yong prompted: Guan Yu and Zhao Yun smiled as they realised the significance.

"...They are, as I am, yes," Zhang Song sighed. "Sadly, the governor is worthless... his father, Liu Yan, would not just be disappointed, he would be *ashamed*!"

"That bad...?" Jian Yong snickered.

"Yes," Zhang Song said with all seriousness. "He is uncharismatic, uninspiring, fails to see talent, and gives high posts to toadying pedants... Fa Zheng and Meng Da, despite their obvious worth, both held low-ranking civil duties in small prefectures, until someone else pointed out that their talents were wasted. ...Both men are extremely disappointed that Liu Zhang could not see it for himself."

"All the same," Jian Yong challenged as Kongming looked on in silence, "that does not warrant the obvious purpose of your visit, does it...?"

"...You are correct," Zhang Song agreed. "But there is worse... as you have no doubt heard, the cult leader Zhang Lu, whom Liu Yan tolerated and received respect from, has no such relationship with my lord. He is trying to form his own state, and has waged open war with Liu Zhang on a number of occasions."

"I see," Liu Bei sighed. "If he is not curbed, your fear is that he will begin another revolt, like the Yellow Turbans."

"Lord Liu, that is unlikely," Zhang Song suggested. "He is a cult leader, yes, but he does not desire the throne... he just wants Yi. He is organised, disciplined... his people respect him. And although Liu Zhang's governance is mild, and generally harmless, it is insufficient in troubled times... Yi Province needs a warlord governor, not a soft-touch prefect."

"I like this man," Zhang Fei whispered to Guan Yu, who nodded agreeably.

"All the same, it *really*...!" Jian Yong began: Zhang Song raised his hand as a request for silence.

"To add insult to injury, he is a faithless coward," Zhang Song continued. "He raised not a finger when Cao Cao was ravaging Xu. He did nothing to help when Lü Bu was causing havoc... he just sits there, as though he thinks the outside world is not his concern. ...But then, he was a toady in the Han court, at the beck and call of the likes of Dong Zhuo and Li Jue for much of his early career."

"But *still*...!" Jian Yong protested.

"Now, with all the current troubles, he seeks an easy way out," Zhang Song grumbled irritably. "I did not come here directly from my lord's capital, Chengdu... I came here from Cao Cao's residence in Xuchang."

"...*Xuchang*...?" Liu Bei exclaimed: his surprise was shared.

"Yes... fresh from being rebuked rudely by Cao Cao, whom I had gone there, on my lord's instructions, to pay homage to, and pledge undying allegiance to," Zhang Song revealed: Zhang Fei sneered with disgust, and the others expressed their distaste, including Liu Bei.

"Such a man will ruin our grand scheme to restore the Han," Kongming said sadly.

"That's why I'm here," Zhang Song continued. "I'm here to ask not, as Lord Lui Xuande thought, for help on my lord's behalf to defend Yi... I am here on behalf of Fa Xiaozhi and Meng Ziqing as well, as we cannot bear to see Yi fall into Cao Cao or Zhang Lu's hands... to ask Lord Liu to work with us to take Yi Province from that idiot before he does anything else."

An awkward, nervous silence descended, as the advisers thought about the offer, and Liu Bei pondered how best to answer.

"I know that what I say is treasonous," Zhang Song conceded, "but a man who serves an unworthy lord is unworthy himself. Please do not refuse."

"...I admit that I am reluctant to take land from a kinsman," Liu Bei sighed, "but..."

"We need to discuss this privately," Kongming interrupted. "I hope you understand, Zhang Ziqiao. We will provide you with hotel accommodation, and ensure you are treated well... while we discuss the matter further."

"Oh, don't worry, I understand," Zhang Song chuckled. "Cao Cao's preparing to invade Jing, he was boasting about it while I was there... thank goodness his arrogance is so vast, else he'd have accepted my lord's grovelling, and not thrown it back in my face, vowing to *conquer* Yi one day instead."

"So he is definitely coming here," Jian Yong mused.

"Take all the time you need," Zhang Song insisted. "I'll decline your hotel: I really should be going home, or my lord will become suspicious... as I said, he readily lends an ear to slander, and I want nothing to affect our plans. I wish you good fortune against Cao's forces... when you're safe again, we should resume this discussion."

With that, Zhang Song got to his feet, made several short, sharp bows of obeisance to his hosts, and took leave of the court.

"...Please don't tell me you're considering turning *him* down as well," Kongming chuckled miserably as he observed Liu Bei's morose expression.

"Mm...? ...No," Liu Bei said frankly. "I should definitely like to take up the offer to visit Yi at the very least... it is perfect, and accords fully with our own plans. I'm just wondering how to proceed, what with everything else that's going on."

"...We're too weak to go there now," Jian Yong suggested. "We'd be seeking refuge, as we are here... if this man is as much of a coward as Zhang Song suggested, he would hand us over to Cao Cao to save himself."

"Agreed," Kongming murmured. "I confess that I have heard a story about Liu Zhang... that he was actually sent to reprimand his own father by the court... and his father kept him in Chengdu, like a naughty child, refusing to send him back."

"...He is some sort of simpleton," Guan Yu suggested. "Unfit to rule anything."

"Sadly, I agree," Liu Bei sighed. "I would not take Jing from Liu Biao because of the politics attached to it... but I would take Yi, since it is doomed to fall into another's hands... exactly as you said to me, Kongming. Once again, your insight was correct, verified by a noted official of that land."

"...Mine was a guess based on facts and hearsay," Kongming insisted humbly.

"Marvellous, all the same," Jian Yong suggested. "You're wasted as an adviser… you should have gone into business as a seer… you'd be rich by now."

"Maybe," Kongming chuckled as he started to fan himself casually.

"…Still, that must wait," Liu Bei said suddenly. "If Cao is definitely coming, we must be ready. Can we blunt his vanguard, delay him, *anything*…?"

"…Unlikely," Kongming admitted. "I'll look at the maps again… if we could fool them with an ambush at Bowang again it would be wonderful… unfortunately not."

"…Okay," Liu Bei sighed. "You should all take leave to see your families, tell them about the move… if Cao Cao is coming, none of our families can afford to be captured. …Go on, you're dismissed."

"Thank you, my lord," the assembly said as one, and then they departed.


"So you're going home…?" Xu Shu supposed as he walked through Fan City with Kongming and Ma Liang. "What will you tell Lady Huang…?"

"*Sorry*, for a start," Kongming sighed. "I haven't been home since I joined Lord Liu… not once. I've been so caught up… so busy… and it's too far away to go home every evening…"

"Yes," Ma Liang scolded. "I've been meaning to talk to you about that, Kongming… while you were a farmer, you worked a full day, and then studied for hours at night by lamp light… now, at court, you do the work of three officials without rest, and you work twice the hours of the rest of us… you'll make yourself ill if you do that all the time."

"Jichang," Kongming said with a laugh, "I have a heavy burden on my shoulders! How can I not work as hard as I can for the cause…? …I will be fine. But yes, I owe my wife an apology… and besides, I miss her."

Xu Shu and Ma Liang smiled sadly.


✱✱✱✱✱✱✱✱✱✱✱✱

## 19

"...Liang...!"
Yueying ignored etiquette and rushed to Kongming as he entered the living quarters, throwing her arms around him.
"...I've missed you," Kongming whispered.
"...Why haven't you been back...?" Yueying sobbed weakly.
"This isn't like you," Kongming said with amusement.
"...Never mind, I'm just happy to see you," Yueying insisted as she continued to hold onto him with all of her strength.
"...I wish I could say that I'm not going back," Kongming admitted as he stroked Yueying's hair gently. "But... in fact... I am here to tell you that we have to go, all of us."
"I thought as much," Yueying sighed as she released her grip, and backed away from her husband slightly. "How long do we have...?"
"It depends," Kongming said frankly, "on how badly Cao Cao wants Lord Liu dead, to be honest. He could fast-march, like he did on the northern campaign, and be here very quickly. ...But he has new regiments to assimilate into his army, rations to prepare, medicine supplies to acquire... he'll be a while. But Sun Quan has launched an attack on Jiangxia... it was starting just as I was packing to leave. Liu Biao is in a state of distress... he'll probably be dead by the time we get back, and then... Liu Cong is our master, and only the Heavens know what he'll do with us to appease Cao Cao's wrath."
"So many enemies... so much intrigue... and now, you're in the middle of it," Yueying said as she traced a finger down the side of Kongming's face. "You've aged, in so short a time... I'm not surprised, but..."
"I know," Kongming interrupted miserably. He now had permanent rings under his eyes, and had lost the youthful exuberance he had once had. In addition, the days spent in rooms and tents, rather than under the sun, had left his skin dry and pale.
"You look so poorly," Yueying said frankly. "You should rest for a couple of days... no work, you understand...?"
"Yes, my lady," Kongming replied with a weary laugh. "I won't argue... I need it."
"...Your brother will probably be back soon," Yueying supposed.
"...He'll have to come with us," Kongming mused.
"*Leave... the arrangements...* to **me**," Yueying insisted emphatically.
"...Sorry," Kongming snickered.
"I mean it, rest," Yueying said sternly. "You're no good to me, your family or Lord Liu if you're a wreck. And you don't want another bout of depression, either."
"...True," Kongming said worriedly. "I do need to be strong... very well, I shall remain at ease... perhaps I shall play the qin later."

Zhuge Jun returned later that day: Jun and Kongming sat alone in the living quarters while Yueying went out onto the grounds to discuss plans with the servants on her husband's behalf.
"...Jun," Kongming said sadly, "you look older."
"I *am* older," Jun replied with a puzzled expression.

"No, I mean... like me, you've had to take on a lot more," Kongming explained as he struggled with the urge to take up his fan. "You're older inside and outside... I'm sorry that my leaving placed such a burden on you."

"I'm a grown man," Jun suggested. "I will soon be getting married myself, and... well... all that."

"...There's something I don't know, isn't there...?" Kongming supposed.

"No," Jun answered immediately.

"...*Oh, I am so sorry*," Kongming sobbed as he realised the cause of Yueying's uncharacteristic show of tears.

"Damn... she said you might guess if I said anything... you mustn't, brother... you mustn't say I told you," Jun pleaded as Kongming's eyes welled up with tears of his own at the thought of Yueying's anguish.

"...She didn't want me to know she was with child, in case it affected my decision to go to Lord Liu... that's it, isn't it," Kongming realised. "I am a wretched, wretched man."

"...No!" Jun insisted with a nervous laugh. "Please... don't blame yourself. She told me it was not in any way your fault... she was sure about that... don't be upset at yourself, brother."

"But... stress can cause these things," Kongming suggested. "The stress of my not returning, not letting her know I was alright... this is my fault."

"No, no, it isn't," Jun insisted again. "Brother, please... say no more, or she'll guess that you know, and blame me, and..."

Kongming had reflexively taken up his fan some moments before: he used it to gesture that Jun should be silent.

"...I'll say no more," Kongming said weakly as he lowered his arm. "...She is very strong... she hid it from me so that I might rest... she is every bit my match, as her father said. ...And we will overcome this."

"That's what *she* said," Jun revealed.

"...Fine... fine," Kongming said: he inhaled sharply, wiped his eyes with his sleeve, and smiled with feigned cheer.

"So when do we all leave the cottage...?" Jun asked.

"We might as well go now," Kongming supposed. "By now, I mean 'in the next few days'... we'll go to Fan City, where Lord Liu is camped... we'll be ready to move from there."

Later that evening, Kongming strummed the strings of his qin, while Yueying listened, hoping to see in his playing a sign of his state of mind.

"...You are unreadable," Yueying said as Kongming played with a relaxed, eerie calmness. "I cannot tell what you're thinking at all."

"I realise now," Kongming said as he continued to play, "that in this chaotic world we live in, there are two types of men... those that wear their emotions on their sleeves, who cry and weep, like Lord Liu, at the first sight of trouble or misery... and then there are the men who must be impossible to read, so that they may strike terror into their enemies, who will not know what they are thinking... because they must *never* know what you are thinking..."

"You are right," Yueying conceded. "But now that you have shown that you can be so cold, even in the warmth of your own home... can you not now tell me what you are thinking...?"

"...It serves no purpose," Kongming insisted as he came to the end of the tune he was playing: he strummed the last few notes, and sat back, exhaling calmly.

"... ... ...Jun told you," Yueying realised.

"My love," Kongming replied, "I would have realised eventually anyway. And while it has left me feeling as though I am to blame... I am also very sad because the little stability you had left – this cottage, the home I brought you to live in – will soon be torn out of our lives too. ...And I cannot just blame Cao Cao, or Liu Xuande for that..."

"You blame yourself, and also your reputation, and your brother," Yueying supposed. "But this was inevitable."

"Yes," Kongming said bitterly. "No matter what I had chosen to do, I would have to abandon my home now. I'm 'Master Crouching Dragon'...! I'm the brother of one of Sun Quan's advisers! I'm related by marriage to the governor of Jing Province! Being in Lord Liu Bei's service is just another reason for Cao Cao to hunt me down, and give me an ultimatum: be his new Guo Jia, or be the next Hua Tuo."

"...So the rumours in town were true, then," Yueying remarked with anger. "He killed one of the most outstanding minds of the age."

Kongming lowered his head and exhaled fiercely.

"Now, I am an open book again," Kongming lamented. "I am yet to learn how to control my anger for long periods... I *must learn*."

"For now, rest," Yueying insisted again. "Play something else."

Kongming looked up, smiled feebly, nodded, and started to play again. Again, the sound was calm: he closed his eyes, and thought about the things that were to come.

Three days later, Kongming stood on the far side of the bridge, watching sadly as his servants and workers waved goodbye to the Zhuge family. Yueying was already sat on a large, open-backed transport cart with their most precious belongings, and his brother Jun was sat on the horse that would pull it.

"...Father will visit from time to time," Yueying said reassuringly.

"Our people are good, honest and trustworthy," Kongming said numbly.

"Cao Cao has a reputation for being a monster, but he was acting out of rage in Xu Province, husband," Yueying suggested. "He has established some marvellous things to make the lives of the people better as well... he wouldn't strike down the people of Jing without good reason."

"I hope so," Kongming said wearily. "Okay... let us depart."

After one last farewell to his family home, Kongming got onto the cart, and Jun got the horse moving with a soft tap of his foot. Kongming watched the thatched cottage disappear from view, and lowered his head sadly.

"At least you got a rest," Yueying suggested.

"Now we are about to see unbridled chaos," Kongming chuckled. "By now, Xiangyang and Xinye... will be falling apart."

************

## 20

By the time that Kongming had returned to Fan City, events had taken a dramatic turn. As soon as he had settled his family into the care of the family of his sworn brother Ma Liang, he hurried to the court to meet with his lord Liu Bei.

"Ah, Kongming," Jian Yong hailed. "I was worried you were going to miss all the fun we've been having. ...You look rested."

"Thanks," Kongming replied, returning Jian Yong's gestures of respect and smiling at the man's ability to maintain a sense of humour in such troubled times. He noted that all of Liu Bei's most trusted vassals were present, and made reciprocated gestures of respect to them.

"...Worthy nephew," Liu Bei pleaded: Kongming looked to the other end of the room, where Liu Bei was apparently arguing with Liu Qi, eldest son of Liu Biao and supposed inheritor of the region.

"He has won, worthy uncle!" Liu Qi said angrily: he appeared to be intoxicated. "I have no choice... but... fight...!"

"...It might seem that way," Liu Bei protested, "but..."

"My lord," Jian Yong hailed. "Master Kongming has returned."

"Oh, *thank the Heavens*," Liu Bei muttered. "Kongming, please, come forth and greet Liu Qi, my worthy nephew."

"...My pleasure," Kongming hailed as he reached the two leaders, and took a seat to the left of Liu Qi, facing Liu Bei.

Liu Bei had ceded the host seat to Liu Qi as a sign of submission to him as the son of the regional governor. Kongming reviewed the young man's ghosted appearance: in most ways, he was more prematurely decrepit and weak than his father was.

"This is a waste of time!" Liu Qi insisted. "Sun Quan... he's... attacking Huang Zu! I have to go to Jiang... to Jiangxia, and help him... but...!"

"You cannot help Huang Zu now," Kongming insisted. "Sun Quan's forces are going to win... good counsel for the future ruler of Jing Province would be for you to keep your forces in the capital... yet you speak of Jiangxia."

"He cannot remain here," Liu Bei said with a mournful sigh. "Even though Liu Biao is still alive, the shock news of Cao Cao's impending invasion – and Huang Zu's impending defeat at Jiangxia – have stressed him, and confined him to his bed: his health, his vitals are fading..."

"...And my step-m-mother and her brother... have seized c-control of the court," Liu Qi said angrily. "I... they...!"

"They've made Liu Cong the heir," Kongming supposed, "as everyone thought they would... because Liu Cong has Lady Cai's niece for a wife, Lady Cai for a stepmother, and Cai Mao as head of his navy. Liu Cong will serve the Cais, whereas you will not."

"Yeah... yeah!" Liu Qi slurred. "You... you're right!"

"...So Liu Qi has to go to Jiangxia so that he is no longer a threat to Liu Cong," Kongming noted. "...If that is what has been decided... young lord, go to Jiangxia: get out of the Cai family's reach. There will be opportunities to regain what is rightfully yours."

"...Okay," Liu Qi agreed, to the surprise of all. "Anyone... that sounds as calm and clever as you... has to know what they're doing..."

Liu Qi got up, made clumsy shows of obeisance to Liu Bei and his retainers, and staggered into the scenic courtyard to begin his journey.

"...He comes to us drunk," Jian Yong scoffed. "That'll impress nobody."

"It isn't just drink," Kongming noted. "Did you see his wasted face, his complexion, his eyes...?"

"...Never mind that," Liu Bei said dismissively, and also with emotion. "Liu Biao is dying... for that, I cannot help but weep."

With that, Liu Bei raised his right arm to his face, and made a visible show of grief for Liu Biao: Mister Sun, Mi Zhu and Xu Shu were touched, while Jian Yong and Kongming were cynically cold to the display.

"...So what now...?" Zhang Fei said impatiently. "Can I go back and sort out my troops now that we've spoken to that boy...?"

"...Yes, yes," Liu Bei said through impassioned sobbing. "Go, Yide, Yunchang, Zilong... go, get ready..."

The generals took their leave.

"My lord," Mister Sun prompted, "we must prepare to depart, but... with the Cais running the court, aren't we in danger of being sent as a vanguard to fight Cao Cao, or as reinforcements to Jiangxia...?"

"No in either case," Kongming insisted. "We are not trusted by the Cais, who would fear our presence in Jiangxia, especially with Liu Qi there as well. And if we were sent as a vanguard to fight Cao Cao, that would be a declaration of war..."

"...Insinuating that you think Liu Cong will...!" Liu Bei realised.

"...Surrender...? Most likely," Kongming sighed woefully. "The Cais will take the easy way out... like Liu Zhang of Yi has."

"So we are in danger," Jian Yong supposed.

"Let's put it this way: Fan City will be resisting alone," Kongming replied.

"...He... he wouldn't," Liu Bei said as he wiped his eyes and brought an end to his show of tears for Liu Biao. "...But then, if he did... what of the villagers..."

"Uh... my lord," Mister Sun chuckled nervously, "what *of* the villagers...?"

"We can't leave them here to suffer the same fate as the good people of Xu Province if we retreated!" Liu Bei suggested. "We would have to protect them!"

"...There are over a hundred-thousand civilians in this region," Kongming protested desperately. "If we took them with us, we'll be going so slowly that Cao Cao could catch up to us even if he *walked* from Xuchang."

"You're the one that constantly reiterates to me the fate of the people of Xu Province," Liu Bei retorted. "How can you now advocate abandoning them...?"

"I don't," Kongming insisted, "but... my lord, leaving them here as surrendered subjects will guarantee their lives... taking them with us is what condemns them."

"...We'll see what the people want to do," Liu Bei conceded. "But if they wish to follow, Kongming, then I will hear no more protestations."

"...Very well," Kongming sighed sadly. "Are we going to try and get an audience with Liu Biao...?"

"Not worth trying," Mister Sun lamented. "The Cais are denying all visitors."

Kongming pondered it, nodded silently, and awaited further instructions.

As the weeks passed, Huang Zu died fighting Sun Quan's forces, and Jiangxia fell into the hands of the southern Sun family. Not long after that, Liu Biao, governor of Jing, passed away at the age of 65. His second son, Liu Cong, succeeded him.

************

## 21

"Something is wrong..."

Kongming was once again sat in counsel with Liu Bei on the roof of Fan City, overlooking the northern capital city of Xiangyang that lay across the river. Liu Bei got up from their rooftop meeting and walked to the battlements, sighing heavily. It was a dull day, and cold winds blew mercilessly, cutting at the skin.

"...Are you intending to seek an audience with Liu Cong...?" Kongming asked.

"I have little choice," Liu Bei decided.

"And if he won't see you...?" Kongming asked.

"...Your counsel is barbed," Liu Bei scolded. "I cannot cut down a kinsman."

"You think Liu Cong has any allegiance to you...?" Kongming suggested with a laugh. "Though Lady Cai is not his true mother, and Cai Mao not his uncle, they might as well be! He's a puppet, a pawn... my lord, we have under our command some able generals, good officials... several of Liu Biao's vassals have already defected to us since he died. We have over ten thousand soldiers..."

"...A deliberately up-scaled estimation," Liu Bei scoffed. "I have much less than that, Kongming... and again, I stress that I will not kill my own nephew."

"He isn't your nephew," Kongming insisted. "And who said you have to kill him...? I am suggesting that you attack now, take the Cais unawares, remove their presence, and, if needs be, exile Liu Cong... remember, he has an elder brother whose office he has stolen."

"You're married to the daughter of a Cai," Liu Bei noted.

"But I serve the Liu family," Kongming retorted, "as does my wife."

"...I cannot risk it," Liu Bei sighed. "No, Kongming... we shall go to Xiangyang and politely ask for an audience... if we do not get one, we shall move on."

Liu Bei took his main bodyguard force, led by Chen Dao, and his general Zhao Yun, and led them to Xiangyang, leaving Kongming to station at a temporary encampment near the River Han. All that anyone could do was await the outcome: Liu Bei's hurried, tense return revealed the truth of the matter.

"**Call a meeting! NOW!**" Liu Bei barked to his nearest aides: a team of messengers ran to fetch the advisors to council.

"My lord..." Kongming prompted.

"That... that *miserable cur*!" Liu Bei growled.

"...Liu Cong...?" Kongming supposed.

"He did not even have the decency to speak to Lord Liu in person," Zhao Yun said angrily. "He sent someone to shout the situation over the walls of the city... he has surrendered to Cao Cao, who is on his way to Xinye to receive the seal of office and take official control of Jing Province."

"**AIEE...!**" Liu Bei screamed with hurt and rage.

"...Fool," Kongming murmured. "He has handed his father's hard-fought territory over to a wolf... he has extinguished all that-"

"Enough fancy rhetoric!" Liu Bei seethed. "I... ... ...sorry, Kongming, I am angry. I even drew my sword on the man, but... ... ...I cannot be so reckless."

"I don't blame you for being angry," Kongming said irritably. "He had no intention of warning us... we were being left to die. He's even going to receive Cao Cao in Xinye, our base... we were going to be turned over to him."

"...You're right," Liu Bei realised. "I did not... ... ...*he was going to let me die.*"

"We are no longer welcome here," Kongming suggested.

"I agree with Master Zhuge," Zhao Yun declared. "My lord, we must leave this place immediately."

"Many have followed us back to camp," Liu Bei said numbly. "A lot of the people of Xiangyang have abandoned the city... now we must return to Fan, warn the people, gather your families...!"

"Cao Cao's advance is truly fast, faster even than I had assumed," Kongming murmured. "I thought we had less to fear with the death of Guo Jia... indeed, his successor, Jia Xu, is formidable."

"Fine, fine, fair enough!" Liu Bei barked. "There's time enough for that at the meeting later!"

"...Yes, my lord," Kongming conceded.

The emergency meeting took place in Fan City later that day.

"...So is everyone in agreement...?" Liu Bei asked as soon as he had finished outlining the situation.

"...Kongming...?" Jian Yong prompted. "...What's your esteemed view...?"

"You all know what I think," Kongming sighed wearily. "We should not flee... we should take all those defected soldiers and generals we have just gained, annex them into our own forces, turn right around, go back to Xiangyang, and take Jing Province from Liu Cong before he gives it to Cao Cao... then, we can consolidate in Jiangling and coordinate defence against Cao Cao. If Liu Biao has successfully held this region for all this time, why can't we...?"

"...Yes, we all know what you think," Liu Bei said sternly, "and you all know what *I* think; that I could not face Liu Biao in Heaven if I was responsible for the death of his son!"

"...We can capture him," Mister Sun suggested.

"No," Liu Bei insisted, "we cannot... the Cais will simply kill him, say *we* killed him, and take over Jing themselves if it looks like he cannot hold. And besides... ...I see no mention of *Liu Qi* in your plan, Master Zhuge."

"...No," Kongming replied. "He *would* kill Liu Cong if he could... and all the Cais, perhaps even those outside the conspiracy, like my wife and mother-in-law. I am trying to avoid that as much as you are."

"...There's no winning a debate with you," Liu Bei sighed. "...But I will not yield to my vassals on the matter. I will not usurp Liu Cong."

"So we must flee," Mister Sun murmured.

"We have no choice," Kongming said bluntly. "Liu Cong cannot now be talked out of surrendering, and he is surrounded by people intent on doing so. We cannot go to Liu Zhang, because he is now helping Cao Cao. We cannot surrender, because Lord Liu is part of the Emperor's conspiracy to execute Cao Cao for treason, and Cao wants him dead for it. So we must resort to the only one of the thirty-six stratagems of war that applies... run away."
The room was silent.
"...Very well," Liu Bei said, exhaling wearily as he spoke. "We could discuss this a thousand times... once again, the only option is to run. Very well... let us run."
The advisors looked at each other with a sense of discomfort: Kongming was especially uncomfortable, since he knew that his plan would not be popular.

**"AAAAAARGH! ...I knew it! Bloody pedants, always wanting to run away! Always, always 'run away'...!"** Zhang Fei screamed as he was told the news.
"...Calm down," Guan Yu scolded. "We have no choice."
**"I'm sick of running away!"** Zhang Fei retorted as he threw a heavy halberd across the room, narrowly missing an officer.
"...So am I," Guan Yu replied calmly, "but this time I understand the odds. After this time–"
**"You said that the last time! ...And the time before that!"** Zhang Fei shouted. **"We *always* end up running away! ...Always! ...We ran from Anxi, we ran from Xu, we ran from Xu *again*, we ran from Runan... we ran from Cao Cao, from Yuan Shao, from Lü Bu! In years to come, artists won't know how to draw our faces, only our backs!"**
"...Yide," Liu Bei said after what had been a long, painful silence.
**"No!"** Zhang Fei screamed. **"I want to FIGHT!"**
Kongming and Jian Yong smiled uncontrollably as Zhang Fei raved, but kept their faces hid behind their sleeves.
"Cao Cao has two-hundred-thousand men," Guan Yu protested. "We have about six to eight thousand, probably. Yide, even *I* do not want to fight."
"Really, Yide," Zhao Yun pleaded, "no more... we cannot fight."
Zhang Fei screamed, **"AIEE!"** and stormed out of the room at great speed, mouthing curses.
"...So he can run when he wants to," Jian Yong quipped.
Kongming followed Zhang Fei silently, leaving the others to bicker.

"...**GO AWAY!**" Zhang Fei screamed as he saw Kongming approach him.
"No," Kongming said sternly. "General Zhang, please understand that this decision makes me as sick as it makes you."
"How so...?" Zhang Fei growled.
"I wanted Lord Liu to destroy Liu Cong and seize Xiangyang, use it to attack Cao Cao," Kongming noted. "I pleaded with him... but he will not go against his own ethics. With Liu Cong betraying us, we cannot fight... we are hopelessly outnumbered, under-resourced, and surrounded by enemies and traitors."
Zhang Fei grunted.

"…I did not leave my home to run away," Kongming insisted with a laugh. "I left home with a plan… a plan to attack Cao in Xuchang and restore the Han to glory. I read all of the books on warfare that I could… what am I gaining from running away…? I am a military strategist… what employer wants a strategist that only knows how to run away…?"
Zhang Fei grunted again, but this time it was more like a laugh.
"…We'll have a chance to fight while we're retreating… we won't win, we *can't*: but we must fight regardless," Kongming said sadly. "That is when you will get your chance to show what you're made of… mine too. And once we're safe, we can plan our next steps… Yide, there will be no more running after this… so long as Lord Liu listens to me, there will be no more running."
"…Okay," Zhang Fei said tersely. "I'll run, this one last time. But I warn you, 'Crouching Dragon'… this had better be the last time: I have pride."
"So do I, so does Lord Liu," Kongming suggested. "…One last time, I promise."
Zhang Fei nodded briskly, flexed his shoulders, and returned to the meeting room: Kongming smiled silently and followed at a distance, fanning himself casually as he walked.

Liu Bei and his followers completed their hurried trip to the city of Xinye, where Liu Bei's forces were stationed. The fugitive warlord had his soldiers make proclamations throughout the city, saying that Cao Cao was on his way, that Liu Cong had surrendered, and that there would be no resistance. Panic was widespread: but further to that, Liu Bei had offered to escort any that wanted to flee. The result was a shock to all, even to Liu Bei himself: the number of civilian refugees from Xinye would number in the tens of thousands.
"…*Aiee*," Zhang Fei exclaimed as he watched the sea of people leaving the town walls. "Cao Cao'll be lucky if he finds a dog or a chicken that hasn't packed up and run off. …Elder Brother, how are we gonna protect all these people…?"
"We'll improvise," Liu Bei retorted sharply. "I won't abandon them."
"We'll be going so slowly…" Mister Sun fretted.
"…Yunchang," Kongming hailed: Guan Yu nodded to indicate that Kongming had his attention, but his gaze was icy. "…Yunchang, you should go ahead, take the warships, sail down the River Han, meet with Liu Qi in Jiangxia, and bring help to us… we'll rendezvous later, at Jiangling," Kongming ordered.
Guan Yu awaited approval from Liu Bei.
"…Good idea," Liu Bei agreed.
Guan Yu left hurriedly to carry out his orders.
"My lord," a woman called from an approaching carriage: it was the beautiful Lady Gan, Liu Bei's principal wife, and mother to the infant A'Dou.
"…My lady," Liu Bei responded. "Are you set to leave…?"
"We are," Lady Gan replied.

Liu Bei peered into the carriage, and saw Lady Mi – the sister of Mi Zhu and Mi Fang, and Liu Bei's second wife – and Liu Bei's two adult daughters – who were both fine in appearance – sat together silently. Lady Mi was cradling A'Dou, who was sleeping silently.

"...Very good," Liu Bei proclaimed. "...**Zilong**...!"

Zhao Yun rode up on his grand white horse, and bowed with deep respect toward his lord.

"...Zilong," Liu Bei ordered sharply, "you will guard my family."

"No harm shall befall them," Zhao Yun promised.

"...**Come**," Liu Bei barked: with bitterness and rage evident in his voice, he began the largest and most humiliating retreat that he had yet suffered. Chen Dao led Liu Bei's elite guards in a protective shield around him, and together they prepared to flee northern Jing, which had been their base for almost 8 years. Zhang Fei reluctantly followed after casting one last look at Xinye's walls.

"...And so it begins," Xu Shu sighed as he stood next to Kongming.

"We have a long journey ahead of us all," Kongming supposed.

"We do," Ma Liang agreed.

"... ... ...Let's get going," Kongming sighed as he stirred his own brown steed into action, and rode after Liu Bei.

Inside Fan City, the people awaited the return of their lord. At the northern battlements of the castle town, a hooded Yueying stared into the distance, imagining her husband Zhuge Liang and his lord Liu Bei at the northeast town of Xinye, and wondering what fate now had in store for them.

"...Good luck, my husband," Yueying whispered. "...Good luck."

************

## 22

### "COME ON! KEEP MOVING, KEEP MOVING!"

The words were echoed by the generals of Liu Bei as they ushered a mass of troops and civilians out of the Jing prefecture of Xinye. They were to rendezvous with the civilians that had chosen to abandon Xiangyang City, and together they would move south, towards what was hoped would be safer territory in Jiangling, the capital of Nan Prefecture in southern Jing Province.
"…We can't go on like this," Mister Sun whined as he stood next to a silent, morbid Kongming, who was fanning himself slowly. Further down the road, Liu Bei – atop a magnificent white horse – was giving words of comfort to his flock of followers.
"…It is fate," Kongming replied coolly. "If we're meant to survive, we will."
Kongming was watching the people as they passed him, and thinking.

Cao Cao had now, upon learning of Liu Bei's retreat, made the announcement that everyone had feared: his first legions had already marched out of Xuchang on what he called a "punitive expedition to rout the traitors to the Han". Word was that Cao Cao was personally leading the army, despite recent lapses in health: his reputation as the scourge of Xu Province preceded him, and as soon as word spread, Liu Bei's offer of accompanying the retreating army was adopted by a large proportion of northern Jing's civilian population.

The ensemble dwarfed the size of Liu Bei's army, numbering well in excess of 100,000: they brought with them livestock and possessions, the sick and the disabled, the old and the young, and that meant that the procession was ambling along at a painfully slow pace, while Cao Cao's armies marched at lightning speed, intent on a battle to the end with Liu Bei.

"Cao Cao made it clear," Mister Sun noted wearily. "Those that were not with him were his enemies… if the people had *stayed*…!"
"…Do not believe everything the man says," Kongming retorted. "He was attempting to divide Liu Bei's forces with those comments… not scare the populace. And if blame must be levelled at anyone for this… blame the Cai family, and Liu Cong. It is their treachery, disloyalty and cowardice that led to this."

Jing Province was a hub, a road into all other places of influence, by land or by sea: some said that whoever controlled Jing Province controlled the doorways of the land. From Jing, you could go into Jiangdong, Sun Quan's provinces, by travelling south; you could go to the capital in the north with relative ease; you could enter the lands of Yi by travelling westward. It had been part of the plans of Cao Cao, Liu Bei and Sun Quan to have a foothold in Jing, whatever form that took: now it was Cao Cao, and there had not even been a struggle. That added the forces of Jing Province to Cao Cao's army, and gave him a clear path to Liu Bei as well.

**"COME ON, MOVE!"** Zhang Fei shouted as he raced about on horseback. His voice was somehow like that of a giant, and echoed above the terrified murmurings of the peasant refugees.

"...We have so few generals of any worth," Mister Sun sighed. "How can we stand up to Cao Cao...?"

"Have courage, Mister Sun," Kongming said warmly. "Those generals we do have are very brave... with sound planning we can make that work for us."

A lesser general rode up to Kongming and Mister Sun, wearing an expression that betrayed concern.

"General Liao Hua," Kongming hailed. "Is there a problem...?"

"Cao Cao's men are already at Wan City, and will be upon us in a few days," Liao Hua reported fretfully. "He sends five thousand elite cavalrymen as a vanguard."

"...Damn," Mister Sun groaned. "We're doomed."

"We have only a few thousand infantry spread across the travel party," Kongming noted. "At the most, with volunteer forces, ten thousand... Cao Cao's elite cavalry can mow down men as a scythe cuts wheat, and we're heavily divided... I must speak to Lord Liu. Come, Mister Sun... General Liao, keep us informed."

Kongming and Mister Sun found Liu Bei guiding a group of peasants, and asked him to move away from the road so that they could speak privately.

"Cao Cao is already at Wan City," Kongming reported. "Where are Lady Gan, Lady Mi, and your daughters, my lord...?"

"I honestly don't know," Liu Bei bleated. "Zilong is with them, I know, but will he be enough...? ...They should be up ahead, but maybe something stalled them. ...But enough of that, Kongming: are your family safe...?"

"Like you, I am unsure where they are," Kongming admitted. "...They have no guards... but I am sure everything will be fine."

"...You said they're coming, Kongming... how many, and how soon...?" Liu Bei asked reluctantly.

"Five thousand riders, in advance of the main force," Kongming replied uneasily. "We have had a fair head start, but with so many people... we'll not reach Jiangling. We'll get maybe two-thirds of the way there, by my estimation..."

"...Where will that be...?" Liu Bei asked impatiently.

"...Steep-slope, near Dangyang," Kongming explained. "I know a bit about the topography, I studied it, since I knew we were going that way... my lord, it isn't suitable for a standoff with Cao Cao."

"My lord," General Chen Dao hailed. "We should not stop for long."

"You'll need to explain as we ride, Kongming," Liu Bei suggested. "We should keep going."

The party were forced to cross the River Han, which not only slowed them, but also led to many deaths as those that travelled by smaller boats – all hastily acquired – were either at risk of sinking, capsizing or being besieged with the disorderly acts of desperate civilians trying to stay alive in cramped conditions. By the time the boats had reached the opposite shore – which was near Xiangyang City – a hundred or more had lost their lives, and Liu Bei openly wept for them. Others travelled over on larger boats, taking animals and heavy carriages: Liu Bei's family was amongst this group.

"Such suffering," Liu Bei sobbed theatrically. "I am to blame!"

"My lord," Mister Sun said encouragingly, "you are not to blame… you are a victim of circumstance, as they are."

"…Let us keep moving," Jian Yong suggested. "We cannot stop here."

"Destroy the boats," Kongming ordered. "They must not be used to aid Cao Cao."

As the troupe continued toward the refugee camp east of Xiangyang, a blanket of fire along the shoreline indicated the demise of dozens of seafaring vessels.

"Do you suppose that Liu Cong has gone to Xinye…?" Jian Yong asked as he rode alongside Kongming.

"…By another route…? …I would say so," Kongming replied. "He cannot afford to upset Cao Cao… he will go in person. Any opportunity we had to unseat him will be gone now. Xiangyang will be on alert… we daren't go back there."

"…What a mess," Liu Bei sighed sadly.

Once the two groups of civilians and military forces were united, the march toward Jiangling began. The River Han ran from west to east between Xiangyang and Fan City, but its course turned a right angle toward the east, running from north to south, parallel to Liu Bei's southern retreat: Guan Yu's fleet was at the same moment travelling on the north-to-south stretch of the river, toward Jiangxia, the prefecture that was on a border with Sun Quan's Jiangdong provinces.

The River Han turned again, running from west to east and eventually joining the great Yangtze River that separated the north and south of China: directly west of this junction and south of Xiangyang was the city of Jiangling. Dangyang County lay between the cities of Xiangyang and Jiangling, and in that county, there was a place known as Steep-slope: this was soon to be a pivotal location in Liu Bei's career.

The march was slow, and yet everyone's pulses were racing, as the inevitable became a matter of days, and then hours. Finally, the first of the weary, desperate hordes – mostly civilians and infantry – reached Steep-slope, and had to rest.

"Such a place is unsafe to remain in for long," Liu Bei supposed.

The land was uneven, and there were numerous hills and groves of trees that made it near impossible to maintain a defensive position.

"…Cao Cao will attack the rear of our forces first," Mister Sun said with a strange aura of bravery. "I volunteer to go and keep him busy."

"Nonsense," Jian Yong scoffed. "You're an old man, and more use for words than as a pincushion. ...Besides, guarding the road east of the Great River is more important."

"And the road that leads to Mai City...?" Liu Bei asked.

"...I don't know," Jian Yong admitted. "...Shall we send Mi Zhu...?"

"He may be right for that," Liu Bei sighed. "Master Zhuge, is Mi Zhu...?"

Kongming was thinking, and had not been paying attention to the discussion.

"...**Hey, 'Water'!**" Zhang Fei growled. "**Your fish asked you a question.**"

"Mm...? ...Oh... sorry," Kongming said apologetically, while Liu Bei scowled at Zhang Fei's rudeness. "I was pondering how best to keep Cao Cao away."

"So were we!" Jian Yong quipped. "What did you decide...?"

"This area is treacherous, having mountains and hills to the west, and forests and hills to the east," Kongming mused. "Cao Cao's advance will try and converge on us in a pincer, most likely, attacking from the north, northwest and northeast simultaneously. We need to guard the Great River road that lies to the west of here, the Mai City road to the northeast of here, and we need a strong contingent as a rear guard to deflect the main attack."

"So we're agreed," Jian Yong declared. "Mister Sun and Chen Shi shall take the western path, Mi Zhu and Mi Fang shall take the east path, Kongming, Chen Zhen, Xu Shu, Yi Ji, and Ma Liang shall guide the crowds, I'll take rear defence with Lord Liu, Zhang Fei and Liao Hua..."

"We should use some of the new recruits," Liu Bei suggested. "Wei Yan looks to be a very promising general: we should have him accompany Mister Sun."

"...I concur, my lord," Kongming said quietly. "Although I wonder if I should assist in the defence of the rear."

"You are gifted as an orator and a statesman," Jian Yong suggested. "You can placate the people, keep them reassured. An advance of cavalry is something that Lord Liu, Yide and I can deal with, Kongming... never fear."

"...I should be with the rear guard," Kongming complained as he rode alongside the throngs of resting refugees with Xu Shu, Ma Liang and Yi Ji.

"Mister Jian and General Zhang will be fine," Yi Ji suggested. "Don't fret."

"Besides," Xu Shu added, "the enemy forces aren't in large enough numbers for showy formations, and the land is unfavourable for an ambush: it will be a plain, simple standoff, something that Mister Jian and Zhang Fei are old hands at."

"In other words," Kongming sighed, "they have no need for me."

"...Pretty much," Xu Shu chuckled. "Seriously, we'll be okay."

"...*Famous last words*," Kongming muttered.


************

## 23

For a few hours, there was a strange peace at the Steep-slope rest encampment.

"We really should start to get moving again soon," Kongming fretted.

"...I'll go and start motivating the people at the front," Ma Liang said numbly.

"Do you think we're okay, Kongming...?" Xu Shu asked as Ma Liang rode away. "...Have you spoken to your family...?"

"Yes, and no," Kongming replied. "I don't even know where my wife and brother are... I cannot afford to show favouritism."

"My family are near the rear, north of Steep-slope," Xu Shu said sadly. "I want to get them closer to the front."

"...What for...?" Kongming chortled. "If we're in danger, it won't matter where they are... everyone will suffer the same calamity."

"My mother is frail," Xu Shu protested.

"...So is everybody else's mother of the same age," Kongming countered disappointedly. "Yuanzhi, I'm concerned for my own family... but they wouldn't thank me if I abandoned my responsibility to everyone here and worried only about them, regardless."

"All the same, I want to go and find them, make sure my mother is still well," Xu Shu said thoughtfully. "I can start getting the rear groups moving."

"...Very well," Kongming sighed disappointedly.

As Xu Shu departed, Kongming exhaled noisily, and exclaimed, "*Aiee.*"

"...Why do you sigh so mournfully...?" Yi Ji asked.

"Our position is desperate," Kongming replied miserably. "Cao's forces are going to set upon us at any moment, and Lord Liu's family is near the rear of the crowd. ...Even guarded by Zilong and his elite riders, I fear the worst if the enemy resoundingly defeats Lord Liu... and they most likely will."

"Why do you say that...?" Yi Ji wondered.

"The men are tired, the terrain is unfavourable to infantry, we are without Guan Yu, and Cao's cavalry are notoriously efficient," Kongming said ominously. "It does not bode well."

"Then why send Guan Yu to Jiangxia...?" Yi Ji asked.

"...Because Guan Yu commands respect from Liu Qi, and if the youth needs intimidating before he will lend assistance, Guan can do that," Kongming explained clinically. "If Cao Cao sends men down the river to intercept, Guan has the expertise to harry or even rout them. I could have said Zhang Fei should go, but his ferocity will come in handy for us later, whereas his recklessness as a messenger could have undone our cause."

"You thought it through well," Yi Ji praised.

"Yes," Kongming said as he started to fan himself. "Now, all we can do is hope that Lord Liu does not meet with more misfortune: his life and ours are now irrevocably entwined, and if he falls, so do we."

"Cheery thought," Yi Ji chuckled ironically.

At the rear of the multitude, Liu Bei and his forces were just in time to meet with Cao Cao's cavalry – led by General Wen Ping – whose numbers were noticeably less than the 5,000-strong force that had been reported.

"They're up to something," Jian Yong said worriedly.

**"Ah, you're being too cautious!"** Zhang Fei bellowed. **"They were boasting about their numbers to scare us!"**

"No, the scouts reported five thousand," Jian Yong insisted. "There're maybe fifteen-hundred riders there."

**"...All bones, rotting bones!"** Zhang Fei cried: his men – roused by his words – cheered and prepared to face the enemy.

"The terrain... we cannot see what's beyond the forest on either side of us, or behind Cao's forces, or...!" Jian Yong protested, but it was to no avail. Zhang Fei led a contingent of around a third of Liu Bei's 3,000-strong force – which was mostly comprised of infantry – toward the advancing riders, their spears levelled.

**"Idiot!"** Jian Yong despaired: as he spoke, his worst fears came true, as from the east and west, two more contingents of enemy cavalry, numbering around 300 each, charged the advancing men and cut them off from Liu Bei's main force.

"*Damn it!*" Jian Yong cried with anguish. "We're split, and...!"

From behind Liu Bei's main force, two more parties of enemy riders – each numbering around 500 – cut off the retreat, and tore into the unprepared units with unbridled ferocity.

**"...WE HAVE TO FALL BACK!"** Jian Yong screamed, hoping beyond hope that Zhang Fei would hear him. The order of Liu Bei's forces started to disintegrate: the men scattered in all directions, leaving them open to being easily cut down by passing riders, who slashed at their unprotected backs and heads with their glaives.

"We're being routed!" Liu Bei said desperately. "We must do something!"

"There's nothing we can do," the bodyguard general Chen Dao said as he repulsed two riders with his spear. "My lord, your survival is vital. We must retreat immediately."

Liu Bei reluctantly agreed. His bodyguards formed a protective circle around him, repelling the riders as best they could while Bei himself started the move southward with Jian Yong.

"I'll ride ahead and warn the people," Jian Yong suggested. "This is my fault... the least I can do is give people a chance to flee."

"Good luck!" Liu Bei said sincerely.

Jian Yong roused his horse to gallop at full speed and fled southward, with only a half-dozen riders as an escort.

**"We're in pretty deep!"** Zhang Fei shouted as he joined his furious master.

"... ... ...You **belligerent oaf!**" Liu Bei scolded. **"You should not have charged!"**

**"...I'm more interested in getting out of this!"** Zhang Fei retorted as he toppled an enemy rider with his snake-tongued pike. **"You can tell me off later!"**

Liu Bei's remaining forces began a gradual retreat, with enemy riders circling them like vultures and making random attacks on their position.

Mister Sun, meanwhile, was besieged by a group of around 200 riders as he tried to hold the western front.

"Another contingent has slipped past us and gone toward the civilians!" General Wei Yan – a tall, stocky warrior with hard features and cold, serious eyes – reported to Mister Sun with concern. "We should send assistance!"

"We're pinned!" Mister Sun retorted. "We can only hope that they are ready!"

Wei Yan grunted irritably at the helpless situation, and continued to hack down any that approached their beleaguered position.

And on the eastern front, the situation was much the same: Mi Zhu and Mi Fang, however, decided to give up their pointless defence and return to the refugee encampment, where they felt their help would be needed. Many soldiers were lost as they retreated westward, but catching up to the riders that had gone straight toward the multitude was the priority.

"...Jian Yong," Kongming said worriedly as his colleague galloped toward him an hour later, covered in gore, and with only two of his escort riders still alive and present. Kongming frowned, saying, "What... where is Lord Liu...?"

"**ENEMY ATTACK!**" Jian Yong screamed desperately: in the distance, the noise of panicked villagers started to fill the air.

"...What do we do...?" Yi Ji fretted. "Where are they???"

"They're attacking... all sides... I... rode through... but...!" Jian Yong explained wearily: he was wounded, though not seriously.

"We have to go," Kongming insisted. "Where is Xu Yuanzhi, did you see him...?"

"No, I... they're attacking the people...!" Jian Yong wheezed.

"I'll round up some soldiers," Yi Ji declared as he turned to gallop in a random direction, hoping to find help.

"...Where is he...?" Kongming asked again. "Where is Lord Liu...?"

"It... it was a rout!" Jian Yong revealed with shame. "They split their forces... pincer attack... split us, and...!"

Kongming lowered his fan and exclaimed, "*Aiee*... is Chen Dao taking Lord Liu to safety...? ...And did you see Zilong...?"

"...I... no, I didn't see Zilong!" Jian Yong replied desperately. "Come on, come with me!"

Kongming spurred his horse to action, and followed Jian Yong and his men northward, where the screams of confusion and agony were intensifying.

The scene that greeted Kongming as he rode south was one of chaos and carnage: the bodies of soldiers and civilians alike were strewn this way and that, the result of recently completed flash raids by the enemy cavalry. The cries of desperate people broke his heart, but he continued after Jian Yong regardless.

"...**Lord Liu!**" Jian Yong shouted suddenly: in the distance, Liu Bei was visible, atop his now gore-covered white horse and still protected by his elite bodyguards.

"...**Xianhe, Master Zhuge!**" Liu Bei hailed: the two groups met, fighting their way through a small group of Cao's elite riders and fending them off as they went.

"...Where is Yide...?" Kongming asked worriedly as soon as the last of their attackers were forced into retreat.

"Alive, but… he's holding them off," Liu Bei replied sullenly. "Kongming, it was awful… we were *destroyed*."

"I know," Kongming sighed. "We must hasten our retreat: we must go east."

"*East*…?" Jiang Yong said painfully.

"I noticed that Mi Zhu and Mi Fang abandoned their position," Kongming reported. "The enemy will now be concentrated here… if we do this right, we can begin an eastward retreat, and cross the River Han at Steep-slope Bridge."

"…But the people…!" Liu Bei protested. "What about *them*…?"

"We… we have to leave them," Kongming said with great reluctance and anger in his heart. "We must rely on Cao Cao's understanding of how to treat the people…"

"…This is *not* how you treat the people!" Liu Bei protested as he gestured at the dead bodies of ordinary villagers that lay about them on the ground like piles of blood-stained rags. "How can we trust him???"

"We have no choice," Jian Yong agreed. "But we can at least tell the people to scatter, and let them know where we're headed."

At this point, Mister Sun and Wei Yan's forces appeared from the west, having finally defeated their attackers and put them to flight.

"…Mister Sun!" Liu Bei said with relief. "And General Wei… you made it."

"General Wei Yan is an exceptional man," Mister Sun praised. "Were it not for him… I might not have survived."

"You overrate me," Wei Yan said with a gesture of respect.

"…My thanks to you, General Wei," Liu Bei said gratefully. "We must…"

"**ELDER BROTHER!**" Zhang Fei bellowed: he was being pursued by a group of around 30 enemy riders, and had only a small group of infantry and riders with him. Wei Yan and Chen Dao charged, and once he saw this, Zhang Fei turned to face the enemy with a wild expression on his whiskery face, and cut down two men in a single twirl of his pike: the remainder of the enemy cavalry – fearing for their own lives – decided to retreat and regroup.

"**THAT'S RIGHT!**" Zhang Fei shouted after them as Wei Yan and Chen Dao rode forward and stopped on either side of him. "**YOU DARE RUN, YOU DOGS??? NO GOOD IN A FAIR FIGHT, UH…? COME BACK, YOU WORTHLESS SCUM, AND FIGHT ZHANG YIDE OF YAN!**"

"…What a man…!" Jian Yong quipped painfully.

"We should begin our retreat now," Kongming urged, "before they regroup. Yide, General Wei, General Liao, I have a plan. Listen carefully…"

************

## 24

Liu Bei led his retainers south in the hope of passing on their plans before they started their eastbound retreat, but all was not well. Yi Ji spotted Xu Shu, who was running around desperately, and the group descended on his position. There had obviously been another score of flash raids by the enemy cavalry, and the cost had been high.

"**LORD LIU!**" Xu Shu cried as Liu Bei approached him. "**LORD LIUUUUU!**"

"...**Xu Yuanzhi**," Kongming hailed. "**Are you hurt...?**"

"**I was with Liu Feng, Ma Jichang, and Zilong**," Xu Shu wailed, "**but...!**"

Liu Bei spotted the smashed remains of the carriage that had been carrying his family, and screamed, "**Where is Zilong???**"

"**There... was... they just...!**" Xu Shu wailed. "**We got some men together to fight them off, but they were too fast!**"

"...Where is my family...?" Liu Bei wondered as he looked this way and that, lost in a daze.

"**Where are they, Yuanzhi???**" Kongming screamed desperately. "**Where are our families???**"

"**I... I...!**" Xu Shu sobbed, but his voice trailed, as he was distressed to the point of breaking down altogether.

"**They're gone,**" Ma Liang reported as he passed through a swathe of civilians and walked toward the group. He was covered in blood and clutching a sword: at his side were Liu Bei's wife, Lady Mi, and Liu Bei's adopted son, Feng. "**A General 'Cao Chun' seized Lord Liu's daughters... Zhao Zilong was with Lady Gan and A'Dou...**"

"...**Where are they...?**" Liu Bei asked again.

"**Zilong went north,**" Ma Liang replied numbly. "**Pursued by...**"

"...**North???**" Kongming exclaimed. "**Back toward...?**"

"...They have my A'Dou," Liu Bei whispered almost inaudibly.

"**Pardon...?**" Kongming asked.

"...**THEY HAVE MY SON!**" Liu Bei screamed: he had yet to even acknowledge the presence of Liu Feng, who was visibly hurt by it.

"...**Yuanzhi, where are _our_ families...?**" Kongming sobbed. "**Where is my brother, my wife, the Ma family... the Yi family... your own family...?**"

"**They... I don't know about your family,**" Xu Shu admitted. "**There was so much going on, I... I don't know, Kongming, I don't know!**"

"**They fled south,**" Ma Liang reported.

"...**Father...?**" Liu Feng hailed.

"...**WHAT???**" Liu Bei screamed: Liu Feng drew back in fright, and said no more.

"...**Kongming... they have my mother,**" Xu Shu said at last. "**They have my family... I can't stay with you anymore.**"

"...**How can you know?**" Kongming pleaded. "**How can you be sure???**"

"**I'm sure,**" Xu Shu sighed. "**I saw them taken... so I have to go.**"

"**And serve Cao Cao???**" Zhang Fei barked as he raised his weapon and prepared to lunge at Xu Shu.

"**NO, Yide, NO!**" Liu Bei sobbed angrily. "**Has he not lost enough???**"

"...He'll... but he'll...!" Zhang Fei whined as he reluctantly lowered his pike.

Xu Shu touched his chest, and said emotionally, "**My heart will always be with all of you... but I must beg your leave now. I swear, I will never be used against you... you have my word.**"

"*Yuanzhi...!*" Ma Liang said weakly.

"...**Kongming,**" Xu Shu hailed: Kongming nodded to indicate that he accepted his friend's decision, even if he did not agree with it.

"...**We'll not meet again,**" Xu Shu said as he made a ritual obeisance to all. "**I have failed you today, Lord Liu... you do not need the likes of me.**"

"*Yuanzhi...!*" Liu Bei said hoarsely.

"**Good luck!**" Xu Shu shouted as he ran northward and gradually disappeared from sight.

"...**You should have let me kill him,**" Zhang Fei growled. "*I have lost MY FAMILY... do you see ME GO RUNNING TO CAO CAO???*"

"**He has made his choice, Yide,**" Liu Bei said calmly. "**Now we must flee.**"

Ma Liang helped Lady Mi onto Zhang Fei's horse, while Liu Feng stared at his adopted father with a sudden sense of rejection and betrayal.

"**My lord, *please*!**" the bodyguard-general Chen Dao shouted desperately. "**This position is untenable!**"

"...Zilong...?" Lui Bei said weakly. "Where *are you*...?"

"**The bulk of Cao's forces must have passed Xiangyang by now,**" Kongming supposed worriedly.

"...**And???**" Liu Bei shrieked hysterically.

"...**You two,**" Kongming said to Generals Liao Hua and Wei Yan, "**Gather whatever men you can find... and spread the word as you go. Meet us at the place we agreed, and be ready.**"

The two generals did as they were told.

"**What are you...?**" Liu Bei asked.

"**Please, my lord!**" Chen Dao shouted worriedly.

"...**RETREAT!**" Liu Bei shouted yet again.

Once again, Liu Bei fled, leaving behind the throng of trusting civilians, who pleaded with the soldiers to stay: their pleas were reluctantly ignored.


The retreat took Liu Bei's remnant forces through treacherous, uneven paths surrounded by trees and dry foliage. In addition to the last of Liu Bei's infantry, some civilians followed, having decided that they had little option.

"**You think we can escape...?**" Jian Yong asked Kongming as they watched the rear for another possible attack.

"...**I don't know,**" Kongming admitted. "**If my plan works... we should buy some time. It won't be enough, really, but... well, I don't know, it might be. It depends entirely on Cao Cao.**"

"...**On Cao Cao...?**" Jian Yong prompted.

"**I'm hoping he isn't too enthusiastic,**" Kongming replied.

Jian Yong looked at Kongming with puzzlement: he was not sure what the young man was thinking, but quietly hoped that whatever he had in mind would save them all from certain defeat.

Meanwhile, Generals Liao Hua and Wei Yan had finished their sweep south and returned to the north. They advanced beyond the position of the majority of the refugees, and commandeered any soldiers that they found.

"...The people are dispersing," Liao Hua noted with relief.

"This plan is foolish," Wei Yan complained. "If it doesn't work, if they work out what we're doing, like I would, and just pass us by..."

"Do you have a better suggestion...?" Liao Hua asked pointedly.

"We should have remained together," Wei Yan said bluntly. "But... what's done is done. Let's just hope the enemy is as stupid as Zhuge Liang thinks that they are."

The small battalion then waited for the next attack by the enemy cavalry: it came after an hour of impatient waiting.

"...Here they come...!" Liao Hua exclaimed.

Wei Yan rode forward to do battle with them, cutting down two of the riders that directly challenged him with frightening ease. The riders temporarily fell back and regrouped: Wei Yan returned to his line and smiled contemptuously, stroking his thick whiskers with his gloved hand.

"...We're supposed to lose!" Liao Hua scolded.

"I won't let them have it that easy," Wei Yan replied with a laugh. "We can lose now... I just needed to feed my hungry pride first. Go on then, General Liao... go and lose for us."

Liao Hua scowled, rode forward, and made a feeble challenge with his spear that failed to hit the leader of the enemy cavalry. Wei Yan then made a follow-up pass that was equally poor: the cavalry suspected panic and charged, allowing Wei Yan to lead a retreat into an isolated section of forested land to the east of the sloping road. Some of the riders halted as memories of the defeat at Bowang six years before suddenly haunted their thoughts: it was only when Liao Hua fled as well that the majority pursued.

"...**Where are they???**" the cavalry leader exclaimed as he reached the centre of the dense greenery: the next thing that he heard was a series of commanding calls, followed by the anguish of his men as flames licked up around them, turning their pursuit into a fight for survival. On the east side of the forest, Wei Yan and Liao Hua smiled with satisfaction: what remained of Cao's cavalry retreated to join the main force, which was now approaching rapidly.

Some distance away, in a hilly region to the east of Steep-slope, Liu Bei's forces waited patiently for a sign of progress. As they waited, refugees filed past them, groaning with agony or anguish, and giving the army quiet distress at what they felt was suffering that they were partly responsible for.

"...How much longer can we afford to wait...?" Mister Sun wondered.

"Give them time," Kongming insisted.

"Perhaps I should go and help," Zhang Fei said impatiently.

"No, wait; look...!" Jian Yong urged. "...Smoke! They did it!"

"Well done, Master Zhuge," Liu Bei praised.
Kongming fanned himself slowly, replying, "Until Generals Liao and Wei return, assume nothing: and Yide, you must remain here, since we need you to…"
"Okay, **okay, alright!**" Zhang Fei complained. "…I *know*."

An hour later, Generals Liao Hua and Wei Yan reached Liu Bei with their small infantry force.
"…Cao's forces are almost at Steep-slope," Liao Hua reported worriedly. "They are aware of our retreat eastward… some captive civilians must have told them."
"We don't know that," Jian Yong suggested.
"They are slowing, as if they intend to change direction," Wei Yan reported. "And they have been taking prisoners… we freed some captives before we came here."
"So we do not have long," Kongming supposed. "My lord, whoever has not already come this way, I'm afraid, is to be considered lost: we must continue east immediately, and get to the river."
"B-but… but Kongming," Chen Zhen protested, "we have only recovered some of our families… we have yet to find yours. Surely, you can't…?"
"It is not a decision I take lightly," Kongming retorted calmly. "We must think of the great cause before we think of ourselves. Our families would not thank us if we surrendered, or if we allowed ourselves to be captured for their sake… we would all die then, and what good would that serve…?"
Murmurs of uncomfortable concurrence could be heard: Kongming remained stony-faced and continued to look to the west, quietly hoping to see one last group of people, and wishing to the heavens that the group included his own kin.
"Zilong…" Liu Bei murmured weakly.
"…That faithless traitor," Zhang Fei – who was stood next to his friend and lord – growled angrily. "If he's gone over to Cao Cao, and taken A'Dou with him, I swear, I'll…!"
Zhang Fei's voice died away as he awaited the likely rebuke from Liu Bei.
After a long pause, Liu Bei said, "He would never do that."

Not long afterward, Kongming gave the final nod to Liu Bei that they should wait no longer: after posting spies to watch for Cao Cao's main forces, Liu Bei ordered the full retreat, and the last of his followers started toward Steep-slope Bridge, which crossed the River Han and led to the western boundary of Jiangxia. Zhang Fei held the rear guard with a group of 20 cavalrymen, a role he had discussed earlier with Kongming. His would be the last action of the retreat: a risky manoeuvre that would either work brilliantly or bring swift death to Liu Bei's depleted forces.


************

## 25

Liu Bei's retreat across the River Han was slower than his retreats from Xiangyang City and Steep-slope: it was as though some were having second thoughts about surviving, and were deliberately reducing their pace so as to be caught, and bring a swift end to their misery.

"...**Please, people, hurry!**" Mister Sun urged from his position at the centre of the crossing bridge. Many of the refugees shuffled along slowly and complained bitterly.

"I heard one man whinging that he'd lost his cattle," Jian Yong sighed as he watched from the safety of the east bank with Kongming and a silent, traumatised Ma Liang. "...Some people really are completely without the power of objectivity, and cannot see beyond their own nose."

"As I have often said before," Kongming replied coldly, "it is the human condition: did not Confucius ask only about the people, and not the animals...? ...How many of these people claim to know his teachings, and still think only of their wealth and possessions. ...I might have lost most of the people that I love with all my heart and soul... I would give *anything to*...!"

Jian Yong looked at Kongming, whose eyes were moist.

"...You're suffering," Jian Yong realised. "I'm sorry... you were trying to be strong, weren't you...?"

Kongming exhaled noisily, and replied, "Perhaps I should just do as my lord does."

"...It doesn't suit you," Jian Yong replied frankly. "Xuande... stirs others to tears when he cries, yet he inspires with it, somehow... whereas you, I think, would just lower our morale. You seem like a man who only cries when the end is at hand."

"...Can we change the subject...?" Kongming pleaded. "...Tell me, what do you think of General Wei Yan...?"

"A braggart," Jian Yong replied immediately.

"Not entirely," Kongming suggested. "I think his deeds will match his words... but I think we will not get on very well, which is a pity... and General Huo Jun...?"

"Already a favourite of Xuande's, like Chen Shi," Jian Yong said despairingly. "Still, Huo Jun seems to be sensible, unlike–"

"We're almost over," Yi Ji reported as he rode up to the three advisers and mopped his filth-covered brow with his blood-covered sleeve. "Then it's all up to Yide."

"We should move away from the bank," Kongming suggested emotionlessly. "Tell Lord Liu to hurry over to this side of the bridge now... it's dangerous."

"He's coming," Yi Ji promised. "He wanted to speak to Yide first."

"I suppose that's to be understood," Kongming sighed. "Let's get to our horses."


A short time later, only Zhang Fei and his 20 riders were on the west side of the river: slowly, gradually, the ensemble of refugees moved east and disappeared from view. Zhang Fei stood in front of the bridge and waited, while half of his riders moved along the riverbank, destroying all of the smaller bridges within the area.

That evening, the remnants of Liu Bei's army stopped on hills that lay within the relative safety of the lands inside the Jiangxia border. They sat on the cold ground, caked with dirt, sweat and blood, and sobbing pitifully at what had been a complete defeat. Zhao Yun and most of their families were missing, the majority of the civilians had been left to fend for themselves, and Zhang Fei was yet to return. Kongming watched Liu Bei wailing, and felt his own composure start to falter.

"...We *abandoned them*...!" Liu Bei sobbed. "We *left the people*...!" Others that had lost family and friends wept: Kongming fanned himself quietly, and said nothing.

Cao Cao's main forces arrived at Steep-slope and captured any of Liu Bei's surviving men, many of the civilians and their belongings, and the military supplies that were left along the roads. Cao Cao himself was present: he was stocky and stern-faced, with a long, well-kept beard. He wore a magnificent yet aged suit of segmented armour that he obviously preferred to wear, and his hair was hidden under a war helmet brushed with gold. At his side was his adviser Jia Xu, who wore blue robes, kept his hair bound under a decorated hat, and had a short beard dotted with prematurely grey hairs.

"...A complete victory...?" Jia Xu said as a prompt.

"Not at all," Cao Cao said in a husky, bitter voice. "I cannot sleep soundly while Liu Bei is alive. ...What are the reports...?"

"We've acquired around thirty-thousand men from the Jing forces stationed in Xiangyang, and we expect to acquire another thirty thousand at Jiangling: we have captured near to three thousand of Liu Bei's men here at Steep-slope, that we also hope to impress into our own forces," Jia Xu recounted. "In addition, around eighty-thousand civilians, and a considerable amount of goods and livestock have been requisitioned."

"The people fled in fear of me," Cao Cao said with what appeared to be regret.

"Liu Bei told them you would massacre them," Jia Xu explained with a tone suggesting disagreement.

"...*Liu Bei*," Cao Cao declared, "I will *kill you*. I will kill you this *very day*...!"

"They retreated east, toward the River Han," Jia Xu continued. "I do not advise pursuit, at least not without advance parties to sound out their plans... they managed to make one small ambush on our cavalry that killed a good few men, and the riverbank is grassy with forest pockets, making it easy to hide flammable-"

"Send Xu Huang, Li Dian, Xiahou Yuan and Xiahou Dun with an advance force of thirty-thousand to advance on Steep-slope Bridge," Cao Cao commanded. "If there are no obstructions, I will advance personally, hunt down Liu Bei, and worry about Jiangling later. If the bridges are down, we will first take Jiangling and then pursue with pontoon bridges. If there are any suspicious signs... well, then, we retreat, and just take Jiangling."

"A sound strategy, my lord," Jia Xu praised.

"...I hope that Guo Jia would have recommended the same," Cao Cao replied.

Across the River Han in Jiangxia, the general mood in Liu Bei's camp was one of painful contemplation.

"...Where is Zilong...?" Liu Bei asked emotionlessly as he toyed with a blood-stained hand axe: it was far from the first time that he had asked that question.

"...We don't know," General Liao Hua insisted. "My lord, we really don't know."

"...Find him," Liu Bei replied coldly. "He has my son."

Liu Feng, who was sat nearby with Lady Mi, scowled angrily.

"Someone said they saw him flee northward," a soldier commented tactlessly.

"...What?" Liu Bei prompted.

"...Someone... in another regiment... said they saw him and his men go north, toward Cao Cao," the soldier continued.

"...**NONSENSE!**" Liu Bei screamed irrationally: he threw the axe he was holding at the soldier, who narrowly avoided it, and ran away in terror.

"Xuande, *please*...!" Jian Yong protested emotionally.

"...**Zilong would NEVER betray me!**" Liu Bei bellowed. "He had a *reason*... he would never do such a thing... *never*... not *Zilong*..."

Liu Bei collapsed into a heap, weary and emotionally broken.

"...Would he...?" Kongming asked as he slowly waved his fan back and forth, despite the chilling wind that was blowing. His audience was Liu Bei's senior bodyguard, Chen Dao, and his fellow advisers, Ma Liang and Yi Ji.

"Would he *what*...?" Ma Liang asked wearily.

"...Defect to Cao Cao," Yi Ji supposed.

"...I have been with my lord since he was in the service of Tao Qian," Chen Dao declared. "Lord Liu met Zhao Zilong before he met me... Zilong was a trusted vassal of Gongsun Zan. The two were almost brothers... Zilong sought out Lord Liu to serve him when Lord Gongsun was defeated by Yuan Shao. Zilong is valiant, noble and trustworthy: no, I do not believe that Zilong could ever betray Lord Liu."

"...Then Zilong is rescuing the daughters of Lord Liu, or trying to find some way to keep the lord's son safe," Kongming suggested. "...We must hold firm."

"I would never have expected Xu Shu to defect," Ma Liang murmured.

"...Why do you not call him Yuanzhi...?" Kongming asked.

"Are you serious...?" Ma Liang asked. "He has betrayed us... he's fled and joined Cao Cao! How can I call him by a familiar name...?"

"I agree," Yi Ji admitted. "I can never call Xu Shu a friend now."

"His decision hurts me... we were good friends, longer than I have been friends with both of you," Kongming sighed. "But I suppose I never swore brotherhood with him... because I knew he was not entirely to be trusted. ...Sadly, I was right... and Pang Shiyuan warned me too, he *knew*. Xu Shu was looking for an excuse to leave... he did not fully devote himself, as we have... a pity."

Meanwhile, Zhang Fei waited at the site of the Steep-slope Bridge: Zhang Fei's riders were concealed, ready to follow Kongming's instructions.

"...Come on, Cao Cao...!" Zhang Fei whispered. "Where are you...?"

A short while later, a group of riders approached.

"…**WHO DARES TO FACE ZHANG YIDE OF YAN???**" Zhang Fei bellowed: the men did not stop, but instead raised a torn, blood-spattered banner belonging to Liu Bei's forces, and one of the spotters gave a signal that the riders were friendly.

"…Zilong…?" Zhang Fei supposed. "…**ZILONG!**"

Zhao Yun approached, accompanied by Mi Zhu, Mi Fang, and a small group of weary cavalry, one of which had custody of Liu Bei's wife, Lady Gan. Cradled in Zhao Yun's left arm was a bundle of rags; in his right hand, he carried a spear; the reins of his exceptionally well-trained horse were tucked under his left armpit.

"…A'Dou…?" Zhang Fei supposed as Zhao Yun stopped in front of him, smiling wearily: Zhao Yun nodded, indicating that the child was safe under the rags.

"…I thought you'd left us," Zhang Fei admitted with embarrassment. "I will never doubt you again, Zilong, I promise."

"I understand," the gore-covered Zhao Yun insisted. "I only wish that I had recovered the lord's daughters as well… for that failure, I'm ashamed."

The equally gore-laden Lady Gan was weeping for her two missing girls: Zhang Fei could not help but be moved by it.

"…We were told that Lord Liu fled east," Zhao Yun explained. "Is he in Jiangxia?"

"…Oh, yes, quickly, get going," Zhang Fei said with sudden urgency. "Cao Cao is coming, so get over the bridge… I'll destroy it when you're across."

Zhao Yun led his rescue party over the bridge, leaving Zhang Fei to resume his vigil.

Cao Cao's advance forces approached the Steep-slope Bridge an hour later: what met them was a bizarre sight. By now, Zhang Fei's men had destroyed a large part of Steep-slope Bridge and sought cover, so all that was left was a single warrior – Zhang Fei – riding back and forth along the river bank where the bridge had once stood intact.

"What… the…?" Li Dian exclaimed.

"**I AM ZHANG YIDE OF YAN!**" Zhang Fei shouted with a voice that cut through the air. "**IS THERE ANY MAN THAT WOULD FIGHT WITH ME???**"

"…What do we do…?" Xu Huang wondered.

"**I AM ZHANG YIDE OF YAN!**" Zhang Fei bellowed again. "**IS THERE NOT ANY MAN AMONGST YOU THAT WOULD FIGHT WITH ME???**"

"What is this man *doing*…?" Xiahou Yuan said with bewilderment.

"Shoot him!" Xiahou Dun urged. "Take your bow and **shoot him**!"

"No…!" Xiahou Yuan said cautiously. "…No… something isn't right here."

"So what do we do then…?" Xu Huang asked again.

"…Get the Prime Minister," Li Dian suggested: a rider was despatched to bring Cao Cao to view the scene for himself.

A few hours later, as the sun was setting, Cao Cao arrived, accompanied by his adviser Jia Xu and another 10,000 of his men. Cao Cao rode to the front and stopped, whereupon an assistant rode alongside him and raised a yellow parasol above his head. A standard-bearer then ran to Cao Cao's side, carrying a flag bearing his name and the title 'Commander of Chariots and Cavalry'."

"...**CAO CAO!**" Zhang Fei boomed. "**HAVE YOU COME TO FACE ME...?**"

Cao Cao turned to the standard-bearer and grunted: the standard-bearer withdrew, and was quickly followed by the parasol-bearer, who needed no further hint.

"**WHY ARE YOU HIDING, CAO CAO...?**" Zhang Fei heckled. "**ARE YOU SCARED OF ME...? ...FINE: WILL ANYONE ELSE COME AND FACE ME, THEN...?**"

"...Who is this man...?" Cao Cao asked.

"Zhang Fei, a close friend of Guan Yunchang," Xu Huang explained. "When he was in your service, Guan spoke very highly of Zhang Fei as a warrior."

"...Oh...?" Cao Cao replied thoughtfully: he noted the slight movement in the foliage behind Zhang Fei, and looked at Jia Xu, who shook his head silently. "...This is an ambush," Cao Cao decided. "...Retreat for now."

"But...!" Xiahou Dun exclaimed.

"You were burned at Bowang by Liu Bei," Cao Cao scolded angrily, "and lost one eye to Lü Bu: what do you want to lose here...?"

No further dissent was heard: reluctantly, Cao Cao's force retreated westward.

"**COWARDS!**" Zhang Fei bellowed. "**WILL NOBODY CHALLENGE ME???**"

Zhang Fei remained at the bridge for some time, as Kongming had instructed: as soon as it was nightfall, he retreated using hidden rafts, having bought his master Liu Bei some much-needed time.

************

## 26

As dawn broke, a blood-soaked Zhao Yun rode up the hill toward Liu Bei's encampment in Jiangxia, with A'Dou in his arms. Behind him, Liu Bei's long-time sponsors Mi Zhu and Mi Fang rode alongside a group of cavalry: one of the riders had Lady Gan clinging to him with all of her strength. Liu Bei leapt to his feet and ran toward them with newfound vigour.

"Zilong…!" Liu Bei sobbed. "*Zilong*…!"

The riders stopped at last, and dismounted their tired horses.

"…My lord," Zhao Yun said with deep regret, "I was unable to save your daughters… I could not find Cao Chun."

"…*Husband*…!" Lady Gan sobbed: Liu Bei took her in his arms and comforted her on their shared loss of their two daughters. Lady Mi walked up to the group, and looked at Zhao Yun, who still held the infant A'Dou in his arms.

"…A'Dou…!" Lady Mi whispered through tears.

Kongming noted that Liu Bei's adopted son, Liu Feng, remained conspicuously distant from the reunion, and silently awaited an action from Liu Bei that could restore amity with the youth. Meanwhile, Mi Zhu and Mi Fang embraced their sister gratefully.

"…My son…!" Liu Bei exclaimed: he and Lady Gan turned their full attention to the child, who was sleeping soundly.

"No amount of gratitude can ever repay what you have done today, Zilong," Liu Bei sobbed. "My friend… my good, good friend…!"

"My lord, you overpraise me," Zhao Yun said humbly.

"Zilong, your bravery is beyond question," Kongming praised. "And my lord… you are indeed fortunate that *both your sons* survived this day."

"…**Feng'er**," Liu bellowed at Liu Feng, who was stood by a tree, sulking miserably. "**Feng'er… I have neglected you in a moment of tension. Come, join your family.**"

Liu Feng walked toward his adopted father with little enthusiasm, but he was grateful for the attention nonetheless.

"Thank you, Kongming," Liu Bei said sincerely. "You helped me remember myself at a critical moment."

"…So once Yide returns, we can go east, and meet up with Yunchang and Liu Qi," Jian Yong supposed. "…But then, what about *our* families…?"

"We will return to the roads, and see if we can find anyone," Liu Bei suggested.

"No," Kongming said suddenly. "…I meant what I said before. I will not be another Xu Shu… nor will I die searching for the lost. We should press east, meet reinforcements, and *then* return… if Cao has released the people to feign benevolence and pacify the district, they can then join us."

"Can we risk that…?" Mi Zhu asked worriedly.

"Do we have a choice…?" Jian Yong conceded. "Kongming is right. If we return a military presence to the area, we may be harming people, not helping them."

Liu Bei exhaled noisily as he pondered it: after a few moments, he asked his family to step aside, and prepared to address his advisers.

"...When Yide returns, we'll move east," Liu Bei said simply and frankly. "We can't do anymore at present."

Time passed, and eventually, Zhang Fei and his gang of riders returned to the main army.
"Well...?" Liu Bei asked as he cradled his son. "What happened...?"
"...Cao retreated," Zhang Fei reported. "Is A'Dou well...?"
"Yes," Liu Bei said gratefully. "But-"
"We still had to leave the villagers," Jian Yong said bitterly. "Still no word on anyone else yet... Lady Huang, the Ma family..."
"We can't hold here any longer," Kongming suggested. "Cao's men must be pressing toward Jiangling if they didn't follow Yide... that's our good fortune. We'll need to go east, meet with Guan Yunchang and Liu Qi, and from there... well, we'll see."
"...Fair enough," Zhang Fei said with respect. "You're in pain, like me, but you're not showing it... you're not so soft after all."
"...I value your respect," Kongming replied with a calm smile.

Reluctantly, Liu Bei's forces continued the retreat eastward, toward northern Xiakou – the port city that Guan Yu's forces had been told to sail to by Kongming. Liu Bei insisted on Zhao Yun's presence at his side during every moment of the journey, and he lavished him with near-endless praise for his earlier exploits.

Cao Cao, meanwhile, regretted his earlier hesitation.
"...We are almost back at Steep-slope," Jia Xu protested. "Why have you stopped the march, Prime Minister...?"
"... ... ...Turn back," Cao Cao commanded.
"But the ambush...!" Jia Xu implored.
"There was no ambush," Cao Cao realised. "This was a child's trick, a bluff, and I fell for it. I had forty thousand men, and I *still* fell for it! No, we march back now, and we destroy Liu Bei!"
"Prime Minister," Jia Xu protested further, "we must take Jiangling. Leave Liu Bei now! We can pursue him later!"
"I cannot allow him to find allies and shelter, not again," Cao Cao insisted.
"And who will he shelter with...? ...*Sun Quan*...?" Jia Xu retorted.
"He is a wily owl," Cao Cao countered. "He has fooled the best of us: only Guo Jia saw him for the threat he was. I won't let him go, not again... we turn around, now!"
"...If you insist, Prime Minister," Jia Xu sighed. "But surely, he will be long gone."
"With that gaggle of peasants he still has with him, he will not have gotten far," Cao Cao suggested. "This time, I go at the vanguard. Let him send 'Zhang Yide of Yan'... I will have my Xu Chu grind his bones to powder."
Xu Chu, the mighty bodyguard of Cao Cao, smirked at the idea: the army turned and started back toward the Han River.

"No... **no!**" a farmer exclaimed as he scurried up and down the bank of the River Han, desperate for a way across. He was part of a large throng of civilians that had finally evaded the forces of Cao Cao and travelled at great pains to the river, where – they had heard – salvation could be found.

"The bridges... all gone," a blood-spattered Yueying sighed miserably as she held the reassuring left hand of Zhuge Jun tightly in her own right.

"**But they said to come here!**" a woman wailed. "**We've been tricked!**"

"**No!**" a youth – Ma Su, the younger brother of Ma Liang – said surely. "They'll come back!"

"I only see one army... Cao Cao's," another woman said fearfully: many turned their gaze to the western dust cloud that signified an approaching force of considerable magnitude.

"**We're going to be slaughtered!**" a second farmer screamed.

"...Be brave, sister-in-law," Zhuge Jun said as he tightened his grip on Yueying's hand.

"I fear nothing now," Yueying insisted.

The battered refugees wailed with self-pity and fear as they waited for the inevitable.

Liu Bei met with Liu Qi – the exiled eldest son of the recently deceased Jing governor – at a temporary camp that lay halfway between Xiakou and Lu Bei's forced retreat from the River Han.

"Esteemed honorary uncle, why are you here in this awful state...?" Liu Qi said as he looked at the mass of battered soldiers and civilians.

"Not now: where is Yunchang...?" Liu Bei asked angrily.

"He sailed ahead, down the River Han, to meet you at Jiangling," Liu Qi replied nervously. "Why did you not wait as we agreed...? ...Were you routed...?"

"We'll explain as we go," Liu Bei replied impatiently. "Are you ready to mobilise, worthy nephew...?"

Liu Qi nodded silently, and the two small armies of Liu Bei and Liu Qi prepared to turn around and pursue Guan Yu.

"...**HALT!**" Cao Cao said as his army caught sight of the people at the river bank.

"Oh, **come now, Brother Mengde!**" Xiahou Dun protested, using Cao Cao's familiar name. "**It's just some peasants!**"

"...Another trick...?" Cao Cao asked of Jia Xu, who shrugged silently.

The refugees huddled in fear.

"So," Cao Cao pondered, "what shall we-"

"...**Prime Minister, ships approaching!**" General Yu Jin announced: several ships – each bearing Liu Bei's standard – were sailing toward the riverbank from the south.

"**Back, back, retreat!**" Cao Cao said with urgency and fear in his voice.

"**But it's just some SHIPS!**" Xiahou Dun protested.

"...**I will not be fooled into destroying myself!**" Cao Cao insisted. "**Retreat, RETREAT AT ONCE!**"

As Cao Cao's massive army turned tail for the second time in as many days, Lady Huang Yueying, the wife of Zhuge Liang, was not the only one to smile and sigh with relief. She turned to look at the approaching ships: at the helm of the command ship was the unmistakable sight of the green robed, ruddy-faced Guan Yu, carrying his custom-made 'Green Dragon' pole sword.

"...It's like a miracle," Zhuge Jun whispered as the people started to cheer and celebrate their relatively good fortune.

"Plucked from the jaws of death," Yueying said with a morbid laugh as Ma Su walked to her side, smiling boldly.

"...**BROTHER!**" Guan Yu hailed as his forces met with Liu Bei's near the eastern bank of the River Han. "Brother... Brother, I wish I could have been with you...!"

"...I'm just glad we all survived," Liu Bei conceded. "Had Kongming and others not recommended this, we would all have been routed at Steep-slope."

Kongming bowed slightly and silently.

"Did the other people manage to get across?" Guan Yu asked. "Did others not...?"

"Yunchang," Zhang Fei said with misery, "we... we...!"

"We will go back," Liu Bei insisted.

"The people know this was the place to come to," Jian Yong said sadly. "Whoever is not now here is a captive of Cao Cao... the families of the generals and lords are mostly accounted for, so it is the soldiers and people of Xinye and Xiangyang that have been captured. They will be alright: he will gain nothing with genocide."

"But Cao Cao's forces *won*...?" Guan Yu said angrily. "So... so Jiangling is *lost*...?"

Liu Bei nodded silently.

"...*Aiee*," Guan Yu exclaimed with frustration. "We should have moved faster!"

"It's not your fault," Liu Bei insisted. "It's mine... I have ignored sound advice. If I had heeded Kongming's sound counsel and captured that traitor Liu Cong, whose evil plotting has caused this suffering to the people... we would now command Jing, and be repelling Cao Cao with Liu Qi."

Guan Yu turned to Kongming, gave a sincere, yet slight, bow of obeisance, and said, "Senior Adviser... what shall we do now...?"

Kongming returned the gesture of respect, and replied, "We cannot take Jiangling... Cao Cao has brought his entire force of two-hundred-thousand from Xuchang, the main objective being to seize Jing Province and destroy us. We must retreat to Xiakou for now... and plan from there."

"But... maybe if Jiangling resisted...?" Wei Yan said pointedly.

"They won't," Kongming said surely. "Will they, Lord Liu of Jing...?"

"No," Liu Qi grunted. "They won't. They'll surrender: Cao has the provincial seal of office, willingly tendered by my fool brother."

"Cao will be anxious to avoid too much unrest now that he has secured Jiangling, he has to reassure the populace of his magnanimity," Kongming supposed. "He will not fight so readily, not if his adviser, Jia Xu, is as smart as he seems to be. Yes, we must give up on the parts of Jing Province to the west of the River Han for the moment, and retreat to Jiangxia... *regardless of who owns that*."

"...Understood," Guan Yu replied: he did not look to Liu Bei for approval this time.

"...I'm sorry," Kongming said as he shared a carriage with his wife Yueying and his younger brother Jun: they were spattered with blood, caked with sweat and dirt, and were visibly tired.

"...Brother, I thought we were dead," Jun admitted weakly. "I... I saw people killed... I wasn't ready for that."

"Neither was I when I first saw it," Kongming confessed in an effort to repair his brother's damaged pride. "It is something that should never be seen."

"...I understand that Xu Shu is gone," Yueying said quietly.

"Yes," Kongming replied coldly. "Xu Shu is gone."

"But if they had captured us," Yueying prompted, "you would have gone over to Cao Cao... wouldn't you...?"

"No," Kongming replied instantly. "It would not be the right course... Lord Liu has lost his daughters, but has kept going, since that is all he can do. He has had to accept their loss. They will either be given to Cao Cao's subordinates and be their wives or concubines, or they will be killed: whichever fate Cao decides is the more damaging to their father. Lord Liu could have surrendered, but he would have died, and they would still be beyond rescue. Sometimes... sometimes, you have to make difficult choices."

"...I am glad to hear you say that," Yueying declared. "I could not live with the knowledge that I had been used as bait to trap you... I would rather die."

"Apologies, Senior Adviser," a messenger said with kindness as he approached the carriage, "but I have been asked by Lord Liu to request your presence."

"...Very well," Kongming said numbly. "I shall be along shortly."

The messenger smiled apologetically and rode back to Liu Bei.

"...He could at least...! ...But... no, I do understand," Kongming conceded.

"Go," Yueying ordered, and Kongming nodded compliantly.


"...My lord," Kongming said as he rode to Liu Bei's side.

"We will be nearing Xiakou soon," Liu Bei reported. "But... what next...?"

Kongming looked at Jian Yong, Mister Sun and Mi Zhu – who had survived their own failed attempts to prevent the attacks at Steep-slope – and sighed woefully.

"...They will be fine," Liu Bei insisted. "Master Zhuge Kongming, when we reach Xiakou, what then...?"

"It depends on how well I have read the situation," Kongming admitted sadly. "If I have read the diplomatic situation as it stands, and I am right... we should soon receive a visit from Mister Lu Su of Jiangdong."

"*Lu Su*...?" Mister Sun exclaimed. "...You expect another attack from Sun Quan???"

"...Not so," Kongming said with a reassuring smile. "Rather, a trip to pay condolences to Liu Qi for the death of his father."

"Nonsense," Liu Qi scoffed. "Why would that rat Sun Quan want to mourn my father's death after he's tried to kill him all these years...?"

"...Diplomacy," Kongming replied. "You shall understand soon enough, provided of course that I am right."

"But if you're wrong...?" Liu Bei asked. "What then...?"

"If I'm wrong," Kongming said honestly, "then we must flee far, far away, and hope that the barrier of great distance is enough to end the chase."

"So it will be over, then," Jian Yong supposed.

Kongming did not reply.

"Still: we survived Steep-slope," Liu Bei said with sudden cheer. "I'm sure that from here, things can only improve for us."

There was more than one cynical thought that met that observation.

************

# ACT III: THE BATTLE OF RED CLIFFS

## 27

After a short space of time serving the warlord Liu Bei, Zhuge Liang and his family were now exiled from his homeland of Longzhong in Jing Province. Liu Qi, the eldest son of the last governor, was also a fugitive, after his younger brother – who seized power upon their father's death – had tendered the seal of office to the Imperial Prime Minister, Cao Cao. Liu Bei was a fugitive because he had been implicated in a plot to assassinate the Prime Minister, a plot that had, supposedly, been initiated by the Emperor, to whom Liu Bei was related by blood: now, all of Liu Bei's followers and any who dared show allegiance to him were enemies of Prime Minister Cao Cao, and therefore – since Cao Cao controlled the court – the state. Cao Cao had now made that very clear by pursuing Liu Bei, Liu Qi and all of their followers as they fled the surrendered territories of northwest and southwest Jing.

Now Liu Bei and his small army were in Jiangxia, the eastern region of Jing, and the only part of the province that was not under Prime Minister Cao Cao's control. However, the region was still unstable, as it had recently suffered an attack by the southern warlord Sun Quan. Sun Quan had attacked under the pretext of revenging his late father, who had died at the hands of followers of Liu Biao, the recently deceased governor of Jing: some suspected, however, that Sun Quan wanted Jing as part of his growing territory, as it offered significant tactical advantages to a would-be conqueror. Regardless of his motives, however, Sun Quan of Jiangdong was the only warlord that could now oppose Cao Cao in any way, and was therefore the only credible – if unlikely – ally that Liu Bei could potentially turn to.

After a sombre journey across western Jiangxia, Liu Bei and Liu Qi's combined forces arrived in the port of Xiakou, which was located in an area where the River Han joined the great Yangtze River. South of the water, a second place named Xiakou stood: this was the former stronghold of Huang Zu, lost to Sun Quan five years before. Jiangxia itself was battle-scarred, having been, only months before, the scene of the final encounter between the forces of Huang Zu and the forces of Sun Quan of Jiangdong. That had resulted in victory for Sun Quan, the death of Huang Zu, and a very short-term occupation by Jiangdong that ended when Sun Quan realised he had neither the spare forces nor the popular support to remain in the region. Now it was a base – albeit with questionable ownership – for the exiled rightful heir of Jing, Liu Qi, and his honorary uncle, Liu Bei.

"I've been thinking," Liu Bei said to Kongming as they sat in conference with all of the courtiers that Liu Bei had. "I *do* have someone I can go to."
"That's good," Kongming replied. "Just remember *not* to mention it to Lu Su."
"...*That* again," Liu Bei scoffed. "Master Zhuge Kongming, I have to confess, this is where I am afraid that with regard to ideas, and even blind optimism, you and I part company. Lu Su of Jiangdong is not going to come here and pay condolences."

"That's right," Mister Sun agreed. "The idea is preposterous."
"...After everything that has happened in the last thirty years,"
Kongming chuckled as he fanned himself, "you – a man that has
been at Lord Liu's side for a decade and witnessed most of it first
hand – have the audacity to use the word 'preposterous'...? If you
consider *anything* that has happened, Mister Sun, why is it such a
far-fetched thing...?"
Mister Sun sneered silently.
"...Maybe," Liu Bei conceded, "but it still pins hopes on Sun Quan
having good counsel around him... Zhang Zhao, his main adviser,
is, I hear, a wretched pedant, who would suggest continued
discord with the Liu family of Jing and capitulation to Cao Cao, and
there is only his like."
"...We'll see," Kongming replied. "Now... might I ask that I can
spend some time with my family...? Whatever happens now, we
will be busy..."
"... ... ...Very well," Liu Bei agreed. "I will allow everyone a day or
two... we have been through a lot. Thank you, Master Zhuge,
Mister Sun, all of you..."
Kongming got to his feet, paid respects to Liu Bei and left the
meeting, followed by an anxious Mister Sun.
"...You really harbour this ridiculous idea that Lu Su will...!" Mister
Sun protested angrily. "Kongming, have we not suffered enough
without enduring such taunting falsehoods???"
"Don't be so narrow-sighted, Mister Sun," Kongming scolded. "We
cannot surrender, and right now, it is the only alternative to
running away that we have. We can either run to one of Lord Liu's
old friends in some small state that will soon fall to Cao Cao or
Sun Quan... in which case, we will need to run *again*... or we can
hope for an alliance with Sun Quan."
"...'Hope' is all we can do," Mister Sun countered. "It won't
happen!"
"...As I said, we'll see," Kongming retorted. "But for now... let us
enjoy a brief respite from war."
Mister Sun nodded briskly, sighed desperately, and walked away.
"You'll see, all of you," Kongming whispered. "I know I'm right to
trust Lu Su."
"...**Kongming**...!" a voice called: it was Kongming's long-time
friend and sworn brother, Ma Liang.
"...Brother," Kongming said as he exchanged polite bows with Ma
Liang and smiled gratefully. "Everyone is settled, now...?"
"Yes," Ma Liang said wearily as he mopped his brow. "Everyone is
tired... my brother Su, unsurprisingly, is excited by war... he is
writing down things as we speak, and he is hoping to talk with you
about *his having actually seen Cao Cao*."
"I'm sure he is," Kongming chuckled as he started to fan himself
slowly.
"...We were lucky," Ma Liang realised.
"Cao Cao was more reserved than I expected," Kongming
admitted reluctantly. "He didn't relentlessly pursue us, ignoring all
dangers: instead, he abandoned the chase and marched on
Jiangling, putting military and official matters before personal...
that isn't just due to sound counsel, but also a personal
willingness to abide by sound counsel."

"...That was a swipe at Lord Liu," Ma Liang said as he and Kongming walked toward the encampment where their families were living. "You're annoyed that he ignored your advice."

"...Naturally, yes," Kongming admitted. "I am not a callous man... I do not crave the death of others... I simply act according to circumstance. From the moment that Liu Cong colluded with Cao Cao, he ceased to have ties to us. To fight him, to kill him then becomes a matter of military urgency... kill, or be killed. Had we attacked Xiangyang, we would not now be in this mess."

"...And if Lord Liu were like Cao Cao, he would listen to his Guo Jia," Ma Liang said with a smile.

"...Yes," Kongming replied wearily. "But I'm no Guo Jia... no Jia Xu... I will need to hone my skills a little, and insist on training for Lord Liu's forces so they can take part in formations. The Steep-slope battle was a shambles... they were torn apart."

"While Cao Cao's forces were well-organised: they were a product of strong collaboration, and good training, that you respect," Ma Liang supposed.

"...I am not going to defect," Kongming chuckled. "As I have said often enough, especially to arrogant types like Guan Yu, you must know your enemy, and respect them, even if you hate them. ...To beat Cao Cao, we will need to know him, and respect him... never underestimate or despise him."

"...Xu Shu..." Ma Liang mused.

The decision by their mutual friend, Xu Shu, to surrender and essentially defect to the forces of Cao Cao had left its mark. Despite his promise that he would never serve Cao Cao in any real capacity, the act of surrendering alone was enough to hurt both men, who had risked similar losses but remained loyal to the lord that they had pledged to serve. Many of their other friends – such as Shi Tao, Pang Degong, and Cui Zhouping – had never joined Liu Bei and did not join the flight from northern Jing, while Pang Tong – the so-called 'Young Phoenix', who was considered to be Zhuge Liang's intellectual equal – was in the surrendered southern capital Jiangling. All of them had most likely capitulated to the Prime Minister as well, so feelings of bitterness, betrayal and isolation were inevitable.

"Say no more of Xu Shu," Kongming insisted as calmly as he could. "What's done is done."

Ma Liang nodded sadly, and the two continued their walk toward the encampment in silence.

"...You still have your books," Yueying said as she sat with Kongming in their own patch of the camp.

"...I shall need to get you and Jun out of here, and into better accommodation," Kongming suggested as he looked about him at the wretched conditions: there was little space, and the smell of the unwashed and untreated was unpleasant, if not unbearable. "Perhaps I'll see about moving you to Three Rivers."

"People are resting, for now," Yueying replied. "We can worry about moving soon enough... we have only just arrived, and for now, we're just glad that we're alive."

"...But still," Kongming began, but Yueying hushed him.

"We are people, like everyone else here," Yueying insisted. "No special treatment, husband... we will be fine."

"...I don't suppose my qin survived...?" Kongming asked with a little humour.

"Sadly, no," Yueying replied with a smile. "It's a pity: you could play to soothe the pain the people are feeling."

It was only now that Kongming truly noticed the sounds of sobbing, complaining, and lamentation amongst the civilians and injured soldiers that shared the encampment.

"...Will things get better...?" Yueying asked.

"If I am right, then yes," Kongming replied.

"...Lu Su...?" Yueying recalled. "Lu Su will come here...?"

"Hopefully," Kongming sighed. "If not, all of the land will belong to Cao Cao, and his progeny."

Yueying was silent and thoughtful at this point.

"...But still," Kongming replied encouragingly, "whatever Cao Cao does to me if we lose, we have seen that he can be fair when he chooses..."

"Tell that to those his men slaughtered at Xu Province, and at Steep-slope," Yueying retorted. "Tell that to the men who will be forced to fight for him, or be his slaves. Tell that to Lord Liu Bei's daughters, to all those captured daughters, sisters and wives who will now be the whores of an enemy's vassals for the rest of their miserable days."

"...I am trying to be optimistic," Kongming insisted. "If we lose-"

"You can't afford to lose," Yueying retorted sternly. "...You have to *win*."

Kongming embraced Yueying gently, and the two enjoyed the moment.

"...I will," Kongming promised. "I'll find a way... if none presents itself, I'll find a way... but Lu Su will come here... I know he will."

"So do I," Yueying said surely. "You are wise, and Lu Su is too... he will see things as you do, and he will come."

Within a few days, a small boat moored in Xiakou, and an ambassador from Jiangdong disembarked, and requested an audience with Liu Bei and the rightful governor of Jing, Liu Qi.

************

## 28

A day later, Kongming and Mister Sun watched from the outskirts of a training ground as the unthinkable came to pass: several men wearing the green uniforms of the south were escorting a short, slim man in blue robes and a black cap toward Liu Bei's command tent, which was also some distance away. Although there was visible discomfort and resentment among Liu Qi's men, the spectacle had, so far, been without incident.
*"Well, I'll be...!"* Mister Sun whispered with genuine surprise.
"...It is good to see that circumstances are clear," Kongming declared.
"I owe you an apology, Kongming," Mister Sun suggested.
"Nonsense, Mister Sun," Kongming insisted. "Your view was sound in a time of order: who is at fault when the unlikely occurs?"
Kongming then gestured to Mister Sun that the two should greet Lu Su: Mister Sun nodded compliantly, and the two started their approach.

"...Greetings, Mister Lu," Zhao Yun hailed as Lu Su reached Liu Bei's command tent. "My master, Lord Liu, would very much like to welcome you."
"That is an honour," Lu Su said diplomatically. "I see two advisers approaching... might the man carrying the fan be Zhuge Liang, younger brother of one of my own lord's advisers, Zhuge Jin...?"
"It is," Zhao Yun confirmed as Kongming and Mister Sun reached Lu Su and Zhao Yun, and exchanged respectful bows. Many soldiers and officials gathered around the tent to observe the meeting with curiosity and trepidation.
"I come to offer sincere condolence for the death of Liu Biao, governor of Jing Province," Lu Su explained to a surprised audience. "I was on my way to Jiangling, when I was informed that Cao Cao is now in possession of it... is this true...?"
"...It is," Kongming reported calmly as he fanned himself.
"...I see," Lu Su murmured. "Well... what, then, is the current situation...?"
"Ah...!" Liu Bei hailed before Kongming could answer: Liu Bei and Liu Qi both came out of the command tent to receive Lu Su.
"...I'm sorry, I'm afraid that since we've never met..." Lu Su prompted.
"I am Liu Bei, former governor of Xu Province," Liu Bei said pleasantly.
"I am Liu Qi, rightful governor of Jing Province," Liu Qi said with bitterness.
*"Rightful...?"* Lu Su noted. "Then... has...?"
"...We should talk inside," Kongming suggested.

The exposition of current events was brief and to the point.
"...So, then," Liu Qi asked cuttingly from his seat at the head of the command tent, "the situation is now explained: what is the purpose of your visit, ambassador of Sun Quan of Jiangdong...?"

"I come to pay my respects to you, Governor Liu, and also pay my condolences, and also the condolences of my lord Sun Quan, with respect to the passing of your esteemed father," Lu Su replied cordially as Liu Bei took a courtesy seat to Liu Qi's immediate right, and the rest of those present – Jian Yong, Mister Sun, Kongming, Guan Yu, Zhang Fei, Ma Liang, Yi Ji, Huo Jun, and Jing officials Xiang Lang and Liao Li – sat in a line to the right of Liu Bei, facing the visitor. Lu Su's men were kept from entering the tent by most of Liu Bei's bodyguards: Chen Dao, their leader, stood at the rear of the tent with Zhao Yun, watching Lu Su.

"The Suns and the Lius have fought without pause or regret since your lord's father invaded my father's province as a vassal of Yuan Shu," Liu Qi retorted angrily. "Now, you come to express condolence...?"

"...Your mood toward me is not unexpected," Lu Su said with a sigh. "I am one of those that has vigorously campaigned over the years to end the dispute between the families of Sun and Liu... it is only in recent times, having the support of Chief Commander Zhou Gongjin, that I have been able to gain influence and hope to finally sway my lord's mind on the matter."

"Where does his *heart* lie...?" Jian Yong asked. "That, after all, has been his only drive for the last eight years that he has ruled over the south."

"Do you not see the hate in the faces of the men of Xiakou...?" Xiang Lang said as he leant forward and pointed at Lu Su. "It is only months since your master came again to this region and took the head of Huang Zu, and occupied this place! The Huang family's influence is the only reason why this place is not now part of your master's already ridiculous empire!"

"...*Empire*...?" Lu Su chuckled nervously. "M-my lord desires nothing like an empire... he is simply stabilising the region."

"...Is that what you call 'invasion' where you come from, then...?" Liao Li asked aggressively. "I really didn't know that."

"...Remember that this entire feud began because your lord, together with Huang Zu, conspired to murder the father of my lord!" Lu Su protested.

"Oh, I *see*, so we should be *grateful* that he is *forgiving us*," Xiang Lang said with mock understanding in his tone.

"...Really, you are being too aggressive," Lu Su protested. "Perhaps murder is the wrong word... perhaps, as an invading general, serving Yuan Shu, Sun Jian was leaving himself open to attack... but it is generally felt that his destruction was unnecessary. Could he not have been captured...?"

"You don't capture a hungry tiger when it enters your home," Kongming said coldly. "You kill it."

"...Mister Zhuge, I hardly expected you to take their side," Lu Su scolded.

"Sun Jian killed a lot of notable generals and rendered some astonishing service in his lifetime," Kongming suggested. "When such a man as that attacks you, a man that once bested *Hua Xiong* and *Lü Bu*, what *do* you do, exactly, if you want to live...?"

"...Strange though it is, it would please my lord to hear you say that," Lu Su said with sudden thoughtfulness. "After all, I am here not to fight, but to make peace... and perhaps it is not just the young governor that still has open wounds."

"...Venerable uncle," Liu Qi said as he turned to Liu Bei, "this man from the south comes here seeking accord... what should I do, in your own opinion...?"

Liu Bei looked at Kongming before replying, "I really do not know. That is why we are sat here now."

"...Lord Liu Bei, you are also in a dilemma," Lu Su said nervously.

**"Are you trying to piss us all off???"** Zhang Fei barked: Guan Yu reluctantly restrained him whilst glaring at Lu Su.

"...I meant no offence," Lu Su insisted. "I am saddened by the events at Steep-slope, and am personally aggrieved at the outcome."

Liu Bei bowed slightly, and said, "My thanks."

"...None needed," Lu Su insisted as he returned the gesture. "Anyone with a soul would be stricken with fear by Cao Cao."

"Ah, *finally*," Kongming chuckled, "we get to the true matter."

"Cao Cao's power is now immense," Lu Su explained. "He has written to my lord, boasting of having an army of eight-hundred-thousand men..."

**"Eight-hundred-thousand???"** Yi Ji exclaimed.

"...Only if he has some magic power to grow soldiers out of beans," Kongming said as he fanned himself casually. "...I wouldn't mind being able to do that myself."

"You do not believe the number...?" Lu Su prompted.

"It is false," Kongming promised. "If he had numbers like that, he would not have left us to retreat at Steep-slope. ...No, I would say less than half of that, possibly only a third. ...That said, they are well trained... he may be being boastful..."

"As in 'one of my men is worth two or three of yours'," Jian Yong supposed.

"Arrogant bastard," Zhang Fei grunted. "Next time I see him, I'll...!"

"Yide," Liu Bei scolded. "...However many soldiers he has, we are freshly defeated, and cannot hope to oppose even the smaller number Kongming suggests."

"Neither can my lord," Lu Su sighed. "...So all options are being examined... tell me, Lord Liu, what your plans are. Do you intend to stay here and hold Jiangxia with the young governor...?"

"No," Liu Bei said sadly. "I am a curse... if I remain here, I only give Cao Cao cause to harm him. My forces are destroyed... I have generals, but many of my men were seized, as well as much of my wealth and supplies. Therefore, I can only go to another, like I have been forced to do so many times before, and throw myself on their mercy... somewhere distant, where Cao's eyes cannot see, and live out my years in obscurity..."

Liu Bei's eyes welled up in a theatrical show of grief.

"...Brother...!" Zhang Fei exclaimed.

"...Brother, control your feelings," Guan Yu pleaded.

"Yes, Lord Liu, please, do not sadden yourself," Lu Su implored. "If you were to seek shelter, to where would you go...?"

"...I have a friend from my younger days, Wu Ju, that has done well, and now governs Cangwu County..." Liu Bei replied emotionally: Kongming frowned disapprovingly at his lord's refusal to take his advice yet again.

"*Cangwu*...?" Zhang Fei seethed. "That's the middle of nowhere!"

"...I agree with your 'brother'," Lu Su said with a laugh. "Not to mention that Wu Ju is an average sort that cannot hope to maintain independence. Come now, Lord Liu, don't give up on your career now, just because of a minor setback!"

"You consider annihilation at Steep-slope to be a minor setback...?" Mister Sun scolded. "...And you insult a friend of the lord...? You are a very poor emissary."

"You mistake encouraging words for underestimating a dilemma, Mister Sun," Kongming said with a laugh. "Lu Zijing meant no offence."

"Thank you, Kongming," Lu Su chuckled. "You saved me repeating myself. Lord Liu, my own lord has long observed you as being a man of upstanding loyalty and good faith, a man of virtue and talent. In the face of a great enemy, one can succeed only by knowing not only one's enemies, but one's allies. Remain here at Xiakou... my lord has no intention of continuing hostilities with the young governor, and no desire to. We will see what we can do to work together."

"...*Seriously*...?" Liu Qi scoffed.

"*Seriously*, young governor," Lu Su replied sincerely. "Enough blood has been shed now... in my view, the feud died with your father and my lord's father... we should look to the future now, an alliance to launch an offensive against Cao Cao."

Murmurs of disbelief met the statement.

"...An *offensive* against Cao Cao...?" the Jing official Liao Li exclaimed. "A *defensive* alliance, *perhaps*, but... *offensive*??? ...Together or apart, we can't go up against him: he is unstoppable! Even the famous Yuan Shao was destroyed easily by Cao Cao, and he had half a million men! ...Are you insane???"

"It's worth thinking about," Liu Qi suggested. "My spineless brother surrendered, and now he is an exiled laughing stock. ...I would rather die fighting, to be-"

Liu Qi's statement ended abruptly as he broke into a fit of coughing: Lu Su noted it with interest, and Kongming noted Lu Su's interest with worry.

"Let us have a recess for now," Liu Bei said as he placed a comforting arm around the pain-wracked Liu Qi. "...Mister Sun, please ensure that Ambassador Lu is given good accommodation, and well looked after, while we think things over."

Mister Sun nodded agreeably.

"Before he goes with you, Mister Sun," Kongming interrupted, "I think you and I might have some things to discuss, Zijing."

"Agreed," Lu Su said with a slight smile.

With that, Lu Su and Kongming started to walk toward Kongming's office, which was another military tent located nearby.

"What's Kongming up to now, I wonder...?" Jian Yong chuckled.

"I'm sure his plan is sound," Liu Bei said as he continued to comfort Liu Qi.


************

## 29

"You are certainly a man of writing, as your brother told me," Lu Su noted as he looked about him: Kongming's tent was filled with his collected studies. He walked to Kongming's map of the proposed 'tripod of power', and hummed thoughtfully, before saying, "This map... it looks very familiar."

"It should," Kongming said with a smile. "But enough of that: you are here for a very good reason."

Kongming's servants brought tea for the two advisers, and Lu Su started to feel a little more at ease with the younger man.

"...I shall be open," Lu Su declared as soon as he and Kongming were sat down and drinking tea. "My lord Sun Quan has a dilemma. Cao Cao commands a fearfully large army, one that even makes ants out of lesser giants like Lord Sun. If Cao Cao were to decide to attack Jiangdong, we would not stand a chance."

"And if he were to set upon my lord again, especially while his forces are disorganised and scattered, we too would be crushed," Kongming sighed. "And then, my friend, what would become of the dream of the restoration of the Han... or of our mutually shared intermediate vision of three independent states...?"

"I am glad we see eye to eye," Lu Su said with a smile. "Our lords will... if only temporarily... need to put aside their differences and ally to oppose Cao Cao."

"Of course," Kongming replied pointedly, "my lord is without a base... the tripod you proposed, of Lord Sun, Liu Biao and Cao Cao... will not now be possible."

After a cautious pause, Lu Su said, "If Cao was, by some miracle, crushed, then your lord would have a multitude of options for a base... perhaps Yi Province to the west."

"...Your lord covets Jing," Kongming suggested.

"As reparation, and as security," Lu Su retorted. "Kongming, you know as well as anyone what my lord's family has suffered at the hands of Liu Biao."

"If it is said once, it is said a thousand times... your lord's father, Sun Jian, was a hired vassal working for Yuan Shu when he was killed in battle," Kongming said with a scolding tone. "Had he succeeded in taking Jing Province from Liu Biao, it would then have been handed over to Yuan Shu... who would, then, as fate has played out, been devoured by Cao Cao, and we would be where we are now anyway. Jing was never intended for Sun Quan by the will of Heaven... why do you deny your own prophecy of a tripod of power by denying Lord Liu the use of those – formerly *family-held* – lands as his base...? ...How does that differ from their being the lands of Lord Sun's 'hated enemy' Liu Biao, for whose death you visit here today offering 'sincere condolence' on Lord Sun's behalf...?"

Lu Su sipped his tea and seethed silently.

"There's no point being angry," Kongming suggested. "You know that I'm right. The tripod depends on *your* lord, *my* lord and Cao Cao's successor... who will, most likely, be his eldest son, the inexperienced youth Cao Pi... governing lands of equivalent wealth and strength."

"Liu Zhang and Zhang Lu govern Yi Province, a land of great wealth and magnificent natural defences," Lu Su retorted irritably. "Yi offers a similar foothold to Jing Province... perhaps better. Jing is too dangerous strategically to be in the hands of another, even an ally. No, for my lord to feel secure, all of southern Jing – not just Jiangxia – must belong to the Sun family."

"...Sadly, I think that Jing will be what breaks our ties," Kongming sighed woefully. "But... but that is for the future. What matters is the present. Cao Cao has a quarter-of-a-million men at his disposal..."

Lu Su smiled sadly and said, "That is what concerns my Lord Sun. Zhou Gongjin, the chief commander and a man of great wisdom, sees things as we do... but Zhang Zhao, one of the lord's most trusted advisers, is gently steering our lord toward seeking peace with Cao Cao."

"...Fool," Kongming scoffed. "Who would that serve? Cao Cao is one of the few men who would *execute* Zhang Zhao for the treachery he showed toward his lord, not *reward him for it.*"

"But war with Cao would destroy us," Lu Su countered. "I confess... he has made some valid points that have even compelled *me* to waver a few times."

"But what is better, to fight and fall a man of conviction, or be slowly eroded, forced to kneel to a man who will kick dirt in his face...?" Kongming suggested.

"That is exactly the sort of language my lord must hear," Lu Su said gratefully. "It would be better if he did not know the true extent of Cao's power... even Zhang Zhao hides those facts from him for now... but to rile him by reminding him of the loss of dignity and power... yes, that is what my lord needs to hear."

"...And you want *me* to do this," Kongming supposed as he sipped his tea.

"Kongming, I will not lie... your name is little known in the south, except for your kinship to Zhuge Jin," Lu Su explained hesitantly. "To those that do know of your service to Lord Liu, your record amounts to no more than barely surviving, and that is met with derision by many of my lord's advisers and scholars. But there are those that *do* appreciate what you have achieved, against near-insurmountable odds... and see that your lord's continued resistance represents a chance... no matter how slim... to face and fight Cao Cao, and win."

Kongming nodded sombrely.

"I do not think that any other man could do it," Lu Su suggested. "You are a man that weaves words well, a man that can antagonise or placate at will. You have sustained the morale of your lord and held a giant at bay with twigs. Your youth and confidence will sway my young and confident lord, because he will empathise far more with you than he will with an older, more cautious man like Zhang Zhao that only seeks to keep his own head on his shoulders. ...So will you do it, Kongming? Will you visit my lord Sun Quan, and inspire him to take up arms...?"

Kongming sighed theatrically, and sipped his tea silently.

"This is not the time for playful musings and pauses, Kongming," Lu Su scolded. "I come to ask for your help... you probably knew I was coming, such is your insight into what must be done... will you do it, or not...?"

"Of course," Kongming replied with a smirk. "But only if I know that you, Zhou Yu and the generals of Jiangdong are united in their conviction... pedants like Zhang Zhao can be shouted down, but not generals, and certainly not Zhou Yu."

"Zhou Gongjin is determined," Lu Su promised.

"But then, why can he not sway Sun Quan...?" Kongming countered pointedly. "He is the best friend of your late lord Sun Ce, married to the sister of Sun Ce's widow. He commands great respect, and his words carry immeasurable weight, surely...?"

Lu Su hesitated.

"...He too, has doubts," Kongming sighed disappointedly. "You expect me to go to Chaisang... *alone*... and antagonise Sun Quan to battle, when his entire advisory and his chief commander are afraid of the odds...? ...That will lead to my death, surely, Zijing."

"I...!" Lu Su exclaimed.

"They would inform Sun Quan of the numbers as soon as he swaggered boldly into court," Kongming suggested, "and then they would say what you have yet to raise... that I am there seeking the alliance to protect my lord from extinction, and that it only serves Lord Liu to have an alliance, and that capitulating to Cao Cao would only hurt my Lord Liu... and Sun Quan will believe it, and my head will separate from my body, and Lord Liu will be left to die alone while Zhang Zhao assists your lord in writing the terms of surrender."

"...You are, unfortunately, quite correct," Lu Su admitted.

"So you would have had me walk into a trap," Kongming snickered.

"Of course not," Lu Su insisted. "I... I intended to broach the subject of strengthening Zhou Gongjin's resolve on the way there, since it is a trifling matter compared to Lord Sun."

"You'd better hope so," Kongming suggested coldly. "A miscalculation will be very, very costly, and I guarantee you that the hot-headed vassals like Zhang Fei and Guan Yu will want your lord's head before they die, if Lord Liu is compromised, and they both know men that could make it happen."

"...I am aware of that," Lu Su sighed. "I do not wish to lose a second lord to vengeful assassins, and neither does Gongjin. No, I promise that we can force Gongjin to see things our way."

"...Very well then," Kongming sighed with resignation. "I would accompany you to see your master... and see where that gets us... I shall ask my lord's permission."

"No."

Liu Bei's answer was immediate and apparently final.

"...My lord," Kongming said in response, "you should not dismiss this idea."

"No," Liu Bei said again. "You cannot go there alone."

"What are you afraid of...?" Kongming asked.

"...Do I have to be afraid...?" Liu Bei retorted.

"Three things scare you," Kongming supposed. "The first is my safety: you fear that I may be killed by opponents of Lu Su's ideas. The second is *your* safety: you are concerned about possible attacks by Cao Cao, or tension between Liu Qi's forces and your own, and worry about losing a confidante at such a time. The third is my loyalty: even after the first two points, there is a part of you that fears I will not return... after Xu Shu, my long-time friend, abandoned you at Steep-slope, and with my brother being in his service already... I can understand that concern."

"...You read me well," Liu Bei replied irritably. "Now address those points if you will, Master Zhuge."

"Lu Su is safe... therefore I am safe," Kongming began. "That addresses the first point. To elaborate, Lu Su may be a benefactor of Chief Commander Zhou Yu, but Zhang Zhao and his brother have been unchallenged in the court since the days of Sun Ce. If they have not already had Lu Su assassinated, then they will not harm either of us."

"...Fine," Liu Bei noted. "The second point...?"

"Cao Cao has only just secured Jiangling... events are moving at a fast pace. He is unpopular in northern Jing... he cannot afford to move too quickly," Kongming suggested. "He has made boasts... but why...? ...Because he wants Sun Quan to surrender without a fight, that's why. If he had near to a million men, Cao Cao would do what he did to us at Steep-slope: he would cross the river and grind Sun Quan into the ground. When Cao Cao has power, he uses it."

"...And internal tension...?" Liu Bei prompted.

"Liu Qi is ill... and he's also young, and he needs you to assist him in affairs of governance," Kongming replied. "He knows your intentions are good, because... and I hate to admit this... I was wrong about killing Liu Cong. It was your sparing the lad that affirmed you in Liu Qi's eyes as a benevolent man. I still believe that he should have been dealt with, but yes, I concede that he should have been spared."

"...So now you see that sometimes, my reasons for things are well thought out," Liu Bei retorted. "I know hearts as you know minds. ...Carry on, Kongming."

"The majority of Liu Biao's generals and officials that followed you here are actually more impressed with you than they are with him," Kongming continued. "So... it is more the case that Liu Qi might have to fear you, rather than the reverse, were you not so honest, my lord."

"...Fine," Liu Bei said with a smirk. "...And the third point...?"

"My brother tried to coerce me to join Sun Quan years ago, before you and I even spoke in my cottage for the first time," Kongming revealed. "You know what I think of Sun Quan... that view is unaltered. My family is here; my loyalty is to your cause; I vowed that to you, and I am a man of my word. Xu Shu... really disappointed me. While I understand his need to honour his mother, he left with so little hesitation that I suspect a life of enduring defeats without victories was not for him anyway."

Liu Bei laughed, placed his hand on Kongming's shoulder and said, "You are as enlightened as always, Master Zhuge. ...Very well, go to Jiangdong: you might be able to get Sun Quan to serve *me* with that wily rhetoric of yours!"

Kongming smiled, bowed, and turned to leave: Liu Bei gestured for him to remain for one last question.
"...How does your family feel about this...?" Liu Bei asked.
"I have not consulted them," Kongming replied.
"...Fine," Liu Bei said quietly. "I was just wondering."
"Don't worry, my lord," Kongming insisted. "The legendary 'ugly daughter of Huang Chengyan' is not going to dissuade me. Even if she beats me black and blue, I'm going to Chaisang."
Liu Bei laughed out loud as Kongming left his presence, fanning himself casually.

Despite Yueying's requesting the opposite, Kongming had already arranged for Yueying and Jun to be relocated to a house near the encampment.
"...I see," Yueying said numbly as Kongming finished explaining his intention to travel to Chaisang, the capital of Jiangdong, and meet the ruler of the region, Sun Quan.
"I am going alone because it is diplomatic business," Kongming insisted.
"...And you don't want Liu Bei to suspect you of defecting, of course," Yueying supposed.
"That as well," Kongming admitted. "Don't worry... I will be quite safe."
"I don't doubt that," Yueying replied with a smile. "...Do you think Sun Quan will agree to what you're being asked to suggest...? ...On second thought, don't answer that... you wouldn't be going if you didn't think it was possible."
"And that," Kongming said with a laugh, "is why I love you."
Kongming embraced Yueying, and continued to smile.
"Bring me back something nice," Yueying quipped.
"I'll see what I can do," Kongming chuckled softly.

∗∗∗∗∗∗∗∗∗∗∗∗

## 30

After another small period of diplomatic niceties, Kongming accompanied Lu Su on his boat ride back to Jiangdong. As the boat travelled eastward on the Yangtze River, Kongming pondered his future, and fanned himself slowly.

"…You're nervous," Lu Su supposed.

"Not at all," Kongming insisted. "In fact, I'm quite looking forward to it. I have met Lord Liu, and also Liu Biao… I have not yet seen Cao Cao, though I have no desire to anyway… no, the only person I have not willingly met that will be a major factor in the future of the land is your lord Sun Quan."

"He is misunderstood," Lu Su insisted. "Some see him as narrow-minded, governed by his mother and the Zhang brothers, paying no heed to good advice, fearful of confrontation: in truth, he is much like Lord Liu… a victim of circumstance, forced to compromise to avoid needless conflict."

"…So explain the feud with Liu Biao to me again," Kongming challenged.

"Uh," Lu Su replied awkwardly, "well… uh… there was a lot of pressure."

"State Mother Wu, the memory of his father, needing to look strong, his generals forcing his hand… I see," Kongming chuckled softly.

"It *was* personal to him, don't get me wrong," Lu Su protested, "but my lord knows when a feud is less important than the affairs of the day… else we would not be here now, would we…?"

"…But I thought your lord craved Jing as reparation," Kongming noted.

"That… was said in a moment of tension," Lu Su countered. "He has no ambition to seize any more of Jing from the young governor… Jiangxia will do."

"…But if he were to die, which is bound to be soon, as you noticed…?" Kongming challenged. "…What then…? Will Jiangxia 'do' then…?"

"…Then," Lu Su replied, "the matter of ownership of Jing Province as a whole is a matter of *honour*, I would say. …Your lord would need to use Jiangling to launch an attack on Yi Province, so we would need to negotiate that."

"Who says that my lord intends to attack Yi, the seat of another kinsman…?" Kongming chuckled.

"…So he intends to seek shelter there, gain popular favour, and wait forty years for Liu Zhang to bequeath it to him on his deathbed, does he…?" Lu Su retorted. "That plan, surely, relies on Lord Liu being a timeless immortal… yet he is already fifty, or thereabouts, and quite obviously so."

"Mm," Kongming said with a smirk, "it seems that it is more a case of you not respecting my lord than the other way around."

"…I-I…!" Lu Su stammered.

"…Meant no offence," Kongming teased. "Lu Zijing, you really are an appalling diplomat, you know. Learn to control your temper when others tease you."

"I'm older than you," Lu Su replied. "I need no schooling."

"...If you say so," Kongming snickered. "But returning to my Lord Liu... no, he does not wish to attack Yi... perhaps there are other ways to win a foothold in a territory other than seizing it by force."
"Sadly, that is nonsense," Lu Su retorted. "A guest cannot rule the house. Don't try and deceive me, Kongming: we both follow the same ideas. I know how to seize Yi: it is just that I always thought that Liu Biao would do it, not your own master."
"...Well, let's see how we go with Sun Quan," Kongming replied. "Who knows...? ...Maybe we're both wrong... maybe the tripod will be Cao Cao, Sun Quan, and Liu Zhang."
Lu Su laughed dismissively, saying, *"That I would like to see."*
The two men both laughed at the expense of Liu Zhang, the ruler of Yi Province, whose fate, each man felt, would be decided very soon.

Once they reached Chaisang, Lu Su installed Kongming in a hotel that was located near to the palace of Sun Quan, the ruler of the Jiangdong provinces, which was also known by some as the land of 'Eastern Wu'. From there, he went to see his lord alone.

"...Zijing, you have returned safely!" Sun Quan hailed as Lu Su entered the palace courtroom: Sun Quan's officials were lined up in rows on either side of the hall, and Sun Quan himself sat upon a mat at the far end, fanned by two beautiful servant girls, while a musician played a qin for entertainment. In front of Sun Quan was a table covered with dishes of cooked meats and vegetables: to his left, a smaller table held a wine jug and a cup.

Sun Quan – the second actual ruling Sun of Jiangdong – was a man in his thirties with shining eyes, a short, coarse, purplish beard, and a regal air. He wore robes that suggested kingship at the very least, their being emblazoned with dragons and other auspicious emblems of the day.
"My lord," Lu Su said with a low bow. "As requested, I have brought back with me Zhuge Liang, the brother of Zhuge Jin."
"Very good!" Sun Quan beamed.
"...My lord!" an elder near Sun Quan hailed dramatically. "This man 'Zhuge Liang' has come to talk nonsense to you!"
"...As always," Lu Su sneered, "you make trouble before it is necessary, Zhang Zhao. The man is not even here with us yet."
"...Indeed," Sun Quan noted, "he is not with you now... why not...?"
"I know, my lord, that you asked me to bring him here immediately," Lu Su said apprehensively, "but... I needed to be sure that things had not changed."
"My lord," Zhang Zhao protested, "we are wasting valuable time. Cao Cao's envoy cannot be delayed forever: a decision must be made, and quickly."
"...Envoy...?" Lu Su said disappointedly. "...I knew it. Zhang Zhao wants us to surrender."
"He does," Sun Quan revealed: the generals along the right side of the room expressed their displeasure with grunts and curses.
"...It was my desire to see the options that were open to us before I made a decision," Sun Quan declared, "and now, Zhuge Liang of Longzhong has come to speak with us."
"...And who *is* this 'Zhuge Liang'...?" Zhang Zhao said with contempt.

"My brother," Zhuge Jin proclaimed as he stepped out into the centre of the hall to be seen. "He is a genius of the age, and cannot be taken lightly."

"Oh...?" Zhang Zhao snickered. "Tell me, Ziyu, what merits this man has got, what achievements he has made, that we should call him a genius...?"

"He is a man of brilliant insight, and excellent at debate," Zhuge Jin answered politely, despite his anger.

"...And this is enough to call him a genius...?" Zhang Zhao mocked. "Well then, are not all the men in this line a genius... except maybe *you*...?"

The other scholars laughed derisively, and Zhuge Jin reddened with anger.

"...This young man is hailed – by men of *Jing Province*, no less – of being one of the great talents of the age," Zhang Zhao continued contemptuously. "Those that laud him include Sima Hui, who is renowned throughout the land as 'Mister Yes', a man that applauded the news that a fellow townsman's son was *dead*, as though he were some sort of simpleton! ...Zhuge Liang is also known by the Taoist name of 'Crouching Dragon'! ...Tell me, Ziyu, when this dragon intends to stop cowering, and get up, and do something of merit...?"

The majority of the scholars continued to laugh, and Zhuge Jin conceded, retaking his place amongst them and saying no more.

"All we have," Zhang Zhao continued, "is the praise of a few fools, and his great record as a persuader, as an adviser, and as a strategist. As a persuader, he failed to secure for Liu Bei a stake in a land governed by family: in fact, his persuasive powers were so effective, that Liu Cong betrayed Liu Bei to Cao Cao, and he was forced to flee the province!"

The scholars were now joined by a few of the generals in derisive laughter.

"As an adviser, his record is even more exemplary!" Zhang Zhao continued. "I myself could not do better: when faced with imminent danger, he allowed his lord to lose his base at Fan, leave Xinye and Xiangyang, and to top it all, take the entire populace with him to slow him down! So slow was their advance that Cao Cao's men reached their quarry before they had passed the halfway point of their journey, despite having had to travel over twice the distance from the capital!"

The laughter intensified.

"And then, in the one battle he has ever taken part in, he showed his true worth as a strategist," Zhang Zhao sneered. "Faced with an enemy whose numbers were *half* that of his own army, he succeeded – through having no formation, no weapons, basically no plan at all – to be completely routed, and lose all of the men!"

"...**That's enough!**" Lu Su shouted: the laughter died down eventually, save a few snickers, but the confident smirk remained on Zhang Zhao's face.

"...You say that is enough," Zhang Zhao continued. "I haven't even *started*. I will not let this walking catalogue of failures come in here and ill-advise my lord, whom I cherish, to go up against an enemy that would crush us the way they crushed his own lord's forces... just to give him time to flee to Nanzhong and hide with the barbarian natives."

"...All of what you say is true for Liu Bei," Lu Su conceded, "but it is not true of Master Zhuge! You bend the truth, Zhang Zhao, as you always do... not one of the failures you mention was down to Master Zhuge."

"But he is a *genius*," Zhang Zhao retorted. "He is the man on whom Liu Bei relies for counsel... so the situation is therefore clearly one of only two opposites: he is a *genius*, as you say, that commands no respect and has no influence on Liu Bei whatsoever... or he is a useless fool that has Liu Bei hanging on his every word, no matter how much grief it brings to him. Which is it, Lu Zijing...?"

"...I have to say, Master Zhang has made some fair points, as always," Sun Quan sighed. "...This man Zhuge Liang will have to come here and state his case, but... after that appraisal, I cannot say that I expect to be impressed at all."

Zhang Zhao looked at Lu Su smugly: Lu Su bowed to his master and said, "Should I fetch him now, my lord...?"

"No," Sun Quan replied. "Let us recess for today... and meet this fellow tomorrow. I have had enough entertainment for one day."

Lu Su bowed again, turned, and left, amid snickering from some of the scholars that agreed with Zhang Zhao's views.

"...We're in trouble," Lu Su said as he met with Kongming and his brother Zhuge Jin that evening.

"I know," Kongming replied. "My brother has already told me."

"...Zhang Zhao is smooth-tongued, and very dangerous," Jin suggested.

"Zhang Zhao is known to me," Kongming said with a dismissive gesture of his fan. "He fawns on the State Mother like a palace eunuch, and in some ways, he helped bring about Sun Ce's downfall by encouraging his mother to spend so much time listening to that 'Taoist saint', Gan Ji, and infuriating Sun Ce with his popularity with the common folk. If Prefect Xu Gong's men had not killed Sun Ce, followers of Gan Ji, upset with his execution, would have killed Sun Ce instead."

"That isn't a hypothesis that I would talk about if I were you," Lu Su said nervously. "Gan Ji was very popular... many people followed him... many besides Zhang Zhao still hold him in high regard. And Sun Ce's death is still a touchy subject for the veteran generals like Huang Gai."

"I am not an idiot, Zijing," Kongming scolded. "I know all that."

"So then how are you going to deal with him...?" Jin asked.

"...The way you deal with all men like him," Kongming replied.

As Zhuge Jin and Lu Su left the hotel, Lu Su said, "What do you suppose he will do, Ziyu...?"

"...I don't know," Jin sighed. "I find him unreadable, I always have. But I'm sure he will certainly give it his all."

Kongming, meanwhile, sat quietly, slowly fanned himself, and thought about the challenge that lay ahead of him.

************

## 31

The next day, Sun Quan held court, and Kongming attended, dressed as always in white Taoist-style robes, a white silk turban over his hair, and carrying his feather fan. Lu Su led him into the court: the reaction was generally one of disbelief that a young man in eccentric dress could be the man that would sway their lord's mind.

"...Master Zhuge Liang, my lord," Lu Su hailed.

"So this is the fabled 'Crouching Dragon'," Zhang Zhao said derisively.

"...Lord Sun Quan," Kongming hailed, making slight obeisance.

"You have travelled a long way," Sun Quan supposed. "You must be very tired."

"I will never tire of fulfilling my lord's will," Kongming replied: Zhang Zhao scoffed, and sneered at the young man.

"...You are here to represent your lord, Liu Bei," Sun Quan prompted. "I should like to hear your appraisal of the situation."

"Perhaps," Zhang Zhao said, "we should first hear another recital of the situation of the lord of young master 'Crouching Dragon'!"

"Perhaps not," Kongming retorted. "I expect their ears are still ringing with the sound of yesterday's session of self-indulgent cruelty at my lord's expense."

"You...!" Zhang Zhao exclaimed.

"You stand there, old man, talking about me as though you know me," Kongming challenged. "Would you like me to tell you what I know of you...?"

"...I have nothing to hide!" Zhang Zhao said angrily.

"No...? ...And neither do I," Kongming insisted. "I know all about your 'appraisal' yesterday... and before we continue with urgent matters, it saddens me to say that we must first refute your childish claims that my lord and I are both incompetent, else there is no point in my being here."

"...Go on," Sun Quan said with interest.

"I have been in Lord Liu's service for a year and a half... that is all," Kongming began. "In that time, Lord Liu has been the guest of Liu Biao, who gave him shelter after he was defeated by Cao Cao. For eight years, Lord Liu has served Liu Biao diligently, and defended the region from both large and small enemies. In fact – as Mister Zhang failed to note – he successfully repelled Xiahou Dun at Bowang, destroying that force and seizing Xiahou Lan as a captive... the man now works within Liu Bei's service as a civil administrator. Such is Lord Liu's good nature that a member of Cao Cao's extended family now willingly works against him."

The generals and less biased scholars murmured with approval.

"...It was around that time that I first met Lord Liu," Kongming explained, "and I found him to be of good character, though perhaps too prone to trusting others."

Zhang Zhao snorted a laugh, and said, "Your lord is a cunning owl, whose history of defections and double-crosses is renowned."

"Really...?" Kongming said. "Relay this history to me."

"...No," Zhang Zhao retorted. "You tell me your own interpretation."

"Very well, although it wastes time," Kongming said dismissively. "Lord Liu has served Gongsun Zan – who he left without malice. He then served Tian Kai and Tao Qian in succession – each bore him no malice at the end of his service, in fact Tao Qian bequeathed his prefecture to my lord on his deathbed. The 'famous defection' you speak of is, no doubt, my lord capitulating to Yuan Shao, which was to spare Xu Province another ravaging by Cao Cao. Had it not suffered enough...?"

"...*Go on*," Zhang Zhao grunted angrily.

"From there, Lord Liu worked tirelessly against the traitor Yuan Shu, and there is not a warlord in the land that could have dealt with Lü Bu any better, especially in a disadvantaged situation. Cao Cao then took Lord Liu to Xuchang, where he learned the extent of Cao's evil... hence his next 'famous defection', spurred by an imperial decree to execute Cao for treason. Is there a better reason to turn on a man...?"

"...*Go on*," Zhang Zhao growled again.

Kongming smiled, saying, "From there, my lord fled the capital, was allied temporarily with Yuan Shao until he too proved his lack of true character... that is when my lord settled in Jing.

"But Jing was truly ruled by the Huang clan in Jiangxia, and the Cai clan in Xiangyang. The Cais despised Lord Liu, and sought a way to turn him over to Cao Cao in exchange for rewards... something Liu Biao objected to, but when he died, and the puppet Liu Cong took his place, fate was already written. He did not even tell Lord Liu of the plan to surrender to Cao Cao, leaving Lord Liu with no time to make plans: the people followed because they did not respect Liu Cong or the Cais, they respected and loved Lord Liu, and they feared Cao Cao, whose reputation for violence is known to all. I advised my lord to seize Xiangyang: he refused, and in doing so, gained the trust of Liu Qi... so he is wise in his own right."

"But then you have made a fool of yourself!" Zhang Zhao suggested. "If the decisions are made by Liu Bei alone, where then does your 'wise counsel' come into things...? ...*Steep-slope*...?"

"...Steep-slope was a disaster," Kongming sighed. "Burdened – if that is the right word – by a horde of a hundred-thousand refugees, we were caught between the dual duties of protecting the weak and fighting our enemies. Topographically, we were at a disadvantage, hemmed in by the River Han to the north and east, most flammable foliage as much a danger to us as our foes and therefore of no value with regard to an ambush; we had no allies in proximity, the only supplies being what we had with us, and they had to be shared with the common people. Our total force in that battle was about three thousand, not double the size of his force, as you claim. ...Three thousand infantry – tired, from days of ceaseless marching – and only a couple of good generals, against five thousand of Cao Cao's elite cavalry, on open ground in alien territory, while protecting a hundred-thousand *unarmed people*: I dare say, Zhang Zhao, that you can tell me how you would have dealt with such a situation."

Zhang Zhao was silent.

"I suspect that your answer would be the same as it is when facing Cao Cao with *thirty-thousand* soldiers, *dozens* of brave and marvellous generals, *dozens* of wise officials, the *Great River* as a barrier, *hundreds* of warships, the best navy in the land, and an ally that would stand tall if Cao Cao sent a **demon from the underworld against them**," Kongming said sternly. "*...Surrender.*"

Zhuge Jin and Lu Su smiled: they could see that their lord, Sun Quan, was now convinced of Kongming's ability, and furthermore, the generals that were lined up along the right side of the room appreciated his positive appraisal of them.

"For my lord, surrender is not an option," Kongming declared. "Not just because he is noble and righteous... but because he has now been implicated in a plot to kill Cao Cao, a plot that has claimed the lives of his co-conspirators within Xuchang. That may *never* be forgiven... while Cao Cao lives, Lord Liu can never visit the Emperor and pay him the respect he wishes to, and that breaks his heart. What must be decided now in Jiangdong is whether surrender is an option for *you*, my lord... and *that*, I am glad to say at last, is what I am ready to discuss."

After an uncomfortable silence – throughout which Sun Quan studied Kongming as though he were observing a priceless vase – the ruler of Eastern Wu got up, slammed his open hand on the empty table in front of him, and said, "Very good... **very good!**"

"...But my *lord*...!" Zhang Zhao protested feebly.

"I should like to hear your thoughts in private, Master Zhuge Kongming," Sun Quan declared: he walked to Kongming, and extended his hand. Kongming took it, and together, the two men walked to a side entrance to the right of the hall, where Sun Quan had a private audience chamber.

"...Well done," Lu Su whispered.

"I was very impressed by the way you dealt with Zhang Zibu," Sun Quan said as he gestured for Kongming to take a seat: he then sat opposite him on a slightly higher platform.

"I did not mean to rebuke him so harshly," Kongming insisted.

"He brought it on himself," Sun Quan said with a laugh. "He is always lofty and confrontational... but enough. You can obviously speak for a long time and fight a good debate: now all I ask from you is a simple summary of where you think I should go from here."

"Well then, in that case, this will be quickly said," Kongming chuckled. "You have but two choices: resist, and surrender.

"Fight, and you will have the assistance of Liu Qi of Jing, and Liu Xuande. They will fight Cao north of the Great River, while you confront him on the water. With the right scheme, he can be defeated: but even if he cannot, you will have at least tried to maintain your dignity, and you can improvise a plan for peace. If we win, then we can destroy him once and for all, restore the Han, and bring peace to the entire land.

"Surrender, and you will be forced to send your son to the capital to serve as a hostage: you will later be summoned to court yourself, and be labelled a dissenter and a traitor if you refuse, justifying a punitive expedition against you that you will face alone. You will lose your land, and be at the beck and call of Cao Cao, who will command you to send gifts and pay respects, and supply him with anything he demands: if you do not believe me, you need only look at Liu Zhang of Yi, who is now nothing more than a supply warehouse for Cao Cao. You will no longer be a master of your own domain: you will be a vassal to another lord...

"That is all there is to say... it is your choice."
Sun Quan pondered the points carefully.
"...My father lived – and died – a vassal to Yuan Shu," Sun Quan said thoughtfully. "My brother despaired at his lack of ambition: all I have is earned, by me or by my brother. I would be a ruler, free of others, and fairly govern all below the Great River. ...But Cao Cao boasts of *eight-hundred-thousand men*..."
"...A boast, nothing more," Kongming insisted. "Forgive my frankness, but only fool pedants who know nothing of the world would believe it."
"Your lord is lucky to have a man such as you in his service," Sun Quan said with a smile. "...Your brother spoke highly of you, and it is deserved."
"I simply do what I can," Kongming replied humbly.

Sun Quan spoke with Kongming regarding many matters for hours after that, and developed a respect for him that would endure through the years.


************

## 32

The next day, Sun Quan invited Lu Su to speak with him once again. The two men sat facing one-another in Sun Quan's private audience room, as Quan and Kongming had done the previous day. Lu Su noted his lord's demeanour, and was quietly optimistic that Kongming has successfully urged him to fight Cao Cao.
"...Zhuge Kongming is a great talent," Sun Quan noted. "It is a pity that he has chosen to serve a future rival of mine."
"You do not need to fear Kongming," Lu Su insisted. "He is trustworthy, as is his lord. Both have been given a bad reputation by people like Zhang Zhao... they are doing their best in difficult circumstances."
"Zhuge Kongming has suggested that I can only fight or surrender, which is obvious enough," Sun Quan said plainly. "He has pointed out that I will be reduced to a worthless nobody were I to surrender... but still, to *fight*... what do you think...?"
"I hear that Gongjin is on his way here to discuss this matter with you in person," Lu Su reported. "But you know what I think...? ...I think that it's easy for Zhang Zhao and the others to surrender... *you* can't."
"How so...?" Sun Quan prompted.
"It's very much as Kongming has already said," Lu Su replied. "You may be called to court... you may be exiled... you certainly wouldn't live as you do now. You would have to live as a vassal of the court... you might even be eliminated."
"...True," Sun Quan supposed.
"While your officials – yes, like Zhang Zhao – may keep their positions, or even be rewarded by Cao Cao for convincing you to surrender," Lu Su suggested further.
"...Again, you are right," Sun Quan murmured. "It's just that... it is a big decision to make, one that could result in a massive loss, death... suffering to my people..."
"Talk to Gongjin," Lu Su urged. "He'll be here soon enough."

A few days later, Lu Su visited Kongming once again, and the two moved to the hotel garden to discuss their progress.
"...So how goes the court...?" Kongming asked.
"The lord is almost stirred," Lu Su sighed, "but... it's all up to Gongjin now."
"...Gongjin... *Gongjin*... oh, right, *Zhou Yu*," Kongming said in a show of feigned forgetfulness. "...Is he on his way here, then...?"
"He wants to meet you," Lu Su revealed, "before he speaks to Sun Quan."
"Ah... he wants to see if the Liu-Sun alliance has any real promise," Kongming said with amusement. "...And, of course, he would like some encouragement."
"He has almost resolved himself," Lu Su said cautiously, "but... well... sometimes, standing alone is not easy. He wants to see that Liu Bei is committed, and you have to convince him of that. ...Then he'll speak to Lord Sun."
"Fine, fine," Kongming insisted, gesturing with his fan. "But-"
"So this is the visitor, then."

Kongming turned to see an attractive young woman who was wearing trousers and a shirt rather than a lady's dress: she wore a sword at her waist, and she had with her a retinue of at least a dozen women in similar attire, also armed with swords.

"…L-Lady Sun," Lu Su hailed nervously.

"This is the man from Jing," Lady Sun prompted.

"I am, Madam," Kongming replied courteously.

Lady Sun studied Kongming at great length in total silence, walking around him ominously as she did so.

"Uh… *Lady Sun*…!" Lu Su exclaimed fretfully.

"…Don't make trouble," Lady Sun warned: she then gestured to her attendants, who followed her out of the garden and out of the hotel.

"…That was strange," Kongming admitted.

"She has the run of the city," Lu Su sighed. "She is tolerated because she is the lord's sister."

"…Quite a strange woman," Kongming said with amusement. "Somehow, I think my wife would like her."

"Your wife is a bit of a handful, then…?" Lu Su supposed.

"No," Kongming replied, "she is high-spirited in an intellectual way."

"I see," Lu Su sighed sympathetically. "That would annoy me no end, having to debate with my wife. It must tire you out: was it a convenience marriage, then…?"

"…You really are tactless," Kongming chuckled disbelievingly.

Lu Su smiled apologetically, saying, "I…!"

"I know," Kongming interrupted. "And the answer is 'no'. Now, where were we…? …Oh, right, 'Gongjin' is coming here. So he will be in Chaisang soon…? You never told me."

"Tomorrow," Lu Su reported. "I shall take you to his Chaisang residence once he and Lady Qiao have settled in."

"…His famous wife," Kongming noted; "It is said that there is no fairer-looking woman in the land, other than perhaps her sister."

"Like you, Gongjin has but one wife, one partner," Lu Su explained. "He is completely in love with her, and she with him… they can spend hours sitting together, just talking, or sometimes she listens while he plays a tune…"

"Oh…?" Kongming said with interest. "What instrument does he play…?"

"…Like you, Gongjin is… *what's the word*… … …'multi-faceted'," Lu Su replied. "He can play the qin, primarily, and he composes music, and also poetry."

"…I shall look forward to meeting him, then," Kongming said with cheer. "He sounds like a person that I can relate to."

"He is also enviably handsome," Lu Su complained. "So he and Lady Qiao are like two objects of perfection… she is not, however, like *your* wife… she is not known for her wisdom, only her beauty and good nature. So – unfortunately for him, I suppose you would say – debate is restricted to his friends. Lady Qiao wouldn't ever question Gongjin, for fear of upsetting him."

"…Such people in this land!" Kongming declared. "I felt I was among the only clever people in the world when I lived in Jing… I see the world has its share of worthy people wherever you go. …I should like to see Lady Qiao as well."

"So would every man!" Lu Su replied with a laugh that quickly died away: he then added, with obvious embarrassment, "But then... mm... maybe that was tactless as well."

"...I meant it as more of an observation of two people... togetherness," Kongming continued. "Perhaps... perhaps Gongjin can be stirred by passion, if not by reason."

"What... tell him Cao Cao wants his wife...?" Lu Su supposed.

"No," Kongming said dismissively. "Well... not exactly, anyway: maybe make him see that her safety is part of the victory... that her fate may mirror the daughters of my lord if he is defeated. I don't know though, maybe you're right: Cao Cao once took the aunt of the governor of Wan City as his unwilling mistress, provoking an attack on him... Cao is lecherous, in addition to being cruel, and it is unlikely that Gongjin has not heard of it."

"Just don't annoy Gongjin," Lu Su warned. "If you annoy him, you'll make an enemy of him... that isn't wise."

"With us being so similar, I cannot see that," Kongming insisted. "Trust me."

Lu Su hummed cynically.

The next afternoon, Lu Su took Kongming to meet Zhou Yu in his large, luxurious home. As Lu Su led him up the steps, Kongming could hear the sound of a qin being expertly played.

"A beautiful sound," Kongming whispered.

Lu Su hummed quietly in agreement.

Kongming stopped reflexively when he reached the court room that would be used to host the meeting. Sat in the host's chair was a clean-faced man of handsome appearance that may or may not have been older than Kongming by sight: he was locked in deep concentration, playing the qin with a strange combination of tranquillity and passion. To his left – and absorbed completely by the music – was a woman whose beauty was, as her reputation had stated, near unrivalled. Kongming's guard dropped momentarily, and he let out a quiet gasp of exasperation at Lady Qiao's beauty, an act which amused Lu Su.

"...My apologies," Zhou Yu said as finished his piece and sat upright: Lady Qiao smiled at the visitors, and Kongming smiled awkwardly in return.

"...Shall I leave you to speak, my lord...?" Lady Qiao asked with a voice that was elegant and wispy.

Zhou Yu smiled at her with boundless love, and nodded, saying, "We shall be discussing banal things... yes, why not retire...?"

"I shall fetch some tea first," Lady Qiao suggested: she got to her feet, and Kongming admired her poise and grace as she left the room to ready some refreshments for the guests.

"...So, Zhuge Kongming," Zhou Yu hailed with a slight yet respectful bow, "it is good to meet you at last. Was your journey pleasant, and how do you find our land of Jiangdong...?"

"...Beautiful," Kongming replied thoughtlessly.

"...The journey, or the land...?" Zhou Yu asked pointedly, while Lu Su continued to be amused at Kongming's youthful weakness.

"...Uh... the land," Kongming replied. "I was surprised by the humidity... it has been some years since I visited the land with my brother some years ago. ...Oh, and the journey was fine, thank you... the Great River was calm, thank goodness...!"

"Unlike the times we live in," Zhou Yu said with regret. "Please, friends, do not just stand there... be seated."

Kongming and Lu Su took seats opposite each other, and on opposite sides of Zhou Yu. Kongming was impressed by the demeanour of the slightly older man, whose military exploits were already considerable.

"I understand that your lord Liu Bei is taking refuge in Jiangxia at the moment, after an unfortunate loss in the Steep-slope region of Dangyang County," Zhou Yu sighed sadly. "Cao Cao is a force to be reckoned with... after so many successful victories against so many opponents whose strength vastly exceeded his, one might wonder who could stop him."

"...I think the answer lies in numbers," Kongming replied as he glanced at Zhou Yu's beautifully carved and decorated qin. "Not just soldiers, but also the number of heroes willing to face him together."

"But what heroes do you speak of...?" Zhou Yu asked as Lady Qiao returned with the tea. "Once, there was not just my own lord and yours, but Yuan Shu, Yuan Shao, Liu Biao, Liu Yan, Ma Teng, Gongsun Zan... now, Ma Teng is a willing lackey of the court, and the rest are dead, and their sons are either dead as well or willingly bent at the knee, grovelling to Cao Cao and ceding their territories."

"Liu Qi, eldest son of Liu Biao, will fight to regain what is rightfully his," Kongming insisted. "...The question, then, since my lord Liu has no choice but to fight... is what your lord Sun will do."

Zhou Yu was silent: in an effort to avoid leering at Lady Qiao, Kongming was aiming his gaze at Zhou Yu's qin and fanning himself slowly.

"Do you play...?" Lady Qiao asked of Kongming: he reluctantly raised his eyes and looked at her as she started to pour tea.

"...I do, my lady," Kongming replied uneasily, "though not as beautifully, I regret, as Zhou Gongjin."

"Sometimes, it is not the beauty of the playing, but the *content*, and the *intent*," Zhou Yu suggested. "Would you like to play a tune now...? I have another qin... we can harmonise... or at least, we can try to."

Kongming understood the meaning of the challenge: he smiled, nodded, and put his fan to one side. Zhou Yu walked to a table – where another qin was placed near inconspicuously – and took it in his hands, saying, "This qin was my first... but then I acquired another. The new one is more elaborate in design yet less hardy, but then, it is still a qin, and only as good as the notes one chooses to play. Each has its own qualities, like the lords I have served."

Lady Qiao took the tea tray to one side, so that her husband could present the qin to Kongming: Zhou Yu set it down in front of his would-be-ally, and then returned to his own seat.

"...Well, then, shall we...?" Zhou Yu urged.

Kongming nodded, and the two started to play.

Lady Qiao took her seat next to her husband and watched as the two expert players quickly harmonised, finding a common thread in their work that married calmness, dedication, tumultuous strides, rousing crescendos, and short, continuous rhythmic strums that evoked the march of thousands to battles unknown. Lu Su and Lady Qiao watched and listened in silent awe for the many minutes that the two men played: when Zhou Yu finally started to wind down the melody, Kongming followed, and the piece came to a graceful halt, having told a story without words.

"Magnificent," Lu Su praised. "...Simply magnificent...!"

"...You are very good," Zhou Yu said to Kongming with sincerity. "Your mind and mine are, I think, in accord on what must be done. My thanks for your visit, both of you: it has been most productive."

"...Wait, *what*...?" Lu Su said with confusion. "But... what about...!"

"I will speak with Lord Sun," Zhou Yu promised, "and I will enthuse – in the strongest possible terms – the need for our cooperation – Sun, and two Lius – in facing down the tyrant Cao Cao."

Kongming nodded silently, and took up his fan.

"Now," Zhou Yu chuckled calmly, "let us discuss some of our shared learning!"

Kongming fanned himself and laughed agreeably: once tea was served, the two men started to talk about stratagems and poetry, music and politics, as Lu Su and Lady Qiao looked on, wondering what was really going on behind the words.

************

## 33

The next day, Zhou Yu travelled to the Sun family court.
"Gongjin!" Sun Quan hailed gratefully.
"May we speak privately...?" Zhou Yu asked as he looked at the angry and worried faces of Zhang Zhao and the other officials.
"...Yes," Sun Quan replied: he gestured to the courtiers, and they filed out of the room silently. As soon as the two were alone, Sun Quan said to Zhou Yu, "Shall we go to the private audience room...?"
Zhou Yu nodded agreeably.

"It is good of you to travel here, brother-in-law," Sun Quan said with relief as he sat in front of his low writing table. "I rely on you even more than my brother did for guidance in all things beyond my domain..."
Zhou Yu smiled, and as he took a seat to the left of Sun Quan, he said, "My lord, I've come here to discuss the matter of Cao Cao."
"A worrisome matter, indeed," Sun Quan sighed. "Speaking frankly, Gongjin... I am scared. Cao Cao boasts nearly a million men in his letter, where he calls for us to submit graciously, promising no..."
"Cao Cao is a liar," Zhou Yu interrupted. "He lies while promising to be honest! ...A *million men*, indeed. My lord, I have been sending spies to learn of the true situation, and the estimations are, I understand, less than a quarter of a million... and seventy thousand or so of that are former Jing forces that will not fight with heart, especially if their first opponent is the son of their former governor. Cao's men are unaccustomed to the south, and will fall victim to disease... many are not veterans of sea battle, and will suffer sea-sickness. Cao's forces will fall apart, and then it is a matter of sweeping them away."
"You make the challenge sound almost too trivial," Sun Quan suggested.
"My lord," Zhou Yu declared, "Cao comes here only because he feels that the north is pacified. Is it...? Ma Chao of Xiliang still lives, and he would go against Cao at the first opportunity. Liu Zhang of Yi might bow to Cao Cao, but his former vassal Zhang Lu refuses, so where is the peace in the north *or* the west...? ...And Cao Cao speaks of his mighty cavalry... what use will they be, in a land of high mountains and wide rivers...?"
Sun Quan nodded agreeably.
"My lord," Zhou Yu implored, "give me the word, and I will march thirty-thousand troops into battle, and give you not only victory over Cao, but dominion over Jing Province as well!"
Sun Quan looked into the steadfast gaze of his late brother's best friend, and realised that the words were no empty boast: after shaking his fist in premature triumph and crying out, "**Very good!**" with sudden cheer, Sun Quan got to his feet, and shouted to an official in a nearby room, "**SUMMON THE COURT!**"

An hour later, Kongming received a visit from an agitated Lu Su. Kongming laughed quietly, and started to fan himself slowly.
"Master Zhuge...!" Lu Su panted wearily. "I... the...!"

"...So am I dead or alive...?" Kongming asked with a smirk.

"No... don't know," Lu Su replied. "I... came to... warn you... verdict..."

"He's going to decide now," Kongming sighed. "Am I to attend...?"

"No," Lu Su replied. "Just... just be ready to... to go back..."

"I have never been anything but ready," Kongming chuckled. "I would not be fool enough to be comfortable when even my brother will not welcome me fully. ...So will *he* be attending this verdict...?"

"Yes," Lu Su said wearily. "...He'll come with me to talk to you if-"

"I should really be there," Kongming suggested.

"You can't go in there!" Lu Su exclaimed. "Why would you...?"

"...I simply wish to see from a distance what Sun Quan has decided," Kongming replied calmly. "Is that a problem...? ...After all, if he has decided not to fight, I am doing him a favour, surely, by delivering myself to the court for orderly disposal, and he will be grateful!"

"Your sense of humour is perverse," Lu Su complained. "Wait here... when he has spoken... I will tell you what he said."

"I shall await your return with amusement and dread," Kongming said with a smile.

"...You're *insane*," Lu Su retorted as he turned to leave.

Within another hour, all of Sun Quan's officials and generals were gathered, ready to hear their leader speak: Sun Quan sat in front of a wooden writing desk, which was conspicuously cleared of any objects.

Among the generals that sat along the hall to the right of Sun Quan were the veterans Huang Gai and Cheng Pu, who had also served Sun Quan's father and brother; the virtuous Ling Tong; the pirate Gan Ning; Zhou Tai, whose valour in difficult situations was as calculated as it was reckless, and loyal as it was madness; and Lü Meng, whose reputation was growing from valiant fool to genius strategist. These generals, and indeed all of Sun Quan's generals, were of a united mind: they should resist Cao Cao at all costs, and preserve their honour to the last, regardless of whether they had allies or not.

Among the officials who sat along the hall to the left of Sun Quan, Zhang Zhao stood as the voice of the majority; of the dozen or more that attended, only Lu Su and Zhuge Jin were in favour of an alliance with 'The Two Lius of Jing' against Cao Cao. Zhou Yu was sat to the right of Sun Quan, which led Lu Su and Zhuge Jin to suspect that Zhou Yu had spoken to Quan as a general.

"I am glad to see you all here," Sun Quan declared as soon as everyone had paid their respects. "...We are now at a turning point. When my father lived, he fought for justice and honour, battling the likes of Dong Zhuo in a quest to rid the land of suffering and build a land of peace. When he died, my brother took it upon himself to pacify the region. He won the hearts of the people, and earned the respect of men like Taishi Ci, who sadly passed away only a few years ago... and, of course, Zhou Gongjin, whose genius is unparalleled in all the realm.

"Before my brother died, he did all he could to serve the realm, but he was felled before he could achieve his greatest dream: to smite Cao Cao, and liberate the land from his tyranny. He would have allied with the indecisive Yuan Shao to battle Cao, and perhaps he might have won some glory... perhaps not. That, sadly, we will never know.

"From him I inherited a vast realm, but also work unfinished: to settle our lands, I opted, reluctantly, for peace with Cao Cao, and left Yuan Shao to fight – and die – alone. While some may question my loyalty to the throne, I question the chance of our success with such an ally, whose superior numbers meant nothing when his slander-prone ear and truth-blind eyes prevented him from following sound advice and having good judgement. Instead, I focussed on ridding us of Liu Biao and his henchman Huang Zu... our forces took Huang Zu, and victory was ours: but then, not unexpectedly, the heavens took Liu Biao, and his unambitious son and heir-by-usurpation drove the true heir from his lands and then conceded to Cao Cao without a fight."

"And received from him the title of Inspector of Qing Province," Zhang Zhao suggested as his master took a pause for breath.

"...That is correct," Sun Quan admitted. "He was granted modest rank, and lives quite comfortably... as I could, no doubt, in some far-off place, if I too surrendered to Cao Cao. Then I, too, could be a **laughing stock, a target for the world's scorn and disdain, and watch from a safe distance as Cao Cao makes my homeland his playground, my people his slaves, while I live a carefree life of luxury!**"

Lu Su and Zhuge Jin smiled with relief.

"...**I will not, and cannot!**" Sun Quan proclaimed: he jumped to his feet, turned to his left, and took from its horizontal pedestal his sword of command.

"My lord...!" Zhang Zhao protested. "Cao Cao commands near a million men!"

"Let him *bring* a **million men!**" Sun Quan boomed. "Let him bring **one, two, or TEN MILLION MEN! I'll drown them all in the Great River! I will fight him to the last man, and the next person that speaks to me of surrender will be answered as I tell this table!**"

With that, Sun Quan slashed his wooden table with his sword, shearing off one corner: the officials shuddered at the thought, and reflexively touched their necks, as the generals grinned and bowed in respect of their valiant master.


"...So there *is* another tiger ruling Jiangdong," Kongming praised cautiously as his brother Jin and Lu Su finished relaying the events of the meeting.

"His orders were clear," Lu Su said. "I am to escort you back to Liu Bei, then you and I will plan the first phase of our counterattack... once we are prepared, my lord will send an official response to Cao Cao, and then it begins."

"...Yes," Zhuge Jin said apprehensively. "It does, doesn't it."

"When you frown like that, you look like a donkey," Kongming scolded. "How many times have I told you to smile as much as you can...?"

Lu Su laughed uproariously as the long-faced Jin replied, "Why do people mock me so...? ...Even the lord teases me this way!"

"...Calm yourself," Kongming chuckled. "Now, Zijing: now that things are settled, are we to head back straight away...?"

"...Yes...!" Lu Su replied amid laughter as he looked at the dour Zhuge Jin.

"Right," Kongming declared, "I am ready, I have always been so... shall we depart for the harbour...?"

Later that afternoon, Kongming and Lu Su sailed back to Xiakou, ready to begin a new chapter in the history of the land.

************

"Oh, thank goodness...!" Ma Liang said as the boat carrying Kongming sailed into northern Xiakou.

"Greetings, brothers," Kongming hailed as Ma Liang and Ma Su met Kongming at the pier. "Have you been here long...?"

"We'd heard you were being returned," Ma Liang said as he eyed Lu Su. "We didn't know in what condition you would be returned, however."

Kongming smirked, replying, "Well, my head and body are still joined, as you can rightly see, and all is well."

"Have some faith," Lu Su suggested. "Where is your lord...?"

"He is waiting in his camp," Ma Liang reported. "Are we...?"

"We are," Kongming revealed. "We have two days before Cao Cao knows Lord Sun's decision... we have much to do. Have the soldiers been training in the manoeuvres I recommended...?"

"They have," Ma Liang replied, "but are we not supposed to *lose*...?"

"...With minimal casualties, yes," Kongming scolded. "Come, let us go to Lord Liu, and inform him of the situation."

For the next few days, the training was extensive, as the joint forces of Liu Qi and Liu Bei knew that they would be facing the full wrath of Cao Cao upon his arrival in Jiangxia. What mattered was how they met that massive force, if they were to succeed in the end.

"We're moving again...?" Zhuge Jun complained as Kongming arrived at the Zhuge family home in Three Rivers one morning with a full complement of soldiers.

"No, no," Kongming insisted. "They are with me for my safety... Lord Liu's orders. I think he fears Lu Su might forcibly abduct me, or something."

Jun laughed at the notion.

"...So why are you here...?" Yueying asked. "Has Sun Quan not...?"

"He agreed to the alliance," Kongming said calmly. "Call me sentimental, but... but it is likely that I will be gone a while and... I wanted to see you both. I thought we might spend some time together, just for a day, the family as a whole I mean."

"...Okay," Yueying agreed.

The day was spent talking, sharing anecdotes, relaying the military situation, and enjoying Kongming's calm playing of the qin. He spoke of his time with Zhou Yu, Lu Su and Sun Quan, and of the expectations for the coming days and weeks ahead: eventually, as darkness closed in on the winter day, Kongming departed, unsure as to when he would next see his family.

A day after Kongming's return to Xiakou, the first reports of Cao's movements came into Liu Bei's tense court.

"His vanguard numbers thirty-thousand," General Liao Hua reported nervously.

"...So are we going to fight them...?" Zhang Fei asked.

"Of course," Jian Yong said calmly.

"It is part of the overall scheme," Kongming added.

"Where's the emissary from Sun Quan, that little man 'Lu Su'...?" Zhang Fei asked further.

"He is quartered in a hotel," Kongming reported. "He may attend the battle to see its outcome, but he will most likely return to Jiangdong now that preparations are complete."

"And when can we expect help from Sun Quan...?" Zhao Yun asked politely.

"We will be alone in this battle, Zilong," Kongming reported.

The statement provoked gasps of surprise from the ensemble.

"What sort of alliance is this...?" Guan Yu asked rudely.

"There is a plan: never fear," Kongming insisted. "All we have to do is face Cao Cao north of Wulin. Once that battle is fought, we will withdraw, and Sun Quan's forces will take it from there, and then-"

"Whoa, wait a minute," Zhang Fei grunted. "So we're being used to soften him up???"

"Not at all," Kongming insisted. "Please, Yide, trust in the alliance."

The grumbles of discontent amongst the generals and some of the less-well-informed officials were notable.

"We will use the formation 'Eight Gates', with a few minor modifications that Kongming has devised as a surprise," Jian Yong added. "That will ensure that Cao Cao is initially humbled: the outcome, sadly, will be altogether a different story, but that is intentional."

"What are we committing to this...?" Guan Yu asked. "We have now got around ten-thousand troops, Governor Liu Qi has about the same under his command... we will still be at a disadvantage, yes, but-"

"Oh, we won't be committing more than five thousand of Lord Liu's forces to the first encounter," Kongming explained. "The rest of the forces, including Governor Liu Qi's soldiers and navy, will remain out of it."

"...*What*...?" Zhang Fei barked. "*Five thousand* against *thirty thousand*...? ...What sort of deal did you strike for us, 'Kongming'...? Did you and your brother cook up some scheme to get the rest of Jing for Sun Quan???"

"Yide," Liu Bei scolded, "do not insult Master Zhuge."

"Phooey!" Zhang Fei exclaimed. "He sold us out!"

"...Will you stop making a show of yourself...?" Jian Yong chuckled. "If we had been 'sold out', Yide, Kongming daren't show his face. Now, orders..."

"...Guan Yunchang, Zhang Yide," Kongming hailed: Guan Yu and Zhang Fei nodded silently. "...You will each have three hundred horsemen, and take distant, out-of-sight positions to the left and right of the main force. Zilong..."

Zhao Yun bowed respectfully, and said, "Ready to take orders."

"...Zilong," Kongming ordered, "you will be in charge of the main force of three thousand, who will be arrayed in the 'Eight Gates' formation. Huo Jun, Wei Yan, Liao Hua and Chen Shi will provide supporting roles as required."

"... ... ...I understand," Zilong replied reluctantly.

"Such a formation with so few soldiers will be barely effective against such a large enemy," Mister Sun protested. "Won't Cao break it by sheer force of numbers...?"

"Of course, yes," Kongming replied with a smile. "However, I intend to show 'Prime Minister Cao Cao' that there is more to be done in the world of warfare... let him break the formation, but he will lose many a good man doing so."
"...So will that be all...?" Liu Bei asked.
"Yes," Kongming replied calmly.
"Then let us prepare," Liu Bei said without fear. "Let us repay Cao Cao for his heartless actions at Steep-slope!"
The generals gave a rousing roar, and the court as a whole bowed in respect of their master, Liu Bei, before departing to make their own preparations for the upcoming confrontation on the plains north of Wulin.

A day later, the forces of Liu Bei had sailed up the Yangtze River and moved west, toward a plain that was located north of the city of Wulin. Once they had arrived at the intercept point and set up their camps, Jian Yong and Kongming took up coloured flags, and gestured to the commanders of the infantry and cavalry forces that would comprise the Eight Gates array.

Lines of soldiers armed with arrow and spear-repelling shields formed the 'walls' of the array, which were mostly inclined to the battlefield line: at varying points, deliberate gaps and 'paths' were formed between the soldiers to provide 'lanes' for enemy forces to pass them and enter what was a human maze of soldiers that would either move in circular chains or form walls of shields and spears that would block enemy attacks and lunge at passing forces. Forces of infantry and cavalry would provide sudden strike forces within the array.

The eight deliberate entrances to the array – known as the 'gates' – could be 'locked' by closing the gaps between the rows of soldiers, trapping the attackers within the living maze of men. Designated commanders armed with coloured signal flags would alert the soldiers as to their next required manoeuvres: they may be expected to attack, alter their lines, close gates, or allow deliberate openings to lure and further trap, or even release, the enemy. Some of the gates were 'death gates', where attempts to enter or exit at that point would result in catastrophic casualties for the attackers: others were 'safe openings', purely due to a fault in the array, which could not be perfect, and knowing these allowed the attacker to pass through or break the array with minimal losses. Other gates were designed to force the attackers into other directions of travel, or inflict average losses.

Someone versed in the Art of War could form the array in such a way that only another, equally-versed strategist could ascertain the method of breaking it: the key was the variations. By using different flag colour combinations, having better-trained and more agile soldiers, or by altering the ordering of the gates, two strategists could confound each other. However, most strategists could only commit a few of the variations to memory, and therefore were reliant on the enemy strategist not being aware of that particular variation: now, Zhuge Liang was about to go up against the minister and strategist Cheng Yu, who was also aware of formations such as Eight Gates, and would therefore be a dangerous adversary.

"I hope that you know what you're doing," Mister Sun sighed as he stood with Kongming, Jian Yong, Ma Liang and Yi Ji, awaiting the arrival of Cao Cao's vast advance force of infantry and cavalry. "We're boxed in by the Great River and sodden marshland in all but one direction."

"...And I have to say that I don't recall this formation having all-black flags," Jian Yong joked. "Did we study the same Eight Gates, Zhuge Kongming...?"

"...As I said, I believe in variation," Kongming replied as he waved his fan back and forth slowly. "Cheng Yu is no ordinary strategist... but then, neither am I."

"Well, I hope that this works," Yi Ji said. "The winter days are short, so we cannot afford this fight to go on for long. ...Is that Cao's forces approaching now...?"

"...It is," Kongming confirmed as he looked at the mass of shapes that appeared in the distance, moving north from Wulin. The numbers were initially terrifying, and many of the soldiers started to panic: however, with Zhao Yun – the hero of Steep-slope – to boost their morale, the majority were calmed before the storm arrived.

Cao Cao's men arrived within an hour. The rows of horsemen were well-disciplined, and Liu Bei noted their perfect deployment with silent fear.

Cao Cao rode to the front of the force, and Kongming was finally able to get a glimpse of the infamous warlord: he sat under a yellow parasol, next to a standard-bearer that carried a flag bearing his name and the title 'Prime Minister of the Han'."

Mister Sun harrumphed, and said, "He's nothing but a traitor."

Cao Cao and Liu Bei rode into the no-man's-land between the disparate forces so that they could state their intentions. Each man took a small retinue of bodyguards, but left their advisers with their armies.

"**Liu Bei,**" Cao Cao bellowed, "**you're late in coming to me to beg for my forgiveness, and for your life.**"

"**...Cao Cao, you are a traitor to the Han, a wolf in the fold,**" Liu Bei retorted. "**I'm late in coming to kill you.**"

"**... ... ...Wretched sandal weaver!**" Cao Cao screamed angrily. "**I took you as a friend, even after all of your worthless exploits and defeats, and welcomed you into my home, fed you, gave you troops! Yet you slandered me, stole from me, and entered into fraudulent pacts to ruin the integrity of the imperial house of Han! You are nothing but a traitor, unworthy of the royal name of 'Liu' that you carry! ...And now you dare to confront me with this pathetic force, and speak so belligerently after the defeat I inflicted on you last time...? You inherit only your *dis*inherited ancestor's failings as a man!**"

"**And you sully the name 'Cao'!**" Liu Bei retorted. "**You, son of a man adopted by a eunuch, a false son to the Cao line, who fled from Dong Zhuo, slaughtered the innocents of Xu Province, betray and killed your friends, seduce widows and aunts, fraternise with whores, kill outstanding men of virtue and talent, and terrorise the court! The Emperor fears your evil ambition, and calls on others to righteously exterminate you! Were I only strong enough, I would tear you limb from limb and feed you to the dogs!**"

Cao Cao screamed furiously, and raised his arm: his adviser, Cheng Yu saw the signal, and ordered one of Cao Cao's best generals, Xu Huang, to ride forward for a duel. Liu Bei and his retinue retreated, and met with Zhao Yun on their front line.

"Zilong…" Liu Bei urged: Zhao Yun rode forward to confront Xu Huang, and Cao Cao retreated to his own lines at last.

Once Xu Huang and Zhao Yun were within earshot of each other, Xu Huang smiled politely, and asked, "**Where is Guan Yunchang…?**"

"**He is not here,**" Zhao Yun replied as he raised his spear defiantly. "**Today, you face Zhao Zilong!**"

"**It is an honour!**" Xu Huang cried.

Xu Huang raised his long handled axe, and the two men started their charges, passing each other with a resounding clang as their weapons met. They passed each other twenty times before Cao Cao had the battle gong sounded to recall Xu Huang to his line.

"**Prime Minister…!**" Kongming called as he rode to the front line. "**…Dare you try and pass my formation of Eight Gates…?**"

Cao Cao leant to his left, where another charismatic middle-aged adviser watched the proceedings intently.

"… … …Who is this imbecile…?" Cao Cao asked contemptuously.

"I don't know," the adviser, Xun You, admitted. "Perhaps this is Jian Yong."

"No, I've met Jian Yong," Cao Cao scoffed.

"…Then perhaps this is the 'Crouching Dragon', Zhuge Liang," Cheng Yu suggested with sarcastic wonderment.

"Mm," Cao Cao replied uneasily. "The men of Jing say this young man is a rare talent of the day. Have we a need to be cautious…?"

"…Considering this man has been in Liu Bei's service for a time predating the battle at Steep-slope," Cheng Yu snickered, "I doubt he is as marvellous as the men of Jing proclaim him to be. …In fact, this 'formation' is a poor example of the Eight Gates. He has used the wrong flags, and a very small number of soldiers… it should also be noted that Liu Qi's Jing standard is absent amongst this rabble. He has abandoned the cause, evidently, and left Liu Bei to die alone here."

"**Do the 'great men of the north' know only how to talk…?**" Kongming taunted.

"…**What…!**" Xiahou Dun seethed.

"**Come, and break this formation, if you have courage!**" Kongming urged. "**Or is the 'Prime Minister of the Han' afraid…?**"

"…This bumpkin has vexed me!" Cao Cao said angrily. "Xu Huang, Xiahou Dun, Li Dian, Yue Jin… break the formation, and kill them!"

The four fearsome generals took their brigades – numbering two thousand men in all – and charged, while Kongming retreated behind his own army: the Eight Gates formation sprang to life, and the living walls shimmered as soldiers interlocked their weapons and formed their barriers, blocking the way to the leaders of the force. The 'gates' along the walls of the formation opened, and Cao's men charged back and forth, awaiting orders.

"...What is this...?" Cheng Yu exclaimed. "This... I do not understand what is going on at all...!"

"What do you mean...?" Cao Cao growled.

"This... this is like no variation I have ever encountered!" Cheng Yu said worriedly. "The... the flags are all alike! They react to unique gestures, and not colour! These men are so well-trained... I... I cannot recognise the safe gates!"

"...**We cannot just retreat!**" Cao Cao cried in anger.

"We can't send them to their doom either!" Cheng Yu retorted, but it was too late: Cao's forces rode into the formation, and the flag-bearers gestured in ways that Cheng Yu still did not recognise, causing the walls of men to close ominously behind the last of the cavalry and front line soldiers. The rest looked on helplessly as their leaders vanished behind a wall of shields that reacted with lunging spears every time it was attacked in any way.

"**It must be overwhelmed... send another force!**" Cheng Yu implored: Cao Cao angrily gestured to two of his prized generals, Zhang He and Yu Jin, to provide reinforcement with their own forces of a thousand men in all: as they charged, Cao Cao was then forced to retreat as a hail of arrows from Liu Bei's archers sailed over the formation and into his own lines, felling dozens of his poorly protected infantry.

"**This is ridiculous!**" Cao Cao fumed. "**Destroy them! ...ATTACK!**"

"We... we cannot, not until the formation is broken!" Cheng Yu protested.

Cao Cao screamed with anger and embarrassment.

Within the formation, the four generals hacked at the shielded walls, and dodged desperately as spears jutted out from between the shields, killing horses and men at random. Flag-bearers continually signalled for changes to the mini-arrays within the walls, causing confusion for the conspicuously giddy and weary soldiers trapped inside, since there was no clear way to escape.

"Magnificent," Liu Bei exclaimed. "We might even defeat them!"

"We must force a retreat soon," Kongming insisted. "If Cao orders a full charge, or his generals break the lines within the formation, then...!"

"Fine," Liu Bei said. "We shall signal to Yunchang and Yide...!"

"No," Kongming ordered. "They are best placed to provide emergency cover for our retreat now, my lord, and we must tell them as much."

"*Retreat*...?" Liu Bei exclaimed. "But... but he is routed!"

"Hardly," Kongming insisted. "See now that Cao, Xun You, and Cheng Yu have already reordered Cao's battle lines out of our archers' range... the shield-charge that is coming will smash this tiny formation, and come straight for *us*."

"...We must withdraw," Liu Bei conceded at last.

"Yes," Kongming said plainly. "Right now…!"

Liu Bei signalled to Zhao Yun, who ordered the withdrawal of the rear line of archers and infantry: Cao's entire vanguard descended upon the formation like a human tidal wave, as the soldiers within it finally started to break from the relentless attacks by the six generals within and without. Shields buckled, spears were angrily pulled from their owners' hands, and gradually, the flimsy defensive lines disintegrated under the pressure.

"**KILL THEM ALL!**" Xiahou Dun – who was now on foot, his horse having been killed – screamed angrily, as he ran one soldier through with his sword.

"**No: let them run!**" Cao Cao said with laughter as the formation broke apart.

"Liu Bei has already fled," Cheng Yu lamented.

"Let him run, there's nowhere for the fool to *hide*," Cao Cao chuckled. "He's a tiny speck of sand before my army of stones… once the main army arrives, we'll avenge the men we have lost today, and send Liu Bei's head back to Xuchang for the Emperor to have one last look at the man that he begged to 'save' him."


"**Why didn't you have us attack???**" Zhang Fei asked angrily as Liu Bei and Kongming led the defeated army back to the temporary camp on the west bank of the Yangtze River.

"Not now, Yide," Liu Bei scolded. "We must cross the river immediately. Cao's force is unstoppable… we must retreat."

"**NO!**" Zhang Fei pleaded angrily. "**No more retreats! You promised, Xuande! …You promised there would be no more retreats!**"

"**…I said not NOW, YIDE!**" Liu Bei cried with anguish. "**We lost perhaps a thousand men in that battle: can we not needlessly lose any more???**"

Zhang Fei looked at the battered, bloody faces of some of the soldiers that had taken part in the formation: he whined miserably, adding to the groans of suffering among the surviving soldiers.

"Cao will not pursue, my lord," Kongming suggested. "His arrogance is peaked: he will return to Wulin and issue a challenge to Sun Quan now, and save you for last."

"A final victory to savour," Jian Yong supposed uncomfortably. "So now, as you said before, it is up to Zhou Yu now…"

Kongming looked to the south – toward Wulin, the town where Cao Cao would now be stationed – and nodded silently.


************

## 35

Once Liu Bei's forces were settled on the east bank of the Yangtze River, Jian Yong turned to Kongming and asked, "What now...?"
"The arrangement is it stands is that I will now accompany Lu Su back to Chaisang to give details of the engagement to Sun Quan and Zhou Yu," Kongming replied.
"So," Zhang Fei said angrily, "you are now going to flee to the east, leaving us to die here on the banks of the Great River...? ...**I knew it! I KNEW IT!**"
Zhang Fei lunged at Kongming, but he was checked by Guan Yu, who said, "*No*, Yide... his family are in Three Rivers."
"**Yeah, well, perhaps he doesn't care!**" Zhang Fei barked. "**Isn't his wife ugly...? Perhaps Sun Quan's promised him something better if he defects!**"
"...How *dare* you," Ma Liang said with hurt while Kongming just stood silently, fanning himself slowly. "...How... *how dare you.*"
"**How** *dare* **I...?**" Zhang Fei fumed. "**He sold us out, you pedant!**"
Kongming averted his gaze and exclaimed sadly, "*Aiee.*"
"**Are you going to cry now...?**" Zhang Fei taunted. "**Cry, then, for the thousand men you just let Cao kill, and cry again for the twenty thousand more that are going to die because of you, you TREACHEROUS...!**"
"...Yide, *no*," Liu Bei implored. "Kongming, I... I apologise for what he has said to you in a moment of anger."
"But this plan makes no sense, my lord," Wei Yan protested. "What if Yide is right, and Zhuge Liang really has betrayed us, as his wife's family has already done...?"
"...You are a defeated general from Jing Province... what do you know of Zhuge Kongming...?" Ma Liang said angrily. "He and I pledged our lives to Lord Liu! We would never betray him! There is a plan, and all of you have to have faith!"
"...Didn't your best friend 'Xu Shu' also pledge his life to Lord Liu...?" Zhang Fei asked pointedly: the statement was met with a short silence, save mournful groans and sobs from the defeated soldiers.
"...I will return ahead of you to Xiakou, meet with Lu Su... go back to Sun Quan," Kongming relayed again with a subdued tone. He could sense that there were many that now doubted him, especially since his formation had done little against Cao's enormous vanguard force. "You should sail back to Xiakou, my lord... don't remain here."
"...Very good," Liu Bei said with a warm smile. "Kongming... I trust you."
Kongming looked at the angry Zhang Fei, cynical Guan Yu and sneering Wei Yan as he replied, "Thank you, my lord."

"...I am not popular," Kongming said with tears in his eyes as he finished relaying the battle to a saddened Lu Su. "To lose, and lose *lives*..."
"But your formation killed maybe five hundred of Cao's men...?" Lu Su recalled.

"Yes, and we actually lost about a hundred men, not a thousand," Kongming reported. "So it was not as dismal a failure as it initially seemed... all the same, it was an act of collateral damage, deliberate sacrifice of good men to feign weakness... a crime that I will no doubt be guilty of more than once in my lifetime."
"Cao will now be convinced that Liu Qi has abandoned you," Lu Su supposed thoughtfully. "And further to that, he'll believe that Liu Bei's forces are weak and small in number... and that there is no coherent alliance between Liu and Sun either, so he'll focus on us."
"He marched straight back to Wulin, exactly as planned," Kongming replied. "He will not bother to pursue my lord here to Xiakou, he so undervalues his threat... so the battle will be right where we want it to be."
"Right, so now Gongjin will engage him on the water, and test his strength," Lu Su confirmed. "Your lord Liu Bei should now remain out of harm's way, and ready for the pincer attack once Cao is defeated on the water."
"Yes," Kongming said, "but... how exactly does Gongjin intend to defeat Cao's naval force...? I have had reports from settlements near Jiangling and Wulin that Cao's fleet is immense... the impressed Jing naval forces number seventy-thousand, his own men around a hundred-and-fifty thousand... the ships and boats number in the hundreds, and the north bank of the Great River near Wulin is now covered by a blanket of wood and flags."
"...You blunt our morale at a critical moment," Lu Su admonished. "Chief Commander Zhou will know all this! ...And he will have a plan!"
"...Like *what*...?" Kongming asked flatly.
Lu Su could not respond.

"...I ask again," Kongming said as he sailed across the Yangtze with Lu Su.
"And I tell you again, for the seventh time, I don't know!" Lu Su whined. "We'll ask Gongjin when we get to Red Cliffs!"
"...Where...?" Kongming prompted.
"It is directly across the Great River from Wulin," Lu Su explained wearily. "It's a port city and a direct journey from the training lake at Ba Qiu, where we have a large facility for drilling our navy. Since we'll be engaging Cao's fleet near there, and Gongjin will no doubt already be there, we might as well head straight there rather than go to Lord Sun."
"Very well," Kongming agreed reluctantly.

When Lu Su and Kongming completed the southbound journey to Red Cliffs City, which lay alongside the southeast bank of the Yangtze, Kongming could not help but gaze in awe at the magnificent navy that Zhou Yu commanded.
"...Impressive, uh...?" Lu Su beamed. "Cao may have superior numbers, but we have the spirit, and the skill!"
"That, I no longer doubt," Kongming said numbly as he looked at the large wooden ships and smaller assault boats, which numbered in the dozens.

"Ah!" Lu Su said as the two finally left the pier, "I see Chief Commander Zhou, and the Assistant Commander, Veteran General Cheng Pu."

Lu Su waved to his friend and commander Zhou Yu, who was inspecting the ships with the imposing elder warrior, Cheng Pu.

"…Old General Cheng must be a handful," Kongming supposed as he watched the two men approach.

"It's true he has disdain for serving a younger man like Zhou Gongjin," Lu Su lamented, "but Gongjin has the sword of command, so Veteran General Cheng must obey, regardless of his… … …**Chief Commander Zhou, General Cheng!**"

"…Zijing, Master Zhuge," Zhou Yu hailed, giving slight bows of respect to both men: Veteran General Cheng Pu's bows were even more slight, and partnered with a sneer of disapproval.

"We have done our part," Kongming confirmed. "The rest is up to you."

"You will be staying, Kongming…?" Zhou Yu wondered.

"I really shouldn't," Kongming said uncomfortably. "My lord has full faith in me, but his vassals…"

"Yes, I imagine that Zhang Fei and Guan Yu are not much fun to work with," Zhou Yu chuckled with amusement. "I hear that both men are arrogant and imprudent."

"That would be a fine description of Guan Yu, despite his bravery," Lu Su said confidently. "Zhang Fei, I would say, is more belligerent and irrational. Would you not agree, Kongming…?"

"…I would not," Kongming replied, noting Zhou Yu's quiet anticipation of his response. "Guan Yunchang is lofty but principled, while Zhang Yide is passionate and honest. Had they been allowed to fight Cao Cao, the casualties would have numbered in the tens of hundreds: sadly, we only scratched Cao without them, since the point was to make Cao overconfident. Their doubts stem from my brother being here, and I can understand that… so really, I should take my leave once-"

"Forgive me," Zhou Yu said with an embarrassed laugh, "but I just realised that it probably won't be possible now… what part of the north bank will be safe now that Cao Cao has arrayed his fleet along it…? We could risk it, but-"

"Uh, Gongjin," Lu Su prompted. "Trapping him here…"

"…Is no fault of mine," Zhou Yu retorted. "Surely, Zijing, you did not bring him here without realising that the way back would be blocked…?"

Kongming smiled and started to fan himself slowly: he supposed that Zhou Yu always intended him to be trapped in Jiangdong, since it was his request that had led to Lu Su bringing him back after the battle in Wulin.

"My apologies, Kongming," Zhou Yu said with an overly saddened expression.

"…Perhaps I can be of service here," Kongming replied pleasantly. "Maybe you, Zijing and I can discuss how to repel such a large force with this – it has to be said – impressive yet inadequate naval fleet you have."

"…**You miserable little pedant!**" Cheng Pu exclaimed. "**I should…!**"

"Please, control yourself, General," Zhou Yu scolded. "Master Zhuge was correctly pointing out the numerical disparity, and I confess, it concerns me. I shall be sending a force to test Cao's forces, see how we do... after that, we'll look at the options, shall we...?"
Kongming nodded agreeably.

"Impressive," Kongming said for what was the third time as he watched the ships of the land of Jiangdong from a high watchtower with Lu Su and Zhou Yu.
"We'll send a small contingent to initiate a battle," Zhou Yu declared. "If what you said was true of the men you fought, Kongming, we're dealing with the signs I hoped for... now is the time to know it for certain."
"...Uh...?" Lu Su grunted unintelligently.
"Cao's vanguard did not number the full thirty-thousand that he had with him initially," Kongming explained. "In addition, his soldiers were slow, unsteady; there were a lot of men stumbling as they charged, their reflexes were poor..."
"...They're sick," Lu Su supposed. "...They're *sick*...!"
"While I should not wish such a thing on a man, this is war," Kongming sighed. "I think that yes, Zijing, the men were sick and tired. So that long trip sailing down the Great River, with no real option to stop anywhere due to the marshlands..."
"His men are seasick at best, or riddled with disease, and good as dead," Zhou Yu said with satisfaction. "...Or, at least, this is my hope... now, we shall see."

The force that would "put its hand in the tiger's mouth" sailed forward, intending to provoke a reaction from Cao Cao's navy: it got that reaction. Several small attack boats containing lancers, swordsmen and archers sailed forth, followed by some large ships which had larger numbers of men aboard.
Zhou Yu's force was outnumbered two-to-one: his generals struck at the small boats, and could not help but be amused at the giddy, nauseous and unsettled northern troops as they flailed about, lunging with their weapons, and the archers, who seemed almost unable to fire a shot, never mind hit a target. Only the numbers posed a threat: soon, another contingent arrived, unbalancing the odds still further. These troops wore not the black and orange of Cao's imperial soldiers, but the grey and orange of the impressed Jing naval forces, and their skills were not hampered by the unstable waters.
"We have only got the Jing soldiers to worry about," Zhou Yu supposed as he watched from afar. "These new boats... they hoist the flags and sails of Jing... I see no clumsiness, no falling overboard..."
Zhou Yu signalled with a lamp, and the southern force retreated, content with the discoveries that had been made and keen to ensure a good outcome.

"They were vomiting!" one naval captain joked with his colleagues as they carried dead and injured comrades to the infirmary. "What idiots!"

"...I find their flippancy distressing," Kongming confessed as he stood near the piers and watched with Lu Su. "Still: we know what we're up against... Cao Cao's men aren't prepared for naval conflict. And if new reports are correct, the hospital facility in Wulin has many hundreds of patients, and the death count from disease is already in the high hundreds."

"Which is all fair and fine," Lu Su replied, "but it still leaves us with the problem you have noted several times... even with all that, he outnumbers us greatly, so how can we defeat them...?"

"Have heart," Zhou Yu said as he approached with Cheng Pu. "We now know that Cao cannot fight an effective battle on the water... that is, I think, a start."

"Do we have a strategic battle map...?" Kongming asked suddenly.

"Of course," Cheng Pu scoffed. "It is not just you northerners that know how to enact strategy, Zhuge Liang."

"...I was speaking obviously, as a friendly prompt, General Cheng," Kongming said desperately. "Can we not put our regional prejudices aside for a moment...?"

"...Indeed, General Cheng," Zhou Yu scolded. "Come, friends, we should go to the war room and look at the plans."

************

## 36

The war room was located on the upper floor of a large palace building that overlooked the Yangtze River to the north. It was night, and the cold, bitter winds were fierce.

"It is not to scale," Zhou Yu joked as he walked to the large model of the area that stood on a table in the middle of the room. At each corner of the room, a lamp was placed to light the area: the fires flickered in the strong winds.

The model depicted the topography of Xiakou in the north, Ba Qiu in the south, Jiangling to the west and Chaisang to the east. Small wooden ships – each representing multiple ships in reality – and small boats representing the strike attack vessels lined the northern shore of the Yangtze, with small figures representing Cao Cao's ground forces placed in and around the small city model representing Wulin. On the south bank, Zhou Yu's obviously smaller force was arrayed neatly, and to the east, units representing Liu Qi and Liu Bei's forces were positioned around the port city of Xiakou.

"...To have had such toys as a child," Kongming sighed with dual intent.

"You think war is a game...?" Cheng Pu grunted.

"...To some, I think it is," Kongming replied. "It depends on how it affects you, I think, Veteran General. ...I see it is placed such that north is north... very good."

"So what are the options...?" Lu Su asked.

"Well," Zhou Yu said with obvious concern, "we can take them down bit by bit with small skirmishes... but that relies entirely on Cao Cao being a fool. If his problem is the condition of his men due to naval engagements, he'll eventually facilitate a crossing and pincer us from the northeast. We don't have enough troops to help the Liu forces hold the riverbank while simultaneously engaging in continuous, costly naval battles."

"Fortunately, he wouldn't dare risk crossing further north or to the southwest, due to the marshlands and hostile resistance forces, so that limits his possible points of surprise attack," Cheng Pu said gladly. "But yes, we have to be concerned about the region north of here, where there are dry plains, suitable for a safe cavalry and infantry march. We have watchtowers, but getting significant ground forces or naval interception there in time, that's another matter altogether."

"Well then," Kongming declared, "a fast, decisive engagement is required."

"Yes," Zhou Yu agreed. "But... how...?"

"He won't be expecting a second battle straight away," Lu Su supposed. "What if we capitalise on our victory and go to him now...?"

"Not so," Zhou Yu insisted. "He will have archery towers and ground-based archers along the river bank and piers, and the Jing force's attack boats are a threat as well."

"But how do we goad him into coming to us...?" Lu Su asked desperately. "Surely, after that last battle, he'll no longer believe he can win a naval engagement and go for the land crossing, at which point we'll be...!"

Lu Su's voice faded away. Zhou Yu stared at the map, as though he were trying to see something that he had not seen before; Cheng Pu grunted with frustration; Kongming lowered his fan, and sighed quietly.

"...Retire for now," Zhou Yu suggested. "We have plenty of time to wonder about this tomorrow, I think..."

Lu Su and Kongming agreed, and they retired without another word.

"Are things desperate...?" Cheng Pu asked.

"...Yes," Zhou Yu admitted. "I worry that we might have to risk going to Cao, accepting the losses we'll inevitably suffer... I see no other way."

Cheng Pu nodded understandably, and left Zhou Yu to ponder the matter alone.

Days passed: word reached the southern alliance that there was frenetic activity in Cao Cao's camp in Wulin. Zhou Yu, Lu Su, Cheng Pu and Kongming received a messenger in their war room, and awaited the briefing.

"**Their soldiers have been ordered to acquire large amounts of giant, wrought iron chains, fixing bolts, and wooden linking bridges!**" the messenger reported. "**Cao Cao has moved the hospital further back from the river bank, and has moved the bulk of his troops, including his infantry, next to the ships! Large supplies of medicine are arriving from Jiangling to cure the minor illnesses!**"

"*Chains*...? ...What is he up to...?" Lu Su wondered as Cheng Pu politely dismissed the messenger.

"A land invasion, it has to be," Zhou Yu supposed worriedly.

"Yes, but the *chains*...?" Lu Su reiterated.

Kongming smiled.

"...Something has occurred to you, Kongming," Zhou Yu said with a worried expression. "It has occurred to me too, yet I see nothing to smile about."

"I smile only at the ingenuity, Gongjin," Kongming replied sadly. "What will you do to confirm this new and unexpected turn of events...?"

"Test him again," Zhou Yu supposed miserably. "What else can I do...?"

"What's going on...?" Lu Su asked obliviously. "What would he need chains f- ... ...wait a minute: chains, bolts, bridges... what, he isn't going to...!"

"Ingenious," Kongming conceded. "It will solve the seasickness issue, and allow him to have cavalry and stable archery lines aboard his ships."

"But it will leave us helpless!" Lu Su exclaimed. "Linking the ships to stabilise them...? ...He has the will of Heaven supporting his-"

"Zijing, *please*," Zhou Yu sighed as he walked to the large model battlefield in the centre of the room, which Kongming was already stood next to.

"...Interlocking ships..." Kongming pondered. "That will not be easy to counter."

"I know, I know," Zhou Yu fretted.

"Can you not, between the two of you, think of *something*???" Lu Su asked desperately. "Can't we send men to sabotage the ships...?"

"Not likely," Zhou Yu sighed. "This plan... so, he intends to sail directly across to us, not at all passing us by... he intends to attack us head on."

"...Which is what we wanted... though not quite like this," Kongming added.

"We might need to smuggle you back to Lord Liu to change the plan, suggest that they sail from Xiakou and pincer Cao's ships while they are in the water," Zhou Yu pondered. "We'll lose a lot of lives... particularly with Cao's superior numbers and archery support... but it would take a miracle now to avoid that."

"Such a battle could result in mutual destruction," Kongming said flatly. "Would that have a point to it, all of our men drowning at sea...? ...And Cao has more men that he could send... we'd lose all of ours, and lose in the end anyway."

"No!" Lu Su exclaimed. "Zhang Zhao... will laugh at us!"

"I doubt that he will *laugh*, Zijing," Zhou Yu scolded. "He hates capitulation as much as any of us: he just accepts the necessity of it in dire circumstances more readily than we do."

"...Some of the ships must be linked by now," Kongming supposed. "We should do as you say, Gongjin, and test his mettle."

"I intend to, this very evening," Zhou Yu confirmed.

As dusk approached, Cheng Pu ordered another assault on the enemy fleet. Zhou Yu, Kongming and Lu Su were once again forced to watch the unfolding events from a high watchtower.

"I wonder how quickly he can respond," Zhou Yu murmured.

"Linked ships might be slower," Lu Su supposed.

"Will it matter...?" Kongming countered.

The southern ships sailed out to sea, and within half an hour, the worst fears of the southern alliance were confirmed, as five groups of enemy ships appeared. They were connected together in small groups by chains, with bridges linking them so that the troops and cavalry could go back and forth between them at leisure. Since the boats were linked, they did not constantly bob and sway in the water, which made them as stable as walking on land: the comfortable, composed northern soldiers – freed from the threat of seasickness – were ready for a battle this time.

The result was a complete reversal of fortune: Zhou Yu and Lu Su watched in horror as enemy archers picked off some of their men before they even reached the ships, and the attempts to board them were easily thwarted by the overwhelming numbers of enemy spears and swords that met them.

"...I must order a retreat...!" Zhou Yu declared: he grabbed the signal lamp, and started to wave it desperately, despite Cheng Pu and the assault leader, Huang Gai, having already realised the situation at ground level, and given similar instruction.

"We're... we're finished!" Lu Su whimpered as the distant cries of triumphant northern soldiers rang out. "Is... is there **NOTHING we can do???**"

"...How... how can this be...?" Zhou Yu asked as he looked to the sky.

"...It would seem that this is so, and that is that," Kongming suggested. "But... perhaps we have overlooked something, Gongjin."

Zhou Yu watched as the arrogant northern forces retreated, leaving the southern force to limp home and count their dead and wounded. Bodies littered the water, and the resentment was almost tangible.

"We should return to the war room, Gongjin," Kongming suggested softly. "We should look again at our options... we shouldn't stay here now."

"Yes," Zhou Yu said with a shudder. "I'm cold... though that might be *fear*."

Kongming hummed ambiguously, and started down from the tower.


"It can't end like this," Zhou Yu insisted as he poured over the battlefield model, searching desperately for something. "There has to be a way... there has to be."

Cheng Pu and Huang Gai were now present in addition to Lu Su and Kongming: it was night on the third day of deliberating, and the lamp fires danced in the wind.

"They're going to go out," Lu Su murmured as he watched one of the lamps.

"We cannot stay here all night," Cheng Pu implored.

"We... we have no choice," Zhou Yu retorted.

"Chief Commander," Huang Gai said with anger, "there is no point to this! I won't lose any more men to these futile stick-poking actions! We know his strength, so let's just have it out with him!"

"Brave, but suicidal," Zhou Yu insisted. "There... there must be something we can do... maybe... maybe a surprise march through the marshes... he won't expect that, will he...? If we sailed to Ba Qiu, crossed the Great River there, took a straight route northward to Wulin..."

"That is desperate and futile," Cheng Pu proposed. "Trudging through the mud to fight a vast force that specialises in land battles... once their inevitable signal towers spotted us, we'd be finished. Even Cao's forces located in other regions could be sent to intercept us while he sailed south and hit Red Cliffs."

"You're right, you're right," Zhou Yu sighed. "There *must* be some way to destroy his fleet... there must be."

"It would help if you could see," Lu Su chuckled as he took a nearby lamp from its stand and walked to the model. "Here, I'll hold it for you."

"...My thanks," Zhou Yu replied. "Now... we're back to the pincer idea again. If Liu Bei attacks from the north..."

Zhou Yu gestured at the model of Xiakou: as Lu Su lowered the lamp slightly to get greater focus, a gust of wind blew the fire of the lamp from where it hovered over the model of Red Cliffs City, setting fire to one of the sails of the model southern fleet that sat directly south of it.

"...Sorry...!" Lu Su said with embarrassment.

"It matters little, since it is just a model," Zhou Yu said before he picked the model up and blew the flames out. "But in reality such a northwest wind is lethal for us..."

"...Ah," Lu Su realised. "Such a wind can rush their ships to our shores with the sails hoisted, and rout us without warning. And if they used *fire*..."

"...Then such a wind is most inconvenient," Kongming said casually: Zhou Yu turned to the smiling Kongming and stared at him with intent.

"B-but... if Cao Cao knows this... and he must... then...!" Lu Su fretted.

"Calm yourself, Zijing," Zhou Yu pleaded. "Sometimes, war seems as though it has an inevitable conclusion... what we must not do is lose heart. Master Zhuge, I think it best for you to return to your lord and prepare for the land battle... this matter of the wind should not be broached, lest it cause panic... I promise, all of you... this will have the positive outcome we seek."

Zhou Yu looked at his veteran generals, and smiled encouragingly. Cheng Pu nodded reluctantly in response, while Huang Gai was conspicuously unmoved.

************

## 37

Once again, days passed, and a small boat carried two men – one elite soldier, and one young adviser – along the Yangtze River, disguised as fishermen. Having travelled in the dead of night, it evaded detection by Cao Cao's forces and settled into Xiakou without incident. However, the forces of Liu Bei that were stationed there were made aware of its arrival, and a squad of men led by Zhang Fei met the two men at the pier, weapons drawn and ready for use.

"...You...!" Zhang Fei exclaimed as Kongming removed the wide-brimmed fisherman's hat that covered his white silk turban, and smiled wryly. "...They let you go, Kongming...?"

"Ah, Yide," Kongming said gratefully as he stepped off of the boat, "you have finally accepted my integrity, it would seem."

"I get it now, yeah," Zhang Fei admitted as he gestured for his men to put down their arms; the disguised soldier in the boat started to sail back to his masters in Jiangdong without a word of farewell. Zhang Fei smiled, and added, "What's happening...?"

"Expect Cao's fleet to be destroyed within ten days," Kongming replied.

"*Destroyed*...?" Zhang Fei said with surprise.

"We have time to talk about this later," Kongming insisted. "We must hurry to Lord Liu, so that I can report."

Zhang Fei nodded briskly, and ordered the squad of soldiers to escort Kongming as quickly as they could.

Meanwhile, in Wulin, Cao Cao was sat reading a text on the principles of good governance in his personal tent, when a messenger suddenly interrupted him.

"**Prime Minister!**" the messenger hailed boldly as he knelt in penitence to begin his report. "**Urgent! Veteran General Huang Gai of the southland wishes to surrender to you!**"

"Mm...?" Cao Cao grunted with surprise as he looked up from his reading. After taking a moment to understand, Cao asked, "...What did you say...?"

"**Prime Minister!**" the messenger hailed again. "**Urgent! Veteran General Huang Gai of the southland wishes to surrender to you!**"

Cheng Yu – who had noticed the messenger hurrying to his lord – now entered the tent and heard the repeat of the unexpected message.

"...Has he presented a letter of submission...?" Cao Cao prompted: the messenger got to his feet, pulled the letter from his sleeve, and moved forward to present it to Cao Cao, who took it enthusiastically.

"...I wonder if this is to be believed," Cheng Yu said as the messenger stepped back and knelt in penitence once again. "...Messenger, you may retire for now."

The messenger got to his feet and left the tent.

"... ... ...He speaks of humiliation in our last battle, and the inevitability of defeat," Cao Cao mused as he finished reading: he passed the letter to Cheng Yu, who also read it carefully. "What do you think...?" Cao Cao prompted.

"… … …Things we want to hear are said," Cheng Yu noted. "He accounts for sending his family later as a point of avoiding suspicion… understandable, if he is so close to Sun Quan and Zhou Yu; he speaks of futile schemes, disorganisation, putting men at risk; he speaks well, indeed. He is obviously disgruntled, since he talks of glory under Sun Jian and Sun Ce that is not reflected in this new ruler… he speaks of general discontent among the veteran generals regarding the new Chief Commander, Zhou Yu… it is very likely that this is genuine."

"Are you sure…?" Cao Cao asked cautiously. "Can we be sure that there is no scheme in this…?"

"How can one be *sure*…?" Cheng Yu retorted as he handed the letter back to Cao Cao, who read it again with disbelief. "This man is known for his fiery disposition, and probably finds the style of leadership and military disposition unbearable. He speaks of other generals that would also defect once the right amount of damage was done to Zhou Yu… of senior advisers that advocated surrender… I would say that is quite possible."

"…Still… it is too good to be true," Cao Cao decided. "We should… … …but then, what if it really is true…? It is entirely and logically right that this old soldier should fear me, I think…"

"My lord, you know my thoughts," Cheng Yu replied dangerously.

"…Again, you sow doubt," Cao Cao growled. "Jia Xu now holds Jiangling because I cannot rely on his counsel to inspire… and since we arrived, you have veered between fawning and floundering. But I can see I will have no peace while you are silent… speak."

"It is as I have said before," Cheng Yu insisted bravely. "Firstly, something about Liu Bei's feeble resistance makes no sense, especially since they have now disappeared, yet the courtiers of Liu and Sun have been in strong diplomatic contact. Secondly, as Jia Xu correctly predicted, disease is rampant, and we have lost many men to it… and even with the boat-connecting plan in place to combat seasickness, we still have many sick soldiers. Thirdly…"

"*Thirdly*…?" Cao Cao scoffed. "How many objections do you have???"

"…Thirdly," Cheng Yu continued tenaciously, "I am worried about the weather in these parts… the winds…"

"The winds are north-westerly," Cao Cao replied irritably. "I am aware that the direction of the winds can sometimes change in these parts… but what do these southern fools know of it, mm…? Can they predict the exact days that this phenomenon occurs, and work with it…?"

"Is it worth risking…?" Cheng Yu protested. "My lord, you hold lavish parties and drink heartily, singing songs and reciting your own poetry that mocks the south for their stupidity. We have connected boats… a fire attack assisted by a southeast wind would wipe out our fleet."

"Nonsense!" Cao Cao proclaimed. "I know of all that you say, and it is all too chancy for them to exploit! They cannot even *pray* for such miniscule odds to be in their favour! ...Now, I think that this man, on second reading, surrenders sincerely. The only bitter wind that blows, blows for Zhou Yu... let this old general come here. We will interrogate him carefully, ascertain his honesty, and if he is genuine – another Zhang He, or Zhang Liao – we will have him be the vanguard! Get the messenger back! We will reply immediately!"
"Very well, Prime Minister," Cheng Yu said: he left to retrieve the messenger while Cao Cao took up a piece of writing material to compose a response.

Zhou Yu and Lu Su, meanwhile, stood in the war room, and looked out onto the Yangtze reflectively as the sun set on another tense day of waiting.
"...Veteran General Huang Gai concerns me," Lu Su said suddenly.
"He will be fine," Zhou Yu insisted. "He was just upset about the loss of some men that were with him for many years... I understand that."
"No," Lu Su said desperately, "I think that it's worse than just the loss of the men... he resents your young leadership... like General Cheng."
"Zhuge Liang, Liu Bei, Cheng Yu and Cao Cao worry me more than Huang Gai," Zhou Yu replied uneasily. "Will Liu Bei honour his side of the bargain...? Will Zhuge Liang relay things as I have told him, or will they fear defeat and surrender, and ruin all of our plans...?"
"Trust the fates, and trust our allies, Gongjin," Lu Su pleaded.
"...I want to," Zhou Yu insisted. "But... as Kongming said often enough... this is war, and in war, is trust an option...?"
Lu Su exhaled noisily, and nodded in reluctant agreement with the point.

Later that night, Huang Gai and a small group of his men waited by the river for a response from Cao Cao: they got what they were waiting for. The messenger – disguised as a fisherman – produced a letter from his sleeve and handed it over to the veteran general.
"...What does it say...?" one old soldier asked as Huang Gai read the letter with initial apprehension, and then obvious satisfaction.
"...In three days," Huang Gai declared, "we go to Cao Cao."
The men smiled, and nodded agreeably.


************

Encounters between the fleets of Cao Cao and Zhou Yu were kept to a minimum over the next three days as Cao Cao prepared for the arrival of his first defected general, and what he hoped would be one of many. On the evening if the third day, Cao Cao travelled to the docks in person, dressed in his full military regalia, and ready to greet the arrival of this important addition to his forces. All of the ships were now chained together in groups, ready for a full assault.

"In ten days," Cao Cao said with satisfaction, "I will destroy these southern rats, and finally reunite the lands above and below the Great River."

"It will be a great day indeed, Prime Minister," Cheng Yu replied numbly.

The soldiers lined the banks, and as a precaution, rows of archers were ready to fire, destroying any ambush party that may surprise the proceedings. Since it was dark, lamps lit the entire docks, so that Cao's flags and soldiers could be seen for miles.

"...It's cold!" Cao Cao chuckled. "Oh well, at least we won't need to be here for much longer. ...It's almost time, isn't it...?"

"It is," Cheng Yu replied with sudden discomfort.

"Well," Cao Cao said as he clutched his throbbing head, "I... I shall retire and read, since this cold does my condition no good. Let me know when this fellow arrives."

"Very good, my lord," Cheng Yu replied.

Cao Cao retired to his command tent, followed by his giant bodyguard, Xu Chu.

**"Chief Commander! ...Terrible news...!"** Lu Su cried as he ran into the war room, where Zhou Yu and Cheng Pu were making final preparations for an imminent naval battle with Cao Cao.

"Oh...?" Zhou Yu prompted. "What terrible news, Zijing...?"

"Veteran General Huang Gai... has defected to Cao Cao!" Lu Su sobbed.

"Ah," Zhou Yu said with a smile. "So he has departed as expected."

"As *expected*...?" Lu Su exclaimed. "You... you knew he was...?"

"Come here, Lu Su," Zhou Yu said calmly: he beckoned Lu Su toward the centre of the room, and had him look at the model ships.

"...Nothing is different, is it...?" Lu Su said with confusion.

"Not at first glance," Zhou Yu said with a smirk. "...Or perhaps it's dark. Bring a torch, will you...?"

"Aiee," Lu Su sighed. "You want me to set fire to our ships again?"

"Just get a torch," Zhou Yu insisted.

Lu Su did as he was told: Zhou Yu gestured that he should examine the map more closely. Lu Su reluctantly lowered the torch as he had done before, and again, the wind picked up the flames.

"*Ayah*! Why are you making me do this...?" Lu Su whined. "I...!"

Before Lu Su could lift the torch high enough, the flames licked the sail of one of the model ships that represented Cao Cao's fleet.

"...Do you see...?" Zhou Yu whispered.

"See what…?" Lu Su said with embarrassment.

Zhou Yu slowly reached out and picked up the affected model.

"…Put it out!" Lu Su pleaded as he looked at the burning sail.

"…Watch," Zhou Yu replied emotionlessly: he returned the model ship to the table, and pushed it toward the model representation of Cao Cao's fleet slowly and mechanically, as though he were no longer in control of his own body.

"What are you doing…?" Lu Su asked with panic: as if to answer him, another strong gust of wind blew the flames on the tiny sail, spreading them to the models of Cao Cao's fleet and setting them alight, one by one.

"What are you…!" Lu Su admonished: and then, suddenly, he understood. He smiled, and said, "A southeast wind…! …Blowing from our position, directly to *his*…!"

"A fire attack," Cheng Pu concurred. "It's perfect… and Cao has even chained his ships together to make it easier for the fire to spread. …We've won."

"We *have*…?" Lu Su asked with bemusement. "But… but how to get the fire ships close enough to *his* ships to start this 'chain reaction'…? We cannot simply sail toward him with attacking boats full of kindling!"

"Can't we…?" Zhou Yu chuckled.

"…Huang Gai…!" Lu Su realised. "But… why was I excluded…?"

"Some things are best left unsaid," Zhou Yu sighed. "I was hoping you'd understand, as Zhuge Kongming obviously did. With his knowledge of seeing the signs and predicting the weather, he knew exactly what I had in mind. Now, let's prepare: Cao Cao is about to be destroyed!"

Cheng Yu remained at the pier with the rest of Cao Cao's generals: he gazed at the vast Yangtze River in front of him, and something did not seem right. He looked about him: the men were now organised, and most of the rampant disease was dealt with, though the losses had been significant. The flags were in perfect array, and fluttered in the night winds, which blew toward the northwest. The lamps flickered as the southeast winds buffeted them: Cheng Yu suddenly realised what his deep-rooted concern must be.

"…The… the wind…!" Cheng Yu whispered.

"What's the matter…?" General Li Dian asked apprehensively.

"The wind," Cheng Yu fretted. "If… if they have come with fire…!"

"They're in sight," General Yu Jin noted.

Yu Jin pointed to a large number of approaching ships bearing Huang Gai's standard: now Cheng Yu was terrified.

"**No!**" Cheng Yu exclaimed. "They must not be allowed to…!"

"What…?" Li Dian said with confusion.

Huang Gai's ships continued their approach, carried by the strong southeast wind. A few of the more astute spotters noted that there did not seem to be any visible crew.

"…No… **NO!**" Cheng Yu exclaimed. "**We have to STOP THEM!**"

But it was already too late.

Veteran General Huang Gai had sent the ships – unmanned – to travel directly toward Cao Cao, the large sails taking the ships exactly where they needed to go. In a small craft that had long since left the lead ship, Huang Gai smiled silently.

The ships were packed with kindling, reeds, and jars of oil and fat: fires had been started before the crews jettisoned, and now the crafts travelled toward the northern bank – and Cao Cao's own fleet – like homing incendiary devices.

The result was a spectacle to behold: the fires were doing their awful work, igniting the treated wood hulls of the ships and boats, and setting the clothes and hair of their crews alight as well. The screams of agony overtook the whistling winds and futile shouts for calm by the commanders as the mood went from confident optimism to a sudden, desperate fight for survival.

**"WE HAVE TO GET OUT OF HERE!"** Li Dian screamed as Cao Cao – who had left his tent to discover the source of the commotion – stared at his once magnificent fleet, which was now a funeral pyre for at least ten thousand of his men.

**"…PRIME MINISTER!"** the one-eyed general Xiahou Dun shouted. **"PLEASE, PRIME MINISTER, WE HAVE TO FLEE!"**

"I… I…!" Cao Cao said hoarsely: he could not, and would not believe what he was seeing.

Xu Chu – Cao Cao's towering bodyguard – took the initiative, grabbing Cao Cao and hoisting him onto his shoulder in order to take him to safety. Ship after ship was sinking, and it seemed that for every ship or boat that sank, another caught alight.

**"With me…!"** Cheng Yu ordered: the ground forces fled the scene, abandoning their sick comrades in the hospital and the men that were trapped on the burning vessels. They fled toward the north of the city.

**"We must escape!"** Cheng Yu shouted as they escaped the worst. **"We can…!"**

**"REPORT!"** a messenger screamed over the sounds of suffering. **"The forces of Liu Bei and Liu Qi are now gathered along the east bank, ready to cross to Wulin, along with several thousand Jiangdong forces! The Great River is blocked to the north by Liu Qi's naval forces! The…!"**

"I… … …D'AAAAAGH…!" Cao Cao screamed as one of his crippling headaches suddenly beset him: Xiahou Dun and Xu Chu hurried the ailing Cao Cao away from the ships, which were now a single wall of fire along the river.

**"Where can we go…?"** Li Dian asked desperately.

**"…The marshes, we have no choice!"** Cheng Yu decided, and so the decimated forces of Cao Cao abandoned Wulin City altogether, moving west and north toward the safe city of Jiangling. Xu Chu carried Cao Cao, who was now semi-conscious and muttering near incoherently as he struggled to rationalise the sudden, absolute destruction of his mighty army.

"We should not have come here," Cheng Yu complained. "I said, I insisted that we should not come here…!"

"What good is that now?" Li Dian challenged angrily.

"Oh… Guo… *Guo Jia*…!" Cao Cao rambled feebly. He was holding onto Xu Chu for dear life as the bodyguard-general steered his horse awkwardly across the waterlogged Jiangxia marshlands.

"…Keep moving," Cheng Yu ordered as he struggled to stay atop his horse: the ground was sodden and uneven, causing many to slip and fall into the mud.

"We did it!" Lu Su exclaimed as he stood at the helm of the southern command ship with Zhou Yu, watching the blaze from the port at Red Cliffs. "I... I don't believe it...! We defeated him...!"
"...Arrogance," Zhou Yu insisted as he shook his head slowly. "Arrogance defeated Cao Cao, not us. But there's time enough for praise later; **let us pursue!**"
That pursuit, however, would not go according to plan.

A Jing-affiliated messenger approached the vanguard forces of Liu Bei and Liu Qi, who were camped on the east bank of the Yangtze River, opposite Wulin.
"**REPORT!**" the messenger hailed as he reached the camp gates.
"...Yes...?" Jian Yong asked wearily.
"**There are insufficient numbers of ships and boats to cross!**" the messenger continued. "**There are**... uh..."
"Oh no... what in the...!" Jian Yong exclaimed: another messenger – who had been wounded by some sort of blade – staggered toward the camp, and fell to one knee.
"What happened to you...?" Jian Yong wondered with concern.
"Re... report," the Liu Bei-affiliated messenger hailed weakly. "F-fighting... has broken out between our forces over commandeering vessels f-for... the crossing."
"**AIEE!**" Liu Bei exclaimed. "How will we be able to pursue Cao Cao now???"
"Get this man to safety... get him water," Jian Yong ordered: two of Liu Bei's soldiers took the battered messengers away.
Kongming fanned himself silently, and offered no suggestions.
"We should flag down our fleet, take some down toward Red Cliffs," Jian Yong suggested. "We can-"
"The north bank is a fire zone," Kongming volunteered with a sigh. "The south bank will be entirely maintained by Zhou Yu... so if Cao Cao is alive and retreating, it will be on land, marching west, across the marshes to Jiangling."
"We must pursue!" Jian Yong protested. "After all this-"
"Let him go," Kongming insisted.
"What...?" Liu Bei exclaimed.
"Are you mad...?" Jian Yong scoffed. "He's-"
"**Think!**" Kongming retorted. "*Think*, Xianhe!"
Jian Yong did not know what Kongming meant, and frowned with bewilderment.
"...We've done all we can here," Kongming suggested.
"I can't let my enemy survive!" Liu Bei protested.
"... ... ...Very well, then, my lord... Huarong Trail is where a trap must be set for Cao Cao," Kongming explained reluctantly. "Despatch forces there, if you must... but you'll not be likely to get there in time now... even with fast boats to cross and faster riding across the drier land to the north to make ground, you will most likely get there in time to see his shadow, no more than that."
"...**Why didn't you suggest this before???**" Liu Bei exclaimed. "**We could have had men...! ... Never mind! Yunchang, Yide, Liao Hua, Chen Shi...!**"
The four generals understood their mission without further explanation, and travelled west to accomplish it as best they could.

"Now," Kongming said, "we must return to Xiakou, and hope that we are still welcome there now that Cao Cao is put to flight."
"What do you mean by that...?" Jian Yong asked pointedly.
Kongming did not reply.

Cao Cao, meanwhile, continued his retreat west, having little of his once proud forces left at this point. He had regained some composure, and was now barking orders: he had old, weak and sick soldiers gather straw and tattered clothes to make the sodden path easier to traverse. When that failed, Cao ordered the men to lie on the ground, and rode over them, killing many of them in the process. Eventually, the party reached Huarong Trail, where Cao Cao let out a boisterous laugh.
"Prime Minister," Cheng Yu bleated, "we have just suffered the most embarrassing defeat since Yuan Shao's fall at Guandu. What is there to laugh about...?"
Cao Cao was looking at the high hills and slopes that surrounded them as he replied, "Liu Bei, he's an old friend. But he isn't that bright. If I were him, I'd have placed an ambush here: coming here, as I am now... I'd have been finished!"
Cao Cao then started to laugh again: none of the soldiers and generals shared his amused appraisal.
"Prime Minister," Li Dian asked desperately, "why do you curse us so...?"
**We have survived!**" Cao Cao boomed suddenly. "**We will endure! We will return here, one day, and avenge ourselves!** ...One day..."
Cao Cao stopped talking: his joyous visage darkened, and he started to ride his horse toward Jiangling, with Xu Chu at his side for protection.
"...We were destroyed," Xiahou Dun sighed. "It...! ... ... ..*Aiee.*"
As Cao Cao rode slowly toward safety, Cheng Yu rode to his side and said, "Their plan was infallible, Prime Minister... we-"
"No, Cheng Yu, it *wasn't*," Cao Cao scolded. "Guo Jia... he'd have seen through it and *persuaded me*. If Guo Jia were here... he would not have let this happen to me."
Rebuked by the statement, Cheng Yu dropped back slightly, and allowed Cao Cao and Xu Chu to take the lead alone.

Many hours later, Guan Yu, Zhang Fei, Liao Hua and Chen Shi reached Huarong Trail with their small army of riders, and as Kongming had said, they only found evidence that Cao Cao had already been and gone.
"...*Aiee*," Guan Yu exclaimed angrily. "We were too late."
"We'll have it out with 'Crouching Dragon' when we get back," Zhang Fei said with irritation. "He was the one that deliberately didn't send us here quickly enough."
Guan Yu nodded in agreement, and the four generals returned to Xiakou with their forces, frustrated that they had missed a marvellous opportunity.


************

## 39

"**This is an outrage!**" Liu Qi fumed as he settled into a camp of military tents outside the city of Xiakou, where the flag of Sun Quan now flew from the city masts, rather than that of the governor of Jing.

"This is what you meant," Jian Yong realised as he confronted the casual Kongming. "Cheng Pu retaking Jiangxia... you *knew*...!"

"No, I *realised*," Kongming insisted. "General Cheng was Assistant Commander, and yet I didn't see his flag during the rout at Wulin... nor did I see Zhou Yu's."

"So where is Zhou Yu...?" Liu Bei asked angrily.

"If Cheng Pu has seized Jiangxia Prefecture," Kongming mused, "then Zhou Yu... has perhaps sailed west and north... to Jiangling."

"**He means to steal my Jing Province!**" Liu Qi fumed, though he attracted little attention for it.

"Does Zhou Yu intend to break faith...?" Mister Sun asked worriedly.

Before Kongming could answer, a familiar roar of discontent heralded the return of Zhang Fei and the group that had travelled to Huarong Trail.

"...Ah," Ma Liang murmured.

"**Where is Zhuge Liang???**" Zhang Fei boomed: he entered Liu Qi's command tent, pointed at Kongming, and said, "**You had better have a bloody good explanation for what's going on...!**"

"...Welcome back, Yide," Jian Yong hailed cheerfully as Guan Yu joined Zhang Fei in the command tent. "...Welcome back, Yunchang... I take it you were both unsuccessful in apprehending Cao Cao...?"

"...**D'AAAAAGH!**" Zhang Fei roared: he lunged for Jian Yong, but was restrained by Guan Yu. "**All of you... pedants... I will... eat your flesh...!**"

"Don't be like that," Jian Yong chuckled. "...Kongming, I do think he's right that you owe us all an explanation."

"**Why did you let us miss a chance to get Cao Cao???**" Zhang Fei asked angrily, as he continued to struggle to break free from Guan Yu's grip.

"It is good that Cao Cao survived," Kongming replied calmly, to the surprise and horror of everyone else.

"How can you *say that*...?" Liu Bei asked with evident offence.

"If he had died," Kongming retorted, "we'd have a vengeful Cao Pi to deal with right now, and that would be worse, since Cao has around a hundred-thousand soldiers left, at least, though they are currently scattered around the regions he still controls. This humiliation will resonate through the rest of Cao Cao's career: he won't forget it, as Liu Biao never forgot his own defeat at Luoyang. Cao Cao will hesitate and give us opportunities, despite still being in a very strong position: his son Cao Pi, quite correctly, would not.

"Or, alternatively, Cao Pi would immediately be drawn into a battle for succession with his brothers, and many of his vassals would desert, leaving the north harmless and exposed. In that case, we'd be up against an unstoppable Zhou Yu... having met him, I can tell you *that* would be our *doom*."

Liu Bei hummed thoughtfully.

"So... so this was so *Zhou Yu* couldn't be stronger...?" Zhang Fei asked.

"Yide, even at his current level of strength, he has burnt forty-thousand men to death at Wulin, and reoccupied Jiangxia," Kongming challenged. "He exceeds Guo Jia: would you want him to have nobody else left to target but us...?"

Zhang Fei stopped struggling, and said, "You knew he wasn't to be trusted... all along... didn't you...? ...But that... there was nothing we could do about it."

Kongming started to fan himself silently, and did not reply.

"Okay," Zhang Fei muttered, and Guan Yu released him, content that he was placated.

"...Cao Cao may also be open to negotiation now," Mister Sun supposed.

"Never," Liu Bei insisted. "Cao and I can never live under the same sky, not now that he is a traitor to the Han Empire."

"Well, Zhou Yu doesn't need to know that," Kongming suggested calmly. "But I'll now come to the matter of Jing Province: Cheng Pu is not receiving visitors to discuss this, which means that both Zhou Yu *and* Lu Su are at this moment on their way to Jiangling... to seize it, as Governor Liu Qi fears."

"That *would* be a breach of faith, surely...?" Ma Liang chuckled uneasily.

"I doubt they care," Kongming scoffed. "Zhou Yu wants the best outcome for his lord, as I do mine, and sees the annexation of Jing as border security, reparation, and compensation for past disputes as well as for the battle we just fought together."

"So what do we do...?" Mister Sun asked. "We can't just let them steal any more of Jing from the young governor, can we...?"

"Legally, Jing Province really isn't his anymore, Mister Sun: he lost it to Han's Prime Minister, Cao Cao, when his brother ceded it," Kongming noted.

"...I've lost *everything*...!" Liu Qi exclaimed desperately.

"Relax," Zhang Fei said comfortingly. "We'll get it back for you."

"We'll certainly try," Kongming promised.

"But why is Zhou Yu breaking faith with us and trying to seize Jiangling after so short a time...?" Mister Sun wondered. "Could he not have at least *tried* to make our alliance work...?"

"Perhaps his estimation of Kongming, and us as a whole, matches Kongming's own shrewd estimation of the south," Jian Yong suggested. "Perhaps he fears us, and acts to protect his lord from a future threat from us... or the exact *opposite*, that we are no threat *at all*."

"If I were to regain my rightful place as governor of Jing," Liu Qi said, "I would not be looking to do anything other than repay my debt to Uncle Liu, and maintain the peace in the region."

Kongming and Ma Liang looked at one-another knowingly.

"The poor man," Kongming chuckled sadly as he walked through the streets of Xiakou with Ma Liang a short time later. "Liu Qi will *never* govern Jing: it is another's, his branch of the Liu clan are finished here now."

"Ethically..." Ma Liang began, but before he could make a point of any kind, Kongming gestured with his fan and laughed.

"Forget ethics, Ma Jichang," Kongming insisted. "We're beyond such things now."

Ma Liang nodded regretfully.

The Battle of Red Cliffs – as it came to be known – changed the face of the military and political map for many years to come. The immediate effect was the reduction in Cao Cao's power, and the rise of Sun Quan as a serious competitor to power in the north, something that Kongming had reluctantly planned for. But while Liu Bei was militarily weak, he was far from finished, and the next few years would see him rise to heights beyond even his most unrealistic expectations.

************

# ACT IV: THE SIEGE OF JIANGLING

## 40

In the aftermath of the 'Battle of Red Cliffs', Cao Cao's forces –
having lost thousands of men and ships to disease and firestorms
– took a reluctantly defensive posture, using the southwest capital
of Jing, Jiangling, as a stronghold to keep the newly emboldened
forces of the southern warlord Sun Quan at bay. This effectively
freed the whole of southern Jing from Cao Cao's control, and
placed it in the hands of his enemies – Sun Quan, the landless
warlord Liu Bei, and the disinherited governor of Jing, Liu Qi. Now
that Cao Cao had been defeated, Sun Quan's senior strategist,
Zhou Yu, had apparently decided to proceed alone, and had split
his forces between consolidating in the southeast of Jing, and
besieging Cao Cao's defenders in the southwest. This threatened
the alliance that had repelled Cao Cao, and brought concern to
Sun Quan's weaker allies, Liu Bei and Liu Qi, who would lose
everything if Sun Quan and Zhou Yu betrayed them.

After a three-day session of imparting advice to his lord, the
weary Kongming left Liu Bei's headquarters outside the city of
Xiakou and returned to his family's new home in the town of Three
Rivers. Zhuge Jun and Yueying led the welcome that consisted of
around a dozen family members and household staff in all.
"...I really wish he'd get himself another adviser sometimes,"
Kongming chuckled as he hugged his brother Jun.
"Are you sure you want the competition...?" Kongming's father-in-
law, Mister Huang, teased. "...Anyhow, it was a well-won battle."
"I don't think it's too much to say that it was history in the
making," Kongming replied as he greeted his wife with a subtle
embrace. "Not since Cao's victory over Yuan Shao at Guandu has
the fate of the entire land been so decided by one event: in fact, I
wonder if this wasn't the most important battle of our time."
"Truly incredible, to win against such odds," Jun said surely.
"As I said to Lord Liu," Kongming replied, "it is proof that 'Even a
powerful arrow cannot penetrate a silk cloth at the end of its
flight'. They were exhausted, sick, and diseased: against a fresh
force of a significant size, they stood no chance of a lossless
victory, even without the fire attack."
"So what happens now...?" Mister Huang asked as everyone
entered the house and Kongming took the host seat.
"Now," Kongming said, "we wait for the smaller pockets of
resistance to spring up. There are many that are dissatisfied with
Cao's regime: Ma Chao in the northern region of Xiliang; Liu
Zhang's subordinate Zhang Lu in Hanzhong; the Wuling tribes;
and Xi Su in Yiling... the last of those will soon be attacked by
Zhou Yu, and I cannot see Xi Su trying that hard to hold the city."
"So Zhou Yu will take Yiling...?" Zhuge Jun pondered. "What does
all this mean for Jing Province, brother...? Are we going to have to
move again...?"
"We may need to follow our lord Liu to many places," Kongming
replied. "But then, it is not true that a bird nests in the same tree
each year: sometimes, he must fly to other, safer branches, and
not mistake complacency for stability."
"Nice analogy," Mister Huang said, "but do birds have luggage...?"

"… … …*No*," Kongming replied as his wife and brother laughed.

"Well then," Mister Huang added, "it would be nice to have *some* stability for a while, yes…?"

"I'll ask Lord Liu to temporarily suspend his ambitions for your sake, Father-in-law," Kongming retorted playfully.

Later that evening, Kongming played his new qin while Yueying listened.

"This one is not as good as my old one," Kongming lamented. "It isn't as good as Zhou Yu's either."

"Zhou Yu has a beautiful qin… not a tired, ugly one," Yueying sighed pointedly.

"…Which, of course, is not a comment made to discuss the musical instrument, but his beautiful wife," Kongming supposed.

"Was she as beautiful as people say…?" Yueying asked.

"More so," Kongming replied as he continued to strum the strings of the qin with skill and grace. "She was the most beautiful woman that I have ever seen… a pity she has chosen to marry such a man. For all his enviably handsome looks, creative genius, and remarkable wisdom, he serves an unjust cause: he will come to a bad end, and she will be a young widow, like her sister."

"A cruel thing to say," Yueying scolded.

"…What…?" Kongming replied with a laugh. "That she is beautiful, or that she chose a bad husband, or that he is doomed, or…?"

"That she is doomed to be a widow," Yueying retorted miserably. "Such things… you should not wish on people."

"Is it because you fear that Liu Bei's grand ambitions will make *you* an early widow…?" Kongming asked knowingly as he continued to play. "Is it… because you almost feel like one *now*…?"

"…We spend no time together now, not even a little, like before," Yueying declared, her point having been correctly deduced. "I have seen you twice in the space of five weeks: how is that going to work…? How can we be a family…? …Now, you will be going to Yi Province, and-"

"Am I…?" Kongming chuckled as he finally stopped playing.

"Your style of playing is rich with open spaces, vastness, and journeys," Yueying suggested plainly. "Where else can you be going but to Yi…?"

"…Possibly, in a couple of years," Kongming admitted. "But at the moment, we're having trouble holding onto Jing, and without Jing, we cannot take Yi."

"Oh," Yueying murmured.

"…*Chief Commander Zhou Yu* is attacking Jiangling and Yiling, while *Assistant Commander Cheng Pu* has retaken Jiangxia," Kongming sighed. "You'll find out sooner or later, since the green-uniformed soldiers – of what shall henceforth be known as '*Eastern Wu*' – that will soon be patrolling Three Rivers will somewhat give it away."

"We're under occupation…?" Yueying realised.

"We are," Kongming replied. "I can't believe they've achieved it: presumably, Cao's treatment of Wulin has made people grateful that a lesser tyrant won the day."

"But I thought the Huang clan of Jiangxia would never allow it," Yueying mused.

"Obviously the Huangs of Jiangxia are not as resilient as we thought," Kongming replied. "It'll be fine, though: do remember that my brother is very influential in the Wu court now, so we're perfectly safe."

"That isn't the point though, is it…?" Yueying suggested. "You serve Liu Bei… who in turn aids the true successor to this region, Liu Qi… will this not mean that good relations with either Sun Quan or Liu Qi have to be severed…?"

"This is *politics*," Kongming replied with a smirk. "With the right rhetoric, and enough compromising of morality, ethics, and rational reason, Lord Liu can be friends with them all and still have ambitions at the same time."

Yueying's gaze wandered as she pondered it.

"I hope you *don't* understand," Kongming sighed, "because if you do, then you're one of *us*… and then you know a part of you is gone."

"Is that how you feel…?" Yueying asked. "…That a part of you is gone…?"

"Of course it is!" Kongming chortled. "I… I've not only had to treat subterfuge and duplicity as acceptable, but also death, *murder*, on a grand scale: over *fifty-thousand men* died at Wulin and Red Cliffs… when you can say you had a hand in that, can you really say you're human anymore…?"

"… … …No, I don't suppose you can," Yueying replied honestly.

"Zhou Yu accepts it… while I don't, not fully," Kongming continued. "I do it because I'm left with no choice… or at least, I have no choice so far as my choice of calling is concerned. My business is lies, and death, and intrigue… Pang Tong said he couldn't do it… maybe that's why. Maybe, for all my accusations that he was colder and more cynical than me… perhaps he's the one that made the right choice. All he has to do is say that people are nice, even if they aren't… I have to lie to people, have people killed…"

"*Okay*… okay," Yueying interrupted weakly.

"… … …Sorry," Kongming said sadly.

"Husband," Yueying said plainly, "you… you made your choice. If you had remained as a farmer, and tried to avoid this, we would now be dead, killed by Cao Cao *just in case* you were going to be a threat later. You knew that. And so did I."

"…I'm sorry anyway," Kongming continued adamantly. "Sorry that I have to go again… that… that I will probably not be back for a while, and that when I do return, it will be to collect you and move you to Yi Province or Nan Prefecture."

"…Nan Prefecture…?" Yueying noted. "I thought Zhou Yu was sieging that."

"Yes, well," Kongming said with a smile, "even if he's successful… that doesn't mean he'll keep it."

"…What are you planning…?" Yueying asked with sudden amusement.

"Mm… I suppose it won't hurt to tell you," Kongming said thoughtfully. "What I am going to do is go back to Lord Liu, and…"

************

## 41

"You want me to grovel to Zhou Yu...?"
All eyes in the tent-based makeshift court in Xiakou turned to Kongming as Liu Bei made the accusing statement.
"...Understand, Master Zhuge, that I can be courteous to even the most undeserving knave should the need arise," Liu Bei added. "But... you want me to go on bended knee to this callous thief, this hireling robber that steals my nephew's lands without even having the decency to acknowledge he exists...?"
"You're having a laugh, 'Water'," Zhang Fei grunted. "Even if Elder Brother agreed to this cheeky scheme o' yours, I wouldn't let him do it. He has to have some **pride!**"
"...I did not say 'grovel'," Kongming replied calmly. "I said 'politely request'."
"Why should I 'politely request' to be given back my own land...?" Liu Qi asked Kongming desperately.
"Because," Kongming replied honestly, "we're in no position to argue with this new super-state of 'Wu' right now."
"...That, I have to concede," Liu Bei sighed miserably.
"If we don't ask nicely," Kongming suggested, "it will have two direct consequences, possibly three: firstly, we will lose Yiling and Jiangling, which will mean losing the gates to the realm. Secondly, we will have to sit back and watch as the four counties south of that become Wu's as well. Thirdly – although, I confess, this is personal opinion, nothing more – we will invite suspicion, since a failure to react to what will be a second blatant act of theft will cause Zhou Yu to wonder what we're thinking... that could lead to anything, even an assassination attempt on either or both of you, my lord."
"He wouldn't *dare*," Liu Qi seethed. "Jing would rise up and-"
"My apologies, young governor, but you were right before: Jing wouldn't rise up and do anything," Kongming interrupted. "Jiangxia has not risen up against Zhou Yu... not even after the rule of the popular Huangs in the region. I doubt Xi Su of Yiling will oppose Wu either, and why...? ...Because Wu isn't Cao Cao, and right now, they'll tolerate anything that isn't Cao Cao. You've been forgotten, young governor... through no fault of your own, maybe, but you have, nonetheless."
Stunned by the blunt truth, Liu Qi was silent and mournful.
"...Now," Kongming continued, "if we stand any chance of restoring order in Jing, getting things back to as they were, with Liu Qi as governor, we must be clever, and yes, that may involve some 'grovelling' if I'm honest. But initially, I would like to try a more proactive, confident, 'friendly' approach... we go to them as allies, as we were supposed to be, and tender our services in the cause against Cao Cao."
"...Alright," Liu Bei agreed.
"Good," Kongming said coldly. "Now, since we have now been requested to attend a meeting with Zhou Yu, they must have some 'use' for us. That, I think I can guess: Yunchang..."
Guan Yu nodded respectfully.

"Yunchang, you'll need to get ready for another naval expedition and a siege, if my suspicions are correct," Kongming explained. "Lord Liu, we'll need to coerce Lu Su, and also make polite suggestions to Zhou Yu if possible, regarding all of the ways in which we can 'help'. We must ensure that this remains an alliance, no matter what Zhou Yu has decided that he wants, and that all parties benefit."

"...What must we do...?" Jian Yong asked.

"To correctly establish ourselves, we need a base, and also a through-route to the Yi Province," Kongming explained further. "To fully elaborate my understanding of the situation: directly after the battle at Red Cliffs, General Gan Ning sailed to Yiling, where he secured the sincere surrender of Xi Su. Sun Quan has taken a force of over ten thousand to attack Hefei Castle and Jiujiang in the northeast, while Zhou Yu – capitalising on Gan Ning's securing of Yiling – has taken a force of thirty-thousand and camped on the banks of the Yangtze south of Jiangling, obviously intending to take Nan Prefecture by first defeating Cao Ren's force in Jiangling, and then – as was initially discussed prior to Red Cliffs – forcing the tolerated independent governors of the four counties south of Jiangling – Changsha, Lingling, Wuling and Guiyang – to surrender, thus ensuring that Wu control the most important part of Jing Province militarily."

"...We cannot allow that," Jian Yong suggested.

"I know we can't," Kongming chuckled calmly. "I've heard that Zhou Yu has been communicating with Zhang Lu of Hanzhong – who is now estranged completely from his lord Liu Zhang – and Ma Chao, the son of Xiliang governor Ma Teng, whose ambition is to gain complete independence from the northern court."

"How *nice*," Zhang Fei grunted sarcastically. "What's the point...?"

"An alternative alliance," Liu Bei supposed. "If he has said nothing of these moves to us, then he intends no good...!"

"My thoughts exactly," Kongming lamented. "He obviously doesn't want to work with anyone that has more of a right to Jing than his master."

"Can't we attack Zhou Yu...?" Liu Qi asked angrily.

"No!" Liu Bei scoffed. "Young governor, you cannot be serious!"

"...I cannot believe I must sit back and watch others bicker over my father's land, ignoring me as though I do not exist!" Liu Qi protested. "Curse my brother for what he did to us! If he were not so far away in Qing Province, I would...!"

"Enough please, nephew," Liu Bei implored.

The suspicion – and, in a way, hope – had been that Cao Cao would renege on his deal with Liu Qi's usurper brother, Liu Cong. But Cao Cao had granted him titles and made him the Inspector of Qing Province, which was on the north-eastern edge of China, far away from any possible recriminations for his actions. This had sent a message to others who might consider resisting the court: submit and be rewarded, or resist and be destroyed. The second part of that message had been somewhat lost after the rebel victory at Red Cliffs, but that did little to quell the belief that Liu Cong had betrayed his allies, his brother, his father, his people and his family name, and suffered no punishment.

"No!" Liu Qi wailed. "He has been rewarded, and will live the rest of his days in comfort, having sold his soul to Cao Cao, and left us to die homeless! He should spend an eternity in the underworld for his treachery, and if I ever get the chance, Uncle, I will... send... him there...!"

The last part of the rant was interspersed with painful coughing: Liu Bei comforted Liu Qi as best he could while the discussion continued.

"We must ingratiate ourselves with Zhou Yu," Kongming suggested. "We should ask him to give us chances to help him, and then exploit them."

"How so...?" Jian Yong asked.

"Well," Kongming said, "we should..."

************

## 42

"Welcome, allies, welcome," Zhou Yu hailed as Liu Bei, Guan Yu, Zhang Fei, Zhao Yun, Mister Sun, Jian Yong, Xiang Lang and Kongming were ushered into his command tent near Gong'an City. Chen Dao remained outside the tent with the rest of Liu Bei's bodyguard forces, who were watched in turn by Wu forces.

"Our congratulations to you," Liu Bei replied, bowing in obeisance.

"...It was our joint victory," Zhou Yu replied diplomatically.

To Zhou Yu's left, Lu Su stared at Kongming suspiciously, while to Zhou Yu's right, General Lü Meng quietly made his own mental observations.

"So tell me," Lu Su asked Kongming, "how is the young governor Liu Qi...?"

"He is fine, Zijing: just fine," Kongming lied.

"We are making good progress," Zhou Yu said pleasantly. "As you are no doubt aware, Xi Su of Yiling surrendered without conflict, so General Gan Ning is now in control of that city. Our lord is at this moment besieging Hefei in the east. We're now in the middle of carrying out some preliminary military manoeuvres against Cao Ren and of course, if you have any helpful advice to give, we would like to hear it, since you probably know more about this region than we do, as former residents."

Resisting the urge to scream, Liu Bei replied, "My thanks for your gracious words regarding the outcome at Wulin. I only wish I had been more help militarily. ...But that is why we are here now, is it not...?"

"It is, Lord Liu," Zhou Yu replied. "But most of the assistance we need is actually best managed from Jiangxia, so once we have spoken, you really should return there, Lord Liu, and-"

"And go back to our *tents*...?" Zhang Fei barked: Guan Yu pinched his nose-bridge and exhaled noisily with embarrassment.

"...*Tents*...?" Zhou Yu said with surprise. "Why are you in tents...?"

"**Don't give me...!**" Zhang Fei began: Liu Bei gestured to Guan Yu, who – together with Zhao Yun – escorted Zhang Fei from Zhou Yu's command tent. Lü Meng got up and followed the three generals.

"...My apologies, Chief Commander," Liu Bei said with an ingratiating laugh. "I am afraid that age has not mellowed my friend and brother at all."

"If you are all in tents, then his anger is understandable," Lu Su said with genuine concern. "Has General Cheng thrown you all out of your homes in Xiakou...?"

"...Not as such," Liu Bei replied uneasily, as he noted Zhou Yu's expression. "We preferred, since the city appears, like Yiling, to have been occupied in the name of Eastern Wu, that we-"

"...'Occupied'...?" Zhou Yu noted with disdain. "Lord Liu, you misrepresent the situation. Cao Cao successfully annexed Nan Prefecture after he defeated you at Steep-slope, so all of our current actions are not an attempt at 'occupation' in the way you seem to indirectly imply, but 'liberation', by adding Nan Prefecture to the territories that are liberally and fairly governed by my lord Sun Quan."

"And Jiangxia…?" Mister Sun challenged. "What of that blatant occupation…?"

"I do not so far see any resistance, which you would expect from an occupation… why, have you seen some…?" Zhou Yu retorted. "Besides, you speak of the region as though you want it… but could you defend it…? Both Steep-slope and Wulin suggest that not to be the case."

"We lost at Wulin intentionally," Mister Sun reminded Zhou Yu disapprovingly.

"…As part of our joint plan to rout Cao Cao, I concede that point in part," Zhou Yu retorted. "But if you had not had our help, would that rout not have been a genuine one, however, and resulted in your total annihilation…?"

"That, we will never know," Kongming declared. "The matter now, Gongjin, is whether we will share the burden of liberating Jing, so that it is seen as just that by the world… or if you will monopolize the retaking of Jing against the wishes of its former governor and also its people, turn down the help of the allies that fought alongside you and shared your suffering at Red Cliffs, and be held up by the world as a seditious conqueror in the months and years to come."

"…I dislike that accusation, Mister Zhuge," Zhou Yu replied irritably.

"I make no accusation," Kongming insisted. "I simply point out that when you have an army of twenty-thousand men, led by a popular lord and the son of the beloved former governor, who are ready, willing and able to assist you in stabilising the region, and you turn them down, thereby making your lone task a harder one to achieve, well… tell me, what other conclusion will historians draw…?"

Zhou Yu was silently seething: Kongming started to fan himself slowly as he awaited the response.

"We want no quarrel," Liu Bei promised. "We just want to help you. Say, for example, with regard to the matter of the four counties of Changsha, Lingling, Wuling and Guiyang: why not allow us to take control of those territories, use them as our base, so that Jiangxia is no longer a point of contention…?"

"…Those counties are also on a border with Eastern Wu," Zhou Yu replied calmly. "I do not think it would be wise to let them fall into weak hands, as it were, lest they give an enemy easy passage into our domains… no disrespect intended."

"… … …None assumed," Kongming said calmly as Liu Bei hid his rage. "But I think that we can genuinely be of service in that endeavour, since young governor Liu Qi is popular in those counties, and peaceful surrender in all four cases is guaranteed, whereas otherwise… especially since those counties know of his current plight… that may not necessarily be quite so guaranteed."

"…I see," Zhou Yu murmured: he knew that Kongming's words were laced with a threat of sorts. "…Okay, perhaps you *can* assist me in that 'endeavour', after all, and act in our name… but once I am done with Jiangling, I expect them to be given over to Eastern Wu for collective governance."

"You demand another's territory…?" Jian Yong scoffed.

"Is it Liu Qi's now, or Lord Liu's...? ...No, it is Cao Cao's, surrendered to him by Liu Cong," Zhou Yu retorted sharply. "By all means, if you think you can defeat Cao Ren in Jiangling, best Man Chong in Dangyang, rout Yue Jin in Xiangyang, *and* hold Yiling, *and* liberate the counties, and *then* hold off the inevitable reprisals by Cao Cao on your own, well, then we will leave..."

"And you'd return Jiangxia...?" Mister Sun prompted.

"We took Jiangxia from Huang Zu before Cao Cao invaded the region," Zhou Yu replied casually. "We were forced to remove our military presence and reallocate it to Red Cliffs because of that invasion: Jiangxia was already ours when you fled there from the rout at Steep-slope. All that Veteran General Cheng Pu has done, Mister Sun, is ensure that there is no more lack of clarity on the matter."

Liu Bei, Mister Sun and Jian Yong looked to Kongming for some inspired retort: Kongming continued to fan himself slowly, and said nothing.

"...You think that I am unfair," Zhou Yu supposed. "This is war... and in war, one can only be sure of oneself, and even then, that is a luxury. You are probably very sincere and righteous, but militarily, you have done nothing but fail at every turn, and therefore, you are unfit to hold the land. If you were strong as well as just, like Lord Sun, then of course I would give more credence to the idea... but you are a weak partner, and I cannot trust a weak partner with key strategic locations. Even if you were my friends, I would not trust you with such responsibility."

Liu Bei fumed silently, but did not respond: instead, he lowered his gaze.

"By all means, if you can take the counties without a fight... go, take them!" Zhou Yu chuckled with what seemed to be condescension. "But now, I would like to discuss the matter I invited you here for. I wonder, perhaps your marvellous general Guan Yu can do Wu a service, as he has done in the past for you and for Cao Cao."

Liu Bei raised his angry gaze and stared at the pleasantly smiling Zhou Yu.

"If I could borrow Guan Yu's might... he could sail down the River Han to Xiangyang and attack there: a pincer would not only cut supplies from the north, it would surely terrify Cao Ren into an early retreat," Zhou Yu said warmly. "The town is guarded, as I said, by Yue Jin, with support from General Wen Ping, and who knows what advisory assistance... but Guan Yunchang is a champion, and with his record for crossing hostile territory and besting the likes of Yuan Shao's fearsome general Yan Liang, he is probably the only man for the job."

"That's a dangerous mission, but I am sure Yunchang would jump at the chance for such an adventure," Liu Bei replied with as agreeable a tone as he could muster.

"My thanks," Zhou Yu said with apparent sincerity. "I will, of course, give him troops and a second to support him... because I believe that if we find the right ways to work together... we can genuinely achieve great things."

"Very well then," Liu Bei agreed reluctantly.

"Excellent!" Zhou Yu proclaimed. "Now, you must all be tired from such a long journey... please, go and get some rest and refreshments: our home is your home."
Liu Bei bowed respectfully, and gestured to his party that they should leave. Kongming cast Lu Su an icy gaze before he paid the expected respects and left the command tent.

"...I have never been so humiliated in my entire life," Liu Bei said with anger and frustration as his contingent left Zhou Yu's camp and started the journey to their own temporary camp to the south, joined once again by Guan Yu, Zhang Fei and Zhao Yun.
"Take heart," Kongming said kindly. "He's enjoying a moment of power... I wonder if he is so bad a person, but that the pressures of his position have made him our reluctant rival."
"I don't care if he gives money to the poor every day," Liu Bei retorted. "He spoke to me as though I were a child! He patronised me, ridiculed my defeats, and rubbed Guan Yu's forced subjugation to Cao Cao in my face!"
"There is some humiliation that a man can and must bear, but this, Kongming, is too much to ask, surely," Mister Sun scolded. "He asks to borrow Guan Yunchang as one asks to borrow a cup, and-"
"We are permitted to take the four counties," Kongming interrupted. "And as for his other comments... I hazard he will regret those badly chosen words. We will not be militarily disadvantaged forever... as I said, take heart."
"So will I be carrying out this 'labour'...?" Guan Yu asked calmly.
"...Yes, I think so," Kongming replied. "Take Ma Liang, Mi Fang, Shi Ren, Liao Hua and Zhao Lei with you... that should be enough to do the job. Obviously, be wary... since it is the formidable Yue Jin that guards Xiangyang. Just harass the city... if Yue Jin is forced to retreat, then Cao Ren will also retreat, and Jiangling..."
"...Will fall into the hands of Zhou Yu," Jian Yong interrupted. "Don't rush, Yunchang... don't rush...!"
"Xianhe has a point," Liu Bei supposed. "...Kongming, if Yunchang succeeds, then we lose the four counties..."
"I know," Kongming replied with a wry smile. "That's his plan... but we don't have to stick to it. Yunchang should do as good a job as he can... we'll do our job, but I suspect that Cao Ren is not to be so easily moved. Even with Yunchang's victory at Xiangyang... Zhou 'Gongjin' has a very long stay here ahead of him."

The next day, as preparations were being made by Liu Bei's forces to make their five separate manoeuvres, Lu Su paid a not entirely unexpected visit to Kongming's 'office'.
"I saw that look yesterday," Lu Su said as he walked into the tent, where Kongming was sat with Ma Liang, Ma Su and Yi Ji.
"...Ah, Zijing," Kongming hailed. "...Did you want to speak privately...?"
"Nothing I have to say is private," Lu Su retorted. "Kongming, you consider us to be faithless, am I right...? ...I suppose you all do."

"You've stolen Jiangxia from Liu Qi, you now move to steal the rest of Jing from him as well," Yi Ji suggested. "A fine deal indeed, Sun Quan and Cao Cao sharing the province, while its true protectors must suffer condescending statements like 'Our home is your home'. A real man would be ashamed of himself."

"...If Cao Cao had stayed where he was, and there had been no great move south, would there be a Jiangxia for Liu Qi...?" Lu Su proclaimed pointedly. "No, there would not... as Gongjin has said, it was taken, it was ours!"

"...Ah, I see," Kongming chuckled. "And if Cao Cao had not marched south, I suppose that Liu Cong would have ceded Jing to Sun Quan instead, as 'reparation' for the 'great crime'."

"There is that likelihood, yes," Lu Su replied.

"Aha! ...Not so," Kongming retorted. "Liu Cong feared Cao Cao because Cao Cao represents the imperial court... itself a Liu family faction, with Emperor Xian being a Liu... he was ceding not to Cao Cao, but to the *Emperor*, as Guan Yu did when he 'served Cao Cao'. But Liu Cong would not have surrendered to your lord... why, he sent Liu Qi to reinforce Jiangxia, and take it back. And he would have, if not for Cao Cao's interference... for Lord Liu could have travelled south and helped him retake it, and then Jiangxia, at least, would be Liu Qi's, I think, if not the whole province in the end."

"...Supposition!" Lu Su challenged angrily.

"Is it any more 'supposition' than your ludicrous claim that Jing would surrender to Sun Quan...?" Yi Ji chortled. "Go away, you insufferable man: it is bad enough that we must kneel to your lord, than we have to listen to your bleating as well."

"*Please*, Boji, we should be courteous to Mister Lu," Kongming suggested sarcastically as Lu Su seethed silently. "...But I do agree, however, that all things which are events that did not transpire are open to supposition, since they are dreams of another reality. The *truth*, however, is *this*: Jiangxia was abandoned for fear of the Huangs, who ruled that prefecture, not for fear of Cao Cao, since Liu Biao still lived then, and had no intention of surrendering anything to your master. It is only now your master's domain through subterfuge: you exploited the weakness of Liu Qi's grip. I wonder... once this obvious ruse of contention ends, does Sun Quan intend to send Cao Cao tribute, to thank him for his assistance...?"

"**You...!**" Lu Su shouted angrily, pointing at Kongming.

"As I already said: go away, little man," Yi Ji growled. "We have things to do."

"...**Aiee!**" Lu Su exclaimed miserably: he left the tent in a hurry.

"You shouldn't have done that, Boji," Ma Liang scolded. "He'll go and tell 'Gongjin' you were rude to him."

"I don't understand those two at all," Ma Su admitted. "They, and General Lü Meng now that I think of it, do not seem... well..."

"...Compatible...?" Kongming chuckled. "...And you'd be right. Lu Su was once a wealthy granary owner... not a courtier at all. When Zhou Yu came into his town, desperately seeking support, Lu Su sold one of his granaries to buy military supplies, and opened the other to Zhou Yu's troops to feed them. Zhou Yu now owes Lu Su a great deal... that is why those two unlikely men are a team.

"Lü Meng, now that's more complicated: I heard from my brother Jin that he was once derided as A'Meng, his infant name, for his attitude to learning... that has now changed, by all accounts. Lü Meng was once scolded by Sun Quan himself for his lack of interest in strategy and literature, his belief in strength over skill..."

"Like Zhang Yide," Ma Liang suggested.

"Yes," Kongming agreed with a sad sigh. "However, A'Meng rose to the challenge, and is now a Confucian scholar who is possibly a match in wit for any of us."

"So he is to be feared," Ma Liang said numbly.

"Definitely more than Lu Su... perhaps more than Zhou Yu in the long term," Kongming replied. "But that, friends, is the future: *now*, we have things to do..."

************

## 43

"I'm sure that Zhuge Liang was joking," Zhou Yu chuckled as Lu Su relayed the encounter that he had just endured. "I doubt he'd dare say such things and mean it. His lord is in a very weak position right now, and Zhuge Liang is no suicidal fool."

"…Yes, yes," Lu Su said with an awkward laugh that indicated embarrassment. "They're irritated at their predicament, no doubt."

"I feel for Kongming, actually," Zhou Yu admitted. "I really, genuinely respect him, Zijing… his intellect equals or perhaps exceeds mine, for he knows as much as me, yet is several years my junior. It is a real, genuine pity that he chose to serve Liu Bei, a real shame."

"…But 'war is war'…?" Lu Su supposed.

"Yes," Zhou Yu replied. "And to that end, I cannot afford to show pity, as he cannot show weakness. We both have difficult jobs: such is life."

"So what will happen now…?" Lu Su asked.

"The situation in Hefei is not ideal, but could be worse," Zhou Yu said wearily. "I spoke to Zhang Zhao and Zhang Hong before I left Chaisang, and as my lord's seconds on that mission, their job is to contain his newfound valour, and prevent him making critical errors of judgement. Zhang Hong is attempting to take nearby Jiujiang, since that divides Cao Cao's forces even further… but we must still be cautious. Cao Cao still has enough men to outnumber both of us simultaneously, even after Red Cliffs."

"We must act quickly, then," Lu Su supposed thoughtfully.

"Yes," Zhou Yu replied. "This siege must end, and end quickly."


Two eventful days later, Kongming and Ma Liang clasped hands as they prepared to depart on their separate missions for Liu Bei and Sun Quan's joint attack on Cao Cao's forces: Ma Liang would join Guan Yu in attacking Xiangyang, while Kongming would accompany Lord Liu in approaching the four counties.

"…Good luck, brother," Ma Liang said with unease.

"We neither of us need luck," Kongming insisted as he drew back and bowed slightly in respect of his sworn brother. "Guan Yunchang will succeed in his mission, especially with your help, while my task is as easy as taking something out of a sack. And then, brother Jichang, we will show Zhou Yu and Lu Su how to play war properly."

"Well then… farewell, for now," Ma Liang said quietly.

With that, he turned and made his way toward the ship that would now sail back to Xiakou. From there, he would journey northward on the River Han to Xiangyang City, a place that was once the home of banter and debate for both men, and the residence of the late Liu Biao, but was now an enemy stronghold that they would have to attack.

"…I wish you all the luck in the world," Kongming said with emotion as Ma Liang vanished from sight. "I wish it for us both, Jichang, for in truth, we sorely need it."

Kongming joined Liu Bei for the discussions on the march on the four counties that they would be taking control of: Wuling – the capital of which was west and south of Jiangling, near the River Yuan; Changsha, which was more or less directly east of Wuling, south of Dong Ting Lake and Sun Quan's naval training facility of Ba Qiu; Lingling, which lay far to the south, halfway between Wuling and the free region of Cangwu, where Liu Bei's friend Wu Ju governed independently; and Guiyang, which lay to the southeast of Lingling.

"...I hate southern Jing," Zhang Fei complained bitterly as he studied the map of the region. "Everywhere is so far apart... this is going to take *months*, Elder Brother... bloody *months*."

"Alas, yes," Liu Bei sighed. "Our meagre forces will do nothing to impress the independent governors of these regions either. We must call on the young governor, and insist he joins us on this campaign."

"...That'll kill him," Xiang Lang suggested. "I advise against it."

"What does he need to do...?" Jian Yong scoffed. "This isn't a military expedition: it's a righteous request that these minor warlords stand down and return their counties to Liu Qi. Liu Biao allowed them to govern themselves in order to reduce his responsibility: Cao allowed it to continue because he doesn't need the hassle. But now, the time for niceties is over."

"...Do you want to maybe write that down in a letter, and we'll shoot copies over the walls of the cities...?" Xiang Lang retorted. "Xianhe, we cannot afford to be belligerent! ...And we can't put Liu Qi's life at risk either! I confess that he is a poor governor-to-be, and that I have little faith in him, but regardless of that, I won't put his life at risk!"

"...These debates are quite pointless," Liu Bei chuckled to Kongming wearily.

"I agree with Mister Xiang that the strain may harm his health," Kongming admitted, "but I also agree with you that we really cannot do this without him. ...I suggest we halt, and ponder our options. Zhou Yu is in no position to take these counties... I wonder, in fact, if we might be wise to be cautious, and find out a little more about the situation on the northeast front."

"Hefei and Jiujiang...?" Jian Yong supposed.

"If I were Cao Cao," Kongming said, "I would not wish to be attacked on two fronts like this... it would mean certain defeat."

"...That's the whole essence of the tripod theorem," Liu Bei recalled. "Only Sun Quan and Zhou Yu are arrogant enough to think they can do it on their own."

"They can't," Kongming scoffed. "Zhou Yu tried to freeze us out, yet at the same time he knows he needs us... the same way that we'll need them."

"...Why did he single out Yunchang for the naval attack...?" Zhang Fei asked.

"Easy enough to answer," Kongming chuckled as he started to fan himself casually.

"... ... ...He wonders if he might induce him to join Wu...!" Mister Sun realised.

"Ridiculous!" Liu Bei exclaimed.

"Yes, but you can't blame 'Gongjin' for trying," Kongming snickered. "It won't work… but Zhou Yu has, apparently, assigned Su Fei, a former Jing general that served under Jiangxia prefect Huang Zu, to assist in the attack on Xiangyang."

"…Su Fei was a friend of Gan Ning, also a defector to Wu," Jian Yong recalled.

"Yes," Kongming confirmed. "He is a man chosen for his skill in naval warfare, and also his decision to 'turn to a wiser lord': sneaky, but pointless."

"…Zhou Yu, the bastard," Zhang Fei growled. "…Trying to break up our family, to serve his river-rat master…!"

"He'll fail, so think no more of it," Kongming insisted. "As I said, it's the northeast front we should be concerned with. Sun Quan's forces there are thin, but hoping to capitalise on the equally poor numbers of soldiers in the region. …Or rather, *supposedly* poor. Cao Cao's no idiot. Expect to hear of Sun Quan's retreat within a few months, or maybe even a few weeks from now."

"But then… won't everything Cao has be directed on Jiangling…?" Liu Bei said with some discontent.

"I expect so," Kongming replied casually. "And then… well, poor Gongjin will have quite a dilemma, won't he…? …While we, on the other hand, will then have a stronger bargaining position, since we will be sorely needed, my lord."

"…So what should we do…?" Mister Sun asked as Liu Bei started to slip into deep thought about Kongming's proclamation.

"Hold here, for now: consider returning to Jiangxia, as Zhou Yu said originally," Kongming suggested. "Let's see what happens in Hefei and Jiujiang… and then we can act when we know the final outcome."

"But we've already told him that we'd take the counties!" Zhang Fei protested angrily. "…We'll look weak!"

"Is that such a bad idea…?" Kongming said with a smile.

The smiles of the majority concurred that it was not.

Lu Su entered the command tent at Jiangling a few days later, and found Chief Commander Zhou Yu studying a map.

"Liu Bei is holding his position," Zhou Yu said wistfully: he had his back to his benefactor, and did nothing to change that. "They're even considering withdrawing to Jiangxia."

"…Why…?" Lu Su asked curiously.

"They want to fetch Liu Qi, they say," Zhou Yu scoffed.

"But Guan Yu will still take part in the raid on Xiangyang…?" Lu Su prompted.

"Yes," Zhou Yu confirmed coldly. "As an officer of Liu Bei… yes."

"…Ah," Lu Su murmured.

"Why, Lu Zijing, does this faithless sandal weaver command such loyalty…?" Zhou Yu asked desperately as he turned to face Lu Su at last. "Why do such wise, courageous men follow such a whining, treacherous old owl…?"

"...There are some that may say that we are fools for serving Lord Sun," Lu Su countered. "Opinions, Gongjin, are opinions: theirs are high with respect to Liu Bei, and remember that Guan travelled across treacherous terrain to flee Cao Cao and return to Liu Bei, forsaking all manner of gifts bestowed on him. If Cao Cao could not buy the man with titles from the Emperor, what is there to say...?"

"...*Sometimes*, you are wise," Zhou Yu chuckled as he turned to look at his map of Jing Province once again.

"...Something else concerns you," Lu Su supposed.

"...And *sometimes*, you are insightful, too," Zhou Yu replied with a mournful, weary laugh. "I have had word that Cao Cao has significant forces near the city of An Feng."

"...*An Feng*...?" Lu Su fretted. "That... that could seriously threaten our lord...!"

"Let us hope not," Zhou Yu replied uneasily.


*************

## 44

As soon as Guan Yu's forces reached Xiakou, they then turned and sailed northwest on the River Han, headed for Xiangyang.

"We could have saved valuable time and effort if he'd just written my lord a letter and told us what he wanted us to do," Guan Yu complained to his subordinates Ma Liang, Liao Hua and Zhao Lei, and his co-commander, Su Fei.

"Chief Commander Zhou had his reasons for summoning Lord Liu in person," Su Fei suggested. "You should not doubt his genius."

"...I don't doubt that he's a *dishonest sort*," Guan Yu scoffed. "Anyhow... we are going up against Yue Jin and Wen Ping... I fear neither of them."

"We should be cautious," Ma Liang insisted. "We're going to be deep into enemy territory, Commander Guan."

"A short time ago, Xiangyang was your home, Ma Liang," Guan Yu chortled. "Now you call it 'enemy territory'...? ...Many may gladly turn to us."

"Anyone that wanted to join the cause or escape Cao Cao fled with Lord Liu on that day," Ma Liang retorted. "Anyone left... will do as they're told. And Cao Cao will have repopulated the city with the families of his soldiers. Be mindful of that."

"I'll be mindful of whatever I choose to be mindful of," Guan Yu scoffed. "These dishonest, unjust men of Cao Cao's will fall to my Green Dragon Sword."

"It was not so long ago that you *served* Cao Cao," Su Fei said bravely. "Truly, you are unique in your opportunity to serve every great lord in the land."

"...Perhaps Green Dragon needs a taste of blood *now*," Guan Yu replied with seething anger.

"I only suggest that you consider, as I have, the idea of...!" Su Fei protested.

"I'll serve no scruffy-bearded river pirate like Sun Quan," Guan Yu insisted. "If you are content with it, then fine... but keep your suggestions to yourself. I'll serve my lord Liu Bei, and the cause of restoring the Han to their full lustre, until my dying day... and that, General Su, is final."

"*Commander* Su," Su Fei retorted. "We're equals on this mission."

"...You are not worthy to be called my 'equal', you inconstant wretch," Guan Yu said with menace. "Your only famous actions are convincing a lowlife pirate to betray your lord and his employer, and then betraying him yourself. Now ask yourself: 'Who has *Guan* betrayed'...?"

Su Fei said no more, but anger was burning within him as Guan Yu walked away fearlessly and returned to the cabins of the ship.

"...Guan Yunchang is overly principled, highly judgemental, and easily vexed, and not at all afraid to show it," Ma Liang said to the humiliated Su Fei. "I would do as I do: ingratiate yourself."

"... ... ...He'll die a miserable death," Su Fei growled furiously.

"That I don't doubt," Ma Liang sighed. "Won't we all...? ...But if we could just survive this mission, and lose our lives later, at a less urgent hour: that would be ideal, Commander Su."

Su Fei nodded silently but agreeably, and returned to the cabins.

"...Well played," Zhao Lei praised.

"Wouldn't it be nice if every situation could be resolved that way...?" Ma Liang chuckled sadly.

As the initial intention was a surprise strike, Guan Yu and Su Fei had their men disguise themselves as civilian sailors, and the generals and advisers clothed themselves as merchants. What few defences there were along the River Han were either quickly surprised and defeated, or bypassed altogether.

As soon as the stretch of the River Han that Xiangyang and Fan stood near to came into view, Guan Yu and Su Fei prepared for the siege.

"We'll disembark some forces here and continue on foot, and send some further downstream as river assault teams," Su Fei suggested.

"...Agreed, Co-commander Su," Guan Yu said reluctantly.

"Since you're an expert at land battles, and I a veteran of naval engagements," Su Fei continued, "you can lead the land contingent... I'll front the pincer attack from the river. This way, our success is guaranteed."

"...I concur," Guan Yu said numbly. "Very well, then: well, good... ... ...good luck, Co-commander Su. I hope that we shall soon meet for victory wine."

Su Fei bowed low to show deep, ingratiating respect for Guan Yu, as Ma Liang had suggested: Guan Yu repaid the gesture with a slight, yet acknowledging bow. With that, Su Fei jumped across to an adjacent ship, and started ordering the sailors on board to press ahead.

"...Prepare for ground assault," Guan Yu ordered emotionlessly.

"...Sir!" Zhao Lei replied obediently.

"You're not going to believe this," a captain told Xiangyang's commanding general, Yue Jin, "but it's true all the same: we've got Guan Yu attacking us!"

"Guan *Yu*...?" Yue Jin exclaimed disbelievingly. "Is this man a fool, or a god???"

"Their forces are small in number," the captain stressed.

"And ours???" Yue Jin countered angrily. "We need reinforcement... get despatches to Man Chong and Wen Ping, immediately! Xiangyang is a critical supply route to Jiangling! It must not even be besieged, never mind fall!"

"Yes sir," the captain replied: he turned and hurried from the room.

"...*Guan Yu*... what madness possesses you...?" Yue Jin wondered.

"**REPORT!**" a messenger hailed suddenly: Yue Jin shuddered.

"...What *now*...?" Yue Jin asked irritably. "Is Lü Bu risen from the dead and attacking the west gate...?"

"Uh... no," the messenger replied unintelligently. "A Wu general, Su Fei, is attacking Xiangyang from the water!"

"How did they even get this far into our territory...?" Yue Jin wondered. "I don't... ... ...never mind. Go, now, and tell the garrison captains to deploy archers to the north wall as well, if they have not had the initiative to do so already."

"Yes sir!" the messenger replied, before he too scurried away to follow instructions.

"...Guan Yu... you'll *die here*, you fool...!" Yue Jin seethed.

News of Guan Yu's successful infiltration rocked the defenders at Jiangling, and gave hope to the besiegers.

"...Truly a god among men," Zhou Yu said with respect as a messenger delivered the report of Guan's siege, many days after it had started.
"This is marvellous news," Lu Su said excitedly. "We will surely win, with so many attack fronts! Liu Bei's forces have taken Linju already!"
"It seems that Heaven may be on our side," Zhou Yu said cautiously. "However, it pays to avoid complacency. We shall press Cao Ren, and hope for the best."

However, Cao Ren's determination was far from dented. Rather, it made him focus more diligently on defence, and that unbreakable resolve started to take its toll of the besiegers. Day after day, Zhou Yu held long and tiring sessions with his generals to discuss how best to weaken Cao Ren, and all the while, news poured in on the status of all of the battle fronts: not all of that news was good.

"...**Re... REPORT!**" a filthy, tired messenger hailed as he entered the command tent at daybreak. "**Cha... Zhang Zhao... has... has failed to take Jujiang, and has withdrawn!**"
"What, *already*...?" the tired Zhou Yu groaned. "...We *needed* Jujiang... ... ...okay, okay. Anything else to report from that region...?"
"**No... no more news,**" the messenger continued wearily. "**No... further news known at this time... c-commander.**"
"Okay... get some rest," Zhou Yu replied kindly.
"Thank you, commander," the messenger said quietly.
"**REPORT!**" another messenger shouted, before the first had even left the tent.
"D'aaagh... **what NOW???**" Zhou Yu exclaimed.
"Gongjin, please remain calm," Lu Su murmured.
"**Gan Ning and Xi Su are besieged at Yiling by six thousand cavalry sent covertly by Cao Ren to rescue the city!**" the messenger reported.
"**How???**" Zhou Yu screamed desperately.
"...That explains the disturbance at the east gate during the night," General Lü Meng said thoughtfully.
"It was a distraction, to allow these men out of the *west* gate," another man in robes concurred: this man was very young in appearance, fresh-faced, and drew expressions of disdain from the older generals for daring to speak.
"Quite so, Lu Boyan," Lü Meng praised in reply to Lu Xun, an administrative colonel in the army whose twenty-six years of age earned him little respect from the older warriors that had seen warfare. "You suspected as much."
"I agree with you both," Zhou Yu said sadly. "I overlooked it... I was tired, but that is no excuse... it was obvious, that was foolish."
"General Gan Ning only has a thousand men," Veteran General Cheng Pu – who had now come from Jiangxia to aid Zhou Yu – noted worriedly.

"And three hundred of those are Xi Su's men," General Han Dang noted.

"...He might perish," General Ling Tong noted with a smile.

"This isn't the time for personal feuds!" General Huang Gai admonished.

"We will have to rescue him," Lu Su supposed.

"No!" Ling Tong exclaimed. "...Forgive me, but feuds aside, that would be foolish: to break the siege of Yiling, we would need to send everything we have there, and Cao Ren has enough men left here to destroy us if we divide our forces to rescue one scabby little pirate!"

"I regret that I agree, for different reasons entirely than hating the man," Cheng Pu said sadly. "I agree that we cannot divide our forces... it is worth losing Yiling to gain Jiangling. We are better off using Cao Ren's reduced retinue to our advantage and taking Jiangling now."

"I feel the same way," Huang Gai admitted, to Ling Tong's delight.

"As do I," Han Dang said ruefully. "I admire Gan Ning's bravery, but would not risk a greater cause for him."

The other generals present – Sun Quan's cousin Sun Ben, the laconic Zhou Tai, and Pan Zhang – expressed their own reluctance to risk losing Jiangling for the sake of Gan Ning. Lu Xun said nothing, while Lü Meng shook his head slowly.

"Regrettable," Lü Meng said sadly.

"...You have an opinion, A'Meng...?" Lu Su teased.

"Zijing," Zhou Yu scolded, "this man is-"

"I know his talent," Lu Su insisted. "My apologies, please, Ziming, tell us your plan."

All eyes turned to Lü Meng.

"...We can turn this around, and with the greatest of ease," Lü Meng suggested. "I have a plan, but... it requires courage."

"The men here are made of courage," Cheng Pu proclaimed. "Speak."

"We can all go and rescue Gan Ning, leaving one general to hold the camp," Lü Meng suggested: the generals murmured uneasily. "General Ling Tong, would you be prepared to hold the camp for ten days, with aid from Lu Xun...?"

"Yes," Ling Tong replied, "but no more than that."

"Excellent!" Lü Meng said cheerfully. "Now that's settled-"

"Ziming," Lu Su said awkwardly, "I don't-"

"I will need three hundred men to cut logs," Lü Meng added.

"...Uh... fine...!" Zhou Yu said with a smile. "I might sound like a child saying this, but... I'm almost excited to see what you're up to."

＊＊＊＊＊＊＊＊＊＊＊＊

## 45

To the north, in Xiangyang, the siege continued, and Guan Yu's confidence of a total victory grew, despite the odds.

Guan Yu's forces numbered only a few thousand: so, too, did Yue Jin's. But Guan Yu was the attacker, and Xiangyang City's formidable stone walls – while not as sturdy as those of nearby Fan City – were not simply going to disappear. Along the top of the walls, archers pelted the besiegers with arrows, while Guan Yu's front force desperately tried to cross the dry moat around the city using their multi-purpose siege ladders. For those that got across with the siege ladders, the worst was yet to come: while they were no longer in danger from the sniping shots of archers, they were now the potential victims of rocks and boiling oil being thrown from the walls as they tried, defencelessly, to scale them.

"We can't afford to lose too many men!" Ma Liang stressed to his commander as another day of taunting and random strikes went into the afternoon.

"...Do you know of a lossless way to siege a city...?" Guan Yu retorted. "I, too, risk my life here... that is life! Death, for me, is like going home!"

"We'll *lose*," Ma Liang protested. "Death doesn't bother me either, but losing does. I could never face Lord Liu or Brother Kongming if I lost here."

"Commander Guan, we are losing too many men!" a captain reported desperately as he ran from the front line. "We must pull back and try again later!"

"They must not be allowed time to gather more rocks and arrows!" Guan Yu replied angrily. "Continue the assault!"

"...The moat is already lined with corpses," Zhao Lei lamented.

"The Great River runs red with the blood of Cao's men from the rout at Red Cliffs!" Guan Yu barked. "What part did we play in that, uh...? The role of *bait*, deceiver with a show of weakness! This is our chance to show our strength!"

"**GUAN YU! WILL YOU CHALLENGE ME...?**" a voice shouted from the top of the city walls: Guan Yu was too far away to hear it, but a captain soon reported it.

"...Yue Jin dares to think he can best me...?" Guan Yu scoffed.

"This is an opportunity to win without more significant losses," Ma Liang suggested. "We should stop, allow our men to recover, and have this duel."

"I agree," Mi Fang said sternly.

"I daren't ignore the challenge," Guan Yu chortled. "I am a warrior, a general, a god among men on the battlefield. To refuse to face Yue Jin is as a phoenix yielding to a chicken. ...Tell him I accept."

Mi Fang, Shi Ren and Zhao Lei exchanged weary glances.

"**Guan Yu...!**" Yue Jin barked as he rode back and forth along his front line an hour later, brandishing a spear. "**How have you been, general, since you departed the capital all those years ago...?**"

"...**Well,**" Guan Yu replied reluctantly. "**And you...?**"

**"You and your lord played your parts in the battle at Red Cliffs, where the Prime Minister and I might have lost our lives,"** Yue Jin replied angrily. **"Now you come here to seek my life again! Is it not insolent and ungrateful to attack your old benefactor? Where is the Confucian sense of right and wrong in that, Marquis of Shou Ting...?"**

**"Enough talk,"** Guan Yu retorted. **"You serve a traitor: therefore, you are also a traitor. Now die like one."**

Yue Jin screamed angrily, and charged at Guan Yu: the two made several attack passes, striking at each other with their pole-arms but neither gaining ground.

"This is ridiculous," Mi Fang scoffed. "Commander Guan is weary from the journey, while his opponent is well-fed and pampered. How can this end well...?"

"We should bang the gong and sound a retreat," Shi Ren added. "We can't afford for Commander Guan to come to harm. Lord Liu would have us executed if we allowed a favourite general to die here."

"...He's winning," Ma Liang noted.

"Impossible...!" Mi Fang exclaimed. "Has age not lessened his strength...?"

"Apparently not," Ma Liang said with a smile.

The forces of Liu Bei watched with satisfaction as Guan Yu pressed on Yue Jin, and the enemy general started to visibly tire. After another five passes, it was Yue Jin's forces that sounded the gong, and Yue Jin retreated, protected by a wall of shields and spears and a hail of arrows. Guan's own archers and infantry pressed the enemy, taking a few lives on the ground as Yue Jin fled to safety. As soon as Yue Jin was inside the city, the barrage of arrows intensified.

**"Coward!"** Guan Yu exclaimed as he backed away to avoid being shot. **"Come back here, and surrender your head!"**

The defences were too strong to attempt a charge on the open drawbridge: Guan's forces had to watch powerlessly as Yue Jin's infantry retreated, covered by the archers along the city wall.

"Their morale will be lowered by that humiliation," Ma Liang supposed as Guan Yu returned to his advisers and generals to receive praise for his exploits.

"A magnificent display of skill, Father," Guan Yu's eldest son, Ping, said gladly.

"I will take his head next time," Guan Yu growled. "...*Coward*."

"We'll give the soldiers some rest, and then we'll resume the siege," Ma Liang suggested calmly.

"...Agreed," Guan Yu grunted. "Even if it takes an eternity, I'll smash those walls and pull that wretch from them, kicking and screaming."


"...General," a senior captain hailed as a tired Yue Jin reached his quarters.

"No need for the sombre face," Yue Jin said with a smile. "All is going according to plan. Guan is at the heights of his arrogance, and General Wen is about to arrive with our naval force. We'll see how this self-proclaimed hero fares then...!"

Meanwhile, atop the walls of the city of Jiangling, General Xu Huang and Chief Clerk Chen Jiao watched the Wu camp with curiosity.

"Their camp has shown little or no signs of activity for two days now," Xu Huang noted thoughtfully. "The attacks are small and slight, the troop movements noticeably less intimidating... what do you think...?"

"They've all gone to protect Yiling," Chen Jiao supposed. "They've found out."

"We could strike their camp... defeat them in a stroke," Xu Huang said surely.

At that moment, Cao Ren joined them at the wall, and noted their optimisitic expressions with disdain.

"...I see no joyous occurrence," Cao Ren scolded.

"The entire enemy force has moved, by the looks of things," Xu Huang reported.

"Oh...?" Cao Ren said with worry. "That bodes ill for my rescue of Yiling... we need that route open for supplies and reinforcements from Yi Province. Can it be that they already know about the cavalry assault...?"

"We should strike their camp," Xu Huang urged. "We can take it, and destroy their supplies... what good will Yiling be to them then? They'll be caught between us and the Yi forces... it would be a rout."

"...A sound idea," Cao Ren decided. "...Yes, very good! ...I'll join you, and we'll both attack the camp at nightfall."


"How many weeks has it been now...?" Jian Yong asked Kongming as the two sat in Kongming's tent that same night, enjoying heated wine. "The siege, I mean."

Liu Bei's forces had barely been called upon, and so – despite a gradual transfer of forces into the region – the mood was calm, since there was little to do.

"...I don't even bother counting anymore, Xianhe," Kongming chuckled. "Not many, though, maybe three or four... five...?"

"How long do you think that Cao Ren will hold out for...?" Jian Yong asked flatly.

"...You really want to know...?" Kongming replied ominously.

"Seriously," Jian Yong said, "how long...?"

"...Based on what I know," Kongming replied as Jian Yong put his cup to his mouth, "I would say... perhaps six months to a year."

Jian Yong almost spat the wine from his mouth at this estimation.

"Are you serious???" Jian Yong exclaimed.

"Cao Ren has access to over a hundred thousand men," Kongming explained casually. "Zhou Yu makes poor use of us, though even if he did, our combined forces aren't even half that number. It doesn't matter how many farcical attempts we make to cut supply routes and suchlike: this is a matter of exhausting Cao Cao's patience more than it is his resources."

"But what of Yunchang and Jichang, and their expedition north...?" Jian Yong asked worriedly. "With numbers like those you speak of... you seem to think they're doomed to failure."

"Even with strategy, they would not fare well," Kongming admitted. "Guan will get them out, but that's all we can hope for, I'm afraid."

"…A *year*…?" Jian Yong exclaimed. "Six months to a *year*…?"

"Jiangling is very important," Kongming replied. "Wouldn't we hold onto it for as long as we could, especially if we had supplies and reinforcements coming from three of the four directions…? It's not a proper siege, really: a proper siege is like… well, it's like two men pushing at either side of an unstable wall. In the end, the man that pushes first – the attacker – has the advantage unless the defender can push back harder than he's being pushed. This, it's more like trying to patch holes in a leaking boat. The water just keeps coming… if you patch the holes, then you survive… but only just. If you can't…"

"…You drown," Jian Yong sighed miserably. "So even if we win, we–"

"Even if *they* win," Kongming said as he took a sip of wine. "Wu has only asked for infiltration assistance… the siege is entirely their own operation, and to their own cost, while we, the 'rejected'… well… wait and watch."

"You're smug about something," Jian Yong noted, provoking a smirk from Kongming. "What is it you think is going to happen…?"

"I don't know," Kongming insisted. "Not specifically… I don't even think I can say that Zhou Yu will definitely win here, sadly: it's all open to chance. But… yet, I think that we will come out of it all in a much stronger position, overall."

"…Do you think that Cao Ren will retake Yiling…?" Jian Yong asked plainly.

"No," Kongming said with certainty. "He is a staunch defender, yes, and a bold warrior, yes, and even, I think, somewhat of a hero of the age: but he's no strategist. He's cautious, he ponders things, but that isn't the same as knowing the pattern of changes, the seasons, the moods and minds of men: he is matching wits with not only Zhou Yu, but Lu Su and Lü Meng, and he raises his sword against not one or two generals, but many, veterans like Huang Gai and courageous new blood like Ling Tong. He'll win only by overwhelming numerical advantage if he is to win at all, and Yiling will return to him only by forcing Wu to retreat altogether."

"He could strike Wu's main camp," Jian Yong suggested. "Fools should have asked our help to defend it. Zhou Yu is arrogant beyond belief! Should we not send forces to…?"

"When Zhou Yu needs our help, he'll ask for it," Kongming replied. "I think you'll find the camp is well defended… this day is Wu's."

Xu Huang and Cao Ren launched their attack on Wu's camp in the dead of night: after sneaking toward the camp with bits in their mouths and coverings on the hooves of their horses, they struck at the gates of the wooden-fenced military base with sudden strength, only to find that the defender, Ling Tong, was ready for them.

As Xu Huang led the vanguard into the camp, he noticed that the way was relatively clear: the tents inside were lit with torches, but as the attackers roared in triumph to unnerve the defenders, no tell-tale shadows within the tents – of scrabbling, half-asleep soldiers hastily readying themselves for battle – could be seen, nor could the confused issuing of orders by surprised generals and captains.

"They've retreated altogether…?" Xu Huang wondered as Cao Ren rode to his side.

"Perhaps," Cao Ren agreed hopefully. "If that is the case, then-"

"**CHARGE…!**" Ling Tong cried: from within the unlit centre of the camp, and from around its unlit perimeter, the forces of Wu launched their assault on the larger but unprepared intruder force.

"*Aiee!*" Cao Ren exclaimed. "We've been deceived!"

"**Cao Ren!**" Ling Tong challenged. "**See Ling Tong here! You've come here to deliver your head to me…?**"

From within the tents, archers and infantry appeared: the force of less than two thousand trounced the attackers, felling many a man and forcing Cao Ren and Xu Huang to turn about and retreat. Ling Tong attempted to directly harass the leading enemy generals, but neither was interested in duelling while their lives and reputations as defenders were at stake.

"**We must return to Jiangling!**" Cao Ren screamed. "**What if they have struck the city while we were here, walking into this child's trap…?**"

Xu Huang said nothing in response.


"Will they return…?" Ling Tong wondered as Cao Ren's forces fled altogether.

"Unlikely," Lu Xun supposed. "They know now that even our lightly defended camp is no match for their full forces. Their morale will be at rock-bottom now… and the outcome of their futile strike on Yiling will break them altogether."

Ling Tong smiled at the notion.


＊＊＊＊＊＊＊＊＊＊＊＊

## 46

At Yiling, Zhou Yu's massive, nearly-thirty-thousand strong force routed Cao Ren's six thousand cavalry, killing half of them and putting the rest to flight. As an added bonus, Lü Meng's loggers had used those felled trees to build a blockade across the road the cavalry needed to use to return to Jiangling: they fled on foot, leaving Wu's forces with hundreds of horses and supply bags, which they retrieved with amusement and newfound confidence that victory was near.

"Ziming, you're a genius," Zhou Yu said with a cheerful laugh as the Wu forces travelled back to their camp near Jiangling.
"You flatter me," Lü Meng insisted.
"Not at all!" Zhou Yu insisted. "What need have we for the likes of that old owl Liu Bei and his band of misfits…? I should have sent *you* to Xiangyang… perhaps we'd have heard of a victory by now if I had, and that matters more than Yiling."
"I'm sure that General Su and General Guan can deal with the likes of Yue Jin," Lü Meng said encouragingly. "Cao's men are chaff, to our finely nurtured wheat. Even if you had sent Masters Zhang Liang, Jiang Ziya and Sun Tzu of olden days to Xiangyang, I would not expect a victory in such a short time."
"Well, a blockading siege is enough," Zhou Yu conceded. "So long as Cao Ren can get no support from that grovelling cretin Liu Zhang of Yi, nor from Yue Jin in Xiangyang… how can he hold out…?"
"There is Man Chong, a shrewd man whose base is Dangyang, halfway between Xiangyang City and Jiangling," Lü Meng noted with concern. "Someone must be sent to harry him, else he can pincer Guan Yu or bolster Cao Ren at his leisure. Dangyang is not the best place for large military confrontations… Liu Bei was defeated at Steep-slope, east of Man Chong's position… but Guan could inspire some rebel activity, I hope, in the area…"
"That's partly why I sent him," Zhou Yu admitted. "The man is respected by law-abiding citizens and lawless cutthroats alike: such a man would be an invaluable asset to us, gathering us land-based bandits in the same way that men like Gan Ning inspire pirates to join us. If only he'd see sense and join Lord Sun…!"
"His time in the Cao camp also earned him the respect and fear of the generals in Xuchang," Lü Meng noted further. "They would be reluctant to engage him with all their martial bravery since he is their friend and former ally."
"It is a pity that Zhang Liao and Xu Huang are not stationed in Xiangyang," Zhou Yu sighed. "Those two wouldn't fight with any heart, then: and so far as Zhang Liao goes… that would be a blessing from Heaven."
"Perhaps we should have Guan Yu siege Jiangling next," Lu Su suggested eagerly. "Perhaps they might surrender in fear of him, and yield the city."
"Not likely," Zhou Yu lamented. "Or wouldn't Xu Huang have joined Liu Bei by now…? Xu Huang may be disinclined to fight Guan… but he won't betray Cao Ren as a matter of honour… so Guan will be little use here in Jiangling."

"Liu Bei's men, however, might be of general use," Lü Meng suggested bravely.

"I am reluctant to use them," Zhou Yu admitted. "They are small in number, but using them against Jing... while it might inspire some defections... those defections would be to the side of Liu Bei, and the objective here is to seize Nan Prefecture for our Lord Sun, not that mat-weaving pretender."

"All the same," Lü Meng challenged, "this is an alliance... we were happy to abandon Gan Ning, after you yourself just said that he inspires pirates to join us... that point you forgot only days ago is the reason I insisted on rescuing him."

Zhou Yu was silent.

"Great minds do not always think alike," Lü Meng continued, "else why would great rulers have advisers by the bushel...? We think differently, but work toward the same ambition... when you thought only of maintaining the siege of Jiangling, I thought of securing Yiling to prevent Cao Ren getting help from Yi, and saving Gan Ning to keep the respect of the pirate forces we command. Would losing good men and reopening an enemy supply route maintain the siege at Jiangling...? ...No, quite the opposite, in fact. But it doesn't mean you were wrong: it means you were focussed on certain critical matters – the defeat of Cao Ren and Xu Huang, the siege at Xiangyang, and controlling Liu Bei – while I took other matters off your busy hands to help you. That's what I'm here for."

"...And to think that six years ago, you were an idiot," Zhou Yu joked as he smirked at the words of Lü Meng and took them to heart.

"I'm a slightly wiser idiot, that's all," Lü Meng replied with a vague smile.

"So with Yiling secured, and Xiangyang blockaded," Lu Su declared, "we can now siege Jiangling freely... while our lord seizes Hefei on the eastern front. Victory may be just a sunrise away!"

"...We'll see," Lü Meng said before Zhou Yu could reply. Zhou Yu added nothing to that, since it was his own thought anyway.

The situation in Xiangyang was going relatively well. Guan Yu had, as Zhou Yu anticipated, inspired uprisings amongst the Jing people against their northern occupiers, and groups of bandits – whose respect of Guan Yu's strength served as their drive – attacked small military encampments belonging to Cao across the entire region from Xiangyang to Dangyang. Guan Yu himself was now camped with some degree of steadfastness near the city of Xiangyang, making regular raids on Yue Jin's weakened position without incurring much of a response.

"Something isn't right here," Ma Liang said to Mi Fang one day as they inspected the camp together. "We've intercepted messengers trying to get to and from Dangyang... the messages are coded, and I suspect Man Chong has a plan. Further to that, we seem to be getting no more word from resistance groups in Dangyang, so their messengers must be being intercepted by the enemy. We need to advise Commander Guan against trickery."

"*Commander Guan* is too *arrogant* to listen to *either of us*," Mi Fang scoffed. "He listens to Zhao Lei, and occasionally to Liao Hua, because they're warriors… 'Real men'… that's it. He has more respect for Su Fei and Yue Jin than he does his own officials. When my brother and I entered Lord Liu's service… little did I ever guess it would be to work with such a man as Guan Yu."

"The sad thing is, he's not a bad person at all," Ma Liang said regrettably.

"No, but he's holier-than-thou," Mi Fang sneered. "All men are faulted… not one man alive is without some mark on his soul, however slight. Yet Guan Yu acts as though he is heaven-sent, faultless, and that he can judge others on even the tiniest mistake! And yet while he is scathing and intolerant to all others, for everything dishonourable he does, he fantasises some honourable reason why he strayed unwillingly from the light! He even has an excuse for yielding to Cao Cao!"

"Don't get angry," Ma Liang pleaded. "Remember, he's a vassal of Lord Liu, same as us… don't lose sight of serving Lord Liu just because Yunchang is intolerant."

"…You're right, and I know you're right," Mi Fang admitted. "But my sister is married to the lord! I, along with my brother, financed Lord Liu when he was starting his campaign! Does that not entitle me, Ma Jichang, to at least being treated with some *respect*…?"

"Of course not!" Ma Liang joked. "Guan Yunchang respects Lord Liu, Zhang Fei, Zilong, Chen Dao, Xu Huang, Zhang Liao… that's it, I think. But there's nothing we can do about that… we have to help him. Where is he…?"

"Playing chess with his son Ping, I think," Mi Fang scoffed.

"I'm going to try and talk to him," Ma Liang declared.

"Good luck," Mi Fang said without a shred of optimism.


Guan Yu dismissed Ma Liang's concerns, as Mi Fang had predicted: within a day, reports started to come in, panic started to spread, and the outcome was inevitable.

"**REPORT!**" a messenger cried desperately as he arrived at Guan Yu's command tent, where Guan Yu was sat in a hastily assembled council with his advisers and generals. "**Enemy general Wen Ping has launched a naval attack on Commander Su Fei with superior numbers, and Commander Su Fei has been forced to retreat eastward, pursued by General Wen!**"

"**What???**" Guan Ping exclaimed: Guan Yu was silently fuming.

"**Reinforcement from Counsellor Man Chong in Dangyang has marched double-time with a force of five thousand and arrived at Mount Jing!**" the messenger continued. "**All civilian and military resistance in Dangyang has been brought under control! General Wen has despatched reinforcement forces on the ground to assist General Yue Jin! These forces, numbering three thousand, will arrive in…!**"

"**ENOUGH!**" Guan Yu shouted angrily as he leapt to his feet: there was not even a murmur from his associates. The messenger quietly withdrew without being instructed to, which alerted Ma Liang.

"My lord," Ma Liang hailed, "we should seek further…!"

"…I said '*enough*'," Guan Yu retorted weakly as he turned to his right as stared at his Green Dragon pole sword.

"But...!" Ma Liang protested: a stern stare from Guan Ping silenced him.

"...Commander Guan," Mi Fang protested, "we cannot win now..."

"I know that," Guan Yu replied numbly. "If Su Fei had held his ground, kept them busy, then maybe... but now... Wen Ping pursues him, and we will soon be overwhelmed, caught in a pincer, with no hope of reinforcement... we cannot hold here now."

"We must go, now, before Man Chong's pincer force arrives," Shi Ren fretted.

"...This mission was doomed from the start," Mi Fang said quietly.

As the meeting broke up, Ma Liang wandered alone around the camp, looking for the messenger that had brought the terrible news.

"He brought news from both fronts," Ma Liang noted sombrely as he searched, despite there being nobody to hear him. "Would there not be *two* messengers to bring news from north and south...?"

Ma Liang suspected a trick: he hurried to Guan Yu once again, and once again, his advice was not even heard. Despondent, Ma Liang retreated to gather his own belongings, and prepare for an inevitable defeat.

Guan Yu ordered the retreat, but as the army sped toward the northeast to their ships, Yue Jin charged out of Xiangyang, dealing Guan Yu's unprepared and demoralised forces a hefty blow. Wen Ping followed with an attack from the water: Guan Yu's remaining forces limped away, humiliated and utterly routed.

"**Magnificent!**" Yue Jin said as he watched Wen Ping's forces return from a short, violent pursuit of Guan Yu's retreating forces.

"We didn't even need the approaching reinforcements from Man Chong!" Yue Jin's senior captain noted.

"...What reinforcements...?" Yue Jin replied with a smirk: the two men enjoyed a laugh at Guan Yu's expense as the general fled, the victim of false information.

"**Co-commander Guan!**" Su Fei hailed as the defeated forces of Guan Yu finally caught up to his own routed fleet on the River Han.

"**Why did you flee???**" Guan Yu admonished.

"**What did you want me to do, stay there after you got thrashed???**" Su Fei exclaimed. "**Why send a messenger to tell me you'd been routed if-**"

"What...?" Mi Fang exclaimed. "We sent no... ... ...*no*...!"

One and all realised the situation: one and all were suddenly very ashamed.

"...We...? ... ... ...**D'AAAAGH!**" Guan Yu screamed with rage as he realised that both he and Su Fei had been the victim of a simple 'false messenger' ruse.

"...*Forgive me*, Kongming," Ma Liang said quietly.

＊＊＊＊＊＊＊＊＊＊＊

## 47

Yue Jin and Wen Ping decided to give the Liu-Sun alliance no more opportunities: Wen Ping pursued Guan Yu and Su Fei along the length of the River Han, dealing two further naval defeats, and taking control of the route into Xiangyang. Yue Jin, meanwhile, stormed southward, eliminating the smaller pockets of infiltrators that Guan Yu had sent that way in order to assist Man Chong and restore the supply route.

Finally, Guan Yu and Su Fei reached Xiakou, where a stubborn defence from the larger Wu naval presence eventually repelled Wen Ping. However, the mission had been a total failure, and it would not be the only thing to go wrong.

"...Well," Zhou Yu declared as he met with his generals in his command tent a few days later, "they say that war is a constantly changing thing, like nature... we have lost – quite significantly, in fact – at Xiangyang... but we have won at Yiling, and dealt a blow to Cao Ren that will make him think again about blindly charging at Yiling or at us. We've shown him that *we* have thinkers... a pity Guan Yu had none."

"What now, though...?" Huang Gai protested. "It is all well and good throwing words at Guan Yu... with Xiangyang restored, Linju and Xinyang lost, and the River Han fortified against repeat attacks, does that not mean that Cao Ren has unlimited supplies from the capital now...?"

The murmurs of worried agreement angered Zhou Yu.

"Veteran General," Zhou Yu scolded, "do not, for the sake of morale, say such things! There is no such thing as 'unlimited supplies'! Food and wood has to be grown, and men born and raised! Cao Cao still has the eastern front to occupy his mind, and our lord's actions in Hefei are so far brave and commendable! If we are courageous, tenacious, and continue to thwart the efforts of the enemy, then we can defeat them! *You*, Veteran General, were the one that ignited the flames that destroyed the 'unbeatable' fleet at Red Cliffs not a few months ago, and yet now you speak as though the situation is desperate...?"

Zhou Yu's words were met with uncomfortable silence. The recent reports from Hefei had not been good as Zhou Yu suggested, with Sun Quan's 'brave and commendable' actions almost getting him killed on more than one occasion, due to his insistence on leading charges against the enemy personally. Sun Quan's adviser Zhang Hong was even contemplating a retreat, since enemy reinforcements were on the way: the siege at Hefei could fall apart at any time.

Guan Yu, meanwhile, had returned to Liu Bei's camp, broken and bitter.

"...Take heart, General," Kongming said as Liu Bei and Zhang Fei gave up trying to ply him with consolatory wine. "War is like that... wins and losses are a matter of course. You fell for a ruse... I'm sure it was unavoidable."

"It was," Ma Liang said before Guan Yu could reply: the older general smiled feebly, grateful that Ma Liang had no intention of adding to his shame.

"...There: it is said, and it is so," Kongming declared, noting the expressions on the faces of not only Ma Liang and Guan Yu, but also Mi Fang, Shi Ren and Zhao Lei. "What we must do now is await the request for more help from Zhou Yu, and-"

"What nonsense is this...?" Guan Yu whined angrily. "I have just been routed by a childish trick! I am the laughing stock of Jing! Why would Zhou Yu want our help again, when I have failed so miserably...?"

"...It does have to be said," Liu Bei proposed thoughtfully, "that we have been made to look rather foolish... Master Zhuge, we may be ridiculed... Yunchang's reputation may be irreparably sullied by this. How do we defend ourselves if his performance in the naval battles is questioned...? What do we say...?"

"...We say," Kongming replied, "what is the truth of it: Guan Yunchang is a tiger, not a duck, and tigers fight best on the land, do they not...?"

Many faces contorted into irrepressible smiles.

"And Su Fei had a mind of his own, yes...?" Kongming continued. "Let Wu harangue us... they are not faultless in this. What fool sends such a small force on such a dangerous mission without ensuring they can receive reinforcement...? Where was your naval escort should things go wrong...? Wen Ping was able to chase you halfway down the Great River, unimpeded, and burn your supply depot... where were Wu, the 'Masters of the Great River'...? Easily answered: they did not appear until their capital was under threat, and only *then* was he repelled! *Some alliance*...! They owe you a supply depot, Yunchang... and an apology."

"Damn right!" Zhang Fei exclaimed. "You tell him!"

Guan Yu was shocked at Kongming's magnanimity: he gave a needless – though still slight – bow of respect, and said no more.

"Zhou Yu is in dire straits... he has retaken Yiling, yes, but the threat of another attack looms large, and he will always have a detachment force ready to aid them... that will not be on hand for the siege. So he has reduced numbers," Kongming explained. "He'll need more help on the ground... and he'll be aware that the Xiangyang siege was a flawed enterprise of his own invention, regardless of how much he tries to blame us. I expect word on the retreat from Hefei at any moment, but yet there is the small matter of the governor of the unstable region of Lujiang being ill... when Heaven enacts its will, we will rise from the pond and ascend to the sky. One man's failure is another man's victory, and in this case, not only Cao but Liu will benefit. Watch and wait..."

"You keep saying that," Jian Yong chuckled. "I hope you're right."

Liu Bei, who had been silent until now, finally spoke.

"...We will aid Wu in whatever capacity we can, but we will not be treated like vassals. We must be careful, as Kongming has said in recent days, not to be too eager to pander to them. I watch the current situation with interest... and with a quiet belief that we are soon destined, as Kongming said, to rise up from Wu's shadow and continue our journey to Xuchang."

One and all agreed.

"...But what if they ask us to take up another naval battle, my lord...?" Mister Sun wondered. "Whom do we send...?"
"...Elder Brother," Zhang Fei said to Liu Bei with mischief, "perhaps next time, *you* should go... since, if I remember, you said you were a fish."
"Control yourself, Yide," Liu Bei said with a smile.

"Sorry, Kongming," Ma Liang bleated as the two reached Kongming's tent after the meeting had concluded.
"For what...?" Kongming chortled. "You can shout all you want, and still not be heard by a man as stubborn as Guan Yunchang."
"The Mi brothers aren't too happy with his behaviour," Ma Liang said as they took seats inside the tent.
"Uh... Mi Fang doesn't like him," Kongming retorted with a laugh as he pointed at Ma Liang with his feather fan. "Be careful in your assumptions and statements, brother. Mi Zhu is the more reserved, and he understands Yunchang, as I do."
"I understand him too," Ma Liang insisted, "but... Mi Fang is right: sometimes his condescension goes too far."
"He admitted his folly today," Kongming noted. "By the way... that was very good of you, sparing his feelings."
"What was the point of humiliating him...?" Ma Liang replied. "A sulking tiger is of no use to us, is it...?"
Kongming grinned toothily, and started to fan himself slowly.
"Will Wu really ask our aid again...?" Ma Liang enquired.
"...Of course," Kongming replied. "When the Hefei siege is broken, all of Cao's power will descend on Jiangling... to add to what Yue Jin already throws at us. Zhou Yu will want a friend then, particularly a stupid one to stand in front of him and get hit by the arrows and rocks in his place."
"Which we wouldn't do, of course," Ma Liang supposed.
"No...!" Kongming chortled. "We're almost set to take the counties to the south... just a little longer now...!"

A week later, the siege of Hefei Fortress did end. Liu Fu and Jiang Xi, the defenders of Hefei, received word of reinforcements of 1000 men from Cao Cao, led by one General Zhang Xi. Faced with armies led by an unrelenting Sun Quan, intrigue was once again the only way to win. False communications between the 3 enemy generals gave Zhang Hong, Sun Quan's deputy and adviser, the impression that Zhang Xi led 40,000 men in reinforcement, and that the 1,000 seen by spotters were just a vanguard force. Terrified by this, Sun Quan retreated, burning his camps as he went. Not long after that, however, the governor of the region, Liu Fu, died of an illness: this would have consequences that were almost universally unexpected.

Many days later, within the Liu camp, the planning was still going on despite the recent announcement of the loss at Hefei. Liu Qi retired early from fatigue, but the discussions continued regardless: and near the end of that day, a messenger came from Yang Province – located to the northeast of the land – with some news that would one day turn the tide of Liu Bei's fortunes.

**"REPORT! Chen Lan and Mei Qian of Lujiang have rebelled against Cao Cao!"** the messenger said. **"They hold the city with a force exceeding ten thousand... no support has been offered by Wu! Cao Cao is despatching forces led by Zhang Liao and Zang Ba to defeat the rebel leaders in the city!"**

Liu Bei turned to his assembled advisors and generals with excitement.

"My thanks," Kongming said to the messenger. "Go and rest for a while now, and then go back to Lujiang, and keep us informed."

The messenger retreated from the court tent and tried to find somewhere to get some refreshment and rest.

"So the men of Lujiang have rebelled...!" Liu Bei exclaimed joyously.

"...So what...?" Zhang Fei grunted cynically. "Who're these fellows, anyway...?"

"Vassals of the recently deceased prefect of Lujiang, Liu Fu: it's a county city south of Cao Cao's near-impregnable Hefei Castle, which is far to the northeast of here," Kongming answered wearily. "Liu Fu was a great man, very benevolent, and he did a lot to develop the region... which was on the verge of collapse after Sun Ce had the previous governor murdered. Cao Cao sent Liu Fu there to tame the angry people... he turned Lujiang into a centre of health, education and agriculture, and he was greatly loved for it. Chen Lan and Mei Qian were the leaders of a bandit uprising... they then became loyal vassals, as I said. Obviously, they weren't too impressed with Cao Cao's ideas for the region now that Liu Fu is dead."

"I'm surprised at you, Yide, for not keeping up with these things," Liu Bei scolded.

"...Why should I care who is prefect of Lujiang???" Zhang Fei barked.

"This is significant, because this is a blow to Cao Cao's rule in the north, Yide, and we will benefit immensely," Kongming explained. "This man has not asked or received any help from Sun Quan! That means that they have not forgotten Sun Ce killing their old master... they want no alliance with Sun Quan, but *perhaps*...!"

"I'm not as clever as you, 'Water'," Zhang Fei said snidely, "so I still don't get it. Why should we get so excited, since Lujiang is way off to the northeast, and we're squatting in tents, like unwanted nomads, here in Jiangxia...?"

"They have over ten-thousand men under their command, possibly as many as twenty-thousand," Liu Bei said irritably. "Yide, stop chiding Master Zhuge at every opportunity, and start being more knowledgeable about the world we live in! Now say these men decided to join forces with *us*...!"

"...We'd be as strong, if not *stronger*, than Sun Quan," Guan Yu mused.

"Why didn't you just say that in the first place...?" Zhang Fei complained.

"It is a pity we cannot help, but we are so far away... all we can hope is that the siege on Jiangling divides Cao's forces and aids the rebellion that way," Kongming sighed. "We shall just have to write to the rebels, telling them that they have our moral support, and then they will know where to go if the rebellion fails."

"Why would we want them here if they lost...?" Zhang Fei asked irritably.

"...Because they will still have soldiers to bring with them, hopefully," Jian Yong answered for his weary colleague. "Even if they don't bring many, it is another general or two for our forces, isn't it...?"

"Goodness knows, we need more of them," Zhang Fei retorted. "Finally, we're thinking about more fighting men, instead of more sleeve-flicking bookworms."

"...There is much to be said for the scholar-warrior, like myself, and Huo Jun, and Guan Yunchang," Wei Yan suggested.

"I agree," Guan Yu said sternly. "Yide, might is not always enough."

"Indeed, and it's a relevant point: we must hope that these men and their followers survive, and they can only do that by having a plan of some sort," Jian Yong said sadly. "Unfortunately, even if they have a plan, Cao Cao is a hero of the age for a reason... he will not have left such a key territory completely undefended."

"...Well, we can do nothing about that," Kongming said frankly. "So we should return to worrying about matters we *can* influence."

"Yes," Liu Bei agreed. "Let us ponder our options in Changsha..."

"...**RETREAT! ABANDON THE CITY!**" the rebel leader Chen Lan's assistant, Lei Xu, ordered desperately from atop the walls of Lujiang: the rebellion had faltered after a small number of days as the elite generals Zhang Liao and Zang Ba pressed the city with barely any impedance or restraint, and supplies ran low.

"We're going to run...?" one of Lei Xu's captains asked desperately. "Chen Lan and Mei Qian are dead... it's over!" Lei Xu retorted desperately.

"...Fleeing south is fine," one of Lei Xu's advisers countered, "but to *whom* can we go...? We won't survive alone!"

"We can't go to Sun Quan," another adviser mused. "But then again, he holds most of the land south of the Great River... and Sun Quan's Chief Commander, Zhou Yu, is a native of Lujiang and the hero of Red Cliffs..."

"Sun Ce's brother will never have our allegiance!" the first adviser protested. "No, we should go to Liu Qi of Jing!"

"...No... to Liu Xuande," Lei Xu sighed. "He is the benevolent hero of the age..."

The citizens of Lujiang screamed and cowered as the forces of Lei Xu and the forces of Zhang Liao and Zang Ba had one last pitched battle in and around the walled city, as the only remaining rebel leader tried to keep his forces alive, together, and loyal. Against all odds, Lei Xu not only survived the encounter, but his forces were almost completely intact. Within a month, they crossed into Jing Province, and joined Liu Bei: these forces effectively doubled the size of his army, a fact that pleased neither Cao Cao nor Sun Quan in the slightest.

************

From the moment that the news of the end of the siege at Hefei had reached the Wu camps in Nan Prefecture, the morale of Wu's vanguard was shaken, and the activity at the front line diminished. Day after day, Zhou Yu and his generals started at dawn and planned their next manoeuvres into the night, desperate to bring about a change of fortune.

"...I am at a loss, Zijing," Zhou Yu admitted as he sat with his former benefactor Lu Su in his personal tent one morning, drinking tea. "Months... *months...* and still, there is no sign of Cao Ren's defences cracking. ...And now, Yue Jin is behind our lines, harassing us from all directions. We have killed so many men, yet they still hold on... what to do...?"

"Well..." Lu Su began.

Zhou Yu pointed at Lu Su accusingly, and said, "No! Not... not Liu Bei. I don't want to hear about Liu Bei."

"...He has the men of Lujiang now," Lu Su protested. "Liu Bei's forces now equal our own... he does not even need Liu Qi anymore."

"You think I don't see that...?" Zhou Yu bleated. "But... we *cannot* ask his help!"

"We haven't a choice," Lu Su maintained. "Gongjin... if we made a fierce push on the city... our own men with their bolstered forces..."

"They're moving as though they intend to take the four counties!" Zhou Yu whined desperately. "After all we have expended here... will they just...!"

"I... I don't know what to..." Lu Su began.

"**REPORT!**" a messenger hailed from outside the tent.

"...Is there anywhere else left to fall...?" Zhou Yu asked sarcastically and desperately. "...Never mind... **COME IN AND REPORT!**"

The Wu messenger entered the tent and proclaimed, "**Jiang Gan of Jiujiang is here to see the Chief Commander!**"

"...*Who*...?" Lu Su wondered.

"...Thank you... where is he...?" Zhou Yu said to the messenger.

"**He is currently waiting in a visitor tent near the entrance to our camp!**" the messenger reported.

"...Fine," Zhuo Yu said ambiguously. "I'll speak to him privately in here. Go and tell him that, please."

"**Yes sir!**" the messenger replied as he turned and ran to fetch the visitor.

"...Who is Jiang Gan...?" Lu Su asked with bewilderment.

"An old acquaintance of mine," Zhou Yu replied, "though certainly no friend. He is handsome, charismatic, has a good way with words... but he is shallow, and he serves Cao Cao as an adviser, though perhaps he does not know that I am aware of that. Or perhaps he *does*...!"

"...And you're going to have a private chat with this man...?" Lu Su said with worry. "...Gongjin, you...!"

"He's no assassin," Zhou Yu chuckled. "More a persuader, I imagine. Cao Cao has sent this smooth-talking snake here to induce me to leave or defect."

"Why *now*...?" Lu Su wondered.

"The siege of Hefei is broken; Lujiang, my hometown, has fallen; the Xiangyang infiltration plot failed; Yiling barely holds; why *not* now...?" Zhou Yu retorted.

"...Surely this meeting should be held publicly," Lu Su suggested. "A private chat with an agent of Cao at such a critical moment... what if others suspect your loyalty to Lord Sun...?"

"*Dare they*...?" Zhou Yu scoffed.

Lu Su remained silent.

"Now *go*, Zijing," Zhou Yu urged. "This is a private discussion between me and this man from Xuchang..."

Lu Su left the tent, and walked straight into an anxious Lü Meng.

"Don't bother," Lu Su chortled, guessing exactly why Lü Meng had come to see Zhou Yu. "...He's going to talk to him."

"...Even he's a spy from Xuchang...?" Lü Meng mused. "...I wonder..."

"You cannot suspect his loyalty, surely...?" Lu Su asked as he took Lü Meng out of earshot of the guards around Zhou Yu's tent.

"No," Lü Meng replied honestly. "He's the sworn brother of our lord's late brother... he sees Lord Sun as his younger brother. No, I wonder why he would not just turn this man away... perhaps he feels this man should be allowed to put his case and have it firmly rejected. ...But I hear that Jiang Gan is matchless in debate in the region he hails from."

"That's worrying," Lu Su replied as he watched Jiang Gan being escorted toward Zhou Yu's tent. The adviser wore beautifully decorated blue robes and wore an elaborate hat: he was extremely confident in his stride, and seemed to be drawing the attention of many of the soldiers with his charismatic appearance.

"...We have to hope that the Chief Commander can outwit this arrogant pedant and send him crying back to Cao Cao," Lü Meng sighed. "But what if he's come here to offer an alliance, or surrender terms, or withdrawal terms...?"

"We'll accept none of it," Lu Su insisted. "Even if all Cao wanted was for us to withdraw... we won't do it, even just to prevent giving Liu Bei a shot at Jiangling."

"Ah, yes," Lü Meng chuckled softly, "I see that Liu Bei has acquired himself quite a force now... near to thirty thousand men he has now, some say. My friend Zijing, does it not worry the Chief Commander that they are mostly stationed in and around key positions in Jiangxia...?"

"What...!" Lu Su exclaimed.

"I wonder if their strategists have something planned," Lü Meng snickered. "I wonder... should we not encourage Liu Bei to move them into Nan Prefecture, in preparation for action against the southern county governors, and away from our newly acquired prefecture...?"

"I'll talk to Gongjin as soon as this 'visitor' is gone," Lu Su promised.

"So," Zhou Yu said to Jiang Gan after the ritual greetings were exchanged, "what can I do for you, Ziyi, after all these years...?"

"Gongjin," Jiang Gan said softly as the two men were seated, "you cannot be ignorant of that. I will not deceive you, mislead you, or patronise you. I will be concise, and to the point."

"My thanks," Zhou Yu said with a smile.

"You are a hero of the age," Jiang Gan continued, "but you are now in a dilemma. I shall explain. Your family has long served the imperial court, and has earned respect and favour for it. But one day, you met a man called Sun Ce, and together, you decided to break away from the bonds of your allegiance to the house of Han, and seek fame and glory in the south.

"You both married beautiful women, and conquered vast regions, quelling bandits and even subjugating lords and governors appointed by the imperial court... a romantic adventure, but not entirely filial, so far as serving your family name goes, nor loyal, so far as serving the Emperor goes.

"There was, however, still hope: when Yuan Shao, the treacherous conqueror of the north, asked your lord and sworn brother Sun Ce to aid him, he was reticent, and his successor, Sun Quan, refused him outright, and paid proper tribute to the imperial court, leaving Yuan to his fate. But then the Prime Minister requested your lord's help in bringing true stability to the south by officially swearing loyalty to the court, and ceding all territories unlawfully seized by Sun Ce... and your lord, supposedly on the advice of yourself and others, refused and declared war.

"The Prime Minister gave you many chances to reconsider, but you entered into a doomed alliance with Liu Bei and Liu Qi, who were rightfully dispossessed when the righteous Inspector of Qing Province, Liu Cong, surrendered his inherited land of Jing to the Emperor. Those two rebels were chased into Jiangxia and routed, and at that moment, if not for your 'advice', peace would now be ours.

"Instead, you still hungered for those heady days of wine, women and adventure, and you opposed the Prime Minister at Red Cliffs, winning only because the Prime Minister's forces – in strange and foreign territory, with no medical supplies or adequate immunity – fell victim to rampant disease, and the Prime Minister was forced to burn his fleet to contain the disease, and retreat.

"Now, you capitalise on a stroke of good luck, and you pursue this folly of facing down the Prime Minister to the Han Emperor, attempting to seize imperial lands from our majestic forces despite being under-resourced and outnumbered! But Heaven is obviously against you, Gongjin. Your sieges at Xiangyang and Hefei have failed: the rebellion in your home region, come to nothing... all you have to hope for now is a relatively graceful conclusion to this debacle here in Jiangling. ...Back home, we were acquaintances... nay, *friends*, and I do not want to see you come to harm. Please... see *sense*, Gongjin, and do the right thing...!"

Zhou Yu was smiling politely as Jiang Gan spoke. As soon as the visitor finished, Zhou Yu coughed to clear his throat, and replied tersely, "What's the right thing?"

"The right thing," Jiang Gan explained, "is to lay down arms here in Nan Prefecture, return to Jiangdong, allow the Prime Minister to apprehend the felon Liu Bei, and see if he can placate the disgruntled son of Liu Biao and find him some territory as compensation for his loss, as he did for the younger brother. Further to that, tender your services to the Prime Min- no, to the *Emperor*, and show *loyalty*, as your ancestors did! Turn away from this false king, Sun Quan! He can only come to a bad end! ...Do you wish to come to a bad end also...?"

"So," Zhou Yu replied calmly, "I should order a withdrawal, and join Cao Cao...?"

"...Yes," Jiang Gan insisted. "You must, to save yourself from ruin."

"...I would *die* for my lord Sun Quan," Zhou Yu declared without regret. "He and I are brothers, as his brother and I were sworn brothers. That is that."

Jiang Gan smiled uncomfortably and silently: Zhou Yu got to his feet, and Jiang Gan followed his lead.

"Sorry, but you wasted your time," Zhou Yu chuckled. "I have no quarrel with you, Ziyi: we serve different masters, our fates cast in different directions. I hope we never have to match wits on the battlefield... I would rather we keep to exchanges of words. Please, ensure you get some rest and refreshment before you go... and please, my friend, take care."

Jiang Gan nodded politely and bowed with respect, but he did not speak: Zhou Yu returned the respectful gesture, but said nothing more.

Later in the day, Jiang Gan left the camp under escort from two soldiers: Zhou Yu watched the man depart and sighed deeply.

"...You are sad that he serves another master, Gongjin...?" Lu Su – his only company – asked curiously.

"No," Zhou Yu replied. "I wonder how such an inflated ego, such a worthless excuse for a grovelling pedant, could ever have been an acquaintance of mine. 'Concise'...? I would hate to hear his idea of 'detailed': it may be enough to bore me to death. ...But still, I heard him out for a reason... he was anxious to portray himself in a strong position, which betrays Cao Cao's true position."

"Cao Cao is *weak*...?" Lu Su exclaimed disbelievingly.

"Not at all," Zhou Yu replied, "but this campaign is draining his resources. If we persist, he will eventually break... that, I now know for sure. It may take weeks... it may even take months... but he will eventually break, and Jing will be ours."

"...Uh," Lu Su bumbled, "I, uh... I should say, now that meeting's over, that-"

"...That Liu Bei's military manoeuvres in Jiangxia are suspicious," Zhou Yu interrupted. "I know it... Lü Meng is not the only one with eyes. I'm going to approach Liu Bei and request his devoted cooperation to subjugating Nan Prefecture... we may be forced to wrangle for it afterwards, but it's better than the crafty old devil stealing Jiangxia while we're stuck here, under the dishonest pretext of 'helping Liu Qi'. ...Further to that, he can keep Yue Jin busy for us."

Lu Su nodded agreeably, saying, "I'll go and talk to them for you."

When Lu Su reached Liu Bei's camps, he was taken aback, and left feeling quite intimidated. Liu Bei now had an organised navy, his soldiers were obviously well-trained and highly disciplined, and the forces seemed to be better financed as well, with dedicated crossbow divisions, and illustrious cavalry.

"Greetings, Lu Zijing," Kongming hailed as Lu Su entered the command tent.

"Indeed, Mister Lu, it is good to see you again," Liu Bei proclaimed from his command seat at the far end of the tent, past the assembled officials: Liu Qi was sat next to him, and the young man's pallor suggested that he was continuing to deteriorate.

"...Congratulations on your recent acquisition of forces," Lu Su said. "You are blessed to have received such support from the region that Zhou Yu hails from! ...I must admit I was quite surprised when I heard that Lei Xu joined you. Where is...?"

"Lei Xu is currently poorly," Kongming reported. "The journey south took its toll, as did the pain of losing his friends, Chen Lan and Mei Qian... we wish him speedy recovery. But he has pledged unconditional allegiance to my lord, and allowed his forces to be completely annexed into our existing army."

"...I see," Lu Su said hesitantly. "So, are the estimations that this brings your forces to forty-thousand, in combination with the young governor's remaining forces, to be believed, Lord Liu...?

Liu Bei laughed dismissively, and replied, "I have not counted them personally, but I suspect the number may be right, give or take five thousand."

"So why are you here...?" Kongming asked plainly.

"...For your help," Lu Su replied coldly. "Your help to take Nan Prefecture and manage the action being taken by Yue Jin behind our lines."

Liu Bei and Kongming exchanged glances, and smiled agreeably at Lu Su.

"You're going to say it was a guess," Ma Liang said with a laugh as he left the meeting with Kongming, "but again I say 'Good guess'...! ...It is all falling into place, as you hoped that it would."

"I hear that Zhou Yu received a visit from Jiang Gan, one of Cao's advisers," Kongming replied. "Cao fears a prolonged engagement will exhaust him, and if it were better planned, it would. The siege of Hefei failed because of poor planning and inadequate deployment; Lujiang, because they fought alone against heavy odds. Were a proper, coordinated pincer against Cao carried out..."

"...Like the one proposed by you and Lu Su...!" Ma Liang noted.

"My lord and Sun Quan as equal partners, striking from two fronts, would destroy Cao Cao, and he knows it," Kongming insisted. "Zhou Yu persists with this alternate plan of allying himself with Zhang Lu and Ma Chao, but it cannot succeed. The allies he seeks are too small, and are too close to enemies and rivals that can be used against them. He failed to court Lei Xu, a man from his own region, and lost a sizeable number of reinforcements as a result. My lord now has the men to fight: now, all he needs is a base from which to fight. And by deploying our new forces in a suspicious way around Jiangxia, we have forced our friend Zhou Yu to accept that fact and give us a clear run at the four southern counties, which will be our first base, from which we can move on Yi."

"But for now, we must follow Zhou Yu's orders," Ma Liang supposed.

"Sadly, yes, else he might become antagonistic," Kongming said sadly. "Well, I expect we'd better ready ourselves, and pay him another visit..."

************

## 49

Zhou Yu received Liu Bei and his officials once again, but this time, the mood was more subdued. Liu Bei had brought with him Kongming, Mister Sun, Mi Zhu and Jian Yong, while the rest of his officials waited outside the Wu camp.

"We have been here now for so long that I worry I might take root," Zhou Yu joked feebly to the ensemble of Sun and Liu vassals. "This has to end soon for all our sakes. Even though our losses have been minimal, the toll it is taking on grain supplies is ridiculous... I can only imagine what it is doing to the north."

"Do you have a proposal for us, Chief Commander...?" Liu Bei asked plainly.

"I do, Lord Liu," Zhou replied humbly. "Your now considerable might is needed to bolster us... forgive my remarks about your weakness at our last encounter, but even you have to admit that at the time, the point was sound, if not so much now."

"It was," Liu Bei replied calmly. "Now, as you say, not so much."

"...Quite," Zhou Yu sighed. "So... have you any suggestions as to how you would prefer to deploy your forces...?"

The Wu generals were wracked with despair that their situation had now deteriorated to the point that Liu Bei could dictate the actions of his own forces: there were noticeable groans and grunts of displeasure that Zhou Yu did his best to silence with angry glances.

"I have no suggestions at this point beyond those already made," Liu Bei said with conviction. "If you are still happy with the idea, Chief Commander, I would like to confront Yue Jin's saboteurs, and try and seize the four counties now, so that Cao Cao cannot rely on those for support. I have, despite the risk to his health, asked Liu Qi to join us in Nan Prefecture, so..."

Liu Bei paused, awaiting a confirmation from Zhou Yu.

"...Fine," Zhou Yu said after an uncomfortable pause.

"We shall set out immediately," Liu Bei proclaimed. "Now our numbers are considerable, we can march on and secure all four in a stroke, and then return to you and see how we can support you further."

Zhou Yu nodded silently and repeatedly for a few moments more than was normal.

"...We shall depart," Liu Bei said again: Lu Su got up to say farewell, since Zhou Yu appeared to be in a daze. The generals of Wu paid slight respects to the officials of Liu Bei as they departed the tent.


Liu Bei and his 4 vassals joined the rest of his forces at their own camp some time later. The short yet eventful meeting was relayed to Ma Liang, Yi Ji, Mi Fang, Guan Yu, Zhang Fei, Zhao Yun, Wei Yan, Huo Jun, Chen Zhen, and Li Qi's Jing contingent, which was comprised of officials including Liu Bei supporters Liao Li and Xiang Lang.

"...He looked like a ghost," Kongming said with a grin.

"Enough, enough!" Liu Bei chuckled. "We shouldn't mock the man, as you yourself said. Now... how best to proceed...?"

"Ma Jichang and Yi Boji are the two men you need to talk to about southern Jing," Kongming replied. "I am not an expert in the politics and specifics of this region."

Liu Bei turned to Ma Liang and Yi Ji and smiled expectantly.

"Oh! ...Uh," Ma Liang began, "well... Jin Xuan commands Wuling, Han Xuan governs Changsha, Zhao Fan governs Guiyang, and Liu Du governs Lingling..."

"As men of the region, Liao Li, Xiang Lang, Ma Jichang and I should visit one of these places each, aided by a general," Yi Ji added. "The most remote is Guiyang, the nearest, Changsha... the capital of Changsha is south of Zhou Yu's Ba Qiu training facility, and sits nearest the border with Jiangxia Prefecture. The other two are to the west and southwest, requiring a long journey in each case."

"...Governor Liu Qi can travel with me to Changsha," Xiang Lang suggested. "I have met the governor, Han Xuan, and know him to be most agreeable. We might not even need to take a senior general, since I can take my son Chong as my general, and it is a short journey back toward Jiangxia, where Governor Liu can be resettled and rested if things did not go well."

"Very well," Liu Bei agreed, "but I shall assign General Wei Yan to you, since he seems to be a high-minded man with good sense. What of the other three...?"

"Because of the long journey, and also a possible family connection, I recommend Zilong travel to Guiyang to challenge Zhao Fan," Ma Liang said surely. "Either myself, or Yi Boji, may be the selected emissary."

"...It is better that I go," Yi Ji suggested. "Jichang, you should accompany Lord Liu to Lingling, which is governed by Liu Du. The Liu name may help in securing surrender, and you will have Chen Dao's bodyguard force as well, but take either Yide or Yunchang for added strength, just in case... Lord Liu is too important to put at heavy risk."

"So then I am to go to Wuling, far to the west, and where Yue Jin's infiltration force is most heavily concentrated," Liao Li supposed. "Who will be my assistant general, since I shall sorely need one...?"

"I suggest Yunchang, for he is resolute, high-minded, and surely the best man to convince Jin Xuan to stand down if he has other ideas... his son Ping, also," Ma Liang said in response. "Further to that, I imagine Yunchang has a score to settle with Yue Jin. Yide will accompany Lord Liu, Chen Dao and me to Lingling City."

"...So what are *we* doing...?" Jian Yong asked as he gestured toward the silent, thoughtful Kongming.

"We're staying on centre ground to provide extra support in the event that any of the administrator governors of these counties decides to fight back," Kongming declared. "Acting Officers Sun Qian, Mi Zhu, Mi Fang and Chen Zhen, and Generals Huo Jun, Chen Shi, Liao Hua, Shi Ren, Zhao Lei, Zhang Da, and Fan Qiang can each manage a contingent of archers, infantry and cavalry, ready to be despatched where they are needed... or even help *Chief Commander Zhou Yu*, should he suddenly need the support. The navy can also be on standby."

Those mentioned by Kongming murmured acknowledgement of the arrangements.

"Right then," Liu Bei proclaimed, "we should begin as soon as possible, so we can be on hand to help defeat Cao Ren and retake Jiangling!"
The generals gave rousing cheers to their lord.

"Kongming tells me that the forces have set out to take the counties," Lu Su reported to Zhou Yu the next day. "They departed together this morning."
"Which one are they taking first...?" Zhou Yu asked wearily.
"They've gone in four directions to seize all four counties at once, rather than one at a time," Lu Su reported further. "Each group has one emissary, one significant general from Liu Bei's four best field generals – Guan Yu, Zhang Fei, Zhao Yun and Wei Yan – and several well-trained archers, cavalrymen and infantry."
"Mm... and 'Lord Liu' is where...?" Zhou Yu prompted.
Lu Su replied cynically, "Accompanied, 'as always', by his bodyguard force of *over a dozen expert swordsmen, archers and cavalrymen, led by Chen Dao* – as you can tell, that was emphasised – Lord Liu will be going to Lingling, since it is governed by Liu Du, a possible relation. Liu Qi is on his way to Changsha."
"...What can I say...?" Zhou Yu chuckled miserably. "You say Zhuge Liang told you this... so where is *he*...?"
"Camped in a position where he can send forces in any one of the five directions... to assist the four raids, or us," Lu Su said ominously. "He has almost a dozen well-organised crack forces led by individual generals or officials of respectable merit, and says that they are ready, *always*, to go into action. Messenger units are placed along all key routes to 'give advance warnings' and 'detect incursions'."
"...Which means that in addition to aiding us, he can also defend himself from us," Zhou Yu noted. "What can I say...?"
"...General Lü Meng wants to know if we are going to intensify our attacks on the city now that we have rear support from Lord Liu," Lu Su prompted.
"...We should," Zhou Yu sighed: he was now starting to become depressed by the prolonged and apparently unending siege of Jiangling. "...We should."

Within a few days, Guan Yu, Liao Li and Guan Ping arrived with their forces at the boundary of Wuling County, and found the border patrols to be fearful. Messengers carried the news of the arrival of 2,000 men nervously, as the city had less than 300 able men that might take up arms.
"...**Alert the governor!**" a city clerk urged as he ordered archers to take up offensive positions along the wall. Two captains on horseback rode out of the capital city, their spears levelled for a challenge, while a small number of infantry formed a line behind them. The drawbridge was half-raised, blocking their retreat and also any possible charge by Guan Yu.
"**HOW DARE YOU ATTACK US!**" one captain bellowed.
"What can two-dozen poorly trained scraps do to me...?" Guan scoffed as he brandished his Green Dragon pole sword.
"Have pity, Father," Guan Ping urged. "Do not kill them unless you have to."

The soldiers that guarded the county were volunteers, and not well armed or protected: they quailed at the sight of Guan Yu's custom-forged Green Dragon, and realised that this must be a man of some reputation.

"**We come here to speak with the county governor on the orders of Provincial Governor Liu Qi!**" Liao Li pleaded. "**Do not fight!**"

"**Who speaks with a sword...?**" one of the two generals retorted: he charged, and was painfully unseated from his horse by a violent flat-edged blow from the Green Dragon. The other general hesitated: Guan Yu loomed with menace as the first general clutched his bruised arm and rolled around in agony near the front hooves of Guan Yu's horse. On the wall above, the order to fire was not given to the archers: there appeared to be some commotion, and after several minutes, the archers stood down and a middle-aged man in elegant robes appeared at the wall.

"...**W-wait...!**" the man shouted. "**We... we yield...!**"

Sensing that Guan Yu could have killed his comrade easily, the second general jumped from his horse and fell to one knee in silent penitence: his terrified soldiers did the same.

Within a few hours, Governor Jin Xuan was tendering the Seal of the County outside the walls of the county capital. The first of the 4 targets had fallen bloodlessly.

To the east in Changsha, a similar scenario was unfolding. Wei Yan stood in front of the city and shouted upward at the governor, Han Xuan, who was stood on the wall of the city. To Han Xuan's left was his best general, the veteran Huang Zhong, who stood tall and proud despite the moment of the day. Huang Zhong rubbed his grey-bearded chin and hummed thoughtfully.

"I have no desire to fight," Han Xuan said as he looked at the array of 2,000 soldiers that accompanied Wei Yan. "But what about the people...? Have they come to kill us, or...?"

"My lord," Huang Zhong replied, "these men fly the banner of Provincial Governor Liu Qi, and this bold warrior below us is not yelling insults or challenges... he is asking us to surrender to Governor Liu, to yield the city. Perhaps we should, for the sake of the people... it is their honour that is at stake if they harm the people, not yours."

"...As always, Veteran General, you speak wisely," Han Xuan sighed. "Very well... since this place was only mine to protect... let's return it to Governor Liu Biao's son now to govern. **Open the gates.**"

Huang Zhong led Han Xuan outside the city: Han Xuan carried the Seal of the County, intending to proffer it to whoever represented Liu Qi.

"...Young Governor...!" Han Xuan exclaimed as Xiang Lang and his son, Xiang Chong, guided the horse carrying the emaciated Liu Qi toward the city governor. "Can it be you...?"

"I... I am poorly," Li Qi said quietly. "But... I wanted to come here, Governor Han... so that you know... we're here to free you from Cao Cao."

"To see such a young man in such terrible condition makes me feel guilty to be so old and so well," Huang Zhong declared, as he stood to one side with Wei Yan and Xiang Chong, while his master tendered the city seal to Liu Qi and Xiang Lang.

"How old *are* you, exactly...?" Wei Yan asked rudely.

"...Old enough to beat you like a child," Huang Zhong hissed. "Show respect!"

"Now, Governor Liu," Han Xuan said, "you need to rest, I think... come into the city, please...!"

Liu Qi passed the seal to Xiang Lang and replied, "I... really need to sit down...!"

Xiang Chong ran forward to help Liu Qi back onto his horse: Wei Yan and Huang Zhong both followed, the imposing Zhong displaying strength belying his 60-or-thereabouts years of age as he hoisted Liu Qi back onto the horse.

"Veteran General," Wei Yan said politely, "it has to be said that you are wasted as a bodyguard to a county governor, inasmuch as your governor's benevolence is wasted on a remote place such as this. Surely you should both be in the closer service of Governor Liu Qi, or even Lord Liu Bei...?"

"...I confess that I feel I could do more in the world," Huang Zhong said as he watched Han Xuan, Xiang Lang and Xiang Chong guide Liu Qi into the city. "But would your lord, Liu Bei, want some old man...?"

"You're a veteran general, not 'some old man'," Wei Yan insisted. "I think that he will be very grateful for your service."

Huang Zhong lowered his head, smiled, and said with a laugh, "And I thought this day was my last... in fact, it might be my first."

************

## 50

It would take twice as many days at least for Liu Bei to get to Lingling and for Zhao Yun to get to Guiyang, so reports of the speedy acquisitions of Changsha and Wuling arrived at Cao Ren, Zhou Yu and Kongming's camps before the other two counties had even been reached.

Cao Ren, meanwhile, was sat in conference with his elite generals, Xu Huang and Niu Jin, and his chief clerk, Chen Jiao.
"We're now surrounded by infantry on three sides, and by naval forces on the Great River," Cao Ren sighed miserably. "What can we do…?"
"The lord has forces that he can send to provide flash support," Xu Huang recalled eagerly. "Yue Jin is occupying Guan Yu and the natives in Wuling, Li Tong is stationed near Xinye, Wen Ping also: I am sure that they will despatch forces to assist us. Man Chong can also send support from Dangyang, can he not…?"
"Hopefully, that may be possible," Chen Jiao said quietly.
"…*Aiee*," Cao Ren exclaimed. "…What can we do…?"
"**REPORT!**" a messenger hailed as he hurried into the room and fell to one knee.
"…Go on," Cao Ren said wearily.
"**Wu's General Han Dang is issuing a challenge in front of the drawbridge!**" the messenger reported. "**He requests a battle with General Xu Huang!**"
"My thanks," Cao Ren said coldly: the messenger retreated.
"…I am willing to go, Commander," Xu Huang said respectfully.
"No," Cao Ren replied with a smirk. "General Niu, I would like you to lead three hundred volunteers to face the enemy and blunt their morale."
"Yes sir!" Niu Jin replied enthusiastically. "I shall depart now, and prepare!"
"*Volunteers*…?" Xu Huang exclaimed. "Commander, I…!"
"This is a senseless strategy," Chen Jiao admonished. "Zhou Yu sends thousands of dogs of war as his vanguard, and we're replying with three hundred pups?"
"You overestimate this young man Zhou Yu," Cao Ren insisted. "And when our small force – inspired, brave and valiant – defeats the larger force, it will give the men morale, and make them fight harder… and then we can break the siege!"
The statement was met with cynical silence.
"After Red Cliffs, is it not true to say that a confident small force destroys a larger, overstretched one…?" Cao Ren challenged.
Again, Chen Jiao and Xu Huang did not reply.
"…Let us wait and see what happens," Cao Ren suggested irritably. "We'll see… I have every faith in Niu Jin."
"So do I, he is a promising hero," Xu Huang praised needlessly. "But even the greatest hero cannot smash a rock with an egg."
"…We'll see!" Cao Ren said again, this time angrily.

The volunteer force led by Niu Jin charged out of the city, their naïve courage proving an excellent source of adrenalin: however, it was not to be. Within the hour, they were hopelessly surrounded by baying, taunting soldiers of Wu.

"...I did say it was a bad idea," Chen Jiao sighed as Cao Ren paced back and forth, wondering what to do.

"This is going to be exceptionally bad for morale," Xu Huang suggested.

"It may even cause us to lose the siege, especially since we no longer have our northwest side covered by Yiling," Chen Jiao complained.

"... ... ...I'll have to rescue them," Cao Ren decided.

"Commander," Xu Huang protested, "if someone must go, let me! You are the commander of the defence of Jiangling!"

"I'm also the reason that man is surrounded and near death!" Cao Ren retorted with anger and guilt. "How can I expect others to atone for my mistakes???"

"...This is extremely unwise," Chen Jiao protested. "You do not correct one mistake by making another, larger one! If you die, this place is lost! The indigenous population will open the gates, and-"

"**Be SILENT!**" Cao Ren screamed. "...I shall get my armour, and I shall save my comrade... and his men also... and then we will do something about Yiling."

Commander Cao Ren left the room to make preparations and gather a rescue force of elite cavalry, leaving Xu Huang and Chen Jiao to wonder whether the situation could deteriorate any further.

Cao Ren made his charge out of the gate to save Niu Jin, and the shock of the second attack completely threw the besieging Wu forces. Cao Ren cut through the bewildered enemy and found Niu Jin, who – with a small group of his three hundred volunteers – had been completely surrounded by spear-wielding infantry. The two generals, once reunited, fought their way back toward the drawbridge of Jiangling City with their forces, leaving the enemy forces behind them, embarrassed and wondering what had happened.

"...I don't believe it...!" Chen Jiao exclaimed as Cao Ren steered Niu Jin and the small group of rescued volunteers toward a group of soldiers inside the gates.

"The other men that are still out there... I'm going back out," Cao Ren panted.

"No, no!" Xu Huang protested. "You're spent; let *me* go!"

"Nonsense!" Cao Ren replied breathlessly. "It is... my error!"

With that, Cao Ren gestured for the gates to be reopened: once again, the general charged, flanked by his cavalrymen, and struck another position where the volunteer forces were desperately holding on. Han Dang attempted a charge on Cao Ren, but was rebuffed by the cavalrymen: Ren found and joined the remaining volunteers, and fought his way back to the city gates yet again.

"...I...!" Xu Huang exclaimed as Cao Ren returned a second time: less than twenty of the three hundred volunteers had been lost, and the soldiers within the city were obviously touched by the risk that their commander was prepared to face for them.

"You... are sent by Heaven!" Chen Jiao proclaimed.

The soldiers and rescued volunteers kowtowed to their commander, Cao Ren.

"Now," Cao Ren panted, "we... must push forward, out of the city." The cheers of the soldiers rang out, while outside, the forces of Wu were solemn and demoralised: they retreated to rethink their options.

"**Fools!**" Zhou Yu shouted angrily as the messenger from the front lines relayed the events of the day. "**Fools, and cowards!**"

"Calm down, Gongjin," Lu Su pleaded.

"You're... you're right," Zhou Yu agreed. "Thank you, Zijing... I should remain calm. But... this is terrible. The men are completely confused and scared: they think Cao Ren is some sort of super-man now. We cannot... we cannot leave things as they are. But... but what to do...?"

"...The generals are suggesting bringing the forward positions back a bit to avoid any more rushing strikes, since they seem to be severely hurting morale," Lu Su said softly. "I don't know, if-"

"Do it," Zhou Yu interrupted sombrely. "Just... just get the lines pulled back, out of range... and we'll rethink things... go."

Zhou Yu stared blankly: Lu Su hovered for a moment, unsure if he should say something encouraging, before he thought better of it and left the tent to carry out his orders.

A week or more went by, and the forces of Liu Bei finally reached Lingling, where the governor gave up without a struggle. Likewise, Zhao Yun met with no resistance when he reached Guiyang: and so, in the end, all 4 counties had surrendered without serious incident. Messengers brought this news not only to Kongming, but to Zhou Yu, who began to despair, and Cao Ren, who was now seizing upon Wu's low morale and building defensive mounds and towers around the city to advance his position.

Days went by, and the siege went on. On one eventful morning, Cheng Pu, Huang Gai and Han Dang rushed into the command tent to report another unfortunate setback.

"**Chief Commander!**" Cheng Pu said with urgency. "They're moving their defensive positions forward again!"

"I know," Zhou Yu murmured. "We need to push them back."

"What are your orders...?" Cheng Pu asked obediently.

Zhou Yu got up and said emotionlessly, "I will personally lead the troops forward to strike their positions and stop this gradual advance. Let's force them backwards, force them back into the city."

That same day, Zhou Yu rode to the front line in his magnificent armour, riding a white horse. He roused the soldiers as well as he could, and ordered two changes to the offensive: in a mirror of events that had taken place during the Battle of Guandu, Zhou Yu had siege catapults built from local timber to rain rocks on the enemy siege towers and hills, while his archers followed that up with precision volleys to hit any soldiers that tried to rush down the man-made hills to stop the catapults. The mission was an eventual success: the forces of Cao Ren slowly moved back toward the city walls again as Zhou Yu's men destroyed or occupied the hills and siege towers and reversed the enemy advance.

"So, Zhou Yu finally forced them back behind the walls of Jiangling again," Jian Yong noted as a messenger, his report made, left the command tent. "Yue Jin is being contained, and Lord Liu has seized the four counties... what now...?"
"With Cao Ren back on the defensive, I'm going to take the opportunity to rendezvous with Lord Liu and do a tour of the counties," Kongming replied. "We'll need to decide who governs what, and see whether there are any worthy men who might join our ranks. I will be going to Guiyang first, gradually moving north: it would be useful for Mister Sun and you to join me. Who would you suggest as a defender of this camp until Lord Liu returns...?"
"I think Mister Sun should stay," Jian Yong replied. "He is looking a little frail these days, and besides, he is an old master of defending positions."
"Very well," Kongming declared. "We'll depart tomorrow, then...!"

With Lingling pacified, Liu Bei advanced southward to Guiyang, where he was eventually joined by Kongming and Jian Yong, many days later.
"Congratulations are in order, I hear, Zilong," Kongming chuckled as he and Jian Yong entered the meeting hall of the city governor's house, where Liu Bei, Ma Liang, Yi Ji, Zhang Fei and Zhao Yun were already seated. Zhao Yun was noticeably agitated, while the others were noticeably amused.
"Ayah!" Zhao Yun exclaimed miserably. "Please, Master Zhuge, do not mock me as well!"
"But I fail to understand why you would turn down a beautiful wife," Kongming prompted.
"*Aiee*... you *know why*!" Zhao Yun said uncomfortably. "Such incest is unjust!"
"...You really are far too much, Zilong," Jian Yong joked.
"Besides," Zhao Yun protested further, "for the governor to not only surrender, to not only swear brotherhood due to our shared family name, but to offer his brother's widow to me for a wife, all on our very first meeting...? Does that not incur some small amount of suspicion...?"
"...I am only teasing, Zilong," Kongming insisted with a grin. "Your suspicions are rightly justified, in fact... I have just received word that former governor Zhao Fan has fled the city."
"Fled...?" Liu Bei said with sudden seriousness.

"A man does not flee after making such overtures without being ill-intended," Zhao Yun declared. "Besides, I am a warrior-vassal of my lord first and foremost. I would not jeopardise his enterprise for the want of a woman. There are many women in the world."

"Well said," Liu Bei said with a satisfied nod of approval.

"So we shall need to place a temporary governor here," Jian Yong supposed. "Who should we leave here...?"

"I suggest Zilong remains here," Kongming said surely. "If Zhao Fan fled, then this is an unstable place compared to Changsha and Wuling."

"So they are taken...?" Liu Bei said with cheer.

"Completely, and without bloodshed," Kongming confirmed. "Han Xuan of Changsha is such a man of sincerity that he is best left to continue to govern the county. Jin Xuan was initially hesitant, and if needs be he can be replaced... though, hopefully, it shouldn't be necessary."

"Excellent news!" Liu Bei exclaimed. "And my old friend Wu Ju is going to come up to Guiyang from Cangwu to pay respects... all quite magnificent!"

"My lord, *please* do not involve Wu Ju in our affairs at the moment," Kongming said desperately. "It is bad enough that his name is known to Lu Su as a friend of yours: please do not now accept tribute from him. He gives tribute to Sun Quan in exchange for autonomy... but if you associate him with us too much..."

"Do not fear so much!" Liu Bei insisted. "What can happen...?"

Kongming fanned himself slowly, exhaled miserably, and declined to reply, as Liu Bei made a toast to the future success that he felt was now his destiny.

************

## 51

After Liu Bei had very conspicuously received the Cangwu governor Wu Ju and spent a day discussing old times, he took his entourage back to the city of Gong'an. He settled in a large house that he designated as his main headquarters, and started to meet his new recruits, many of which – to the delight of Zhang Fei – were generals.

"So," Liu Bei said with triumph," I have got some wonderful new talent!"
"And some weathered, old, worn-out talent," Zhang Fei grunted quietly as he looked at the elder stalwart, Huang Zhong.
"With the likes of Wei Yan and venerable veteran Huang Zhong among my generals, bringing their knowledge of warfare new and old, how can we lose?" Liu Bei declared. "We have taken the four counties... now, I think, our wings are finally starting to spread."
"There is one noted talent that we have yet to acquire from Jing Province, Lord Liu," Mister Sun noted.
"Oh...?" Liu Bei prompted. "Who is that...?"
Kongming flinched as Mister Sun said, "It has come to my attention, and not entirely recently either, that Pang Tong, styled Shiyuan, Taoist name Young Phoenix, has long been residing in Nan Prefecture in a civil official post."
"...Young Phoenix...?" Liu Bei said with enthusiasm. "Master Zhuge, your contemporary resides here and you have not sought him out...?"
"...No," Kongming replied, as all eyes fell on him.
"*Why*...?" Zhang Fei snickered. "You worried he'll outdo you...?"
"Yide," Liu Bei scolded, "do not be rude."
"If he were better than I – and I believe him to be, in fact – and he wanted to join us, Yide, that would be to our advantage, and be not a curse but a blessing to me," Kongming insisted. "I have not been evading the issue... on the contrary, I have tried to find him several times, but his office is in Jiangling. Not that it matters, to be honest, my lord... Shiyuan once told me, long ago – on two separate occasions, both before and after I entered your service – that, sad to say, he feels as I once felt... that the business of war was not something he wanted to be a part of, and that he was happy in a civil post."
"...*Aiee*," Liu Bei sighed. "Then we will not have this man's help. That is a pity."
"You said that about *him*," Zhang Fei noted as he pointed rudely at Kongming.
"As Yide has just said," Kongming concurred, "do not lose hope of his one day deciding otherwise. We-"
"**REPORT!**" a messenger wearing Eastern Wu's green uniform hailed as he ran into the hall and stopped near the door, escorted by two of Liu Bei's own soldiers.
"...Zhou Yu," Kongming supposed quietly.
"My lord," Jian Yong hailed, "it is obvious what this will be."
"...Speak, messenger, speak," Liu Bei urged.

**"Chief Commander Zhou Yu has requested your presence for an urgent discussion of the military situation,"** the messenger reported.

"I'll *bet he has*," Zhang Fei chuckled.

"Well!" Liu Bei said with notable enthusiasm, "let us go and meet him, then!"

After the considerable journey to the front at Jiangling, Liu Bei took his officials to Zhou Yu's large base camp. The camp – which was laid out according to the ideas of the age – was gigantic: it was a sea of tents, surrounded by a wall made of sharpened stakes and logs, with a high front gate and a wooden portcullis. Kongming noted the apparent newness of the structure, and said to Ma Liang as they approached the command tent, "They've had no peace here."

Ma Liang nodded sombrely.

"My thanks to you for coming, Lord Liu, and congratulations on securing the four counties so quickly and easily," Zhou Yu hailed as Liu Bei's men entered the camp. Chen Dao remained outside with Liu Bei's bodyguards, as always, so that they were ready for any possible situation.

"Not worth mentioning...!" Liu Bei said with confidence as he and his followers took their seats.

"...We have been going back and forth with Cao Ren now for far too long," Zhou Yu sighed miserably. "This... stalemate... has *got to end soon*."

"Perhaps we should try raiding his supply routes again," Liu Bei suggested.

"...Did you have a stratagem in mind...?" Zhou Yu asked pointedly.

"The enemy can transfer goods by river if they please," Liu Bei continued, "but they must still get them to Jiangling by road... perhaps if I deploy forces under Guan Yunchang and Zhang Yide, simultaneously striking the supply roads from the north and west, it might be enough to break Cao Ren's spirit."

"...Perhaps," Zhou Yu replied as he and Lu Su exchanged tense and wary glances. "It is a sound idea, but the-"

"Excellent!" Liu Bei said with cheer. "Together, there's nothing that Yunchang and Yide cannot accomplish!"

"...You seem committed to the endeavour," Zhou Yu noted. "Very well... we'll launch a simultaneous attack on all sides of Jiangling, in order to prevent Cao Ren sending aid. Good luck, then... I suppose that's all there is to say about that. Now, there are some other matters..."

The meeting continued, but the Wu leaders were notably unnerved.

Hours later, Liu Bei and his vassals returned to their Gong'an base: Ma Liang and Jian Yong met with Kongming in his office.

"They didn't like that suggestion at all," Kongming noted uncomfortably.

"How so...?" Ma Liang whispered uneasily.

"...Didn't you see...?" Kongming chortled. "Zhou Yu and Lu Su... we offer assistance, and they balked! ...They don't really want our help with the Jiangling blockade at all... so that they don't have to share Jiangling with us. They still resent the alliance."
"...Ah," Jian Yong mused. "Perhaps that's true. But will the blockades even work...? I can't see Cao Ren not being prepared, to be honest."
"I've advised caution, and both commanders will retreat if the odds overwhelm them," Kongming insisted. "And once again I have to say that I just don't think it bodes well for the future if Zhou Yu and Lu Su are still so hostile towards cooperation..."
Jian Yong and Ma Liang hesitantly agreed.

The supply routes from Yi Province and Xiangyang City were commanded overall by Li Tong, Cao's appointed Administrator of the region. Once forces had been sent to pin Yue Jin in Wuling, Guan Yu would press northward from Jiangling, placing log and stone blockades along the roads from central Dangyang County, Mai City and Xiangyang City. Zhang Fei, meanwhile, would strike westward, in an attempt to block land and river supply roads from neighbouring Yi Province. Although both were initially successful, the venture was still, overall, a failure.

The tenacious Li Tong chased away Guan Yu's northern forces and dismantled the log barricades, restoring that supply route with relative ease. Zhang Fei, despite being in command of more men and generals than he had ever been assigned in his life, was forced into a tactical retreat by the sheer determination of the enemy.

One unwanted outcome was yet another surge of morale among the defenders at Jiangling; they started to capitalise on the momentum and before long, they were back in control of mounds and towers outside the city.

Guan Yu and Zhang Fei returned to Liu Bei's court in Gong'an to report the outcome in person: they were visibly battered, angry, and demoralised.
"Another military failure," Liu Bei mused as he looked the miserable generals up and down, "but even the mission was less taxing, the outcome of this was even worse than last time... how can this be, I don't understand."
Guan Yu and Zhang Fei eyed the advisers angrily in anticipation of harsh criticism of their performances.
"Look, Xuande," Jian Yong began, "we shouldn't be so-"
"My lord," Kongming interrupted calmly, "last time, we asked a tiger to be a duck: this time, we demanded that two rivers be dammed with twigs. When one asks for the ridiculous, one should not be surprised when the result is a farce."
There was barely a face in the room that did not wear a smile: only Liu Bei – who was embarrassed – had a solemn expression.
"We sent insufficient forces against a desperate enemy that have nothing to lose and everything to gain," Kongming continued. "If Guan and Zhang had been successful, my lord, then I might have suggested that we move straight onto Xuchang, since Cao Cao was obviously without capable men. We lost because we lost... let's say no more about it."

"Perhaps," Liu Bei replied quietly. "I think only about the reputations of two men whom I consider to be like brothers to me. I would not want the men of Wu to scold us."

"Neither man has reason to be ashamed," Kongming suggested. "Would Zhou Yu be right to be scathing, when he has spent nigh on a year staring up at this man Cao Ren, high on the walls of Jiangling, with nothing but a stiff neck to show for it...?"

"Like I care what Zhou Yu thinks, anyway," Zhang Fei grunted. "This whole thing is stupid, anyway: I didn't come here to build blockades and go sailing... I came here to fight! Tell him that, too, if he asks!"

"...Perhaps we should let this sorry matter drop," Liu Bei conceded. "Master Zhuge is right... the Wu high command has no right to castigate us, not when considering their own poor rate of success, and I'm sure that they know that."

"I think we should stick to giving Zhou Yu ground support," Jian Yong said dryly, "unless any of our new acquisitions are veterans in naval warfare or blockades... in which case, my lord, *they* should be leading such things...?"

Liu Bei smiled, and nodded apologetically.

Further attempts were made to sabotage Cao Ren's supply lines, although they were never sufficient to completely break them. In Zhou Yu's camp, this brought despair.

"...We need to do something to fight back against this decisively," Zhou Yu said angrily as he looked at his maps. "...Tomorrow, I will go out again and rally the men personally."

"You shouldn't keep doing that," Lü Meng warned. "At least change your horse, if you insist, and wear duller armour... you're too obvious a target."

"...Fair enough," Zhou Yu grunted. "...But this has to end."

The next day, Zhou Yu went to the front, at the head of a raid on one of Cao Ren's external camps.

"He's here again," Xu Huang noted as he watched from the city walls with Chen Jiao. "He's on a brown horse this time."

"He is too strong a presence to hide with poorer decoration," Chen Jiao said with a callous laugh. "The demeanour of his men while they're in his presence does much to reveal it is him..."

Cao Ren approached the wall at this point, and smirked.

"...Today," Cao Ren declared, "Zhou Yu dies."

With that said, Cao Ren raised a small flag, and from various points in the camps below and the walls around him, extra archers appeared, firing relentlessly into Zhou Yu's vanguard.

"**Stay calm!**" Zhou Yu protested as his infantry dashed about, desperately trying to avoid being struck. "**Place our own archers in a line at the rear! Infantry, pull back to the-**"

The next noise to come from Zhou Yu was a pained, resigned groan: he slumped forward, and fell from his horse, landing face up, his eyes open but dull.

"**CHIEF COMMANDER!**" Cheng Pu screamed: he had his best men rush to Zhou Yu's position to defend him from the continued volley of arrows.

"We got him!" Cao Ren realised as he saw the panic in the Wu lines. "Xu Huang: finish them off!"
Xu Huang left the city wall and led a charge on the Wu army, who were now retreating. Their commander, Zhou Yu, was now laid across a horse, an arrow embedded in his chest at the base of his rib cage. He was alive, and murmuring orders as best he could, but as far as his generals were concerned, the battle was over.

"He's alive," Xu Huang reported as he returned to Cao Ren.
"...Not for long," Cao Ren insisted. "With Zhou Yu wounded, this is now as good as over! We'll start hounding their base camp, every day... we'll curse him until he dies of grief and indignation, and then Nan Prefecture will be recovered, and victory will be ours!"
"And Liu Bei...?" Xu Huang asked.
"What *about* Liu Bei...?" Cao Ren scoffed. "He is nothing without Wu... he'll turn and run once Zhou Yu's dead! This is over!"
Xu Huang and Chen Jiao nodded in agreement, and with relief. But in the Wu camp, the mood was as desperate as it could be. The doctor frantically worked to save Zhou Yu, while Lu Su, Cheng Pu, Huang Gai and Lü Meng looked on with decreasing optimism.

************

## 52

Kongming visited the Wu camp a few days after Zhou Yu's injury at Jiangling: he was escorted by an elite force that was forced to hack its way through the confident enemy lines that now hounded the Wu camp on a daily basis.

"...How is he...?" Kongming asked Lu Su as the two sat alone in Lu Su's tent: the latter was shakily consuming a cup of heated wine in an attempt to calm his nerves.
"...It went through the armour, through the bone...!" Lu Su bleated. "The rib, it is shattered... the flesh... he coughs blood, and...!"
"At least the arrow wasn't poisoned," Kongming suggested. "I'm sure he'll be fine, Zijing... Gongjin is very stubborn, and he'll not let this go unfinished."
"He'll not ride a horse again this year," Lu Su lamented. "He's unfit to remain here, and now, he insists that I'm in charge until...!"
"...You'll make a fine Chief Commander," Kongming promised. "But you really should do something about those men that come and taunt the camp. That could worsen his condition."
"He knows," Lu Su sighed. "He doesn't care... he isn't superstitious. It's annoying the generals, but... I don't think we should be attacking them, not until we know whether... whether..."
"Stay calm," Kongming insisted. "You cannot retreat just because Gongjin is injured... you could not if he *died*, even, because your lord's cause is at stake. If you need any assistance, we will do all we can. We'll continue to harass the city, but we're thinly spread, so there's only so much we can do alone."
"Remain in your camps for now, Kongming," Lu Su insisted. "And... thank you."
Kongming smiled feebly, and left Lu Su to brood alone.

Liu Bei convened a meeting the next day to discuss the situation.
"Since the Chief Duck has been shot," Zhang Fei said with amusement, "does that mean you're in charge of the army now, then, Xuande...?"
"Nonsense," Liu Bei scoffed. "How can I command Wu's army? Sun Quan does not even want me to command my own!"
"We have less to fear in the future if that man is hurt," Mister Sun suggested.
"...Mister Sun," Kongming scolded, "even if we *should* fear him in the future, we should not fear him *now*! Right *now*, he is our ally, and without him, Cao Ren may turn the tide of this battle and break the siege... and then Steep-slope, Wulin and Red Cliffs may all have been for naught!"
"But we have an army now," Mi Zhu suggested. "An army the size of Zhou Yu's, bigger if you count the forces of Liu Qi... if *he* could defeat Cao at Red Cliffs, then why should *we* worry?"

"Cao Cao was defeated by circumstance and luck, not numbers or strategy," Kongming suggested angrily. "With the wrong wind direction, or better training for his forces, or better management of the rampant epidemics, that would have ended in a rout, not a victory. And if he'd listened to Jia Xu, he'd never have gone to Red Cliffs at all. You will never see the like of it again in our lifetime."
"So what can we do...?" Liu Bei asked desperately.
"Hope that Zhou Yu has a plan," Kongming sighed. "Even from his sickbed, he will be commanding the forces... Lu Su is only serving as a mouthpiece for Zhou Yu's orders. We just have to wait and watch... be ready to assist or retreat as the situation demands."

The ritual Cao Ren enacted every day was commonplace as a demoralising tactic. His force descended on the camp each day, wheeling out giant war drums that would be used in conjunction with the chanting. After a few hours of abuse, the army would then relax, discard their armour, and take up leisurely postures: Cao Ren would, to Xu Huang's distaste, insist that the two of them sit in the open and drink tea or wine, while eager spotters watched for any activity at the gate or in the archer towers inside the Wu camp. At the end of the day, they would slowly retreat, laughing theatrically and deriding the weakness of their enemies.

Zhou Yu was bedridden for the next few weeks, helplessly listening as Cao Ren's forces camped outside the walls of his base every morning, spending the entire day chanting curses and willing Zhou Yu's early demise. He took the abuse stoically, resting and reading as the military doctor tended to his injury as best they could. But as time wore on, so Zhou Yu's patience started to run out.

"Day after day, all I hear is their wishing for my death," Zhou Yu complained as he convened a bedside meeting with Lu Su, Lü Meng, Cheng Pu, Huang Gai, Ling Tong and Han Dang. "This cannot go on."
Zhou Yu was sat up, but he was in obvious discomfort: his entire chest was bandaged under his silk pyjamas, and every move that he made was excruciatingly painful.
"Chief Commander," Cheng Pu replied emphatically, "we would gladly go out and fight, but Acting Chief Commander Lu Su insisted we put up a sign of battle-refusal, and remain in the camp... stating that any who disobeyed would be executed."
"...You tattle on me like a whining child," Lu Su admonished angrily. "What else can I do? The men are demoralised, and we do not know what other schemes Cao Ren may have in mind, do we...?"
"If we leave him be," Cheng Pu said angrily, "he'll build mounds and towers right outside the camp, and rain arrows down on us."
"We have archer towers," Lu Su reminded Cheng Pu sternly. "Letting him chant and pontificate is one thing... of course, if he started building assault points, we'd retaliate! I'm not *that* stupid!"
"Please... stop arguing," Zhou Yu said painfully. "They are convinced that I am dying... else he would not be doing this. There is only one way this is going to end besides my death..."

Zhou Yu's face contorted in agony as he turn his body sideways
and moved his legs off the bed as if to get up.
"...Chief Commander!" Cheng Pu exclaimed.
"Gongjin," Lu Su pleaded, "you mustn't...!"
"This is... the only... way," Zhou Yu insisted. "Someone... get my
armour ready. Someone... help me up."
"Gongjin...!" Lu Su whimpered.
Zhou Yu looked up at his benefactor, and said, "You... gave me,
and hence my lord... your entire fortune, Zijing, for... the sake of
peace... so what's my life...?"
"Your life is worth more than some granaries!" Lu Su implored.
"Don't be reckless! You do not need to do this!"
"...Yes I do," Zhou Yu said with a laugh.

After weeks of getting no response, Cao Ren and his soldiers were
becoming generally complacent: it was not unusual for the
spotters to be drunk or asleep, and the men became more and
more blatant in their idling, which distressed the disciplinarian Xu
Huang to breaking point.

A week before, Cao Ren had ordered a captain to smash
the battle-refusing sign: that now lay broken in the dust outside
the camp, an extra insult to the enraged men that were forcibly
contained within the base. Cao Ren did not fear Zhou Yu at all
now, and was completely relaxed as he rode to the camp, drank
heartily, and occasionally rallied the insults on his injured
counterpart.
"This is dangerous," Xu Huang pleaded as Cao Ren sat without
armour, sipping a cup of heated wine.
"Every day, every single day, you say that, General, and what has
happened...? ...Nothing," Cao Ren snickered. "Zhou Yu is good as
dead. ...**Men, shout some more! Shout some more!**"
A group of young soldiers laughed and chanted repeatedly,
**"YOUR LIFE IS AT ITS END, ZHOU YU! GO TO YOUR GRAVE,
AS HEAVEN DEMANDS!"**
**"Drums, drums!"** Cao Ren chuckled. **"DRUMS!"**
The drummers started their slow, rhythmic beat, done in time with
the chants.
**"Your life is at its end, Zhou Yu...!"** Cao Ren said almost
musically: he laughed, and continued to drink without fear.
Xu Huang noticed that the Wu camp's gates – which were usually
manned by dozens of angry infantrymen – were conspicuously
clear.
"...Something's going to happen," Xu Huang realised: he got up,
and picked up his heavy, long-handled war axe.
"Coward!" Cao Ren mocked. "You're afraid of a dead ma-"
Before Cao Ren could finish, a drummer yelped with pain and fell
from the wheeled podium he was stood on, and his drum fell
silent. As the men around him pondered the event, another drum
fell silent, and then another, as the men in the Wu archer towers
– which the spotters had been too busy idling to monitor – took
down one drummer after another with arrows. Just as the men
outside the camp realised that something was going on, the camp
gate was hastily raised, and a mass of Wu infantry and cavalry
descended on their poorly defended position.
**"QUICKLY...!"** Xu Huang urged. **"WE MUST ORGANISE!"**

"What the...? What's going on...?" Cao Ren murmured: he looked about for his armour, and started to panic.

**"WE HAVE TO RETALIATE!"** Xu Huang screamed. **"RALLY AT ONCE!"**

The imperial force, however, was not prepared for the Wu assault, and man after man crumpled as spears and hooves slammed into them. The men of Wu had weeks of rage to expunge, and killing their tormentors was the perfect remedy.

"This can't be happening...!" Cao Ren exclaimed: but even as he struggled to comprehend how the Wu forces could so suddenly be taking the advantage, he saw among the charging hordes a familiar general adorned in shining armour, wielding a gleaming sword, and riding a white horse.

**"See Chief Commander Zhou Yu here!"** Zhou Yu declared as he charged at the enemy commanders. **"Do you come to deliver yourself into my trap, Cao Ren?"**

Cao Ren was not sure if this was a man or a ghost: his courage left him, and he fled the field on foot, parts of his armour hanging off of him unceremoniously, while Zhou Yu pointed his sword and laughed boisterously.

Xu Huang found a horse and tried to make a stand, but the Wu generals were too many in number, and – faced with duelling Lü Meng, Ling Tong and Han Dang at the same time – he reluctantly followed his commander in retreat.

"We won!" Lu Su exclaimed as the last of the enemy withdrew. "Gongjin, we...!"

Zhou Yu was still atop his horse: he slowly lowered his sword until his arm was vertical, at which point the sword fell from his hand and landed with a shrill clang on the hard earth.

**"Chief Commander!"** the generals said as one: they all rushed to Zhou Yu, who was staring blankly toward the city of Jiangling.

"...Gongjin...?" Lu Su whispered as he looked up at Zhou Yu.

Without looking down, Zhou Yu said, "They're... they're gone...?"

"Yes," Lu Su said with emotion. "They're gone."

**"Chief Commander!"** the generals exclaimed again.

"Get... me inside," Zhou Yu pleaded weakly: his followers hastily complied.

Cao Ren did not dare come out and fight again, and his defences once again receded into the city, which put up only minimal defence against the few coordinated sorties by Wu and Lui Bei. Within a few weeks of that, Cao Cao decided – after a year of Cao Ren holding Jiangling – that enough resources had been wasted on an enterprise doomed to failure. Yue Jin quietly returned northward, and Cao Ren and Xu Huang retreated to Fan City and Xiangyang City. What had been deemed unthinkable had come to pass: Eastern Wu took control of Nan Prefecture, in southern Jing.

************

# ACT V: ESTABLISHING A FOOTHOLD

## 53

The forces of the southern warlord Sun Quan - whose vast responsibility below the Yangtze River was now widely known by the name 'The state of Eastern Wu' - had dealt a second humiliating blow to the ambitious Imperial Prime Minister Cao Cao by chasing him out of his recent acquisition of southern Jing Province. They had not achieved this alone: the forces of renegade warlord Liu Bei and disinherited governor of Jing Liu Qi had played their part, though their precise role in things to come would now be an urgent matter of discussion for the Wu leadership. Liu Bei – who had, prior to Cao Cao's first defeat at Red Cliffs, forces numbering less than 5,000 at his nadir – now had an army of approximately 30,000 men under his command, and Liu Qi still had his own sizeable force of around 10,000: the two Lius could not be ignored anymore, and they were keen to stress that to their Wu allies at every opportunity.

The wounded Zhou Yu returned to Chaisang to recuperate following the defeat of Cao Ren, leaving the matter of stabilising Nan Prefecture to the Acting Chief Commander, Lu Su, and his deputy, Lü Meng. The two remained in the city of Jiangling, wondering how best to approach their allies, Liu Bei and Liu Qi.

"Those four southern counties that Liu Bei took with such ease while we shed blood in the siege of Jiangling should now be returned to us," Lü Meng insisted.

"No," Lu Su replied. "I am aware that there is a lot of mistrust, but we also have to consider the size of Liu Bei's army here... Lord Sun has written to express concern at the possible threat Liu Bei now poses to our future enterprise, and wonders what we can do to placate him and maintain the alliance."

"...A regrettable but understandable stance," Lü Meng said sombrely. "Perhaps we need to consult the Chief Commander."

"Let poor Zhou Gongjin rest," Lu Su insisted. "I'm in charge, and I think that Lord Sun is correct. Liu Bei has helped us to get rid of Cao Cao, the least we can do is help him establish a temporary base for himself and his followers."

"But we must get from Liu Bei an assurance that he understands exactly who it is that now governs Nan Prefecture," Lü Meng countered. "He cannot stay in Jing as a warlord king... he'll have to remain here as a guest-subject, or go elsewhere."

"Yi Province," Lu Su revealed. "My lord supposes Yi to be the next target, as does Gongjin, and why should Liu Bei not take that?"

"The Chief Commander does not want Liu Bei to have Yi either," Lü Meng challenged. "He has already said that he sees Zhang Lu and Ma Chao as allies, sharing Yi with our Lord Sun."

"...So where does Liu Bei go...?" Lu Su asked desperately.

"That isn't my concern," Lü Meng said assertively. "So long as he isn't in Jing, or Yi, I do not care where Liu Bei goes."

"...I'm going to go to Gong'an and speak with Liu Bei," Lu Su sighed wearily. "Perhaps we can resolve this without incident."

"Do not be fooled by Zhuge Liang," Lü Meng warned. "Your shared 'dream' of 'Tripods of Power' should not take precedence here."

"It won't," Lu Su promised. "But I argue again that Zhuge Kongming is an ally... he will help me find accord, I'm sure of it."

Lu Su travelled to the city of Gong'an. Liu Bei was in the governor's house – protected as always by his bodyguard force led by Chen Dao, and speaking with Kongming as he often did – when Lu Su entered the meeting hall for an audience.
"Ah!" Liu Bei hailed. "Mister Lu: a pleasure, a pleasure!"
Liu Bei and Kongming rose from their seats so that the three men could ritually exchange slight bows of respect: that done, they then sat down to talk.
"...I'll come straight to the point," Lu Su said as Liu Bei and Kongming stared at him with probing, curious expressions on their faces. "I have travelled here on behalf of Lord Sun to thank you for your part in the annexation of Nan Prefecture."
"No need to mention it," Liu Bei said with a kind smile. "After all, we have all benefitted: Liu Qi has regained some of his territory, Lord Sun has greater security, and I have a base from which to plan the defeat of Cao Cao, even if Lord Sun no longer wishes to challenge him personally."
"...That is perhaps the problem," Lu Su continued tonelessly. "You refer to bases and regaining territory... understand, Lord Liu, that the four counties you currently occupy are Wu's domains, taken by you on our behalf, and we would like to see the seals of office tendered to me for safekeeping, so that there is no ambiguity."
Kongming started to fan himself slowly, and looked at Liu Bei.
"...No," Liu Bei replied flatly. "We took these counties with our own forces, with no help from Lord Sun, and under no direct rule of Lord Sun. I am not his vassal, I am his *ally*, or at least, I thought I was... why do you now renege on a clearly understood relationship between our forces...?
"Far from it," Lu Su insisted as Kongming stared at him silently. "It is *you* that reneges on the deal by seizing these counties. We *saved you*... we lost lives to rescue you and your rabble of followers from Cao Cao! What would you own if you were not helped by Lord Sun Quan? You would not even have possession of your own head!"
"...Get out," Liu Bei said quietly.
"Lord Liu, you...!" Lu Su continued angrily.
Chen Dao walked to Liu Bei's side and glared at Lu Su, who got to his feet and hastily took his leave.
"...If you'll excuse me," Kongming said as he rose to follow Lu Su.
"I shall," Liu Bei replied with a smile.
Kongming left the hall and found Lu Su a short distance away, arguing frantically with two guards that were blocking his path.
"You and I should go to my study, and speak further," Kongming suggested.
Sensing that he had little choice, Lu Su agreed with a terse nod.

Lu Su glared at Kongming as the latter invited him to take a seat.
"...I don't know what you think gives you the right to try to intimidate me, Zijing," Kongming said calmly. "Remember, it is your master that went against our covenant and laid siege to Jiangling first."

"I told you, long before Red Cliffs, "Lu Su admonished, "that my lord wanted to secure Jing Province as a safety measure. Nothing that has occurred should be coming as any surprise to you!"

"...I'm not surprised, but I *am* disappointed," Kongming retorted. "Zijing, we are both proponents of a Sun-Liu alliance, and yet this act goes against it completely."

Lu Su seethed, but the cause was not fury: it was frustration.

"... ... ...Ah, I see," Kongming murmured after a pause to probe Lu Su's expression. "Your Chief Commander, 'Gongjin', still has other ideas."

"Lord Liu is not trustworthy," Lu Su protested.

"How so...?" Kongming countered. "What has he done to wrong your lord...?"

Lu Su frowned theatrically, and said, "His past record shows-"

"You now use Zhang Zhao's arguments against me...?" Kongming chortled contemptuously. "He has a 'past record', Zijing, regarding the likes of Lü Bu, and the Yuans, and Cao Cao! Does your lord have sinister ambition, then...?"

"You...!" Lu Su exclaimed, pointing angrily at Kongming.

"That's it, isn't it...?" Kongming chuckled softly. "*Your* lord sees *my* lord's resistance to bending at the knee to previous conquerors and usurpers, and fears for his own career. ...So, then, what is it, I wonder...? ...'Gongjin' targeted Jiangling before securing Lingling, Wuling, Changsha and Guiyang, despite knowing that those four counties are strategically important... would that be because Jiangling is the road not just to the north, but to the *west*...?"

Lu Su was incriminatingly silent.

Kongming laughed, saying, "Zhou Yu intends to dismiss our alliance as one of convenience in a perilous moment, conquer Jing... and then Yi."

"...He seeks an alliance with Zhang Lu and Ma Chao," Lu Su confessed.

"He'll use them to defeat Liu Zhang," Kongming supposed.

"And cut Cao Cao's supply lines!" Lu Su blurted. "Zhang Lu and Ma Chao could divide Yi Province between them, and be our allies in attacking Xuchang!"

"A sound plan," Kongming conceded. "But with Jing in the hands of your two-faced master, and Yi divided up between cultists and barbarians to the west... where, then, according to this unholy design, does *my* lord go...?"

"...He could seek shelter with my lord Sun," Lu Su said uncomfortably: the derisive laughter that met the statement was expected.

"...A fine betrayal!" Kongming congratulated sarcastically. "...An act of truly brilliant treachery, a marvellous sleight of hand! You use my lord as bait to defeat Cao at Red Cliffs, and then steal the land from his relatives, and then you use his kin's land to conquer the heartland and seize the throne, while my lord is reduced to an unwanted guest in a foreign land! ...Tell me, what other humiliations has your high-minded Zhou Yu got planned for us...? Am I to tend the rice for his fields, and Lord Liu can weave his shoes and mats...? ...Or perhaps he would like to castrate us both, and have us as eunuchs in his master's new imperial palace...?"

"And what was *your* plan...?" Lu Su retorted angrily. "You always planned to seize Jing and use it to threaten us, continue Liu Qi's family feud with the Suns! Your lord has coveted the throne from birth! You talk of 'betrayal'; we shed our lifeblood fighting Cao when we could have surrendered and let him hunt your lord down like a rat! And you use our weakness as an opportunity to-"

"To *what*...?" Kongming replied calmly. "Really Zijing, stop it. There is no argument you can offer that will give just cause to your lord. He is a shameless thief, and your friend Zhou Yu is a would-be kingmaker, and that is all there is to it."

"...These are chaotic times!" Lu Su protested. "The Han is weakening! The Mandate of Heaven is shifting! It is time for others to-"

"So that is the treasonous rhetoric that 'Gongjin' has placated you with," Kongming supposed. "He sullies the loyal family name he carries: generations of service to the imperial house, disregarded in favour of personal ambition... it is disgusting. The man is shallow, arrogant, and vain: he talks grandly of beautiful songs that lack real content or good intent... and that is, indeed, a fitting description of *him*. He is, in fact, exactly the same as Cao Cao... both are guilty of the same fault."

"*You*...!" Lu Su seethed.

"...Between us, Zijing, I have long known that the Imperial house of Han is weak, and on the brink of collapse," Kongming admitted. "But I have chosen to *support* the ailing house, to provide my meagre knowhow to helping it *recover*, and if that ultimately means Lord Liu – a recognised relative of the imperial house – taking the throne, then that is perfectly right, since he has the love of the people, and therefore perhaps the 'mandate to rule' that you speak of. However popular your lord, Sun Quan, might be in his domain of jungles and disease-ridden hamlets below the Great River, he is not a Liu, and therefore not a legitimate heir to the imperial throne. He is the meritless second son of a feudal vassal whose domain was seized, not earned."

"A man of learning, resorting to class bigotry," Lu Su heckled. "You disappoint me, Zhuge, you really do. Liu Bang, the Han founder, was a peasant!"

"Lord Liu weaved mats and sandals," Kongming retorted. "You accuse me of contradiction, while deliberately missing my point... Sun Ce conquered your domain... the four southern counties of Jing willingly surrendered to Lord Liu because he is known to be virtuous. He has Liu Qi's affection as an honorary uncle because he is upright. Yet Jiangling held out for a year against Zhou Yu... not only Cao Cao's men, but men who once served Liu Biao! They held out as one against their besieger, yet when those same men faced Lord Liu in Jiangxia, they fought half-heartedly, and some even deserted Cao Cao. What does that say...?"

"This is pointless," Lu Su muttered bitterly.

"Only because your argument has no ethical basis," Kongming suggested pointedly.

"Ethics...?" Lu Su scoffed. "This is a time of...!"

"Chaos," Kongming chuckled. "I know, Zijing... I had this very same discussion with Ma Jichang only the other day. But even in chaos, there must be some semblance of order for the forces to balance. You go back to Jiangdong and think that over... you ponder the matter, and wonder if Zhou Yu is really right..."
"It doesn't matter what I think," Lu Su retorted. "Zhou Gongjin has the willing ear of our lord... what can I do...?"
"I am thinking of the *future*, Zijing," Kongming said ominously.
Lu Su looked at Kongming's cold gaze and slow, rhythmic fanning, and wondered what he meant by that for a few moments: and then, in a flash, it hit him, and he frowned disapprovingly.
"...Not a word, Zijing," Kongming insisted. "Just... ponder what I have said."

"You were a little harsh, methinks," Jian Yong said half-jokingly, as Kongming relayed his conversation with Lu Su to the other officials several hours later, and after the flustered Acting Chief Commander had long since fled the city.
"...Really...?" Kongming replied with a smirk.
"He's a sick man," Mister Sun scolded. "What if your comments aggravate his condition, Kongming...? Do we want to be accused of killing him...?"
"...He will die of his wound, not my words," Kongming chuckled. "Since when did anyone ever die from harsh words...?"
"We both know that stressing a sick man can kill him, Kongming," Mister Sun scolded further. "Why under Heaven did you do it...?"
"They exhausted the diplomatic options," Kongming suggested calmly. "But never fear... when Lu Su replaces Zhou Yu as Chief Commander, things will change."
"So you hoped to accelerate the inevitable," Jian Yong sighed. "Cruel, but... well, it couldn't happen to a nicer man."
"Nothing I said is untrue, and that is why it would aggravate him," Kongming said without regret. "He claimed to value verity... so I have given him only my honest beliefs, unfettered by diplomacy."
"...Okay," Jian Yong said with a smile. "So what happens now, then...?"
"Well," Kongming chuckled, "I suspect that, in the interests of keeping the peace... Zhou Yu will actually realise that he cannot argue..."
"That, or we're about to find out how Cao Cao felt at Red Cliffs," Mister Sun said ominously. "We're not that strong, Mister Zhuge... this is folly."
"But Lord Liu had already refused the request to cede the seals of office!" Ma Liang protested. "Kongming was only serving Lord Liu's wishes! What would *you* have done, Mister Sun...?"
"...*Aiee*," Mister Sun said weakly. "I pray this is not our doom."


************

## 54

Lu Su did not go back to Jiangling: instead, he went to Chaisang, the current capital of Eastern Wu, intending to speak firstly with his friend Zhou Yu, and then his lord, Sun Quan.

"Zijing… welcome…" Zhou Yu hailed feebly as he turned his head to face his visitor and smiled. Zhou Yu was confined to his bed, and his condition had improved little in recent weeks.
"You… … …are you better…?" Lu Su asked nervously.
"You have… come here to talk," Zhou Yu said with a painful laugh. "It must be important… for you to come all this way, Zijing. …Speak."
"I only come here to see if you are well," Lu Su lied.
"Lying was never… something you were good at," Zhou Yu chuckled weakly. "I insist… that you tell me… what Liu Bei said to you."
"What…!" Lu Su exclaimed.
"Lord Sun… has asked me about it," Zhou Yu explained. "It can only be that… Zijing… so out with it! Is it… about Yi…?"
"No," Lu Su said quietly.
"…Jing, then," Zhou Yu sighed miserably. "Liu Bei… pleads to be allowed… to remain in Jing…?"
"…Not exactly," Lu Su replied uncomfortably.
"…Then… what…?" Zhou Yu wondered.
"He… uh…" Lu Su mumbled.
"Just *tell me*…!" Zhou Yu said angrily.
"He has refused to cede the county seals," Lu Su said anxiously. "He threw me out of Gong'an."
"**Faithless rogue…!**" Zhou Yu cursed furiously. "We should…!"
Before he could finish, Zhou Yu's face contorted in pain, and the heartbroken Lady Qiao, who had been watching from afar, rushed to his side.
"…Rest yourself," Lu Su pleaded. "There will be time to deal with them later."
"Please, listen to Mister Lu Su's advice," Lady Qiao said worriedly.
"… … …You haven't finished, have you…?" Zhou Yu supposed after the wave of extreme pain passed. "What else… did *Zhuge Bumpkin* say to you…?"
"Nothing," Lu Su promised falsely.
"…You're not fooling me," Zhou Yu said with an uncomfortable laugh. "Zijing, we are friends… what did he say…?"
"He accused us of being the ones to break faith, not Liu Bei," Lu Su explained reluctantly. "He called Sun Quan the 'meritless son of a feudal vassal', and…"
"…*And*…?" Zhou Yu prompted angrily.
"He… he said you were shallow, and vain, a 'beautiful song without true content or good intention'," Lu Su recalled with distress. "He… he…"
"He…? … … …**AAAUGH…!**" Zhou Yu cried with pain: but, as Lu Su gestured that he would not continue, Zhou Yu gestured that he should.

"He… he cited your family's service to the Han," Lu Su bleated. "He said you had betrayed your ancestors for personal ambition… he said that… that… that you were… … …'disgusting'… and… no better than Cao Cao…"

"…**BUMPKIN!**" Zhou Yu raved, despite unbearable agony: Lady Qiao gestured meekly for her husband to calm down and compose himself. "…**Wretch! …Bare-footed cow-herder!**"

"…I refuse to continue," Lu Su said foolishly.

"…He dared say *more*…?" Zhou Yu seethed. "You… you *continue*, Lu Su…!"

"…I daren't!" Lu Su sobbed fearfully.

"You *must*!" Zhou Yu groaned painfully. "Just… just *tell me*!"

"…He deduced your scheme to ally with Zhang Lu and Ma Chao," Lu Su sighed miserably: he had decided to reveal all and be done with it. "He said that, with your 'unholy design' to put Jing in the hands of our 'two-faced master', and Yi in the hands of 'cultists and barbarians', he…"

Lu Su paused: Zhou Yu was shaking violently, his expression was one of irrepressible fury, and his eyes were bulging wildly. Lu Su did not continue, but an anguished grunt from Zhou Yu forced him to go on.

"…He jeered me, asked me if we intended to make peasants or eunuchs out of them in our master's imperial palace… that we had always had 'sinister intention' to usurp the imperial throne and belittle the Liu house… that we were treacherous, and that we had played a sleight of hand against them, and that you… that… that you were a 'would-be kingmaker' for a 'shameless thief'."

"… … …I… *swear*," Zhou Yu said as rage filled him, "that I will personally gut that fan-waving pedant… and Liu Bei…? No simple castration or… or servitude for *him*! I'll… dismember them *both*…!"

As Zhou Yu writhed in pain, Lu Su bowed his head sadly and mumbled.

"Wha… *what*…?" Zhou Yu prompted with disbelief. "There… is *more*…?"

"…Kongming told me to return here and think about what he had said," Lu Su continued reluctantly.

"*Please*, Mister Lu Su!" Lady Qiao begged. "*Don't*…!"

"My lady," Zhou Yu interrupted, "this… this is business. Please… let him speak."

Lady Qiao wept without restraint, and walked away.

"…He asked me to reconsider the Sun-Liu alliance, implied that we should be keeping to his and my plan of a tripartite state," Lu Su said with an almost pleading tone. "He… that was all he said."

"No, it… *wasn't*," Zhou Yu urged. "Your… plan… is not to my liking… you know that, and… *he* knows… that… and as the lord's… c-confidante, it will never be so, Lu Su, n-not s-so long as I… … …that's it, isn't it…? …He… told you to… think about it… f-for… *future*…!"

"…*Gongjin*…!" Lu Su sobbed. "I… do you see why I did not want to…?"

"…Soulless **cow herder…! …Deviant r-rice p-picker…! …Heartless, w-wicked pedant…!**" Zhou Yu said with anger and upset. "He… wishes *death* on me??? He will… *he* will die… for this… Lu… *Su*…!"

Zhou Yu started to convulse as the pain in his side became unbearable: Lu Su got up and shouted, "A doctor... **GET A DOCTOR!**"

Hours later, Zhou Yu was settled, and lay silently in his oom, bathed in the moonlight. Lu Su sat at his side, breathing noisily.
"...He's right, though," Zhou Yu said suddenly.
"*Gongjin*...!" Lu Su exclaimed: Zhou Yu had said nothing for hours, and the sound of his voice was music to Lu Su's tired ears.
"He's right, but what can I do...?" Zhou Yu continued emotionally. "He and I... why can we not be as you and I, and serve the same lord...? Why must we be enemies...? Why has fate condemned us both to be bitter enemies for the sake of others' ambitions...?"
"I... do not know," Lu Su replied numbly.
"...What can we do...?" Zhou Yu asked weakly.
"We... have no choice," Lu Su sighed miserably. "I... cannot fight this fight, nobody else can but *you*: for now, we must concede, for the sake of stability. I must go to Lord Sun first thing tomorrow, and tell him..."

"...That we must cede Nan Prefecture to Liu Bei???" Zhang Zhao exclaimed.
"No, no, ridiculous," Zhang Zhao's brother, Zhang Hong, said not just to Sun Quan and the increasingly uncomfortable Lu Su, but also the entire retinue of officials and generals that were at court. "That would never do."
"...I said 'lend', not 'cede'," Lu Su protested. "My lord, Gongjin is seriously injured... he will take a long time to recover, and that means he is no fit state to keep the wolves from the door. This plan pits the wolves and tigers against each other."
"... ... ...Mm..." Zhang Zhao mused. "Perhaps... perhaps, seen like that, my lord... ... ...Shall we retire to the private chamber to discuss it further...?"
"...Very well," Sun Quan agreed: Zhuge Jin was quietly worried.

A short time later, Sun Quan, Lu Su and Zhang Zhao were seated in Sun Quan's private audience chamber, having dismissed the rest of the court.
"...I understand your reasoning now, Zijing," Zhang Zhao said pleasantly. "It really could have marvellous benefits if played correctly."
"Really, Zibu, I am not a fool," Lu Su said emphatically. "Remember that my original plan saw only a temporary tripartite situation, until we could isolate Cao by setting him against enemies from barbarian states, and then we would annex Jing and fight Cao as the stronger of two parties. I only placate Liu Bei and Zhuge Liang with my other rhetoric."
Sun Quan nodded agreeably.
"...So then Liu Bei would become an unwitting shield...?" Zhang Zhao supposed.

"Exactly so," Lu Su confirmed. "My suggestion is not, as Zibu obviously thought, an act of folly... if we put Liu Bei in Nan Prefecture he will then be seen as the intended beneficiary all along. That will placate the people – who are afraid that, due to the previous enmity between you and Liu Biao, you may mean them harm – and it will also direct any retaliatory action at Liu Bei, not us.

"It will be Liu Bei's troops, not ours, that will be pitched against Cao Cao... weakening him so that he will not be a threat in the future. It is a case of 'pitting two tigers against each other'... where only *we* will benefit in the long run. Once we are strong again, fully recovered from Red Cliffs and the sieges at Jiangling at Hefei, and Gongjin is back to full health... if we really want to, we can take it back."

"But still, Liu Bei is very strong now," Sun Quan fretted. "His troops now number close to forty-thousand... he has acquired strong generals, and able advisors."

"...What is your concern...?" Lu Su asked plainly.

"With that much borrowed territory," Sun Quan supposed, "he may try for Yi himself, jeopardising our own plans for managing that province."

"Well then, in addition to loaning him part of Nan Prefecture," Zhang Zhao declared, "I think we should enter into a marriage alliance with him."

"...*What*...?" Lu Su exclaimed.

"Your sister, Lady Sun, is not yet married, my lord," Zhang Zhao noted. "Now-"

"No, no!" Sun Quan protested. "That won't do! He is an old man, near sixty, my sister in the flower of her youth...!"

"My lord," Zhang Zhao said, "she has often spoken of wanting for her husband a true hero: why not the 'hero' Liu Bei...?"

"I expected an idea like this from *Zhuge Jin*, but not *you*!" Sun Quan groaned desperately. "If I am to lend him Jing and my sister, why not let him borrow all of Jiangdong, and the clothes on my back...?"

Lu Su had been pondering Zhang Zhao's suggestion: now, he understood.

"...Ah, I see," Lu Su said with an ominous laugh. "Very good, Zibu, very good."

"...*No*!" Sun Quan implored. "No, no, why do you venture to ruin me...?"

"This has three advantages to you, and no disadvantages," Lu Su realised. "The first advantage – while it is the least meaningful in our grand plan – is obvious to all, and will obscure the other two from even the likes of Zhuge Liang."

"...Explain," Sun Quan asked with tense curiosity.

"First," Lu Su began, "you will be married into the Liu family: he currently lacks a wife, Ladies Gan and Mi having both passed away in recent times, which will ensure Lady Sun – who is young and beautiful - is of high status and priority. Therefore, producing more children will be uppermost in Liu Bei's mind, and any children born of the marriage will be distant – yet significant – heirs to the imperial house."

"...So even if Liu Bei won out at first, we would still win in the end," Sun Quan mused. "...Very good... very good...! ...What are the other two advantages...?"

"Secondly," Lu Su said with a smirk, "Lady Sun's loyalty to you exceeds all else... even if, by some unwanted miracle, she actually came to love Liu Bei, she would still hold the interests of the Sun family foremost... making her an ideal contact that will provide us not only with general information, but perhaps also court proceedings and pillow talk that could have us knowing what Liu Bei intends to do even before his most trusted vassals find out."

"...Marvellous... marvellous...!" Sun Quan exclaimed. "I am convinced already... but still, what is the third advantage...?"

"In addition to being loyal, Lady Sun has the courage of a tigress, the spirit of a warrior... almost matching any man," Lu Su ventured.

"...It is true," Sun Quan sighed, sensing the true meaning of Lu Su's words. "Her antics are sometimes embarrassing."

"...Think, then, what havoc she will cause for Liu Bei...!" Zhang Zhao cackled.

"...Indeed...!" Sun Quan chortled. "Oh, we must make these things happen as soon as possible...! ...Zibu, Zijing, your plans are wonderful, and accord well with my own thinking. Go, quickly, and begin negotiations...!"


************

## 55

"...I... what can I say...?" Liu Bei said hesitantly as he absorbed the words relayed from Sun Quan's court in Jiangdong. Present in his Gong'an court were Mi Zhu, Jian Yong, Mister Sun, Chen Zhen, Xiang Lang, Yi Ji, Liao Li, Huo Jun, and Kongming.

"Sun Quan is scared," Mi Zhu supposed. "He wants a marriage alliance to ensure we won't attack him later, and he 'lends' us these counties to avoid the embarrassment of us taking them from him."

Kongming and Jian Yong both remained silent.

"We should accept the 'loan'," Mister Sun said surely. "The marriage... well... it would force some greater cohesion... but it is obviously just Sun Quan 'edging his bets', trying to make sure that he will at least be related to the royal house if he cannot seize the throne himself. A nephew born into the Liu family... would be very useful to him."

Kongming and Jian Yong remained silent.

"...All the same," Ma Liang supposed, "it would not hurt to form such an alliance... it would remove the threat of Sun Quan betraying us."

Kongming and Jian Yong both smiled conspicuously, but remained silent.

"...You two have said nothing," Mister Sun complained as he looked at Jian Yong and Kongming. "Normally, it is a trial to shut you up, Kongming... why do you now sit in silence while we debate urgent matters...?"

"There is nothing to say," Kongming insisted. "Mister Sun, you have already decided matters with great care."

"...*Ayah*," Mister Sun groaned. "You are more suspect than ever with your kind words! What is really on your mind???"

"Nothing," Kongming insisted. "I cannot speak for Mister Jian."

"Like Kongming, I am without original contribution," Jian Yong said. "What has already been said by Mi Zizhong and your good self, Mister Sun, is quite right, and Ma Jichang also states the truth."

"Then... I am to marry this young beauty, Lady Sun...?" Liu Bei prompted.

"And take ownership of much of Nan Prefecture, yes," Kongming chuckled, amused at Liu Bei's obvious but incorrect priorities.

Since there was now a lull in hostilities, many of the officials decided to take the time to visit their families. Kongming, Ma Liang and Ma Su travelled to Three Rivers, visiting the Ma household and then the Zhuge household together as brothers.

"So Lord Liu will marry Lady Sun, it seems," Kongming sighed regretfully.

"...And you didn't talk him out of it...?" Yueying said with surprise as she presented tea to Kongming, Ma Liang and Ma Su.

"...No," Kongming chuckled as he fanned himself slowly.

"Kongming," Ma Liang scolded, "if you had reservations, you should have-"

"It is also to our advantage to have Lady Sun here, am I right...?"
Ma Su asked plainly. "...After all, she can be used to feed false
information back to her brother, she makes a good hostage, and
her behaviour will give us ample warning of Sun Quan's motives."
"...Well said," Kongming praised. "Your knowledge extends beyond
the battlefield, Youchang! Yes, it is obvious that Sun Quan has had
at least two advantages pointed out to him, since Lady Sun is
treasured by State Mother Wu, and she would need to be
consulted on this. But even though a spy can be deceived... my
greater worry is her boisterous reputation."
"...'Boisterous'...?" Yueying giggled. "How so, husband...?"
"When I was in Chaisang," Kongming revealed at last, "she
entered the hotel where I was being kept, guarded by a retinue of
twenty armed women, and-"
"Armed *women*...?" Ma Su chortled.
"She herself was armed," Kongming continued. "She wears not
ladylike dresses befitting a southern princess, but the trousers and
shirt of a serving maid, a farm hand, or a lady monk."
"Wait, wait... *she* was armed...?" Ma Su chuckled. "With *what*...?"
"...A sword," Kongming replied dryly.
"And her women, they carried swords...?" Ma Liang asked
excitedly: Kongming looked at Yueying with a glazed and weary
expression, and she giggled silently.
"...Her handmaidens are, apparently, like her, trained sword
fighters, martial artists and crack archers, and they act not just as
servants, but as guards," Kongming reported calmly.
"Women with *swords*...?" Ma Su chuckled incredulously. "...Women
as *guards*...! Women that can *fight*...!"
"...That will certainly be the talk of the land," Ma Liang snickered.
"I do not see why this is the first I've heard of it."
"She is... an embarrassment to her brother," Kongming revealed.
"...Because she has taken up interests reserved for men...?"
Yueying asked pointedly, and with a small hint of empathy.
"Not specifically," Kongming sighed, "rather... that she is... well...
you see, she came to the hotel not to greet me – which would be
enough of a breach of protocol. She came to the hotel to..."
Kongming coughed awkwardly, and stopped talking.
"...To what...?" Ma Su asked curiously.
"...To *threaten me*," Kongming admitted: Yueying used her sleeve
to hide her smile from the three men, who were obviously
uncomfortable with the notion. "She came to me with hand on
hilt, telling me not to make trouble," Kongming added soberly.
"That won't do," Ma Liang fretted.
"Apparently, she has the free run of the city," Kongming explained
further. "She is, to use Lu Su's description: 'rowdy and
unrestrained'."
Yueying only just held in a laugh: Ma Liang and Ma Su groaned at
the thought, and frowned worriedly.
"We can't let this lawless force of nature marry Lord Liu," Ma Liang
protested desperately. "She will bring his house into disrepute!
...This casts the marriage in a whole new light, Kongming: they
mean to offload a troublemaker onto us!"

"Lord Liu *craves her*!" Kongming chuckled miserably. "You saw him, Jichang… he longs for a wife since Lady Mi and Lady Gan passed away. This girl is half his age, it appeals to him completely. He'd marry her tomorrow if he could."

"But… but if he knew she was 'rowdy'," Ma Liang suggested: Yueying was again forced to stifle a laugh.

"I don't think that'd make any difference," Kongming said sadly. "Let us just accept this thing as an unavoidable event, and plan instead for how to keep her contained as best we can."

"Perhaps Lord Liu can tame her," Ma Su suggested.

"…She's not a horse," Kongming scolded.

"She may try to be more restrained to impress him, and win his respect," Yueying proposed. "…Sometimes, you would be surprised what someone would supress to earn a person's love."

"…You mean your secret proficiency at playing the qin…?" Kongming replied, taking Yueying by surprise. "I still do not know why you thought I would be threatened or angered by it… to think that you and I could play together, harmonise as I did when I played alongside Zhou Yu…"

"…Lady Huang, you play the qin…?" Ma Su exclaimed.

"Enough," Kongming chuckled: he could see Yueying was too stunned to say any more. "We must plan our movements carefully… regardless of the outcome of the marriage, we have Nan Prefecture and the worries that go with that too."

"…I had thoughts about that," Ma Su admitted. "Are they not offloading a problem onto us with Nan as well…?"

"Well spotted," Kongming lauded. "We'll be alright, though… in fact, it will give us the doorway into Yi that our lord so badly needs: so whatever their schemes portend, we will outwit them, and win in the end."

Night time arrived, and Kongming sat with Yueying while she played the qin: he listened to the melodies that she played with interest.

"…So what else have you 'supressed' to 'earn my love'…?" Kongming asked as Yueying finished playing.

"My passion for astronomy and astrology is known to you," Yueying replied. "I am interested in inventions, as you also know… and I have read every single document you left here, and every one of them enlightens me."

"…You should not have kept your love of music from me," Kongming scolded.

"I did no such thing!" Yueying insisted. "I have always enjoyed hearing you play… I simply refrained from sharing my own knowledge of playing."

"And you are a wonderful talent indeed," Kongming suggested. "I am very lucky to have you in my life… a pity, then, that we have always been so far apart until now."

"Until now…?" Yueying prompted excitedly.

"...I have had reports that suggest we have nothing to fear from Sun Quan at present," Kongming explained. "Cao Cao appears to be consolidating his positions in the west and southeast, intent on removing the threats of Ma Chao and Sun Quan before he starts harassing Jing again. That may change... but I doubt that will happen while Cao Cao only sees an alliance of eighty-thousand waiting for him every time he sets foot near Jiangling."

"So...?" Yueying prompted with even greater excitement.

"So," Kongming declared, "I think it's safe for you to come with me, you and Jun and his family, and settle in Jing. Lord Liu has taken Gong'an as his temporary capital, and has had Liu Qi appointed Inspector of Jing Province. I have... mm. I did not think about the magnitude of it until now."

"The magnitude of *what*...?" Yueying asked impatiently. "Come on, husband, tell me your news, please...!"

"...I have been appointed 'Military Adviser General of the Household', and Governor of Changsha, Lingling, and Guiyang counties," Kongming admitted hesitantly: Yueying's eyes welled with tears of surprise, joy, and fear.

"It's ridiculous, isn't it...?" Kongming chuckled.

"Liang...!" Yueying whispered: she threw her arms around Kongming and sobbed emotionally, while Kongming struggled to ascertain her true feelings.

"...Are we happy, or sad...?" Kongming asked as he embraced Yueying gently.

"Both," Yueying replied.

"...Are we optimistic, or afraid...?" Kongming asked further.

"Again, both," Yueying replied.

"I see," Kongming murmured. "But... you will be coming to join me...?"

"Of *course I will*," Yueying said gladly. "I... will finally be able to spend more time with you... at long, long last."

"...I'll make sure and acquire a second qin," Kongming chuckled softly. "It shall be waiting for you when you arrive. But in the meantime... which of us shall play...?"

"...I shall," Yueying insisted: the two ended their embrace, and Yueying turned once again to the qin. Her playing was contented, optimistic, and gentle: Kongming fanned himself slowly as he listened, and smiled gratefully.

The marriage between Liu Bei and Lady Sun of Wu would take place in Jiangdong, where the two warlords, Liu Bei and Sun Quan, would finally meet face-to-face after years of conversing through their vassals. Zhou Yu started to recover slightly as the weeks wore on, and Liu Bei continued to consolidate his position in Jing. Jiangling and Yiling were still under Wu's control, which impeded Liu Bei's mission to take Yi Province from his distant kinsman Liu Zhang. As the day of the wedding drew closer, it became apparent to all that the matter of Jing and Yi would need proper resolution, as steps taken so far were far from enough.

************

## 56

As the year drew to a close, life drew to a close for the young Inspector of Jing Province, Liu Qi.

Liu Qi had been stationed in Changsha since the county had been tendered to him, and Liu Bei was forced to hurry from his base in Gong'an in order to be by his kinsman's bedside at the end. Liu Bei insisted that all of his most important generals and officials join him on the journey, so that Liu Qi would understand the level of respect that he had earned. Kongming insisted on having Yueying accompany him, and as governor of the county, he could install her in his local residence while he attended the final vigil for the dying inspector.

Kongming watched silently and emotionlessly as Liu Bei rushed to the side of Liu Qi, tears streaming from his eyes.
"Oh, nephew...!" Liu Bei exclaimed as he knelt next to the frail, gaunt man in the bed: Liu Qi was breathing only faintly, and he seemed to be blind as well.
"...Oh, how can there be a Heaven...?" Liu Bei sobbed as the officials gathered around him. "How can Heaven be just when it steals away a young man, a dragon yet to reach his prime... and leaving only old bones like mine...?"
"Mm... uh...!" Liu Qi exclaimed: he could not form words, and the end was very near.
"...But I swear, nephew, that I will safeguard your lands, and honour the promise I made to your father," Liu Bei declared. "You may rest easy... Jing will continue to thrive in the hands of a Liu, and your spirit will live on in me."
Liu Qi smiled faintly.

"...A sad and pathetic end," Kongming said as he entered his home in the city, accompanied by Ma Liang and Ma Su.
"Yes," Ma Liang agreed emotionlessly.
At that point, Yueying entered the room from the direction of the garden.
"Welcome back," Yueying hailed warmly. "...You look sad."
"Liu Qi has finally succumbed," Ma Liang declared.
"...He 'succumbed' a long time ago... that was the cause of his malady," Kongming scoffed as he sat in front of his qin, and the Ma brothers took seats as guests.
"I suppose we shall have to acquire white clothes to wear, then," Ma Liang noted.
"We shall," Kongming replied. "We will be expected to assume full mourning attire, and sob for the man until our eyes bleed."
"Riddled with the consequences of overindulgence as he was, I am surprised he lasted as long as he did," Ma Su suggested with contempt. "...But that means..."
"...That Jing no longer has a 'rightful heir'," Kongming sighed. "Zhou Yu is bedridden, and cannot discuss this with us himself... but I know full well that Lu Su will be on a boat as soon as the death is made public."

"What, and insist Jing be ceded...?" Ma Liang said incredulously. "How can he do that...? ...It is disgraceful enough that he has seized Yiling, Jiangling and Jiangxia Prefecture without daring to come and demand the counties we have."

"...I imagine that they are still scared of our military capabilities," Kongming replied surely. "They won't demand anything... I have already suggested that Lord Liu should advance to the provincial governorship, and I think that they will accept."

"Would they...?" Ma Liang chuckled. "Kongming, they only lend us parts of the region to placate us while they wait for 'Gongjin' to recover."

"He won't recover," Kongming insisted. "He'll be dead before the end of next year, Jichang... he knows that, that's why he doesn't contest any of these plans."

"So what do you think will happen...?" Yueying asked.

"Lord Liu will become Governor of Jing Province, Sun Quan will accept it and marry his sister to Lord Liu, and – hopefully – he will also cede Yiling and Jiangling to us, so that we can advance on Yi Province in the next year," Kongming supposed. "As soon as Provincial Inspector Liu Qi has been mourned sufficiently, I will be travelling to Jiangdong with Lord Liu, Jian Yong and Mister Sun to finalise the arrangements for this marriage."

Ma Liang shuddered.

"...I saw that," Kongming joked as he pointed at Ma Liang with his fan. "Really, Jichang, this young woman will not be so much of a handful!"

"I hope not," Ma Liang fretted.

"Does Liu Qi's death really not affect any of you at all...?" Yueying asked.

"Lady Huang," Ma Su replied, "he was not a man worth mourning. His illness was his own fault, and when he knew he had such responsibility to bear... shameful."

"Agreed," Kongming said reluctantly. "But all the same, mourn him we must..."

For a month, Liu Bei insisted that all of the officials, generals and soldiers wear colourless garments and paid several visits to the shrine of Liu Qi. Once it was deemed acceptable to do so, mourning ended, and Liu Bei prepared for a journey to Chaisang to meet the brother of his future bride.

"So Liu Bei will soon be in Jiangdong," Zhou Yu said as Lu Su sat as his bedside, relaying important news of the day.

"He will be bringing Kongming, Mister Sun Qian, and Mister Jian Yong," Lu Su elaborated mechanically. "We have agreed to the suggestion that Liu Bei should be made Governor of Jing..."

"I disagree strongly, Zijing," Zhou Yu admitted. "You cannot lend a man the signs of kingship, and then complain when he calls himself a king. By appointing him governor, you make him Liu Biao's legitimate successor, something Bei himself was not prepared to do for Liu Qi when he only recommended him as an inspector. Why do we do this for a man we only loan the province to...?"

"We are going to make him the target for Cao Cao's wrath," Lu Su insisted.

"You're opening the way for him to take Yi as well, Zijing," Zhou Yu retorted. "I am fearful of the man *now*: if he also had Yi... he would become a true king, with domains greater than ours, and *then* what...?"

"Kongming insists that he has no intention of taking Yi," Lu Su replied: Zhou Yu writhed in pain as he struggled to contain contemptuous laughter.

"...You... *idiot*...!" Zhou Yu spluttered. "You *believe*... him...?"

Lu Su lowered his head guiltily.

"He is... danger... *danger*...!" Zhou Yu insisted. "*Zijing*...!"

"I will do what I can to keep them from becoming a threat to us," Lu Su promised.

With that, Lu Su departed, and Zhou Yu sighed with despair.

Sun Quan sat in his exalted position at the end of the palace hall and watched Liu Bei stride into the Chaisang court with his head held high. Jian Yong, Mister Sun and Kongming followed him at close distance, while Chen Dao and the rest of Liu Bei's bodyguards respected Sun Quan's request that they wait outside the hall, watched by elite officers and soldiers led by the Wu General Zhou Tai.

"Greetings, Governor of Jing Province," Sun Quan hailed, as Zhang Zhao and Zhang Hong – who led the line of officials – looked Liu Bei up and down contemptuously.

"And greetings to you, Governor of Jiangdong and founder of Eastern Wu," Liu Bei replied politely: he made a slight bow as a restrained gesture of respect. "I am glad to see that you are well, and take the opportunity to wish a speedy recovery to Chief Commander Zhou Yu."

"Please, be seated, Governor," Sun Quan said as he reciprocated the bow from his seated position, though he made the gesture even more slight. "I am glad that the situation in Jing is finally starting to stabilise..."

"The last of Cao's puppet governors is removed, and the region is now safe," Liu Bei replied. "I only wish... that Inspector Liu Qi, my nephew, could have lived a little longer to enjoy the moment."

Liu Bei wiped a tear from his eye.

"...My condolences to you and to the people of Jing for the loss," Sun Quan replied emotionlessly. "It is regrettable that the feud between our families prevented peace in the land... I appreciate Liu Qi's desire to see that feud ended, and can now say that it has. But Jing Province is still divided, Governor, and that cannot change while things remain as they are."

"I concur," Liu Bei replied calmly. "Feuds between men are a poison... if only every man showed such high-mindedness, and realised that the needs of the many outweigh the needs of the few."

"But you do agree," Sun Quan prompted with less subtlety, "that things cannot remain as they are in Jing Province."

"Quite," Liu Bei replied tersely.

"...Chief Commander Zhou Gongjin retains his position as Administrator of Nan Prefecture, and controls Jiangling and Yiling," Sun Quan noted. "You, Governor, are the *figurehead* governor, while a more permanent solution is sought. I hope that the proposal of a union of our families will solidify your position, build our trust, and inspire you to succeed in your own ambitions..."

"...My only ambition is to destroy Cao Cao and rescue the Emperor," Liu Bei insisted: the words incited quiet, derisive snickering from some of Sun Quan's officials. "Jing is governed by me in the name of the Emperor... I see no ambiguity, no lack of clarity, and no need to speak of solidifying positions... I am solid as a rock in those parts of Jing that I now control, and it suits me well as a base from which to carry out Heaven's will."

Nervous coughing and awkward murmuring met Liu Bei's bold statement.

"...I understand that our officials have been discussing ideas such as lending you the use of the rest of Nan Prefecture," Sun Quan noted. "Tell me, Governor Liu, what ideas you have concerning the fate of Yi Province...?"

"I have no ideas, Governor Sun, besides making Provinicial Governor Liu Zhang of Yi turn away from the darkness," Liu Bei replied. "What are your own thoughts...?"

"...We have considered attacking Liu Zhang, I confess," Sun Quan sighed. "Our main reservation is his kinship to you, Governor Liu... and, it goes without saying, his kinship, however distant, to our sovereign. I wonder, would you object to his being removed as a threat to Jing Province and the land as a whole...?"

"Before I would ever seize Yi Province, I would rather unbind my hair, become a recluse, and retire to the mountains!" Liu Bei insisted. "I make that vow to all the land and men under Heaven, and I'll never break that vow!"

"Your benevolence is known throughout the land," Sun Quan replied with a mournful sigh, "and today, it is known to me. Very well: I shall speak with Chief Commander Zhou, and consider alternative ways of resolving the crisis in Yi."

"My thanks, Governor Sun," Liu replied, making a needless but slight bow of respect from where he sat.

Later that evening, Sun Quan invited the officials Zhang Zhao, Zhang Hong, Zhuge Jin, Lu Su and Lü Fan to a meeting in his private audience chamber in order to discuss his first encounter with the infamous warlord and possible rival that would soon – according to intrigue-driven design – be his brother-in-law.

"I must say," Sun Quan admitted, "that Liu Bei seemed very upright, an outstanding man... is there no way we can find accord with this man, since I see in him none of the 'crafty owl' I've heard so much about...?"

"Well," Zhuge Jin – who was grateful to be included in discussions – said cheerfully, "I have talked at great length with my brother Kongming, and he assures me that Liu Bei has no desire to contend with you... he simply wants the land to be at peace, and for all men to have the land that should be theirs."

"Nonsense," Zhang Zhao scoffed. "While I may not always agree with Gongjin, I do agree with one thing... Liu Bei should be left out of any long-term plans we have for Jing or for anywhere else."

"Then why do you want to marry Lady Sun to the man...?" Zhuge Jin countered irritably. "Is this some farcical attempt at a 'Beauty Trap' then...?"

"...You are not thinking about the lord!" Zhang Zhao retorted. "Why should he not have Jing...? The marriage is a means to several ends...it ties our families together, so that any act of Liu Bei that is not in our mutual interest will earn him the scorn of future historians; it ensures that any aforementioned act of ill-will is known to us before it can harm us; it ensures that he can be governor, since he will then be related by marriage to the true ruler of the province... our own Lord Sun."

"Petty, nonsensical subterfuge: unprovoked, needless backstabbing!" Zhuge Jin admonished angrily. "You are a schemer for scheming's sake, Zhang Zhao, and you plot against a good man that has done nothing but help us!"

"...You should cross the river now, brother of Zhuge Liang," Zhang Zhao replied ominously. "You obviously have no desire to serve here any longer."

"Oh, I'm going nowhere," Zhuge Jin scoffed. "Someone has to keep your snake's tongue closely watched."

"Can we... have some calm...?" Lu Su pleaded. "Zhang Zibu, Zhuge Ziyu, I see both of your arguments... but my heart is with accord between the families of Sun and Liu. Let us see this marriage not as petty subterfuge, but as a way to set things right, and also as a means of reducing risk if we are wronged."

"And if Liu Bei is content to remain in Jing, building trust and respect amongst his leased vassals, until he is one day ready to seize it...?" Zhang Zhao asked pointedly.

"Liu Bei will invade Yi, brother," Zhang Hong insisted. "He yearns for that land of prosperity... how could he resist snatching it from feeble hands and claiming it to be 'the righteous passing of lands from Liu to Liu' when he's challenged, like he is doing in our own Jing Province...?"

"If Liu Bei says he will not invade Yi, then I believe him," Lu Su said sternly. "He defends Jing as an uncle to the late Liu Qi, not as a thief."

"And so, Zijing, now *we* are thieves...?" Lü Fan chortled.

"You...!" Lu Su said angrily.

"Ziheng makes a fair point," Sun Quan added. "You imply we are thieves when you state that Liu Bei is not."

"...Jing was fairly rescued from Cao Cao," Lu Su conceded.

"The matter of who belongs on a piece of land is a matter of opinion," Zhang Zhao said with a condescending, explanatory tone. "The truth is that there are none with an eternal right to land... the strongest, most able, wisest and most productive will always win out, because it is the will of Heaven.

"Once, parts of Yi belonged to the barbarian Nan tribes... did they build roads, reap the silk, till the fields, and build bridges to cross into other lands, and share the bounties of their land...? No, they fought us and each other, and enacted pagan ceremonies, and disrespected the law of the land. When the Han people took those lands, they took them rightly, to make proper use of them, where the ignorant Nan 'masters' of the land could not! Man's purpose is to grow, and to do that, we must use all things as best we can... not live like animals!"

"What have the Nan tribes got to do with Jing...?" Zhuge Jin said angrily.

"Righteous governance," Zhang Zhao insisted. "We now rule Jing because we are righteous: once, Jiangdong was unfit for purpose, now it is a thriving nation in its own right. What we have done is take a piece of worthless clay, and make a valuable pot from it. Jiangdong was stagnant, so is Yi... we'll help them find their true worth, in ways that the imperial court has never tried to do!"

"Are you saying...?" Zhuge Jin exclaimed.

"Uh... let's end the discussion there," Lu Su chuckled nervously. "Jing is ours, Liu Bei is the governor in name only, at our discretion... if he will not seize Yi, then we must do it, else we must find someone who can, or Liu Zhang will continue to act in Cao Cao's name and aid attempts to take Jing back from us."

"Agreed," Sun Quan murmured uneasily. "...For now, let's retire... is Liu Bei in good accommodation...?"

"Since he is marrying Lady Sun," Lu Su explained, "he has been placed in the best hotel in Chaisang... pending a better solution, should one exist."

"Very good," Sun Quan said with a weak smile. "Tomorrow, I am going to visit Gongjin, and see if he is well. ...Lu Su, please feel free to attend."

"I shall," Lu Su promised: with that said, the meeting ended.

"So, Zhang Zhao has imperial designs for Sun Quan," Kongming chuckled as he sat with his brother in his own hotel room. "I'm not surprised... well, at nothing but his foolish blatancy. It is true that Sun Quan has done remarkable things south of the Great River... and if there were no worthy Lius left to take the throne... then I might agree with him."

"You derided him once," Zhuge Jin challenged. "Now, he is a worthy inheritor of the Mandate of Heaven. Could it be, younger brother, that you are reconsidering your own allegiances...?"

"You once spoke of despairing for me choosing to serve Lord Liu," Kongming reminded his brother sternly. "Now, you concede that he is a benevolent lord. A man should not be inflexible in his thinking."

"And, as Lü Meng once said to Lu Su, 'When you see a man that you have not seen for three days, you should view him again, with a new eye'," Zhuge Jin said with a laugh. "Very true... yes, I concede, younger brother, than Liu Bei is worthy. What a shame that two such worthy men should appear at the same time... else men like us would have no trouble knowing where we should be."

"...Quite so," Kongming sighed miserably. "Would we all be lurking in darkened rooms, plotting to entrap and kill each other's lords and each other, then...?"

"...'Kill'...?" Zhuge Jin fretted. "Why do you say such things...?"

"Can I trust Zhou Yu and the Zhang brothers not to try and murder my lord Liu while he is here, far away from his own army...?" Kongming prompted.

"Of course!" Zhuge Jin insisted desperately. "The men of Jiangdong would never-"

"But I see that plans are being made to put Lord Liu in a palatial home, adorned with beauties and luxuries," Kongming accused. "Would I be right in thinking that Zhou Yu hopes to soothe the soaring dragon into slumber by plying it with wine and women, hoping that his poor childhood and background as a sandal weaver has made him fond of wealth and leisure...?"
Zhuge Jin was silent.
"I am powerless if this 'Luxury Trap' works... and it might, since Lord Liu is well known to be fond of wealth and leisure, sadly," Kongming admitted. "But be warned... his vassals in Jing will not be placated. Even if Lord Liu abandons them for a life of vice, and becomes another Liu Qi or Liu Cong, that is not the end of the story. Zhou Yu plays with fire... sick men shouldn't do that."
"Honest as always," Zhuge Jin sighed miserably as Kongming started to fan himself casually. "I'll be off now... take care, until we meet again."
"Soon, I hope," Kongming replied: Zhuge Jin departed, and Kongming sighed sadly.

************

## 57

The wedding of Liu Bei and Lady Sun was treated as a magnificent state affair. Red flags adorned the streets of Chaisang, and in the palace of Sun Quan – where the ceremony would take place – red flags and tassels hung from every mast and spear. There were thousands of guests, including the entire court of officials, and many of Wu's generals, even the ailing Zhou Yu. State Mother Wu and Sun Quan oversaw the proceedings from two elevated seats.

As was the custom, Liu Bei and Lady Sun arrived separately but walked from the palace gates to the podium together. Lady Sun – who was dressed in an array of magnificent red and patterned robes – moved with such grace and elegance that Kongming wondered if this was the same woman that had once threatened him with violence. Liu Bei was dressed in finery that outshone even Sun Quan, and his headdress – a black hat topped with a long, flat piece of reinforced cloth, from which rows of beads dangled at the front and back – made him look like an emperor.

A priest blessed the two as they arrived at the podium, and were made to sit opposite the designated matchmakers, Mister Sun and Lu Su. They then paid respects to State Mother Wu, Lady Sun's mother, and to the heavens: once one last set of vows were uttered, the two were married. Sun Quan observed the whole affair with cold eyes, as the enormity of the event dawned on him at last.

"I've just wed my sister to Liu Bei," Sun Quan murmured as he convened a meeting with his advisers in his private audience chamber once again. "I've just forced my sister to marry that-"
"My lord," Lu Su interrupted, "nobody forces Lady Sun or State Mother Wu to endure anything. Both were perfectly happy with the arrangement... State Mother Wu is shrewd and clever, she sees things as we do, and Lady Sun understands her role perfectly."
"What, to sleep with Liu Bei and steal secrets...?" Sun Quan retorted angrily. "I could have asked one of *you* to yield a daughter for that!"
Zhang Zhao and Zhang Hong blanched: Lu Su and Zhuge Jin were silent.
"I have just married my tigress sister to an old snake, a lofty owl," Sun Quan lamented bitterly. "He came dressed to *outshine me*, to portray a man whose destiny is to rule the land... even my mother said he looked like the next Emperor!"
"...But then," Lu Su suggested apprehensively, "is it so bad that you are now the brother-in-law of a possible future emperor...?"
**"Is that supposed to be funny...?"** Sun Quan asked cuttingly. **"What of MY ambitions??? Did I pit thirty-thousand men against Cao Cao at Red Cliffs, and did my brother lose his life building the state of Eastern Wu, all in order to put that sneaky old peasant Liu Bei on the throne???"**

"...My lord," Lu Su replied carefully, "you must be assured that your tone matches your intent. Were you to say such things in front of the wrong people... those people might say that you had ideas about taking the throne yourself."

Zhang Zhao and Zhang Hong looked at one-another uncomfortably; Sun Quan's eyes, which had practically bulged out of their sockets with rage, suddenly receded and turned to look at the floor.

"Liu Bei has the right, however indirect, to claim succession: you do not," Zhuge Jin continued. "As Zijing said, the main reason that Cao Cao is reviled is the same reason that your father's lord, Yuan Shu, was so hated... for coveting the throne."

"You are both right," Sun Quan realised. "I risk damaging my reputation as a benevolent statesman by speaking of Liu Bei in that way. It is true that the mandate can legitimately pass to one of greater worth, but for that to be so, there has to be no worthy successor to the line of Liu. ...I shall choose my words and thoughts with greater care in future."

"We should now focus on keeping Liu Bei in comfort, my lord, to reassure him that we have no wicked intent, as Gongjin suggested," Zhang Zhao said eagerly.

**"A supposed act of reassurance that is, of course, being done for entirely the opposite reason!"** Zhuge Jin accused. **"You have nothing BUT ill intent! You want to trap Liu Bei, keep him here in Jiangdong!"**

"If he does not want to stay, he can leave," Zhang Zhao replied casually. "Nobody will make him stay and enjoy the palace we will give him, or the magnificent treasures, or the beautiful serving maids, or the fine food and well-brewed wine..."

"...*Treachery*," Zhuge Jin hissed.

"If he ignores his vassals and his mission, and he stays, then he only proves that he is a greedy peasant that craved nothing more than fame and wealth, and that he never had a true heart," Zhang Hong added. "If such a thing were proved... then no more worthy Lius live... *do they*...?"

Zhuge Jin looked at Lu Su: Zhuge Jin was worried, but Lu Su seemed to be completely comfortable with Zhang Hong's statement, and simply smiled.

Weeks passed: Liu Bei remained in his new palace at Chaisang, wandering the halls and enjoying the relentless torrent of expensive gifts that Sun Quan lavished on him. Kongming, Jian Yong and Mister Sun had long since returned to Jing, but Liu Bei showed no signs of returning.

"Liu Bei appears to be feeling very comfortable," Sun Quan sighed as he visited Zhou Yu in his home: the latter was playing his qin – albeit with slowness and discomfort – and smiling self-assuredly.

"...Tell me," Zhou Yu said, "has Mister Bu Zhi returned from his wanderings...?"

"You know that he has, Gongjin," Sun Quan replied with a smile. "What are you up to now...?"

"I would ask you, my lord, to grant Bu Zhi with the title of a general of the field and give him special permission to act as he sees fit," Zhou Yu declared as he continued to play with clinical precision. "Give him a special elite force of men, and send him southward... to collect tribute from the independent southern rulers."

"...Do we need to take such steps...?" Sun Quan wondered.

"Furthermore," Zhou Yu said, "give him permission to discipline – to any degree, as he sees fit – lower-to-middle-ranking officers."

"...Gongjin, that would give him the right to discipline the governors themselves, 'as he sees fit'," Sun Quan noted.

"It would," Zhou Yu replied casually. "He could even *execute them*, if he saw fit."

"...I shall do it, although I do not know why," Sun Quan said apprehensively.

"My lord, these independent rulers cannot, like those in the four Jing counties, remain independent forever," Zhou Yu explained. "Rulers whose allegiances may not be reliable... must be dealt with to ensure your safety and your authority. I like it no more than any man would... but for my lord, I will compromise any 'principle' to ensure his success."

"I am lucky to have you to rely upon," Sun Quan replied gratefully.

"...I wonder, Lord Sun, if you might rely upon me to make another suggestion," Zhou Yu said calmly.

"Speak, Gongjin," Sun Quan chuckled. "Say whatever is on your mind."

"...Liu Bei is, at present, free to leave whenever he chooses," Zhou Yu began.

"And that will remain so," Sun Quan interrupted. "I... I appreciate your deep-rooted concerns about the man, for I have many of my own: but we cannot be seen to break faith. So far, he seems contented to stay... but when he wants to leave... let him."

"This is a golden opportunity to remove him as a threat," Zhou Yu insisted. "We could keep him where he is, living as he does... is that such a crime...?"

"His vassals would not stand for it," Sun Quan countered. "Leave him be."

Zhou Yu sighed regrettably, and nodded in compliance.

Weeks later, in Jiangling, Kongming convened the officials for an urgent meeting.

"I'm worried," Kongming admitted. "Chen Dao has written to me yet again... he took my advice, and... and...!"

"And what...?" Jian Yong prompted uneasily.

"... ... ...*Aiee!*" Kongming exclaimed after a long and painful pause. "I almost find it impossible to say it...!"

"Just say it," Yi Ji insisted. "If the worst has occurred, we can plan where we will go from here... who we will serve."

"...Don't talk nonsense: Lord Liu is our one true master!" Mister Sun said angrily.

"Yours, maybe, Mister Sun," Yi Ji retorted. "But if he is another Liu Biao... I will not waste my life serving a fool."

"Kongming," Jian Yong urged. "Please, speak."

"Last time, I asked Chen Dao to remind Lord Liu of his obligations, such as administrating Jing and saving Emperor Xian from Cao Cao... Lord Liu replied that 'There will be time enough for all things when the fates are on our side'," Kongming said with despair. "This time, I told Chen Dao to ask him if he ever thought of returning to Jing... and he... he replied, 'I am at peace, and hardly think of Jing'...!"

"*What*...?" Jian Yong and Mister Sun exclaimed in one voice.

"He *must* have been drunk," Ma Liang insisted.

"Jichang, that's *worse*!" Kongming replied desperately. "An intoxicated man speaks more honestly than a sober one! Look, drunk or sober this is his *true mind*, not some fabricated placation! He thinks *nothing* of Jing... *nothing*!"

"Then the cause of Han is lost," Yi Ji grieved. "I have wasted nearly three years in this man's service, and all for naught!"

"We can't let him do this to us, Kongming," Jian Yong growled as Mister Sun started to sob quietly. "I've been his friend for forty years... I know there's more to him than this! It's the women, the drink, the money... he's muddle-headed, and needs to be brought back to reality."

"You think I'm not trying...?" Kongming replied angrily. "I... I have one last idea... please, trust me."

"Zhou Yu is better, and he's back in Jiangling, planning something," Ma Liang noted with concern. "Lord Liu has to return... what if morale starts to plummet, and our followers – especially those won from Lei Xu – start to turn to Zhou Yu?"

"I expect that's the scheme," Kongming sighed. "Fortunately, we have even had people joining us while Lord Liu has been pampering himself in Chaisang... so we have not lost faith yet. I'll write again... and if it works... then Lord Liu will be back here with us before the month is out."

The other officials nodded agreeably and hopefully.

In Jiangling, Zhou Yu was starting to acquaint himself with the officials under his command: one such official was the Officer of Merit, Pang Tong.

"You summoned me, Administrator Zhou...?" Pang Tong said as he reached Zhou Yu's office.

"Yes, Master Pang... please, enter, sit down!" Zhou Yu hailed enthusiastically.

Pang Tong made a strong bow of obeisance, and took a guest seat to the left of Zhou Yu, who bowed slightly, saying, "I would prostrate myself on the ground to welcome such a man as you, were I not still nursing a wound, Master... please, forgive my inability to show you the respect you deserve."

"Hardly," Pang Tong insisted. "I am a mere pedant... not worthy of your time or such shows of respect."

"You," Zhou Yu replied, "are Young Phoenix... one of the talents of the age! Why do you work as an Officer of Merit, when you could hold high office, like your friend Zhuge Liang, the Crouching Dragon...?"

"...Perhaps I take my Taoist name too literally," Pang Tong replied. "While all a crouching dragon must do is come out of the shadows, can a young phoenix really hope to fly...?"

"...An interesting response," Zhou Yu said with a laugh. "How would you rate yourself when compared with Zhuge Liang...?"

"Kongming and I are equals," Pang Tong replied. "Or, perhaps, he exceeds me... or I exceed him... I do not truly know."

"Or is it that you don't want to find out...?" Zhou Yu replied. "Master, your skill and knowledge would be of immense value to the cause of Eastern Wu... would you condescend to helping us...?"

"I am content to remain in my current post," Pang Tong replied. "Here, I appraise people, and harm not a hair on a person's head, in accordance with my wishes to live a peaceful, benevolent existence. Of course, I am aware that this may be more of a demand than a request..."

"Not at all!" Zhou Yu insisted desperately. "I would not dare to harm a man such as you, Master... never."

"I am lucky," Pang Tong snickered. "Now, Cao Cao's agents and yourself have spared me, despite my refusal to do service... most who refuse Cao Cao, like the venerable Hua Tuo, meet an early death... yet here I am, alive to refuse another hero of the age... I wonder, then, what will become of me...?"

"Is it that you do not wish to contend with your friend, Crouching Dragon...?" Zhou Yu asked plainly. "If so, please be aware that his lord and mine are allies... surely you have heard that they have now secured their everlasting friendship with a marriage between Governor Liu and Lady Sun."

"I have," Pang Tong replied. "A great boon for the people of Jing, indeed: there has been no peace here since the death of Liu Biao. To once again know that wonderful time when men of learning could go from county to county, town to town, debating and lyricizing, composing and pondering... alas, the times since Liu Biao's demise have been dark ones, indeed."

"I hope the recent stability has brought those times back," Zhou Yu said numbly.

"It is too early to say," Pang Tong replied. "The signs are good, however, as are the signs that good relations between the houses of Sun and Liu at all levels, from the meek to the mandated, will be sound. Let us hope that those signs point to the truth, shall we...? ...I wonder, were you interested in hearing about the worthy men of the city, so as to know what great minds to employ? What I do not already know, I can find out, Administrator Zhou."

"Uh... no, not for now, thank you," Zhou Yu said miserably. "In fact, I expect that you are very busy, as I am... I shan't keep you any longer, Master."

"Feel free to call upon me anytime for advice on worthy men to serve your administration," Pang Tong said kindly. "Good day, Administrator Zhou."

With that, Pang Tong rose from his seat, bowed low, stood tall, and left.

"...Such men are free spirits," Zhou Yu supposed as he watched Pang Tong leave his presence. "...Who am I to trap him...?"

Chen Dao received another letter from Kongming, and – as Kongming had hoped – Liu Bei was back at his base in Gong'an with Lady Sun by the end of that month, to the relief of all of his demoralised officials and generals.

"That was a cruel trick, Mister Zhuge," Liu Bei said as he held his first official meeting: the assembly were laughing uproariously. Even Chen Dao, whose presence at court was as a silent living statue protecting his master, could not help but smile slightly.
"A necessary deception," Kongming replied. "Were you intending to live there forever, Lord Liu...?"
"...I confess that I might have spent longer there than I had intended," Liu Bei retorted, "but it was in the name of diplomacy! Could I really refuse those gifts and run straight away, snatching Lady Sun from all that she knows without first giving her the chance to know me...?"
"...No, perhaps not," Kongming said dryly.
"I feigned intoxication with their gifts and treasures to ingratiate myself with their court, and maybe see if there were men that might join me," Liu Bei continued. "Alas, there were none... but seriously, Master Zhuge, to tell me that Cao Cao had attacked Jiangling...? How could you do that...? What if I had not become suspicious as to why Sun Quan had not told me, and told him what you said...?"
"That was never likely," Jian Yong chuckled. "Although his sister will have told him why you left, surely...?"
"I insisted in the letter that Lord Liu hurry back," Kongming explained. "So you did not have time to tell her why you were leaving until you were halfway back here, my lord... am I right...?"
"As ever, yes," Liu Bei grunted. "But all the same... there is no threat...?"
"Does it matter...?" Kongming chortled. "If there was, where should you be...?"
The officials murmured amongst themselves, a fact that was only made obvious by Liu Bei's silence.
"Lord Liu," Kongming continued, "we have a mission, an objective... to restore the house of Han to its former glory. That cannot be achieved miles away in Jiangdong, indulging in the treasures of the south."
"Do not scold me," Liu Bei retorted. "Remember who is lord and who is vassal."
"...I do," Kongming replied awkwardly. "I simply remind you that you should be among your followers, not among people who mean you no good. Zhou Yu has been in Jiangling these past weeks, negotiating with Zhang Lu and Ma Chao... did you know that in Chaisang...?"
"...No," Liu Bei admitted. "No, I did not, Master Zhuge... but I should have known, it is my responsibility if they are threatening my kin... my apologies to you all, I have let you down."
"Enough of that," Jian Yong said dismissively. "The important thing is to be ready, since Cao Cao and Zhou Yu both seem to be preparing for manoeuvres..."
Kongming fanned himself slowly, and nodded in agreement.

Chen Dao paid Kongming's Gong'an office a visit as the scholar was finishing his administrative work for the evening.
"...You'll kill yourself working so hard, Master Zhuge," Chen Dao hailed as he stood in the office entranceway.

"General Chen...?" Kongming said with tension as he looked up and saw Liu Bei's near-inseparable bodyguard. "Is... the lord unwell...?"

"He is fine," Chen Dao replied as he entered the office at last. "I have been granted leave, which I rarely accept, since the lord's wellbeing is my life's work."

"Please, sit," Kongming urged.

Chen Dao took a seat, chuckling softly, "I stand guard all day, so this feels very strange, Master Zhuge!"

"You must tire of watching Yunchang, Yide and Zilong taking all the glory," Kongming said sadly.

"My role is the most important, if not the most famous, Master Zhuge," Chen Dao replied humbly. "To be truthful, I fear combat, because it means that – as my lord's last line of defence – the hour is desperate."

"...A wise general, indeed," Kongming mused. "What can I do for you...?"

"I wanted to thank you," Chen Dao declared, "for your help in forcing Lord Liu to return to Jing. There was not a moment that my fellow guards and I were not fearful for the lord's safety..."

"And he *was* in danger," Kongming admitted. "The lord is yet to know... I myself have only just learned... that Wu Ju, Lord Liu's friend, and the governor of independent Cangwu, has been executed for 'treasonous activity' by Administrator General Bu Zhi of Wu... and the territory has now been annexed by Sun Quan."

"I see and hear everything, as Lord Liu's shadow," Chen Dao said sadly. "You warned him many a time that openly courting the man and opening political channels would result in mishap... your prediction has come to pass."

"Lu Su must have told Zhou Yu that my lord and this governor were old friends, and that there was potential trouble there," Kongming mused. "Lu Su must carry equal blame for this man's death, I think."

"...Do we have to fear Lady Sun, Master Zhuge...?" Chen Dao asked honestly.

"I think so," Kongming admitted. "I mean politically, of course... although I suspect some other discomfort exists within the lord's mind...?"

Chen Dao smiled, and lowered his head.

"...Speak," Kongming snickered. "I think I already know, though."

Chen Dao looked up, and said, "She allowed the lord one night after the wedding to become acquainted with her... but she has never since invited him to her presence, which should not even be necessary. But..."

"*But*...?" Kongming prompted.

"He fears her," Chen Dao confessed at last, and despite his best efforts to be serious, his tone betrayed the amusement that he found in the situation. "He would often approach her room, and on spying her armed maids, turn tail and flee, making excuses that he was tired. He spent more time carousing with the beauties offered to him by Sun Quan as gifts... although I do not know to what extent."

Kongming grinned, and chuckled, "This could be very amusing, if nothing else."

"But she is a spy, part of a scheme by Zhou Yu and Lu Su," Chen Dao supposed. "As his last line of defence, I felt it right to enquire from you the extent of the threat, so that I can be of best service to our lord and ensure his continued safety."
"Oh, certainly, she is a spy," Kongming concurred. "But let them scheme… it will do them no good, for our lord is destined for greater things, and they cannot stop that. When it is a man's moment, or his allotted time, or span… *nothing* can oppose it."
Chen Dao nodded sombrely.

Indeed, all men have an allotted span: while planning his own northern and western manoeuvres, Zhou Yu's health suddenly deteriorated, and he was rushed back to Ba Qiu, in the west of Jiangdong. And within weeks, he was dead, at the age of 35.


************

## 58

When the news of Zhou Yu's sudden death reached Kongming in Changsha, his fan fell from his hand: while some of his colleagues celebrated the fact that the most dangerous adviser in Eastern Wu was dead, Kongming found no peace in the news at all, and started to fall into a mild depression, retreating to his home at the end of every day to avoid conversing with his peers.

"…You have not played the qin since Zhou Yu died," Yueying protested as she sat with Kongming, several nights after the funeral of his rival had been held in Jiangdong.

"It doesn't seem right, somehow, to play during the mourning period," Kongming said numbly. "He… Gongjin… was a magnificent player."

"I suspect you mean that of the game of war, and not just the qin," Yueying sighed as she looked into her husband's face and searched for a glimmer of his usual determination. "I never expected his death to affect you like this."

"You *knew* he would die…?" Kongming asked weakly.

"…You *said* he would die," Yueying reminded him gently.

"Oh, yes… I did say that, didn't I," Kongming recalled miserably.

"His poor wife," Yueying realised suddenly. "She… she must be so lonely now, so lost, and… … …it isn't fair."

"I pity them both, the dead and the living," Kongming sobbed. "Is this the fate of men that mean to do the right thing by the lord they chose…?"

Yueying was silent. In that silence, it was impossible to miss the sound of trusted visitors being admitted into the house by one of their servants.

"…Kongming," Ma Liang hailed: his younger brother, Ma Su, was with him.

"Ah… Jichang, Youchang… please, come in, and sit down," Kongming said mechanically, and with none of his usual warmth.

"I don't understand," Ma Su admitted. "We were stony-faced when Liu Qi died, and rightly so… why are you so upset, and my brother too, at the death of this duplicitous enemy of ours…?"

"…Perhaps you still have much to understand," Kongming chuckled ironically. "I mourn because this man was like us: he lived like us… he died as we will, leaving widows and orphans to lament his passing! How is that the benevolent will of the heavens, Youchang, to take a loyal and studious man so soon…? Less than forty again, too, to 'ill health', while danger-seeking men like Guan Yu and Huang Gai live to grey old age, not a sniffle of sickness nor a scratch on them! First Guo Jia, now Zhou Yu: when will it be *me*…?"

Yueying fled the room in tears: Kongming regretted his badly chosen words.

"…That sounded selfish," Kongming realised. "That… did not convey what was intended at all. I… I owe her an apology."

"Maybe you need to take some time away from your official duties, Brother," Ma Liang suggested. "Why not rest a few days, and allow Youchang to get some experience? I can oversee him, and-"

"I have to keep busy," Kongming insisted. "I'll be fine, Jichang... though your idea of Youchang shadowing me is a good one."

"I would appreciate the tutelage, Master Zhuge!" Ma Su said gratefully.

"...My brother Jun is now a junior official," Kongming noted. "Will his own fate mirror mine, and mine, Zhou Yu's...?"

"You're being negative again," Ma Liang scolded. "Don't do this to yourself."

"...You're right," Kongming replied. "Really... I'll be fine."

Kongming finally got over his depression, and things started to return to what was considered as normality. Another shock to come, however, was the announcement of Zhou Yu's successor as the Chief Commander of Wu's armies and the Administrator of Nan Prefecture.

A few weeks later, Lu Su invited Kongming to a meeting in Jiangling City.

"Congratulations, Zijing," Kongming said with a vague smile.

"...You win," Lu Su sighed. "The fates are with your master, Mister Zhuge Kongming... you win."

"I am sad that Gongjin has passed away," Kongming replied. "It was never my desire for such a gifted genius to leave the world so soon."

"I thought you said he was 'disgusting', a 'would-be kingmaker', a blight on his family name," Lu Su recalled bitterly. "...Perhaps I am confused."

"Remember that my words were part of heated argument," Kongming retorted. "I did respect Gongjin... even if I did not always agree with him. Surely, Zijing, you are not trying to tell me that your own relationship with the man was one of consistent, total accord...? ...Perhaps *I* am confused."

"...Alright, alright!" Lu Su groaned. "I'm here to discuss the future, Mister Zhuge. I have spoken to my lord and – although he has rightfully strong reservations – I am expanding the deal with regard to Jing Province. We will be withdrawing to Lukou, and we will *loan* everything west of Jiangxia Prefecture to Liu Bei, so all of Nan Prefecture... including Jiangling and Yiling... is under your *temporary* jurisdiction now. We'll withdraw our own forces as soon as yours are installed."

"...That is a very sensible decision," Kongming praised, making a slight bow of respect as he spoke. "Now, I think, we can restore good relations between our two houses and return to the true business of restoring the glory of the Han."

"This will, of course, mean that we are abandoning our plans to ally with Ma Chao and Zhang Lu," Lu Su said pointedly. "...So now, Kongming, the future of Yi Province is entirely in your lord's hands. He can either help Zhang Lu take it, or aid Liu Zhang in keeping it... although I'm sure you have something even more fanciful in mind."

"I already told you, Zijing: my lord has no ambitions to seize Yi Province, and neither do I," Kongming replied. "...And I meant what I said... Zhou Gongjin was a marvellous talent, and one of the greatest regrets of my life is that my last words to him were so harsh and intolerant. Had I known that he was truly going to die so soon, Zijing, I would not have been so cruel, and I would certainly have made it my mission to restore accord between us while we were all in Chaisang, rather than avoiding him as I did."

"...Lady Qiao was blaming your words for worsening his condition," Lu Su admitted. "It was Gongjin that placated her... he told her that you and he were alike, and that he would have done the same in your position. He knew your words were intended to incite thought and debate... not his early death. Whatever bad blood might still exist between our lords, rest assured, Kongming, that he bore no true grudge against you."

Kongming nodded thankfully.

And so, over the next few weeks, the forces of Wu disappeared from Nan Prefecture, and Liu Bei's forces took over the region completely, even if it was only temporary in the eyes of Sun Quan and Lu Su.

"This is truly wonderful!" Liu Bei declared as he sat in his Gong'an court, looking at the newly acquired officials and generals. "This is slowly starting to take shape, at last! Soon, we will-"

"...Be attacked by Cao Cao, and for real this time," Jian Yong interrupted. "Xuande, anyone can see that Lu Su is weak and ineffectual... but he isn't stupid. When Zhou Yu lived, Cao Cao was afraid... he sent Jiang Gan to win Zhou Yu over, and he stayed away from the borders, just in case Zhou Yu had another pocketful of tricks to rout his armies. But in the same way that we have relaxed since the man's passing, so has Cao Cao: soldiers are being drilled near Hefei Castle in the east and Xinye City north of here, *and* there is talk of Cao targeting Zhang Lu and seizing Hanzhong. It's obvious what's going on here..."

"Is it...?" Zhang Fei grunted. "Go on then, Mister Jian... 'obvious' it for me."

"...Kongming," Jian Yong sighed, "you tell him."

"Lu Su is setting us up," Kongming declared. "By putting us in charge of the entire prefecture and retreating to Lukou, he leaves us as the only recipients of Cao Cao's wrath. If Cao Cao sieges Jiangling, can we afford to take the same losses that Zhou Yu inflicted on Cao Ren...?"

Anxious murmurs filled the hall.

"Furthermore, Cao Cao targets the northern Yi region of Hanzhong," Kongming continued. "To get to that he must pass through Ma Teng's territory, Xiliang. Ma Teng is at court, paying obeisance to Cao Cao, so it is his violent, neurotic son Ma Chao that governs in his stead, aided by Teng's former Qiang tribal enemy, Han Sui."

"...Will Ma Chao allow that...?" Liu Bei wondered aloud.

"Only if he's a fool," Guan Yu suggested.

"Yunchang speaks true," Kongming said surely. "This is, as we both know from our knowledge of the classics, the ruse of 'passing through on the way to take Guo'."

"...Which *is*, for the stupid and uninformed...?" Zhang Fei grunted.

"In the *Spring and Autumn* era," Guan Yu explained, "the King of Jin asked for peaceful passage though the kingdom of Yu in order to take over the kingdom of Guo... he succeeded, but he then conquered Yu on the way back."

"If he had first attacked Yu, Guo might have helped, as in the modern case, Zhang Lu would help Ma Chao, who is easily the more dangerous of the two," Kongming explained, to make the tale more relevant to the cantankerous Zhang Fei. "By first eliminating Zhang Lu, it facilitates a pincer attack on Ma Chao: the grateful governor of Yi Province, Liu Zhang – who fears that Zhang Lu will one day seize all of Yi Province – will aid Cao Cao in eradicating Zhang Lu, and then the two would beset Ma Chao from all sides, vanquishing him... then all of the north and west would be Cao's, and we would be alone... very alone, since I cannot see the meek Lu Su doing anything else but surrendering."

"So Ma Chao has to figure this out and fight, or we're all stuffed," Zhang Fei realised. "But you said he was a madman... is he clever as well as mad?"

"I said that he's neurotic," Kongming replied, "and hopefully, that will do it."

"And then," Liu Bei supposed, "Zhang Lu would attack Liu Zhang to stop him aiding Cao Cao... what then, my advisers, should *I* be doing...?"

"That," Kongming said, "is going to be a decision you must make quickly... since we will soon have visitors from Liu Zhang's court begging help... and Zhang Song is probably already on his way here to speak with us once again about taking the province from his master. We will need to give him an answer this time, as the outcome of our whole endeavour depends on it."

Liu Bei nodded slowly. He had already sworn, in front of Sun Quan and his entire court, that he would never take Yi Province by force. Now, he would be asked – by trusted vassals of the Yi governor, no less – to do just that. A dilemma was once again placed at his feet, and he had little time to concoct a solution to a very difficult diplomatic problem.

Kongming shared the burden, as the principal adviser to Liu Bei. He had already, in his own mind, allowed Liu Bei to lose Jing Province to Cao Cao and Sun Quan by not being forceful enough, and allowed him to lose a friend and ally, Wu Ju, by not stressing secrecy enough. Now, Yi Province beckoned, and a third mistake would hand Yi Province to Zhang Lu, Cao Cao, or Sun Quan, and guarantee that Liu Bei would never achieve anything. He needed to convince Liu Bei unreservedly, and that, he felt, might be a task that he could not complete alone.


************

## 59

Before Zhang Song of Yi Province arrived, another man invited himself into Kongming's presence as he sat in his governor's home in Changsha one evening.

"Oh...!" Yueying gasped as she walked from the kitchen: a man in dark brown robes and a wide-brimmed hat was stood in the entrance hall.

"Who...!" Kongming exclaimed as he looked up from his reading and saw the ominous shadow cast by the lamp in the front hall.

"Your brother let me in as he was departing," Pang Tong said as he removed his hat, placed it against the wall, and bowed courteously. "You must be Lady Huang... forgive me, madam, if I scared you."

"Shiyuan...!" Kongming said with surprise. "Pang Shiyuan...!"

"...The Young Phoenix," Yueying said nervously. "I am glad to meet you at last."

"And I, you," Pang Tong replied, bowing again. "I know you to be a woman of extraordinary talent... Kongming once told me he'd find such a woman as you, and he was right, as he very often is."

"...Pang Shiyuan...!" Kongming said again. "Wha... why are you...?"

"Here...?" Pang Tong chuckled. "Why, to visit you, why else...?"

"No, I mean, in Changsha!" Kongming asked.

"...Because you live in Changsha," Pang Tong replied. "It is where you are the governor, Kongming... you have done well for yourself, as I expected."

"When we last met, I was recently installed in Fan City... before Cao Cao routed us," Kongming recalled. "My... has it been three years...?"

"It has," Pang Tong replied. "Three years... I have enjoyed hearing of your exploits from the wanderers in Jiangling."

"Oh, of course... you were in Jiangling!" Kongming realised. "You were there when Cao Cao conquered the prefecture!"

"It really wasn't as bad as all that," Pang Tong insisted. "It was more unsettling than anything else, to be honest."

"Oh, wait, sorry... take a seat, take a seat!" Kongming chuckled with embarrassment. "Please, Shiyuan, sit down...!"

"I'll fetch tea," Yueying declared as Pang Tong sat down as a guest.

"...A marvellous woman!" Pang Tong suggested as Yueying left the room. "The wisdom... it burns in her eyes, you can see it. What need have you for peers...?"

"I agree," Kongming admitted. "...But please, tell me of Jiangling... did Cao Cao treat the people well...?"

"Very well," Pang Tong revealed. "Jia Xu sought my service for his lord... I declined, and he left me be. He asked about you... but you'd gone, and I didn't know where you were anyway."

"You refused an offer... and Cao Cao spared you...?" Kongming noted with surprise. "But... why then, did Cao Cao kill Hua Tuo...?"

"Cao Cao is a funny creature," Pang Tong chuckled coolly. "His headaches, his strange turns: that's what makes him dangerous. Most of the time, he is a model statesman, an example to us all: the agricultural and legal reforms, the improved conditions for the poor, the tax on excess wealth for the rich... he even forbids ostentatious funerals, for he feels the money is better spent on the needy living!"

"...He *does*...?" Kongming said with even greater surprise.

"...Speaking of funerals, I attended Zhou Gongjin's recently," Pang Tong declared, to Kongming's continued surprise. "It was a quiet affair, really... the sort of thing Cao Cao wouldn't mind too much. Gongjin insisted that the officials on important duty remain at their posts, and not return to Chaisang... very professional, amazing man, Gongjin was. He asked me to join Wu, but I refused, and he let me be."

"...He *did*???" Kongming exclaimed.

"...I feel like I'm going to kill you by surprises, Kongming," Pang Tong teased cheerfully. "Yes, I refused him too... and then, after all that, I was invited to his funeral, since he held my work in high regard... I met many generals and officials, even Lu Su... a very nice man, very nice indeed, if a little too timid for his own good, but then I'm sure you know that."

"...Yes," Kongming replied cautiously, "I do."

At this point, Kongming started to fan himself slowly: Pang Tong noted it and grinned toothily.

"You can trust me, Kongming," Pang Tong insisted. "You always could, and you always can. I spoke to the officials and generals of Wu, and they all agreed on what I'm sure you also agree: Lu Su is timid, and ultimately unfit for purpose. He is an excellent statesman – if a little tactless – and good for civil affairs... but he makes for a poor Chief Commander."

"...I agree," Kongming said thoughtfully: he stopped fanning himself, and relaxed slightly.

"It puzzles me as to why Gongjin would appoint him as his successor," Pang Tong admitted. "It is well known that he detested the idea of allying with Lord Liu Xuande, and that he would rather seize Yi and Jing in alliance with Zhang Lu and Ma Chao... so why, on his deathbed, when all other matters were dealt with so delicately and carefully, did he assign this meek man to take his place...? ...Even now, it perplexes me."

Yueying was stood at the partition between the kitchen and living area, watching the conversation between her husband, Crouching Dragon, and the eccentric, visually unappealing Young Phoenix, with curiosity and fascination.

"My belief initially," Kongming confessed, "was that Gongjin wanted to appoint Lu Su to repay the favour to his benefactor, and perhaps because the real shining light of Wu – Lü Meng of Fupo – is not yet fully fledged. But *now*..."

"...Now, you suspect that Lu Su is a front, concealing the true threats in the shadows," Pang Tong supposed, and Kongming nodded sadly. Pang Tong smiled, adding, "Then we concur... Lü Meng is the one to fear right now – and perhaps Lu Xun, who I have also met – in times ahead. Lu Xun is also very clever, Kongming: only a year or two's age difference from yourself, and every bit the scholar-minister for the future. We'll see more of that one in years to come. But the ceding of Jiangling provides a magnificent opportunity to seize Yi... what will Xuande do...?"

"...Nothing," Kongming replied cautiously.

"Don't start fanning yourself again, Crouching Dragon," Pang Tong teased. "I told you, I'm not here to deceive you. Zhang Song is on his way here from Yi... a second visit, no doubt, to discuss taking the province, now that you have a base to operate from. Liu Zhang is weak and timid, worse than Lu Su... such men are fish bait, worthless in a time of chaos. To stabilise the land, and restore the ruling house to its former glory, a real hero is needed: only one save Cao Cao exists, and that is Liu Xuande. Xuande must hold Jing, seize Yi, contend with Cao Cao for Hanzhong, and then – only then – can the tripartite theorem be realised... only then will there be Liu, Sun and Cao, equals or near enough, and only then can there be a chance to restore the Han. Surely, Xuande knows this...?"

"...'*Xuande*'...?" Kongming noted warily. "I... I don't believe...!"

"I am not done," Pang Tong declared. "I am a cautious man, Kongming... that you have always noted, and it is true. I have seen the true aura of all the great leaders, and my final analysis matches yours, at least in terms of my conclusion.

"Cao Cao is ultimately benevolent at heart, a creative man, a poet and scholar, whose mind has been poisoned by illness, affliction and bitterness at the cruel necessities of politics and government: hate burns in his heart, he is twisted and sadly irredeemable, and his progeny will one day harm the throne. He is prone to killing good men and punishing unwanted counsel, which in turn has led to his being surrounded by loyal, unquestioning generals and fawning, greedy pedants, and that can only lead one day to a coup. I'll not serve such a volatile man.

"Sun Quan is a thinker, a planner, who truly yearns to finish the amazing work that his brother started. He seeks a prosperous south, not the stagnant wasteland that it once was, ruled by complacent pedants that saw its governance as a necessity, but made no effort to improve conditions. But a man is a man, and his motives for the consolidation and development of the south are suspect. Even if he himself were a man that sought nothing more than comfort and stability, he is, like Cao Cao, surrounded by pedants who entice him to expand his frontier and covet the throne... he is only a man, and is therefore weak, and not to be entirely trusted when greedy vassals are always the ones that will find his ready ear before virtuous ones, and cautious men are tamed with swords, not words. I'll not serve such an easily corrupted man.

"Liu Xuande is not perfect – he is a man, and as I said, all men are weak – but in him, I see a man whose intentions are just, unmarred by afflictions like Cao Cao, and he is ready to hear righteous counsel, unlike Sun Quan. Yes, I am aware that he can be tempted by comforts, and that he can sometimes allow emotion to dictate his actions, rather than good sense. But that is true of all men, and it is the way in which a man conducts himself otherwise that is most important. He does not seize land, even when it is offered, if it goes against the way, and that shows that he is not boundlessly covetous. He does not betray his allies, even when they are themselves untrustworthy, which shows that he adheres to principle, and does not readily allow weak examples to become excuses for poor conduct. And he truly regrets his mistakes and publicly atones for them, which shows a willingness to accept that he is a man with faults, and nothing more, and that is the mark of a man that is truly worthy to govern others. ...All men must have a master in times of chaos, Kongming, and in Liu Xuande... I see a man I can follow."

"...A-a-are you...!" Kongming stammered: he could not believe his ears.

"Tomorrow," Pang Tong said, "I should like you to introduce me to Lord Liu, so that I can tender my services. It's time for the phoenix to fly...!"

Kongming's response was to grasp Pang Tong's arms and laugh hysterically; Yueying found that she could not stop herself from weeping. *Now*, Kongming thought joyously, *Liu Bei would have Crouching Dragon and Young Phoenix, and soar to the greatest heights*.


************

## 60

Pang Tong spent the night in Kongming's guest room, after an evening of lively debate between the two scholars: and, at times, Yueying was invited to join them as an equal. The very next morning, Kongming and Pang Tong left Changsha together, and went to Gong'an to meet Liu Bei.

**"Oh, no, no, not AGAIN!"** Zhang Fei exclaimed as Jian Yong relayed the news that Kongming would now be announcing Pang Tong. **"We don't need any more pedants! Aren't we invading Yi…? Well then don't we need GENERALS???"**
"Yide," Liu Bei scolded, "you do this every single time I recruit someone. And I am *not invading Yi.*"
"Oh…?" Pang Tong said as he walked into court ahead of the smiling Kongming, and stopped in front of Liu Bei. "But if you do not take Yi… who will…?"
The assembly viewed Pang Tong with unfortunate disdain: he was dressed in plain, washed-out blue robes and had his hair kept in place with a plain silk turban. He now carried a small wooden fan, although he kept it pressed to his chest. He grinned toothily, exposing his disordered teeth. Many also noted his dark, pockmarked complexion and ape-like forehead with cruel amusement.
"So you are Young Phoenix," Liu Bei remarked coldly.
"…He's ordinary," Guan Yu suggested as looked the scholar up and down.
"You see, with cynical eyes, a phoenix as a chicken," Kongming chuckled. "But to eyes that see truth, that phoenix fire burns brightly all about him."
"…All I'm seeing is a scrawny little chicken in a fire," Zhang Fei scoffed, "cooking in its own juices. He's a silly little man, and if you trust him, Elder Brother, he'll hand your head to Cao Cao, one way or the other."
"Why do you say that, Zhang Yide of Yan…?" Pang Tong asked with a smile.
"Don't 'Yide' me, you ugly little turd!" Zhang Fei retorted angrily. "You spent three years hiding in Jiangling, kissing Cao Cao's shoes, and refused to see your mate 'Crouching Dragon'… why? Alright, maybe it was occupied, you couldn't leave… but you spent the last few months freely serving Zhou Yu: I hear you even got to go to his funeral! You crawled up *his* arse too, and even though your city was occupied by our allies, you *still* ignored your *friend*! Now you're *here*, 'Young Cuckoo', and for *what*…?"
Pang Tong lowered his head, but continued to smile.
"…Yide," Kongming implored, "he is finally won over… and now you push him away. Why…?"
"Cao Cao approached me, and yet I live despite refusing," Pang Tong suggested. "I expect that is enough to make a man wonder if I was left in Jiangling to act as a spy for Xuchang… or, perhaps, I am a spy from Jiangdong."
"That's about right," Zhang Fei growled. "Why else would you mess us all about? Your friend joined us, but you didn't… why?"

"I am a man that likes to assess a situation thoroughly," Pang Tong chuckled, "and until now, it has sometimes been difficult to tell the good from the bad. Lord Liu, however, has shone brighter with time, while Sun and Cao have dimmed as their darker nature has surfaced. Now it is clear that while Liu is militarily the weakest, and he possesses no land of his own, he is the purest in terms of motivations, and should be the one that stands tall among the warlords of the day."

"...Alright," Zhang Fei grunted, "but what use are you...? What can you do...?"

"Pang Shiyuan is my equal in his knowledge and wisdom," Kongming declared. "I will say now that if there is a man to deliver the realm to its rightful owner, it is Pang Shiyuan... I may be considered his equal, but he is perhaps my superior, having five times more in his head than me."

"That's good enough for me," Jian Yong said with a laugh. "When can you start?"

"...Indeed, Master Pang, you are a difficult one to get accustomed to," Liu Bei admitted awkwardly. "But you are a great mind, and they are always hard for the common man to fathom. If you would lend me your support... then I shall be eternally grateful for it."

To Kongming's surprise, Pang Tong kowtowed to his new master, saying, "I, Tong, shall serve you most diligently, my lord."

Liu Bei got up, rushed to his newest sage, and helped him to his feet.

"Your eyes are like pools filled with knowledge beyond a normal man's capacity," Liu Bei said with surprise. "In you I see a man wise beyond his years. Perhaps, if I had heeded the words of your scholar-peer, Crouching Dragon, I would already be at the side of the Emperor, and good men like Wu Ju of Cangwu would still be alive... so with both of you providing sagely counsel to my ready ear... there will be no more mistakes."

Both Pang Tong and Kongming bowed in respect of Liu Bei, and hoped that he meant the humble words that he had now said.

From that moment Pang Tong and Kongming were equals in the court, and the two spearheaded the continuing overhaul of Liu Bei's civil and military administration. Soldiers were trained and drilled regularly, and taught how to take part in all the elements of the most common arrays and formations. Liu Bei's army grew in size and skill with every passing day, until it was a fluid machine where no man worked alone. News of this reached the courts of Sun Quan and Cao Cao, but in the latter's case, there were more pressing concerns.

Spring brought forth new growth and new threats of war. Cao Cao finally made it official – with imperial sanction – that he would be marching on Zhang Lu of Hanzhong, intending to make him surrender and return that region to a form of government that was not 'unholy'. Zhang Lu's advisers gathered for meetings, and decided to put up a defensive front against Cao Cao. Furthermore, they intended to seize Yi Province from Liu Zhang in order to prevent a pincer attack.

At the same time, Ma Chao and the other leaders in Xiliang and surrounding regions met to discuss Cao's true motives, just as Liu Bei's advisers had predicted. Because the imperial army did indeed have to travel through their region to reach Hanzhong, they suspected subterfuge, and rose up as one against the Prime Minister of Han and his forces. The size of the rebellion even surprised the cynical Cao Cao: 100,000 men had taken up arms to fight for the coalition of western leaders, which included Ma Chao and Han Sui of the Qiang.

"Apparently, Cao Cao was warned this would happen, but you know Cao Cao and heeding advice on military matters," Kongming joked as he sat with some of his ever-growing group of peers and friends – Pang Tong, Ma Liang, Ma Su, Yi Ji, Liao Li, and Jiang Wan – in his office.

"If I were Jia Xu, I'd have retired a long time ago," Yi Ji suggested.

"Cao ignored him when he warned about going to Red Cliffs, didn't he...?" Jiang Wan recalled hazily.

"And Cheng Yu," Liao Li snickered. "And more, probably... he has about twenty advisers, and their only purpose seems to be to make suggestions he can ignore."

"Cheng Yu advised cannibalism once, when the army ran out of grain," Ma Su recalled clearly and with disgust. "I wouldn't listen to him either."

"That's hearsay," Kongming chuckled as he pointed at Ma Su with his fan.

"Both Jia Xu and Cheng Yu are clever men," Ma Liang mused. "To ignore them again, after all the times that it has cost him..."

"It wasn't Jia Xu or Cheng Yu this time," Kongming chuckled; "It was Gao Rou."

"...Well, he was going to get ignored, then," Jian Yong joked. "He probably hasn't offered ignored advice yet."

"Seriously, though," Yi Ji said, "regarding his long-time adviser Xun Yu... if nothing else shows Cao has evil intent, I don't know what does, more than this: someone – and I suppose it's some pedant like Wang Lang or Dong Zhao – has suggested Cao Cao take the grand title 'Duke of Wei'."

"...Have his own *duchy*...?" Ma Liang exclaimed.

"I heard that too," Kongming admitted. "It's inevitable that he will advance to a duke, and then a prince, and then a king... and from there, perhaps an emperor. ...It is utterly inevitable. Do go on, Boji."

"Xun Yu – who has supported Cao for decades – opposed it," Yi Ji explained. "And Cao Cao rebuked him... he has now fallen completely out of favour."

"Worse than that," Kongming replied ominously. "He was sent to inspect some troops and 'fell ill suddenly'... he is now bedridden with a mystery affliction that erodes his vitals... many expect it will kill him."

"Poison," Jiang Wan supposed.

"It is suspicious," Kongming agreed. "It would not be the first man Cao killed."

"...Cao Cao is a monster!" Ma Su exclaimed.

"A very clever, very creative and divided monster," Pang Tong declared. "What a pity that a man of such genuine intent should be plagued by a second, diseased part of his soul that sows chaos and destruction."

"Aren't all great men summed up that way...?" Jiang Wan said suddenly.

"...Even Lord Liu...?" Ma Liang asked pointedly.

The ensemble fell silent as Jiang Wan raised an eyebrow and smiled to indicate that nothing was beyond consideration.

The meeting broke up, and only Kongming and Pang Tong were left.

"...What Jiang Wan said... it bothered you," Pang Tong supposed.

"Naturally," Kongming replied uneasily. "Jian Yong has, on occasion, spoken of Lord Liu's 'other side'... very reluctantly, I might add. While Lord Liu had to flee Anxi to escape the slander of a corrupt official, many neglect to mention that he tied the said official to a post and beat him senseless with a short whip before he left the town... which hardly helped his defence."

"But it isn't as though it is a secret," Pang Tong noted with amusement. "I heard that story countless times in one tavern in Xiangyang... twice in one week, in fact."

"Yes, but then there is his tendency to speak out of turn while drunk," Kongming continued. "He does, I've seen it... and I understand that he once jeopardised his place in Jing Province by arrogantly telling Liu Biao that 'if he had a base, the Nobodies of the age' – in other words, every other warlord, including Liu Biao – 'would not concern him in the slightest'. Hearsay, *maybe*, but..."

"Mm... that's interesting, if it isn't just slander spread by Lady Cai," Pang Tong replied ponderously. "But not exactly damning, Kongming... so he disguises his true, ambitious nature with tears and rhetoric; what warlord – what *man*, in fact – doesn't conceal his true feelings?"

"He also resisted returning to Jing when Sun Quan lavished him with wealth," Kongming admitted. "He wanted to stay and indulge himself... and dismissed his responsibility to Jing and to the Emperor as 'Things of no urgency'. ...And once... though he later sobbed publicly... he revealed to me privately a cold interest in seeing the early demise of Liu Biao, so that he might find accord with his sons. And then there are those that wonder if his true intention in bringing the peasants of Xiangyang and Xinye with us on that ill-fated retreat through Steep-slope..."

"...Was to use them as a human shield to protect his inadequate forces, and force Cao Cao into the role of a heinous villain...?" Pang Tong chuckled calmly. "Possibly... it depends what you choose to believe. Why did you urge me to join this man if you think so little of him, and ponder your own place...? Why do you tell me these things now, after I have already pledged public loyalty to him...? Is it that you now want me to flee, like Xu Shu...?"

"Of course not," Kongming said dismissively.

"Liu Xuande is a man who – as you yourself have often stated – acts according to circumstances, "Pang Tong suggested. "Why should he always be honest, and condemn himself, when others freely lie? Bar the last, every 'wrong' you mention is a moment of simple honesty.

"He considers himself a hero... I agree that it does not make him modest, but then he *is* a hero! Cao Cao told him so! You and all of his other vassals tell him so... and yet you castigate him for secretly believing it?

"He craves a base... what else have we all done, and what else do we all do, but constantly convince him to betray his kin, and Sun Quan too, and seize Jing and Yi? We want him to have a base, and get angry that he refuses to act, yet you castigate him for secretly wanting a home?

"...And as for his whipping of the inspector in Anxi... well, if he had not done it, Zhang Fei would have, or Guan Yu.

"His only 'crime' is self-indulgence... Cao Cao has a palace, fine art treasures, and over a dozen women at his beck and call, one of them a live-in prostitute that some say he shares with one of his bodyguards. ...And Sun Quan...? ...He lives in a palace too, he acts like a king, and his idea of wealth and status was what he gave Xuande, so is he any better? Our master spent his youth as a sandal weaver and a peddler, and then he was a roaming warlord, friendless, running from place to place, his daughters snatched at Steep-slope and married to men in Cao Cao's gentry... his body and mind continually battered by enemies, a victim of intrigue and suspicion, his friends slaughtered just for knowing him. A moment of leisure, however dangerous... receipt of kindness, however feigned... really, Kongming... can you blame him...?"

"...And I never believed that he was using the people as shields, either," Kongming said with a smile. "We didn't need to... without them, we had a head start... but then every man would have lost his family, and would he have loyalty then...? If anything, it was a risky attempt to keep his followers loyal... nothing more. ...But onto other, more pressing matters... do you agree that Ma Chao's rebellion is doomed...?"

"If the alliance continues to funnel all of their men and resources into Tong Pass and the surrounding area instead of fortifying their own domains... then yes, within a year, they will lose," Pang Tong replied. "There are so many leaders... so many ways for them to be divided through bribery and intrigue... I pity them for what they will suffer at the hands of Jia Xu. The real question, Kongming, is whether this northwest rebellion will be the end or the beginning of trouble in that region."

Meanwhile, Zhang Song once again departed Yi Province: this time, he was bound for Gong'an in Jing Province, intending to continue an old conversation, and install Liu Bei as his governor.


************

## 61

**"Zhang Ziqiao!"** Liu Bei hailed with dramatic enthusiasm as Zhang Song of Yi was escorted into his court in Gong'an. Liu Bei leapt from his seat and met the visitor before he had even walked half the length of the room: he bowed low, angering his generals and distressing Zhang Song.

"P-please, Lord Liu," Zhang Song protested. "I do not deserve this courtesy!"

"You are a friend as well as a guest!" Liu Bei said he straightened up. "Please, be seated, Ziqiao, be seated!"

Zhang Song noted the two men sat to the left of Liu Bei's place, and smiled.

"Master Crouching Dragon!" Zhang Song exclaimed. "And that must be Young Phoenix, Pang Shiyuan...!"

"A pleasure," Pang Tong said kindly, and he bowed slightly from his seated position.

"We expected to hear from you sooner," Kongming admitted. "Did Liu Zhang not allow you to travel...?"

"He was floundering, as usual," Zhang Song complained as he moved to sit down in the guest seat offered by Liu Bei. "He wanted to-"

"We really should discuss this in a private audience chamber," Pang Tong interrupted. "These are matters of great delicacy."

"...Quite right," Zhang Song realised.

Zhang Fei harrumphed angrily.

"Don't be offended, Yide," Liu Bei suggested. "It is just a precaution."

"Like I wanted to sit and listen to six hours of prattle anyway," Zhang Fei grunted.

Liu Bei dismissed his court and moved proceedings to his private audience chambers, which were similarly modelled to those of Sun Quan in Jiangdong. The only attendees would be Kongming, Pang Tong, Jian Yong, Mister Sun, Bei himself, and the visitor from Yi.

"...As I was saying," Zhang Song said as soon as all the men were seated, "my lord Liu Zhang is a weak fool, too muddle-headed to decide what to do. I suggested he break ties with Cao Cao, but he did not... as you know, he aided Cao Ren throughout the siege of Jiangling. Zhou Yu of Eastern Wu is dead because of my lord... would an arrow have struck him nine months into a siege that, without Liu Zhang, might have been over in four...?"

"I'm hesitant to agree," Kongming admitted. "Zhou Yu... should be left out of this. He was a general of Eastern Wu... his fate of no concern to any of us at this moment. I appreciate your point about your lord aiding Cao Ren, however... any help he proffered for any length of time breaks faith with good men."

"I reluctantly concur," Liu Bei declared.

"My lord desires an alliance," Zhang Song said at last. "He asks that you come to Yi as a kinsman, and that together, you defeat Zhang Lu and secure Hanzhong."

"But for whom...?" Pang Tong asked pointedly. "Liu Zhang is a vassal of Cao Cao, so wouldn't we be working for Cao if we helped Liu Zhang...?"

"...A fair point," Liu Bei noted. "If so I would be betraying my covenant with the Emperor, and colluding with my nemesis. That won't do."

"Such an alliance may ingratiate you with Cao Cao, but how will Sun Quan read it...?" Pang Tong added. "After all, Lord Liu, you pledged never to take Yi... so if you enter the province, it will be to aid Liu Zhang... against Zhang Lu, a man that his beloved Zhou Yu planned an alliance with. You'd be opposing Zhang Lu and Ma Chao... surely inviting Eastern Wu's indignation, especially since they loaned you Jing to help *them*, not Cao Cao."

"But...!" Zhang Song protested.

"...No... no, no, that won't do at all!" Liu Bei proclaimed. "My wife will divorce me, and my alliance with Wu would end... I would have to fight them for Jing, and perhaps end up homeless, a guest of Liu Zhang, who serves Cao... who would no doubt demand my head... which Liu Zhang would gladly trade for his own independence! No, no, this is not at all agreeable!"

"I...!" Zhang Song exclaimed.

"Well then," Jian Yong said plainly, "we must decline."

"B-but that's a pedant's course!" Zhang Song retorted bluntly. "Just tell him you'll help him, and I'll work with Fa Zheng to destroy his court from within... if we coordinate, we can be rid of this traitor in a year or less, and Lord Liu will be Governor of Yi Province!"

"...If we do this, we must do it quickly," Pang Tong said frankly. "If we dally, we will face the ire and ridicule of all men, and Lord Liu will lose everything. On the other hand, if we are successful... then Sun Quan will never bother us again, and the imperial capital will be in sight."

"We would secure Yi, and from there, we could advance on Hanzhong if Zhang Lu insists on hostility rather than accepting us as allies," Kongming supposed. "With the support of the remnants of the rebel armies in Xiliang... and Sun Quan... we could finally oppose Cao Cao!"

Liu Bei was silent and ponderous.

"...This is a magnificent opportunity, admittedly," Jian Yong sighed. "We would be fool pedants, as Ziqiao said, to simply ignore it."

Liu Bei hummed ambiguously.

"So we are going to go into Yi after all...?" Mister Sun asked hoarsely.

"...Yes, Mister Sun," Liu Bei replied. "I think so. In what capacity, I am not sure, but... yes, we will be going to Yi."

"Excellent!" Zhang Song cried. "Excellent, excellent! ...Ah, but perhaps I have gone too far... it isn't my place to invite you, I have only come to tell you how things stand. It is Fa Zheng that you must now converse with... I've done my part. I shall now return to Yi... Fa Zheng will soon come here as Liu Zhang's official envoy, or at least, he should... yes, I'm sure he will. Liu Zhang *must* agree..."

Zhang Song rose from his seat.

"Is there any need for you to rush, Ziqiao...?" Liu Bei asked cheerfully.

"Time is of the essence," Zhang Song insisted. "My role is now in Chengdu... as I said, Fa Zheng will soon be here... yes, I really should be off."
"We shall see you to the road," Liu Bei insisted.

Zhang Song left Gong'an, and started the long, laborious journey to Chengdu, the capital of Yi Province.

With Jing now surrendered to Liu Bei and the southern warlords under his control, Sun Quan could have his own forces – now a considerable 80,000, or thereabouts – mainly consolidated around his capital, Chaisang, ready for an attack from Hefei, to the north. Since his successful defence of Hefei, Cao Cao had set up military settlements along the north bank of the Yangtze River, placed several of his best generals – Xiahou Yuan, Zhang Liao, Zang Ba, Yue Jin, and Li Dian – in the area, and relocated the civilians; this suggested quite clearly that his next target, once Ma Chao's alliance was defeated, would be Eastern Wu. The only question left to answer was when that attack would come.

In Jing Province, Fa Zheng of Yi arrived at the court of Liu Bei. All of the officials and generals were assembled to receive this second guest from Yi Province.
"...There's no need to look at me like that," Zhang Fei said to Liu Bei. "I'm not going to say anything."
"Yes, well, that would be preferable," Liu Bei scolded.
**"My lord,"** Jian Yong hailed as he entered the hall, **"Fa Zheng of Yi approaches."**
Fa Zheng – a charismatic man of 35 years, with a well-kept beard and moustache, elaborately decorated silk robes, and his hair covered by a square hat – walked into the hall, passing numerous generals and officials, and bowed graciously before Liu Bei, saying, "Fa Zheng pays most humble respects to Lord Liu Bei, benevolent governor of Jing Province."
"...Very good, very good!" Liu Bei said with cheer. "I hope that your journey was without incident, Mister Fa...?"
"I departed Chengdu with optimism in my heart, and travelled though the rich, plentiful countryside of my master's domain on Yi," Fa Zheng replied, "enjoying the sights, and imagining that nothing could equal the splendour of the 'River lands'... but my journey through Jing, Lord Liu, was an education. The fields are tirelessly worked, the soldiers well drilled, the children well-fed and happy, the land a place of prospect and a testimony to good governance. You are truly as kind and just a ruler as Zhang Ziqiao described."
"You flatter me," Liu Bei said with a laugh.
"Not so!" Fa Zheng insisted. "Flattery is a pedant's business... honest appraisal is my own. And my honest appraisal in this case, Lord Liu, is that such a man as yourself cannot surely be content to toil so strenuously to make bounty for another, such as the ambitious Sun Quan."

"Sun Quan kindly allows my unworthy self a place to rest my head and provide shelter for those that have chosen to follow me," Liu Bei explained carefully. "I am grateful for his assistance, from his rescue of my battered body from the rout in northern Jing to his assistance in purging southern Jing of mutual foes. To be given a little place to quietly plan the downfall of the great villains of the age, when Sun Quan could just as easily hand me over..."

"I disagree," Fa Zheng declared. "Your virtue is renowned throughout the land. Your current position is due to your unwillingness to turn from the path of righteousness... perhaps, when these official discussions are over, you might reflect on how you can expand your influence and save others from an undeserved fate."

"...Perhaps that is something for discussion," Lui Bei replied cagily. "But of course, you are here on business for your lord... please, state your case."

"My lord, Liu Zhang, Governor of Yi Province, inherited the province from his father, Liu Yan," Fa Zheng began. "During the reign of Liu Yan, things were prosperous, because Liu Yan's fame preceded him, and he won the obedience of those that perhaps only understood fear, and not respect.

"Zhang Lu, leader of the 'Celestial Masters' sect, continues the unholy traditions started by his ancestors, ruling by a system of unfair and exploitative taxation. He ensures his rule not by winning over the hard-working and the just, as a good ruler should, but by placating the lazy and those that willingly fail to contribute to society. He collects food and tinder from those that toil, and makes it freely available not only to the elderly and incapable, as is undeniably fair, but also to those who do nothing and expect everything. He accuses the sick of sinning, and – in exchange for false ritual that does nothing to cure the illness – demands rice and other valuables, which he then adds to his considerable wealth.

"Despite possessing the power to crush the Celestial Masters and leave corpses in the fields, Liu Yan tolerated this sect during the years when Zhang Lu's mother was the master, and then when Lu was leader, he tolerated it still further, and in exchange for that mercy, Zhang Lu would control his heart's ambition, and allow those that wanted another way to find it. But when Liu Yan died, my master replaced him, and Zhang Lu – a rude sort that mistakes restraint and generosity for weakness – broke ties with Chengdu, and refused to recognise our rule. My lord tried to show strength, and for Zhang Lu's crimes, he executed Zhang Lu's family that resided in our lands... but that show of strength only deepened the enmity between the two rulers.

"The Prime Minister of the Han ordered my master to the court in Xuchang, and asked him to affirm his loyalty to His Majesty the Emperor... which he did, willingly, and sincerely. Since then, he has enjoyed cordial relations with the imperial court, and has – on occasion – lent it strength in times of need, and in exchange, we would receive support should we need it. But in this instance, the court is busy managing rebellions in the north, east and west, and cannot spare the resource. So, in a time of great difficulty, my lord comes to you, a kinsman, to ask your help, and respect the bonds of family and loyalty to the empire."
Zhang Fei grunted irritably, but very quietly.
"He asks," Fa Zheng concluded, "that you raise an army and go to his aid in this most perilous of moments, when Zhang Lu looms, ready to pounce: he asks that you join hands to face this unholy terror, and together, reclaim Hanzhong for the state. Rewards are sure to follow."
"...I would not seek rewards," Liu Bei replied. "That is not my objective... to see the Han restored is reward enough for my worthless self. Please, Mister Fa, consider my forces at the disposal of your lord... we should now retire to my private court to discuss the details at greater length."
Fa Zheng bowed low, saying, "My thanks and my master's thanks are immeasurable, as is your benevolence and virtue."

After the unavoidable public display of polite political discussion, Liu Bei and his guest moved to his private audience chamber to speak with his trusted inner circle.
"...My lord," Fa Zheng began as soon as all were seated, "now is a truly urgent moment. My master, Liu Zhang, is a poor judge of character, and has made a poor choice of an ally in the wicked, ambitious Cao Cao."
"A somewhat extreme case of 'the pleasantries before the hostilities'," Jian Yong joked. "Out there, he was a restrained but generous governor... now, he's a bumbling idiot."
"While there are sound-minded men at court, in the districts, talented fellows languish in minor roles while fawning pedants and talentless opportunists hold the highest seats," Fa Zhang said with frustration. "That is why a godless, irrational creature like Zhang Lu was able to seize power in Hanzhong so easily."
"Surely, though," Ma Liang said, "there is good in Zhang Lu's governance...?"
"I agree with his policies on welfare for the needy," Fa Zheng replied reluctantly, "no matter how unrealistic they may be in tough times. But he extends that generosity to the undeserving... to win their love, to avoid mass dissent, and to prevent anyone from launching an effective attack on his government. Those that have something to give are overtaxed, overworked and underappreciated... while the very poorest and his elite enjoy lives free of stress."
"And is Liu Zhang a good governor...?" Pang Tong asked pointedly.

"He is competent," Fa Zheng admitted, "but only just. One must possess the ability to govern with a firm hand: punish the wrongdoer, reward the contributor. But Liu Zhang is always looking for the easiest way out of situations... he delegates much of his responsibility to others, hides from urgent matters, and grovels to those he should demand respect from. He kowtows to the 'Prime Minister of the Han' without a hint of shame... at which point, I feel I owe you all an apology for my inability to prevent him lending aid to Cao Ren... I..."

"We hold none of his vassals responsible," Liu Bei interrupted. "This wretched, spineless coward aggravates me with every new revelation that leaves a good man's lips. I once had a strong disinclination to the idea of seizing Yi Province from a kinsman... I could now do it without a scrap of a conscience. My ancestor was disinherited for lesser crimes than this fool! While he enjoys high position purely because his father was an exemplary statesman, I was made to weave mats and shoes, enduring a punishment passed down the generations, atoning for another man's supposed mistakes... so now I think, 'why should I pity this man'...?"

"It pleases me to hear you say that," Fa Zheng declared.

"If I have one wish," Mister Sun said weakly, "it is to see my lord settled at last..."

"And so you shall, Mister Sun," Fa Zheng insisted. "I will guarantee it."

"You are very quiet, Kongming," Pang Tong noted.

"...When wise men speak, wise men listen," Kongming replied. "I am glad that things are finally starting to happen... I can add nothing to the proceedings except my hope for success."

"So you will not be going to Yi, then...?" Jian Yong asked pointedly.

"No," Kongming replied. "Mister Fa and Pang Shiyuan are all you need for the enterprise to be successful... somebody has to remain in Jing, managing state affairs and protecting the borders from Sun Quan and Cao Cao, since neither of them have gone anywhere."

"Zilong, Yide and Yunchang shall remain here to guard Jing with you," Liu Bei declared. "Master Young Phoenix shall be the Director General on this campaign. For warriors, I need only General Chen to protect me, my son Feng, Wei Yan and Huang Zhong to fight in the vanguard... I have Huo Jun, Liao Hua, Chen Shi and many more besides as worthy generals to aid them... yes, it is decided. We depart as soon as possible... Jian Yong shall go ahead as our envoy."

"Consider me already there," Jian Yong joked.

"Excellent," Fa Zheng said with gratitude. "I look forward to the day of success."


"Kongming," Pang Tong hailed as he entered the Gong'an office of his friend, his face filled with gratitude. It was the day before the expedition into Yi Province, and the city was bustling with activity.

"...Ah, Shiyuan," Kongming responded cheerfully as he looked up from his administrative work. "Is something troubling you...?"

"...Kongming," Pang Tong said with a bow, "I... ... ...words cannot express my gratitude to you for your kind and honest friendship."

"Did I miss something...?" Kongming chuckled.

"Only this campaign," Pang Tong replied. "Another man in your position would have feared my accompanying Lord Liu and gaining all the merit... you actually gave way. I... I never doubted your sincerity, don't misunderstand me, but..."

"I am 'giving way' to the better man for the job," Kongming insisted. "You are a more capable tactician than I ever will be, Shiyuan... I am well-read, but there is something within you that allows you to react more readily to the urgent moment. There will be many such moments on this journey... I, meanwhile, have the important role of guarding Jing from dangers within and without."

"By 'within' I presume you mean Lady Sun," Pang Tong said.

"Once Lord Liu is gone, her behaviour will, I think, worsen," Kongming admitted miserably. "And once she tells her brother where Lord Liu is... well, I don't expect matters to improve, let's put it that way."

"Yours, I think, will be the harder, less appreciated role," Pang Tong sighed. "Still, at least Lord Liu leaves Zilong, Yide and Yunchang to help you, and does not idly disregard the threat from Sun and Cao, as we both feared he might."

"You explained matters, and he listened: you are a greater persuader than I," Kongming said truthfully. "I have the ideas, but he won't listen as readily to me as he will to you... I lack the commanding voice of a statesman, maybe."

"Nonsense," Pang Tong insisted. "You are one of his greatest confidantes."

"...Lord Liu respects Fa Zheng greatly... and rightly so," Kongming suggested. "That man is every bit our equal... he will be a pillar of our future state, I think."

For several moments, there was awkward silence.

"...Has someone died...?" Kongming said with a nervous laugh.

"We will be embarking on different journeys now, after such a short time working together," Pang Tong mused. "I suppose, since we will not speak for some months, or perhaps even years... ... ...and I am at a loss for words."

"You could wish me luck," Kongming joked. "I'm going to be spending those 'months or years' chasing a delinquent Lady Sun around the market stalls of Gong'an, and fending off random personal attacks from Zhang Fei. All you have to do is unseat Liu Zhang... how hard can that be...?"

Pang Tong smiled, and replied with a laugh, "Put that way, I pity you."

The two scholars spent that afternoon reminiscing about their shared time in Longzhong and about old friends, including Cui Zhouping, Xu Shu, Meng Jian and Shi Tao. After hesitant farewells, the two parted company; Kongming sat in his office in darkness that night, slowly fanning himself and thinking.

* * * * * * * * * * * *

## 62

Jian Yong travelled immediately to Chengdu, the capital of Yi Province, and Liu Bei's main force of around 60,000 departed Jing Province later in that same month. Fa Zheng led the way: once the vanguard had crossed into Yi, they stopped at the strategic White Emperor City, and General Meng Da – another of the conspirators against Liu Zhang – met Liu Bei with 2,000 troops. Liu Bei ordered Meng Da to take the troops to Jiangling and add them to the forces stationed there, while he continued westward into the Yi heartland.

Pang Tong was the Director General of the army, chief strategist, and adviser: Liu Bei's adopted son Liu Feng, Wei Yan, Huang Zhong, and Huo Jun were the vanguard generals. All of Liu Bei's other senior vassals had been left behind, under the command of Zhuge Liang.

Liu Bei hurried to Chengdu with Fa Zheng and Pang Tong, intent on meeting with the governor, Liu Zhang, and making his own assessment of the man his vassals were so keen for him to remove from power. As he travelled, Liu Bei noticed how well-governed, prosperous and peaceful the region appeared to be, and – to Fa Zheng and Pang Tong's dismay – started to speak of having second thoughts about conquering the territory.

"Xuande!" Liu Zhang hailed as Liu Bei entered his court. "At last, at last!"

Liu Zhang was in his early forties, chubby-faced, with a short beard and long moustache. He wore elaborate robes, and had a mildly distinguished air, but his physique was far from athletic, as he never partook in activities outside of court affairs, and his face had no definition or strength.

Many of Liu Zhang's most prominent vassals were present. Zhang Song, Liu Ba, Huang Quan, Dong He, Hu Jing, Zhang Yi, Wang Fu and Li Yan were the main representatives of the administration, while Wu Yi, Zhang Ren, Ling Bao, Deng Xian and Lei Tong represented the generals. Pang Tong noted that Huang Quan, Dong He, Hu Jing and Zhang Ren were particularly hostile, though none – save Zhang Song – seemed to be particularly glad of their presence. Jian Yong, however, seemed to be very comfortable in his seat as guest and emissary.

"Brother," Liu Bei hailed, "it has been a long time since we were born, and only now we meet."

"Indeed!" Liu Zhang replied. "Please, be seated!"

"…I noticed, while I travelled, how marvellously the land is governed," Liu Bei declared as he took a guest seat alongside Pang Tong. "You have achieved much, Jiyu, and the old governor would be proud."

"I wish everyone saw it like that," Liu Zhang lamented. "I act only according to circumstances, Brother Xuande… and I am not a violent man. When I was forced to order the execution of Zhang Lu's family, my heart was broken… never did I think that, after all my attempts to keep the peace, I would be forced to do such a terrible thing."

"...As you say, we are all victims of circumstance," Liu Bei agreed ponderously. "I once entered the service of Cao Cao, despite-"

"Xuande," Liu Zhang interrupted, "we... should not speak ill of the Prime Minister. Like us, he is bound by circumstance... and in a time of chaos, there is no clarity as to who is right and who is wrong. There is only who is left standing when the smoke of battle clears... I long resisted that awful truth, but now I embrace it. That's why I invited you here. There are some that say there should be bad blood between us, since I aided Cao Cao during the siege of Jiangling, and you, the southern rebel Sun Quan, but-"

"You acted as a vassal of our Supreme Majesty, against men you were told were rebels against the state," Liu Bei interrupted. "Sun Quan has since been proven to have selfish ambition... so your actions against Wu were justified. We assisted them only because we owed them for saving us from Cao Cao at Red Cliffs."

"Ah, yes, for your attempt at seizing Xiangyang and obeying a fraudulent imperial edict," Liu Zhang mused. "But if you were to aid me, I would vouch for you with the Prime Minister, and perhaps this ugly matter could be resolved. He might even petition the Emperor to have you rewarded with Hanzhong or Jing once Ma Chao, Zhang Lu and Sun Quan are defeated, and restore your branch of the family to its previous standing... and then, Xuande, we could rule a peaceful land, side by side!"

"...That would indeed be a fine end to a chaotic time," Liu Bei replied.

"But for now," the adviser Zhang Yi interrupted, "we have to deal with Zhang Lu, else none of this fine rhetoric will have any meaning. Lord Liu Bei, we would like you to place your forces at Jiameng Pass."

"The border with Hanzhong," Liu Bei noted. "Very well. What is our purpose there... to harass the enemy, or put up a staunch defence...?"

"Very much to attack," Zhang Yi ordered. "The only thing the Celestial Masters understand is violence... pressure them as much as you can."

"Very well, we shall," Liu Bei replied politely.

"Magnificent!" Liu Zhang exclaimed. "Now, Xuande, I appreciate that you have just arrived, and would not be so rude as to ask you to set out straight away... please, stay awhile and we will have a feast to raise morale and wish you good luck on your journey. ...Perhaps Mister Jian can entertain us with some of his witty anecdotes, as well."

"Well, I'm sure I can think of something," Jian Yong chuckled cheerfully.

"We shall be honoured," Liu Bei replied.

Pang Tong, meanwhile, had been observing each person carefully, noting who was to be feared, who was to be bought, who was to be disregarded, and who was to be reconciled with. He fanned himself slowly with his small brush fan, and smiled at Zhang Song, who smiled slightly in return.

"I can't betray this man," Liu Bei said as he travelled to Jiameng with Pang Tong, Fa Zheng and Jian Yong riding at his sides, at the rear of the vanguard of the army.

"My lord," Fa Zheng replied, "he seems affable enough now, but... well, if you are slandered, or he dislikes your approach, or he becomes frightened of you, or he becomes frightened by the fear of upsetting Cao Cao... you will regret the mistake from your cell in Xuchang. I almost lost my post once because of the unsubstantiated words of a nobody: because Liu Zhang is an untrustworthy man at heart, he attributes that same lack of faithfulness to others, and so is quick to judge people unfairly."

"Listen to Xiaozhi," Jian Yong pleaded. "I have spent *days* with this man, and I can tell you, he's a bloody *fool*... any good governance here in Yi is a happy accident."

"I think you exaggerate his incompetence to justify your wanting to secure me a base, and that is wrong," Liu Bei countered. "Besides, even if he is just a half-decent governor, it will be impossible for us to win his people over... and eventually, this 'scheme' will be revealed, and I will be forever cast as a mean-minded, opportunistic villain, no better than Cao Cao."

"*Ayah*," Jian Yong exclaimed, "is muddle-headedness some sort of contagious disease in this region? We agreed all this before, Lord Liu, and I suggest we stick to it, or you'll be Sun Quan's gatekeeper for the rest of your life... or until he sends his friend Bu Zhi to 'assess your loyalty', like he did to the governor of Cangwu."

"...I suppose so," Liu Bei conceded. "But how...?"

"My lord," Pang Tong said, "I have not spent years as an Officer of Merit without it leaving a mark. I am quite good at assessing men at a glance... we will get nowhere with Huang Quan or Zhang Ren, but others... such as Wu Yi... can be won over."

"Agreed," Fa Zheng said sombrely. "But for now... and I hope Shiyuan agrees... we should placate and gain favour with the local people when we get to Jiameng, and ingratiate ourselves with the local officials and military... that should be our first objective."

"We shouldn't do that for too long before we act," Pang Tong mused, "but yes... yes, that sounds like the best approach."

In Jiangdong, the news that Liu Bei had marched to Yi Province was met with anger and a distinct feeling of betrayal. Aware that the latest reports were best discussed in private, Sun Quan held a private court session attended only by Zhang Zhao, Zhang Hong, Bu Zhi, Lu Su, Lü Fan, and Lü Meng.

**"That lying, devious, godless mat-weaving WRETCH...!"** Sun Quan cried as Zhang Hong finished making his report. **"He sat out there, in front of everyone, and swore to the heavens that he'd never do this!"**

"I wish I could say I was surprised," Zhang Zhao sighed theatrically. "But this man is an evil, devious owl-"

**"Shut up!"** Sun Quan screamed. **"You convinced me to marry my sister to him, and now you say 'I told you so'???"**

"My lord," Lu Su protested, "I'm sure there is another, entirely rational explanation for this... they wouldn't break faith."

"You're just saying that because you practically stood guarantor for them," Zhang Zhao snickered, "and you're hoping to escape the executioner."

"And your head is safe, is it, matchmaker...?" Lu Su retorted. "My lord, I will go and speak with Kongming... we will get the truth from him."

"...It is true that Zhuge Liang is a wiser man than his master," Lü Fan reluctantly agreed, "but is he even that influential anymore, if his master left him in Jing when he went on this 'expedition'...?"

"Quite the contrary," Lu Su replied. "Kongming has been made acting governor, so Liu Bei has every faith in him. The Director General of the army is Pang Shiyuan, the 'Young Phoenix'."

"So," Zhang Zhao scoffed, "that ugly little man fawned on Cao Cao and then Zhou Gongjin – even having the audacity to attend Gongjin's funeral – just to gather intelligence for Liu Bei and his friend 'Crouching Dragon'. And you say we can trust the latter when he sends his friend to spy at a *funeral*...?"

"...In this matter, I agree with Lu Zijing," Sun Quan insisted. "Master Zhuge is a good man... like his brother. We will find out what Liu Bei is up to."

"There are only two possible answers to that," Zhang Hong chuckled. "He's either reneged on his word to us and intends to seize the province alone... or he reneged on his entire covenant with us, and has turned to Liu Zhang and his master, Cao Cao, in an attempt to take Jing Province from us."

"Would you blame him in either case...?" Lu Su chortled. "I would be annoyed with Eastern Wu after you sent *that man there* on his 'mission'!"

Lu Su pointed at Bu Zhi angrily.

"That was regrettable," Sun Quan said wearily. "But if Mister Bu says that Governor Wu Ju's behaviour was suspect... he did the right thing executing him."

"*Ayah!*" Lu Su exclaimed. "...'*Execute*'...? Bu Zhi lopped his head off in front of his courtiers without a trial! He was killed because he was Liu Bei's...!"

"**Enough,**" Sun Quan interrupted ominously. "Lu Zijing, it was at Zhou Gongjin's instruction that Mister Bu went to the independent territories... and the end result is that all of the troubles in those areas have been eradicated, and we have stability. If Wu Ju was Liu Bei's friend, well... that's unfortunate. I'm Liu Bei's landlord *and* brother-in-law, and that's *definitely* unfortunate."

"...I'll go and speak to Kongming," Lu Su said with a weary tone.

"Very good," Sun Quan replied coldly. "Perhaps we'll see what Liu Bei's up to."


"...**Governor!**" a soldier shouted as he ran into Kongming's Gong'an office.

"...Yes...?" Kongming sighed with resignation.

"Lady Sun... she...!" the soldier whined.

"*Again*...?" Kongming complained. "Where is she causing trouble this time...?"

"The... the main street near... the meat market," the soldier replied. "I ran as... quickly as... I could... Governor, she...!"

"Okay, okay," Kongming said as he got to his feet, rubbed his eyes, and flexed his shoulder painfully. "Have you alerted Zhao Zilong...?"

"No, I... should I have...?" the soldier asked.

"...I'll do it," Kongming replied.

**"APOLOGISE!"** Lady Sun screamed as she aimed her sword at the neck of a cowering merchant, who was scrabbling backwards on the ground, desperate to escape the humiliating situation he was in. The civilians were watching from a safe distance, and were amused by the sight of Lady Sun and her armed maids; the women and children seemed to be enjoying the moment most of all.

"I really could do without this," Kongming sighed as he arrived at the scene with Zhao Yun and a small retinue of soldiers.

"It is becoming a regular occurrence," Zhao Yun complained.

The cowering merchant spotted the soldiers and shouted, **"PLEASE, HELP ME!"**

Lady Sun stepped back reluctantly and sheathed her sword as Kongming approached with the soldiers.

"Where is A'Dou, my lady...?" Kongming asked Lady Sun pointedly.

"...With an old servant of my household," Lady Sun replied bluntly. "Are you against women having time outdoors, Acting Governor...?"

"Not at all," Kongming replied. "In fact, my own wife is just over there, shopping."

Lady Sun turned to follow Kongming's gaze; Yueying – who he had moved to his house in Gong'an so that the two could remain close – was indeed stood in the crowd, watching the scene with amusement.

"I do not intend to chastise you, my lady, and could not, since you are my master's wife," Kongming continued. "But these are dangerous times..."

"I can defend myself, as you can rightly see," Lady Sun retorted, drawing her sword once again: Zhao Yun also drew his sword reflexively, at which point Lady Sun's maids – and after them, Zhao Yun's soldiers – all drew their own weapons, and the situation became a crisis. Kongming started to fan himself slowly.

"...I will not be humbled!" Lady Sun insisted.

"As the only person who isn't armed," Kongming replied, "I have little ground to humble you. It is one thing to walk around with armed guards... it is another entirely to look for trouble... is that not what happened to your older brother...?"

**"Don't you DARE BRING HIM INTO THIS!"** Lady Sun screamed: she thrust her sword at Kongming's neck, but Zhao Yun deflected it with his own blade.

"So you'd *kill me*...?" Kongming chuckled casually. "How utterly childish."

"I... I only intended to scare you," Lady Sun retorted nervously.

"...Which is even more childish," Kongming sighed. "Lady Sun, you are a married woman now, the sister of one great man and the wife of another. Do you not think that a busy marketplace full of flailing swords is the perfect place for an *assassin*...? ...And this is *Jing*, my lady..."

"Eastern Wu's domain, governed by my husband," Lady Sun replied confidently. "Why should I fear *Jing*...?"

Kongming leant forward and whispered, "Because there are many that may want to avenge Huang Zu, or Liu Biao, and they may be all around us, right now. And their killer's sister... perhaps makes a very good target."

Lady Sun suddenly realised her error, and sheathed her sword: her maids followed her example. As Zhao Yun and his men also sheathed their swords, Kongming turned his attention to the merchant that Lady Sun had been threatening.

"...What was the dispute about...?" Kongming asked coldly.

The merchant replied, "M-my silk... she said it was... too expensive, so I said... she was a... a...!"

"...I can sense you do not wish to say," Kongming said quietly. "Apologise to the lady, and then be gone."

"A-apologies, Lady G-Governess," the merchant said pleadingly.

Lady Sun grunted irritably.

"...Now *go*," Kongming ordered.

The merchant ran to his stall-full of wares, grabbed as much as he could, and fled; his assistants grabbed what they could and followed.

"Zilong, escort Lady Sun back home," Kongming said calmly.

"I need no bodyguards," Lady Sun insisted. "I can find my own way home."

"...Very well," Kongming conceded. "One last thing... my lord values A'Dou very much... please ensure that he is often in the care of his mother... which is now, since his birth mother has passed, a title that has fallen to you. And please, Lady Sun, be careful... my lord has no desire to lose a third wife."

Lady Sun nodded tersely, and gestured for her maids to follow her from the marketplace. Kongming then nodded to Zhao Yun, who followed the band of women at a discreet distance with half of the soldiers, leaving the rest with Kongming. Slowly, the people started to go about their business once again.

"...*Aiee*," Kongming exclaimed: he forgot his surroundings for a moment, and clutched his aching head with his left hand.

"Husband," Yueying said worriedly as she approached him, "are you alright...?"

"Honestly...?" Kongming chuckled as he lowered his hand from his face. "*No.*"

"...Please finish work on time today," Yueying implored. "Don't work late."

"Would I argue with a woman right now...?" Kongming joked miserably.

Yueying smiled, and Kongming walked away with his soldiers.


A few days later, Kongming received a visit from Lu Su.

"...Have you come for Lady Sun...?" Kongming asked as Lu Su sat down. "You can have her back if you want... really, *seriously*, take her back."

"...That's not funny," Lu Su replied angrily. "You're making things very tough for me, Kongming, you *and* your master!"

"I wondered when Sun Quan would send someone to harass me over the expedition into Yi," Kongming sighed as he resisted the urge to clutch his aching head. "I know what you're going to say, it's obvious."

**"Yes, well, I'll say it anyway!" Lu Su barked. "I lost count of how many times you told me that Liu Bei definitely wouldn't go into Yi! Liu Bei himself pledged to the entire court in Chaisang that he'd rather be a bloody *hermit* than invade Yi! You LIED, Kongming! You both LIED!"**

302

"Can you... not *shout*...?" Kongming pleaded. "...I know I lied."
"I...! ... ... ...Wait, *what*...?" Lu Su said with confusion. "You *admit* it...?"
"Lu Zijing, our business as envoys and diplomats is to lie," Kongming chuckled miserably as he finally gave up and placed his left hand to his forehead.
"...Are you unwell...?" Lu Su asked worriedly.
"It's just a headache... I get little time to rest," Kongming insisted. "Mister Lu, we have done nothing but lie to each other for the entire time we've known each other... but at the same time, we've also told the truth. I said Lord Liu would never *invade* Yi Province... he has been *invited there* by Liu Zhang."
"B-but... Liu Zhang is a vassal of Cao Cao!" Lu Su exclaimed. "Are you saying that Lord Liu has decided to try and make amends with...?"
"*No*," Kongming insisted. "You have to trust me on this... Lord Liu is trying, as we all are, to play a very complicated diplomatic game... which, if he succeeds, will earn him Yi bloodlessly, for it will be *given to him*."
Lu Su pondered it silently.
"My lord vowed never to harm Yi... and yes, he'd sooner be a hermit than harm a hair on a person's head in Yi," Kongming continued. "But the situation at the moment is delicate... the ideal would be for Sun, Liu and the forces under Zhang Lu and Ma Chao to unite and destroy Cao Cao... but we know that cannot happen. Sun Quan must protect Jiangdong... my lord must protect Jing, and Cao Cao has enough forces and defences now to fight us both at the same time. Zhang Lu must protect Hanzhong... and the forces at Tong Pass will lose because they have put everything into their offensive, but left no guards in their home territories.
"If Zhang Lu attacks Yi, and Liu Zhang gets no help from Cao Cao or from us, he'll move into Jing as he retreats, and we'll have to repel him by force... losing Yi to Zhang Lu, risking Jing, and shedding needless blood for no personal gain."
"What you say is true," Lu Su murmured thoughtfully.
"My lord, with Young Phoenix, has entered Yi to find some way to resolve the crisis, as he tried to do in Jing," Kongming continued. "Zhang Lu and Liu Zhang are just like Sun Quan and Liu Biao... Liu Zhang killed Zhang Lu's family, so the two can never be reconciled, not without massive reparation. My lord will pursue all diplomatic channels... and if that fails... well, we may have to fight, but it will be to stabilise the region, as you did with Jing."
"...It all sounds very upright, but we both know that you're up to something, one way or another," Lu Su said miserably. "Okay, Kongming... I'll give Lord Sun your version of events... but if you don't hear from me again... you'll know why."
With that, Lu Su left, and returned to Jiangdong.


＊＊＊＊＊＊＊＊＊＊＊＊

## 63

While Kongming maintained the peace in Jing as best he could, Liu Bei did what he could to avoid conflict in Jiameng, rather than follow the instructions given to him by Liu Zhang's advisers. He started to cultivate a relationship with the people of Jiameng as soon as he arrived, and his only military manoeuvres were responses to attacks made on the region. This was noticed by Liu Zhang's supporters and reported to the seat of power in Chengdu, but Liu Zhang was not suspicious: at least, not at first.

Summer turned to autumn, and the battle at Tong Pass between Ma Chao's alliance and Cao Cao's imperial forces dragged on. The number of rebels increased dramatically with every month that passed, as tribe after tribe and village after village sent everything they had against the Han Prime Minister, yet Cao Cao was said to have rejoiced at every new army that was announced. Even Cao Cao's most intimate confidantes were perplexed, but in the sixth month of confrontation, it suddenly became obvious as to why. If all of their enemies were in one place, all that was needed was a single decisive victory, and once again, it was obtained through stratagem, not direct conflict.

Ma Chao's 'uncle', Han Sui, was invited to a parley, where only trivial matters were discussed by Cao Cao, to Han Sui's confusion; this, followed by Han Sui's receipt of a letter from Cao Cao containing errors and corrections, was enough to make Ma Chao wonder if something was being concocted between Cao and Han Sui. The suspicion was enough to break the alliance, and before long, Ma Chao and his closest aides fled Tong Pass, resoundingly beaten in a sudden a relentless attack by the imperial army. Ma Chao's tribal allies, Han Sui and Yang Qiu, were defeated and forced to flee, and most of the other leaders had been killed during the rout.

It was by no means the end of Ma Chao – he would soon return – but Cao Cao felt at ease enough to completely divert his attention elsewhere, since he considered the rebellion in the west to be definitively broken.

"I am unnerved," Sun Quan admitted to his assembled vassals in the main court.

"Be at ease," Zhang Zhao insisted. "Surely, Cao Cao will first turn his attentions to Zhang Lu of Hanzhong, his originally stated target."

"*This*," Lu Su scoffed, "is why you are in charge of internal affairs, Mister Zhang... because you know *nothing* of the world outside this court. My lord, Cao Cao has left the western front and returned to Xuchang... he seems to have no intention now of attacking Zhang Lu... perhaps he never did."

"...You mean, 'borrowing passage to destroy Guo'...?" Lü Meng supposed.

"My thoughts exactly," Lu Su replied. "And now, Zhang Lu is locked into fighting Liu Bei... Cao Cao obviously doesn't want to inadvertently help his hated enemy in any way, so he's staying away from Hanzhong."

"I confess, it adds credence to Liu Bei's claim that he is there to seek a diplomatic solution," Sun Quan said begrudgingly. "Had Cao Cao attacked Zhang Lu, then I would have certainly marched on Jing, and wrested it back before Liu Bei betrayed me further and handed it to Cao Cao."

"Perhaps, however, it might be wise to recall Lady Sun," Zhang Hong suggested suddenly. "After all, if we are reading the signs wrongly, and he does suddenly turn to Cao Cao, he would have your sister as a hostage… that would hardly be ideal."

Sun Quan silently pondered the idea.

"No, no!" Lu Su protested. "If we recall Lady Sun, that effectively divorces her from Liu Bei, and ends our alliance!"

"When Liu Bei conquers Yi and refuses to hand back Jing, as he inevitably will, does that not also end the alliance…?" Zhang Zhao countered.

"But this is all cause and effect!" Lu Su retorted. "If you recall Lady Sun, of *course* he will refuse to return Jing, out of bitter *spite*! Why do you do everything you can to bring us harm???"

"**How DARE you!**" Zhang Zhao growled. "I went along with your fool idea to befriend this treacherous peddler, and where has it got us, mm…? Red Cliffs was several years ago now, and all we have to show for it is a parasitic squatter!"

The majority of the officials murmured agreeably.

"…My lord, *please*…!" Lu Su protested.

"I… I cannot risk my sister becoming a bargaining tool in a prolonged dispute between myself and Liu Bei," Sun Quan decided. "If Liu Bei chooses to see her return to Jiangdong as grounds for terminating the marriage, then, well… so be it. It is quite obvious that we will have a dispute over Jing anyway… and his current activity in Yi is very suspicious. No, I agree with Zhang Hong… get her back, get her back at once."

Lu Su's arms hung limply at his sides, and his head fell forward slowly.

"…My lord," Zhuge Jin implored, "can we not contact my brother and let him know our decision, rather than send soldiers to retrieve her…? Guan Yu, Zhang Fei and Zhao Yun have been left as protectors alongside Kongming, and they may overreact and think that we're invading."

"…No," Zhang Hong insisted. "We do not need an angry Liu Bei returning from Yi, and causing all manner of havoc in the west. If she's gone before he hears about it, he'll stay where he is and complain about it on his return."

"And if Zhuge Liang *does* somehow find out," Zhang Zhao threatened, "and Lady Sun's freedom of movement is compromised… it will not be looked upon lightly."

Zhuge Jin lowered his head and said no more.

"…My lord," Zhang Zhao said further, "I have an idea…!"

"…Can it be said here and now…?" Sun Quan asked.

"…No," Zhang Zhao replied.

"**The court is concluded,**" Sun Quan declared. "**You may all depart.**"

Lu Su watched Sun Quan, Zhang Zhao and Zhang Hong disappear into Sun Quan's private meeting room, and shook his head bitterly.

"The alliance is over, isn't it…?" Zhuge Jin supposed.

"...I pray it isn't," Lu Su replied. "Cao is amassing forces near Ruxukou... we'll need all the allies we can get."

Within a week, the Zhang brothers' plan was put into motion.

"...*Ayah*," Kongming muttered as he returned home from a day of work that he would gladly forget.
"I heard there was commotion down at the river," Yueying said as Kongming collapsed to his knees in front of his qin, and let the fan fall from his right hand.
"...Lady Sun has gone," Kongming reported anxiously. "I should never have joked about it with Lu Su."
"*Gone...?*" Yueying exclaimed. "How do you mean 'gone'...?"
"She has returned to her brother in Jiangdong," Kongming continued. "That is not at all well-timed... I will have to arrange a meeting to smooth things over before Guan Yu and Zhang Fei take an army down the river to Chaisang."
"...What happened...?" Yueying asked with confusion. "Why did she leave?"
"Her brother's advisers, of course," Kongming chortled. "They advised him to recall her, and he agreed because they have convinced him that our movements in Yi Province are treacherous, and that she might become a hostage if she stayed... which would be bad enough, only someone also recommended that she take A'Dou with her: a classic 'reverse hostage and captor' scheme."
Yueying gasped with surprise, as she knew the potential implications of the events.
"Fortunately," Kongming sighed with relief, "somebody vigilant alerted Zhao Zilong, and he and Zhang Fei were able to stop her and recover A'Dou... but they had to 'negotiate' with her escorts, which means that she will not be reporting a favourable departure to Sun Quan."
Yueying gazed vacantly as she absorbed the news.
"I've written to Ma Liang in Jiangling," Kongming continued, "to urge him to pacify Guan Yu... since Guan is very, very protective of Lord Liu's interests..."

"...**That weasel!**" Guan Yu bellowed as he pondered the attempted abduction of Liu Bei's son. "...Sun Quan will forever be an enemy of mine!"
"General Guan," Ma Liang protested, "you cannot seek reprisal. In fact... Kongming has suggested that I travel to Chaisang and attempt to repair the damaged relationship between our houses."
"And look *weak*???" Guan Yu suggested angrily. "I will not abide this! Yide is like my brother, since we go so far back... but I cannot believe he didn't slay the witch for treason, right then and there!"
"...I do believe that he considered it to be an option," Ma Liang said wearily, "but we cannot afford to be so rash. As Kongming has pointed out..."
"Zhuge Liang is a wretched pedant whose brother serves the lord of Wu!" Guan Yu retorted. "I care nothing for his duplicitous wrangling!"

"...As Kongming has pointed out," Ma Liang began again, "there are some in Wu that see our excursion into Yi Province as an act of deceit or hypocrisy. At the very least, General Guan, they may see us as hypocrites, for we openly criticised their own intentions for Yi, citing them as without basis or righteousness... at worst, well, since Lord Liu once vowed – in front of the entire court of Chaisang, no less – that he would never to step foot on Yi soil to invade it – which would constitute the greatest of deceit in their eyes, of course, if he then has – the only other reason that he would take an army into Yi - to *aid* Liu Zhang – is, by the very nature of it, to aid Cao Cao, and betray our covenant entirely... in which case they attempted to 'reverse hostage and captor' by having Lady Sun take A'Dou to Chaisang."
Guan Yu noted the hypothesis quietly.
"...That is a sound observation," Guan Yu conceded. "I would be a hypocrite myself to ignore it. So how does Mister Zhuge intend to resolve this matter...?"
"He is busy with state affairs," Ma Liang explained, "and Mister Sun is unwell, so he has asked me to travel to Chaisang and act as envoy. He has asked that I depart as soon as possible."
"...Good luck, Jichang," Guan Yu replied respectfully. "Although if Mister Zhuge has faith in you to restore amity in such a difficult moment, then so do I."


************

## 64

Within a week, Ma Liang was presented to the Wu court in Chaisang. Sun Quan invited the scholar-envoy to speak privately.

"Lu Su tells me that you are the sworn brother of Kongming," Sun Quan said as he took his seat in his private audience room. "Hence, Mister Ma, I have spared you a harsh deconstruction by the Zhang brothers."

"My thanks, Lord Sun," Ma Liang replied politely, bowing as he spoke.

"...Is Kongming well...?" Sun Quan asked courteously. "I understand that he works very hard... I hope that he does not work *too hard*."

"He is diligent, and perhaps, Lord Sun, a workaholic," Ma Liang replied sadly. "We often criticise him for it... but he only replies that he is serving his chosen lord as well as he can. We both took our pledge to Lord Liu very seriously, and despite the hardships, we do not regret the decision... since, despite outward appearances, Lord Liu means well for the land, Lord Sun."

"...Very well approached," Sun Quan chuckled softly. "Perhaps you would explain to me this 'trip' to Yi Province that your lord has undertaken."

"The politics in Yi is, as with all the land, complicated," Ma Liang replied. "Lei Xu of Lujiang chose to join my lord because of past grievances with the Sun family, not for any sound tactical reason. Lord Liu joins Liu Zhang for similarly unorthodox reasons... he hopes – however unlikely it is – that Cao Cao's obvious abandoning of the Yi governor to the mercy of Zhang Lu of Hanzhong will make Liu Zhang reconsider his allegiances... join us, and oppose Cao Cao. He currently sits on the Hanzhong border, attempting to make peace with the local populace."

"Is that so...?" Sun Quan sniggered. "Well, my advisers think that he is simply wooing the populace before a takeover... is that not the true state of things...?"

"Yes and no," Ma Liang replied. "Liu Zhang must understand his precarious position, see the light, and switch his allegiance. If he does not, and persists in his destructive and – it has to be said – selfish and personal feud with Zhang Lu... then there are some within the Yi administration that would assist a regime change."

"...Well put," Sun Quan said soberly. "I cannot fail to note that you criticise my own feud with Liu Biao of Jing, however."

"Wasn't the loss of family your pain to suffer...?" Ma Liang countered. "Zhang Lu is the wronged party, Lord Sun. There are some that advocate a ceding of territory as a bloodless solution, but Liu Zhang will not hear of it."

Sun Quan smiled, and said, "You're Kongming's equal, and no mistake. You understand the nature of lords and their ways, and the difference between justice and natural law. A pity that you also serve another lord... I would be glad of both of you in my court. ...So now that you have 'explained' Liu Bei's journey to Yi, what is his stance on my sister returning to my homeland...?"

"Jing was dangerous," Ma Liang replied. "There are many that bear grudges toward the Sun family for the troubles there, and the only way to guarantee her safety was to imprison her at home... hardly fair, when she rightly enjoys freedom to move as she desires. Lord Liu's current strategy is admittedly reckless and untried, and if there were a mishap, Lady Sun should be with her family. ...There... there was some discomfort over the attempt to bring the lord's son to Jiangdong as well... for while it is right that the child be with its mother... Zilong is his appointed guardian since the battle at Steep-slope, and he must protect both Jing and the young master."

"...So Liu Bei desires a continued peace between us...?" Sun Quan realised.

"Lord Sun, he desires nothing else," Ma Liang insisted. "We knew that this expedition to Yi would look suspicious... we prayed that it would not lead to bad blood... your caution is entirely understood, and we ask that you understand our actions... for while they seem duplicitous, they are meant sincerely. In fact... my lord has stressed that as and when Cao Cao does attack you at Ruxukou, we will try and provide support to divide Cao's forces, involving Liu Zhang if that is possible... or, at least, we will prevent Liu Zhang from supporting Cao Cao."

"Splendid," Sun Quan praised. "Truly splendid... it was not my desire to end our truce at all... I am glad that we have reached this diplomatic point. Tell Kongming and your lord Liu Bei that if that is so... they have my word that peace will endure."

Ma Liang bowed humbly from where he sat; Sun Quan continued discussions, and found Ma Liang to be as agreeable as Kongming. It would not be the last time that Ma Liang would visit Wu, and Sun Quan would have deep respect for him until his end of his days.

"Ma Jichang handled Sun Quan very well," Mister Sun said to Kongming as he read a letter sent by Ma Liang a week later, upon his return to Jiangling. "Very good, and a real boon to us: we did not need Sun Quan attacking Jing."

"Jichang is a natural statesman," Kongming said as he fanned himself slowly. "He is my equal, if not my superior in that. So, with Wu pacified, and that dispute diffused... we can focus on Yi. Wu didn't want a fight with us, since Cao Cao is converging on Ruxukou. In fact, this has turned about nicely.

"We are rid of the troublesome Lady Sun, which – I would presume unwittingly – has them removing a spy from our midst: how foolish the Zhang brothers are to go to great lengths to install her here, and then remove her when she is at her most useful! Secondly, we have now pledged support against Cao Cao, which would indebt them to us, and reinforce our position in both Jing and Yi. Thirdly, by aiding Wu, we will be forcing Liu Zhang to make a swift choice about where his allegiances are... even a slimy coward like him will not be able to find a way out of picking a side, and if he picks Cao Cao, he is as good as defeated."

"Kongming," Mister Sun said hoarsely, "I have been with Lord Liu since the early days in Xu Province... for nearly eighteen years. In all that time, I have watched him suffer, struggle... hah, I remember when we reached Xinye, and he met your friend Xu Shu... and that day he brought you to that banquet... I remember you, waving your fan, and thinking you were an opportunist, another one trying to exploit him... when you refused to serve him, I then thought you were some sort of time-wasting eccentric... now, when I see all that you've achieved, I...!"

"I have done nothing to speak of, Mister Sun," Kongming insisted. "When I joined Lord Liu, he was on the way to becoming strong, and my guidance has done nothing other than reinforce the inevitable."

"Rubbish," Mister Sun scolded. "You helped coordinate at Steepslope, you helped to placate the late Liu Qi and retain his support, and you anticipated that Lu Su of Jiangdong would come to us for an alliance! You were one of the men that achieved what everyone thought was impossible: an alliance between the lord of Jiangdong, Lord Liu, and the governor of Jing! You negotiated the lease of Nan Prefecture, you coordinated the takeover of the four independent counties, and you were the one that made that crucial diplomatic step of suggesting we speak to Sun Quan after he tried to steal away our lord's son... even I, a dedicated peacemaker, would not have tried to seek accord after such an affront, but you were right. If Lord Liu did not have you, Kongming... I wonder, would we have anything at all, even our lives...?"

"You are very kind," Kongming said with a bow of gratitude. "To receive such words from the man that has been Lord Liu's sword and shield in all matters for so long... I am truly touched."

"I shall be travelling to Jiameng, now that I am a little better," Mister Sun revealed, "since Lord Liu feels he needs more advisers around him. Oh, Kongming... to see Lord Liu in Yi... and to think that I may live to see him finally get the power and influence he deserves, and be able to finally confront that villain Cao Cao...!"

"We all wait for that day, Mister Sun," Kongming replied. "May that day come soon."


************

## 65

Cao Cao continued the movement of his armies into the east, and along the north bank of the Yangtze River. Both Liu Bei and Sun Quan watched this development with nervous interest: while Cao Cao's public announcement that Xiahou Dun had 26 *juns* – where a single *jun* was a force of 12,500 men – was met with understandable cynicism, word was that Cao Cao's use of the *tuntian* system for social development and agriculture had given him considerable stocks of food and an army of 400,000, a number that dwarfed his army at Wulin three years before, and coincided nicely with the force attributed to 'Blind Xiahou'. Sun Quan had already diverted all of his forces – which only numbered around 70,000 in comparison – to the riverbank that lay directly south of Cao Cao's camps, and he awaited the conflict apprehensively. It was around this time that Xun Yu – Cao Cao's trusted adviser of many years – died aged 49 from the sudden and inexplicable illness that he had succumbed to after his opposition to Cao Cao becoming the Duke of Wei.

Liu Bei, meanwhile, continued his peaceful activity in Jiameng, but as the weeks turned to months without any sign of meaningful confrontation, Liu Zhang started to become impatient and then suspicious of his kinsman and supposed ally. The conspirator, Zhang Song, was also starting to worry: he wrote letters to Fa Zheng in Jiameng, urging swift action, as – spurred by increasingly hostile advice and observations from his inner circle – Governor Liu Zhang's mood turned from grateful cheer to bitter anger.

"Another letter," Fa Zheng said to Liu Bei as he walked into the warlord's command room in Jiameng. Liu Bei, Pang Tong and Jian Yong were conferring when the Yi envoy made his entrance, and his announcement was unsettling.
"He should be careful," Pang Tong warned. "...But I understand his fear. Huang Quan and Zhang Ren are stirring trouble for us. We really are now a point where we can dally no longer. My lord... I have a suggestion - or rather three suggestions – that I want to make to you, if you would listen."
"...Very well," Liu Bei replied, "I shall certainly listen."
"The time is now upon us to make a move," Pang Tong explained. "We are getting nowhere in our efforts to find a peaceful solution to this mess. This cannot go on. Liu Zhang is a fickle fool that will soon turn on us, regardless of what we do, had done, or intended to do; and Cao Cao will eventually turn his attention to Jing, not to mention the need to support Sun Quan and save our alliance. There are three ways to progress, and only those three.
"Firstly, we advance quickly on Chengdu, without warning, and seize power, making use of our support within Liu Zhang's inner circle. If we act very quickly, even Zhang Ren will not be able to act in time to stop us.

"Secondly, we take control of the armies here in the north of the province, buy whoever we cannot inspire, and gradually take control, moving toward Chengdu, where we try and persuade Liu Zhang to surrender.

"Thirdly… … …thirdly, we retreat to White Emperor City, near the Yi-Jing border, as quietly as we can, and await new opportunities."

"…I dislike the first idea," Liu Bei replied, "as it is too hasty, and leaves us open to all manner of mishaps. The third idea… is no longer even a slight option for me, since I cannot and will not leave Yi under the rule of a puppet governor that serves Cao Cao. We will adopt the second plan… but how shall we go about it…?"

"Finally," Jian Yong snickered, "some action."

"Cao Cao is about to attack Ruxukou," Pang Tong explained, "if he has not done so already. We must force Liu Zhang's hand… ask him to provide us with support for the defence of Jing Province. Since we have sixty-thousand men embedded here in Yi, surely the least he can do is provide ten thousand good troops and some provisions to us…? That will reduce his forces in the south and east of Yi, and give us greater strength… we can then win over his men in the north, as I said, and press on Chengdu. If he refuses, that's grounds for a rightful cessation of our alliance."

"Excellent," Liu Bei praised. "Xianhe, let us get the discussion started as soon as possible."

"I'm ready to get started," Jian Yong promised.

Soon enough, a messenger was on his way to Chengdu: the reply was as swift as it was politically final.

"**REPORT!**" the returning messenger hailed as he entered Liu Bei's makeshift court at Jiameng. "**Governor Liu Zhang has agreed to supply four thousand stalwart soldiers and a measure of provisions to bolster the defences of Jing Province! He regrets that further support is currently impossible!**"

"…The…!" Liu Bei exclaimed: Pang Tong gestured with his small fan in order to remind the angry warlord that he should choose his words carefully while the messenger was present.

"…Messenger, go and rest," Jian Yong ordered.

As the messenger retreated silently, Mister Sun – who had only recently made the arduous journey to Jiameng – said, "My lord, stay calm. I-"

"We should talk privately," Pang Tong suggested.

On Pang Tong's suggestion, Liu Bei, Jian Yong, Mister Sun, Fa Zheng and Tong himself moved to a private room.

"*Stalwart*…?" Mister Sun chuckled.

"We all know that means 'old and weak'," Jian Yong snickered. "What a cheeky man he is… but stay calm, my lord, we-"

"Faithless fool!" Liu Bei growled. "I bring my entire army here to save his worthless, craven hide… risking betrayal by Sun Quan, invasion by Cao Cao… and he repays me by refusing to send me help in an emergency…? …Now I am determined to see him removed… Master Pang, what do we now do…?"

"We should assess potential allies in this area," Pang Tong replied. "We're going to have to move now... unfortunately, Yang Huai and Gao Pei, the generals that guard the strategic Boshui Pass, are not for turning. That means a critical communication channel is under the command of two men that are loyal to Liu Zhang."
"From now on," Fa Zheng added, "we should have all discussions in secret... this plan of ours must not leak out."

Liu Bei and his advisers quietly pondered how best to deal with Liu Zhang, while in the east, the battle at Ruxukou raged between Cao Cao's imperial forces and Eastern Wu. Sun Quan's forces achieved a surprising number of small victories during the initial skirmish, forcing Cao Cao's massive army to retreat to the north bank and assume a defensive posture. The Wu forces hailed it as another Red Cliffs, while Cao Cao bore the humiliation with little stoicism. It was now winter again, and almost exactly four years since Cao Cao had fallen for Zhou Yu's fire attack: the bitter reminder of that day made Cao Cao reluctant to take risks, just as Kongming and other observers of the hour had once predicted.

Before anyone realised it, time had flown by, and the spring season was approaching. As Liu Bei conferred with his group of advisers in private for yet another day, a nervous Liu Feng appeared at the doorway.
"Feng'er," Liu Bei scolded, "this is a private meeting."
"An urgent despatch from Chengdu," Liu Feng replied, handing a small tube to Pang Tong. Within the small, hollowed wooden cylinder was a silk letter, which Pang Tong removed and started reading immediately. Liu Feng expected that, as Liu Bei's adopted son, he might be allowed to stay; a stern stare from Liu Bei said otherwise, and he retreated, inwardly indignant and distressed.
"...Oh...?" Jian Yong exclaimed. "What could...?"
Pang Tong was nearing the end of the letter, and was visibly agitated.
"...What is it...?" Liu Bei asked worriedly.
"Zhang Song has been discovered," Pang Tong said as he passed the letter to a fretful Fa Zheng. "...The plot is leaked, and we do not have much time."
"Ziqiao... has been discovered...?" Fa Zheng murmured as he started to read the letter with growing horror. "But... he'll *die*...!"
"What...!" Liu Bei said with tears in his eyes.
"...Zhang Su... his own brother... his own *brother* betrayed him???" Fa Zheng whined as he read the letter and learned the truth. "A fool: a **worthless, miserable FOOL!** Zhang Ziqiao will die for this... he will already be cold bones! What sort of brother does this to his own blood???"
"Ziqiao... Zhang *Ziqiao*...!" Liu Bei sobbed as he covered his face with his hands.
"We acted too slowly," Pang Tong lamented. "I consider myself partly responsible for that. His death – if he dies – is my fault, as much as any man's."
"Your caution... was necessary," Fa Zheng said emotionally. "...I only hope Liu Zhang shows leniency... but I do not think he will."

"So we are now exposed...?" Jian Yong asked impatiently: Fa Zheng handed him the letter, which he started to read immediately.

"...We still have the advantage, despite our loss," Fa Zheng continued. "If we move quickly, attack Boshui Pass... before Liu Zhang's agents get here and tell them that we are no longer allies."

"Better still," Pang Tong said, "I suggest we invite them here... Lord Liu...?"

Liu Bei was still sobbing pitifully.

"...Lord Liu," Pang Tong prompted irritably. "We have not got time for tearful lamentations... Mister Fa was the dearest friend of this man, and yet he controls his feelings for the sake of our important cause. Please, regain yourself: we need to act quickly, if we aren't to join him in early death, and for the same regrettable reason... needless procrastination."

Liu Bei looked at Pang Tong: his eyes were swollen and red.

"...Lord Liu, *listen to me*, for you are key to our next move," Pang Tong urged. "What we must do, is..."

************

## 66

"...My lord, two generals approach," Jian Yong declared to Liu Bei and his assembled court. "Here are Yang Huai and Gao Pei."

The two Yi generals advanced toward the stony-faced Liu Bei without fear, as no word had yet reached them from Chengdu, and they knew him as an ally. Many of Liu Bei's vassals were also unaware of the true situation, and sat wondering why the two generals had been summoned from their key post at the strategically important mountain checkpoint known as Boshui Pass. Liu Bei was slowly sipping from a cup of wine; to Liu Bei's immediate left, Director General Pang Tong stood quietly, fanning himself slowly.

"...Commander Liu," the Yi General Yang Huai hailed after an awkward silence. "Why have you summoned us here...?"

**"Worthless cur!"** Liu Bei retorted angrily, as he leapt to his feet and noisily threw down his wine cup; the two generals – and most of Liu Bei's own vassals – were taken aback by the outburst. **"You two dare to address me with such a contemptuous tone???"**

"But...!" Gao Pei protested: but before he could say any more, swordsmen appeared from behind the curtains that lined the walls of Liu Bei's court, and descended on the two Yi generals. As Liu Bei's vassals struggled to understand what was going on and drew their own swords in reflex, sharp blades flashed, and the heads of Yang Huai and Gao Pei fell to the floor, while their bodies fell backwards to the ground.

"...Lord Liu," Wei Yan said nervously as Gao Pei's head came to a rest near his legs, "why did you just kill two good generals...?"

"Do not question me," Liu Bei replied. "Just listen, all of you: after an act of faithless treachery, the two Liu houses that I tried to bring together are irreconcilable, and we are now at war with Liu Zhang. Zhang Song, the wise man who twice visited my court to make my family whole again, is as dead as these two men... and Liu Zhang now tries to cut our communication lines and retreat routes. Boshui Pass would have been our grave, had I not taken the steps you now review with such groundless cynicism."

"...So... we were lured here, as part of Cao Cao's actions in the east, to prevent us aiding Sun Quan...?" General Huo Jun supposed.

"Hard to ascertain," Jian Yong replied. "Regardless the circumstances, we now have to begin urgent retaliation, and fortify our position. We must secure Boshui Pass, annex Yang Huai and Gao Pei's men into our own regiments, and move immediately on the strategically important city of Fu."

"Your orders are prepared, and there's no time to lose," Pang Tong added. "Huang Zhong, Wei Yan... you will set out for Fu City with an advance force of ten thousand as soon as you can."

Huang Zhong and Wei Yan got to their feet, stepped over the bodies of the dead generals, passed the swordsmen, and left the court.

"General Liu Feng," Pang Tong continued, "you will move immediately to Boshui Pass with five thousand to gather and organise Yang Huai and Gao Pei's forces."

"Understood," Liu Feng said obediently, and with that said he departed.

"Huo Jun," Pang Tong continued, "you will remain here in Jiameng Pass with a force of three hundred to guard Jiameng City and the pass. We don't expect any problems from Zhang Lu once he hears that we are now in opposition to Liu Zhang... but if he does come here, send a messenger, and hold fast."

"I shall," Huo Jun promised.

"My lord," Pang Tong concluded, "we will take the main force and move on Fu as soon as we are sure that this area is secure."

"Very good," Liu Bei agreed.

In the east, Sun Quan's battle with Cao Cao at Ruxukou was reaching a sudden and surprising conclusion. Once again, Cao Cao had been prevented from achieving a victory by the Yangtze River and Wu's bold strategists. But as spring arrived, another announcement shattered his resolve: Ma Chao had returned, and after a devastating march across Longxi County – during which every city surrendered or fell – he was now laying siege to Ji City, north of the mountains of Hanzhong. It was not long before Cao Cao retreated from Ruxukou, since this new western threat – coupled with his desire to start building the Duchy of Wei – dulled his interest in a fruitless standoff with Sun Quan.

"So Cao Cao has retreated," Sun Quan said as he held his first peacetime court since the early winter. "However, we're far from done here, I think... we should press our offensive."

"We should be cautious," Zhang Zhao protested. "We should maintain defence... every time that we have attacked our enemies, it has cost us dearly. Our best strategy is to sit quietly."

"A pedant's talk," Huang Gai scolded. "Did the late Chief Commander Zhou Gongjin, *and* the late Assistant Commander Cheng, not win a magnificent victory at Red Cliffs, and then at Jiangling...? If either man were alive now, they would take you outside and lash you raw with a whip for being so craven!"

"I do agree that we should be cautious," Lü Meng admitted. "We are receiving reports that Liu Bei has decided to fight Liu Zhang after all."

"He sent no help during this siege we've endured!" Zhang Zhao barked. "Yet another empty promise... he used our plight to make a play for Yi Province!"

"...Not so," Lu Su insisted. "I am reliably informed, from correspondence with Zhuge Kongming and Ma Jichang, that their dispute was ignited by Liu Zhang's cold refusal to commit any troops to reciprocate Liu Bei's total support... troops that were intended for a front in Jing Province, to be spearheaded by Guan Yunchang, against Fan City."

"Yet conveniently enough," Zhang Zhao sneered, "Liu Zhang refused... weakening us, and giving Bei the excuse to break faith!"

"*Aiee*," Lu Su exclaimed irritably. "I give up trying to reason with you."

"Ma Jichang is on his way to Chaisang to meet with you again, Lord Sun," Zhuge Jin reported. "My brother is anxious that we maintain cordial relations."

"I will see him," Sun Quan promised. "...But nonetheless, I want Liu Bei's actions watched carefully... and the second that Yi falls, I want Jing returned to me."

"My lord...!" Lu Su exclaimed.

"No, Zijing," Sun Quan interrupted, "I am not to be dissuaded. I asked Liu Bei if he wanted to take the province together with me... he swore never to take it. I do not care if current events are genuine circumstance or cunning contrivance... though, since he now employs both 'Crouching Dragon' *and* 'Young Phoenix' to do his plotting, I very much suspect the *latter*... I will not stand by and watch while this man annexes province after province, while I act as nothing more than some sort of elaborate, unrewarded distraction."

Lu Su and Zhuge Jin exchanged nervous glances.

"Now," Sun Quan continued, "we must look at the possibility of another attack on Hefei Castle... while I detest the extra assistance it unavoidably gives to Liu Bei, we can't afford to let Cao Cao rest. Ma Chao now provides us with the perfect opportunity to seize the capital... so while Liu Bei takes care of himself, let's do what he keeps saying his own true mission is, shall we...?"

Cao Cao founded his duchy, and from that moment on, his faction was now known as Cao Wei, or simply Wei. He now had bestowed upon him the 9 dignitaries, which gave him a number of privileges reserved only for the most respected in the land: unfortunately – as Cao Cao's adviser Xun Yu had, to his own detriment, pointed out – most, if not all, of the men in history that had been awarded those 9 dignitaries went on to usurp the imperial throne, or if not them, then their descendants. To those that already resented Cao Cao, this bestowment – and the fate of the loyal adviser that opposed it – only proved what they had long since suspected.

"There's no going back now," Kongming said to Yueying as they sat in their Gong'an residence. Kongming was playing his qin: his playing was energetic, and almost boastful. "Beware, Duke of Wei... soon there will be a Lord of Yi."

"...You are certain that Liu Bei will take Yi," Yueying noted.

"My only concern," Kongming replied calmly, "is the price that we'll pay."

With that said, the notes he played became mournful, and almost chilling.

************

# ACT VI: THE BATTLE FOR YI PROVINCE

## 67

Ma Liang arrived at the Wu court several weeks after Liu Bei began his takeover of Yi Province, and spoke to Sun Quan in his private court once again.

"When we last met," Sun Quan chuckled casually, "you said that this outcome was a possibility... now that it is a reality, how do you feel...?"

"Firstly," Ma Liang replied, "I would like to congratulate your forces on another astounding victory over Cao Cao at Ruxukou."

"Cao Cao retreated before real damage could be done to either side," Sun Quan insisted.

"Nevertheless," Ma Liang praised, "you held out against an army almost five times the size of your own... again. Truly, Wu is a great power, and not attacked lightly. Cao Cao, Duke of Wei will hopefully realise that, and also start to see that his days as a dictator in the Han court are numbered."

"He gives himself titles," Sun Quan replied. "I doubt, therefore, that he agrees... I wouldn't either, if I had an army of four hundred thousand. ...But if we may return to discussing Yi...?"

"...Lord Liu deeply regrets Liu Zhang's refusal to turn to the light," Ma Liang sighed woefully. "My lord requested ten thousand men and ample provisions to aid Guan Yunchang in an attack on Fan City... Liu Zhang supplied less than half of the requested supplies, and the supplied soldiers – less than four thousand - were old, sick, or weak. This was deemed an insult... and then, a communication between the Yi adviser Zhang Song and my lord was interpreted as a plot to oust Liu Zhang, and he turned on us."

"...*Interpreted*...?" Sun Quan snickered. "I thought that Zhang Song *invited* Liu Bei to overthrow his master."

"Admittedly, yes," Ma Liang replied. "Zhang Song was dissatisfied with Liu Zhang's governance, and wanted my lord to remove him, but my lord refused to do it, reiterating what he said to you... and on speaking to Liu Zhang, he became even more determined to give peace a chance... but Liu Zhang broke faith, and now we are where we are now. My lord only hopes that you see this as an unfortunate turn of events, and not a breach of faith on his part. Had Liu Zhang been a different man, Lord Sun..."

"...Then we might now be allies against the Duke of Wei," Sun Quan lamented. "I will agree with your version of events, since it accords with Chief Commander Lu Su's own feelings. ...Tell me, what does Zhuge Kongming think about the actions of Ma Chao...?"

"It is truly marvellous," Ma Liang replied. "With Longxi County now in the hands of Ma Chao's alliance save for one stubborn city, the Duke of Wei is threatened on all fronts. By finally realising there can be no rationalising with Liu Zhang and turning on him, my lord has freed Zhang Lu to assist Ma Chao... the west is now completely isolated, with forces loyal to Wei on the decline, and all those in opposition acting as one. It was one possible outcome that Director General Pang Tong, the Young Phoenix, predicted... whatever my lord's wishes in regard to Yi, I think that the Director General always saw this as the logical end... visit as a friend, and then keep the door closed from inside."

"Mm," Sun Quan sniggered. "Well, as you said, this is the way things have turned out. When Liu Bei has taken Yi, will we have Jing returned to us without incident...?"

"Lord Liu is not as soft as Liu Zhang, but he does allow his followers – particularly Guan Yunchang – autonomy," Ma Liang replied cagily. "There is a genuine feeling brewing within his ranks that for our alliance to continue, certain notable figures need to have certain key locations from which to operate, and-"

"That isn't what I want to hear, Jichang," Sun Quan admitted sadly. "Jing Province is on loan... that was what your master agreed to. I don't care if Guan Yu likes having a base in Jiangling, it isn't his, nor is it his lord's domain to give."

"I... I am aware of that," Ma Liang replied hesitantly. "All I can say is that once Yi is taken, there will be a united western front commanded by Lord Liu, and a united eastern front commanded by you, Lord Sun, while all domains south of both fronts fall under your jurisdiction."

"The four counties of Wuling, Changsha, Guiyang and Lingling do not fall under my *full* jurisdiction, as they should," Sun Quan retorted. "Moreover, Zhuge Kongming is named as governor of three of them, and they are heavily guarded by Liu Bei's generals, Zhao Yun and Zhang Fei. Why are Guan, Zhang and Zhao in Jing, and he takes old bones like Huang Zhong, pups like Liu Feng, and untested men like Huo Jun and Wei Yan into Yi...? Doesn't that suggest he wants to keep Jing from me more than he wants to take Yi from Liu Zhang...?"

"As we already stressed, the expedition into Yi was never intended as anything more than a diplomatic mission, an attempt to make Liu Zhang see sense, and neither Lord Liu nor Director General Pang felt it required our best forward generals," Ma Liang replied. "Hopefully, that will continue to be the case. So far as keeping Jing from *you* goes, well... since it already *is* yours, it is more a case of keeping Jing from the Duke of Wei. A guest should take care of his host's house as best he can."

"...Quite...!" Sun Quan snickered. "Well, you seem to have the situation under control... once again, you've entertained me with your spontaneity and sound judgement, Jichang. Once I have given you a banquet to welcome you properly, you may return to Jiangling, safe in the knowledge that we will only be moving against the Duke of Wei, and not against Jing, since, as you say, it is ours, and will soon be returned without incident."

"I shall pass on that information gladly," Ma Liang replied.

Ma Liang stopped in Gong'an upon his return, and visited the office of his sworn brother, Kongming, to relay his meeting with Sun Quan in person.

"...Well played once again," Kongming praised as Ma Liang summed up the discussion. "But our position is starting to become tenuous... while Lord Liu haggles with a kinsman for his territory, we are in danger of being eclipsed by Ma Chao of Xiliang and Sun Quan of Jiangdong, who now enact a pincer on Cao Cao, living out the tripod theorem I envisaged. If they successfully defeat Cao Cao without Lord Liu's direct help, won't they both turn on him...?"

"Let's hope not," Ma Liang replied. "Still... does Ma Chao really stand a chance of taking Ji City once Cao Cao sends proper reinforcement...? Sun Quan is dallying, and hasn't done more than send a few sorties to sound out Cao Cao's defences. Cao could deploy his four hundred thousand to Ji and wipe Ma Chao out."

"Which is why we needed a third front from Jiangling to pressure Cao at Fan City," Kongming stressed. "Liu Zhang's stubborn defence is prolonging a needless war, and costing lives. ...One thing, Jichang... did Sun Quan... sound like he was becoming impatient about recovering Jing...?"

"Very," Ma Liang said worriedly. "He is, as you know, very cunning, and puts on a front of being amused... when in fact he was seething. He knows Lord Liu is going to refuse to return Jing, and I think he would certainly take it by force when that refusal occurs. ...We'd have ample warning to relocate our families, however, since he will not act until Cao Cao is no longer a threat in the east, and we have actually secured Yi Province... and if we failed to take Yi, he would probably capture it for himself."

"And then what... *loan it to us*...?" Kongming scoffed. "We cannot afford to lose Yi *or* Jing... if Sun Quan controlled Jiangling, the entire southern front would be his, and any expeditions against Cao Cao would have to pass through Wu's territory or through Zhang Lu's... Yi alone is pointless to possess, if the aim is smiting the Duke of Wei and preventing others, such as Sun Quan, from taking his place as a threat to the house of Han."

"And Sun Quan has sounded out our defences," Ma Liang fretted. "His comments about Zilong and Yide guarding the four counties... Kongming, we must also hope that Lord Liu does not need reinforcement generals."

"I have every faith in Pang Tong," Kongming insisted. "With him as Director General, Lord Liu will make no mistakes... but perhaps speed, if not haste, is important. I may write to him stressing that, but he already knows, I'm sure."

While Ma Chao's violent takeover of the northwest continued, Liu Bei advanced his own, more passive campaign, all at the instruction of Pang Tong and Fa Zheng.

"Fu City has fallen at last," Liu Bei said to his assembled officials and officers. They were convened in a command tent near the next military target of Mianzhu County, west of the vast mountain range that walled Yi Province.

"We are thinly spread now," Jian Yong noted. "We cannot rush to Jiameng now if there were problems. We must act quickly, and hope for the best."

"This western trail is the fastest way to take Chengdu, the provincial capital," Pang Tong insisted. "Speed is everything."

"Yes, but always remember the difference between speed and *haste*, Director General," Fa Zheng urged. "Haste cost Zhang Ziqiao his life."

"*Impatience* cost Zhang Ziqiao his life," Pang Tong replied, "as did my unwillingness to act quickly. But enough of that: Liu Zhang has sent much of his forces to reinforce Mianzhu, and although we outnumber him two-to-one, he has the advantage of full awareness of topography and support of some of the populace."

"…I was hoping that the people would be grateful for my arrival here," Liu Bei said miserably. "Instead, Zitong shut its doors, Fu held out for many days… and now we face stubborn defence from Mianzhu."

"Many people have shown gratitude for our coming here," Jian Yong insisted. "It's just that… well… it isn't everyone that likes to see their street on fire."

"We're treating the people – and even the captured soldiers – well, excluding officials and generals that we know are not redeemable," Pang Tong added, "and that is received very well. My lord, many in Yi don't want war with Zhang Lu, and they want to be ruled by Cao Cao even less. When many of those that arrive in Mianzhu to resist us are approached with reason… I think we'll see a lot of surrendering."

"Why would they…?" Mister Sun asked. "Wouldn't they fear Liu Zhang killing their families, Director General…?"

"Liu Zhang is desperately trying to look fair at the moment," Pang Tong chuckled contemptuously. "He has promised not to punish the families of surrendered men. More fool him… it only makes our job even easier."

"…He is now lenient to his men… even when they surrender to us…?" Liu Bei noted nervously. "Such a man… is hard to fully judge, or truly defeat, surely."

"It's weakness, not benevolence," Pang Tong insisted. "He does it to *look* fair. Was he fair to Zhang Song?"

"If I may…?" Fa Zheng interrupted: all eyes turned to the former Yi envoy and conspirator. "Liu Zhang is sending, under the command of his most trusted aide and general, Wu Yi, a number of his valiant generals, the probable aim being to hold the strategically important fortress city of Luo. We must pass that place to reach Chengdu, and it therefore has to fall to ensure safe passage and a storage facility."

"Well then," Liu Bei said plainly, "we will have to siege the defenders… regardless of the villain it makes of me. All I ask is that we show mercy."

"We can buy many of these men," Pang Tong insisted. "This will not be as bad as you assume, my lord."

"I hope not," Liu Bei replied.

Wu Yi advanced on Mianzhu with thousands of men and five strong generals under his command: Zhang Ren, Liu Gui, Deng Xian, Lei Tong, and Ling Bao. The defence was indeed solid, and Liu Bei was terrified that the potential bloodshed would make a mockery of his benevolent reputation. Pang Tong, meanwhile, was calm: he could often be found sitting and observing the enemy forces while he fanned himself slowly, or drank tea.

"How can he be so calm…?" Mister Sun said to Jian Yong one day.

"He knows he's already won, I suppose," Jian Yong replied.

************

## 68

The Yi forces intercepted Liu Bei before he reached Luo City, and set up a large field encampment. Their commander, Wu Yi, observed the advancing forces of Liu Bei and grimaced. He then retreated to his command tent within the fenced camp and called for an urgent meeting. His closeness to the embattled governor guaranteed him respect from some of the generals, but others – such as the belligerent Zhang Ren – despised his cautious approach and obvious reluctance to engage the enemy.

"...We can't face them directly," General Deng Xian suggested. "Shouldn't we ask for more forces to meet this massive threat...?"

"If their entire army is here in Mianzhu," General Zhang Ren supposed, "their defence of Jiameng and Boshui must be very small and weak."

"With all due respect, General," Wu Yi retorted, "how does that help us...? They do not need a strong defence, because Zhang Lu isn't going to attack! If anything, he'll send Liu Bei help as soon as he knows that Ma Chao doesn't need it!"

"I propose that we hold Luo," Zhang Ren insisted. "We face them here, blunt their morale by showing a bold front, and then wear them down, as Cao Ren and Xu Huang did at Jiangling. Let Pang Tong scheme all he wants... is he Zhou Yu...?"

"No, no more than I am Cao Ren and you are Xu Huang," Wu Yi scolded. "Cao Ren had us helping him, he had support from the north, and he had forces in excess of double those that Wu had... while we are half in number, and closed in at all civilised sides... nowhere to run, except to the barbarians of Nanzhong. And I doubt that the lords of Nanzhong would help us, since they see us as thieves that live on land stolen from their ancestors."

"So you suggest *surrender*, then...?" Ling Bao accused.

"...No, no, don't be ridiculous," Wu Yi protested. "I... I just..."

Generals Zhang Ren, Ling Bao and Liu Gui glared at Wu Yi suspiciously; only General Lei Tong seemed to be hesitating in his condemnation of Wu Yi's weak stance.

After the meeting, Lei Tong visited Wu Yi in his personal tent.

"...General Lei," Wu Yi hailed.

"My colleagues are harsh," Lei Tong sighed, "but they are correct in the fact that we must resist these odds with all our might. Mianzhu must not fall."

"Agreed," Wu Yi replied hesitantly, "but at the same time, we have to be realistic. I have written to the lord for reinforcement... let us see what he says."

Days passed, and the letter from Chengdu came as Wu Yi had expected. Wu Yi was holding a meeting in the command tent when it arrived, and he was forced to accept it publicly.

"...Well...?" Ling Bao asked as Wu Yi read the contents carefully.

"We... must hold out with the resources we have," Wu Yi groaned.

"Why do you react so weakly?" Zhang Ren scolded. "This man we fight is a master of holding out against larger, stronger opponents… yet look at Cao Cao! When he fought Yuan Shao, his force was small, and isolated, and low on supplies, and yet he won… it was at Red Cliffs, when his army and resource were vast, and Ruxukou, where he had even more, that he met with his most bitter defeats! Let them fight us as some bloated beast… our small, nimble force will beat them easily!"

"This isn't Red Cliffs!" Wu Yi retorted, laughing desperately as he spoke. "Cao fought across the Great River with sick men and no naval training, and with linked boats, downwind! That was a farce! This… this is something else entirely! Their men are trained by Crouching Dragon and Young Phoenix, who are said to be the two geniuses of the age! They have perfect battle order, knowledge of formations, understanding of how to manage a perfect siege, advantage of numbers…!"

"…I have heard enough," Zhang Ren growled: he got up and left the meeting, followed by Ling Bao, Liu Gui and most of the lesser generals and captains.

"…*Aiee*," Wu Yi exclaimed. "Perhaps I *am* being weak."

Lei Tong was still present, along with a couple of lesser generals, although they sat in morbid silence as Wu Yi walked to the easel where the battle map was mounted.

"**REPORT!**" a messenger shouted as he ran into the command tent. "**General Zhang Ren has taken to the field to fight the vanguard of Liu Bei's forces!**"

"…Without my orders…?" Wu Yi noted angrily. "…*Aiee!*"

"**WHERE IS LIU BEI?**" Zhang Ren screamed at the front line of Liu Bei's intimidating forces: he rode back and forth on his steed, his spear aimed at the surprised and uncomfortable infantry. Behind him, thin rows of infantry, cavalry and archers stood patiently yet nervously.

"This man is another Zhang Yide," Liu Bei noted to Pang Tong from the safety of the rear of the force. "What a shame it is that he isn't to be won over!"

"We need to chase this man off the field, and set up a parley with Wu Yi," Pang Tong suggested. "We shouldn't set up a formation, he'd die trying to get out of it… we want this hero of the age alive. No, have Wei Yan challenge him… if this man is all boast, we'll pursue with an emphasis on capturing rather than killing the soldiers. If he is really as powerful as he thinks he is… have Wei Yan feign retreat, and bring Liu Feng and Huang Zhong in from the sides to encircle and capture him."

"Fine, fine," Liu Bei agreed enthusiastically. "Go to it."

A short time later, Wei Yan rode out to confront Zhang Ren.

"**WHO ARE YOU?**" Zhang Ren shouted as he pointed his spear at Wei Yan. "**I WANT TO SEE THE FAITHLESS TURNCOAT LIU BEI, NOT SOME SCRUFFY MINION OF HIS! BE GONE!**"

Wei Yan snorted a laugh and replied, "**I AM WEI YAN… ARE YOU SCARED?**"

Zhang Ren bellowed like a wild animal and charged: the two generals met time and again as they rode past each other, clashing their weapons.

"Zhang Ren is no boaster," Liu Bei noted sombrely as Wei Yan struggled to gain an advantage over the Yi general.

"…Yes, and Wei Yan is stalling his planned retreat," Jian Yong complained. "The man is too bold."

"Don't be concerned," Pang Tong insisted.

Before Wei Yan could stage his own retreat, it was Zhang Ren that fell back, crouching low to his horse's back to avoid any possible swipes or arrow shots from Wei Yan as he fled. Wei Yan smirked, and pursued.

"His lines are very thin, and he isn't getting any cover fire from the archers," Mister Sun noted.

"They're drawing him in…!" Liu Bei realised.

"…No, **no!**" Jian Yong protested pointlessly. "He's going to pull a reversal on us!"

"Entirely within my expectation, Xianhe," Pang Tong promised. "Let him."

It was around this time that Wei Yan – whose adrenalin had now passed – realised he was being led into a trap, albeit too late. As he turned his horse to ride back to his own line, horns sounded and two forces – Ling Bao on the left, Liu Gui on the right – descended on his position. At that point, Pang Tong raised a black flag, and two forces – Liu Feng on the left, Huang Zhong on the right – converged on the rear of Ling Bao and Liu Gui's forces, reversing their fortunes. As Wei Yan reached his line, Chen Shi rode forward and joined him in rushing back to Zhang Ren's forward position, which crumbled under the pressure of the four generals that served Liu Bei.

"Magnificent," Liu Bei praised as Zhang Ren's demoralised forces fled the battlefield and withdrew to their main camp.

"Not really," Pang Tong insisted. "Kongming and I studied this kind of thing as a trifling matter… there was no deep strategy here."

Many of the Yi soldiers had been wounded or separated from their commanders; the healthy men prostrated themselves and pleaded for mercy, while the wounded groaned and whined for help.

"**Get the wounded men of both sides medical treatment, and respectfully bury any dead,**" Pang Tong ordered. "**Give any surrendered man the choice to remain with us, return home, or return to their commander.**"

"Is that wise…?" General Chen Shi asked.

"It's a sound plan," Wei Yan declared. "That will break their morale completely."

"Yes, well, it's a pity you keep letting your battle lust muddle your brain," Mister Sun scolded. "After our service together at Steep-slope, I thought you were a wiser man, Wei Yan, and yet you blundered straight into an obvious trap! I mistook you for a Zhao Zilong, when you are nothing more than a Zhang Fei or a Xiahou Dun!"

Wei Yan smiled and laughed coldly.

"Do not stress your-self, Mister Sun," Liu Bei pleaded. "And don't insult our Zhang Yide by comparing him to the likes of Cao Cao's right hand man."

"General Wei, you played an excellent part, regardless your intentions," Pang Tong said with a smirk. "…Now, Mister Jian… it is time for us to see if Wu Yi wants to talk to us."

Zhang Ren, Liu Gui and Ling Bao reported to the command tent to explain and justify their actions.

"**That was a blatant disregard for military law!**" Wu Yi shouted at an indignant Zhang Ren. "**Now we are demoralised, and only YOU, General, are to blame!**"

"**Wrong, wrong, WRONG!**" Zhang Ren screamed in retort. "**YOU are the one that has broken our morale by insisting we sit here and await death! Had you, Lei Tong and Deng Xian been on the field, we would have won this day!**"

"...*Aiee!*" Wu Yi exclaimed. "This... is pointless!"

"I won't sit here and let them laugh at us!" Zhang Ren declared. "If we fought them, showed courage and will... these men who live on loaned land would run back to Jing, their tails between their legs!"

"...I'll let this matter go, General, since there is sense in what you say," Wu Yi said soberly. "But General... if we fight each other, we all lose."

The meeting broke up, and later that day, a messenger arrived with an offer to discuss the situation. Wu Yi agreed, and the next afternoon, Jian Yong travelled to the camp to speak privately with Wu Yi. The two sat in Wu Yi's personal tent, while the other generals looked on and wondered what the outcome would be.

"...I prefer this," Jian Yong said with humour. "No smell of blood, no spears in my face... very civil, much better than meeting on the battlefield."

"Governor Liu may have been amused by your antics in peacetime," Wu Yi scolded bitterly, "but even *he* would not find you funny now. What are the terms you have come here to offer...?"

"None whatsoever," Jian Yong replied with a smirk.

"Then what...?" Wu Yi exclaimed. "Have you just come here to waste my time, like some sort of mad clown...?"

"Hardly," Jian Yong chuckled. "I come here with a proposition from Lord Liu Bei, or Xuande, as we like to call him. I've been with him over thirty years now, you know."

"...That's quite a long time to serve a lord," Wu Yi noted. "You don't even look that old."

"I've been his friend as well as his adviser," Jian Yong explained. "He and I, we joined forces to fight the Yellow Turbans... those were the days."

"My lord... didn't participate in that campaign, but his father did," Wu Yi said reflectively. "My lord... is often frowned upon for not doing more for the state, but to those that criticise, I say-"

"I'm not here to criticise Liu Zhang," Jian Yong insisted. "After all, if you're honest, you know why so many officials are loathed to work for him now, or ever. I'm here to talk about what comes next... because we know he is doomed."

"...You end your statement by contradicting the introduction, Mister Jian," Wu Yi scoffed. "You *are* a demented clown."

"His fate and an appraisal of his character are two different things," Jian Yong countered. "Look at the facts: he has a lot of people that willingly follow him, like Zhang Ren, and you… but Zhang Song risked his life, and Fa Zheng his reputation, in order to facilitate Liu Xuande becoming the new governor. And outside the province, Zhang Lu, Ma Chao, Cao Cao and Sun Quan all hunger for his land: do you really think he can keep it…?"
Wu Yi was silent.
"Think it through, Mister Wu," Jian Yong implored. "You serve a lord on borrowed time, a man whose allegiances and actions have earned him universal indignation, regardless of his motives. This isn't about whether he governs Yi Province well anymore… if his 'good governance' is dependent on being at the beck and call of a murderous tyrant that is killing other people, is that truly righteous and good…?

"If Liu Xuande is the victor in our confrontation, he will grant Liu Zhang a lavish household in Gong'an, give his sons prominent roles in the administration, and reward all those that facilitated the regime change; those that 'failed to see the changing times' might find their fortunes take a downturn… although, admittedly, Lord Liu has a record for paying good men proper respect even if they do not reciprocate… if you know anything about him, you should know *that*.

"If, however, your lord is successful in repelling mine, then there will be severe consequences, I think, and not just for Liu Xuande. Cao Cao will one day demand that he hand over the province: I can promise you that, and you *know* that, because Zhang Song was once told by the Duke of Wei himself that the province would one day be seized, if only for fun. And that is if Zhang Lu, Ma Chao, or Sun Quan do not come here for it first. He *will* lose this province, Mister Wu: the question is how, and I am sure that you agree that giving it to a good man is better than losing it to a tyrant."
"You're asking me to betray my lord," Wu Yi whined, "but my family is in the capital! What if he harms them…?"
"He won't," Jian Yong insisted. "He *should*… but he won't."
"…No, never," Wu Yi insisted. "I won't join Liu Bei."
"If that is the case, Mister Wu," Jian Yong posed, "why did you ponder the fate of your family…? …You know that it is the only sensible option… but I'll leave the decision with you. Xuande hates people making him take tough decisions under pressure… and so do I, actually. I'll be off now… you think about it."
Jian Yong got to his feet, bowed slightly, and strolled casually from the tent and then the camp, smiling cheerfully at the soldiers and generals as he went: his armed escort were bemused and even frightened by his demeanour. Wu Yi, meanwhile, sat and thought about what he should do.


************

## 69

"**My lord, guests are announced!**" Jian Yong said with a proud smile as he entered Liu Bei's command tent a few days later.
"Oh...?" Liu Bei exclaimed. "Who...?"
"My lord," Jian Yong declared, "Senior General Wu Yi and General Lei Tong of Yi Province approach."
The assembly was startled with the exception of Pang Tong, who fanned himself slowly and smiled as Wu Yi and Lei Tong entered the tent, walked to the centre, and kowtowed to Liu Bei.
"...I, Wu Yi, humbly surrender to Lord Liu Bei," Wu Yi announced.
"And I, Lei Tong, surrender to Lord Liu Bei," Lei Tong said humbly.
"...Excellent... excellent, excellent, marvellous!" Liu Bei praised: he got up, walked to the two men, and helped them to their feet. "This is magnificent! Please, do not be so humble... I find it regrettable that we have come to this. General Lei, please acquaint yourself with your peers... Venerable Mister Wu, I think that we need to speak privately."
Wu Yi smiled nervously, and agreed.

"...I am astounded that the man said to be Liu Zhang's right arm should now come to me," Liu Bei admitted as soon as the assembly was dismissed and the meeting was a private one.
"I have been fooling myself," Wu Yi chuckled desperately. "Mister Fa and Mister Zhang are... wiser than I, I think. I stayed at his side, and watched him pander to Cao Cao... grow ever more unpopular with the world at large... just so his own populace thought he was wonderful. That isn't how a righteous world works, since to be truly righteous, fairness must be universal: you cannot govern one land well at the expense of forty others."
"I fret for your family, Mister Wu," Liu Bei said with emotion. "Is there some way that we can save them...?"
"He has vowed to spare the families of those that defect," Wu Yi supposed hopefully. "We shall see... but... even if he decides to do as he did to the families of Zhang Song and Zhang Lu, sometimes, a man must act righteously, even if he must suffer for it... is that not so, Lord Liu...?"
"As a man who has lost much because of my principles," Liu Bei replied, "I agree."
"Did you want to know our next move...?" Pang Tong asked.
"Hah... *no*," Wu Yi insisted. "Master Pang Tong, I will remain wherever you put me, and do whatever you say. I will ask no questions, and make no requests."
"I consider your surrender genuine," Pang Tong assured Wu Yi. "We intend to do all we can to spare the province pain... we'll siege if we must, but where conflict can be avoided, it will be."
"I know," Wu Yi sighed. "Your generous care for the wounded men, your return of the defeated and captured... many men decided to follow me and come back here when they saw how harshly Zhang Ren intended to treat them for their 'failure'. You'll win hearts that way... you certainly know what you're doing."
"Please, rest now," Liu Bei said kindly. "We can speak later... and thank you again, Mister Wu, for your support."
Wu Yi nodded, stood up, bowed, and took his leave.

"...Well...?" Jian Yong asked quietly.

"He's gone," Pang Tong noted. "...He's genuine, Xianhe. And his surrender will be of immense use to us. We should not use him, not even to induce others... we must let him be, and not involve him in anything."

"He spares their families... a clever move," Mister Sun reiterated.

"Not at all," Pang Tong chuckled. "As Wu Yi has already realised, Liu Zhang is cruel at heart... he once scolded his father at the court's instruction, which shows his lack of respect for his father, against Confucian values. He slaughtered the family of Zhang Lu at a moment when he should have been pursuing peace, and then expected us to rescue him. When he discovered Zhang Song's part in the plot to remove him, his first instinct was to purge and kill, not forgive... this benevolence he now shows is false, and everyone will see it.

"By sparing the families of those that defect, he puts himself in a precarious situation: foolish men that would remain loyal – out of fear of losing their loved ones – would risk defecting, knowing there was a possible way back, but we know a victorious Liu Zhang would then renege on his amnesty and slaughter without fear. Smart men will see that, defect anyway, but be extra diligent in removing him. And the man they defect to is showing benevolence too... so their moral standing is upheld, and that further compounds the case against Liu Zhang."

"So we'll see a lot more defections, then ...?" Jian Yong asked.

"I think so," Pang Tong replied with a smile.

Liu Zhang was shocked by the defection of Wu Yi, but – despite protests from Huang Quan and Zhang Ren – he did not destroy the defectors' families. Instead, he moved Wu Yi and Lei Tong's families out of the capital, and ordered the official Li Yan and General Fei Guan to replace them.

Pang Tong chuckled as Liu Bei and his inner circle of counsellors received the news of the new appointments from a spy.

"These two men are more meat for our table," Pang Tong suggested. "We can induce them to defect as well, my lord, and with even greater ease."

"What makes you say that...?" Mister Sun asked.

"Li Yan... I've heard that name before," Jian Yong mused.

"Of course you have!" Pang Tong chuckled. "He once served Liu Biao as a civil clerk in Xiangyang... he would have been responsible for some administration or other. This man fled Jing to escape Cao Cao... how unfortunate for him that he fled to serve a man that willingly serves that same Cao Cao!"

"...Shiyuan is quite right," Fa Zheng confirmed. "Li Zhengfang, Prefect of Chengdu is, in fact, a refugee from Jing. I knew that he has never been comfortable with Cao Cao's arrogant control over this province, and Liu Zhang's willingness to be a pawn: I agree that he may be won over."

"Marvellous!" Liu Bei said with cheer. "This man is our good friend, only he doesn't know it yet!"

************

## 70

A messenger carried a letter from Liu Bei to the new defender of Mianzhu County, Li Yan, and it was not long before Jian Yong was announcing another pair of defectors to the court.

"**My lord,**" Jian Yong proclaimed, "**Li Yan and Fei Guan approach.**"

Liu Bei smiled gratefully as the two men kowtowed to him.

"…As a man of Jing," Liu Bei said, "you must be glad to be able to return to the light at last, Li Zhengfang."

Li Yan looked up, smiled, and replied, "My lord, it is like finding my way out of a maze that I have been imprisoned within for four long years or more. I have always wished that I could return to Jing one day, so this is a dream come true."

"Excellent, excellent!" Liu Bei praised as he helped each man to his feet. "You shall be Assistant General to Wei Yan. Fei Guan can, in turn, be your assistant."

"My thanks, my lord," Fei Guan said quietly.

"This second, blatant theft of personnel has really annoyed General Zhang Ren," Jian Yong said with a laugh. "He's marching on our position now."

"Then we should meet him," Pang Tong suggested. "And this time, we'll dent his pride properly. Wei Yan: since you are a man of near-peerless wit and valour, you shall once again be the lead general."

"My thanks, Director General," Wei Yan replied sincerely.

"Huang Zhong, Liu Feng, Li Yan, Chen Shi… you will provide support as dictated by the occasion," Pang Tong continued. "Let's move quickly."

By the time that Zhang Ren cleared two thirds of the distance between his own encampment and Liu Bei's, Pang Tong and Fa Zheng had already arrayed their forces perfectly. Zhang Ren's forces balked at the multitudes of cavalrymen, archers, crossbowmen, spear-wielding infantry, and confident, charismatic generals.

"**WELCOME, ZHANG REN!**" Wei Yan boomed: his words were weighted with laughter. "**HAVE YOU COME TO JOIN US AS WELL…?**"

"**I WILL TAKE THE HEADS OF THE FOUR TRAITORS TODAY, AND OFFER THEM AS SACRIFICES TO THE HEAVENS!**" Zhang Ren retorted angrily. "**BUT FIRST, I'LL TAKE YOURS!**"

Wei Yan and Zhang Ren met in the field once again, and clashed for what seemed to be an eternity to the two assembled armies. Wei Yan's speed and ferocity was matched blow-for-blow by Zhang Ren, and both sides marvelled at the skills and strength of both men, without bias.

"…We really must have this man on our side," Liu Bei insisted.

"My lord," Pang Tong sighed sadly, "Zhang Ren is a man of stubborn, inflexible thought and lofty principle."

"Isn't that true of Yunchang…?" Jian Yong suggested.

"Yunchang is flexible," Pang Tong replied wispily: he was watching the enemy forces, wondering if there was some scheme. "He surrendered to Cao to protect a higher purpose... this man would have demanded death."

"That is true," Fa Zheng said regrettably. "Zhang Ren refuses to see the weakness in Liu Zhang, or the inevitable end of his rule here, in Yi... he'll never join us."

Both Zhang Ren and Wei Yan were starting to tire after hundreds of exchanged – and perfectly blocked – strikes, and the gongs sounded on both sides to recall them to their lines.

"...He is very tough," Wei Yan admitted reluctantly as he rode his exhausted horse to Liu Bei's position at the rear of the battle lines. "I can beat him, but-"

"No," Pang Tong insisted. "It is a case of that oft-used idiom: 'When two tigers fight, both are sure to be hurt', and in this case, one will die. I desire neither of you to be hurt or killed, Wei Wenchang. You are a pillar of our future state, and as for this man, Zhang Ren... while he cannot be induced to defect... his capture will hurt their morale more than his death."

Wei Yan nodded agreeably, and said, "We would be wrong to make a martyr of him, as the Director General says."

While Liu Bei's forces deliberated, Zhang Ren had obtained a new horse and ridden back to his front line, where he now declared, "**I WILL FIGHT THIS DOG, 'WEI YAN', TO THE DEATH! WHERE IS WEI YAN???**"

Wei Yan's face contorted into a furious sneer: he turned to his assistant and shouted boldly, "**Bring me a fresh horse!**"

"No," Liu Bei protested. "Let him curse... Wenchang, you are one of my best generals, and I do not wish to lose you to death or injury. Let this man exhaust his energy shouting insults, and then we'll rush his lines... is that not a sound strategy, Director General...?"

Pang Tong smiled, but did not otherwise move or speak.

"...Well then, what should we do...?" Liu Bei asked desperately.

"My lord," Pang Tong replied, "Zhang Ren must be blunted. This time, he will not run... there is no strategy, as all of his generals are within his battle array. What we must do, if Wei Wenchang condescends to agree, is..."

Zhang Ren started laughing boisterously as the veteran soldier Huang Zhong rode to the front line and levelled his spear.

"**WHAT IN THE NAME OF THE HEAVENS ARE YOU?**" Zhang Ren asked with amusement and contempt. "**DID WEI YAN DIE OF SHAME, AND THEY HAVE NOW DUG UP HIS DEAD FATHER'S BONES TO FIGHT ME?**"

Zhang Ren's men laughed theatrically to mock Huang Zhong and Liu Bei.

"You...!" Wei Yan exclaimed from his place next to Liu Bei.

"...Calm," Pang Tong urged. "You'll have your moment."

"**DON'T BELITTLE THESE OLD BONES, ZHANG REN,**" Huang Zhong retorted ominously. "**OR YOU MIGHT REGRET IT FROM YOUR PLACE IN THE NETHERWORLD.**"

Zhang Ren charged: Huang Zhong met the charge, and the two clashed.

"...I'm impressed," Fa Zheng admitted. "Huang Zhong is truly a general."

"I feel ashamed," Mister Sun said weakly. "I cannot even manage a ride across the mountains... he now puts armour on and fights... he is a true man. Zhang Fei and Guan Yu call him 'worthless old bones', but it is I that are the 'worthless old bones'."

"Despite his impressive strength, his age is still a factor," Pang Tong suggested calmly. "Natural law dictates it."

Huang Zhong seemed to tire, while Zhang Ren could still find strength despite this being his second bout of the day. Eventually, Huang Zhong feigned a reckless strike to startle Zhang Ren, and used the opportunity to retreat.

"**CHARGE!**" Zhang Ren said with triumph. "**HOW DARE LIU BEI SEND HIS OLD GRANDFATHER TO FIGHT ME! I WANT HIS HEAD!**"

Zhang Ren's forces charged: but as Huang Zhong reached his line, Wei Yan rode to his side, and the old general turned to face Zhang Ren with a smirk across his grey-whiskered face. Together, Wei Yan and Huang Zhong charged at Zhang Ren, followed by a chanting mass of infantry. Ling Bao, Liu Gui and Zhang Ren met the two generals in the centre of the engagement: in the confusing melee that ensued, the Yi general Liu Gui lost his life, and Zhang Ren was forced to order a humiliating retreat. But as he retreated, forces led by Liu Feng and Li Yan encircled his forces, knocking down man after man in a show of unrestrained brutality. Bodies littered the field this time, and the victory was absolute.

"**THE DAY IS OURS!**" Liu Bei cried in triumph.

"Director General, that was another magnificent victory," Jian Yong praised.

"...Again, I did little more than observe," Pang Tong insisted. "A pity that men had to perish this time, but... we must be seen to be serious and we must act quickly."

Liu Feng and Li Yan rode to Liu Bei and awaited the opportunity to report.

"Did we capture Zhang Ren...?" Pang Tong asked.

"No," Li Yan said regrettably. "He hacked his way through our lines and returned to his camp. But we did capture General Deng Xian."

"...Regrettable," Pang Tong admitted. "Now, we face a prolonged engagement... which we cannot afford."

"But regardless, this day was ours!" Liu Bei said excitedly. "Victory is certain, Director General... have heart, and do not cover our success in shadow! Tonight, we have a banquet to properly welcome our new acquisitions!"

Pang Tong eyed the near-hysterical Liu Bei and hummed thoughtfully.

************

The celebratory banquet at Liu Bei's camp was lavish, given the circumstances. Pang Tong watched the revelry with silent disapproval that was noted with concern by Mister Sun, Jian Yong and Fa Zheng.

"We... we were magnificent!" Liu Bei said drunkenly. "Wei Yan... you... you are god... I mean *a* god, a god among men!"

Wei Yan nodded agreeably, but did not respond, since he too was very drunk.

"You... are a match for Chen Dao, Guan Yu, Zhang Fei, Zhao Yun," Liu Bei continued. "With all these men, how can I not one day sit in the imperial palace...?"

"...Sit *where*...?" Pang Tong asked pointedly.

"Uh... my lord, you are very lively...!" Jian Yong chuckled nervously before Liu Bei could respond. "Director General, my lord desires a seat *before the emperor*... where else...?"

Pang Tong fanned himself slowly and replied, "Where else, indeed...?"

"...Today," Liu Bei declared, "we have defeated Zhang Ren... and taken the head of one of his worthless minions... forced another to surrender... we'll get them all! We'll kill all of them, if we must!"

The generals murmured in response: most of those murmurs were agreeable.

"...Today, we celebrate!" Liu Bei continued. "We cel... celebrate a victory! One day soon, Liu Zhang will be on his knees, begging for mercy for kissing Cao Cao's feet, and all of Yi will be mine!"

Liu Bei raised his wine cup clumsily, and laughed.

"...My lord," Pang Tong said calmly, "is it really a man of Confucian values, a man of *ren*, that celebrates invading another's territory, and bloodshed and carnage, and pointless loss of life...?"

Before Jian Yong or Mister Sun could intercede, Liu Bei turned to Pang Tong with anger and said, "**Pang Tong, you pedant, you overstep you... your mark! King Wu of Zhou, he... he celebrated his v-victory over King Zhou of Shang. So was he not a 'man of *ren*'? How *dare* you chide me! Get out... GET OUT!**"

"My lord...!" Mister Sun protested.

Liu Bei got to his feet, pointed at Pang Tong, and screamed, "**GET OUT!**"

Pang Tong smiled ambiguously, got to his feet, brushed his clothes down, and slowly walked out of the banquet: he fanned himself slowly as he went.

"Xuande," Jian Yong pleaded desperately of Lui Bei, "recall him."

"...Pedant!" Liu Bei grumbled as he sat down clumsily and took another gulp of wine. "How... how *dare* he...!"

Pang Tong was sat in his tent – quietly reading 'The Spring and Autumn Annals' – when Jian Yong and Fa Zheng came to see him half an hour later.

"...Lord Liu requests that you return to the banquet," Jian Yong said sombrely.

"Oh...?" Pang Tong chuckled. "And for what reason...?"

"Master Pang," Jian Yong continued, "Lord Liu… is a man. He is not entirely perfect, for no man is… you know that, and I know that. We follow him because he does the right thing, regardless of what he truly desires. He always lets his mind lead his heart in important matters, and not the other way around."

"…If I do return to the banquet," Pang Tong countered, "is it to continue the celebrations, continue the argument, end the argument, or end my life…?"

"How can you say that…?" Jian Yong chortled with disbelief. "Yes, Xuande can be haughty when he is drunk, but he would never dare harm you!"

"…So which of the first three is it, then…?" Pang Tong asked plainly.

"Perhaps we should leave this until Lord Liu is sober," Fa Zheng protested.

"We must resolve it now," Jian Yong insisted. "Master Pang… Shiyuan… please, return to the banquet. I cannot genuinely tell you what Lord Liu will say, because I do not know… all I can guarantee is that he will not do you harm."

"…Very well," Pang Tong said as he put his bamboo book to one side. "I shall go back… but I shall not compromise my ethics, Xianhe."

Jian Yong nodded silently, and smiled with embarrassment.

Pang Tong's return to the banquet was met with nervous silence.

"…Take your seat, Director General," Liu Bei said with no emotion: he was holding a wine cup in his right hand, which Pang Tong noted quietly.

Pang Tong walked back to his place – which was directly to the Liu Bei's left – and sat down, as ordered. Pang Tong said nothing, which made Mister Sun, Jian Yong and Fa Zheng very nervous.

"…So tell me," Liu Bei said drunkenly as everyone watched in silence, "When that happened… the… the thing that just happened… whose fault was it…?"

Mister Sun lowered his head silently and closed his eyes; Jian Yong and Fa Zheng frowned; Pang Tong did not immediately reply, rather he stared into Liu Bei's eyes and smiled ambiguously.

"Yours and mine," Pang Tong replied at last.

The general mood was one of surprise at Pang Tong's unapologetic response: many expected Liu Bei to explode with rage, but instead, he stared into Pang Tong's eyes, and his stony expression gradually became one of amusement.

"…My lord…?" Mister Sun whispered inaudibly.

Liu Bei burst into cheerful laughter: he raised his wine cup as a gesture of respect for his brave Director General, and the banquet restarted.

"…I thought he was dead," Mister Sun whispered to Jian Yong as the joviality continued. "…Thank the heavens that Lord Liu is no Duke of Wei."

Pang Tong overheard the comment, and smiled.

************

Zhang Ren's forces abandoned their field camp and retreated to Luo City after repeated defeats, and Liu Bei continued his march through Mianzhu. Until Liu Bei reached Luo, there was little or no resistance: many towns surrendered immediately, since Liu Bei's forces were reputed to be fair, and they had the endorsement of Wu Yi and Li Yan. Luo City, however, would be a different story: Liu Xun, Liu Zhang's eldest son, had come to lead the resistance alongside Zhang Ren and Ling Bao, and there was little hope of breaking the deadlock quickly.

"Pang Tong has written to me," Kongming said as he sat with Yueying one evening in their Gong'an residence. "He's worried."
"They've been besieging Luo now for a couple of months," Yueying noted sombrely. "It is going to be another Jiangling."
"We cannot afford such things," Kongming fretted. "Yes, Ma Chao now holds much of the northwest, but that's only because Cao Cao is too busy being the 'Duke of Wei', and indulging himself. Eventually, he'll want revenge on Ma Chao *and* Sun Quan for making a fool of him, and the court will demand that he act anyway. And we have to be concerned about an alliance between Liu Zhang and Zhang Lu if this drags on for too long."
"...I'd say that was ridiculous," Yueying sighed, "but we have already seen Liu Qi and Sun Quan – whose enmity was born out of similar circumstances – join forces to fight Cao Cao... why wouldn't Zhang Lu help Liu Zhang if there was something in it for him...?"
"Liu Zhang is desperate," Kongming supposed. "He'd rather cede some of northern Yi to Zhang Lu – which is what he should have done in the first place – rather than lose it all to us. And Zhang Lu would rather attack Liu Bei and gain territory than watch us take what he feels is his, yet never had just cause or the resources to seize. And then there is Ma Chao... his violent tendencies will have earned him enemies, since he slaughtered all those that refused to surrender or serve him. I wouldn't be surprised if he's defeated by *that* rather than by Cao Cao."
"...Do you wish you were at the front...?" Yueying asked pointedly.
"Part of me does," Kongming admitted. "But Jing must be defended, and I have been entrusted with that important task. ...And I... I admit, I see what Luo City is turning into, as you do, and I genuinely have to admit that I would rather leave it to Master Pang. I am not Zhou Yu."
"Lu Su's come to visit you, hasn't he...?" Yueying prompted.
"Yes," Kongming chuckled nervously. "What for, I don't know. It cannot be Jing, surely... I've asked Yide and Zilong to be more vigilant, regardless. Whatever he wants... I'll know by the end of tomorrow."

"...We're just interested in the current situation in Yi," Lu Su insisted as he took his guest seat in Kongming's office. "As Chief Commander, I wanted to be sure that we weren't going to be needed for anything."

"You've observed the deadlock in Mianzhu County, and you want to know if we needed Wu's help to take the province," Kongming chuckled. "No, Zijing, we don't need assistance at the moment... what was the intention of asking...?"

"Not for what you suspect," Lu Su replied irritably. "We're making plans for a more concerted strike on Hefei Castle. Cao Cao seems to have lost all interest in fighting us, and spends all his days in his new duchy... truly mad, truly insane. But that's a good thing for us. Ma Chao now holds much of Bing and Liang provinces, so we want to increase the pressure. Might Guan Yunchang assist us with a strike on Xiangyang and Fan City, aided by Zhang Yide and Zhao Zilong...?"

"I never foresaw *five* parts in my plan for the division of the land... I don't know if you did in yours!" Kongming replied with a laugh. "It seems as though there will be Sun Quan, Ma Chao, Liu Bei and Zhang Lu in an alliance against Cao Cao! With all of us attacking him, that is surely the end of the old villain. Certainly, the signs are that Lord Liu and Master Pang are keeping Liu Zhang under pressure, and will at the very least prevent him helping Cao Cao. I don't see why a strike on Fan is unreasonable, Zijing. Just be aware that we are a little understaffed."

"Yes, I know, I've seen your flimsy defences," Lu Su replied tactlessly. "I know you to be more sensible than to place such a small amount of troops on your border unless you had no choice... ... ...I've said too much."

"Only because you know you can," Kongming replied with a laugh. "The border with Wu is lightly guarded, but it really shouldn't need to be guarded at all, should it, Zijing...? Jiangling and Yiling are more heavily reinforced, and rightly so."

"...Very good," Lu Su replied uneasily. "Well then, I'll leave you to write a letter to Guan Yunchang, and I'll be in correspondence to confirm and finalise things."

"Fine," Kongming replied: the two bid farewell to each other, and Lu Su returned to his base at Lukou, east of the Wu capital, to prepare for another attack on Cao Cao's eastern defences.

But as quickly as opportunities come, they can also suddenly disappear. When Ma Chao had taken Ji City after the prolonged siege, he had done so with the aid of the Hanzhong ruler Zhang Lu's trusted aide, Yang Ang. The city had been governed by the respected Wei Kang, and his aides, Yang Fu and Yan Wen. Yan Wen had been captured in battle and then brutally executed for refusing to defect and induce his allies to surrender, and Governor Wei Kang – who had then opened the city once he saw the fate of Yan Wen – was killed by Ma Chao's Hanzhong ally, Yang Ang. While this show of strength and amazing amount of success inspired Zhang Lu and earned Ma Chao the respect and support of Qianwan, king of the western Di tribe, the death of Wei Kang resonated with many of his former vassals. Acting Ji City Governor Yang Fu – who had surrendered falsely – had secretly begun to plan a massive and calculated reprisal.

Within months, that reprisal came. Yang Fu – on the pretext of going to a family funeral – left Ji City, sought and earned the aid of three other minor warlords, and staged a very public rebellion against the furious Ma Chao. The adviser Zhao Qu – also a former vassal of the former governor Wei Kang – recommended that Ma Chao take his forces and crush the rebellion quickly, while he remained in Ji City. Ma Chao complied, and struck out at Lu City, where Yang Fu's forces had gathered. Yang Fu's forces feigned defeat on the field and lured Ma Chao into a trap, where his forces were routed by Yang Fu, his local allies, and Cao Cao's reinforcements led by Xiahou Yuan.

Ma Chao fled to Ji to regroup, but what met him was a sealed city: the adviser Zhao Qu had been in alliance with Yang Fu secretly, and had taken the city as soon as Ma Chao had gone. Ma Chao was subjected to harrowing torment as Zhao Qu had the dismembered bodies of Ma Chao's family held aloft or cast down from the walls, and Ma Chao retreated from Ji City as a broken man. After a brief yet unsatisfying revenge on his enemies' families at Lu City, Ma Chao, his cousin Ma Dai, and his trusted aide Pang De fled with the remnants of their forces to Hanzhong, where they sought shelter with Zhang Lu. Bing and Liang provinces fell under the control of Cao Cao or his allies once again.

"*Aiee*," Lu Su exclaimed as he sat in a private audience with the Wu ruler Sun Quan several days later, when the events in the north were widely known.

"That really is all that can be said," Sun Quan sighed miserably.

"If only he had not been such a brute!" Lu Su despaired. "Cao Cao has ordered the Ma family at court exterminated... so the great Ma Teng is also dead. Ma Chao's family now numbers less than the fingers on a man's hands... he is bound to seek revenge against Yang Fu and Zhao Qu."

"My father knew Ma Teng, and spoke highly of him," Sun Quan recalled. "What a shame... but as you say, Ma Chao was without restraint, and that made him bitter enemies that have laid him low. ...This affects our plans to attack Hefei, and finally unite the land... do we still have support from Liu Bei's forces in Jing...?"

"I don't know," Lu Su replied. "There are fears now about Cao Cao's next moves all across the west... Zhang Lu is now isolated, and Cao Cao will not have forgotten that he helped Ma Chao's takeover of Liang and Bing provinces. Liu Bei's still tied up at Luo City, and the southeast regions of Yi Province are now starting to supply aid to the capital Chengdu and Mianzhu County. That could go a number of ways now."

"Find out," Sun Quan urged. "I don't want to attack Cao Cao if it means I am going up against an undistracted horde of four hundred thousand."

Lu Su bowed and said, "I shall."


✳✳✳✳✳✳✳✳✳✳✳✳

## 73

"You're back again," Kongming said as he urged Lu Su to sit.

"I felt this to be a matter that needed face-to-face discussion," Lu Su replied. "Can we rely on you to...?"

"Zijing," Kongming interrupted, "in the last few days, I have heard that Cao Cao is reinforcing Fan City, moving troops into Bing Province, and pondering an attack on Hanzhong. Further to that, our spies in Chengdu say that Liu Zhang is considering requesting aid from Hanzhong... as I had feared. Worse yet, with Ma Chao defeated, Zhang Lu might well take up the offer, if it means more land and resources to act as a buffer against Cao Cao."

"But can't Liu Bei promise some land to Zhang Lu in order to pacify him?" Lu Su asked desperately.

"Not really," Kongming replied wearily. "It isn't his to offer, is it Zijing, and it would look bad to the residents of the ceded territories... he'd lose masses of support. But if Liu Zhang does it, it *is* his to give, and probably won't hurt his reputation at all."

"...*Aiee*," Lu Su groaned. "Things were so right...!"

"Yes, and now they're not," Kongming said irritably. "Was this how you consoled Zhou Gongjin during the siege of Jiangling?"

"...Sorry," Lu Su murmured. "I... I really thought, as you probably did, that an end to this madness was finally upon us."

"An end for whom...?" Kongming scoffed. "Even if Ma Chao and Lord Sun had successfully defeated Cao Cao together, would either of them have settled for thanks, and the feeling that they'd done something nice...?"

"...I dislike your tone," Lu Su said irritably.

"Enough," Kongming sighed. "I am being unfair, I know. Zijing, we cannot rule Ma Chao out of the affairs of the land just yet: his clan has been reduced to him and his cousin, and the men that committed the atrocity still live. While Ma Chao has reciprocated the slaughter of innocents, he still craves the heads of Yang Fu, Zhao Qu, Jiang Xu, Liang Kuan, and anyone else that played a part in driving him to destruction. He still has support from King Qianwan and other tribal leaders, and if Zhang Lu were to lend him troops... which I'm sure he would, if only to save himself... Cao Cao hasn't seen the last of that man."

"And if he did return...?" Lu Su prompted. "Would we have your support...?"

"Of course," Kongming promised. "But let us wait and watch."

Liu Bei's forces in Yi were starting to tire of the siege of Luo City.

"Ma Chao's defeat increases the urgency of victory," Jian Yong suggested.

"This place must fall, and quickly," Pang Tong declared. "I will personally lead tomorrow's attack on the city, once we have successfully lured their forces into a battle outside the walls."

"No," Liu Bei insisted. "You're the Director General... I'll go."

"I can react to sudden opportunities, my lord," Pang Tong countered. "I'll be fine... Mister Fa can remain with you and coordinate against other surprises, though I very much doubt there will be any."

The next day, Wei Yan and Huang Zhong rode to the front to provoke Zhang Ren to battle. Zhang Ren and Ling Bao rode out to confront the two generals, and a duel ensued once again between Wei Yan and Zhang Ren. This time, however, both sides had schemes: Wei Yan lured Zhang Ren toward a planned ambush by Pang Tong, and the defenders' forces were divided by two forces led by Liu Feng and Chen Shi. Zhang Ren – who had anticipated a trick – feigned an injury and retreated, amid a hail of arrows. At the same time, Pang Tong had launched an attack on Luo, but the defenders were ready.

**"Siege ladders, quickly!"** Pang Tong shouted from his command position. **"More ladders! Keep up the arrows! Don't give them a moment!"**

Arrows flew from the bows of both factions as Zhang Ren's forces returned to the city, and made a sudden turnabout to strike at the pursuing Liu Feng. Pang Tong rode forward to issue commands amid the chaos, but as he bellowed his instructions to his generals, an arrow – and nobody knew from whose side it originated – struck him mortally, and knocked him from his horse. Wei Yan and Huang Zhong ordered a desperate retreat, as Chen Shi hurried the Director General away from the battlefield and to the top of a small mountain road nearby. Liu Bei, upon learning of the event, rushed to Pang Tong's side.

"...Shiyuan...!" Liu Bei sobbed as he reached the temporary hospital – or rather, hospice – that had been set up at the top of the sloping road.

"...Lord Liu... Xuande...!" Pang Tong said hoarsely as Liu Bei knelt by his side and took his right hand; the small fan that Pang Tong liked to carry was still clutched tightly in his left hand. Liu Bei looked at the arrow that was protruding from Pang Tong's gut, and looked up at the military doctor with disbelief.

"There is no point," the doctor replied to the unspoken question.

"...Shiyuan...!" Liu Bei bleated: his eyes were filled with tears.

"Director General...!" Wei Yan exclaimed.

The generals and officials watched sadly as Liu Bei cradled Pang Tong's head in his arms and cried pitifully.

"...Luo...!" Pang Tong said as he stared skyward.

"This should not be how it ends!" Liu Bei sobbed. "Can we not do *anything*...?"

"...I'm sorry," the doctor insisted.

Pang Tong smiled and said, "Luo...!" once again.

"Shiyuan... I'm sorry...!" Liu Bei pleaded.

Pang Tong's eyes wandered about, taking in the surroundings, as he continued to smile with what appeared to be joy.

"Luo...!" Pang Tong chuckled. "Luo... where a phoenix... *falls*...!"

"Shiyuan...!" Liu Bei whined. "*Pang Shiyuan*...!"

Pang Tong – the Young Phoenix - exhaled noisily, and the fan fell from his hand. He had expired in the vicinity of Luo City in Yi Province, aged just 35.

************

## 74

Kongming was at home when a messenger from Liu Bei's headquarters in Yi Province arrived in Gong'an, bringing terrible news and a burdensome request.

"...**REPORT!**" the messenger shouted as Kongming's servant opened the door.

"At home...?" Kongming chuckled. "Can't this wait until tomorrow...?"

"...**URGENT!**" the messenger insisted wearily.

Kongming got up from his desk, took his fan from where it lay, and walked to the door, fanning himself briskly.

"...What is it that is so urgent...?" Kongming asked. "Come in... come in."

The messenger entered the house, fell to one knee in the middle of the living room and said, **"Zhang Lu of Hanzhong has accepted a request to attack Jiameng in exchange for land; Huo Jun holds the pass, but cannot make progress! Southeast Yi has started to rebel against our expedition and provide aid to Chengdu! Ma Chao has attacked Liang Province with aid from Zhang Lu! Sun Quan of Wu has begun action against Cao Cao to the east!"**

"None of this is important enough to come to my home at night," Kongming scolded as he slowed his frenetic fanning.

Yueying entered the room, suspecting that something was seriously wrong, and watched from a distance as Kongming demanded, "Who sent you here?"

"...M-Mister Yi Ji," the messenger replied nervously. "The... there is more to report, Governor."

"...*Oh no*," Yueying sobbed quietly: she bit her hand, and awaited the inevitable.

"... ... ...What else...?" Kongming said with fear. "**What else???**"

The messenger held back tears of fear and pain as he said, "D-Director General Pang Tong has-"

"No," Kongming said with a tone of denial. "I... I won't hear it."

"Director General Pang Tong... has been killed at Luo City!" the messenger reported apprehensively. "Lord Liu requests that you-"

The fan fell from Kongming's hand, and he collapsed to the floor, wailing uncontrollably. Yueying ran to his side and knelt down next to him.

"...Lord Liu requests..." the messenger began again.

"...Please, enough," Yueying ordered. "Lord Liu requests that Governor Zhuge Liang to leave immediately and replace Director General Pang Tong at Luo City!"

The messenger nodded silently.

"Please, go... thank you, but *go*," Yueying said miserably as she tried to get some sort of rational reaction from Kongming.

As the messenger retreated, Yueying whispered, "I always dreaded this day."

"...Luo... Luo...!" Kongming wailed: as he reiterated the word, the sobbing became deranged laughter. "Luo... *Luo*...!"

Yueying noted his point: although the 'Luo' of Luo City meant something else entirely, a homophone of 'Luo' meant 'to fall'.

"...To *fall*, indeed...!" Kongming chuckled maniacally. "First a phoenix, and then a dragon, no doubt...!"

"No!" Yueying scolded: she shook Kongming angrily, and started to cry as she added, "Don't say that! Don't say that! You have to be stronger than that!"

"I do, don't I...?" Kongming snickered. "For *wonderful Lord Liu*...!"

"What do you mean by that???" Yueying asked desperately.

"...Do you know," Kongming chuckled, "what his last letter to me said...?"

Kongming grinned uncomfortably, pulled a silk letter from his sleeve and handed it to Yueying, sobbing, "Go on... read it."

"...He upset Lord Liu...?" Yueying said as she finished reading.

"So what was this, mm...?" Kongming chortled. "Was 'Hongmen' or a 'dropped cup ambush' too obvious, so he had him shot outside Luo City instead...?"

"I... I don't think he would do that," Yueying said emotionlessly. "Not when his cause depends on great men... not when he-"

**He threw Shiyuan out of a banquet, in front of his new recruits!**" Kongming shouted angrily. "**He cares NOTHING about ANYTHING!**"

"Please, do not shout," Yueying implored.

"...Sorry," Kongming said sincerely. "But... if he is *that irrational*, why would he *not* kill Shiyuan later...?"

"For the exact same reason that he didn't kill him at the time," Yueying insisted. "He was sorry... he invited Pang Tong back, he was sorry. Liu Bei is a passionate man, and he lost control... he felt comfortable being himself around friends and allies, that's all it was."

"No, no, I can't be sure of that!" Kongming retorted.

"You're upset," Yueying said sternly. "You need to regain control. Tomorrow, you're going to be preparing for an urgent march west, into Yi Province."

"...You're right," Kongming said with a loud snort. "I... I need to be at his funeral, at the very least. I *want* to be there... I *need* to be there... I *have* to be there."

"Try and rest for now," Yueying pleaded gently. "Tomorrow, you need to-"

"I can't wait until tomorrow," Kongming said mechanically: he gently pushed Yueying away, got to his feet, and walked to the map of Yi that he kept on permanent display. After gently running his finger across a piece of pinned silk with Pang Tong's name on it – placed over Luo City – he turned to Yueying and added, "I have to plan the defence of Jing... since I will no longer be here when Sun Quan demands its return, I have to ensure that the borders are well maintained, and I have to decide who will stay and who will join me."

"...Who will stay...?" Yueying asked. "Who can you trust to sensibly guard Jing Province against Sun Quan...?"

"...With matters so urgent, there is only one man for that task... although Heaven knows I need him in Yi," Kongming replied as he unpinned the silk square bearing Pang Tong's name from the map, and placed the small piece of cloth on a nearby table with care.

"...Guan Yu," Yueying replied.

Kongming nodded silently.

After sending urgent despatches to Zhao Yun and Zhang Fei, Kongming hurried to the Nan Prefecture capital, Jiangling, to meet with Guan Yu and Ma Liang.

"Kongming," Ma Liang said hoarsely as his sworn brother marched into the main audience hall, clutching a small wooden box that was wrapped in a piece of red silk. Both men wore white and dye-free clothes to mourn their fallen friend.

"...Jichang," Kongming replied weakly. "...You know why I'm here, of course...?"

"You're going to replace him," Ma Liang supposed. "General Guan will be here tomorrow, as you requested."

"I'll look forward to it," Kongming chuckled humourlessly. "...I have ordered the immediate attendance of Zilong and Yide, so they'll be here soon as well."

"...Was it really an arrow...?" Ma Liang asked strangely.

"That's how most birds, even a phoenix, are taken down from the sky," Kongming replied miserably. "To die like that, in such a place... at least Gongjin died in the company of his beautiful wife, and in familiar surroundings... not by the roadside, like a penniless beggar."

"...You've brought the seal, I see," Ma Liang noted numbly. "Which of the three generals is it intended for...?"

"Who else but Guan Yunchang...?" Kongming replied.

"...Surely Zilong is more dependable," Ma Liang protested. "Guan Yunchang is very arrogant, and has no intention of being civil to Sun Quan at all."

"I know that," Kongming insisted, "but Guan is more fearsome, and will intimidate Sun Quan more than Zilong will... and I need Zilong to help me advance through the counties quickly. I haven't time for arguing with Yunchang, I need someone who will act as I instruct and not ignore me."

"...So you will be taking Zilong," Ma Liang sighed. "Will you also take Yide?"

"Yes," Kongming replied. "I'd rather have another Zilong, but I don't. Hopefully, he will refrain from his usual antics and just advance as instructed."

"Oh, well, at least Ma Chao and Sun Quan are keeping Cao Cao and each other busy," Ma Liang suggested miserably.

"But Zhang Lu has generals besieging Jiameng Pass now," Kongming said wearily.

"Zhang Lu...?" Ma Liang exclaimed. "He's helping Liu Zhang...?"

"The world is a place of chaos and insanity," Kongming replied. "Why else do the warmongers live, and the peacemakers die in their place? In a just universe, only those that sought death would find it."

"...Are you okay...?" Ma Liang asked pointlessly.

"Not at all," Kongming admitted. "But... I have to be fine, so let's keep that fact between us, shall we...?"

Ma Liang nodded sadly, replying, "He was my friend too."

As soon as the three generals – Guan Yu, Zhang Fei and Zhao Yun – were in Jiangling with their assistants and advisers, Kongming called them together for an urgent meeting.

"As you know," Kongming began, "Director General Pang Tong has perished... I will be replacing him."

The gathered ensemble – who all wore articles of white clothing out of respect for Pang Tong – nodded seriously and silently.
"I intend to take five thousand men, and march to White Emperor City... Yide and Zilong, you will be accompanying me on this trip," Kongming continued. "This general 'Zhang Ren' who holds Luo City with Liu Zhang's son, Liu Xun... he must be eliminated. We also have to pacify the southeast prefectures and counties; otherwise, this will just turn into a prolonged mess, like the siege here in Jiangling five years ago. We have already lost 'our Zhou Yu' to an arrow on the field, as fate weaves its cruel, repetitive web of misery... let's make the Director General's death the only needless loss we suffer."
"So I am to stay and guard Jing," Guan Yu complained.
"Do not take that responsibility lightly, Yunchang!" Kongming admonished. "I have stayed here and watched Jing for the last two, nearly three years because I consider service more important than glory! Sun Quan will come here looking to take this place back when we have secured Yi... what will you do...?"
"...Fight him, what else...?" Guan Yu scoffed.
"With *what*???" Kongming exclaimed. "You will *have no troops*!"
Guan Yu was angry but silent.
"Yunchang," Kongming implored, "you will need to be careful. Until Lord Liu has successfully defeated Liu Zhang, added his men to our own, and returned to Gong'an, Jing will be near defenceless. What you must do is hold out until he returns... say or do anything it takes to stall Lu Su, or whoever else they send here... but for goodness' sakes, *stall them*!"
"We should do as Kongming says, Brother Yunchang," Zhang Fei suggested. "If there's one thing the years have taught me, it's that this man knows what he's talking about... and we can't afford to lose Jing."
"...Very well," Guan Yu conceded.
"Scour the streets, talk to learned men, see if any new talents have sprung up in the area," Kongming continued. "For every shining star like Pang Tong that we lose, our constellation dims... we must replace them, or our cause is as lost as the day that just passed us by."
"...I do know that you're right," Guan Yu insisted. "I respect your insight and knowledge as well, Mister Zhuge... I simply yearn to do more than guard a gate. But you may trust me that I will do my duty well, and I will not let Elder Brother Xuande, our Lord Liu, down. I vow it."
Kongming got to his feet and walked to a nearby table, where the silk-wrapped seal of office was placed: he took it, turned, and walked to Guan Yu, who got to his feet to accept it.
"...With this official seal comes a lot of responsibility, Yunchang," Kongming said as he handed the object over. "You'll have Generals Guan Ping, Liao Hua, Xiang Chong, Shi Ren and Zhao Lei; Officials Xiang Yang, Liao Li, Pan Jun, and Mi Fang; and Ma Liang will remain here to act as an adviser and envoy should you need one at any point."
Guan Yu nodded silently: any present whose names had been mentioned murmured as acknowledgement.

"Mi Zhu, Yi Ji, Chen Zhen, Jiang Wan, Ma Su... you will accompany me," Kongming said sombrely. "General Meng Da: you have 'surrendered' to us, as have your two thousand troops, and we will certainly need them. What we will do is send you to reinforce Huo Jun at Jiameng Pass."

"As you command," Meng Da replied obediently.

"Once Yi province is taken... and as I stand before you now, I swear it will be," Kongming concluded, "we should, as a precaution, have our families moved west immediately... Ma Liang, I hope you will be well assisted in that."

"He will be," Guan Yu promised.

"...Fine," Kongming said emotionlessly. "We prepare immediately... let there be no more delays. We shall march on Yi Province as soon as it is possible."

Ma Chao's newest northern expeditions into Liang Province, meanwhile, ended in another crushing defeat. Upon his return to Hanzhong, he was not met with pleasantries, but with suspicion, since many around Zhang Lu suspected that the born conqueror Ma Chao would seize Hanzhong if he could not take Liang. Ma Chao sensed the suspicion, and travelled with his cousin Ma Dai to the mountainous western region of Wudu, where the Di tribe, led by King Qianwan, were based. His friend and general, Pang De, now broke ties and remained in Hanzhong. Zhang Lu sent a subordinate, Yang Bai, to the Wudu region in order to keep watch on Ma Chao and ensure his continued loyalty.

With Ma Chao finally spent and his allies all but destroyed, the northwest would no longer be a distraction to the imperial forces led by Cao Cao, Duke of Wei and Prime Minister of the Han. Those forces were now entirely free to travel eastward to face Sun Quan of Wu, southward to confront a severely understaffed Guan Yu in Jing, or westward to destroy Ma Chao's ally-turned-landlord, Zhang Lu of Hanzhong. Further to that, the nervous Sun Quan might want Jing under his control if he ever learned that Liu Bei was no longer guarding it well enough to keep it, or he may just want it anyway. Kongming knew that these issues made the need for a quick resolution to the conflict in Yi Province more urgent than ever, and that the responsibility for victory or defeat was now his to bear.

************

## 75

In Jing, the preparations were swift, and the departure was determined. The 5,000-man reinforcements for Liu Bei journeyed west along the Yangtze River toward the Jing-Yi border, and crossed into Yi without incident, since the border was now held by a small force loyal to the defector Meng Da. Those forces disembarked at the region around White Emperor City, and pitched camp temporarily.

"Lord Liu has prepared several battalions for us to take command of," Kongming explained as he held court with his forces. "Meng Da… you will be going north at Jiangzhou, taking the river route into the mountains to Jiameng, to aid Huo Jun. Zilong, you and I will advance west, past Jiangzhou to Jiangyang and then Jianwei, and then you will strike Chengdu from the west while I advance down the river to Luo City. Yide, you will siege Jiangzhou until they break, and then advance up the Dian River to Chengdu."

"…Jiangzhou will be no problem," Zhang Fei said surely.

"Well, be careful," Kongming insisted. "It's guarded by an experienced veteran general, Yan Yan, another loyal stalwart that refuses to give in. Try and take him alive, if you can, and don't hurt the people."

"I promise, I'll go easy," Zhang Fei said with a smile. "I'm getting to be very well behaved in my old age, Crouching Dragon, so don't fret yourself to death."

The three-pronged attack began: Huo Jun received Meng Da and his forces gladly, and together, the two repelled Zhang Lu's generals from Jiameng Pass. Zhang Fei, meanwhile, struck out at Jiangzhou, keeping its determined defenders busy while a second force led by Kongming and Zhao Yun sailed west of the fortress and advanced to Jiangyang.

"Master Zhuge," Zhao Yun asked Kongming as their forces neared Jiangyang, "how will we be helping Lord Liu to lift the siege at Luo…?"

"The obvious answer, Zilong, is division of their forces and priorities, but we will be doing more than that," Kongming replied. "Once Chengdu is besieged, Liu Zhang will panic, and a lot of resources will be transferred away from Luo and back to the capital. At that point, we will leave forces in Chengdu, and move north to Luo: our priority is not the weak, ineffectual Liu Zhang but his son, General Liu Xun, and the champion officers, Generals Zhang Ren and Ling Bao. If we do not defeat those three men, we cannot succeed."

"Can Yide be trusted to *capture* Yan Yan…?" Zhao Yun asked further.

"…Let's hope so," Kongming replied.

"**HEY!**" Zhang Fei shouted as he rode back and forth outside the fortress city of Jiangzhou. "**WHERE IS OLD YAN YAN? LET THE OLD MAN COME OUT AND FIGHT ZHANG YIDE OF YAN!**"

Yan Yan – who was not as old as Huang Zhong, but was still very much a veteran general – frowned with disapproval as he watched Zhang Fei from the ramparts.

"**HOW DARE YOU RESIST!**" Zhang Fei screamed. "**COME OUT AND SURRENDER, YOU OLD MAN!**"

"...Get my armour," Yan Yan ordered.

Yan Yan rode out of the city with his men to confront Zhang Fei, and said angrily, "**How dare *you*, outsider, come here and invade our province! We were prosperous, and enjoyed an era of peace! Now corpses are everywhere, the people starve and suffer... what did we ever do to *you*???**"

Zhang Fei yelled angrily, and charged Yan Yan's position: the two fought briefly, before a gong sounded on Yan Yan's side, and the old general retreated, covered by a hail of arrows from the walls of the city.

"...**You won't escape!**" Zhang Fei boomed. "**Where can you go?**"

"He is a demon of war," Yan Yan panted as the gates closed behind him.

The city of Jiangyang surrendered quickly, after a short confrontation between Zhao Yun and the defending generals.

"Let us hope Yide finds the same swift end to hostilities in Jiangzhou," Zhao Yun suggested cheerfully. "I will now advance... will the Director General be staying in Jiangyang long...?"

"Not at all," Kongming replied. "I have a funeral to attend."

"Of course," Zhao Yun realised. "Well, I hope that you are not impeded, Director General, and that you are not too late."

"My thanks, Zilong," Kongming said sadly. "I'm already too late... he'd still be alive if I wasn't."

Zhang Fei, meanwhile, had started building siege hills outside Jiangzhou, leaving Yan Yan no choice but to lead another attack: however, Zhang Fei's generals, Fan Qiang and Zhang Da, rushed Yan Yan's forces from the left and right as they charged out of the gates, and Yan Yan was routed. Distressed, the old general fought his way back to the safety of the city walls, once again covered by archers atop those walls.

"**Close the gates!**" Yan Yan implored as soon as all of his surviving men were accounted for; but Zhang Fei's forces had braved the arrows, and they were already rushing the city. After a short, futile resistance, Yan Yan was captured, and brought before the victorious Zhang Fei for final disposition.

"...Not so smart now, uh, old man...?" Zhang Fei heckled as Yan Yan stood before him, bound with rope. "You were so confident that you rode out to face me, but how could your old, saggy body cope with a battle with me, the man that shouted down Cao Cao's hordes at Steep-slope Bridge...?"

"...So you're *the* Zhang Fei," Yan Yan scoffed. "Little did I ever guess that a man whose name was a byword for bravery and justice would this day be stood in front of me, belittling my age and service, and serving a lord who covers our green lands with red blood to further his own career!"

**"You DARE say that???"** Zhang Fei challenged. **"You old man! You old, dried up bones! How can you be confident when you're defeated?"**

"So sad," Yan Yan snickered. "All the tales that people tell are truly nothing more than tales... Liu Bei is no man of justice, and Zhang Fei is no man of honour. You're an uncultured thug, serving a wicked tyrant. Kill me and be done with it."

"*You*...!" Zhang Fei exclaimed. **"Guards... DEATH!"**

"...That's all I want," Yan Yan said with a smile.

But as the guards started to drag Yan Yan away, Zhang Fei suddenly changed his mind and shouted, **"WAIT!"**

"...I suppose you want to torture me first," Yan Yan heckled.

"...You're a righteous man," Zhang Fei said with a sigh. "I have no right to deny the world a man like you."

"*What*...?" Yan Yan exclaimed: Zhang Fei untied him, and gestured silently that Yan Yan should sit with him as an honoured guest.

"...No, no!" Yan Yan said desperately. "Just give me death!"

"My lord," Zhang Fei replied, "is a good man, General Yan. I know this must seem unfair... but you haven't been chased by Cao Cao, watched him kill good people... my lord's daughters were captured six years ago, made to marry Cao's men and give them children. My lord was hunted down... just because he wanted to see the Han survive. Your lord helped Cao Cao kill the people of Jing, attack Wu at Red Cliffs, and hurt the people in the north. See it from the *outside*, General Yan."

Yan Yan looked into Zhang Fei's eyes: they were full of sincerity.

"If Lord Liu was what you said he was... I couldn't help him. If people are suffering, it's because *your* lord won't give up and stop," Zhang Fei insisted. "I'm serious... all I want is peace as well. But if I knew the peace I had was only because somewhere else, people were dying... well, I couldn't just ignore that. Can *you*...?"

"I...!" Yan Yan bleated: before he could continue, Zhang Fei surprised everyone by falling to one knee and bowing.

"General Yan," Zhang Fei pleaded, "I want this to end, just like you do. Help me end it sooner. Help me save Xuande, help me make Liu Zhang see sense."

"To bow before a defeated general... you're more than a warrior," Yan Yan said with tears in his eyes. "...You're every bit as legends say...!"

With that, Yan Yan surrendered, and Zhang Fei's path northward was clear. General Yan aided Zhang Fei in reaching Chengdu quickly, and along the way, Zhang Fei spared the populace from harm. This benevolence earned support and praise that was badly needed if Liu Bei was to succeed.

＊＊＊＊＊＊＊＊＊＊＊＊

## 76

After sieging Chengdu and securing essential supply routes, Kongming, Zhang Fei and Zhao Yun travelled to Luo City to join Liu Bei. Kongming arrived first, hoping that he was not too late for the funeral of his friend.

"Kongming…!" Liu Bei said with joy. "Thank goodness you are now here! We have to break the siege! General Huo Jun is-"

"I have already sent General Meng Da to Jiameng Pass to rescue General Huo," Kongming interrupted.

"Oh…?" Jian Yong chuckled. "You already have things under control then, Kongming… I'm not surprised at that."

"What has been done for Director General Pang…?" Kongming asked: he noted – and appreciatively so – that everyone, from the lowliest infantryman to Liu Bei himself, was wearing at least one article of white or non-dyed clothing to commemorate Pang Tong.

"…Kongming," Jian Yong replied, "can the answer to that not wait until later…? We need to deal with Zhang Ren-"

"We need Yide and Zilong before we can deal with Zhang Ren," Kongming countered. "Xianhe… what has been done…?"

Jian Yong started to reply, but Liu Bei hushed him.

"I intend to build a shrine near Luo City, by the road where he died," Liu Bei proclaimed. "I wish that sloping road to be called 'Valley of the Fallen Phoenix', so that all of the people of the world are forced to remember him."

"…He would be touched," Kongming replied coldly: he bowed slightly in addition, and Liu Bei noted the restraint with discomfort.

"My deepest regret," Liu Bei continued, "is that… as I am certain you are aware… Director General Pang… no… *Shiyuan*… and I did not see eye-to-eye during the last weeks of the campaign over a trifling matter. I can never undo that… I can only show Heaven and the earth under Heaven that I truly valued him as an adviser, and as a friend."

Kongming smiled and bowed more penitently, saying, "Your words mean much."


Once Zhang Fei and Zhao Yun had arrived, plans were put in place for a final battle with Zhang Ren. Kongming arrayed the forces in a bizarre fashion, utilising strange battle lines and mismatching flags, such that Zhang Ren and his forces viewed Kongming's efforts with derision.

"Is this the replacement for Pang Tong…?" Zhang Ren jeered. "What a worthless pedant. I could array men better whilst drunk."

"We should be careful," Ling Bao suggested. "That's *Zhuge Liang* organising those men. I've heard folk say that at the battle of Red Cliffs, the winds were seasonally blowing from the northwest, but that he prayed to the stars for a southeast wind, and that without him, Zhou Yu would have lost."

Liu Xun and Zhang Ren stared silently and contemptuously at Ling Bao, who suddenly felt very uncomfortable.

"B-but even if that isn't true," Ling Bao protested, "didn't he once fool Cao Cao with disorderly arrays at Wulin…?"

"He *lost* at Wulin," Zhang Ren replied condescendingly. "So if all Liu Bei now has is this fool, we've won today. We should prepare to march immediately, Commander Liu."
"...I'll decide that for myself, General Zhang," Liu Xun retorted, "but this does certainly seem like a golden opportunity..."

Eventually, it was General Ling Bao that was sent to test Kongming's formation: he did not return. The array swallowed his men, and left nothing but corpses and surrendered foot soldiers. Kongming then ordered the men to retreat to the main camp to rest; Liu Xun and Zhang Ren surveyed the moonlit ground in front of Luo City with sudden desperation.
"...I don't know what sort of training this Zhuge Liang received," Zhang Ren said to Liu Xun, "but it is almost possible to believe that he could change the direction of the winds, his wisdom in variable arrays is so vast. We can't afford another loss like that... before they have a chance to attack us like that again, we must take the fight to them as I tried to suggest before. Their camp is across the gorge... Wild Goose Bridge is the only direct route. Let us storm the bridge!"
"...Risky," Liu Xun suggested.
"I'll go, you stay here and guard the city," Zhang Ren suggested. "If I am victorious, we will share the merit with our lord for ridding Yi of these wicked bandits. If I lose, hold the city and request support from Chengdu."
"Very well," Liu Xun agreed reluctantly. "But be careful, General."

Zhang Ren led his forces to Wild Goose Bridge under cover of night, but upon reaching the bridge, he realised too late that Kongming and Fa Zheng had set a trap for him. Zhang Fei and Zhao Yun met him at the bridge; Li Yan and Yan Yan approached from the left; Liu Feng and Huang Zhong approached from the right; Wei Yan and Chen Shi met the rear of his forces.
"**IT'S BEEN A WHILE!**" Wei Yan boomed. "**I'VE MISSED YOU!**"
Zhang Ren fought furiously, but against such large forces, and with nowhere to go, he was doomed. Eventually, he was wrestled to the ground by infantrymen, bound tightly with rope, and led to Liu Bei.
"...So this is Zhang Ren," Kongming noted coldly.
Zhang Ren glared at Liu Bei with undying hatred.
"Look around you," Liu Bei pleaded. "Fa Zheng, Wu Yi, Li Yan, Deng Xian, Fei Guan, Yan Yan... they have all seen the light, and turned to me to save the Han, defeat the Duke of Wei and restore peace to the land. Why do you – and you alone – continue this groundless vendetta against my imperially sanctioned duty...?"
Zhang Ren scoffed, and replied, "The Duke of Wei is awarded the nine dignitaries, and serves the Emperor loyally... while you, progeny of a disinherited prince, a mat-weaving peddler, are branded a rebel by the court, you and your friend Sun Quan."
"You...!" Zhang Fei exclaimed: Kongming silenced him with a gesture of his fan.

"You are misinformed," Liu Bei insisted. "I was authorised by the Emperor to remove the villain Cao Cao, long before he awarded himself that dukedom... the nine dignitaries you speak of are a precursor to usurpation, and yet your lord still craves an alliance with him, to the indignation of all. General Zhang Ren... you have proved yourself an equal to any of my great generals throughout your defence of nearly a year against the siege of Luo. Such a man as you could make the country great once again if only he served the right lord... can I really not sway you...?"
Zhang Ren smirked proudly and eyed the defectors as he replied, "A faithful man could never serve two masters!"
Liu Bei probed Zhang Ren's face for a trace of flexibility in his stance: he found nothing but indefatigable resolve.
"...*Aiee*," Liu Bei sighed. "*If only I had met you first.*"
"**Guards,**" Kongming barked. "...**DEATH!**"
General Zhang Ren laughed as he was dragged away: he did not stop laughing until his head left his shoulders.

As soon as the capture of Zhang Ren was reported to Liu Xun in Luo City, he started to make preparations to retreat. Within weeks, he deserted Luo, and fled to Chengdu to join his father. Liu Bei now set up an interim court, and started to behave as though he were already ruling Yi Province. He conferred titles on his followers, new and old, and started recruiting new talents, intent on having a fully-fledged government ready for when Chengdu finally surrendered.

************

## 77

Months passed, and Liu Zhang and Liu Xun held Chengdu, with additional help from Zhang Lu of Hanzhong bleeding through and attacking Jiameng Pass at regular intervals. Morale did start to drop as the idea of Chengdu becoming another Luo or Jiangling started to look like a reality: but then, when all seemed bleak, a letter arrived from the Wudu region that might change the course of the siege on the Yi capital. Liu Bei summoned his top generals and officials to his command tent to review this unexpected and important correspondence.

"...Ma Chao wishes to ally himself with us," Jian Yong said with surprise as he read the letter. "With a man like that on our side, we might just turn this around."

"Why should having Ma Chao on our side make a difference?" Zhang Fei complained. "Everyone except Yunchang is now here in Yi... if he doesn't surrender to me, Zilong, Wenchang, or any of the other generals... why would he give in to this lonely Qiang barbarian?"

"...Precisely because of his reputation," Kongming replied uncomfortably. "The man rebelled against Cao Cao while his father was at court, knowing it meant the extermination of his clan. He slayed the governor of Ji City to force his hand, he butchered the families of the defenders of Lu City to avenge his own losses, he commands respect – and fear – from the Qiang, the Hu, the Di... if he came here, Liu Zhang would surrender to escape a violent massacre."

"Your tone insinuates that you have doubts about him as an ally, Director General," Zhao Yun noted.

"Is it," Jian Yong supposed, "that you see in him another Lü Bu?"

"That's no unfair comparison... he is ambitious," Fa Zheng sighed. "The letter speaks of 'conquering Yi together': that does not suggest that he will be coming here as a vassal to tender service, but as a rival warlord to offer an alliance for mutual gain. What will we give this hungry tiger in exchange for his support...?"

"...A promise," Kongming replied after a short pause for thought, "that we will recover Liang Province for him."

"...That's perfect," Jian Yong said with a smile. "We will win Ma Chao, pacify Yi, reassure Hanzhong, and have just cause to march on Liang, all in a single stroke!"

"...But he says that he is under constant supervision by Zhang Lu's subordinate, Yang Bai," Fa Zheng challenged. "Even now, Zhang Lu urges him to attack Jiameng Pass, and with Yang Bai at his side, what can he do...?"

"He would have to kill Yang Bai," Liu Bei said plainly, "which would serve as a warning to Zhang Lu and proof of Ma Chao's sincerity also, since he cannot then betray us and return to Hanzhong."

Nervous silence met the pragmatic suggestion: after an awkward pause, Kongming coughed deliberately and said, "Well, that does seem like the only real choice. After all, he cannot flee Yang Bai, nor can he convince the man to defect... we must see this 'Yang Bai' as another Zhang Ren, and move on from it."

"Fine," Liu Bei proclaimed. "Send a letter: have all we have said put to him."

"We'll need to show our own sincerity, if we're going to suggest he kill a man and burn the bridge that leads back to Hangzhong," Jian Yong suggested. "This letter has to be delivered by a trusted vassal of yours. I'll go."
"No, no!" Liu Bei insisted. "That won't be necessary."
From among Liu Bei's newest acquisitions, a man stepped forward and said, "I will go, my lord."
"...Who are you?" Zhang Fei asked bluntly.
"Family name Li, given name, Hui, styled De'ang," the man replied confidently. "I will go, my lord."
"...You refused to serve in Liu Zhang's administration, didn't you," Jian Yong noted. "But really, you don't have to put your hand in a tiger's mouth to prove your worth! I'm more than happy to go."
"I would also happily volunteer," Mi Zhu said. "I have been idle in Jing, and have not been able to act as ambassador or envoy for some time."
"*Aiee*," Liu Bei exclaimed. "Are you all so desperate to end your lives early...?"
"*I* will go," Li Hui said emphatically. "You have lost enough limbs recently, my lord: allow me to speak with this man Ma Chao. I will even write a military pledge, that I should be executed if I return empty-handed."
"No need for that, Li De'ang," Jian Yong chuckled. "This man's enthusiasm has won me around... perhaps it is better that Mi Zhu and I remain here, in case we are needed to speak with Liu Zhang or Zhang Lu."
"...Fine," Liu Bei conceded. "Go with all haste, and watch your words!"
"I shall," Li Hui promised.

Chengdu was soon alive with rumours of a terrifying force of nature: Ma Chao of the Qiang had arrived in Yi Province. Though his followers were few, his reputation alone – as Kongming and the other advisers had rightly predicted – was enough to put Chengdu on high alert. As the days passed and Ma Chao neared the city, the governor Liu Zhang started to waver in his determination.

A man in his mid-forties left the city of Chengdu as an envoy, and entered Liu Bei's military camp to speak with the officials.
"I recognise him," Zhang Fei growled to Yan Yan as the official entered the command tent. "He tried to block us at Deyang..."
"Zhang Junsi," Yan Yan said quietly.
The man – Zhang Yi, styled Junsi – bowed graciously, and said, "I am honoured to meet with Lord Liu Xuande, Zhuge Kongming, and the other magnificent generals and officials under Liu Xuande's service."
"Does this mean he's surrendering...?" Jian Yong asked pointedly.
"Xianhe...! *Please*...!" Liu Bei scolded.
"I am here to discuss the options we have available to us," Zhang Junsi declared.
"Surrender, or fight Ma Chao," Zhang Fei cackled.
"*Yide*," Liu Bei barked.

"My lord does not wish to see any more bloodshed," Zhang Junsi said graciously. "If that means peace by concession, then so be it, provided the terms are fair and just, and serve the people of Yi."

"I am only doing this for the people of Yi," Liu Bei insisted. "We will harm nobody, and Governor Liu will be treated with respect and courtesy."

"...That being the case," Zhang Junsi said, "after some more clarification... I think I can return to my lord with that proposal."

"My lord, you cannot surrender!" the adviser Huang Quan protested as Liu Zhang paced back and forth in his court hall, sighing desperately. "The people will fight... we cannot allow Liu Bei to take Chengdu!"

"But how can I survive???" Liu Zhang retorted angrily. "Zhang Lu is withdrawing support, many of my most trusted followers have deserted or died... even *Wu Yi* has defected to Liu Bei, and without Ling Bao, Zhang Ren... I am done for!"

"You still have many followers, and the people are willing to fight for you, even they are scared," another adviser, Liu Ba, said reassuringly. "Please, my lord, don't give up yet."

"...Jian Yong has asked to see me," Liu Zhang revealed. "Zhang Junsi has conveyed to me a desire for a peaceful solution, and now Jian Yong will-"

"No!" a third adviser, Hu Jing, pleaded. "That tactless, uncouth man will say whatever it takes to get you to submit, but you shouldn't give him the chance! If anything, lure him here and behead him as a sign of our determination!"

"I'm going to talk to Jian Yong," Liu Zhang insisted. "This... this has gone on long enough. People are dying... and regardless of whose fault that actually is, people will eventually start to blame me, and I already blame myself. ...It's over."

Despite the teary, heartfelt pleas of his remaining vassals, Liu Zhang had decided to surrender. He ordered his forces to stop firing on Liu Bei's siege forces, and accepted the request for an audience from Jian Yong. Once the two had spoken, that was that: Chengdu fell at last, almost three years after Liu Bei had entered Yi Province. The enterprise had been costly to everyone, but now, it was over.

"I... have waited so long for this," Mister Sun croaked emotionally as he waited on horseback – along with all of Liu Bei's other notable vassals – for Liu Zhang to open the gates of Chengdu and present the seal of provincial office to Liu Bei. "Lord Liu... has a base – no, a *home* – at last...!"

"Let's hope he doesn't give this one away," Kongming chuckled coldly as he waited alongside the elder official.

"This... isn't like Xu or Jing, Master Zhuge," Mister Sun insisted hoarsely. "This is-"

"Spare your precious energy, Mister Sun," Kongming said kindly. "Just enjoy the moment quietly, if you must enjoy it at all."

The gates of Chengdu finally opened, and a horse-driven carriage appeared, in which Liu Zhang and Jian Yong sat together, talking pleasantly. Liu Zhang appeared to be completely relaxed, as though Jian Yong's casual humour had made him forget the affairs of the day: it was only when he saw the gathering of officers and officials – with Liu Bei at their helm – that he suddenly lost his smile, and became emotional and bitter. The officers and officials of Chengdu followed the carriage, many weeping and complaining about the event that was taking place.

"...I should feel glad that it's over, at least... but I feel numb," Liu Bei realised as he watched Jian Yong and Liu Zhang depart the carriage and walk toward him. Liu Zhang was carrying the silk-wrapped seal in his shaking hands.

"Go and take the prize," Zhang Fei urged. "Come on, we all worked hard enough for it, didn't we...?"

Liu Bei sneered at Zhang Fei and rode forward slowly, until Liu Zhang suddenly stopped walking toward him. At that point, Liu Bei dismounted his white horse and walked toward Liu Zhang, his eyes filled with tears.

"...Brother," Liu Bei sobbed, "I... I never wanted this."

"You came here to take the province," Liu Zhang replied. "Well... now it's yours."

"No, not at all," Liu Bei insisted. "We two are alone on this patch of ground... what I say now is not for the benefit of anyone but you. I really did not want this. Do you not see that circumstance forced my hand...?"

"What *circumstance*...?" Liu Zhang asked with disdain.

"You lowered yourself to serve Cao Cao," Liu Bei retorted, "who is the mortal enemy of the state. He confers upon himself titles that foreshadow a coup, he kills innocents, he-"

"You have done your fair share of inflicting suffering, Xuande," Liu Zhang said with emotion. "For three years, my people have suffered needlessly...!"

"Others in neighbouring provinces have suffered needlessly for far longer so that yours could prosper, Jiyu," Liu Bei countered. "Was your support of the tyrant villain Cao Cao benefitting the likes of Jing, Liang, or...?"

"*Enough*...! ...Enough," Liu Zhang conceded. "Perhaps, in its own way... my rule was selfish and... perhaps cowardly, too. How do you intend to do better...?"

"I intend to enforce the law more strictly, make good use of all the land, as Sun Quan has done with the former wastelands and jungles of Jiangdong," Liu Bei explained. "I will raise a mighty army, and together with Ma Chao of Liang and my brother-in-law, Sun Quan of Eastern Wu, I will attack the Duchy of Wei and rescue the Emperor from Cao Cao's clutches. Once the throne is saved and restored, I will do all I can to rebuild this country, providing education, agriculture, commerce and law, so that cults like the Yellow Turbans and Celestial Masters can never again claim to speak for the people, since those people will live well and thrive in an era of enduring peace. All I ask, Jiyu... all I ever asked... is that you help me."

Liu Zhang lowered his gaze, and exhaled noisily.

"...Together, think what we can achieve...!" Liu Bei said enthusiastically.

Liu Zhang looked into his eyes, nodded, and turned to his miserable followers, saying loudly, "**All of you... serve him well.**"

With that said, Liu Zhang turned to face Liu Bei once again and fell to his knees, his arms outstretched, to offer the seal of Yi Province.

"...I humbly accept," Liu Bei said as he knelt to take the seal from Liu Zhang's steady, determined hands. "I promise, Jiyu... I won't offend your memory. I will always strive to make the people as happy as you did."

Both men got to their feet, and Jian Yong walked to Liu Bei's side, gesturing that he should now enter the city hand-in-hand with its ousted governor, Liu Zhang.

"...So at last, we are settled," Mi Zhu said with relief.

"You forget that Sun Quan will now demand Jing," Kongming chuckled.

"What are we going to do with Liu Zhang...?" Fa Zheng wondered. "That's *my* main concern."

"He will be sent to Gong'an, where he will be of no further concern," Kongming said coldly. "We'll send Liu Xun with him."

"You don't like him, do you...?" Mi Zhu noted.

"What I think doesn't matter," Kongming replied. "All that matters now is that he is removed as a threat of any sort... without making a martyr of him. Anyhow, his fate doesn't concern me half as much as that of our families... has word been sent to Jiangling of our success...?"

"It has," Mi Zhu confirmed. "Ma Liang will start moving our families immediately, unless we're afraid that there may be uprisings here...?"

"Unlikely," Kongming scoffed as he watched Liu Bei and Liu Zhang walk into Chengdu City. "No, the only things we have to fear now are the Duchy of Wei and Eastern Wu."

Liu Bei finally took up residence in Chengdu, openly declaring himself the governor in an official despatch to the imperial court in the north. He sent out word across the land that any who wanted to see the Han restored to its former glory should find their way to Yi Province. Now there were only four great powers in the land – Wei, Wu, Yi, and Han'ning, the court's name for the region of Hanzhong that Zhang Lu officially governed. Liu Bei conferred more titles on his vassals, and enjoyed – for a very brief period of time – a sense of security.

Ma Chao, styled Mengqi – whose dual Qiang and Chinese ethnicity made him an imposing, unique figure – marched into the Yi court wearing shimmering armour and white articles to show his continued mourning for his family. Behind him was his cousin, Ma Dai, who also wore white articles. The two were now – as far as they knew – the only remaining members of their once extensive branch of the Ma clan.

"Ma Mengqi," Liu Bei said as Ma Chao reached him, "your service in this campaign was as glorious as it was unexpected. I appoint you 'General who pacifies the West': I hope, one day soon, to assist you in avenging your lost loved ones, and in retaking Liang Province."

"My lord," Ma Chao said humbly as he and Ma Dai each fell to one knee, "I will serve you tirelessly, in gratitude for your benevolence and generosity to this man of the mountains and plains of the west... I will do all I can to disprove my brutal reputation, and be an example to the people of this land."
Liu Bei nodded approvingly, saying, "You are a valiant hero of the day. I am very lucky to know you."
"I hope one day soon, you'll spar with me!" Zhang Fei said eagerly. "I want to know if you're really as great as everyone says you are!"
"Yide, control yourself," Liu Bei chuckled as the court burst into happy laughter.
Zhang Fei and Ma Chao exchanged smiles and nods of true respect.

But within a few weeks, Mister Sun's health deteriorated, and the officials gathered at the old man's bedside to bid a reluctant farewell.
"...Sun Gongyou," Jian Yong said sadly as Liu Bei wept uncontrollably, "please, try and fight this. Our cause is not done, and we need you!"
"I'm not sad," Mister Sun said weakly. "I've seen you reach the heights... I always hoped you would. That's enough for me."
"Gongyou...!" Liu Bei sobbed as he clutched Mister Sun's hand tightly. "I have only just lost Pang Shiyuan... please, Gongyou... don't go...!"
Mister Sun looked at Kongming and smiled sadly; Kongming returned the smile, and with a tear in his eye, he said, "We have all been through much together, Gongyou... I'm losing a kindly uncle that I shall never forget."
Mister Sun recalled the voice of contention that he had actually been with regard to the young strategist, and smiled gratefully at his generous choice of memorial to their tumultuous relationship.
"...Gongyou...!" Mi Zhu sobbed. "Not *now*, Gongyou... not *now*...!"
"Take... care... of Xuande... all of you," Mister Sun said softly, and with the last of his strength.
Liu Bei embraced his vassal like a father, and the ensemble wept. Later that same day, old Mister Sun Qian passed away, at an age of 60 or more, after serving as adviser, envoy, ambassador and friend to Liu Bei for 20 years. Pang Tong and Sun Qian were commemorated within a short time, and yet the morale of the new nation remained high, since an end finally appeared to be on the horizon.


************

# ACT VII: REALISING THE VISION

## 78

For Zhuge Liang, the journey was now at a critical yet positive stage. When he had joined the wandering warlord Liu Bei in Yi Province, he had 5,000 soldiers and a death mark against him. Since then, Liu Bei had sunk to new lows at Steep-slope, and risen to new heights when his mortal enemy, the Han Prime Minister and Duke of Wei, Cao Cao, suffered 2 crippling military defeats at Red Cliffs and the southern Jing capital of Jiangling. Now – thanks in part to a tenuous alliance with the southern warlord Sun Quan – Liu Bei had most of the land that Zhuge Liang's tripartite theorem required him to have in order to face Cao Cao and fulfil his promise to Emperor Xian that he would remove the Prime Minister and his followers from court before they seized power completely.

Liu Bei still needed a clear path northward through which to attack Cao Cao, and at present, that path – the former Yi region known as Hanzhong – was governed by the cult leader Zhang Lu. To add to the difficulties, the central attack point in the three-way pincer – Jiangling, the southern Jing capital – was, so far as Sun Quan of Wu was concerned, on loan until Liu Bei had conquered Yi Province, at which point it would need to be returned to full Wu occupation and Liu Bei would have to leave. This would place two of the attack points under Sun Quan's control, and make Liu Bei a secondary player in the confrontation with Cao Cao. For Liu Bei to be the ultimate victor, he had to retain Jing Province, win Yi Province, and ally with or annex Hanzhong.

Although it had been costly, Liu Bei had, after a 3 year campaign, taken control of Yi Province. On the advice of his vassals, Liu Bei sent the former governor of the province, Liu Zhang, and Zhang's eldest son, Liu Xun, to his capital in Jing Province, Gong'an – effectively banishing them from Yi. Ma Liang travelled to the capital from Jiangling and met Liu Zhang at the gates of Gong'an City, so that – it was hoped – the expatriated governor would not feel completely discarded and betrayed.

"…Welcome, Lord Liu, and Master Liu Xun," Ma Liang said, accompanying the words with a low bow of respect. "I hope your journey to Jing Province was not too uncomfortable."

"Why am I 'Lord Liu'…?" Liu Zhang asked with obvious bitterness. "I am, after all, not here to be governor. As I understand it, *General Shi Ren* is in charge here."

"Titles and roles are being finalised," Ma Liang replied diplomatically. "At the moment, we are in the middle of transporting the families of Governor Liu Bei's vassals to Chengdu. In exchange, we want a person of influence in Gong'an, someone that Governor Liu Bei trusts, while we negotiate the 'lease' of this province with Sun Quan."

"So I will be acting as an emissary to parley with Sun Quan of Eastern Wu, then…?" Liu Zhang asked pointedly.

"…No," Ma Liang replied. "As I said, we are trying to get our affairs in order, so all I can do is to ask you to be patient. Now… shall I show you to your residence…?"

"Lead the way," Liu Zhang replied coldly.

Many days passed: the news of Liu Bei's success in Yi Province had already reached Sun Quan, who was busy overseeing a sustained harassment of the imperial border forces in the east. When it became clear that nobody was going to be sent to the Wu court, Sun Quan angrily ordered Chief Commander Lu Su to travel to Jiangling and demand the return of Jing Province.

Ma Liang greeted the frosty Lu Su cordially, and invited him to a private meeting in his office to discuss the return of the province.
"...Should I not be speaking with Guan Yu...?" Lu Su said irritably.
"Chief Commander," Ma Liang protested, "I really do think that your hostility is unnecessary."
"My lord loaned Nan Prefecture to Liu Bei because he wanted to assist him, since his own resources were inadequate for our alliance, even with his additional forces from Lei Xu of Lujiang," Lu Su admonished. "Liu Bei now has Yi... he doesn't need Jing anymore. The time for excuses and delays is over: did you think we would simply sit there and ignore the fact that you have not sent anyone as envoy to us, even out of courtesy to convey your recent victory...? Return Jing, *now*."
"When my lord pacified Yi Province," Ma Liang replied carefully, "it was not without help. I take it that you know from those who informed you of our success that it was partly due to the intervention of Ma Chao of Xiliang...?"
"...I did not," Lu Su admitted. "In what sense did he 'intervene'...? I thought he was indebted to Zhang Lu of Hanzhong, who actively aided Liu Zhang in the latter half of the conflict, and so I therefore see no sense in your words."
"He was allied to Zhang Lu, yes," Ma Liang said with a smile. "But as you just stated, Zhang Lu broke faith with our alliance, and started to supply Liu Zhang with aid in exchange for land."
"...Go on," Lu Su prompted.
"I wonder, did it not concern you that Zhang Lu – a former ally of your predecessor – turned on us, and started helping a man whose allegiances lay with the Duke of Wei...?" Ma Liang challenged. "Did it not concern you at *all*...?"
"Of course it did!" Lu Su exclaimed desperately. "I never expected Zhang Lu to aid a mad barbarian rebellion against Cao Cao in the north, and then aid a hated enemy, a man that slaughtered his family, and who serves Cao Cao in the south! It made no *sense*! But what is it that you want me to say???"
"Nothing," Ma Liang said quietly. "What I want you to *do*, however, is be fair. Zhang Lu aided Ma Chao for personal gain: he hoped to gain land in Liang Province. When Liu Zhang asked for help, he offered part of Yi as a reward and also as reparation for his earlier purge of Zhang Lu's family. With Ma Chao's coalition forces defeated in the north and an angry Cao Cao looming, he saw expansion southward as an option, and took up the offer. He cares nothing for our alliance against Cao Cao... Zhang Lu cares only for his own security."
"Another subtle swipe at Lord Sun," Lu Su supposed irritably.

"If the cap fits, wear it," Ma Liang retorted. "If it doesn't, why complain...? But I have yet to come to the point. After his defeat, Ma Chao fled into the mountains to live with the Di people. Zhang Lu mistrusted him, and had men watching his every move... Ma Chao was no longer a respected titan but another wandering warlord, trapped in another lord's lands..."
"Like Lü Bu, and your own lord," Lu Su said with a smirk.
"Enjoy your petty heckling," Ma Liang scolded. "It serves no purpose. You say that matters are serious and urgent, so why do you interrupt me needlessly...? Ma Chao should rightly govern Liang Province, but was denied by Cao Cao, and the intrigue of selfish independent governors in the region. When he saw how my lord was faring against Liu Zhang, he offered his support, and after irreparably severing ties with the faith-breaking Zhang Lu – a self-harming act that only a man of sincerity would dare risk, I think – he marched south, and helped us placate Chengdu."
"...Because he wanted land as a reward, surely...?" Lu Su suggested.
"We offered an alliance... he would help us secure Yi if we helped him retake Liang Province," Ma Liang explained. "Now that he has kept his side of the bargain, we are bound by honour to-"
"Oh, no, no, no...!" Lu Su chuckled angrily. "You're not fooling me again! You want us to leave you with Jing until you've taken Liang...? Where then: Bing, Qin, Yu...? You've got ample resources now to conduct your activities alone! You don't need to leech off of us anymore! I am not going back to Lord Sun and-"
"...**You'll go back,**" a booming voice said, "**and you'll tell Sun Quan what Lord Liu has plainly and directly said: no.**"
Lu Su turned and saw Guan Yu standing in the doorway of Ma Liang's office, clutching his Green Dragon pole sword in his right hand.
"...When Liang is taken," Ma Liang pleaded, "and we have honoured our debt to Ma Chao of Xiliang... come back *then*, Chief Commander."
"...I'll go back," Lu Su said numbly. "I'll convey what you have said... but do not be surprised if my lord is displeased."
"I don't care if he's 'displeased'," Guan Yu growled. "Be gone."
Lu Su got up, made slight bows of respect to Guan Yu and Ma Liang, and tried to leave; Guan Yu stared him down and smirked before he finally moved aside to allow him to leave.
"...We shouldn't intimidate him," Ma Liang protested as Lu Su fled. "He's the Chief Commander of Eastern Wu's armed forces."
"He's a gullible fool, a granary owner that was given the job as irrelevant thanks for an act of generosity," Guan Yu scoffed. "Would I make a fruit farmer the Director General of our army because he gave me an orange...? Sun Quan is surrounded by sentimental idiots with blurred concepts of justice, that seem to have trouble distinguishing what is theirs from what obviously belongs to another. That man Lu Su is unfit for purpose, and will never be a threat to us. How can I fear them...?"
"All the same," Ma Liang chuckled nervously, "I think we should reinforce the borders at the same time as we let Lord Liu and Kongming know that we've finally had the visit."
Guan Yu harrumphed and walked away proudly.

"*Aiee*," Kongming exclaimed desperately as he sat in his new office in Chengdu, reading a letter from Ma Liang.

"Is something the matter...?" Ma Su asked rhetorically.

"This... this is not good," Kongming complained. "Lu Su was not even slightly delayed or placated... instead, he was sent back to Sun Quan with a stubborn refusal, one which 'came directly from Lord Liu', no less! ...*Aiee!*"

"So what do we do?" Ma Su wondered.

"I'm afraid that 'we' can't do anything," Kongming grumbled. "I'll go and speak to Lord Liu... Wu are not fighting Cao Cao at the moment, so Sun Quan could easily put the necessary elements together to take Jing Province back by force."

"It will be no trouble to repel Eastern Wu, will it, not now we have such a large army...?" Ma Su said surely.

"When Lord Liu took this province," Kongming said ominously, "he inherited its officials, and they now form a large part of the Yi court. Jian Yong, Mi Zhu and I are really leading a 'pre-Yi' faction at court, while Wu Yi, Li Yan, Dong He, Huang Quan, Qin Mi, Peng Yang and others are either neutral, wavering, or very much a 'Yi' faction that we are already in contention with. I don't know their true motivations – especially Peng Yang's, which I have repeatedly warned Lord Liu of – but they might advise against pre-emptive action, and he might agree."

"But I thought that you got on well with Dong He," Ma Su protested.

"Yes, but friendly debate and court matters are not the same thing!" Kongming replied desperately. "Surely, Youchang, you are aware of the universal belief that two men can tear one-another to pieces, discredit each other, ruin each other's lives while working in contention... but that outside of business, they can happily drink together as friends, and that it is not – as it should be – considered insanity...?"

"...Yes," Ma Su said seriously, "I am aware... I didn't think it applied to men such as you and Dong He, that's all. I thought it more a warlord's weakness."

"*Ayah*," Kongming exclaimed, "it applies *even more so* to the likes of us! I considered Zhou Gongjin a righteous man, and would have gladly whiled away summer evenings drinking wine and discussing the affairs of the time with him! But we schemed to destroy each other, and if not each other, each other's lords!"

"...So what will you do, then...?" Ma Su asked. "My brother will want some help, and I for one cannot bear to think of losing Jing or anyone in it."

"I'll hurry to see Lord Liu now," Kongming decided. "The sooner we act... I pray it is not already too late."

＊＊＊＊＊＊＊＊＊＊＊＊

## 79

Unfortunately, by the time that Ma Liang's urgent despatch had reached the remote Yi provincial capital, Chengdu, it was already too late to prevent the forces of Wu from taking action. Before Lu Su had even spoken to Ma Liang, he and his assistant Lü Meng had already started to move their forces west, away from the Hefei border region, and consolidate them around Jing's eastern and southern borders. Soon enough, reports of attacks on 3 of the 4 thinly defended southern counties – Lingling, Guiyang and Changsha – were reported to Guan Yu in Jiangling, with the Wu forces across those counties numbering around 20,000, and led by Lü Meng and Ling Tong.

**"D'AAAGH! How DARE THEY???"** Guan Yu screamed as the messengers carrying the news cowered reflexively.

"They're lost…!" Ma Liang bleated. "I cannot believe they mustered so quickly… unless they were *ready*, they *knew* we'd refuse, and… … …wait, that doesn't matter. Lord Guan, we must send a messenger to Chengdu immediately."

"My brother has informed me that Lord Liu is already sending relief forces," Mi Fang declared. "They won't get here in time to stop us losing the counties, but they'll arrive in time to prevent them taking Jiangling."

"I have a few thousand troops here," Guan Yu said angrily. "I will not let these underhanded Wu rats sneak in and take my brother's lands! They're thinly spread… let's attack them group by group, and show them how real men fight!"

"Lord Guan, our troops are too few in number," Ma Liang protested. "And besides all that, you want to take what little protection Jiangling has and throw it at Wu like throwing an egg against a rock…?"

"Mi Fang and Shi Ren can hold Jiangling, as Cao Ren held it seven years ago!" Guan Yu countered. "Are they not a match for the likes of Cao Ren?"

"Cao Ren had a hundred thousand men behind him," Ma Liang protested. "All that is behind Jiangling now is the Duke of Wei, with four hundred thousand men, poised to strike at the first sign of weakness and leave neither side with Jing. Besides… can we say that they won't guess you'll try and retaliate…?"

Guan Yu tensed, and screamed with frustration.

Ma Liang was proved right: forces in excess of 10,000 men blockaded the River Han and the Yangtze, preventing Guan Yu from moving to rescue the counties.

"Sun Quan, the rebel!" Liu Bei cried with anger as he led a force of 40,000 men to rescue his stake in Jing Province. An advance army of 10,000 sped to Jiangling by way of the Yangtze River to reinforce the beleaguered city.

"Our army has numerous officers and valiant generals now, Lord Liu, enough to match anything that Sun Quan can throw at us," Fa Zheng – who was now the chief military adviser – said reassuringly. "We can easily repel them, even if the fighting becomes unfettered and costly. But Kongming was right, we need to try and find a diplomatic solution to this."

"Sun Quan stole my wife, 'loans' me my own family's lands, and now he threatens my brother Yunchang," Liu Bei growled. "He will see no diplomacy from me, the wretched, covetous...!"

Kongming, meanwhile, was still in Chengdu, far from the action taking place in his old homeland of Jing to the east. He spent most days overseeing administration with his protégé, Ma Liang's brother Ma Su, and a group of trusted new recruits.
"Why did Lord Liu take Fa Zheng, and not you...?" Ma Su wondered.
"Fa Xiaozhi is a better overall strategist than I ever will be, Youchang," Kongming conceded. "The lord has taken the more capable man for the battlefield... I, on the other hand, have all of the affairs of state to coordinate... and I have to watch all of the despatches personally, just in case some important piece of news from the north arrives that changes our entire approach to things."
"You don't have to deal with everything yourself, Master Zhuge," Ma Su insisted.
"Youchang," Kongming chuckled, "your brother and I are sworn brothers, and our families are as one. ...Call me Kongming."
"My apologies," Ma Su said awkwardly. "Since you were and are my mentor in affairs of state and strategic warfare, it-"
"Well, I say nay," Kongming insisted. "And I know what you were going to say... 'Get some rest'. Well, I would love to, but with nothing stable, I can hardly afford to be idle, can I...?"
"Kongming," Ma Su pleaded, "when there was only a handful of worthy men to delegate responsibility to, I would have agreed... but *now*...!"
"...Perhaps you're right," Kongming sighed. "...Thank you, Youchang."
"Go home," Ma Su suggested. "It's already late... and Yi is not as mild on the senses as Jing was. The weather and the altitude... are quite unbearable, at times."
"Agreed," Kongming said with a laugh. "I have barely been home since my lady wife arrived here... yes, you're right."
Kongming and Ma Su parted ways, and Kongming went home.

Within no real time frame at all, Lingling, Changsha and Guiyang fell under Wu control, and those that did not wish to stay and be part of Eastern Wu fled north to Wuling County or Jiangling. Not long after that, the Yi advance force arrived to bolster Jiangling and Yiling, and Guan Yu began his push back, repelling Lu Su and the pirate general Gan Ning on land and water.
"*Aiee*," Lu Su exclaimed as he led the Wu retreat from Jiangling. "Liu Bei's reactions... or rather Zhuge Kongming and Fa Zheng's reactions... were far too quick. Now Guan Yu is in a position to take the counties back, and so quickly...!"
"So we'll not get Yiling back then," Gan Ning supposed. "Pisses me off, that, given how hard I fought t'win the bloody place."
"...Uh... they *surrendered*...?" Lu Su chuckled. "...*Immediately*...?"

"I meant *after*, boss," Gan Ning insisted. "But then, I s'pose that weren't really a whole lot o' work neither. ...Look, gimme a team o' horsemen an' I'll turn this around for us. I'll ride round the side o' Jiangling, scale the walls, and before he even knows it, I'll have shoved a spear up Guan Yu's rosy red backside!"

"No! ...No... I'll have to find a diplomatic solution," Lu Su sighed miserably. "I'll talk to Guan Yu... see if we can't get them to see sense."

"...Don't see it meself," Gan Ning admitted. "Guan's a noble bandit at heart, like I'm a noble pirate... he'll not give back what he holds for a friend in all good faith."

"I have to *try*," Lu Su insisted. "If we can't sort this mess out by the time Liu Bei gets here... it'll be a massacre."

Before Guan Yu could march south and engage Lü Meng and Ling Tong, Lu Su arranged a meeting with him. The two were armed with swords; they met in an open space in front of a Buddhist temple, and remained some distance apart.

"I'm impressed," Guan Yu admitted. "I thought you were a craven, untalented pedant... but you have played this well, Chief Commander."

"I had a good mentor," Lu Su replied coldly, "and plenty of cause to learn quickly."

"So what do you want to say...?" Guan Yu asked plainly.

"Please, see sense," Lu Su implored. "Guan Yunchang, surely a man such as you can see that ours is the higher moral position in this matter...?"

"Quite the opposite," Guan Yu retorted, "which, as a man of supposed virtue, I thought that you would see."

"If we fight, Yunchang, we'll lose thousands of men, and place ourselves at the mercy of the Duke of Wei," Lu Su challenged.

"Then why," Guan Yu countered, "did you attack us without provocation...?"

**"This is OUR TERRITORY!"** Lu Su shouted angrily.

"By whose authority...?" Guan Yu chortled. "The Han court saw this land as belonging to Liu Biao's kin... my lord, Liu Xuande, is Liu Biao's kin. Your predecessor, Zhou Yu, took this place... you've taken it again, by violent force and subterfuge, and neither time were you right!"

"What we discuss now is not righteousness, but natural law!" Lu Su countered. "It is only right that the strongest and worthiest rule this region!"

"But I thought you said you had the moral high ground," Guan Yu said with a contemptuous smirk. "Why do you now retreat to the defence of 'natural law'...?"

"...*Aiee!*" Lu Su exclaimed. "We are right on *both counts*! Liu Biao owed us land as reparation for the death of the lord's father! We rescued this place from Cao Cao! We saved Liu Bei's life at Red Cliffs, therefore *he* owes us reparation! And don't bother telling me he doesn't, he uses the same reasoning when he says he must help Ma Chao take Liang Province! Why can he then not return this place to us as thanks???"

"It is not my lord's to give," Guan Yu said calmly. "The land of Jing desires autonomy from Cao Cao and Sun Quan… the people flocked to Lord Liu because he gives them what they want. The counties you just seized surrendered to us willingly. Lands and men are not gifts… if your lord wants 'reparation', then he should ask for silk and gold, not men's lives."

"And Ma Chao's desire to take Liang…?" Lu Su challenged.

"As far as I am aware," Guan Yu said with a laugh, "his uprising was very popular, and failed only because of the same sort of duplicity and mistrust that you now bring to the table. But Liang really is none of my business… and you have no right to defend a hypocrite with comparisons."

"*You*…!" Lu Su exclaimed.

"Be *gone*, Lu Su," Guan Yu chuckled. "Your arguments are weak and baseless, and I have no further interest in talking to you. We'll meet again on the battlefield… and there, little man, you are not my equal in the slightest."

"…**AIEE!**" Lu Su exclaimed with tears of rage in his eyes: he turned and walked away, without bothering to guard against an attack. Guan Yu, meanwhile, smirked, and watched Wu's Chief Commander walk away silently.

"Brother Yunchang," Liu Bei hailed as he arrived in Jiangling.

"Elder Brother," Guan Yu replied. "I've been despatching the reinforcements you sent me… I want to go south personally, and face this 'Lü Meng' and 'Ling Tong' that dare come here and seize our hard-won counties."

"Take another twenty thousand men and keep the pressure on Lu Su and Gan Ning, they're the real threat since they covet Jiangling and Yiling," Liu Bei ordered. "I will go to Gong'an, and command the forces from there. We'll get the counties back, even if it means killing every man in Jiangdong."

Ma Liang shuddered at the proclamation.

But while Liu Bei was mobilising his troops in Jing, Cao Cao was travelling west by river, toward the Hanzhong border. At his sides were two of his advisers: on one side, a regal man in an elaborately decorated blue robe stood calmly and stared at the scenery, while on the other side, a stony-faced man in plain brown robes stood and stared at the sky.

"Any reports as yet, Ziyang…?" Cao Cao asked as he stroked his long, grey beard.

"No, my lord," the man in blue robes – Liu Ye – replied.

"…Do either of you have any thoughts…?" Cao Cao prompted.

"Not as yet, my lord," Liu Ye replied. "I think we have discussed everything relevant already."

"…Zhongda…?" Cao Cao prompted as he stared at the brown-robed man, who was still staring thoughtfully at the sky. That man was Sima Yi.

"…I wonder if the newly-conquered Yi Province will react in any way to your actions," Sima Yi replied as he turned his gaze to his lord. "After all, my lord, Hanzhong is the gateway to Yi… Liu Bei has fought long and hard for that place, so will he not want to do everything he can to keep it…?"

"It's only newly won, Zhongda, and Liu Bei is a crafty owl that makes as many enemies as he makes friends," Liu Ye suggested. "Will he keep it from his newly-defeated subjects...?"

"...I am not interested in the battles to come," Cao Cao sighed. "Liu Bei is in Jing, scrapping with Sun Quan over which one will have the honour of kneeling before me in two years' time, and tendering the seals of office. What concerns me is the battle now in front of us... we have much to be worried about since we are facing barbarian tribes and a popular cult, all of which have mountain barriers and hideouts that will be hard to besiege."

"The Di people are our first concern," Sima Yi suggested. "Advance on them from the city of Chen Cang, and then remove the threat of the barbarians as a priority, else we will be continually harassed from the west. Once Zhang Lu is without their help, he will retreat southward, and do all he can to hold the region around Yang Ping Pass... it will be difficult to defeat him, yes, but alone, he'll succumb eventually, especially since he cannot go to Yi for help... not with Ma Chao stationed near to the border, and the memory of his inconstancy still raw."

"I concur," Liu Ye said with a smile.

"Very good!" Cao Cao praised. "Soon I'll have one less enemy. Let Sun Quan and Liu Bei fight it out... the only winner will be me!"

Cao Cao's forces arrived at Chen Cang, a strategically important city near the Hanzhong border. From there, he launched an attack into the mountains and forced the Di tribe to retreat; and, with advice from Sima Yi and Liu Ye, Cao Cao was able to drive a wedge between the tribal leaders, who were being led by Ma Chao's former ally, the Qiang leader Han Sui. Han Sui fought unsuccessfully against the advancing Xiahou Yuan, and not long after that – after a brief time contemplating joining Ma Chao in Yi – Han Sui's severed head arrived at Cao Cao's main camp. The tribal support for Zhang Lu disintegrated, and he fled to Yang Ping Pass, where he would make his final, desperate stand against the Duke of Wei.

* * * * * * * * * * * *

## 80

Cao Cao marched mercilessly on Hanzhong, intent on taking the region from its court-appointed governor, Zhang Lu, with whatever force was necessary. Zhang Lu had gone through Yang Ping Pass and set up a staunch defence in the Hanzhong capital, Nanzheng. His brother, Zhang Wei, fortified the region around the pass and held it successfully, but only for a while. Cao Cao's forces eventually broke through, killed Zhang Wei, and advanced on Nanzheng with full fury. Sensing imminent defeat and seeing the lack of mercy shown to his brother, Zhang Lu fled to Bazhong, a fortress city south of Nanzheng. Cao Cao arrived in Nanzheng City to the sound of triumphant chants from his troops, and occupied Zhang Lu's palatial mansion.

A thorough search of the mansion and the surrounding capital was carried out: at the end of that search, a captain entered Cao Cao's court to relay a surprising piece of news.

"**REPORT!**" the captain began. "**The retreating forces of Zhang Lu have not harmed the crops, taken valuable goods, or damaged anything!**"

"Oh...?" Cao Cao said with disbelief.

The captain added, "**Zhang Lu has apparently asked that the Duke of Wei and Prime Minister of the Han be told, regarding all of the resources and treasures of Hanzhong: 'These things belong to the country, not to me'.**"

"...A magnanimous man, indeed," Liu Ye praised.

"This should not go unrewarded," Sima Yi suggested. "My lord, we should see if he will accept terms of surrender..."

"That coincides exactly with my own thinking!" Cao Cao lauded. "Very good, very good! Send a messenger to Bazhong... we will talk with this upstanding man!"

The news of the developing events was not received well in the Yi capital of Chengdu, where the officials held court almost continuously once there were two dangerously close battle fronts in the north and east.

"...This is bad," Kongming said worriedly as he read the latest reports on the situations in Jing and Hanzhong. "Our lord wears down our forces fighting our only ally, while Cao Cao decimates the tribes and forces Zhang Lu into retreat."

"Where is Zhang Lu now...?" Huang Quan asked.

"...His capital, Nanzheng, according to the latest despatch, but this is several days old, at least," Kongming fretted. "Cao Cao is too close for comfort... he's on our border, and Lord Liu is in Jing...!"

"Then call him back, Kongming," Dong He urged.

"It isn't as simple as that, Youzai," Kongming despaired. "If he returns, Sun Quan will seize Wuling, and then Jiangling, and then Yiling... and we cannot afford that right now. No, there has to be a compromise... ... ...I have it. I'll write to Lord Liu, Fa Zheng, and Ma Jichang..."

In Bazhong, Zhang Lu made his decision to surrender, based on Cao Cao's generous terms. He was received in his former capital by Cao Cao, who promised him the title of a marquis: although he would be a house prisoner, he would live out his remaining days comfortably. In a chilling coda to his relationship with Ma Chao, Zhang Lu was given the responsibility of final disposition regarding Ma Chao's one remaining son, whom Cao Cao had kept alive during his purge of the Ma family members stationed within the imperial court: Zhang Lu had the youth executed.

"That went extremely well!" Cao Cao said as he addressed his vassals in the Nanzheng court. "Now, I must return to the capital."
"*What*???" Liu Ye said rudely. "My lord, you cannot-"
"I agree with Ziyang that this is an opportunity that is too good to pass up," Sima Yi declared. "The Yi forces are currently engaged in a bitter struggle with Eastern Wu, far from this place... if we move now, Liu Bei will be homeless once again, and Yi will be ours to govern once again. Jing will be hard to retake without it, and once Liu Bei returns-"
"You are all so hungry!" Cao Cao chuckled: his words were met with universal disbelief. "We have swallowed Liang, Hanzhong, Bing, and northern Jing... what rush is there to devour Yi?"
"My lord," Liu Ye protested, "I really think that you should-"
"Xiahou Yuan, Zhang He, and Xu Huang shall guard the strategic points... Du Xi shall remain here in Nanzheng and oversee the administration," Cao Cao insisted calmly. "I have my reasons... Ziyang, Zhongda, you should both be more aware than most, so I despair at your snivelling. We will depart in all haste."
"...Very well, my lord," Sima Yi conceded. "Perhaps patience is the virtue needed to win the day."

Kongming's letters to Liu Bei, Fa Zheng and Ma Liang had already left Chengdu when the news of the surrender of Zhang Lu reached the court.
"...But Cao Cao *retreats*," Kongming noted as he absorbed the news relayed by the messenger from Hanzhong.
"A ruse, perhaps...?" Zhang Junsi wondered.
"Hopefully not," Kongming replied. "If it is, we're in trouble, because Lord Liu cannot possibly get back from Jing in time, even if Sun Quan agreed to the border treaty I've composed with Yi Ji."
"We have Zhang Fei, Wei Yan and Ma Chao guarding the north," Yi Ji pointed out optimistically. "And Ma Chao alone will fight with the strength of a thousand men, to avenge his family, if Cao Cao attacks us."
"All the same," Kongming said, "that treaty *has to work*."

Ma Liang was once again sent to Chaisang for an urgent meeting with Sun Quan.
"...It is nice to see you again, Jichang," Sun Quan said politely as Ma Liang entered his busy court.
"What brings *you* here...?" Zhang Zhao jeered.
"We'll be speaking publicly today, Ma Jichang," Sun Quan declared, "so state your case, and state it quickly."
"My lord desires a truce," Ma Liang revealed to an angry yet self-satisfied Wu court.

"Is that so…?" Zhang Zhao snickered. "Why should *we*…?"

"Because Cao Cao threatens us both, and benefits greatly from our division," Ma Liang countered. "I… I see that Lu Zijing is not here."

"He is still at the front, fighting Guan Yu," Zhang Zhao explained with hostility. "Indeed, we're at war, so envoys are a little bit late in coming… my lord, send this man back without his head!"

"I'll have no harm inflicted on him," Sun Quan insisted. "He is doing his job… and very well, and very bravely, too. Jichang, you did not come here to propose a truce so that he can retreat from Jing because Cao Cao threatens Hanzhong. You came here to offer more than that, I think, because Changsha, Guiyang and Lingling are now ours, as they should be, and that cannot and will not change."

"Exactly his thoughts," Ma Liang replied cautiously, "but only to a certain degree."

"How dare you come here negotiating???" Zhang Zhao said angrily.

"With all due respect," Ma Liang said, "my lord's army now equals yours: and we could, I think, put up some measure of defiance, and seriously deplete both sides needlessly, while Cao Cao does as he pleases. But this has all grown out of a misunderstanding that I have been sent here to put right."

"…Go on," Sun Quan insisted: he gestured that his advisers should be silent.

"My lord does not want an argument," Ma Liang promised. "He is angry because you threatened Guan Yunchang's safety in Jiangling, and my lord prides his vassals more than land or power. Kongming shares his anger, because of our brotherhood… yet this has all become needlessly personal.

"The proposition is this: my lord regains Lingling, *temporarily*, until Yi is completely stabilised, all those that do not wish to serve Wu are relocated peacefully, and Hanzhong is no longer under threat from Cao Cao. All previous talk of the true ownership of the Jiangxia Prefecture is discarded, and from now on, the general opinion and legal standpoint will be that it is rightly gained territory of Eastern Wu."

Sun Quan leaned forward noticeably, and absorbed the words with delight and thinly-veiled disbelief.

"Further to that, Changsha and Guiyang counties – once all voluntary refugees are safely rehoused in neighbouring territories such as Lingling and Wuling – will fall under your unchallenged jurisdiction," Ma Liang concluded, "and we will set a new border along the River Xiang."

There were murmurings amongst the officials, but no real clarity.

"…Zibu…?" Sun Quan prompted excitedly as he looked at his faithful adviser on home affairs, Zhang Zhao.

"But giving them back Lingling after…!" Lü Fan protested: Zhang Zhao gestured that his fellow official should be silent, and hummed thoughtfully.

"I reluctantly admit that to be an agreeable *short-term* solution," Zhang Zhao replied. "If all others agree, then… well, it *does* stop us fighting and losing lives."

"If you think it amicable... I won't argue," Lü Fan said miserably. "After all, we will get Lingling back *eventually*... along with the rest... that much is explicit."

"It is," Ma Liang promised.

"...Fine," Sun Quan agreed with sudden hesitation. "But... I suspect that such an agreeable-sounding deal doesn't end there."

"You would be right," Ma Liang replied. "My lord hopes that you see the benefits of our continued military cooperation, and..."

"Liu Bei desires us to launch an attack on Hefei again, to divide Cao's forces," Zhuge Jin supposed. "My lord, it would serve both of our nations well."

"...Fine," Sun Quan agreed further. "I will immediately request that Chief Commander Lu Su withdraws his forces and places them back in Lukou, pending an attack on Hefei that I will lead personally."

"My lord...!" Zhang Zhao protested.

"...Liu Bei is nearly sixty, and he commands his forces from the front," Sun Quan said bravely. "Cao Cao, too, commands his forces in person, and carries a sword, and he exceeds sixty by many a year... so am I a lesser man...?"

"All the same," Ma Liang said courteously, "take care of yourself, Lord Sun... for regardless the current and future differences between our nations, I would not like to see you come to harm."

Sun Quan smiled gratefully, and gestured that Ma Liang should be safely escorted back to Jing. Both sides kept to their words, and the tension was diffused.

"And now that the threat of violence in Jing is temporarily passed," Kongming said sadly as he sat with Yueying in their new home in Chengdu, "we will see another chapter of violence take its place. While Sun Quan fights a bitter war of attrition against the fearsome Zhang Liao at Hefei... we might be facing the Duke of Wei himself, and after seven years, Lord Liu and Cao Cao will both be anxious to avenge their historical defeats and bring matters to a close."

"A final battle between Cao Cao and Liu Bei, I suppose," Yueying said quietly.

"It may well be so, although reports suggest that his return to his capital was genuine," Kongming sighed. "...I wish I was accompanying Lord Liu on this expedition, since it is a critical hour... but I must guard Chengdu. I should say, also, that things have changed drastically. The last time we fought Cao Cao, I recommended – nay, *engineered* – that he lived to provide a needed alternate target for Zhou Yu to pit his unrivalled skill and formidable forces against. This time, I think, we should try and kill Cao Cao after we seize Hanzhong, because then, since we'll be stronger than Sun Quan this time... *then*, it can end."

************

## 81

With Sun Quan temporarily placated by the new border treaty, the crisis in Jing was resolved, but Liu Bei returned to Yi Province in a subdued mood. He called for a meeting as soon as he was settled within the city walls of his capital, Chengdu.

"…This feels like a bitter defeat after a great victory," Liu Bei admitted: some of Liu Zhang's former vassals were visibly irritated at his words, but they remained silent, and allowed Liu Bei to continue. "Now that I have returned… having been forced to give away even more of my late kinsman Liu Biao's domains to that thieving rat, Sun Quan… I understand from reports received during my retreat that Cao Cao has left Hanzhong, and that he has no intention of attacking us at the moment."

"My lord," Kongming protested, "we had no way of knowing whether the Duke of Wei was playing one of his cunning tricks. We now understand – from speaking with minor court vassals from Hanzhong that have since fled to Yi – that we are to consider ourselves lucky. Cao Cao's advisers, Liu Ye and Sima Yi, advised an immediate attack on Yi, but Cao adamantly refused to hear them out."

"…We have much to fear from those men," Fa Zheng suggested. "It will be a dark day indeed when their advice is heeded."

"Instead," Jian Yong joked, "it's just another two to add to the list of men whose sound advice Cao Cao has ignored. I guess he'll never learn."

"Is this a time for joking, Mister Jian…?" the official Qin Mi scolded.

"Calm down…!" Jian Yong scoffed. "Stop being such a pedant."

"*You*…!" Qin Mi seethed.

"Now, now," Liu Bei implored. "Xianhe, for once I agree. Mister Qi, forgive my friend this one time for his indifferent attitude. We should be thankful that their advice was ignored, since I was too far away to act, and would have lost both Jing and Yi… I have the officials to thank for formulating a solution. My regrets about Jing are selfish… forgive me."

"My lord, when Cao Cao is defeated, we can wrest the counties back from the faithless lord of Wu," Fa Zheng said encouragingly. "For now, let us bear the insult with our heads held high."

"It isn't like we've not been in worse situations," Jian Yong chuckled. "We didn't have anything at all fifteen years ago… compared to begging scraps off of the likes of Yuan Shao and Liu Biao, and sharing yard space with Lü Bu, this is pretty good, Xuande, and we should-"

"You *dare*…!" Qin Mi exclaimed.

"Mister Qin," Liu Bei interrupted, "my friend is just being a little more familiar than court protocol usually permits… forgive him this second time. …Xianhe, please try and show a little more professionalism at court, mm…? It isn't like you don't know how, is it…?"

"True," Jian Yong sighed. "Guess I'm just enjoying feeling like I'm at home... but to return to the point, I agree that we shouldn't be too bothered about losing face with Sun Quan. The dupe marriage, the 'loaning' to us of our own land, the deceit, and worst of all in my mind, the murder of our allies and the attempts to steal you away from your cause... we'll have our revenge eventually, but right now, we have to deal with Cao Cao. The real question is, really, 'Why did he *not* invade'...?"

"In an attempt to quash the power the Celestial Masters have in Hanzhong, Cao Cao has expatriated half of the populace to surrounding territories," Fa Zheng noted. "I think the answer is simple... he fears the instability of the place, and worries that an attempt on Yi Province could trigger a sympathetic insurrection. He cannot move against us until the region is stabilised, and that will take time."

"So while Liu Ye and Sima Yi appeared to be correct on the surface," Kongming supposed, "they were wrong when examining the situation in detail... or at least, that's how Cao Cao saw it. After all, he blames his failure at Red Cliffs not on his own ignorance, or his failure to heed the advice of Jia Xu and Cheng Yu... he blames his not being convinced to pacify Jing first, and win the populace over."

"Which was part of Jia Xu's ignored advice," Jian Yong snickered. "The man really can't handle losing. It's always everyone else's fault."

"We must watch events carefully," Liu Bei declared. "If Cao Cao now rules Hanzhong, generals Huo Jun and Meng Da, stationed at Jiameng Pass... will be in serious danger."

"We're monitoring the situation closely," Kongming promised. "For the moment, I suspect that Cao Cao has returned to the capital to collect another title... surely the rumour that he intends to be made 'King of Wei' has not passed you all by...?"

"...That heinous...!" Liu Bei growled.

"What a pity that Xun You, nephew of the Xun Yu that opposed the dukedom, was not observant of the past," Kongming sighed. "He opposed the kingship, and was asked if he wished to be like his uncle..."

"Oops," Jian Yong chuckled.

"So he is now rebuked...?" Liu Bei supposed.

"No, he is now *dead*," Kongming replied with a morbid laugh. "Truly, can there be a man alive that does not suspect foul play...?"

"...*Aiee*," Fa Zheng exclaimed. "There will be no men of talent left in the north."

"The last time Cao received a title, he was too busy enjoying the pomp and ceremony to be bothered with anything else," Kongming explained. "So we may have a year or more before he'll act. In addition, we have to remember that Sun Quan is besieging Hefei Castle at the moment... that will be concerning him."

"Let's hope that continues," Liu Bei declared. "...Just please... keep me informed."

Months passed, and Liu Bei's forces quietly steeled themselves for what many felt would be a purely defensive stance.

"…Sun Quan isn't going to like it," Ma Su sighed as he sat in Kongming's home one evening, drinking tea. "That border treaty my brother took to him clearly stated that we were supposed to aid each other on a simultaneous strike, a pincer attack on Cao Cao from two directions. All we've done so far is pontificate."

"Youchang," Kongming scolded as he fanned himself slowly, "don't be so rash. Of course it looks like were reneging on our agreement. But we are not ready, and we can't strike at thin air. We need a target, and motivation to act."

"So we're waiting to be invaded then…?" Ma Su retorted as Yueying entered the room and sat next to Kongming silently.

"…If that's how it needs to be," Kongming admitted. "We don't know what's going to happen in Hefei… if they were to retreat, we'd be marching straight into the maw of the four-hundred-thousand-strong horde. Even though our ranks are bolstered with the men of Yi now, we're woefully outnumbered and we lack resources, especially since we just fought an expensive war with Liu Zhang."

"But if they attacked…!" Ma Su protested.

"Topographical advantage is everything," Kongming replied. "We hold a lot of high ground here in Yi… high ground is *almost* always a huge advantage. Remember how well the Yi forces held out against us… and we outnumbered them by two-to-one. If Cao Cao came here, we would be outnumbered by up to four-to-one, yes, but we would be on favourable defensive terrain… which would make Cao Ren holding Jiangling look like an easy victory for Zhou Yu. If we attack… well, Hanzhong is mountainous, and they hold the high ground."

"…I understand," Ma Su said thoughtfully.

"Cao Cao is coming eventually, though, isn't he…?" Yueying supposed.

"Oh, I'd think so," Kongming chuckled. "Once he's 'King of Wei'… then, and only then, will he march. The real question to be asked is, 'Who will he march on first… Wu, or Yi'…?"

"…Wu, surely," Ma Su said with conviction.

"…Not so," Kongming replied with a slight hint of disappointment in his tone. "I imagine that, after Red Cliffs and Ruxukou, Cao Cao has no desire to be humiliated by Sun Quan's use of the Great River as a barrier again.

"If I were Cao Cao… I would want to strike *us* first, retake Yi as a resource base, and use that to attack Nan Prefecture… Zhang Liao and Xiahou Dun could provide a threat from the east, but the real power lies in an attack from the west, from Jing… that's why Sun Quan does not want us to have the province, in case we turn on him and let Cao Cao through Jiangling. Further to that, Wu would not assist us if we were in serious trouble… they'd just look at it as an opportunity to get Jing back, and maybe a part of Yi as well. But we would be obligated to aid Wu in the opposite case… so of course we would be the first target."

"…I understand," Ma Su said again.

"If I am completely honest, I advocate action, but Lord Liu is hesitating," Kongming sighed. "He fears another attack from Wu, he fears the army of nearly half-a-million men that Cao Cao has… fortunately, Fa Xiaozhi agrees with me… which means that we will eventually act."

"*Ayah*," Ma Su exclaimed. "Why does everything revolve around whether Fa Zheng agrees with it or not these days...?"

"As much as I find it... discomforting," Kongming replied, "at least he is a man who should be listened to. ...But to answer your question, Lord Liu listens to him because he got us Yi Province... which takes precedence over securing an alliance with Sun Quan eight years ago. Lord Liu recently married Wu Yi's sister for the same reason... to forge strong alliances with his new vassals, and honour them."

"But does it not anger you that you have to argue with him vainly, and Fa Zheng can simply make a gentle suggestion and be heard...?" Ma Su asked pointedly.

"...What's the point...?" Kongming chuckled casually. "I am highly trusted... a certain amount of an adviser's role is to convince as well as advise, and I do not currently have the power to convince, even though I hold immense power. I am content to guard Chengdu, and share the burden of responsibility with worthy men like Dong He, Zhang Yi and Fa Zheng: for once, I do not feel like the only man that is trying to do my job properly. I am getting rest, sleep, and days away from work to spend at home with my wife: why embroil myself in a row when the proper outcome will be obtained by another...?"

"...Put that way," Ma Su sighed, "I can see your ease with the situation. ...I should be going, since my own wife will be wondering where I am."

"Off you go," Kongming chuckled warmly. "See you tomorrow at work, Youchang... and please, don't concern yourself with matters like that anymore."

Ma Su got to his feet, smiled pleasantly, bowed to Kongming and Yueying, and left the house. Kongming put his fan to one side and exhaled noisily.

"...Do you think this will last...?" Yueying asked sombrely.

"We have lost Mister Sun and Young Phoenix," Kongming replied, "so I do not underestimate the cruelty of the fates. If it is at all possible to lose everyone else... so that I am left alone to be burdened with it all... well, I don't rule it out."

"...Do you think we will always be childless...?" Yueying asked with sudden honesty and painful emotion.

"...I might think about talking to Jin about adopting Qiao, as he suggested all those years ago," Kongming said thoughtfully. "I know it isn't the same, but... well, it's something."

"...Yes," Yueying said miserably.

"Now isn't the time, not with the threat of war on two fronts," Kongming continued with a great pain in his voice. "But maybe, once this is over..."

"...Yes," Yueying said again, her voice cracking under immense emotional strain.

They sat in silence for several hours after that, thinking their own tormented thoughts.

************

## 82

An urgent report brought every official of importance to the Chengdu court.

"The Ba region, which is dangerously close to us, is currently being evacuated and repopulated under supervision of the Wei general, Zhang He," Kongming explained.

"He was one of the generals that destroyed Ma Chao's forces," Fa Zheng noted worriedly. "Is he also the Zhang He that defended Cao Cao's retreat at Red Cliffs...?"

"Yes, he is," Kongming confirmed.

"What of Huo Jun and Meng Da...?" Huang Quan asked.

"...That's... what the most urgent part of the report was," Kongming admitted. "It appears that – against all advice that Huo Jun proffered – General Meng Da decided to attack Zhang He rather than maintain a tight defence... he was routed."

"Is... is he dead...?" Fa Zheng asked nervously.

"No," Kongming replied coldly. "But his incompetence has cost us dearly. Huo Jun was injured whilst rescuing him... Meng Da is doing what he can to hold the pass but he'll probably lose it. Further to that, of course, is Zhang He's movements since then... he's advanced to Dangqu."

"Dangqu???" Liu Bei exclaimed: the officials were very nervous.

"We can't allow him to stay there," Jian Yong insisted. "That's a choke point of Yi Province... right between Chengdu and the border with Jing Province."

"That's an act of aggression," Huang Quan suggested. "Doesn't that force an immediate response from us...?"

"Zhang Yide has taken an army of twenty thousand to stop him," Kongming reported, "and push Cao Cao's forces back as far as Nanzheng."

"Can he manage that alone...?" Jian Yong wondered.

"Let's hope so," Liu Bei replied uneasily. "Keep me informed of Yide's status... I want to know anything the moment it is known. Yunchang, Yide, Xianhe and I lived in the same house, slept in the same room and ate at the same table in our early days... we're brothers, all of us, by choice, and his life is as precious to me as any with whom I share a bloodline."

"I vow that I shall," Kongming declared.

Zhang Fei, meanwhile, had begun his advance on the Ba region, but he had been intercepted by Zhang He, who had led an army to Dangqu, a city located halfway between Chengdu and White Emperor City geographically.

"This man Zhang He... he comes dangerously close to our domain," one of Zhang Fei's generals, Fan Qiang, noted worriedly. "Isn't he the former champion of Yuan Shao that defended Cao Cao's rear guard as he escaped the fires at Red Cliffs...?"

"I'm Zhang Fei, I stopped Cao's million-man horde at Steep-slope with a roar," Zhang Fei replied. "I don't care who this idiot is."

"So shall we attack...?" another general, Zhang Da, asked.

"I say we should," Zhang Fei's military adviser for the mission, General Fu Rong, suggested. "They don't drastically outnumber us, and we match him in valour."

"Good enough for me," Zhang Fei replied. **"FORWARD!"**

On the morning that his army arrived at Dangqu City, Zhang Fei rode up to the walls and bellowed, **"I AM ZHANG YIDE OF YAN! WHERE IS ZHANG HE...?"**
"...So this is the bridge-guarding champion of Steep-slope, Zhang Fei, after all these years," Zhang He chuckled as he looked down at his adversary from atop the walls. "Seeing the like of him still going strong, it's... nostalgic."
"Will we be challenging?" a captain asked.
"Not yet," Zhang He replied. "Let him burn himself out shouting."

Sunset came, but Zhang Fei had not relented.
"...*Ayah*," Zhang He sighed. "This man has the energy of a god."
**"COME DOWN, ZHANG HE, AND FIGHT A HUNDRED ROUNDS WITH ME!"** Zhang Fei shouted. **"WHAT'S THE MATTER? COME AND FIGHT ZHANG YIDE OF YAN!"**
"...I will, if only to *shut him up*," Zhang He complained. "Get me my armour."
        Zhang He rode out of the city to challenge Zhang Fei.
**"Zhang Fei!"** Zhang He challenged. **"Here I am!"**
**"About bloody time!"** Zhang Fei boomed. **"Were you having trouble finding your sword, or maybe your courage...?"**
Zhang He charged: they clashed more than a hundred-and-fifty times before the natural light became too poor to continue. Zhang He was noticeably concerned, and started to take a more defensive stance.
**"WHAT'S THE MATTER?"** Zhang Fei taunted. **"...TIRED...?"**
**"...Will NOTHING shut you up???"** Zhang He shouted angrily: he resumed his attacks, even though it would soon be impossible to fight without torchlights.
**"I'm impressed,"** Zhang Fei admitted during one clash of weapons. **"You're as good as they say."**
**"I'll prove it by taking your head as a prize for the Duke of Wei!"** Zhang He retorted angrily. **"You won't stop our march!"**
**"March all you want,"** Zhang Fei said with a laugh, **"so long as it's back to where you came from!"**
Zhang Fei broke off his attack suddenly, and rode back to his line; at that point, just as Zhang He supposed something might be afoot, forces led by Fan Qiang and Zhang Da rushed the city, throwing Zhang He's troops into confusion.
**"RETREAT, RETREAT!"** Zhang He pleaded: his forces fled in all directions, while Zhang He himself rode back into Dangqu and had the gates firmly closed.
**"COME OUT!"** Zhang Fei heckled. **"STOP HIDING, ZHANG HE, AND FIGHT ZHANG YIDE OF YAN!"**
"...*Ayah*," Zhang He sobbed angrily.

Zhang He's forces lacked sustainable resources, and were forced to retreat northward. They settled at Ba Xi City, which was surrounded on 3 sides by treacherous mountains and steep valleys where the ground below was almost impossible to see. Zhang He watched from the battlements as a frustrated Zhang Fei – whom he had now been fighting for almost a month – was riding back and forth, issuing curses and challenges as always.

376

"...'**Zhang Yide of Yan!**' ...'**Zhang Yide of Yan!**' ...PHOOEY to **Zhang Yide of Yan!**" Zhang He screamed with anger as he sat in his war room and vainly tried to block out the continual chants from the slopes in front of Ba Xi City.

"...There's no point getting angry," Xiahou Yuan's deputy general, Zhao Yong, said calmly. "I'm going to go and inform Commander Xiahou of your predicament..."

"*Predicament...?*" Zhang He retorted angrily. "What am I supposed to do? That isn't a general out there... that's some sort of wild animal!"

"You and Xu Huang are two of the five great generals of Wei," Zhao Yong said with disdain. "You were both left here to guard Hanzhong... why are you allowing this oaf, this old butcher from the countryside, to get the better of you...? Your reputation as a hero is at stake, General... I say that as a colleague."

"You're right, I know you're right," Zhang He admitted. "He has an advantage of unshakable morale, and he's scaring my men with his ceaseless bellowing. The more superstitious ones think he's some sort of god."

"Shoot him from the walls," Zhao Yong scoffed. "Anyway, I'm going to report to the commander... best of luck to you."

The two generals exchanged bows of respect, and Zhao Yong departed the city and travelled northward. Zhang He returned to the battlements, and whispered, "You won't get the better of me."

For a few days, Zhang Fei's camp fell silent. Rumours abounded of Zhang Fei falling ill, or being drunk from frustration at Zhang He's reluctance to fight. As he was glad of the peace, Zhang He thought it to be a good omen: but one day, after a fortnight or more of holding Ba Xi, a sudden din at the rear of the fortress took the general – and his already terrified men – by complete surprise.

"**WHERE CAN YOU RUN NOW, ZHANG HE...?**" Zhang Fei screamed. "**WHERE CAN YOU HIDE AND COWER FROM ZHANG YIDE OF YAN?**"

"Impossible...!" Zhang He cried: Zhang Fei had somehow reached the rear of his defences and trapped the city in a pincer.

"**He's immortal!**" one soldier screamed.

"**No he ISN'T!**" Zhang He protested. "**We have to fight back!**"

But panic had set in, and the day was lost. Screaming with rage, Zhang He did the only thing he could do: beat a hasty retreat. Zhang Fei laughed maniacally and hurled taunts as Zhang He abandoned his horse and fled on foot with those men that did not surrender out of fear.

Zhang He's retreat from Ba Xi took him to treacherous mountain paths with steep drops that claimed many of his panicked forces; by the time he reached the Hanzhong capital of Nanzheng, Zhang He had less than fifty men left under his command, and Zhang Fei had won the day. The Ba region – which was too close to Liu Bei to remain in enemy hands – had been successfully secured.

************

## 83

"A marvellous victory...!" Liu Bei chuckled as a victorious Zhang Fei relayed his victory in the Ba region to the court in Chengdu.

"I expect that Zhang He will be happy to never, *ever* hear your name again as long as he lives," Jian Yong said with a hearty laugh. "A marvellous exercise in psychological warfare, Yide: many lives were spared because of it."

"...Yeah, well, Zhuge's always going on about 'topographical advantage'," Zhang Fei replied. "I thought, 'Well, there *must* be some road somewhere that goes around the place', and sure enough, a few locals that don't like Cao Cao helped us out. I have never seen a look like that on a man's face, but to see it on so many men's faces... they thought I was a god, or something!"

Many of the officials laughed at the idea.

"Truly a great *first victory*," Kongming praised. "Dangqu was far too close for comfort... we need to keep up the pressure, and stop them gaining ground."

The officials murmured in agreement.

Despite the setback in Dangqu, Cao Cao still had the advantage. But his personal ambitions apparently took precedent over military responsibilities, and one day – before any more incursions took place – the announcement that everyone had expected was made.

"...**We've actually had an imperial messenger from the court come here, would you believe...?**" Jian Yong scoffed as he walked into the Chengdu court. "**We all know what this is.**"

"...Cao Cao," Kongming said bitterly. "He's-"

"**REPORT FROM HIS MAJESTY'S DIVINE COURT!**" a messenger-official in robes shouted as he walked into the hall: everyone, even Liu Bei, was penitent before the announcer, whose presence represented that of their emperor. The official unfurled a document, and proclaimed, "**Prime Minister Cao Cao, the Duke of Wei, shall henceforth be known as the *King of Wei*! A full list of promotions and personnel is now presented to you!**"

Jian Yong received the official proclamation letter from the messenger, who turned and left the court with his head held high.

"...For a minute there, I thought we might be invited to his coronation," Jian Yong snickered as he read through the list of names. "...Mm... Yang Xiu's made Secretariat... surprised at that, since he's related to Yuan Shu... Sima Yi's doing alright for himself..."

"...*That* we don't need to hear," Fa Zheng complained.

"... ... ...Oh," Jian Yong said awkwardly.

"What...?" Liu Bei asked worriedly.

Jian Yong shook his head and replied, "It isn't anything bad, really, just... well... Kongming, do you want to take a look at this for a minute...?"

Jian Yong crossed the room and passed the document to Kongming, who read it with surprise and disappointment.

"...Is something the matter, Mister Zhuge...?" Huang Quan asked.

"...Xu Shu...?" Kongming exclaimed. "*Meng Jian*... ... ...and Shi Tao???"

"So there're three of them on there, then," Jian Yong sighed sadly. "So were Meng Jian and Shi Tao friends of yours as well…?"

"Shi Tao was Xu Shu's friend, the two men came to Jing together," Kongming replied soberly. "Meng Jian… was our friend, too. We… they, Pang Tong, and I… we were… good friends."

"Alas," Liu Bei said dramatically. "We have lost three of five great talents to Cao Cao's coercion, and one to an early death! What an unjust world…!"

As Liu Bei started to sob quietly at the thought of Pang Tong's death, Huang Quan asked, "If they are your friends, Mister Zhuge, and their allegiances do not truly lie with Cao Cao, are they not useful spies…?"

"They will be watched," Jian Yong suggested. "That, and-"

"*Ayah*!" Kongming cried. "Wei already has great men… why do they also have these men, rotting in inconsequential posts, when they could be here, saving the land from a great evil…?"

"…Still, *Xu Shu*, after all these years," Wei Yan chortled. "So he's in the capital… serving Cao Cao."

"He's… he's not done that well," Kongming said reassuringly. "He's underselling himself, and deliberately, I think… he's in a pedant's role, not an advisory one. Shi Tao and Meng Jian, the same… Xu Shu promised he would never betray us, and he's done his best to keep that promise."

"Now that Cao Cao's a king, we'll see him spend a bit of time building his new kingdom, and then he'll come after us," Fa Zheng supposed.

"…We should wait and watch," Huang Quan suggested.

"I… cannot go on today," Liu Bei said with tears in his eyes. "We… can discuss this tomorrow. There is no urgency here…"

Despite objections from the courtiers, Liu Bei retired, and the court session ended.

"…He's stalling," Kongming complained to his wife, Yueying, when he reached his home.

"Oh, you're back early…!" Yueying said with a grateful smile. "Who's stalling, Lord Liu…?"

"He's afraid to go to war, but hesitation cost Yuan Shao everything, and it will cost Lord Liu even more than that, since he has the weight of responsibility for the whole country, and the fate of the Emperor, on his shoulders," Kongming said irritably. "I cannot convince him, and Fa Zheng isn't really trying… though I don't know why."

"Perhaps he's waiting for something," Yueying suggested.

"…Whatever it is, I can't see it, for once," Kongming said sadly. "Perhaps I'm slipping, missing some vital element…"

"Is something else on your mind…?" Yueying asked knowingly.

"…Xu Shu, Shi Tao, and Meng Jian… they're serving Cao Cao, who has just been declared the King of Wei," Kongming reported. "So yes, I am a little clouded."

"Cao Cao is…!" Yueying exclaimed. "…He must intend usurpation within a matter of a decade or less…!"

"Yes, but will it be him, or his chosen heir that will do the deed...?"
Kongming chortled. "I understand that there is an unhealthy war
brewing between his sons, Cao Pi, Cao Zhang, and Cao Zhi: that
started when all there was to fight for was a duchy, but now, Cao
Cao needs a *crown prince*, so there is much to fight for. Cao Zhi is
brilliant but arrogant, and a terrible drunk... he is also, I
understand, a bit of a theatrical dandy, and so not the best man
to front a military nation, although he is Cao Cao's favourite
because of his intellect, and because they share a passion for
intricate, profound poetry and song. Cao Pi is clever and gifted,
though not so much as Cao Zhi... he's the eldest, but Cao Cao is
following the example of Yuan Shao, and forgetting the natural
law. Cao Zhang is less talented, and more of a general, but
certainly isn't as likely to win his father's favour as he wishes to.
...Sense would dictate Cao Pi winning, but Cao Cao is showing the
typical signs of muddle-headedness... in addition, he'll not want to
be remembered for usurping the Han. He'll leave the deed to his
heir... that is certain."
"...I'm sorry about Xu Shu and the others," Yueying said sincerely.
"I'm not," Kongming replied coldly. "I must be pragmatic... they
were weak."
"I know that you feel differently," Yueying said surely. "But... yes,
you are a statesman, and you must be pragmatic."
"...Thank you," Kongming replied quietly. "Perhaps... I'll play the
qin tonight."
The music that Kongming played was sorrowful and resigned.

General Huo Jun – whose service holding Jiameng Pass since the
start of the Yi campaign had been of such vital importance –
finally succumbed to illness and passed away, aged around 40
years. Liu Bei insisted that the general have a large funeral, and
he mourned publicly for several days. Kongming wept at the
funeral, but it was more for the grief of losing so many people that
he had once held close to his heart; he was inwardly hurt by Xu
Shu, Shi Tao and Meng Jian's servitude to Wei, and the loss of
Pang Tong. Soon enough, however, he threw himself back into his
work, and an unhealthy but stable normality resumed.


************

## 84

Despite the public proclamation that Cao Cao – now known as the Prime Minister of the Han Empire and King of Wei – was still deploying forces in the name of the emperor, the states of Yi and Eastern Wu started to refer to those imperial Han forces as the forces of Wei, as they were always led by men that served Cao Cao directly. Those forces continued their defence against Wu in the east, while at the same time holding Hanzhong, poised to strike Yi at any time.

Liu Bei called yet another urgent session of court as unwanted news started to pour in from the eastern front at Hefei Castle.

"...As we had suspected," Kongming said sadly, "Wu have been trying to supress news of an epidemic in their camps. Sun Quan is trying to retreat as quietly as he can... but if *we* know, then there is a good chance the Wei forces know as well, and Zhang Liao will hit them as they flee."

"The most important concern," Fa Zheng insisted, "is the lack of that eastern front... that frees Cao Cao's main army for an attack on us."

"We have maintained a tight defence," Huang Quan said seriously. "All we need to do is hold that defence-"

"Is that enough...?" Fa Zheng proposed. "Cao Cao will come here eventually..."

"And believe me, we've done Steep-slope, and we really don't want that," Jian Yong chuckled ominously.

"So what do we do...?" Huang Quan asked. "Are we to simply sit here and wait for Cao Cao to come here and try to repel him, or do we attack while his hold on Hanzhong is not firm...?"

"Very much the latter," Kongming insisted. "When he was alive, Pang Shiyuan and I would often discuss-"

"Please...!" Liu Bei said with emotion. "Do not... do not say his name here! I cannot bear to be reminded of my failure to protect his sagely life...!"

"...I forgot how it affects you, my lord," Kongming said coldly as Liu Bei's eyes filled with tears. "But I really must finish. We discussed what would happen once Yi was stabilised-"

"I'm sure you *did*," Huang Quan scoffed quietly.

Kongming chose to ignore the remark from the recently surrendered vassal of Liu Zhang and continued, saying, "And we agreed that Hanzhong would end up being an unavoidable next target, since the enmity between the former rulers was as deep as the enmity between Liu Biao and Sun Quan, and they would be a threat even if Cao Cao had not conquered the region. In fact, the pattern is frightening to me in its obviousness: again, we see a state engaged in a bitter personal feud with a potential ally... they surrender to Cao Cao after minimal struggle... my only praise for Zhang Lu is with regard to the fact that he at least *tried* to resist, something which Liu Cong of Jing failed to do."

"Resistance against such a violent man was, however, *futile*, Mister Zhuge," the official Liu Ba suggested.

"...Yes," Kongming sighed: he knew that this second remark from another of Liu Zhang's former vassals was probably aimed at Liu Bei. "But anyhow, we agreed on one thing: if we saw the like of what we envisioned, we would not make the mistake that was made in Jing."

"...But avoiding repeating the mistakes of the past is fair enough in principle," Liu Bei said waveringly. "We criticise Cao Cao for the same, however..."

"My lord," Fa Zheng protested, "we must attack Hanzhong, and we must seize it before Cao Cao has completely tightened his grip. Firstly, we need it as a base to attack Cao Cao, and restore the Han Dynasty to its former glory... which is our main mission, the reason for all of our efforts. Secondly, we can attack Liang Province and other provinces to the west of Cao's sphere of influence, which not only secures those regions, it also contributes to our other, prevailing goal. Thirdly, and most importantly, we need Hanzhong if Yi is to survive... for Hanzhong is Yi's *throat*. When Cao Cao tightens his grip on that region fully, it is *us* that will choke to death."

"...Then should we not already be preparing...?" Liu Bei urged.

"My lord," Kongming replied, "a good strategist never lets his guard down. We were not completely ready, but our mobilisation to Jing was swifter than Lu Su could ever have predicted... we anticipated treachery. Since we also anticipated a strike on Hanzhong, preparations have been underway for some time. Medicine, food, training, topography studies, enemy profiling; it is all underway. My lord, all that is really needed is your order to proceed."

"...Fine," Liu Bei agreed. "Are there any objections...?"

Kongming, Jian Yong and Fa Zheng glared at the officials inherited from Liu Zhang; they remained silent.

"Well then," Liu Bei said bravely; "...Let us strike Hanzhong."

Kongming returned to his home that evening, and threw his fan to the ground as soon as he reached the living quarters.

"...*Aiee*," Kongming sighed miserably. "Though I know it's necessary to ensure the peace we seek... will it ever end...?"

Yueying entered the room and smiled sadly.

"Don't worry," Kongming said. "I'm remaining in Chengdu... Lord Liu trusts me and only me with the task. I would rather be in Hanzhong, but... well... I did go and call myself 'Crouching Dragon', didn't I...? Nine years, I've worked for this man... and most of that has been as a man of the pen, a court official."

"I would rather you were here," Yueying admitted. "It's a selfish thought, but..."

"...But you do not want to see me cut down in mid-flight, like Pang Tong and Zhou Yu... I can understand that," Kongming replied forlornly. "I wonder if I'm any safer in the capital, though... the 'Yi' faction at court really does make me shiver sometimes. They still resent Lord Liu a little, some of them... and I really do not think he can see it. My concern is that we've already lost Mister Sun and Shiyuan. What happens when the 'Yi' faction greatly outnumbers the men that served Lord Liu before that...? Can they be trusted...?"

Kongming sighed miserably as he pondered the inevitable: Yueying sat next to him, and smiled reassuringly.

While Sun Quan's attack on Hefei in the east of the country stalled, Liu Bei once again prepared for a western offensive, this time against the adjacent Hanzhong region, which was now governed by Cao Cao's followers. This campaign would involve all of Liu Bei's most dependable vassals, save Guan Yu and those under his command in Jing. Guan Yu held Jing Province with a considerably larger force than he had been left with on the earlier Yi campaign: there would be no lack of caution taken this time with regards to Eastern Wu.

Fa Zheng and Huang Quan would be in charge of directing the forces and advising strategy; Zhang Fei, Zhao Yun, Ma Chao, Wei Yan and Huang Zhong would be the main vanguard generals.

"Now be careful," Fa Zheng said to Kongming as the officials gathered for their last meeting before the expedition.

"You're the one walking into certain death," Kongming chuckled. "As usual, I'm safe inside a city, counting grain depositories. Why do I need to be careful...?"

"...Well at the very least, don't die of boredom," Jian Yong said with a smirk.

"That I cannot promise," Kongming replied with false joviality.

"We could use the extra brains out there, but you're needed here too," Jian Yong added seriously. "After all, Sun Quan..."

"...May, out of spite, want Jing back," Kongming said wearily. "I know... and it's all the worse with Lu Su being ill at the moment. His chosen substitute – and likely successor – is Lü Meng, and he really isn't anywhere near as amiable. He hates Guan Yu, he hates Lord Liu, he worships Zhou Yu's memory, and he wants Jing Province, *badly*."

"...Maybe we need to reinforce Guan Yu," Fa Zheng fretted.

"No, no, you need everything you can get for Hanzhong," Kongming insisted. "I'm sure Yunchang will be fine... and it'll be months before Sun Quan's forces are fit enough to fight again, by which time, hopefully, Hanzhong will be ours."

Huang Quan approached as Kongming spoke, and said, "Are we ready, Mister Jian...?"

"...Yes," Jian Yong replied coldly. "Are *you*...?"

Huang Quan sneered irritably and walked away.

"I'm glad he's going with you," Kongming admitted.

"We need to keep the 'Yi' faction split at court, we know that," Fa Zheng said reassuringly. "But... Huang Quan is just unsettled. He wouldn't betray us... on the contrary, we can trust him to remain loyal, if only begrudgingly. One day, though, I think he'll be one of us. He's just stubborn, like Liu Ba, and Yan Yan."

Battle horns sounded in the grounds outside the court.

"...Farewell for now, Kongming," Fa Zheng said kindly. "Now remember, if you need any support, talk to Yang Hong."

"...My thanks," Kongming replied. "Good luck to you all."

"One day," Jian Yong said as he started to walk away, "we'll actually get to stay in one place, and I'll get to retire. I plan on growing a garden."

Kongming laughed at the idea, and gestured with his fan, ushering his colleagues on their way.

Weeks passed, and Ma Liang was summoned to the Wu military facility at Lukou by a messenger representing the Chief Commander of the Wu forces. Since the atmosphere was unusually cold, Ma Liang suspected that Lu Su – the only man in Eastern Wu that truly championed the tripartite theorem that Kongming lived by – was no longer in charge. He was correct, as Lu Su had died of illness shortly after the retreat from Hefei Castle, aged just 45.

"...Envoy Ma," Lü Meng said coldly as Ma Liang reached his office: he was wearing white to mourn the loss of Lu Su.

"...You... you should have said..." Ma Liang said apologetically: he was wearing no white articles. "I didn't know, or I would have-"

"It doesn't matter," Lü Meng insisted. "Sit down, please."

Ma Liang took a guest seat, and Chief Commander Lü Meng sat in his own place as host.

"...Why have you summoned me here, Chief Commander...?" Ma Liang asked with fear and tension. "Is this... about Jing Province...? ...I thought it was agreed with Lord Sun that-"

"I just wanted to speak with you... that's all I wanted," Lü Meng interrupted. "You see, I am concerned about the future... Guan Yu was always very hostile towards Lu Zijing, and I just wanted to make it clear that, as a warrior before I was a thinker, I will not be intimidated."

"...General Guan intimidates everybody," Ma Liang snickered nervously. "Even he finally refers to me by my style name, after I don't know how many years, he-"

"He can do what he wants to his subordinates: that isn't my concern, but rather it is your lord Liu Bei's concern. Being frank, he should show more concern about such behaviour in his ranks," Lü Meng interrupted again. "What I want to make clear is that I do not intend to be spoken to as my predecessor was. I am offering you an opportunity to convey that to Guan Yu so, in the event that I am forced to come and take Jing... and I would prefer it was *offered*... we won't have any unnecessary and unfortunate altercations. I'm not some 'little man', to be bullied and harassed... I'm not 'out of my depth' or 'too nice for my own good'... and I can use this sword I'm carrying very well. Is that understood...?"

"...Completely," Ma Liang replied numbly.

"There will be no visits to Jing by me, only messengers," Lü Meng continued. "If there is one thing that is clear when reviewing the past, it is that 'familiarity breeds contempt'. My predecessor treated Zhuge Liang as a friend, and that was a mistake. There will be no familiarity from me... is *that* understood...?"

"...Yes," Ma Liang said sadly.

"Very good," Lü Meng declared. "This one-sided relationship between Lord Sun and Liu Bei has gone on long enough... things are going to be different from now on."

Ma Liang nodded slowly to indicate that he understood.

"...Another one gone," Kongming said as he sat, days later, in his home in Chengdu. He was wearing several articles of white clothing, to show respect for Lu Su. "...Still, he got to his forties: that's encouraging."

"Don't say things like that!" Yueying pleaded.

"...Sun Quan was completely routed at Hefei," Kongming continued obliviously. "He was almost killed... Zhang Liao is now a symbol of terror in the Wu ranks. After such a complete humiliation, and such a loss of life, how can Sun Quan not want Jing back, just to be seen to save face...? And Lü Meng... he didn't want to be even the slightest bit cordial... *aiee*. I really hope that the situation in Hanzhong does not drag on too long, or we really will be-"

"Please, stop it!" Yueying implored. "This is weak talk... you need to be stronger than this...!"

"...I know," Kongming sighed, "but I feel like I'm burying someone I respect or care about on a regular basis now, and the wars, the battles, the intrigue... it never ends, it just gets worse. How can I be optimistic against such odds...?"

"You were strong at Steep-slope, you were strong at Red Cliffs... you were strong during the acquisition of Jing, and you were strong when you took Yi," Yueying challenged. "This is just another battle. You promised me that everything would be okay: keep your promise."

Kongming gazed into Yueying's eyes, and saw only anger and determination.

"...You make me feel ashamed," Kongming chuckled miserably. "You're right, I need to calm down. Lord Liu's forces should be engaging the enemy now, or if not now, then soon. I need to be focussed, watch the despatches-"

"No, no, that's *worse*!" Yueying whimpered. "Don't start working late and-"

"No, no, you were right," Kongming proclaimed, to Yueying's dismay. "I need to go back to the court, and request constant updates from the front... I'll be back soon. Oh... and thank you."

As Kongming left the house, Yueying laughed miserably, and sighed with resignation.


************

## 85

Liu Bei's forces descended upon the Ba region like a living storm, taking the new defenders by surprise with the scale of the attack. Cao Cao's forces had moved against Ba Dong – an eastern city that threatened White Emperor City and the Yi-Jing border – and Ba Xi, a city situated directly west of the Hanzhong capital, Nanzheng. This time, Liu Bei's aim would be to purge the Ba region completely, and begin a proper assault on Hanzhong.

Atop the walls of the main city of Ba Dong, the defending general, Pu Hu, viewed the 30,000 men that were laying siege with fear. Led by Zhao Yun and Huang Zhong, and advised by Fa Zheng, there was seemingly no end to the men in orange uniforms that were storming the walls at their behest.
"...We need to get help," Pu Hu decided. "We've tried holding out, but they keep coming... **send messengers to General Du Huo in Ba Xi, Xiahou Yuan in Yang Ping Pass, and Du Xi in Nanzheng at once!**"
"I don't think we can break through," a captain replied uneasily.
"...We're finished, then," Pu Hu replied soberly.

The situation in Ba Xi was – unbeknownst to Pu Hu – very much the same. Forces led by Li Yan and Liu Feng were besieging the walls of the city, while its protector, Du Huo, looked on angrily from atop the walls.
"Liu Bei is here," Du Huo said to his advisers. "His banner and parasol are at the back of the field, and his son Liu Feng is leading the forces."
"We should try and kill Liu Feng," his assistant general Wang Ping suggested.
"No, no!" an adviser insisted. "We don't want to rile him! Better to let them think we've got no morale, and then make a sudden charge on them!"
"...Perhaps," Du Huo agreed. "We could make a sudden rush at Liu Bei... the King of Wei would reward us well for capturing him!"
"Then let's do that," the adviser concurred. "We'll get ready now."
        At a distance, Liu Bei, Jian Yong and Huang Quan watched the unfolding events with interest.
"...So far, your advice has been faultless, Mister Huang," Liu Bei praised. "What shall we do now, in your esteemed opinion...?"
"My lord," Huang Quan replied, "it seems that the enemy are anxious to engage us. We should refuse combat, save for pinning them in the city... their resources will be limited at this point since they are not organised, and we should find them losing heart in a matter of days."
"I like it," Jian Yong chuckled. "Well, then... let's do that."

Zhao Yun, meanwhile, was accepting a challenge of sorts from Pu Hu, protector of Ba Dong.
"**Worthless dog!**" Pu Hu cursed as he pointed his spear at a bemused Zhao Yun.
"...**People have heard of *me*,**" Zhao Yun replied. "**Who are *you* to call *me* worthless...?**"

Pu Hu screamed angrily, and ordered one of his officers to fight in his stead. The man rode forward with his spear raised, but within less than twenty clashes, he was toppled from his horse by the more skilful Zhao Yun.

"...**Someone else!**" Pu Hu ordered: another officer charged at Zhao Yun, and was easily bested.

"**How many more nameless nobodies do you intend to throw at our great general Zhao Zilong...?**" Huang Zhong taunted as he rode to Zhao Yun's side. "**Let this old soldier waste some more of his old life fighting with these men, Zilong... your talent should be saved for worthy men.**"

The Wei forces started to disintegrate as their morale plummeted: but as Pu Hu turned to flee, a third general charged at his left flank with a group of cavalry, shouting, "**WEI YAN HERE! YOUR CITY IS MINE!**"

Yan Yan appeared with another cavalry force to attack the right flank: despite archers firing volleys from the city walls to assist Pu Hu, the battle quickly turned to a rout.

The siege at Ba Xi proceeded as Huang Quan had predicted: as soon as supplies started to dwindle, morale plummeted and many men – including Du Huo's assistant general, Wang Ping – surrendered to Liu Bei's forces. The situation in the city became so dire that the inhabitants took matters into their own hands, and Ba Xi eventually surrendered to Liu Bei altogether.

Liu Bei entered Ba Xi City and pacified the small civilian populace before he held court.

"...Marvellous," Liu Bei praised as his generals lined up in front of him. "What happened to Du Huo and his advisers...?"

"They're such nobodies that I don't know if we even got them or not," Jian Yong joked. "...But their forces are smashed, that much we do know. The news coming from Ba Dong is positive... we won, which is the main thing. But we can't hope for any more laxity on Cao Cao's part: word is that the big names are on the march now that they're taking us seriously , so no more 'Pu Hus' and 'Du Huos'. Xiahou Yuan is moving significant forces to Yang Ping Pass, Zhang He is now holding Guangshi, and Xu Huang is at Ma Ming Ge. News of Zhang Yide and Ma Chao's progress is not coming through yet, but Wudu is a tad remote, so that isn't any surprise."

"Mm... well, keep me informed, as always," Liu Bei ordered. "I want to know anything that happens as soon as it happens."

"...Of course," Jian Yong promised.

In Chengdu, Kongming made sure to read the despatches as they arrived: Yueying would often sit and watch with dismay as Kongming read and re-read the letters in the evenings.

"You're becoming obsessed," Yueying scolded one night.

"I need to be sure to read thoroughly," Kongming replied emotionlessly: his main focus was on a report from the Wudu region. "...The Di tribes have joined us."

"Is that good...?" Yueying asked desperately. "Can you leave this until tomorrow if something good has happened...?"

"The Di people are not entirely trustworthy," Kongming replied uneasily. "They joined Ma Chao in Liang because he was seen as strong after he killed the Ji City governor... but they'll abandon or even turn on us if we're perceived to be weak."

"But isn't that why Zhang Fei and Ma Chao were sent to Wudu...?" Yueying said pointedly. "Husband, you're really pouring over something for no good reason!"

"...Why... because I'm not needed...?" Kongming retorted ominously.

"No... no, that's not what I meant, and you know that," Yueying replied irritably.

"...It isn't what you meant, but... it's true anyway," Kongming said miserably: he threw the despatch to one side and exhaled noisily, adding, "I am stuck here, an overqualified administrator, shuffling from office to office, bleating about bureaucratic nonsense like a snivelling little pedant, while-"

"Enough," Yueying pleaded. "When Pang Tong died, the thought of taking his place nearly killed you... why do you now wish for it...?"

"I joined Lord Liu to make a difference," Kongming replied.

"You joined him because you had no choice," Yueying countered. "It was him or one of his rivals. I'd understand if you were bored... but it's because you're not sure anyone else can be trusted to complete your grand design, now that you feel that the end is within reach. You see Lord Liu on the verge of taking Hanzhong and completing the tripod, and you cannot bear the thought of it going wrong now, when we are so close."

Kongming smiled, and said, "I suppose so... you're right."

"You didn't know...?" Yueying asked with confusion.

"I'm... tired," Kongming admitted. "I should get some rest, get some clarity. You're right, it isn't as though others don't know the nature of the Di... Ma Chao lived with them, he could pass for one of them if he needed to. And yes, I... I need to trust these men. The tripartite state is almost formed, as you say, and everything is going very well, as you say... yes, I'm being too untrusting, as usual. I'll... I'll get some rest."

Kongming got up and slowly walked toward the sleeping quarters, smiling strangely all the while.

"...This is unfair," Yueying complained miserably.

In Hanzhong, 3 stalemates formed: at Yang Ping Pass, Xiahou Yuan held firm, while Zhang He held Guangshi, and forces led by Cao Hong met Zhang Fei and Ma Chao at Wudu, and prevented them from moving forward. To make matters worse, bandit leaders in the Yi region of Jianwei started a mass revolt that was only just contained by the meagre forces of Li Yan. The weeks wore on, and morale took an inevitable drop on both sides.

✳✳✳✳✳✳✳✳✳✳✳✳

## 86

"This can't go on," Liu Bei complained as his siege of the Yang Ping Pass continued without progress. "Is there any news at *all* from Wudu...?"

"Nothing," Jian Yong replied. "Nothing good, anyway... the Di are getting impatient, and if they don't get to hit something soon, we risk them turning on us."

"...And Zilong...?" Liu Bei asked further. "Where is *he*...?"

"Zilong will be here soon, he was chasing down any Wei forces around the region that might have caused us problems," Jian Yong reported. "A matter of days, one or two at the most, and he'll be here, he says."

"...Fine," Liu Bei acknowledged numbly.

Jian Yong smiled encouragingly, and said, "What are we doing next...?"

"Good question," Liu Bei said as he turned to Huang Quan.

"...We can try cutting Xiahou Yuan's supply route," Huang Quan suggested.

"That would mean attacking Ma Ming Ge," Jian Yong supposed. "Well, when Zilong and Wenchang get here, we'll-"

"General Chen," Liu Bei hailed: to Jian Yong's horror, General Chen Shi stepped forward, and bowed silently. Liu Bei smiled, saying, "General Chen, you will go to Ma Ming Ge, and-"

"Uh... *no*...!" Jian Yong protested. "No offence to General Chen, but he's no match for Xu Huang. The man used to spar with *Yunchang*, so how can General Chen hope to match him...?"

"No general of Wei is a match for us," Liu Bei retorted. "Zhang He turned tail and ran from Yide, and look at what Wei throws at us now! Nobodies, like Pu Hu and Du Huo, and has-beens, like Xiahou Yuan! If they weren't entrenched and hiding, we'd defeat them easily!"

"...Xiahou Yuan and Zhang He defeated *Ma Chao*," Jian Yong protested. "I really don't think we should be underestimating them, Xuande. Really, I think that Xu Huang should be challenged by Zilong, or Wenchang, or maybe even *both*."

"That's giving free morale boosts to the enemy, isn't it...?" Liu Bei scolded. "I'm surprised at you, Xianhe... General Chen is not going to challenge him to a duel anyway, he's going to cut the supply line... all he needs is troops."

"Gongheng, *tell him*...!" Jian Yong implored as he looked at Huang Quan.

"If Chen Shi were being sent to duel, I'd agree," Huang Quan replied. "The purpose of this exercise is to cut the supply line, so all we need is a smart man."

"Xu Huang is no idiot!" Jian Yong protested further.

"Oh...?" Liu Bei chuckled casually. "Zhou Yu made a fool of him at Jiangling..."

"Zhou Yu made a fool of *Cao Ren*, *once*," Jian Yong countered. "Xuande... Lord Liu... listen to me...!"

**"General Chen,"** Liu Bei barked. "**...Get ready for your mission.**"

"...Yes, my lord," Chen Shi responded quietly.

"*Aiee,*" Jian Yong exclaimed as Chen Shi walked away. "Truly, the tiger will laugh at the courageous mouse before he devours it."

Zhang Fei, meanwhile, had started rumours in the Wei camp about his next movements. Cao Hong – a confident, swaggering relative of Cao Cao – called his officials, Cao Xiu and Yang Fu, to discuss the hearsay and decide action, while Zhang Fei and Ma Chao put on a bold, confident front for the enemy and their Di tribal allies.

"**COME OUT!**" Zhang Fei shouted as his forces put on a bold front outside Cao Hong's camp. "**OR ARE YOU SCARED...? YOU'VE HEARD OF ME, UH...? YOU'VE ALL HEARD OF ZHANG YIDE OF YAN...?**"

"**I AM MA MENGQI OF XILIANG!**" Ma Chao screamed as he rode back and forth astride his magnificent white horse. "**WHERE ARE CAO CAO, ZHANG HE, AND XIAHOU YUAN...? ARE YANG FU AND ZHAO QU HERE? I WILL PEEL THEIR SKIN, AND EAT THEIR FLESH! ...I WILL EAT *YOUR* FLESH!**"

Zhang Fei cackled at the thought, and added, "**WHO WANTS TO BE EATEN BY ZHANG YIDE OF YAN...?**"

"This 'Zhang Fei' and Ma Chao are laughing at us," Cao Hong complained as he sat with Cao Xiu and Yang Fu in his command tent. "Zhang Fei acts as though we're stupid, spreading rumours like a child... I want to attack him, but I want to hear your thoughts. Mister Yang, you once bested Ma Chao during his western rampages, so what say you?"

All eyes turned to Yang Fu, the former acting governor of Ji City, whose schemes had indeed led to the complete destruction of Ma Chao, his family, and many thousands of his allies during the great northern rebellion a few years before.

"...The general mood is suspicion," Yang Fu said honestly. "To blatantly tell us that he intends to cut our supply route seems to be an attempt at trickery. If he were really intending to attack our supply route, would he let it slip so easily...?"

"He might be intending to mislead us with a deliberately managed leakage of information," Cao Xiu suggested. "Commander, we really can't afford to miss an opportunity to prepare if they intend to do something."

"...One of their generals, Wu Lan, is stationed at Xia Bian," Cao Hong noted. "I think he should be attacked."

"It looks like bait for a trap," Yang Fu protested.

"Zhang Fei and Ma Chao are all brawn and no brain," Cao Xiu said surely. "They are trying to be clever... well fine, lay an ambush trail, so if they do try an attack our supply route, they'll be routed. As for Wu Lan... if we hit him now, while they're all preparing to make their next movements, we can break their spirit, and hopefully, break their ties with the Di at the same time."

"I like it," Cao Hong praised. "We'll smash them. Okay, get ready for a strike on Xia Bian, and get some ambushes along the supply road. We'll see how 'Zhang Yide of Yan' likes *that*...!"

"**Aiee...! How can this be???**" Kongming cried as he read through the latest despatches in his Chengdu office two weeks later: Ma Su looked on with dread.

"...What is it...?" Ma Su asked.

"The court will have to know, so... so I have to go," Kongming said tensely. "I... I need to go to the court, speak to Yang Hong, get-"
"Master Zhuge, please...!" Ma Su said angrily. "What's happened...?"
"...Come with me, I'll explain as we go," Kongming replied.
"...The fronts are all falling apart," Kongming explained worriedly as he hurried to the court in a carriage with Ma Su. "Zhang Fei tried some sort of scheme that the enemy pre-empted, and it's all gone wrong in Wudu. Cao Hong attacked Wu Lan at Xia Bian... General Lei Tong was killed, and Wu Lan fled to the Di tribes, who killed him and broke ties with us."
"What...?" Ma Su exclaimed. "B-but... have they joined Wei...?"
"I don't know... but Zhang Fei and Ma Chao are withdrawing from Wudu, we've lost there now," Kongming continued with obvious panic. "And Lord Liu sent Chen Shi... *Chen Shi*...! ...To fight at Ma Ming Ge, where Xu Huang was stationed..."
"...*Chen Shi*...?" Ma Su said with disbelief. "Why not Zilong...?"
"I don't know, I don't know!" Kongming whined. "All I know is that he's been routed as well, and now, Lord Liu is stuck at Guangshi!"
"...Guangshi...?" Ma Su said with surprise. "But... wasn't he attacking the Yang Ping Pass...?"
"The... ... ...*look*, I don't know why he did it, but he's attacked Zhang He at Guangshi as well, and now he's stuck," Kongming despaired. "Jian Yong warned him, but he didn't listen, and... and now he's stuck. Now, he's written to me, asking for reinforcements. If he asked for *anything else*, Ma Youchang: supplies, advice, my personal presence, then of course, these things are possible, and it would be done... but *reinforcements*??? Where am I supposed to get *reinforcements* from???"
"*Ayah*," Ma Su sighed. "No wonder you're so stressed. ...We can't protect Yi and Jing, and also send reinforcements to Hanzhong..."
"I *know that*!" Kongming said angrily. "I...! ...He was fine! He was *fine*! Now, because of Zhang Fei's idiot blundering, and Lord Liu's overconfidence, we are completely ruined! I *knew* I should have insisted that I lead the army! I *knew*-"
"Kongming," Ma Su interrupted. "Don't... don't get angry like that."
"What else can I do but get angry...?" Kongming retorted. "It's that, or cry! I'm not a magician! I can't conjure up more men! We can't spare anyone else! We need farmers to tend the fields, officials to manage the administration! We haven't any men to spare for fighting! The only way that I can see is-"
"Let's... just see what Yang Hong says," Ma Su suggested.
"...*Aiee*," Kongming exclaimed. "...This... this is the same, stupid *nonsense* again... what is the point of having advisers if you don't *listen to them*???"
"...Let's just see what the court says," Ma Su pleaded.

"Kongming, is...?" Dong He hailed as Kongming rushed into the court, where many of the officials were sat discussing matters of state.
"...Lord Liu... has requested reinforcements," Kongming declared.
The murmurs of confusion and fear erupted immediately.
"...Has the campaign faltered...?" Qin Mi asked plainly.

"I'd say that's a good description," Kongming replied wearily. "But if you're going to say something caustic, then-"
"Kongming," Yang Hong interrupted, "you need to remain calm."
Kongming was fanning himself erratically as he paced back and forth. "What reinforcements can I send...?" Kongming said agitatedly. "This needs serious thought!"
"Kongming," Yang Hong declared, "Hanzhong is the throat of this province. We have reached a desperate moment: the survival of everything depends on success. If we cannot secure Hanzhong, the independent state of Yi will cease to exist, and this region will fall into the hands of Cao Cao."
Kongming stopped pacing, and stared at Yang Hong.
"The danger is right at our door," Yang Hong continued. "At such a time, drastic measures must be taken... the men can go to Hanzhong and fight for our future, and in their place, tending fields and transporting supplies... the women can do that."
"*What*...?" Qin Mi scoffed.
"No more dallying," Yang Hong insisted. "Tell Lord Liu that reinforcements are on their way, Kongming."
Kongming smiled gratefully: after a short pause, he said, "My thanks, Jixiu... you have saved me from my own short-sightedness. You are quite right... quite right! I'll write back immediately... can you-"
"I will administrate and oversee the labour duty changes," Yang Hong promised. "Dong He and Qin Mi can oversee drafting of the men for the campaign."
Kongming bowed low in great respect of the old politician, Yang Hong, and called for paper, a pen, and a messenger to carry the news to Hanzhong.

"...Is it true that women are...?" Yueying asked excitely as Kongming returned home later that day.
"It's okay, you don't need to go," Kongming replied before Yueying could finish.
"I want to do something," Yueying insisted. "Everyone wants to help: even my parents – old and weak as they are – want to help."
"...I can't allow that," Kongming said desperately.
"I've spoken to Ma Liang's wife, and they're already preparing, all the women of the Ma household," Yueying declared. "This is... this is a wonderful opportunity."
"...You're aware of the reason why this is being done, are you...?" Kongming scolded. "The situation is desperate! How can you call this an opportunity???"
"...Don't be angry," Yueying pleaded. "I didn't mean it like that."
"I... I know," Kongming said apologetically. "I... I always dreamed of a day when we would be able to work together, but... not if it meant things coming to *this*."
"But if the situation turned about, and we won, which we will," Yueying suggested encouragingly, "then... well, the change is made now, isn't it...? Can't things keep on going forward, even when the crisis is over...?"

"...And I thought _I_ was ridiculously optimistic," Kongming chuckled tactlessly. "If we lose, we all die... and if we win... then things will go back to as they were before. This is _temporary_... Lord Liu is not like me, or you, or Jichang, or Shiyuan... he's an old Confucian Legalist, and things will be as they were."
"I suppose I knew that," Yueying said with tears in her eyes. "But... the thought was nice, while it lasted."
"...If you're going to insist on helping, I won't stand in your way," Kongming promised. "Just... just please, don't overdo it."
"Of course not, husband...!" Yueying giggled miserably. "I promise, I'll take it easy, like _you_ always do!"
Kongming walked to Yueying, embraced her warmly, and said, "I'm sorry."
"For what...?" Yueying retorted. "...I've not done farming for years."
"Enjoy it," Kongming chuckled. "One way or another, it won't last very long."

With the changes made to the running of Yi Province, a new fighting force was quickly assembled and despatched to Hanzhong. The women of Yi Province replaced the men, providing the stability that the infrastructure sorely needed, although there were not many officials that agreed with the decision. Kongming would often journey to the places where Yueying was working once his own work was done. Sometimes, he would briefly assist, although it had been some time since he had worked the land and lived simply, and the work was not so easy as it had once been: he smiled as he worked or watched, finding strange contentment.

The reinforcements enabled Liu Bei to regain some ground, but the situation was still critical. Xiahou Yuan held firm, and there were rumours that Cao Cao was now trying to find the time to manage the situation personally. Weeks turned to months, and both sides waited for an opportunity to end the deadlock. For Liu Bei, that opportunity was just around the corner.

************

## 87

Liu Bei summoned his officials to a meeting in his command tent, and urged his officials to consider every available option.

"We cannot stay trapped in this deadlock," Fa Zheng began.

"You can say that again," Jian Yong snickered. "We've been here a year! A *year*! This is worse than Jiangling, worse than-"

"I have an idea to break the stalemate," Fa Zheng interrupted. "With the relief forces from Hanzhong now fully accustomed to battle and the terrain, we need to force Xiahou Yuan into an offensive posture. We must advance and camp on and around Mount Dingjun, where the high ground will enable us to see the enemy positions. This will unnerve Xiahou Yuan, and from there, we wait, see what action he takes, and react accordingly."

"...Fine," Liu Bei agreed. "Put it into motion."


"...Nn...! What now???" Xiahou Yuan exclaimed as a messenger ran into his command tent at Yang Ping Pass.

"**REPORT!**" the messenger began. "**Liu Bei has moved the bulk of his forces across the Mian River, and camped around Mount Dingjun!**"

"...**What???**" Xiahou Yuan cried.

As the messenger retreated fearfully, a mid-ranking general said, "Commander, we cannot allow that to remain the case. We have to stop them taking root in such a tactically dangerous position."

"...You don't think I *know that*, Guo Huai...?" Xiahou Yuan admonished. "...We have to retaliate immediately. General Zhao, is Zhang He still in Guangshi...?"

"No, my lord," General Zhao Yong replied. "He sent a message to say that he was on his way here... obviously he is aware of these manoeuvres, since the pressure has lifted from his own position."

"...Well that's something," Xiahou Yuan complained. "And Cao Hong... I suppose he's still celebrating his promotion...?"

The generals coughed nervously.

"While I'm being besieged, he's watching prostitutes dance barefoot on top of war drums, and drinking himself stupid!" Xiahou Yuan growled angrily. "I need tactical support here!"

"He is sending relief," Guo Huai confirmed, "but remember, Nanzheng is under threat as well, and Wudu must be watched."

"...Yes, I know," Xiahou Yuan sighed. "And His Highness...?"

"The King of Wei has moved to Chang'an, but he is busy with administrative affairs and cannot assist yet," Guo Huai reported. "He will be sending Cao Zhen with a relief force as soon as-"

"He's sending Tubby to help me...?" Xiahou Yuan scoffed. "Oh, well, I feel much better...! What's *he* going to do, sneak into their camp and eat all of their supplies...?"

The generals stifled any replies or expressions that swelled within them: as a relative of Cao Cao, Xiahou Yuan could be so frank and caustic, but that might not be the case for others.

"...As soon as Zhang He gets here, I want him to report to me," Xiahou Yuan ordered irritably. "I won't move until I have his support... someone send a message to Xu Huang, telling him to stay where he is unless I say otherwise, in case this is part of some larger scheme. If I need him, I'll tell him."

"Yes, Commander," the generals replied as one.

Jian Yong entered Liu Bei's command tent on Mount Dingjun, where the mood was uncomfortable but strangely optimistic.
"Xiahou Yuan knows we're here," Jian Yong confirmed. "We're getting reports that he's received Zhang He, and the two of them are on their way to face us."
"Excellent," Fa Zheng said eagerly. "...My lord, when they arrive, they'll want to fight... we should give them what they want."
"...They'll camp on another mountain, won't they...?" Huang Quan supposed.
"If Heaven is with us, they'll camp in Zouma Valley," Fa Zheng replied. "Setting up another mountain camp would take time, and mean a long engagement. They'll want – as we do – a fast conclusion, and so I think they'll set up in the valley."
"So will we send forces to encourage them to think we want to end it quickly...?" Jian Yong prompted.
"I wish that Zilong, Yide and Wenchang were here," Liu Bei sighed. "That would be an option... Zhang He is frightfully strong, and Xiahou Yuan, though no demon of the battlefield, cannot be taken lightly."
"That's a change of stance," Jian Yong chuckled. "Before, you sent *Chen Shi* to fight Xu Huang, and called them all 'nobodies and has-beens'."
"...Keeping discussions to the current situation," Liu Bei countered, "we only have the old general Huang Zhong. Can he really be pitted against the likes of these two men...?"
"...He's perfect for the task," Huang Quan suggested with a smile.
"Agreed," Fa Zheng said surely. "...He should meet them, engage quickly and then retreat... give them an idea or two that will be the ruin of them."

As instructed, Huang Zhong led a contingent of weak, miserable-looking soldiers to set up a defensive line near Zouma Valley – which was at the foot of Mount Dingjun – and awaited the approaching Wei forces.
"...Well will you look at that...!" Xiahou Yuan chortled as he caught sight of Huang Zhong and his men. "So it was no lie that Liu Bei is lacking men to fight for him!"
The Wei forces mocked the feeble forces under Huang Zhong.
"...I sense trickery," Zhang He insisted. "Where are their champions...?"
"Oh, you mean '**ZHANG YIDE OF YAN**'...?" Xiahou Yuan mocked.
"...*Yes*," Zhang He replied irritably, "and Ma Chao, Zhao Zilong, Wei Yan...? Don't you think it is a little strange that he sends this old donkey when he has four fine stallions in his stable...?"
"Not at all," Xiahou Yuan countered. "Zhang Fei and Ma Chao were routed, they may even be dead. Zhao Yun is guarding Guangshi because he doesn't know what might happen there, and Wei Yan... well, I don't know, he's probably still at Yang Ping Pass. All I know is that this is either an insult or a sign of impending victory! We should destroy that old man and make our strength known!"
"Very well then," Zhang He sighed. "I'll challenge."
"Don't hurt him too hard, he might be someone's father," Xiahou Yuan snickered.

Zhang He rode forward and pointed his spear at Veteran General Huang Zhong, shouting, **"ZHANG HE IS HERE! WILL YOU FIGHT?"**

**"AREN'T YOU THE FRIGHTENED DEER THAT FLED FROM ZHANG YIDE...?"** Huang Zhong replied. **"WHY SHOULDN'T I FRIGHTEN YOU OFF AS WELL...?"**

Zhang He snarled, and charged his older enemy: the two clashed as their forces chanted and beat drums to heighten the atmosphere. Huang Zhong was, however, too old to last against Zhang He, who was in his prime, and Huang Zhong and his men quickly retreated, pursued by a handful of eager Wei infantry that were urgently recalled by Zhang He.

"Why didn't you pursue...?" Xiahou Yuan admonished as Zhang He rode back to his own battle line.

"...That was a trap, I know it was," Zhang He insisted. "We need to be cautious."

"You lose one battle, and your nerves give out," Xiahou Yuan mocked. "Honestly, General, you disappoint me. Where is the nerve you showed against the barbarian hordes of the west...? I mean, what trap could these idiots spring on us...? You know the extent of their *brilliance* from all of our other encounters... Steepslope, Wulin, Xiangyang, Wudu..."

"...Bowang, Red Cliffs, Jiangling," Zhang He countered. "We're not invincible, and they're not complete fools, or they wouldn't now hold Yi Province and loan Jing from Sun Quan. I thought that you would recollect Bowang and fear this tactic, especially given the fate of Li Dian and Xiahou Dun."

"... ... ...Nn, well, there is logic in your words," Xiahou Yuan admitted. "We'll pitch camp in the valley, and prepare a strategy for getting them off of that mountain, before they can do us any damage."

"We should keep a stringent watch at all times," Zhang He suggested.

"Yes, and we should wear armour, and carry swords as well," Xiahou Yuan retorted sarcastically. "Should a man that fled from Zhang Fei twice be telling me about how to win a battle...? Was I not also in Liang Province, as your commander...?"

Zhang He gritted his teeth angrily as Xiahou Yuan walked away, barking **"SET DOWN, AND PITCH CAMP!"**

"They've done as we wanted them to!" Fa Zheng said with glee as a messenger ran into the command tent to report.

"We don't know that yet," Liu Bei suggested.

**"REPORT!"** the messenger began. **"Xiahou Yuan and Zhang He have halted their advance and set up a fenced camp in the Zouma Valley!"**

"They... they really fell for it," Liu Bei chuckled as Jian Yong dismissed the messenger.

"They haven't really fallen for anything," Fa Zheng insisted. "We just made them feel more comfortable, that's all. But... ... ...a *fenced camp*...? They're settling in properly, preparing for defence as well as for attacks."

"They wouldn't expect us to attack a properly defended encampment with such poor forces," Huang Quan said surely. "We should take the fight to them, blunt their morale, and then every subsequent battle will be easier."

"We might even... ... ...well, we'll see," Fa Zheng said hesitantly. "I agree with Huang Gongheng... let's take them by surprise."

"How shall we do it...?" Liu Bei asked.

"With fire... how else...?" Huang Quan said with a smirk.

The day passed without incident, but in the dead of night, Xiahou Yuan was woken by the sound of panicked soldiers and the smell of burning timber.

"...What's going on...?" Xiahou Yuan wondered as he sat up and rubbed his eyes.

"**FIRE!**" Xiahou's 13-year-old son, Xiahou Rong, cried as he ran into the tent, dressed in armour and carrying a spear.

"*Fire...?*" Xiahou Yuan said sleepily. "They're... they're attacking...?"

Zhang He pushed Xiahou Rong to one side and entered the tent, shouting, "**Wake up, and get ready, Commander! They're on all sides! We have to retaliate!**"

"Yes... yes! ...Quickly, yes...!" Xiahou Yuan said as he started to regain his senses. "Where are the attacks coming from...?"

"South and east," Zhang He reported.

"You... you take the east," Xiahou Yuan ordered as his son helped him to put his armour on. "I... I will take the south."

"I'll leave you and go," Zhang He said. "...Good luck, Commander." With that, Zhang He journeyed to the east of the camp.

"...Rong'er," Xiahou Yuan said kindly, "try and remain calm."

"I will, Father," Xiahou Rong promised.

Liu Bei's attack had reduced the fences and horse traps to walls of all-consuming, indiscriminate flames. Zhang He led his own forces to the eastern side of the camp, where he opposed forces led by Liu Feng, Chen Shi and Feng Xi; Xiahou Yuan, meanwhile, battled forces led by Yan Yan and Wu Ban.

"We're routing them," Fa Zheng said with disbelief. "Their preparations were pathetic... we've taken them apart! My lord, Chen Shi is reporting that Zhang He is buckling, and Xiahou Yuan has had to send him support... if we now rush the south with everything else we've got, Xiahou Yuan will die."

"Agreed," Huang Quan said surely.

Liu Bei rode forward and shouted, "**Beat the drums, bang the gongs, and shout as loud as you can, men! Veteran General Huang, you may lead the charge!**"

"It will be a pleasure!" Huang Zhong replied: the Yi forces rushed the ruins of the southern gates of the Wei camp, throwing Xiahou Yuan's men into confusion.

"**Stay calm!**" Xiahou Yuan pleaded. "**Stay calm, you fools, STAY CALM!**"

The camp was filled with the screams of men that were burning or suffering from the attacks of Liu Bei's infantry and cavalry that now swarmed the camp. The din and the carnage continued for hours.

Zhang He and Guo Huai led a rabble of survivors from the camp and retreated to the northeast, where the River Han ran from west to east. They commandeered boats, and sailed across, anxious to escape the terrible fate of their comrades.

"...He's dead," Guo Huai said as the men pitched camp on the north bank of the river. "Commander Xiahou is dead... I can't believe it..."

"Are we sure...?" Zhang He asked pointedly.

"...Yes," Guo Huai replied miserably. "He was cut down... his son, and General Zhao Yong as well. It... how can this be???"

"...So do we now go to Nanzheng...?" Zhang He wondered.

"I don't know," Guo Huai replied. "But if someone has to be in charge, then until someone else says otherwise, I say it's you. You knew they'd attack... if he'd only *listened to you*...!"

"He was a good commander," Zhang He insisted. "This... was a flawed moment, like mine at Dangqu. We all get them, General: his was just costlier than some."

Guo Huai and Zhang He said no more: they looked southward, desperately trying to ignore the mournful sobs of their soldiers.

The news was received in Chengdu with relief and hope.

"We've taken everything below the River Han!" Kongming said excitedly as he read a despatch from Mount Dingjun. "...Nanzheng... Ba... we've turned it around!"

"...So the war will soon be over, then...?" Yueying supposed.

"Oh, if that is so, then... then...!" Kongming replied cheerfully. "It says that the Wei forces are regrouping north of the river, and Lord Liu is concerned about the continued threat of Zhang He... but Xiahou Yuan is dead! That... that is an achievement, a truly surprising victory."

Kongming's tone changed as he concluded.

"...Still," Kongming said soberly, "to kill his *son* as well..."

"Son...?" Yueying prompted.

"His son, Rong, died trying to avenge him," Kongming noted. "He was only thirteen or fourteen, by my reckoning... I often think of how sad it would be for my nephews, Ke and Qiao, to fight and die, and they're over sixteen."

"A lot of boys went to fight, initially and in the second draft," Yueying reminded Kongming calmly. "He died fighting for a cause he believed in..."

"All the same," Kongming sighed, "Rong was a noted talent... very bright, very studious, and very promising. Another shining light dimmed and extinguished before its time... does Wei not know how to use worthy men...?"

"Let's be glad they don't," Yueying suggested.

Kongming realised her point, and nodded agreeably.

The victory at Mount Dingjun was not completely decisive, but it did alter the course of events. With the death of Xiahou Yuan, authority passed temporarily to Zhang He, and the Wei forces prepared for a counterattack which – despite the optimistic mood – Liu Bei's forces awaited with dread.

************

## 88

Cao Cao gave General Cao Zhen a force to bolster the defences at Yang Ping Pass, and promised yet again that he would lead a force himself as soon as the opportunity arose: he was even more determined to keep that promise, now that his beloved relative, Xiahou Yuan, had been slain.

Cao Zhen was obese, but it was perhaps due to a medical condition: nobody was really sure. Despite his lack of apparent value in battle, he was still trusted to lead armies by Cao Cao, something that even surprised and irked their relatives.

"...Where is Cao Hong?" Cao Zhen asked as he walked into the command tent at Yang Ping Pass.

"He knows you're here," the official Du Xi reported. "He is still guarding Wudu at present, in case of a second attack by Zhang Fei and Ma Chao."

Cao Zhen sat at the host seat with great difficulty, and replied, "Fine, well, I don't want to work with him, anyway. I suppose he's still enjoying himself."

"Yang Fu and Cao Xiu have both spoken to him, and he is now ready to assist if it is necessary," Du Xi said uncomfortably.

"In other words, they scolded him for his total lack of readiness when Commander Xiahou needed him, and he has been forced to think again," Cao Zhen chortled. "Well, I'm glad I don't need to rely on him. Where is General Xu Huang...?"

"On his way, as you requested," Du Xi replied.

"When he gets here," Cao Zhen ordered, "I want him to launch an immediate strike on the enemy position in front of this pass. If we don't blunt their morale now, it will just lead to more defeats later. They must be shown that we are not done yet."

"...It shall be done," Du Xi replied.

The forces at Yang Ping Pass were now, at Liu Bei's instruction, led by the generals Gao Xiang and Chen Shi: Wei Yan, Zhao Yun and Huang Zhong were all stationed with Liu Bei near the River Han.

"My lord," Jian Yong protested, "we cannot just have Chen Shi and Gao Xiang guarding Yang Ping Pass."

The command tent was busy with hurried discussions and constant streams of messengers bringing news about possible occurrences in Hanzhong, and Liu Bei was unable to focus on any one person for very long.

"...Xianhe, if Cao Cao may be coming here, well then Yang Ping Pass is no longer our priority," Liu Bei replied. "That said, Gao Xiang and Chen Shi are both good generals, and should be able to resist whoever is there. Isn't Zhang He – the true threat – across the river...?"

"*Yes*," Jian Yong retorted, "but *Xu Huang* is reportedly on his way to Yang Ping Pass! He may already be there! *Cao Zhen* certainly is!"

"...*Aiee*," Fa Zheng exclaimed. "Those two generals are outmatched."

"...By a fat oaf and one other fairly notable general...?" Liu Bei scoffed. "Still... if you say there is a danger, Xiaozhi, act as you see fit."

"Well then," Fa Zheng sighed, "we should-"

"**REPORT!**" a messenger cried over the din. "**GAO XIANG HAS BEEN ROUTED BY XU HUANG OF WEI, AND FORCED TO RETREAT FROM YANG PING PASS!**"

"*Routed*...?" Huang Quan murmured. "*Again...?*"

"*Ayah!*" Jian Yong cried. "We're too late!"

"Don't be too worried," Fa Zheng said reassuringly. "It was never ours to lose. We still hold Mount Dingjun, and we're still holding the south of the river. If they launch any serious attack at the pass, we can move troops to the pass to counter it. All this is, unfortunately yet fortunately enough, is a morale boost for them."

"I'll go and inspect the troops, if Cao Cao is coming," Jian Yong suggested.

"I'll join you shortly," Fa Zheng promised.

"...*Aiee*... why does he keep using *Chen Shi*...?" Jian Yong complained as he walked out of the tent.

Cao Cao finally left Chang'an a few weeks later, and personally led another army toward Hanzhong; his advisers were Liu Ye and Yang Xiu, although the latter, as Cao Cao's registrar, was also responsible for general administration.

"I want Liu Bei *dead* this time," Cao Cao insisted. He then ran his finger through his long grey beard and exhaled angrily.

"...Commander Xiahou will be avenged, Your Highness," Liu Ye promised.

Yang Xiu – who, despite his small, thin frame and weak features, was very confident and self-assured – said, "What a shame it is to be away from the capital, away from the marvellous poetry of Cao Zhi. I should have asked him to provide me with some of his latest work to read. Truly profound, truly-"

"If this is a hint about his worthiness as my heir," Cao Cao interrupted, "this isn't the time. All I care about right now is killing Liu Bei and this old man Huang Zhong that killed the man I regarded as my right arm. I will accept surrender by any man of any level of talent but them... they will both suffer slowly."

Cao Cao's forces joined Zhang He's on the north side of the River Han, and the two men planned their first manoeuvres against the Yi forces while Liu Bei and his army watched from their camps on the south bank of the river with nervous interest.

"They've kept their camps away from the bank," Fa Zheng noted. "We were wise to remain on this side after all, my lord."

"So now we're dealing with Cao Cao and Zhang He here, Cao Zhen and Xu Huang at Yang Ping Pass, and Cao Hong at Wudu, with the next strike coming from any of those flash points," Jian Yong surmised. "What shall we do...?"

"Wudu and Yang Ping Pass are not 'flash points', they're blockades, at best," Fa Zheng countered. "Cao Cao's forces are concentrating here for a battle at the river. His supplies are being stored at Mount Bei, and it is there that we must strike next, rather than sit here waiting to be routed."

"...I second that," Huang Quan said emotionlessly.

"I'm not going to argue, we have to hit them while they're unprepared," Jian Yong said surely. "We're outnumbered and, I hate to say it, outclassed... in addition, we're not fighting with a vengeance, and Cao's got far more reinforcements available to him than we do. In fact, we'll need to use women and old men if we run out of personnel this time, and we'll have to train animals and court officials to do the manual labour."

"How under Heaven can you joke at a time like this...?" Fa Zheng chuckled.

"Who's joking...?" Jian Yong retorted. "We're out of men."

"...He's right, as much as I hate to say it," Huang Quan admitted. "Who will attack Mount Bei and destroy Cao Cao's supplies...?"

"Wei Yan and Fu Rong have been despatched to Yang Ping Pass to assist Gao Xiang and Chen Shi in repelling Cao Zhen and Xu Huang," Fa Zheng recounted carefully. "Zhang Fei and Ma Chao are on the Wudu border blocking Cao Hong's advance... that leaves us with Zhao Zilong, Huang Zhong, Meng Da, and Liu Feng, my lord."

"Feng'er and Meng Da are too reckless," Liu Bei said dismissively.

"Well, it was only ever going to be Zilong, and perhaps Huang Zhong," Jian Yong said with a laugh. "What worries me, Xuande, is the men we're dealing with..."

"...Cao Cao and Zhang He...?" Liu Bei pondered. "...Oh, of course... *Wuchao.*"

"Wuchao...?" Huang Quan mused. "Ah, yes... Cao Cao destroyed Yuan Shao's supply depot at Wuchao..."

"That's how Cao Cao won the Battle of Guandu," Fa Zheng realised.

"...By exploiting poor defences," Jian Yong confirmed. "Further to that, Zhang He was one of the many generals that pleaded with Yuan Shao to defend it properly... now he's acting commander of the forces, he doesn't have to reason with anyone, and that's bad news for us now, and in the future."

"So it will have to be both Zilong and Huang Hansheng, then," Liu Bei declared. "Time is against us: have them prepare and depart as soon as possible, and make sure they are aware that they are dealing with veterans of Wuchao..."

In the dead of night, Zhao Yun and Huang Zhong set out for Mount Bei, which was across the River Han. Their seconds were Zhang Zhu and Zhang Yi, the second of three men named Zhang Yi that famously served Liu Bei: his style name was Bogong. The two generals pitched camp on the north bank, to the west of the main forces, and planned their next moves over the next day while their men assembled the log walls, horse traps and archer towers with professional speed.

"I'll go and raid the supplies," Huang Zhong said. "Zilong, you hold the camp."

"No, no," Zhao Yun protested. "Save your precious strength, Veteran General. I am younger, and I rescued A'Dou at Steep-slope with only twenty riders for assistance... I am used to this sort of operation."

"You rescued a helpless child from an emergency," Huang Zhong countered. "Let this old white-haired general spring any traps... then you can try and rescue A'Zhong from his own idiocy, if the need arises."

Zhao Yun laughed and said, "Very well... but be careful, Hansheng. Your forces defeated Xiahou Yuan because he was complacent... Zhang He is altogether different. ...How shall we coordinate...?"

"If I am not back within... mm... a day, at the most... but let us say noon tomorrow," Huang Zhong mused, "then you can consider my position as troubled, and assist me. You can leave Zhang Zhu and Zhang Yi to guard the camp."

"No, no," Zhao Yun replied. "Take Zhang Zhu... you'll need a backup general, Zhang Yi can cope here if I need to come and assist you."

"Very well," Huang Zhong agreed. "I'll set out straight away! See you at noon tomorrow, a little singed but all the happier for it!"

Zhao Yun laughed, and patted the old general on his shoulder.

Noon arrived, and Huang Zhong did not return to the camp.

"...What now, General...?" Zhang Bogong asked.

"What now...?" Zhao Yun chuckled ominously. "I must go and rescue him. He must have come up against Zhang He... guard the camp well, General, and I shall return shortly!"

Zhao Yun was already wearing his battle armour; he mounted his white horse, hailed his elite soldiers, and started the journey to Mount Bei to rescue Huang Zhong.

Zhao Yun advanced to Mount Bei, where he found Huang Zhong surrounded by forces led by Xu Huang and Zhang He.

"Zilong...? ...**ZILONG!**" Huang Zhong cried as he spotted his fellow general advancing on the foot of the mountain.

Zhao Yun levelled his spear and – together with his men – he cut his way through the surprised Wei forces and joined Huang Zhong.

"Are you okay, Veteran General...?" Zhao Yun asked Huang Zhong as the two assessed the situation carefully.

"Yes... did Zhang Zhu reach you...?" Huang Zhong replied.

"No, he didn't," Zhao Yun said worriedly. "But before we can worry about him, we need to escape this encirclement. Are you ready...?"

"Always," Huang Zhong declared.

Both men let out courageous roars, and charged headlong at the terrified infantrymen that surrounded them; to the dismay of Xu Huang and Zhang He, the two generals hacked their way out of the trap and led their men to safety.

"You go back to camp!" Zhao Yun ordered. "I'll cover you, and find Zhang Zhu!"

Huang Zhong reluctantly complied, and led his battered soldiers away from the mountain, as Zhao Yun took his fresh troops back into the fray, intent on finding General Zhang Zhu.

Zhang Zhu was, in fact, trapped by General Wen Ping, the general that had, ten years before, repeatedly defeated Guan Yu's navy after his ill-fated siege of Xiangyang; Zhao Yun engaged Wen Ping directly, fighting him off and scaring him and his soldiers into a retreat.

"Are you okay...?" Zhao Yun asked as he met with the demoralised, blood-spattered Zhang Zhu and his few surviving riders. "Are you hurt...?"

"We... *I* lost some men... I'm sorry," Zhang Zhu whimpered.

"Don't be ridiculous," Zhao Yun chuckled. "Come, let's get back to the camp."

Zhao Yun, Zhang Zhu and their men returned to the camp, and were greeted at the gates by a nervous Zhang Bogong.

"Is Veteran General Huang okay...?" Zhao Yun asked worriedly when he saw that the old warrior was not awaiting his return.

"He is just exhausted, the medic suggested he should rest awhile," Zhang Bogong replied. "I think the same could be said of you, Zhang Zhu."

"Yes, rest, and your men, too," Zhao Yun said to Zhang Zhu: the weary general did not argue, and rode into the camp. Zhao Yun then asked calmly, "Are the enemy in pursuit...?"

"Cao Cao is coming personally, since he has heard that Huang Zhong, 'slayer of Xiahou Yuan', is here," Zhang Bogong reported. "His flag has been spotted."

"I see," Zhao Yun replied thoughtfully.

Zhang Bogong then said, "Well, then we need to close the gates, post visible ranks of archers in the towers, and-"

"No, no," Zhao Yun interrupted. "Take down the flags... and..."

When Cao Cao arrived at the Yi encampment, he surveyed the scene with suspicion and fear. The camp was completely open: not one single flag or banner was flying, and not one single soldier was visible save for Zhao Yun, who was atop his white steed in front of the camp gates. The vegetation around the camp was tall and thick, which added to the possible scenarios.

"...Who is this man that stands alone before us...?" Cao Cao asked uncomfortably.

"I think it is Zhao Yun, styled Zilong," Zhang He said in response.

"Is he the man that fought his way through your combined forces and rescued the felon Huang Zhong...?" Cao Cao asked further.

"...He is," Xu Huang confirmed. "And yes, it is Zhao Zilong... he has aged a little, as I have, but I would recognise him anywhere. He is valiant, strong, and clever."

"...*Clever*...?" Cao Cao mused: he studied Zhao Yun uneasily, and said, "This is a trap."

"I agree," his adviser, Liu Ye, said. "Let's get out of here."

"**RETREAT!**" Cao Cao shouted: but as the Wei forces turned fully to withdraw, archers and crossbowmen appeared from within the vegetation and fired relentlessly on the Wei forces.

"**NOW, CHARGE!**" Zhao Yun boomed. "**A FIEF FOR THE MAN THAT SLAYS THE VILLAIN CAO CAO...!**"

Cao Cao was terrified; he urged his horse to a gallop, followed by his bodyguard Xu Chu, Liu Ye, and the generals Zhang He and Xu Huang. Huang Zhong and Zhang Zhu led two more forces in pursuit of the Wei army as they got out of range of the archers, and pursued them to the River Han. Zhao Yun, Huang Zhong and Zhang Zhu then embarked on a merciless killing spree; many of the men that tried to escape by jumping or falling into the river were drowned instead.

"We have won!" Zhao Yun exclaimed.

"...Alas, not completely," Huang Zhong sighed. "I failed, Zilong..."

Zhao Yun smiled, and said, "Perhaps, if you wish to be hard on yourself: but look at Mount Bei...!"

In the clear daylight, a plume of smoke was visible in the distance: it could only be from Mount Bei, and it could only be a fierce fire destroying Cao Cao's supplies.

"Mister Fa Zheng... must have sent someone else to do it when we didn't come back," Zhao Yun said with cheer. "So we have routed Cao Cao and made it possible for the plan to be realised anyway... so smile, Hansheng... the day is ours!"

Huang Zhong smiled involuntarily, and laughed.

Liu Bei crossed the river with the main forces as soon as it was confirmed that Cao Cao had been pushed back: he then travelled to Zhao Yun's camp, and laughed with glee as 6 generals – Zhao Yun, Huang Zhong, Zhang Bogong, Zhang Zhu, Liu Feng and Meng Da – came out to meet him.

"You are all heroes to match any from history!" Liu Bei praised. "Zilong, you are a tiger among men... and Veteran General Huang..."

"Young Master Liu and General Meng were the ones that successfully burned the supplies, and Zilong is the one that defeated Cao Cao," Huang Zhong said miserably; "all this old fool did was provide bait and distractions."

"You are too hard on yourself!" Liu Bei insisted. "You are a great warrior... you have the death of Xiahou Yuan to your credit. But yes, Zilong... I think we are all agreed that your exploits here were beyond a normal man. Henceforth, you are to be known as the 'General of Tiger Prowess'! You are almost unequalled!"

"My lord," Zhao Yun said with a humble bow, "you overpraise me."

"...Say no more," Liu Bei insisted. "Feng'er, Generals Meng Da, Zhang Zhu, and Zhang Yi... you have all performed admirably, and you will all be rewarded. Cao Cao is broken now... he will not regain ground here, and he knows it. All that remains now is to keep him pinned: the old villain will soon realise that he is better off retreating."

"Agreed," Huang Quan said sombrely.

"Hanzhong... is almost ours," Fa Zheng said surely.

Cao Cao camped beyond the reach of Liu Bei's forces, and began a futile and wasteful series of attempts to regain the area around the River Han. Months passed: his forces were tiring, and their morale was completely gone.

"...Dezu," Cao Cao hailed one day: his registrar, Yang Xiu, responded to the call and looked up from his paperwork.

"Your Highness...?" Yang Xiu prompted.

"How long have we been here, Dezu...?" Cao Cao said as he looked around his large tent; there were wooden tables covered in bamboo scrolls, maps on easels, and weapons on racks in every direction.

"...A long time," Yang Xiu replied cagily.

"I have an order to issue," Cao Cao said. "Summon the officers."

"Very well," Yang Xiu replied with a sense of foreboding.

As soon as the generals and officials were assembled in Cao Cao's tent, Liu Ye said, "Your Highness... what is your order...?"

"...Chicken rib," Cao Cao declared. "My order is 'Chicken rib'."

Yang Xiu exhaled noisily and said, "What a shame it is, indeed."

Noting the confusion of the officials and generals – and not entirely understanding himself – Liu Ye said, "Your Highness... *Chicken rib...?*"

"It is a shame to discard it, for though it has no meat on it, it does have some flavour, some potential, though perhaps not enough," Yang Xiu explained, "very much like this campaign. Prepare to retreat."

"...*Retreat...?*" Liu Ye exclaimed as he looked at Cao Cao, who nodded silently. "...Very well then," Liu Ye sighed. "...Retreat."


Kongming was at home when a messenger arrived from Hanzhong, his face wreathed in a smile.

"Oh my... it...!" Kongming said excitedly as the messenger fell to one knee: Yueying entered the room and smiled.

"**Report...!**" the messenger said with a tone that bordered on hysterical laughter. "Cao Cao's forces have completely retreated from Hanzhong! The campaign is concluded with a victory for our forces!"

"We won... **WE WON!**" Kongming said with laughter: he practically pulled the messenger to his feet, and grasped his shoulders, saying with disbelief, "We've *won*...!"

Kongming released the elated messenger and turned to Yueying, who practically fell into his arms with emotional exhaustion. The messenger stepped back, still smiling, and left Kongming and Yueying alone.

"We... we won...!" Kongming sobbed wearily as he hugged Yueying.

"We won," Yueying replied gratefully.

"Everyone can come home now," Kongming supposed. "We... we have Hanzhong... it... it's finally happened! The three states... the plan that Lu Zijing and I said would come to pass... it's here, it's happened! I promised Lord Liu it would... oh, how I doubted it in recent days, but... but it's here, it's real, it's-"

"Calm down," Yueying pleaded. "You want to go to the court, I can tell, but... let us just-"

Cheers started to erupt along the street outside as the news of the victory spread, interrupting Yueying before she could finish. Ma Su – who only lived a short distance away – ran into the house with Kongming's brother Zhuge Jun, and Yueying's father Mister Huang, shouting, "**WE WON, KONGMING! WE WON, WE WON, WE WON...!**"

"Your 'Longzhong Plan'," Mister Huang croaked, "was a possibility after all, my wonderful, brilliant son-in-law... and now, thanks to you, and all the brilliant men you serve alongside... it's a reality."

Kongming embraced Ma Liang's brother Ma Su, and then his own brother Jun as he said, "I... am speechless!"

"That makes a nice change!" Mister Huang snickered as he hugged his daughter.

"...Cao Cao... now we're Wu and Wei's equal, we can destroy Cao Cao!" Ma Su supposed. "Together with Eastern Wu, we can finally defeat the old villain, break his hold on the imperial court, and save the Han Dynasty...!"
"...And Northern Jing...! ...Longzhong could be liberated... we could go *home*...!" Zhuge Jun suggested.
Kongming and Yueying's teary eyes met, and they smiled hopeful smiles as Kongming replied, "Yes... that's all possible now...!"

As the last of Cao Cao's men fled Hanzhong, the area fell entirely under Liu Bei's control. The mountainous region of Wudu remained, in part, a Wei stronghold, but that mattered little. Liu Feng and Meng Da were immediately despatched to take the region west of Fan and Xiangyang, which would facilitate the recapture of Zhuge Liang's home, along with the rest of northern Jing Province. At last, three states – the Kingdom of Wei, the state of Eastern Wu, and the reunited lands of Yi and Hanzhong – had been formed as a precursor for the final battle that would decide the fate of the imperial house of Han.

＊＊＊＊＊＊＊＊＊＊＊＊

# ACT VIII: THE BATTLE OF XIAOTING

## 89

The mood in Chengdu was one of elation as Liu Bei returned victorious from the Hanzhong Campaign. That campaign had brought the Liu faction to the brink of destruction, but with a few stratagems, some relaxations of legal normalities, and some rare acts of courage and tenacity, the day had been won, and Cao Cao, King of Wei, had retreated to his domains to lick his wounds. Now Yi and Hanzhong – which would thereafter be known collectively as 'Shu' – celebrated as one. Within a decade, Liu Bei had made the transition from homeless warlord-for-hire to the master of over a quarter of the land and peoples of China. But the southeast part of his domain – southern Jing Province – was still, as it had been since those first days of the Liu-Sun alliance, a point of contention. Now, its final governor – Liu Bei of Shu, or Sun Quan of Wu – would have to be decided, by the pen or by the sword.

**"Welcome home, my lord!"** Kongming said as Liu Bei entered the court, followed by the heroes of the Hanzhong Campaign: Zhang Fei, who had scored an initial victory at Dangqu; Ma Chao and Ma Dai, whose forces had allowed a successful initial strike on Wudu, and a fairly graceful retreat from that place when a worse defeat loomed; Huang Zhong, whose assault on Xiahou Yuan's forces at Mount Dingjun eliminated a 'limb' of Cao Cao's kingdom; Wei Yan, whose support manoeuvres throughout the campaign gave Liu Bei more victories than were otherwise possible; Fa Zheng, Huang Quan and Jian Yong, the advisers on the campaign; and, trailing behind the main group, were the other generals such as Zhang Bogong, Wu Ban, Fu Rong and Feng Xi.
"Well, it took nearly thirteen years to get there, but it looks like your tripod theorem wasn't so ridiculous after all!" Jian Yong joked as he approached Kongming and clasped his hand in a show of friendship.
"You seem to have brought everyone here to greet us," Liu Bei noted as he looked at the officials lining left side of the hall. "…I see some unfamiliar faces."
"We've had to have personnel changes to provide your reinforcements," Kongming replied. "We've found some great talents, however, by doing that."
"…Fine, fine!" Liu Bei chuckled as he took his host seat and gazed at the officials and generals before him. "…I really never thought this day would ever come. I can finally rival Cao Cao… I can finally rid the world of the villain, save the Emperor, and restore the imperial house! …Now, my son Feng and General Meng Da are currently attacking Shangyong and Fangling…"
"What about Wu…?" Yi Ji asked.
"What about them…?" Liu Bei snickered. "They're still burying plague victims, I imagine… they're in no fit state to assist us, but I'm sure that when they see our activity in northern Jing, they'll resume the eastern front once they've sorted themselves out."
"They've resolved their domestic problems," Kongming confirmed. "Through our now impersonal communications with Wu, we've ascertained from Chief Commander Lü Meng that there is another attack on Hefei Castle planned."

"Well, they were bound to capitalise on our victory in Hanzhong, so that comes as no surprise," Liu Bei scoffed.

"I... was referring more to the return of southwest Jing Province," Yi Ji said nervously. "After all, we did promise-"

"They won't dare ask for Jing now," Liu Bei interrupted. "Our forces will at least equal theirs at the moment of any conflict... and they have a very large part of Jing already as so-called 'security and reparation' for an old matter, so really, Mister Yi, do they need any more...?"

"...Perhaps," Kongming said thoughtfully, "we should try and maintain good relations, since the tripod theorem does rely on it. Firstly, we cannot risk an attack from Wu right now. Secondly and perhaps most importantly, Cao Cao is currently on the defensive, but that will not last long. Wudu is being repopulated to reduce the risk of insurrection should we strike there again, and Cao Cao will definitely try and strike something... hopefully he'll target Ruxukou, but if he struck at Jiangling..."

"Ah, yes, I se your point: our main force is too far away to assist," Liu Bei fretted. "Further to that, we cannot afford to leave any point unguarded until we know the truth of things..."

"I don't think an attack there is likely," Huang Quan said dismissively. "There is a rebellion going on in Xiangyang and Xinye, so Cao Ren is too busy with that to command an attack on Jiangling."

"That rebellion... which got no help whatsoever from Yunchang, despite written pleas... collapsed months ago, Cao Ren is just clearing up the mess now," Kongming countered. "All they needed was help... have we learned no lessons from Lujiang...?"

"Is that so...?" Liu Bei enquired. "I wasn't entirely aware of these things. Why did Yunchang not help those brave friends of ours in northern Jing, and leave them to die?"

"Guan Yunchang has, at the most, fifteen thousand men to use for an attack, and they might have been needed for Hanzhong, or to repel an attack by Wu," Fa Zheng interjected. "Further to that, the 'rebels' were *Wei generals*, not local people, and their motives were unclear: don't be too judgemental, Kongming."

"That's perfectly true," Kongming sighed. "I should know that."

"You're tired," Liu Bei chuckled. "Anyone can see that. People will speak of our exploits on the front line, but you had to administrate Yi and keep close watch on Jing for the duration of the campaign... that is a huge burden."

Kongming shook his head, saying, "My success is down to the fabulous officials in your service, such as Yang Hong, Dong He, Qin Mi and Zhang Yi... if not for Elder Yang Hong especially, where would we be...? Truly, no man can survive alone... he is as good as his support."

"Mister Yang, you will be remembered for your service," Liu Bei said as he looked at the old politician. "But Kongming... a good support is wasted on a useless man. You had to be of immense value too... your contribution is as great as any man on the battlefield, and it is your plan that began our proper journey. Let no man forget that, my friend, least of all you. Please... rest...?"

"...I will," Kongming promised.

Court continued until the afternoon, at which point the session was ended so that a celebratory banquet could be held. Liu Bei's forces revelled for some time, in order to reward themselves for a difficult campaign.

Time passed, and matters progressed. Reports from Shangyong and Fangling arrived within hours of each other, and were presented to an elated Liu Bei at a court session.

"...We've taken Fangling... and Shangyong has surrendered!" Jian Yong reported joyously. "That's it... Hanzhong is now secured!"

"My lord, the people are grateful for your sagely rule," Huang Quan began unexpectedly. "Since you have been our governor, you have proved yourself to be every bit the magnanimous master, and every bit the wise warrior, advancing to battle for the causes of justice and preservation of the law. When Zhang Lu threatened our borders, he was often asked by the people of his land to take the title 'King of Han'ning', but he refused on the grounds of unworthiness, a view shared by the people of Yi. Now, you hold Hanzhong fairly and justly, having purged the region of Cao Cao and the remnants of the Celestial Masters. The people of Hanzhong hold you in high esteem, and yet you are not considered the equal of the villain Cao Cao, since he is the King of Wei, whereas you are but a governor. Why not do as the people desire, and appoint yourself 'King of Hanzhong'...?"

"*Ayah*," Jian Yong exclaimed. "Is that really going to solve anything?"

"It would reinforce Lord Liu's governance in the region, and send a message to Cao Cao that there will always be a king to face him on equal footing," Kongming said agreeably. "I think it is a fabulous proposal."

"Well, put like that, fine," Jian Yong conceded. "If it's what everybody wants, and it isn't going to cause any trouble... congratulations, Xuande."

"Uh... well, if as you say, it is the desire of the people," Liu Bei said hesitantly, "then who am I to refuse...?"

"We should then prepare for a coronation!" Huang Quan said gladly. "My lord... Your Highness... it will be a great day indeed."

Liu Bei smiled, but tears were forming in the corners of his eyes.

"Why are you crying...?" Jian Yong wondered.

"So many friends have not lived to see this day," Liu Bei said sadly. "My friends of old, Gongsun Zan, Tao Qian, Mister Sun, General Huo Jun, Master Young Phoenix, Wu Ju... I weep for the loss of them, and also with joy, because we made it this far, we are realising the dream that all great men wish for... true peace."

"The people need some colour in their lives after such an awful time," Jian Yong supposed. "A coronation... would be a great boost to morale."

"And a bloody waste of money," Zhang Fei whispered to Wei Yan, who nodded agreeably.

"...This is, of course, all dependent on Hanzhong remaining in our hands for Lord Liu to call it a kingdom," Fa Zheng suggested. "Shouldn't a protector of the region be named now, so that we can safely move forward...?"

"Oh, yes, of course," Liu Bei said with a laugh.

Zhang Fei smiled confidently.

"...Guan Yunchang has guarded Jing exceptionally well," Kongming said as a prompt. "Which of your great generals will be given a domain to rule in your stead, to guard against the looming threat of the King of Wei...?"

"...*Wei Yan* shall rise to the task," Liu Bei replied: the entire court was shocked and surprised, and Zhang Fei's face fell.

Wei Yan got to his feet, walked to the centre of the room, and kowtowed to Liu Bei, saying, "I am honoured by this show of faith in me, Your Highness."

Kongming made eye contact with the miserable – and slightly humiliated – Zhang Fei, who smiled sadly, snorted a laugh, and lowered his gaze to the floor.

"Tell us, please, General Wei," Liu Bei said, "how you will fulfil your role."

Wei Yan got to his feet and proclaimed, "If Cao Cao invaded the province with every man in his army, I will assist you, Your Highness, in repelling them; if a general came with force of a hundred thousand, I will ensure that they are destroyed, Your Highness."

"...Good answer," Jian Yong admitted.

"Splendid!" Liu Bei chuckled. "I knew from our previous conversations that you were the right man for the job: a warrior through and through, who has learned from his mistakes and become a thinker, a man who knows his limitations and acts within them! Only a man such as you can protect Hanzhong... I know you will not let me down, Wenchang."

"Your Highness," Wei Yan said boldly, "I have already formulated a plan for the defence of the region... if it is at all possible, I should like time with yourself and the senior advisers to gain final approval."

Kongming looked at Jian Yong, who shrugged as Liu Bei replied, "Splendid, splendid! We shall *make* the time!"

Court proceedings ended later that day: as many of the officials started to prepare for Liu Bei's upcoming coronation as 'King of Hanzhong', Kongming decided to visit Zhang Fei.

"...What...?" Zhang Fei asked miserably as Kongming entered his living room. "I suppose Xuande asked you to come and make sure I'm not drunk, smashing up the place and planning on going and having it out with him."

"No," Kongming replied. "I'm here of my own volition."

"Right," Zhang Fei grunted. "So what did you want...?"

"There isn't a man in that court, not a man in the land that isn't shocked by his decision," Kongming said kindly. "The fool that lost Xu Province to Lü Bu for the sake of a quarrel is consigned to history... the ignoramus who once prodded me with a chicken wing and called me a 'bastard pedant' is long gone. They have been replaced by a wise owl that earned Yan Yan's respect and outwitted Zhang He. I don't know why he chose Wei Yan..."

"He's the better man, obviously," Zhang Fei muttered.

"I disagree," Kongming insisted. "Wei Yan is arrogant, contemptuous... and unlike you, it is never in jest. But... he is clever, admittedly, and he is well read..."

"Like I said, he's the better man," Zhang Fei said sadly. "The times are changing, Mister Zhuge. When it was me, Xuande, Yunchang, Zilong, Mister Jian, old Mister Sun and those Mi brothers, roaming the land, fighting for whatever we could get... it was all simple, you either lost a battle or you won it, you had food or you didn't. Once everything got bigger, well... an ignorant old pig butcher like me was never going to be able to keep up. This isn't Steep-slope... I can't just yell at half a million men and make them go away, we need strategy. It's not time for brutes like me, Lü Bu, or even Ma Chao anymore... you have to be smart, like Yunchang, Zilong, Wei Yan, and Lü Meng."

"You still have your place," Kongming insisted. "As General of the Right, you will be guarding Yi against invasion."

"But they have to get past Wei Yan or Yunchang first," Zhang Fei retorted. "I'm a last line of defence, like Chen Dao... doomed to spend my last years waiting for a disaster to happen so I can get to do something."

Kongming exhaled noisily, and replied, "I should leave you."

"See you at the coronation," Zhang Fei scoffed.

Kongming left Zhang Fei to brood, and returned to his duties.

The official Fei Shi hurried to Jiangling in Jing Province, his mission being to deliver the news to Guan Yu and his officials.

"**Further to this,**" Fei Shi continued after announcing the coronation, "**there will be promotions and titles assigned! Esteemed General Guan Yu will henceforth be known as General of the Vanguard, and one of the Five Tigers of Shu!**"

"...'Five Tigers of Shu', eh...?" Guan Yu said with a laugh. "With which men do I share this honour...?"

"**You are sharing the accolade with generals Zhang Fei, Zhao Yun, Ma Chao and Huang Zhong!**" Fei Shi replied cheerfully.

"...Brother Yide and Zilong, I understand," Guan Yu said with disappointment. "I also understand the need to elevate Ma Chao, since he is a key figure in our future enterprise, due to his relationship with the barbarian tribes, and the son of a court official... but *Huang Zhong*...? Why do I share this 'accolade' with an old common soldier, a man of no real rank or status...?"

Ma Liang lowered his head and sighed regrettably at the callous observation.

✳✳✳✳✳✳✳✳✳✳✳✳

## 90

Now that the cities of Shangyong and Fangling were secured, the western route into Northern Jing was clear. The southern Jing capital, Jiangling, provided the first and most obvious route, but any attack on the northern Jing strongholds of Xiangyang City and Fan City from there would be impeded by Wei forces stationed in the regions between those cities and Jiangling, such as Dangyang County. Now that the Hanzhong route was clear, however, the Shu invaders could coordinate resources more easily, and force Wei into a defensive posture. This all led to a further consequence: once Xiangyang and Xinye cities were blockaded, there would be no obstruction to an invasion of the northern heartland by the Shu forces. This worried Cao Cao, who called an urgent meeting of his top advisers.

"...I want to strike Jiangling, hit them before they hit me," Cao Cao suggested. "If we do it now, before they have a chance to-"

"That... won't be possible," Liu Ye said uncomfortably.

"The troops are currently demoralised and unfit for service," Sima Yi concurred.

"We should wait until the troops are recovered," Jia Xu proposed. "Your Highness, if we rush into this, it will lead to disaster."

"Yes... and we don't want another one of those again so soon, do we...?" Cao Cao grumbled. "Very well... we'll wait. But I want to be kept informed of every little scrap of news from east, west, south and north! If someone so much as looks at one of our soldiers in a strange way, I want to know about it!"

"...**Yes, Your Highness,**" the advisers said as one.

Liu Bei, meanwhile, was enjoying a tour of Yi Province as the newly crowned King of Hanzhong. He was sat in a grand carriage, accompanied by his friend Jian Yong.

"So how does it feel to be a king, Xuande...?" Jian Yong asked.

"...Shouldn't you be calling me 'Your Highness' now, Mister Jian...?" Liu Bei chuckled.

"Piss off," Jian Yong snickered: the two men enjoyed the humorous interlude.

"All it is all day is 'Your Highness' this, and 'My liege' that," Liu Bei sighed. "I should enjoy it, Xianhe, but... well, I get no time to myself, and at my age, I should be able to spend some time at home..."

"...Managing your garden," Jian Yong teased. "Xuande, you're a soldier at heart, a warlord... you'd get bored, surely...?"

"I don't mind the quiet life if it's comfortable," Liu Bei admitted. "If being the King of Hanzhong meant sitting around all day, surrounded by fulsome beauties, fine wine, fine treasures... nothing's changed at all. The Han is still endangered, I'm still fighting Cao Cao, I'm still having to worry about Jing Province, and Sun Quan..."

"...And this prohibition," Jian Yong complained. "I know there's a shortage of things at the moment, but do you have to hit people where it hurts...?"

"I like a drink, you know that," Liu Bei said seriously. "But we need to save everything to feed people... everyone had a good drink for my coronation, and now we have to be a little more conservative."

"...There's 'conservative', and there's 'stupid'," Jian Yong scolded. "Kong Rong went up against Cao Cao over banning wine, and was even willing to lose his life for it. Surely you're risking rebellion...? You do know there are people that would defect to Wu if they were promised some wine...?"

Liu Bei sniggered dismissively and said, "Nonsense."

"It's not," Jian Yong insisted. "As soon as things were more or less back to normal, you packed the women back indoors and expected war veterans to get back in their fields... that annoyed enough people. But now, you're banning wine...? ...And you do know that there are local inspectors taking it to ridiculous lengths, don't you...?"

"...Like what...?" Liu Bei asked curiously.

"Like arresting people for owning *spoons*," Jian Yong said sincerely.

"...Go away...!" Liu Bei chuckled. "Shut up, you're talking nonsense."

"No, I'm *serious*," Jian Yong insisted. "Spoons, Xuande... bloody *spoons*."

"...Well, the officials are not fools," Liu Bei supposed. "It depends on the context... and if they had the right equipment for the crime..."

Jian Yong glared at Liu Bei, who was now looking out of the carriage at the field to the left of the road. Jian Yong shook his head disapprovingly, and exclaimed miserably, "*Aiee.*"

"...What's that for...?" Liu Bei asked.

"...Nothing," Jian Yong replied: he then looked out of the carriage, seemingly fixated with something. After a short time, he suddenly turned to Liu Bei and said with horror, "Xuande, **stop the carriage! STOP THE CARRIAGE!**"

"What...!" Liu Bei cried. "What is it, what is it???"

"Out there, don't you see...?" Jian Yong said dramatically. "That man... is about to molest that woman! Quickly, we must arrest him!"

Liu Bei leant across the carriage and followed Jian Yong's gaze and frantic gestures: up ahead, an old couple were stood by the side of the road talking, but besides them, nobody was there.

"...I don't see anything," Liu Bei said uneasily.

"No, no, those two, don't you see???" Jian Yong said with fear.

"But... they're just old people talking," Liu Bei said with despair.

"Xuande, I'm an official, and officials are not fools," Jian Yong protested pointedly. "It depends on the context... and if, as a man, he has the right equipment for the crime...!"

"What are you...?" Liu Bei exclaimed: and then, he suddenly realised that Jian Yong – who was patting his own crotch as he delivered his last words – was mocking his stance on the prohibition arrests. As Jian Yong smirked mischievously, Liu Bei leant back in his seat, glared at Jian Yong, and started to laugh uproariously.

"So can we look at the whole prohibition thing again, please...?" Jian Yong asked desperately. "Or at least put something on the statutes to make owning a *spoon* slightly less damning...? ...Else we may as well arrest every man who isn't a eunuch for being a-"

"Okay, *okay*...!" Liu Bei said through his laughter. "I'll... I'll think it over...!"

"Bloody hell, Xuande...!" Jian Yong chuckled disappointedly. "What it takes to make you see sense, sometimes!"

Sun Quan massed his forces for his proposed attack on Hefei Castle, but neither his Chief Commander nor anyone else made an attempt to contact the Shu leadership to coordinate a pincer attack through southwest Jing. However, no attempt was made to discuss or demand the return of southwest Jing either.

"...The lack of communication is disconcerting," Kongming admitted as he led a meeting with some of his fellow officials.

"Not a lot we can do about it, really," Yi Ji said emotionlessly.

"Perhaps my brother should seek an audience with Chief Commander Lü Meng...?" Ma Su suggested.

"He's tried," Kongming said worriedly. "All he ever gets is some guard telling him that Lü Meng is either busy or ill... his assistant, Lu Xun, will not speak to us either at the moment. They're saying that the Hefei campaign is keeping them occupied."

"That's something that we should all be viewing with interest," Fa Zheng proposed. "Is Yunchang watching Cao Cao's movements...?"

"He is," Kongming confirmed. "It's looking very much like Cao Cao might divert his main forces to Hefei to repel Wu... if he does, then we've got him."

"They were thinking about an attack on Jing," Dong He noted. "We're lucky that his advisers talked him out of it."

"...He killed another one, didn't he, for supposedly trying to influence his choice of heir," Yi Ji said derisively. "It was Secretariat Yang Xiu, this time..."

"*Aiee*... he was rather gifted," Kongming lamented. "Oh, old villain, die soon, before you can harm another talent...!"

"...Kongming," Dong He said awkwardly, "do we... know what His Highness intends to do about his own heir...? He was supposed to announce it when-"

"I didn't call the meeting to discuss that," Kongming replied uncomfortably. "Yes, I am being consulted about it, but... I'd rather not discuss it."

"There isn't anything to discuss," Ma Su said plainly. "Liu Feng is the eldest son, he's a war hero, and that's that."

"...But His Highness now has three blood sons, Kongming, born to his wives and concubines," Dong He noted. "Although Liu Feng was adopted before any of them were born-"

"Look, I have to have this conversation with His Highness frequently now," Kongming sighed wearily. "I... I really think we need to discuss Yunchang's stance against Wei before we worry about whether Liu Feng or Liu Shan is the crown prince of Hanzhong."

"I agree," Fa Zheng said sternly. "What if Yunchang needed military aid...? Have we the resources to support him...?"

"No," Kongming admitted. "If he attacks Xiangyang and Xinye now – which he will do regardless of what we think if the notion arises within him – it's with whatever forces that he can muster within the province, and nothing more... in a few months perhaps, we could help... but not now."

"But can he afford to miss an opportunity...?" Ma Su wondered.

"No," Kongming retorted. "It just means he'll have to accept the risk, and show cautiousness... something which, sadly, is not his greatest strength when his arrogance has peaked."

Guan Yu had, as many had predicted, noted the reports of the massing of Wu forces in the east, and also the opportunity provided by the Wei response: he called his generals and officials to an emergency meeting in Jiangling. Ma Liang and Mi Fang reached the meeting room early, and nervously awaited Guan Yu and the other officials.

"This is about an attack on Fan, isn't it," Mi Fang said to Ma Liang with a tone of resignation.

"Why do you speak as though that is a bad thing...?" Ma Liang wondered.

"Who can we rely on here...?" Mi Fang complained. "Lord Liu... or rather, 'His Highness'... cannot spare forces for an attack, so we would be taking every scrap of resource we have on this, leaving ourselves exposed to a hostile and voracious Wu led by Lü Meng, who is every bit as dangerous as Zhou Yu ever was, if not more so. We have only Zhao Lei, Shi Ren, Xiang Chong, Liao Hua... what sort of effective attack could we launch against Cao Ren, a man that held the entire Wu army at bay for a year with a *quarter* of what he can muster now...?"

"He held around half of the Wu army at bay for a year with the aid of a ridiculous personnel and resource advantage, and yet he still lost in the end," Ma Liang countered. "Things have changed since then... their front is Xiangyang, which I know well, and with the cities to the west under our control, with Liu Feng, the lord's own son, and Meng Da, a very capable field general, in charge of them, ready to provide support at a moment's notice... this time, Wu is keeping Cao Cao completely occupied on the eastern front, and there are scores of disaffected Wei vassals – for one, the impressed Jing officials, soldiers and civilians – that will defect when they see that we're on the offensive."

"That's very optimistic," Mi Fang suggested. "What if Wu buckle again...? Even if they are committed, last time the outcome was decided by plague, not swords: what if-"

"We have to try," Ma Liang insisted. "Word from friends in the capital is that Cao Cao wanted to attack us with everything he had, and that he was forced to-"

"I know, I heard that too," Mi Fang interrupted. "My point is not so much that we shouldn't take the initiative... my point is that we have insufficient resources to fight Cao Ren, let alone fight Cao Ren *and* keep Jing from Lü Meng, and that *cannot* be refuted."

Before Ma Liang could give an answer, Guan Yu entered the hall and took his seat: he closed his eyes and seemed to be meditating. Ma Liang studied his face silently, wondering whether the veteran general was planning something grand, or if it was going to be an impulsive, suicidal strike on an overwhelmingly large opponent. The other officials started to arrive, and took their seats: once all were seated, Guan Yu's son, Guan Ping – who had arrived shortly after his father – coughed to indicate that he was about to speak.

"My father has invited you all here to discuss an attack on Fan City," Guan Ping declared. "There will need to be logistical planning, and-"

"We can't attack Wei right now," Shi Ren protested. "We're under-resourced."

Guan Yu opened his eyes and looked at Shi Ren coldly.

"If we leave responsible, sensible officials in charge of the key cities," Ma Liang suggested, "then this plan is entirely feasible. Mi Fang can guard Jiangling, and you, General Shi, can guard Gong'an. Zhao Lei, Liao Hua and I will accompany Commander Guan and General Guan Ping, providing military, administrative and advisory support."

Guan Yu nodded, saying, "My thoughts entirely, Jichang. We shall begin preparations immediately. We will keep forces stationed at key strategic points to guard against Lü Meng, and with our signal beacon network along the river, he cannot hope to surprise us. If they attack, we can rush back and secure the province, requesting emergency aid from His Highness, while Liu Feng and Meng Da keep the pressure on Xiangyang in our stead, until we can resume our march northward. Regardless, the aim is to pressurise the enemy, giving time for His Highness to stabilise Hanzhong and resume the offensive from there… no more, no less. Once His Highness is ready, we will be just another part of a larger attack that will finally see the end of the traitor Cao Cao, and the restoration of justice and order."

The officials made agreeable statements and murmurs, and the decision was made: as soon as it was possible, Guan Yu would lead an army of twenty thousand or more – some from his own forces, some from Liu Bei's own regiments – northward, in an attempt to retake northern Jing and remove Cao's influence from the province.

That march north was carried out with clinical swiftness, and soon enough, Cao Ren of Wei was under siege yet again.

∗∗∗∗∗∗∗∗∗∗∗∗

## 91

Cao Cao anxiously awaited news from Hefei, where he hoped that Zhang Liao would once again succeed in driving Sun Quan's forces away. On one dark and gloomy day, Sima Yi arrived at Cao Cao's palatial home to deliver some unexpected bad news.

"...Zhongda," Cao Cao exclaimed. "What are you doing here...?"

"...Your Highness," Sima Yi reported, "we've received a letter from Cao Ren, it appears to be urgent..."

Sima Yi passed the letter to Cao Cao, who read it speedily.

"...**Ayah!**" Cao Cao cried as he read the letter. "...I knew we should have attacked them before! Now they have the advantage!"

"...Our troops were not ready for an offensive," Sima Yi insisted, "although we might perhaps have reinforced Xiangyang and Fan a little more."

"...We cannot allow Guan Yu to take those cities," Cao Cao mused. "Knowing him as I do, he will not stop... I must send immediate aid."

"Much of our force is taken up with monitoring the border with Hanzhong, and manning the eastern front against Wu... we can only spare General Yu Jin," Sima Yi reported honestly.

"His glory days are far behind him, but if there is one thing to be said about Wenze, one can pick from fair, just, brave, and dependable, and just the right man for the job," Cao Cao declared confidently. "...But his age bothers me... Guan Yu is still a demon, despite his grey hairs, while Yu Jin was never a match in martial prowess, even when he was younger. ...He will need a second."

Sima Yi remained silent as Cao Cao pondered the appointment.

"...To defeat Guan Yu, we need a terrifying man, a man who can match Guan in his skill, and intimidate his followers," Cao Cao decided. "General Pang De will accompany Wenze to lift the siege of Fan. He has already worked with Cao Ren, so that will work very well indeed. General Yu and General Pang should depart for Fan immediately with a force of a hundred thousand... for although I respect Guan Yu, I want him overwhelmed, I need him to be destroyed, or the capital will be endangered. Summon the officers... I'll issue the orders personally."

Sima Yi nodded silently and departed to carry out his instructions.

One night, weeks later, Kongming sat with Yueying in their Chengdu home and mused over the current events with concern.

"Yu Jin and Pang De have been despatched with an army of a hundred thousand to aid Cao Ren," Kongming said soberly.

"Guan Yu cannot hope to defeat such odds," Yueying supposed.

"He could, if he were dealing with idiots," Kongming chuckled miserably. "That's a potent combination... Cao Ren the stalwart defender, Yu Jin the 'cautious thinker', Pang De the valiant savage... Ma Chao is very disappointed to hear that his old deputy is now working so hard for Cao Cao, but the two are irreconcilable, and Pang is not a man that makes decisions lightly, so there is no way to win him over. Our only hope is that the reports on their encampment are correct."

"...What reports...?" Yueying wondered.

Kongming smiled, and said, "If the reports *are* true, then General Yu Jin has made a laughing stock of his own reputation. He has, *if the reports are true*, overridden concerns and put his entire hundred-thousand-man force in one location... a heavily fortified camp along the riverbank."

"...But if there are heavy rains...!" Yueying supposed.

"...Yes, well, I dislike the human cost aspect, but we'll win if that happens," Kongming sighed. "We need some good news, because Cao Cao's forced migration has taken nearly a hundred thousand people away from Hanzhong, meaning that there are severe labour shortages, no men to conscript, and massive administrative overhauls required. That means, obviously, that we can't really move north until Hanzhong is stabilised... there will be no march on Cao Cao from the west, not for a while."

"...Well," Yueying replied, "we should wish Guan Yu luck, then."

Guan Yu continued his siege of Fan and Xiangyang, despite the odds that now faced him: atop the walls of Fan City, Cao Ren and Pang De stood with a group of officials and lesser generals, watching Guan Yu riding back and forth amongst his troops and issuing orders.

"I will blunt him," Pang De promised.

The officials murmured disconcertedly.

"...It appears that I'm not trusted," Pang De said tensely.

"We've worked together before, *I* trust you," Cao Ren insisted. "His Highness would never have sent you here if he didn't trust you, anyway. By all means, do what you can... get rid of him, if that's possible."

"Commander," one official said worriedly, "this man has a brother in Liu Bei's service, and also his former master."

"So it has come to this," Pang De lamented. "Commander, I'll take a detachment of my own troops, and I will fight Guan Yu... I will take an enemy's head, to prove my sincerity to you and your vassals."

Cao Ren nodded silently, and Pang De left the battlements to prepare for a direct engagement of Guan Yu's forces.

Guan Yu and his officials were in their command tent when Pang De started his bold manoeuvres; a messenger ran into the tent and fell to one knee.

"**REPORT!**" the messenger cried. "**The gates of Fan are opening!**"

"What...?" Guan Ping said with surprise. "They're actually going to charge...?"

Guan Yu's forces outside Fan City were awestruck as – despite the activity against the fortress city – its gates were opening to allow a contingent of troops to enter the battlefield. Pang De rode at the front of his force, adorned in intimidating Qiang armour and astride a magnificent white horse. When Guan Yu reached the scene with his officials, he read the general's standard and sneered.

"...Pang De of Xiliang...?" Ma Liang noted with shock.

"**Traitor...!**" Guan Yu barked. "I'll take him on myself!"

"The man is younger than you," Zhao Lei protested.

"I'll break him in two!" Guan Yu snarled as he raised his Green Dragon pole sword and roused his horse to charge. Guan Yu and Pang De matched weapons dozens of times, with neither able to gain the advantage; each secretly admired the strength of the other, though they wished it were not so.

"…Magnificent," Cao Ren praised as he watched the joust from the city walls.

"Are we going to try and shoot Guan Yu…?" one official asked.

"No, we might hit General Pang," Cao Ren replied dismissively. "That man is a champion for Wei's future glory days… this surely quells all thoughts of his supposed lack of sincerity! See how he pushes Guan Yu to the limits!"

The officials murmured agreeably.

Eventually, both Guan Yu and Pang De withdrew to their lines, but with the morale of Guan's forces blunted – as Pang De had intended – the siege had lost momentum, and a sudden rush of troops on Guan Yu's position temporarily ended the assault and forced Guan Yu away from Fan's walls. Pang De returned to the city and received a hero's welcome; Guan Yu, meanwhile, retreated to his camp, angry and embittered.

"**D'AAAAGH…!** How can I be bested by a barbarian oaf???" Guan Yu screamed.

"Pang De is another Lü Bu," Ma Liang suggested.

"Ma Chao is 'another Lü Bu'…!" Guan Yu retorted. "How many Lü Bus does the world need at once??? …Our assault is faltering because of this man!"

"The siege of Xiangyang is also faltering," Ma Liang reported uncomfortably. "Yu Jin has successfully entered the city and is assisting the defenders, and because the city is on the opposite side of the river, we cannot coordinate effectively. Our forces are split into three, and that means that all we have are three ineffective units. If we were to focus on breaking Xiangyang, pushing the enemy across the river to Fan, setting the river as a boundary, a line that-"

"We cannot afford to focus ourselves on Xiangyang alone!" Guan Yu interrupted irritably. "Xiangyang and Fan are mutually supportive, and must be broken together! We-"

"We lack the forces to press both with any real effectiveness, Commander," Ma Liang scolded. "We have overstretched ourselves…"

"You seem to be suggesting, Jichang, that I do not know the rule of 'keeping one's forces concentrated'," Guan Yu retorted. "In this case, we had no choice! My objective here is to harass the enemy, destroying their morale and keeping them occupied! The objectives were surprise and sabotage, and that has now been ruined by this traitor, Pang De! Now this looks set to become yet another Jiangling, another prolonged, exhaustive siege that will break both armies!"

"We should request aid from Wu," Ma Liang suggested. "I-"

"No, no," Guan Yu interrupted insistently. "*Never* will I ask for their help: they have treated us contemptuously, and if we ask their aid, they will want southern Jing as initial incentive, and northern Jing as a reward… we will end up worse off for it."

"It doesn't need to be so," Ma Liang protested. "If we request aid, it will show that we are committed to the alliance, and that is very important!"

"*They*, however, are *not* committed," Guan Yu countered.

"They attack Hefei as a sign of their dedication to our alliance," Ma Liang proposed defiantly. "We must accept that the situation here is exactly as Jiangling was, and there – despite Zhou Yu of Wu wanting sole success – we were recruited to help… let us show the same good sense, and call on help when we need it. If our helping Wu gave no reward save the loaning of Jiangling… how can their helping us earn them Fan and Xiangyang, if we are working by the same rules…?"

"…That's true, Father," Guan Ping suggested. "We do need help."

"I'll contact Liu Feng, Meng Da, Mi Fang and Shi Ren as well, since they should be doing more to assist us," Guan Yu grumbled. "I'll write straight away… and if you really think Wu will send aid, Jichang, then fine: go ahead and approach them. I'll leave it entirely with you."

Meng Da – who was serving as a protector of the recently seized Fangling City – received Guan Yu's call for assistance, and travelled to see Liu Feng in the city of Shangyong.

"…Greetings," Liu Feng hailed as Meng Da marched into the courtroom; Shen Dan, the former governor of Shangyong, was present, having been allowed to remain in court circles as gratitude for his quick surrender of the city.

"Did you receive a letter from Guan Yu…?" Meng Da asked.

"I did," Liu Feng replied. "…I am not sure how to respond. This region is still unstable, so we really cannot spare anyone."

"I have the same dilemma," Meng Da sighed. "But… Guan Yu does not like being refused when he makes a request."

"I am the son of the governor of Yi and King of Hanzhong, and his rightful heir," Liu Feng said confidently. "If Guan Yu makes fuss, I will put him in his place."

"This is a military matter," Meng Da retorted, "and your privileged position – if, indeed, your assessment is correct – doesn't come into it."

"…By that, what do you mean…?" Liu Feng asked.

"…I should leave…!" Shen Dan suggested awkwardly; Liu Feng nodded, and the former governor left the two men to talk.

"It is my understanding," Meng Da reported, "that His Highness the King of Hanzhong has regular conversations with Zhuge Liang and other officials… and, of course, his comrade-vassals from the old days, such as Guan Yu, Zhang Fei, and Jian Yong…"

"…And… what do these 'conversations' concern…?" Liu Feng prompted.

"It is only fair that you know," Meng Da replied, "that His Highness is not entirely sure that he wants to appoint you as his heir… he secretly favours his first-born son, Liu Shan."

"...A'Dou...?" Liu Feng chuckled with disbelief. "He's too young, and an imbecile, furthermore. I might have been born as Kou Feng, but I was adopted at a time when Liu Bei had no sons at all, so what is this nonsense...? I am his oldest son by age, and whether I was adopted or not is irrelevant! I've fought battles for him, proved my worth as a man, earned respect from his most able generals, and needlessly put my life on the line! I know that he has...!"

Liu Feng suddenly stopped talking and fell ponderously silent, as he recalled, involuntarily, the times that Liu Bei had not treated him as a true son. Liu Feng scowled bitterly for a moment, and the fleeting expression was not missed by Meng Da.

"...A thought crosses your mind...?" Meng Da asked.

"No," Liu Feng replied coldly. "...No, no, my friend, it does not. I let weak, stupid thoughts fade and wither, as every man should. Return to Fangling: tell Guan Yu the truth, as I will, and that should be the end of the matter."

"...Fair enough," Meng Da replied emotionlessly; he bowed respectfully, and left the courtroom without another word.


Ma Liang, meanwhile, returned to the front from Lukou – Lü Meng's base of operations – in a sombre mood. He wrote to Kongming, who sat in his Chengdu office with Ma Su, digesting the military situation with some discomfort.

"...So Lü Meng has agreed aid," Kongming noted, "but is slow to actually provide it... and worse still... Liu Feng, Meng Da, Mi Fang and Shi Ren have been privately defamed for not sending aid that they cannot spare... what is Guan Yu thinking...?"

"At least it was private defamation," Ma Su said encouragingly. "At least Guan Yu has not told them what he is thinking publicly to shame them. And as for Wu... well, at least they *have* agreed to help us, and it shows that they still want an alliance, doesn't it...?"

"...Yes," Kongming agreed apprehensively. "It looks as though we need the help... Pang De has forced Guan Yu to retreat half-a-dozen times now, and that's making the men start to fear him. Maybe we do need to send Ma Chao to Fan, and try inducing Pang De to defect... perhaps whatever differences Ma and Pang have can be reconciled... we have to *try*, surely."

"Well, he is still in the capital," Ma Su noted. "He spends a lot of time talking to Peng Yang at the moment, I see."

"...Yes," Kongming replied hesitantly.

"I suppose that would worry you, since you fear Peng Yang," Ma Su said plainly.

"Peng Yang is ambitious," Kongming insisted. "He has ill intent for the future... I have warned His Highness repeatedly, and yet... he doesn't see."

"Are you *sure* that you're right...?" Ma Su asked.

"Absolutely sure," Kongming replied. "The man was never fully won over, not like Liu Ba and Huang Quan... he's got ambition, and he will use whatever rhetoric he can to get what he wants. And he is even being given the ability to do it, despite my protestations... because Peng Yang is being given the governorship of Jiangyang. That is a huge mistake: Jiangyang is near strategic rivers and is far enough away from the capital for such a man to plot unhindered, ingratiating himself with the local populace and stirring up resentment for His Highness."
You sound like you want him done away with," Ma Su chuckled.
"Such a man," Kongming replied, "is a threat to us all."
"...So you *do* want him dead," Ma Su realised nervously.
"I seek only the pacification of the realm," Kongming said calmly. "This region was not obtained easily, so it should not be lost easily. We have wished scores of men dead in order to reach this critical point: what's one Peng Yang...?"
"...I see that, if you're right," Ma Su conceded. "But are you *sure*...?"
"I already said that I am," Kongming insisted. "Unfortunately, Ma Chao does not seem to agree."
"You told Ma Chao that you distrust Peng Yang...?" Ma Su said with surprise.
"...If I must regret it, so be it," Kongming replied. "But yes, I said that the man was best avoided. We must only hope that Ma Chao does not intend to join forces with Peng Yang and try to seize Yi Province, or worse yet, all of Shu."
"I doubt they'd have much success," Ma Su said with amusement. "We have Wei Yan, Zhang Fei, and Huang Zhong."
"But if they were to coordinate with Cao Cao of Wei or Sun Quan of Wu," Kongming fretted, "we'd lose it all...! ...Ah, why does life not get any easier...?"
"...You're tired," Ma Su suggested worriedly. "Get some rest: I intend to."
Kongming was going to reply, but he knew that Ma Su was correct: as always, he had worked far too hard, and now, he was near to breaking point once again.
"I'll rest," Kongming promised: he turned to his busy secretarial staff, Dong Jue and Zong Yu, saying, "But you must both promise to bring any urgent military *or* civil matters to my attention."
"You know that they would," Ma Su replied on their behalf.

Guan Yu's situation became increasingly desperate: besides the lack of haste on the part of the Wu reinforcements from Lukou, Guan Yu's soldiers were now openly fearful of Pang De, and morale was plummeting quickly. Despite the failures, Guan Yu made yet another attack on the walls of Fan, and yet again, Pang De challenged him directly by riding out of the city with a band of cavalry.
**"It's General White Horse!"** one of Guan Yu's soldiers cried: infantry scattered in all directions as Pang De whirled his spear and charged randomly.
"...This time," Guan Yu muttered, "I shall defeat you."
Guan Yu charged at the younger general, but after a few clashes, Guan Yu retreated, determined to lure Pang De beyond the safety of his battle lines.

"**Where are you going, Guan Yu...?**" Pang De chuckled: but instead of pursuing, as Guan Yu intended, he concentrated his attacks on Guan's panicked infantrymen. When Guan Yu realised that there would be no successful trap, he turned and charged at Pang De once again, and General Zhao Lei followed him to provide support. Pang De did not say a word as Guan Yu challenged him again: he took up his bow, fitted an arrow to the string, and released it. Soldiers on both sides were shocked – and none more than Guan Yu himself – when the arrow struck the narrow plume of his helmet with terrifying accuracy. As Guan Yu rode back to his own lines to have the arrow removed, Pang De laughed and shouted, "**Next time, I will hit you between your eyes, Guan Yu! Take that as a warning!**"

The Wei soldiers cheered their champion as Guan Yu's forces disintegrated and fled the battlefield: atop the walls of Fan, Cao Ren nodded approvingly, saying, "This man will make all the land ours to govern. No rebel will last if Guan Yu cannot beat him! See here, today, the beginning of the end of those that would threaten the stability of the Empire! With Pang De and Yu Jin leading the charge here, victory is assured!"

Seizing the opportunity to raise the subject, an adviser said, "Yu Jin should move the camps away from the river bank."

"General Yu is shrewd... he knows what he's doing," Cao Ren supposed as he watched the grand sight of Pang De charging around the grounds in front of the city, cutting down straggling Shu soldiers. "...Truly, this man from Xiliang is incredible... how can Guan Yu win, now...?"

With that said, Cao Ren laughed boisterously, and roused the men on the walls to cheer Pang De as loudly as they could.

************

## 92

As the weeks wore on, the weather started to change. In Xiangyang and Xinye, the threat of heavy rains built with every passing day, and many – including Pang De – made futile pleas to Yu Jin to relocate the Wei camps away from the river bank. Upriver, the waters swelled as the rains increased in their intensity, something which Guan Yu smiled at every time scouts reported the matter to him. In Chengdu, the mood was generally more subdued, but two men – Kongming and Fa Zheng – awaited the impending disaster for Wei with a measure of delight.

One day, as Kongming was working on civil affairs in his office, a solemn Ma Chao paid an unexpected visit.

"...Tiger General Ma," Kongming said apprehensively. He suddenly felt very threatened, since he had no guards to protect him from a possible assassination; he looked at Zong Yu, his only company, who knew his thoughts and sought an opportunity to get near the door without incurring suspicion.

"Chancellor Zhuge Kongming," Ma Chao replied humbly: the use of his style name indicated to Kongming that Ma Chao had come to him respectfully.

"What can I do for you, Tiger General...?" Kongming asked pointedly.

"I am here to discuss an awkward security matter, Chancellor," Ma Chao replied cagily.

"Oh...?" Kongming exclaimed. "What matter...? Is this about General Pang De...?"

"I only wish I could do something about him, but he rejects all communication and desires no accord with us," Ma Chao sighed regrettably. "No, I come about a problem that is somewhat closer to home... Peng Yang."

"...Please, sit down," Kongming urged: Ma Chao bowed respectfully, and took a guest seat in front of Kongming.

"As you know, I have been speaking to Peng Yang recently, since his views on proactivity did appeal to me," Ma Chao began calmly; Kongming started to fan himself slowly. "Forgive my lack of trust in your judgement, Master... but I wanted to see the merits or faults of the man for myself," Ma Chao insisted.

"I fully understand that," Kongming replied quietly.

"I have business to the north, and Peng Yang, to the south, since he will soon be filling the post of Governor of Jiangyang," Ma Chao continued. "He came to visit me to tell me of his departure, and... well... you may decide the meaning of his carefully chosen words for yourself."

Kongming leant forward and awaited the words with curiosity.

"He said to me," Ma Chao continued dramatically, "these very words... 'If you are in charge of external matters and I am in charge of internal matters, the country will not be hard to pacify'."

"*Ayah*...!" Kongming exclaimed without hesitation.

"...So you see it as I do," Ma Chao said with a mournful sigh. "He mistook me for an ambitious traitor, and openly invited me to assist him in a rebellion."

"No doubt about it," Kongming replied surely. "He must be arrested immediately… Mengqi, you have done the state of Shu a great service this day. Come, let us go and gather troops to make an arrest, and deal with this brazen traitor as soon as possible! He must be executed for this!"

Ma Chao smiled, and said, "I shall assist you unwaveringly, Chancellor… please know that I am eternally grateful to His Highness for not only giving me shelter, but by honouring me as a Tiger General, and vowing to assist me in retaking my home from our mutual enemy, Cao Cao… any man who plots against Shu is my hated enemy, and will die for it."

Kongming smiled appreciatively, and – leaving Zong Yu alone – beckoned Ma Chao to follow him to the court to collect troops. The very same day, Peng Yang was arrested, accused in front of Liu Bei, and sentenced to death for treason. As Peng Yang was dragged away from the court to be beheaded, he protested endlessly, while Kongming watched with cold, unsympathetic eyes, and smiled contentedly.

The situation in Xiangyang and Xinye was now beyond rescue by normal means. With the Wei forces still numbering almost a hundred thousand, and Guan Yu's forces at Fan continually put to flight and demoralised by the heroism of Pang De, only a miracle or a natural disaster could change things: and one day, as the rains reached such an intensity that besieging Fan was next to impossible, the entire battle took a sudden turn, entirely due to a natural disaster.

Downstream, the River Han swelled and burst its banks, sending a torrent of water coursing toward Xiangyang, and right over the Wei camps that were stationed by the riverbank. Atop the walls of Fan City, Cao Ren and his officials watched in horror as Yu Jin's camps all but disappeared underwater, and the beleaguered soldiers struggled to get to land. But there was little that the protectors of Fan could do to help; the water was flooding the city as well, and the inhabitants were as trapped as the camps outside were doomed.

Guan Yu ordered his forces – which had escaped the flooding – to take to their ships and sail to the area where Yu Jin's camps had once been. What met them was an unquestionable catastrophe: thousands upon thousands of bloated corpses bobbed about in the rushing waters, and thousands upon thousands of demoralised, broken soldiers lined the land by the side of the swelled river. As Guan Yu's fleet approached, most of the Wei soldiers started to cry miserably, and beg for mercy. The soldiers' surrenders were accepted, and relief ships started to rescue the grateful men and take them to Guan Yu's Xiangyang encampment.

"What a thing this is," Guan Yu admitted as he viewed the scene from the deck of his command ship.

"The heavens must favour you, Commander," Ma Liang suggested. "…I should say that we have yet to find either Yu Jin or Pang De."

"If possible," Guan Yu replied, "I want them taken alive… especially Pang De. I want him to surrender, I want him to join His Highness, and fight for us."

"That would be wonderful," Ma Liang agreed.

Yu Jin was found on a stretch of a broken dam, and he surrendered without hesitation, to the surprise of Guan Yu. Pang De, however, would be a different story. General Pang had also survived: he was stranded on an isolated stretch of higher ground, but he had no intention of surrendering. After killing any men that refused to fight to the death, he engaged Guan Yu's men, killing several before he was finally captured, bound, and brought to Guan Yu's tent for final disposition.

"...Yu Jin surrendered," Guan Yu said as Pang De stood in front of him defiantly, bound with rope. "Why not you...?"

Two guards tried to force Pang De to kneel, but he refused to budge and shrugged them off angrily.

"See sense," Guan Yu urged. "His Highness, the King of Hanzhong, is a benevolent ruler, and your brother and friend serve him loyally. Why must you be the only one to forsake the light and serve a monster like Cao Cao...?"

"...Worthless, long-bearded dog!" Pang De cursed. "I will serve with no rats and pigs! You are all wretches!"

"I will not let you condemn yourself to an early death without your careful consideration of the facts, since your talent is too great to waste," Guan Yu insisted, despite angry pleas from his generals to have the man executed. "I implore you one last time, General... see sense. The King of Hanzhong-"

"...Is a mat-weaver, a land-borrowing, land-stealing thief, a vagabond that is renowned throughout the land for his treachery and hankering!" Pang De interrupted bravely. "He is no king... he is a common talent, a descendant of a disinherited prince that succeeds entirely because he exploits the deeds of others! Why would I forsake a jewel for a lump of dung?"

"...*You*...!" Zhao Lei exclaimed: he pointed at the fearless general angrily, while others heckled and demanded his execution.

"You dare to speak of His Highness in such a way... I know it is because you want an end to it," Guan Yu said miserably. "There really will be no swaying you, I see that... very well. **GUARDS! ...DEATH!**"

"You'll not live long," Pang De said with a smile as the guards started to drag him away. "**I'll see you soon, Guan Yu, in the afterlife! You're doomed!**"

"**DEATH! DEATH!**" Zhao Lei screamed. "**No more from him! DEATH!**"

Guan Yu watched Pang De as he was pulled from the tent, laughing confidently, and said with a sigh, "That is a truly valiant man... such a pity."

"Commander Guan, we now have a new set of problems," Ma Liang reported. "The thirty or forty thousand bodies that are now in the river pose the threat of disease... and the additions to our forces, the surrendered Wei soldiers... we estimate there to be around thirty thousand men that are willing to serve, if only out of gratitude for our saving and sparing them."

"The corpses I agree with you about... but the reinforcements... how is that a problem?" Guan Yu chuckled heartily. "It only makes us more likely to succeed, does it not...? In fact... this great gift from Heaven is obviously sent to give us a clear path to Chang'an! We shall continue to press Fan and Xiangyang, but now, we will not be simply distracting them... with sixty thousand men, we can lead the attack on Cao Cao, and destroy him for our king!"

"*Ayah*...! No, no!" Ma Liang protested. "We must remain within the boundaries of our original mission! Remember the plan! The tripod of power... we must work with Wu, coordinate with Chengdu-"

"To hell with Wu...!" Guan Yu interrupted. "What good have they done here, uh...? Jichang, I respect your efforts, but Zhuge Liang was wrong! Wu is no reliable ally! They are, in fact, as much our enemy as Cao Cao, and should be met only with suspicion and contempt!"

"I...!" Ma Liang began: but before he could finish, a messenger ran into the tent and fell to one knee.

"**REPORT!**" the messenger shouted. "**The Wei-appointed Inspector of Jing Province, Hu Xiu, has surrendered!**"

Guan Yu laughed boisterously, and said, "Very good! That man is the second sign! We are destined to take this place! With Fan flooded, their forces annihilated, and our forces doubled, the day is ours without question!"

"Commander, what will we feed these sixty thousand men with?" Ma Liang protested. "We have only enough food for the thirty thousand we brought, and if we halve rations, our own men may mutiny, and we may lose them all to Wei!"

"Pessimist!" Guan Yu chuckled. "We shall contact Jiangling, and request food!"

"Even if that is an acceptable solution," Ma Liang said, "these floods are only temporary! I am a resident of these parts by birth, and I tell you that this will not last! Once the floodwaters subside, Wei will send more reinforcements, and the stalemate will resume!"

"All the more reason to act quickly," Guan Yu retorted. "General Zhao, we will need to write to Mi Fang and Shi Ren, and request supplies."

Ma Liang stifled the urge to scream as Guan Yu started to issue orders for a sustained assault with a new objective: the conquering of Northern Jing, with a view to advancing northward to the capital immediately afterward.

Cao Cao took the news from Jing Province badly: he wept for the loss of forty thousand men, he wept for the death of Pang De, and he lamented the surrender of not only the thirty thousand troops, but also his long-serving general, Yu Jin. As he cried and wailed, 5 of his advisers – Liu Ye, Sima Yi, Jia Xu, Dong Zhao and Jiang Ji – looked on with dread, and wondered what his final disposition would be.

"...The common soldiers, I understand," Cao Cao said for what was not the first time, "but no matter how many times I mull it over, I do not understand... Yu Jin... *why*...? Why did my prize general – a man I have known and shown respect to for thirty years – show not a hint of courage, while a recently defected barbarian – a man who faced prejudice and mistrust – gave his life for me without hesitation...?"

"Forgive me," Liu Ye said hesitantly, "but we must not dwell on matters beyond our control. What matters now is the recovery of the situation. We are now threatened on two fronts, Jing and Hefei. If we do not do something, we will soon face a third front from Hanzhong, and we cannot defend ourselves from three directions... not when Liu Bei now has thirty thousand more troops, and we have seventy to eighty thousand less."

"...I am aware of that," Cao Cao replied bitterly. "I 'dwell' on the past in order to learn from it, as I always have. I assume you have suggestions for dealing with the new situation...?"

"Guan Yu is advancing north like a rampaging demon," Jiang Ji said worriedly. "His next target must be Wan City, but its protector, Xu Huang, cannot retaliate as his force is made up entirely of new recruits that lack effective training. Hu Xiu has surrendered, Fu Fang of Nan Town has surrendered and opened the gates to Guan, and now we have a peasant rebellion in Luhun that appears to have ended in the loss of the town, if initial reports are to be believed. Further to that, Guan's 'cells' in and around the north are starting to intensify their harassment of the settlements... even if Wu sat there and did nothing, and Liu Bei made no move out of Hanzhong, Guan Yu alone is enough to destroy us."

Cao Cao clutched his head and groaned miserably, saying, "There's nothing else for it... we shall have to abandon some key positions, and move the imperial capital."

"Let's... not act so drastically, at least not yet," Sima Yi suggested. "Wu appear to be stalling their advance on Hefei rather than intensifying it... that suggests that they fear Guan Yu more than they want to fight us. I think we might be able to turn this situation around by the old concept of 'Divide and rule'. Why not exploit the difficulties in their alliance, augment those difficulties with Guan Yu's arrogance, and destroy them in exactly the same way that Ma Chao and Han Sui were destroyed during the battle at Tong Pass...?"

"I agree," Jiang Ji said. "Let's see if we can get Sun Quan to help us... let us offer him the whole of Southern Jing in exchange for a pincer attack on Guan Yu."

"Sun Quan wants Jing Province... and he fears Liu Bei's ambition," Sima Yi proposed. "Even if they fail to take Jing, the alliance between Wu and Shu will be irrevocably broken, and then we can rest easily, for they will fight each other to the death, and then we can eliminate whichever of them is left at the end of it."

"Very good... very good!" Cao Cao chuckled. "I like that idea, it accords with my own designs well. Tell Cao Ren and Xu Huang to defend vigorously, and have a messenger travel to Jiangdong and deliver our terms to Sun Quan... soon, we'll have no more enemies, and the land will be at peace!"

That day, 3 messengers left Chang'an: the first went to Fan City to reassure Cao Ren, the second to Wan City to give heart to Xu Huang. The last travelled far to the south to carry a message to Sun Quan that – if it had its desired effect – would cause another reversal of fortunes, bring ruin to the Wu-Shu alliance, and give a final, decisive victory to Cao Cao.

In Chengdu, Liu Bei's court received an official from Jing Province. Jian Yong declared, **"Your Highness, Yang Yi approaches."**
Yang Yi entered the courtroom, walked toward Liu Bei apprehensively, and kowtowed to the King of Hanzhong.
"General Guan, Governor of Jiangling, sends his greetings," Yang Yi declared.
"Oh...?" Liu Bei said with cheer. "Please, introduce yourself fully."
"Yang Yi, styled Weigong, originally from Xiangyang," the official replied.
"...Xiangyang...?" Zhang Fei grunted. "Took your time joining us, didn't you...?"
"Indeed," Wei Yan mocked. "We're natives of Jing, many of us... yet I don't ever recall seeing you before. What rock were you underneath...?"
"...Now, now, Wenchang," Liu Bei chuckled warmly as he smiled at the tense and uncomfortable Yang Yi. "Sorry, Yang Weigong, that Wei Yan and Zhang Fei are so abrupt. You said that Yunchang sends greetings... are you one of his staff...?"
"I briefly served him, after leaving the undesirable Wei regime," Yang Yi confirmed. "He sent me here to work in the court at Chengdu: he said that was the best place for me."
"...It's not like Yunchang to send us his unwanted rubbish," Zhang Fei said to Wei Yan, who smirked cruelly.
"We shall have to speak properly at some point, Weigong," Liu Bei said politely. "For now, however, we must refer to business: what news is there from the front?"
"The Wei forces are in disarray," Yang Yi reported. "General Guan now has sixty thousand troops under his command, and several towns have surrendered, carrying the number of Shu troops closer to seventy thousand with every passing day. Cao Ren and Xu Huang are keeping to a tight defensive posture, since Fan City is flooded and Wan City has only recruits to defend it. Furthermore, a peasant leader, Sun Lang, has killed Cao Cao's officials in Luhun and handed control to us."
"They're practically defeated," Liu Bei said with cheer. "It looks as though old Yunchang will win all by himself... something which I cannot say surprises me in the least!"
Many officials laughed gratefully at their king's words: only Huang Quan, Fa Zheng, Mi Zhu and Kongming were silent.
"Wu are not pressing Hefei as strongly as they could be, Your Highness," Fa Zheng said with worry. "We must be ready for any possibility at this point."
"And General Guan pressures my brother constantly," Mi Zhu protested. "There is only so much that any man can do, and he is doing his very best... if another man can do better, then please, Your Highness, give him the role of protector of Jiangling, and spare my brother the unfair chastisement he faces."

"It's just Yunchang being Yunchang," Zhang Fei insisted. "Don't be so touchy."

"I regret to say that I agree," Liu Bei said calmly. "Please, Mi Zizhong, do not be alarmed. Even I am intimidated by Yunchang when he is annoyed, but he always means well."

"And you, Kongming...?" Mi Zhu prompted: Kongming was fanning himself slowly and trying to ignore the indignant stares of acquaintances of the recently executed Peng Yang.

"...Yunchang being Yunchang," Kongming said, "is all there is to it, I think. Why is he suddenly so intolerable...? Mi Fang must not lose sight of the matter at hand... bringing stability to the land. If his complaints were about Yunchang's obvious overstretching of his forces, or the resource dilemma that caused the friction he is suffering, then I might comment."

"...With so much local support, I don't think we need fear him overstretching himself," Liu Bei declared dismissively. "However the resource 'dilemma' you refer to, Chancellor, is also a concern of mine... but surely Jing Province has ample resource to supply that many men...?"

"Just about," Kongming replied. "Remember that there has been a shortage of workers, as many men were drafted to fight: remember also the problems here in Yi and Hanzhong... a lot of what is grown in Jing is needed here, as well."

Liu Bei nodded silently.

"Now, Your Highness," Fa Zheng said, "we should plan ahead... we must consider the success or failure of Yunchang's expedition, and have plans ready. We might need to support him, we might be able to launch another front to the north... or we might be forced to repel Wu, however unlikely that may seem."

"I have my own spies in Jing," Liu Bei revealed, "and so far, there is no sign of any untoward activity. We can be content, I think, that Sun Quan is either trustworthy, or scared... sadly, it is most likely to be the latter."

Once again, laughter filled the court; neither Kongming nor Fa Zheng was impressed by Liu Bei's flippancy.


"You seem to agree that we should be worried," Fa Zheng said as he walked out of the court with Kongming later in the day.

"Guan Yu is being reckless and arrogant," Kongming replied. "What sort of fool would I be if I were not to acknowledge that? He has never commanded more than ten thousand men before: now, he commands sixty thousand, maybe more, and men bow low when they see him coming. That will inflate his arrogance to *beyond* its peak... and then, Xiaozhi, we might have just cause to fear losing everything. All it takes is one capable mind to see an exploitable rift... and Wei has many, even after Cao Cao has killed so many talents."

"Jia Xu, Liu Ye, Sima Yi, Man Chong... and many more besides," Fa Zheng noted.

"I've warned Ma Liang," Kongming said, "but... really, we just have to hope."


∗∗∗∗∗∗∗∗∗∗∗∗

## 93

Sun Quan summoned his court in the city of Chaisang for urgent discussions.

"My lord," Zhuge Jin began, "I am hearing disturbing rumours about a letter from… from Cao Cao, the King of Wei."

"That is indeed true," Sun Quan declared. "We have received a letter from Cao Cao, raising the idea of a truce between us."

"He's frightened," Zhang Zhao chuckled. "Guan Yu is destroying his forces in the centre of the land, rising up from Jing like fires from the lowest levels of the netherworld. Cao Cao isn't the only one that should be scared… Guan Yu is a fearsome beast when unleashed, and perhaps we should reinforce our border with Jing, just to be safe."

"For a moment there, I thought you were going to be agreeable, Zhang Zhao," Zhuge Jin sighed sadly. "My lord, we must not break ties with Liu Bei! Together, you and Liu Bei can free the land from Cao Cao's tyranny, and rule your domains with the blessing of the Emperor! Why throw that away to do sinister business with a man who will thereafter destroy you?"

"…Because it is my belief that Cao Cao is not the painted demon that Liu Bei portrays him to be, and Guan Yu, sadly, is a law unto himself," Sun Quan replied matter-of-factly.

Zhang Zhao sneered, and said, "Were my brother Hong still alive, he would happily, based upon his time as our envoy in the capital, vouch for Cao Cao as a shrewder, more refined man than Liu Bei or Guan Yu could ever hope to be!"

"Which is why we fought him at Red Cliffs," Zhuge Jin retorted.

"Back then, men did not know one-another as they do now!" Zhang Zhao countered. "Then, Cao Cao viewed our lord as more chaff, another pretender, a shallow man of limited substance, like Liu Bei! Now, he knows better! As for Liu Bei and Guan Yu… in all our years of 'alliance', have they ever been anything but selfish?"

"Guan Yu made a habit of mistreating Lu Su, and he has made no effort to reconcile with Lü Meng and mend his ways," Sun Quan agreed. "In fact, it is my understanding that – from those few relief troops that did trickle through to the front at Xiangyang – Guan Yu is, if that is possible to comprehend, more arrogant and rude than he ever was… and even less inclined to hear sound advice. He intends to march on Chang'an, now, and no doubt seize the throne for Liu Bei…"

"That's speculation," Zhuge Jin protested.

"What is not 'speculation', however, is the fact that he will not return Jing," Zhang Zhao suggested. "On the contrary, he intends to take Xiangyang and Xinye, and make North Jing part of Liu Bei's domain… but after that, what then…? Will he move northward, as he has declared… or east, into Jiangxia, Changsha and Guiyang, and attempt to take them from us…?"

Zhuge Jin shook his head, saying, "My brother assures me-"

"Your brother is a shameless vassal of Liu Bei, a man that has already confessed to lying to us to support his lord!" Zhang Zhao interrupted. "I would commend his dedication, were it not so misguided! Liu Bei will betray us, whatever your brother wants for our alliance! He will want Jing, mark my words! And if we wait until Cao Cao is vanquished, we will lose not only Jing, but all that our lord's brother and father worked so hard to build!"

"No, no, no!" Zhuge Jin insisted. "You are *wrong*! Liu Bei is trying to put a northern front together, but he is stymied by Cao Cao's cunning expatriation of the inhabitants of Hanzhong! Were the population stable, Liu Bei would be attacking Cao Cao, restoring the throne, and bringing order to the west and north! Liu Bei does not want a war with us: he wants us to cooperate, like we did at Red Cliffs!"

"Red Cliffs was a decade ago, and as I have already said, a lot has changed since then," Zhang Zhao suggested. "Liu Bei was weak, a nomad with no strength that saw us as a crutch to hoist himself above the fog of despair. Now, Liu Bei is a self-crowned king, an arrogant, ambitious man that intends to swallow the land. It is said that Cao Cao once told Liu Bei, 'There are but two heroes in this land... you, and I'... by heroes, he meant would-be-kings, tyrants, conquerors that would one day rule with an iron fist if others – such as Lord Sun – did nothing to stop them. Liu Bei is now a threat to the land, just like Cao Cao: he recruits bandit lords like Guan Yu, heartless barbarians like Ma Chao, and slimy, treacherous pedants like Fa Zheng who would betray their lord in exchange for titles and privilege."

"Ah, so what you *actually* propose, you now admit, is allying with one tyrant to get rid of another...?" Zhuge Jin snickered derisively. "Since we are already in that position, what do we have to gain by swapping the tyrants around...?"

Some of the other officials murmured uneasily, since Zhuge Jin's point appeared to be valid.

"Your argument is baseless and self-defeating," Zhuge Jin proposed further. "Your argument revolves around toadying to Lord Sun, since an alliance with Cao Cao will, I expect, earn him something...?"

"...Cao Cao proposes a pincer," the adviser Lü Fan explained. "We would attack Jing, and in return, we would be allowed to take possession of the south of the province, and be awarded full acknowledgment of our right to the region by the imperial court. Cao Cao would keep everything north of Jiangling, much as it is now... only we would be rid of our loathsome sitting tenants."

"...And you think Liu Bei, with his army of a hundred thousand, will just accept that...?" Zhuge Jin said with a laugh. "When we have Jing, and Cao Cao closes the border, we will be sharing another border with a very angry Liu Bei... a Liu Bei who will stop at nothing to revenge himself upon us! Cao Cao will just have to sit back and laugh while we hack each other to small pieces, ready for his hungry horde to devour at his leisure! Will we irrevocably shorten our lives in order to temporarily extend our borders...?"

Once again, the officials murmured uncomfortably; this time, even Sun Quan was visibly hesitant.

"My lord, think this through carefully," Zhuge Jin pleaded. "Guan Yu is not an easy man to get along with, simply because he is a giant among men, a man who merges lofty principle with gutter survival instincts, a man who judges and yet insists that he himself is beyond judgement... but goodness knows, we have a few awkward personalities among our number, don't we...? Are we going to allow a difficult man to ruin a decade of collaboration...?"

"...Very well, Ziyu," Sun Quan conceded. "I shall give this man another chance."

"My lord...!" Zhang Zhao protested.

"I think it only fair," Sun Quan insisted. "In fact, even Lü Meng and Lu Xun do not seem to object to our giving peace another chance, and they can't stand Guan Yu. ...Because Cao Cao is desperate, he has placed no time limit on responding... we shall exploit that, and detain his envoy in the nicest way possible. Meanwhile, I have a proposal to make to Guan Yu... if he accepts, then the Wei envoy goes back to his master in two pieces, and we continue our alliance with Liu Bei. If not... well, we'll improvise."

"...*Aiee*... again, we make concessions to a brute," Zhang Zhao groaned.

"I think that your decision is wise, my lord," Zhuge Jin praised. "I will lose faith in the alliance myself if this fails."

"Bring me ink and paper," Sun Quan ordered. "I want to send this letter to Guan Yu as soon as possible."


"...A marriage proposal...?"

Guan Yu and his son, Guan Ping, sat silently and thoughtfully as Ma Liang finished reading the message of peace from Eastern Wu.

"...He wants my daughter to marry his runt offspring...?" Guan Yu scoffed.

"Please, do not reject this offer so quickly," Ma Liang whined.

"...Father, perhaps it would be advantageous," Ping suggested. "This would be ideal in fact, since my sister needs a husband, especially one of good breeding-"

"No, my son," Guan Yu interrupted. "For my daughter to marry his son would be to marry a proud tigress to a mangy tomcat."

"Lord Liu married Lady Sun," Ma Liang scolded. "By your words, you imply that you outrank your lord in terms of dignity."

"We knew nothing of his poor ability and treacherous nature when Elder Brother married his graceless, disreputable sister," Guan Yu countered. "Since then, she has fled, revealing her true nature as a spy and saboteur for her brother!"

"...Ah," Ma Liang sighed. "Perhaps you're right..."

"The man knows no sincerity!" Guan Yu continued. "He has annexed southeast Jing, stealing it from its rightful governor, and he has the audacity to tell us he is 'loaning' it to us...? What manner of man lends a friend his own property, property stolen on the flimsy pretext of 'reparation' for another man's so-called 'crime'...? There is nothing in the texts that I have immersed my soul in that justifies his behaviour, no way in which it can be termed 'righteous'!"

"Father..." Guan Ping murmured.

"*No*, Ping'er...!" Guan Yu boomed. "This water rat from the south has given no service to the royal house, and fought Cao Cao at Red Cliffs purely so that he could protect his domains and then expand them, at the world's expense! His father was a hired sword, his brother a thief, and he, nothing more than a scruffy-bearded parasite that lives in his predecessor's shadow, feeding on his dead brother's exploits with no merit of his own to speak of! I have a right to look down upon a man who has never acted altruistically in his life, not even *once*... he has earned nothing but my **contempt**, and that is all that he shall receive!"

"General Guan...!" Ma Liang protested feebly.

"In fact," Guan Yu decided, "I shall not ignore this ingratiating act as I intended to... I shall do what he should have done at least once in his time outside the womb, and be *truthful*...!"

"No, no, don't do *that*!" Ma Liang whined. "He'll...!"

"Where is the man who will be receiving my reply?" Guan Yu barked. "He can have that reply *now*...!"


"...He said *what*...?" Fa Zheng groaned as Kongming relayed a written account of the encounter to Liu Bei's inner circle days later, in Chengdu.

"...He actually made that his reply," Kongming said weakly. "He actually called Sun Quan a hankering dog, his son a runt, and rejected the proposal outright..."

"Oh dear...!" Liu Bei chuckled. "Yunchang really isn't getting to be any better at diplomacy in his old age, is he...?"

"This isn't funny, Your Highness," Fa Zheng said with genuine fear in his voice. "I worry what Lü Meng will do..."

"As do I," Kongming murmured. "...We should see what we can find out about the diplomatic correspondence between Sun Quan and Cao Cao."

"...You don't really think he'd turn to Cao Cao, do you, Kongming...?" Liu Bei said incredulously. "After Hefei, and Red Cliffs...?"

"This is an affront," Kongming said plainly, "that only the highest-minded of men would ignore: Sun Quan would really have to want to make our alliance work to endure this unforgivable act of contempt."

"Sun Quan likes Ma Liang," Fa Zheng suggested. "Why not-"

"No, no," Kongming said emphatically. "If Sun Quan is angry, he'll kill him, and then we'll be forced to retaliate. ...At least Guan was sensible enough not to send one of our men to deliver this ludicrous insult."

"So what do you think Sun Quan will do...?" Liu Bei wondered.


"...My lord, you cannot be serious!" Zhang Zhao protested.

"I know that it looks weak," Sun Quan conceded in front of his small group of advisors – he had left the generals out of the discussion this time – as he took stock of their disapproving and worried stares.

"My lord," Zhang Zhao said, "you must have a plan, surely."

"No," Sun Quan admitted. "Guan Yu looks at me in the same way that most of you view Liu Bei: greedy, ambitious, false, of little proven ability, living off of the successes of others, and lacking in any magnanimity. I cannot blame him for that view: I see myself in that way sometimes. I have always relied on the vassals I inherited from my father and brother, and I have none of their military prowess. My stabilising activity carries on from my brother's work, and it can be seen as ambition to become a king or an emperor. I do have that ambition, as Liu Bang, founder of the Han, once did when he deposed an emperor deemed as having lost the Mandate of Heaven that dictates the imperial line of the moment.

"Everyone can see that the Han's fire has dimmed. One after another, the usurpers line up: the Ten Eunuchs, Dong Zhuo, Li Jue and Guo Si, Cao Cao, Yuan Shu, Yuan Shao, and even Liu Bei, for all his superficial claims that he supports the Emperor. My father died prematurely while in the service of one of those unrighteous men, having rendered great service to the Han; he weakened Dong Zhuo by killing Hua Xiong and repelling Lü Bu, he thwarted rebels, crushed Yellow Turban uprisings, all to preserve an ungrateful royal house... yet he is remembered as a vassal to a traitor, an unambitious tool, and nothing more. ...Is that fair...?

"I stand alone among the warlords for not actively seeking the death of the Emperor, I think. I am happy to govern the land below the Great River, where the north has long held no jurisdiction: to build an independent southern kingdom that trades with the foreign lands beyond the mountains and seas, such as the seat of the scriptures, and the land of Da Qin; I would have peace with the northern capital, regardless of who holds the throne in the end. ...Yet does Guan Yu see any merit in me...? ...No, because he lives in a dream-world unlike the one in which he actually exists: heroes are not perfect, including Liu Bei. But I will forgive him for his beliefs, for though they are unrealistic in this chaotic age, they are righteous, and they are to be commended... I shall maintain the peace."

"And if he oversteps the mark in an 'unrighteous' way...?" Zhang Zhao asked.

"Then he will know my righteous wrath, and suffer," Sun Quan replied.


When no reply came from Eastern Wu, Ma Liang enquired the response to Guan Yu's letter from Zhuge Jin: he then relayed his findings to an ever more buoyant Guan Yu.

"Weakling," Guan Yu scoffed. "We have nothing to fear from Sun Quan... he has realised, since his impending defeat the last time he came into Jing, that he is outclassed, and so he will no longer threaten the border."

"Commander Guan, do not say what I think you're going to say," Ma Liang implored. "We cannot, we *must not*...!"

"Ping'er," Guan Yu hailed: his son nodded in acknowledgment. "Ping'er, we can safely divert some more troops to the front here in Xinye... write to Shi Ren and have him gather forces from the Jing-Wu border."

"No, no, no!" Ma Liang pleaded: Guan Ping noted the fear in Ma Liang's face and frowned thoughtfully.

436

"...Father," Guan Ping said, "I am a man of forty... I know something of warfare, and... well... this is not entirely sensible."

"As a man of nearly sixty, I know even more," Guan Yu countered. "Sun Quan is a craven fool, obsessed with expanding his wealth and territory but lacking the spine to do it. Lü Meng, while competent, is sickly... Lu Xun is a pup that we needn't concern ourselves with. We will use the troops to break Fan and press on to Chang'an... we'll have plenty of time to retaliate if they do try something because we have signal towers, and our force is so great in size that Sun Quan will be devoured if he tries such a foolish thing."

"...Very well, Father," Guan Ping conceded.

"And while you're writing," Guan Yu added, "remind him that I requested supplies from him and that other pedant, Mi Fang, and have yet to receive anything... tell them to hurry up, because men can't live without food."

Weeks passed, and the siege of the flooded Fan City continued without respite for the attackers or the defenders. News was slow in reaching Chengdu, where the atmosphere was becoming increasingly tense: some were optimistic that the end of Cao Cao's regime was in sight, while others feared an impending disaster that would overshadow even the swelling of the River Han.

"You look worried," Kongming suggested as Mi Zhu entered the court wearing a gloomy and fretful expression. Liu Bei was not present, so the few officials that were present spoke freely and without restraint.

"...General Guan," Mi Zhu exclaimed, "is reckless beyond belief!"

"Now what...?" Jian Yong wondered desperately.

"My brother is still stationed in Jiangling," Mi Zhu reported, "and he has just sent a messenger to tell me that General Guan is 'grossly dissatisfied' with his service, and that he intends to punish him for insubordination and failure to carry out orders."

"...After all your family's good deeds for His Highness...?" Fa Zheng said with surprise.

"My brother is uneasy," Mi Zhu admitted, "but it gets worse... General Guan is annoyed because he has run out of supplies for his siege at Fan, so-"

"Then why has he not petitioned Chengdu...?" Kongming asked plainly.

"...General Guan has decided to obtain supplies by... by...!" Mi Zhu stuttered.

"...By *what*...?" Kongming prompted.

"...By raiding one of Sun Quan's grain depots," Mi Zhu reported reluctantly: the revelation was met with groans of displeasure and fear.

"Fool!" Kongming said angrily. "Does he want to ruin our cause???"

"That's it," Fa Zheng sighed. "We will now be at war with Sun Quan."

"He claims that, since Jing should belong rightly to His Highness, he is only taking what is rightly ours," Mi Zhu bleated. "He has no understanding of what this will bring down on him. He is oblivious to the complexity of politics."

"Do we know what Sun Quan's response is to this...?" Kongming asked.

"...**He has now gone TOO FAR!**" Sun Quan screamed: the generals and officials of Eastern Wu were mostly pleased at their lord's newly-found rage, though they went to great pains to conceal it.
"So," Zhang Zhao asked, "should someone be despatched to the Chief Commander to advise him to advance...?"
"...I want Jing retaken," Sun Quan ordered. "I don't care how long it takes, but I want Guan Yu and his son taken – alive – and Jing returned to me. I do not care if this audacious brigand acts alone, or with Liu Bei's blessing, and I do not care about the consequences... this abuse has gone on long enough!"
"My lord...!" Zhuge Jin interjected.
"**He has STOLEN FROM ME!**" Sun Quan boomed. "All his absurd claims of 'righteousness' are **NOTHING to me now!** He is a common thief, and will be treated as one!"
"But my lord, how can we attack?" Zhuge Jin challenged. "...Southwest Jing is heavily fortified!"
Zhang Zhao smirked, and said, "Is it...?"
"...B-but... but the alliance...!" Zhuge Jin whined.
"There is no alliance now," Sun Quan declared. "I control my officers: if Liu Bei cannot or does not control his, that is because he cares nothing for the damage they cause. Summon the Wei envoy... I want a reply drawn up by the time he gets here, so someone bring me a pen and ink."
As the officials murmured excitedly and Sun Quan prepared to write his letter to Cao Cao, Zhuge Jin – who now felt very alone – muttered, "It's all turned to dust."

************

## 94

Kongming sighed miserably as he sipped his tea one evening, a few days later.

"...Husband," Yueying prompted from her seat opposite Kongming, "you are worried about Guan Yu."

"He has brought misfortune on himself," Kongming replied. "I worry about us, about the cause, about Lord Liu, and how he will react if the worst occurs."

"And what is 'the worst'...?" Yueying wondered.

"...Losing Jing province, and Guan Yu," Kongming replied ominously.

"Surely not...!" Yueying giggled incredulously. "How could such a thing happen after all the careful preparation...?"

"Arrogance... the cause of all great disasters," Kongming sighed woefully. "The surrender of Yu Jin's troops meant thirty-thousand new mouths to feed... so he crossed into Wu-controlled Jing, and raided one of Sun Quan's storage depots."

"...He did *what*...?" Yueying said with surprise. "He raided a Wu depot...? He raided the supplies of an ally...?"

"...Which is, yes, an act of gross contempt," Kongming continued. "...And it is such an audacious act, such a provocative act, that it gives me a terrible thought."

"...Like what...?" Yueying wondered.

"...What if, in addition to not respecting Sun Quan's borders, he does not respect Sun Quan's *might*...?" Kongming proposed. "What if he has reduced the security on the Jing-Wu borders...?"

"Perhaps you need to go to Wu, talk with your brother, try and prevent a catastrophe," Yueying suggested.

"It's too late for that," Kongming said sadly. "But... there is something else, something that gives me another terrible thought."

"...Are you sure that there is nothing you can do...?" Yueying interrupted.

"I am sure," Kongming insisted. "...To return to my thought: Mi Fang and Shi Ren have been left in charge of Jiangling and Gong'an... both men dislike Guan Yu for his loftiness and his general distaste for 'pedants'. He does not show them respect... he has always felt that the Mi family bought King Liu's respect rather than earned it, which might be right, but in the name of the Heavens, was His Highness meant to starve???"

"...You insinuate... that Mi Fang and Shi Ren are wavering in their loyalty to the king," Yueying said fearfully.

"No, to Guan Yu," Kongming replied, "and that is enough. Guan requested supplies... he raided the storage depot because he did not receive those supplies. Mi Fang and Shi Ren deliberately hesitated, to spite Guan Yu for his haughty attitude towards them."

"...But they endangered the army," Yueying suggested.

"I know, I do not praise them for it," Kongming groaned. "But Guan... threatened them with military punishment upon his return, and then left them in their posts. ...Do you condemn a man to death and then leave him as acting governor...?"

"...Jing is doomed," Yueying decided.

"So how do we come back from this...?" Kongming asked
desperately. "I cannot send troops that we do not have to bolster
Fan or reinforce Jiangling; I cannot see a way to placate Sun Quan
or make Guan Yu change his ways; I cannot undo the acrimony
between Guan Yu, Shi Ren and Mi Fang; I cannot make His
Highness see the folly in it all; I cannot... I cannot. I just... cannot.
But I *must*. This... this is my dilemma."
Yueying did not volunteer any more words, and the two sat in
sombre silence.

In Fan City, Cao Ren received a reply to a fretful letter that he had
written to the Runan Administrator, Man Chong, and studied it
carefully. He smiled; his adviser, Zhao Yan, entered the otherwise
empty court hall at that point, and frowned.
"Have we had good news about reinforcements...?" Zhao Yan
asked.
"Not really... no, this is from Man Chong," Cao Ren replied. "I
asked him if we should abandon Fan and Xiangyang... he says that
the flooding is only temporary, that Fan will be relieved later, and
that we should hold out, because these cities are too strategically
important to lose. His Highness said much the same thing... so we
will hold on."
"But how do we do that...?" Zhao Yan said desperately. "We're
down to a few thousand men, and morale is non-existent!"
"We will draft everyone to serve," Cao Ren replied calmly. "That
will increase our force by a considerable amount, reduce the
chances of peasant revolts, and give people something else to
think about."
"I can see that," Zhao Yan agreed. "But when will help arrive...?"
"Xu Huang will be coming here soon," Cao Ren promised. "When
he arrives, things will improve drastically, since we served
together during the siege at Jiangling. I've learned a lot since
then... together, he and I can turn this around."

"How can you do nothing about Xu Huang...?" Ma Liang asked
Guan Yu desperately: the officials were gathered around a map in
Guan Yu's command tent, studying all of the units that were
currently fighting.
"He and I were friends when I was working under Cao Cao, I know
him as well as I know my family," Guan Yu insisted. "He has a
small force of raw recruits that are unfit for battle, and he will
refuse combat... he is only coming to Fan to give an impression of
strength, so pay him no mind. Fan will have fallen by the time he
gets here, and so will Xiangyang."
"He's advanced to Yangling Slope," Ma Liang noted. "He is now in
line with your proposed vanguard advancements... which splits our
forces dangerously, Commander Guan. What if the vanguard were
cut off, somehow...? We should not advance so quickly, we need to
keep the forces together!"
"...Pedantic nonsense," Guan Yu scoffed. "We will never take
Chang'an if we dithered, as you suggest, Ma Liang. Why do we
need seventy thousand men to stay in one place, attacking a
handful of soggy, demoralised northerners...?"

"...If we pressure them, we can break them," Ma Liang replied wearily. "If we break them, *quickly*, it opens up the entire northern heartland... Sun Quan can then attack the eastern front with ease, and our way to the capital will be assured. If you do not pressure them now, the water will subside, and Cao Ren will be able to hold out for another year if he has to. All it would then take to destroy us is reinforcements from Cao Cao, or an act of revenge by Sun Quan for your calling him a dog."
"We will proceed as I have designed," Guan Yu said angrily. "This victory is Heaven-ordained... Wei is doomed, and Cao Cao will die. I want a larger contingent to move against Xiangyang, and the vanguard to advance northward, towards and beyond Wan City."
"...*Aiee*," Ma Liang exclaimed. "I... ... ...*aiee*."

Unfortunately for Guan Yu, Xu Huang was joined by a force of thousands of elite veteran soldiers before he completed his advance, and that sudden addition to Cao Ren's forces destroyed whatever advantages that Guan Yu might have had. A simple ruse panicked his rapidly advancing vanguard into a humiliating retreat, and soon enough, Guan Yu was again locked into a seemingly endless siege at Fan, where the floodwaters were now receding. The morale of his forces dropped once again, and suddenly, things were not as promising as they had been only a short time before.

A few weeks later, a self-satisfied Cao Cao received a letter from Eastern Wu that would further improve his already reasonable fortunes. He called his advisors to a meeting, and announced, "Sun Quan is ready to cooperate."
The murmurs amongst the advisers were enthusiastic and excited.
"It is hard to believe," Cao Cao continued, "that a few months ago, the situation was bleak beyond belief: Guan Yu had advanced to the edge of our heartland, Chang'an firmly in his sights, and that I even considered relocating the capital! Now, things are somewhat different. His failure to recognise his old friend Xu Huang as a threat has led him back into a stalemate from which he will find no victory, even if Heaven designed to flood the whole of the north. And this latest development... well, suffice to say that soon, Guan Yu will be a legend... and nothing more."
"What does Sun Quan propose...?" Jia Xu asked.
"He proposes a pincer, a surprise attack into Jing, naturally enough," Cao Cao replied with a laugh. "He would suggest nothing else... his hunger for that place is all that currently drives him, the poor fool. He asks – nay, *pleads* – that we keep our new alliance a secret, so that Guan Yu will suspect nothing until it is too late: he has already started to move troops away from Hefei and into a clandestine base that borders southwest Jing."
"...Your Highness," the adviser Dong Zhao interrupted, "If it is your intention to abide by his preferred stratagem, I disagree."
"...Oh...?" Cao Cao said as a prompt.
"You see," Dong Zhao continued, "we have much more to gain from alerting Guan Yu to this new development deliberately. Shoot copies of the letter into Fan, and ensure, at the same time, that copies find their way into Guan Yu's hands..."

"…He will then have a serious dilemma," Sima Yi concurred. "Guan Yu will be trapped, unable to secure a victory whether he stays or retreats: if he disbelieves the letter or prioritises attacking us, he loses Jing, and Wu and Liu Bei will be forced to fight, giving him no choice but to abandon the siege eventually anyway; if he retreats to defend Jing, we will be relieved, Wu and Liu will fight… either way, we win."

"Whereas a surprise attack, kept a secret by us, will give Sun Quan an easy play for Jing, while we continue to lose men, morale, and resources," Dong Zhao suggested. "He'll gain southwest Jing and have a total advantage over Liu Bei, while our people – starved, afflicted with disease and trapped inside Fan – might lose hope, and that might lead to surrender. Why allow Wu to become a greater menace to us…? Do we want to one day bring another Red Cliffs on ourselves…? Let Guan Yu know of Wu's treachery, and they'll destroy each other for us. Furthermore, this temporary pact with Wu will give the defenders of Fan some hope, if they know of it."

"Very good," Cao Cao agreed. "I shall act according to your idea."


"A letter has been fired into our camp by Xu Huang's archers," Ma Liang reported to a gloomy, demoralised Guan Yu in his command tent near the city of Weitou. "It's not good news, Commander."

"…Do they not wish to challenge…?" Guan Yu chuckled miserably.

"Commander, Wu have broken faith," Ma Liang said desperately as he waved the cloth letter aloft. "They intend to attack Jing Province."

**"They WHAT???"** Guan Yu exclaimed.

"I think it is a genuine concern," Ma Liang said pointedly. "The letter is a copy of official communications between Cao Cao and Sun Quan, with Sun Quan pledging allegiance to Wei and vowing to crush you for your insolence and audacity… Lü Meng has had an army stationed at a secret location near our border, and-"

Guan Yu snatched the cloth letter from Ma Liang's hand and started to read.

"…And it is obvious that Sun Quan has been planning this for some time," Ma Liang continued. "They've completely abandoned the Hefei campaign and turned their attentions to us… the alliance is over."

Guan Yu finished reading the letter and slowly lowered his arms to the table in front of him: tears welled up in his eyes as he contemplated his own very significant contribution to the situation.

"This… this is… … …**D'AAAAGH!**" Guan Yu screamed: Guan Ping ran into the tent to see what was ailing his father.

"…Father, what is it…?" Guan Ping pleaded.

"Wait… wait a minute," Guan Yu said as he tried to salvage some good from the situation. "I… no, wait, Sun Quan is no fool… this-"

"The letter is genuine," Ma Liang insisted: he took the letter from Guan Yu's hands and handed it to Guan Ping, who started to read it. Other copies had found their way into the hands of generals and soldiers in the camp, and the noise of discontent was starting to spread.

"I… I don't doubt that it is genuine," Guan Yu said numbly. "I… I simply doubt that the best course is to retreat."

"Father, that's ridiculous!" Guan Ping said with surprise. "How can we not return to Jing and save it from Lü Meng???"

"Ping'er, Sun Quan is a hungry tiger," Guan Yu replied with feigned calm. "What he wants is *power*... Jing seems a worthy prize, but if I was to take Fan and Xiangyang, he would have more to gain by going into Wei... he will change direction, abandon this petty feud, and go after the true prize: Hefei, and the northern heartland."

"That is too optimistic, and a poor assessment of Sun Quan," Ma Liang suggested. "He is a bitter, petty man when riled... he allowed his feud with Liu Biao to extend beyond logical, rational boundaries, so do you think he will let this barrage of personal insults go...? You insulted *his son*! You insulted *him*! You refuse to return his 'loaned' Jing to him! You chastised his emissary, intimidated his last Chief Commander, and robbed his storage depot! His Highness vowed never to attack Yi, and then conquered it! He married Sun Quan's sister, thus making her forever doomed to rot, a wife with an enemy for a husband! He-"

"I... see your point," Guan Yu interrupted. "The alliance, the tripod your friend Zhuge Liang so firmly believes in... enabled us to rise to power, but it is also needed to finally defeat Wei. I understand that. I understand that it is important to maintain good relations with Wu, with Sun Quan..."

"What good is there in valuing the songbird's call after you shot it from the sky?" Ma Liang asked desperately. "There *is no alliance now*!"

"This... is not solving anything," Guan Yu suggested. "Jichang, Ping'er, I do not think we should go back to Jiangling. We have more to gain by staying here, and completing our takeover of northern Jing. How can Jiangling and Gong'an fall when Mi Fang and Shi Ren guard them...? There are still enough troops to resist, and with the signal towers in place, let Sun Quan have his 'clandestine barracks' on the border... he still has to get those troops into our domain, and that will not be easy for him to achieve at all. We still have our seventy thousand troops... let us do what we came to do, and if Sun Quan is still so stupid as to crave pebbles over jewels, we can send a detachment of thirty thousand to reinforce the defenders."

"We're getting reports that Cao Cao has decided to bring another force – we do not know how large – to break the siege," Ma Liang said soberly. "Xu Huang is also planning something, but we don't know what."

"Father, I don't think we should remain here," Guan Ping admitted.

"...We *stay*," Guan Yu insisted. "We... we *cannot* retreat! I *promised* Xuande that I would do this... I will not break my promise!"

Ma Liang saw no sense in protesting further, and retreated to his rest tent.

Xu Huang took the opportunity to attack the floundering Guan Yu within the next few weeks: Guan's messengers suddenly started to report Wei scouts around Guan Yu's Weitou camp.

"They're planning to attack Weitou," Zhao Lei supposed.

"Our spies seem to be gathering intelligence to that effect, yes," Ma Liang confirmed wearily.

"...What a foolish thing to do," Guan Yu scoffed.

"We should reinforce the Sizhong camp, in case Xu Huang is planning a second attack there that we haven't heard about," Ma Liang suggested.

"Agreed," Guan Yu declared. "Send a-"

"**REPORT!**" a panicked messenger cried as he ran into the tent and fell clumsily to one knee. "**The enemy general Xu Huang has launched an attack on our camp at Sizhong!**"

"I'll rescue the camp personally," Guan Yu said angrily. "How *dare* he...!"

Guan Yu prepared a significant force and began the journey to Sizhong, leaving Zhao Lei in charge of the main camp at Weitou. But as soon as he reached the camp at Sizhong, messengers from Weitou reported that an attack of even greater ferocity was taking place there. Realising that he had been tricked, and that the enemy force at Sizhong was small, Guan Yu turned his army about to rescue Weitou. Xu Huang had a contingent of men smash into Guan Yu's forces as they hurried back to Weitou; and, as Guan Yu arrived, a horde of Wei soldiers rushed the rear of his army, dealing a spectacular defeat.

The Wei defectors, Hu Xiu and Fu Fang, were killed in the attack on Weitou; many of their followers surrendered to their former masters, which significantly reduced Guan Yu's support. Yu Jin's former troops started to desert and defect as well; by the time that Guan Yu finally conceded defeat and ordered a full retreat to Jiangling, his forces were less than they had been when he had begun his expedition.

"...We must hurry back to Jing," Guan Yu said with thinly veiled despair. "Perhaps we can somehow recover ourselves."

"Wei are not pursuing," Ma Liang noted as he looked at the train of troops behind him; some were discreetly falling away from the march and deserting, and the mood was sour and despondent.

"Why...?" Guan Ping wondered. "Why do they not pursue...?"

"That's easy enough to answer," Ma Liang sighed. "They do not want to waste troops attacking us... we're losing men all the time to sickness and desertion, and when we get to Jiangling, we're going to be fighting Wu."

"Our messengers to Jiangling have been gone a long time," Guan Yu noted. "I hope that Mi Fang is not under siege."

Ma Liang knew, deep down, why there had been no word: but he stifled tears of rage and desperation, and he did not reply.

"Sun Quan ruined everything," Guan Yu complained. "We were so close... we were so close."

"...A messenger is coming," General Liao Hua said: a horseback messenger had brought his horse to a halt, fallen clumsily from the saddle, and was now scrabbling along the ground, desperate to reach Guan Yu.

"Oh, no..." Ma Liang sobbed.

"Why does this man stumble all over the place?" Guan Yu wondered. "What could be so urgent that he-"

"**REPORT!**" the messenger cried. "**Jing has fallen!**"

Guan Yu's mouth opened, but the only sound that came out of it was a raspy, painful whine; his forces were suddenly and completely demoralised beyond redemption.

"...But how?" Guan Ping protested. "How could Jing fall so quickly???"

"**Everyone... surrendered!**" the messenger sobbed.

Ma Liang took a written account from the messenger, and started to read it silently. It explained in greater detail what had occurred: he absorbed the information, and stifled further rage at the completely unavoidable situation that they were now in.

"Mi Fang, Shi Ren, Pan Jun...?" Guan Ping exclaimed. "They... surrendered???"

"**Everyone... surrendered!**" the messenger said again.

Guan Yu started to scream: it was a long, vocal lament that broke what little spirit was left in his army. When he finally ceased, he lowered his head and fell silent.

"...Commander Guan, we cannot advance now," Ma Liang said numbly. "You must go east, to Mai City, and make a temporary base there. A messenger should be despatched at once to Chengdu requesting help from His Highness... I will go with this messenger to acquire more immediate support from Liu Feng and Meng Da."

"Go," Guan Ping urged. "Hurry, Jichang."

Ma Liang gestured to the messenger that he should remount his horse and follow him to the northwest, while Guan Yu had his rapidly disintegrating army turn and head east, toward temporary shelter.

Liu Feng received the anxious Ma Liang in his Shangyong office, and awaited the news on Guan Yu's forces.

"...Master Liu," Ma Liang said tensely, "we are at a critical hour. Commander Guan is currently besieged by Sun Quan's forces at Mai City... he had several thousand troops when we parted company, but that may now be far less. Please, you must contact General Meng Da, and both of you must despatch troops to rescue him immediately."

"...General Meng Da and I are not on entirely friendly terms at the moment," Liu Feng replied coldly. "Further to that, neither of us has been able to stabilise the regions we are in control of... and now we'll need every man we have to prevent the rot from the Fan campaign spreading in this direction."

"But Guan Yunchang is besieged!" Ma Liang protested. "This isn't about land: this is about the life of a hero, a great man! Regardless of his failings, he has been a pillar of His Highness' forces since the very first days! He has achieved feats in the past that defy human ability! He cannot simply be allowed to perish!"

"If he is so astounding," Liu Feng retorted, "then he will not need my help."

"...Why are you so hostile...?" Ma Liang wondered. "What is the matter with you...? Do you not understand the urgency of this? If you have some reason to spite him, let it not have fatal consequences!"

Liu Feng harrumphed, and said, "I have fought *tooth and nail* for this army since I was a young boy... ten, maybe fifteen years now, I've been the eldest son of 'His Highness'... now, I am a field general, a *lackey*, while my simpleton brother is named as the crown prince. My only crime was to be adopted... Cao Cao's father was adopted by a palace eunuch, and now he's a king! **Why should I not be a king???**"

"Young Master, *no*...!" Ma Liang pleaded.

"Guan Yu has been speaking to 'His Highness'... and Zhang Fei has, and Zhuge Liang, too," Liu Feng added bitterly. "I'm now unwanted... a *nuisance*... it's only a matter of time before I am exiled, or *assassinated*, because I'm no longer *convenient*! I served my purpose: I was his son until he had a **real one!**"

"...Please, Master Liu... *help him*," Ma Liang said weakly.

"I already told you, I can't," Liu Feng said coldly. "Like me, he's on his own... I wish him luck, of course. I expect that Meng Da will tell you the same: regardless of my feelings, the Empire and the state of Shu come first... I will not sacrifice a part of my adopted father's kingdom to save a fallen hero whose best days are far, far behind him."

"Then... then I must hurry to Chengdu," Ma Liang murmured.

"I'd say that's the best option," Liu Feng replied. "If the situation here improves, I vow that I *will* help... because I would spite him more by indebting him to me."

Ma Liang got to his feet and left the office without bowing: he hurried on to Chengdu, all the time praying to the heavens that Guan Yu would last until help could be mustered.


＊＊＊＊＊＊＊＊＊＊＊＊

## 95

By the time that Ma Liang reached Chengdu, the situation in Jing was already widely known, although the exact details were yet to emerge. Kongming met with Ma Liang at the city gates, accompanied by Ma Su: the three embraced as brothers.

"Jichang," Kongming said, "it has been too long."

"No time," Ma Liang panted. "Guan Yu, he-"

"We know about Jing," Kongming said sadly. "We know the outcome at Fan, and the actions taken by Sun Quan..."

"Kongming, I failed you," Ma Liang sobbed. "Time and again I remonstrated; time and again I pleaded with him to follow the plan, to remember the alliance...!"

Ma Su helped his brother into a carriage that they would all use to get to the court.

"We have both failed... we have all failed," Kongming sighed as he boarded the carriage. "I fear that His Highness is no less stubborn... truly, I begin to understand how men like Cao Cao eventually start to take matters into their own hands, when you see how slow the ruler is to react to a simple problem."

"What happened, brother...?" Ma Su asked tensely as he climbed aboard the carriage and sat opposite Ma Liang.

"...Fan, or Jiangling...?" Ma Liang wondered.

"...Fan first," Ma Su said curiously as the carriage started to move.

"Poor planning, through and through," Ma Liang said regrettably. "Yunchang did not listen to me: once, if at all. He attacked two cities on opposite banks of the river at the same time..."

"...*Aiee*," Kongming exclaimed. "You should *never* split forces that way."

Ma Liang nodded, adding, "He was successful at first because of luck, and nothing more... that flood gave us a heaven-sent opportunity that he crushed with bad judgement. In the end, he ignored a sizeable enemy reinforcement until they were in place, he allowed the vanguard to move so far ahead of the main army that they were almost cut off and destroyed, and then he – well, *we* – fell for a force-dividing ruse that lost us both of our main camps. We started out with twenty or thirty thousand men, Kongming: at our peak, we had seventy to eighty thousand, we had inspired a peasant rebellion in Luhun, and we were within sight of Chang'an. If he had only been *patient*... if he had only *respected Sun Quan*...!"

"...I saw your letter," Kongming said, "and Fa Zheng and I both agreed that something like this was inevitable from that point. So you'll forgive my casual demeanour... you are seeing me after I have already contemplated the worst and been as despondent as was possible."

"...Brother," Ma Su said, "what happened in Jing...?"

"*That*," Ma Liang chortled, "was entirely Guan Yu's fault. There is no other way to see it. He upset Mi Fang and Shi Ren, threatened them both with execution, and then failed to demote them from their posts... and he diverted the border troops to Fan, which left us with nobody to keep Wu out. Not that it mattered... Wu sent thousands through, once the signal towers were disabled."

"...How was that possible...?" Kongming asked plainly.

"Idiocy, what else...?" Ma Liang replied. "Lü Meng feigned illness and passed authority over to Lu Xun; that, and Sun Quan's proposal for marrying Guan's daughter to his own son... Guan Yu thought Wu were no threat, and removed the troops. All Lü Meng had to do was sail over the Xiang River with civilian merchant ships filled with hidden soldiers. The signal tower guards were bribed by the 'merchants' into being allowed to stay on the river bank... the hidden soldiers defeated the tower keepers when they let their guard down, and that was that."

"But that should have been obvious!" Kongming complained.

"You'd think so," Ma Liang sighed. "But that was not the worst... Pan Jun surrendered when he saw the enemy forces, and Mi Fang and Shi Ren... they surrendered too, because it was better than being executed by Guan Yu."

Ma Su was struck dumb; Kongming seethed, and said, "Guan Yu has undone all his good deeds of days past with this idiocy... two good men surrendered a quarter of our territory to avoid undeserved punishment, and it is his burden to bear!"

"Mi Fang... betrayed us...?" Ma Su murmured. "How... how can we look Mi Zhu in the eye again...? His brother has betrayed us in the worst possible way...!"

"Mi Zhu should not be held responsible for his brother's actions," Kongming scolded. "My brother serves Wu, which is worse... Pang Rou's brother was Pang De, which is worse still! Take each man on his merits, not his bloodline, Ma Su!"

"...And besides," Ma Liang said, "the worst of all the betrayers is Liu Feng."

"...*Liu Feng*...?" Kongming exclaimed. "Jichang... please explain...!"

"He didn't send any help," Ma Liang replied to his startled audience. "Not a single man. Not a single scrap of food. He said that he couldn't spare anything, because the region was too unstable."

"...That... ignorant... *ungrateful*...!" Kongming growled.

"He resents *you*, *Guan*, and *Zhang*," Ma Liang continued. "He thinks he was cheated out of being named heir to the kingdom, and that you, Guan, and Zhang are responsible. He said that had nothing to do with his decision, but-"

"And General Meng Da...?" Kongming asked angrily. "Did he compensate for Liu Feng's lack of support...?"

"...He also refused," Ma Liang revealed uneasily: Kongming and Ma Su groaned as the fatal consequences of that refusal of help dawned on them both. "He gave the same reason: that-"

"There is no reason that can justify abandoning Guan Yu to die!" Kongming said desperately. "I may not particularly like his attitude at times, but he is entitled to be confident, since he has lived a remarkable life, and been a hero! ...This isn't right. It cannot end for the man this way. As soon as we have reported to His Highness, we'll join the double-time-march on Jing, to rescue Guan Yu."

"I only pray that we're not too late," Ma Liang whimpered.

When Ma Liang relayed the news to Liu Bei's court, the silence was overwhelming: the enormity of it all was not lost on a single man present. Ma Liang noticed that many prominent figures – including Zhang Fei, Ma Chao, Huang Zhong and Wei Yan – were absent due to illness, or due to postings around the vast kingdom that Liu Bei now controlled.

"I really cannot believe it," Jian Yong said sombrely as Ma Liang concluded.

"...For this... ... ...blood will be shed!" Liu Bei declared angrily. "...Lü Meng, Lu Xun, Meng Da, and *especially* Kou Feng! I gave that ungrateful little bastard my name, and-"

"The only crime committed by Meng Da and Liu Feng," Fa Zheng noted, "was repeatedly refusing to send aid when they had internal disputes to resolve. Your Highness, we were no more readily aiding Guan Yu than they were."

"That is correct," Kongming said. "For now, let us be annoyed, but have an open mind. The main concern now, Your Highness, is rescuing Yunchang from his predicament. I have already issued orders for the assembly of a relief army of thirty thousand: they can march via White Emperor City and into Jing, and then travel northwest to Mai and repel Lü Meng, if he has not already retreated when our forces are seen at Yiling."

Liu Bei lowered his head and said, "Kongming, Yunchang is like a brother to me. We ate at the same table, slept in the same room, fought together for more than thirty years... he... he cannot, he *must not* be allowed to die."

"The army will march double-time," Kongming promised. "We'll send advance forces, we'll employ saboteurs: we'll do whatever it takes to rescue Yunchang."

"...Fine," Liu Bei sighed. "...Someone should notify Yide."

"A messenger is already on his way to Linjiang," Kongming said. "Yide's close to the border, so he can act as vanguard."

"That is how it should be," Liu Bei replied emotionally. "Thank you... Kongming."

"I forgot to ask: where is Mi Zhu...?" Kongming said calmly: some of the courtiers expected the question to rile Liu Bei, and murmured uncomfortably.

"...I wonder the same of my friend," Liu Bei said wistfully.

"He is preparing to present himself before Lord Liu," Fa Zheng said hoarsely. "He will be approaching shortly."

"Why does he delay his arrival...?" Liu Bei wondered.

As Liu Bei spoke, Mi Zhu entered the hall alone, bound with rope: the spectacle surprised and horrified the assembled courtiers.

"**What are you doing???**" Liu Bei exclaimed.

"Your Highness...!" Mi Zhu cried as he fell to his knees in front of Liu Bei. "Your Highness, my brother has committed a great wrong against you! How can I not demand death to atone for his wretched behaviour?"

"...Stand up, Zizhong... someone untie his bonds!" Liu Bei urged: Jian Yong stepped forward to untie Mi Zhu, who was visibly distressed and mortified.

"You are my benefactor, and my friend, Zizhong," Liu Bei said honestly. "A man should be taken as a man... his heart before his blood. I do not feel obliged to suffer for any crimes my kin commit... I expect no other to, either."

"But Your Highness, what he has done, it is shame that cannot be borne by one man alone...!" Mi Zhu sobbed. "His acts have shamed my entire family! All the good that I have done, it is *meaningless* before this...!"

"Would you shut up, please...?" Jian Yong chuckled softly. "None of us blame you for your brother's actions: besides, Zizhong, he surrendered when he was faced with overwhelming odds, and even Yunchang had to do that once. Calm down."

"...I... I cannot live with myself...!" Mi Zhu whined.

"Go home," Jian Yong suggested: Mi Zhu nodded mechanically, and started to walk away from Liu Bei slowly. Jian Yong took a seat next to Kongming, and exhaled noisily.

"He moves like a man with a terminal illness," Kongming murmured.

"...It's terrible," Jian Yong whispered. "He's dying of shame."

"...*Aiee*," Liu Bei exclaimed. "We are again in a crisis... will it ever end...?"


For four days, Kongming remained at court and personally oversaw the organisation of the army; when the force seemed to be ready to march, Kongming finally returned home and collapsed with exhaustion as soon as he was indoors.

"Husband...!" Yueying fretted as a servant helped Kongming into the living quarters. "Where have you been? There are rumours that-"

"...Whatever you've heard, it's probably true," Kongming replied wearily.

"You need to get to bed," Yueying pleaded.

"I've done all I can," Kongming chuckled. "I've pacified Liu Feng and Meng Da, I've reassured His Highness, I've sent letters to all the generals, I've listened to every stupid argument for doing absolutely nothing from some of the ridiculous pedants I work with-"

"Yes, you've done all you can," Yueying said surely. "Now come on... you need to rest, now."

"...He's dead, you know," Kongming said suddenly.

Yueying froze for a moment, before dismissing the servant helping Kongming to his feet with a gesture of her eyes: she collapsed to her knees and levelled her eyes with Kongming's.

"...Guan Yu...?" Yueying whispered.

Kongming nodded sadly, saying, "Sun Quan is already in the region, inspecting his acquisition... Guan Yu is trapped in Mai City, between the forces of Wei and Wu, with maybe two or three hundred men, and no food."

"His entire army deserted...?" Yueying exclaimed.

"Deserted, surrendered, or died," Kongming replied. "Guan Yu, Guan Ping and Zhao Lei are now waiting for death... they could try breaking out of the city, but where would they go...? There isn't a friendly place in any direction. They're deep in enemy territory with two hungry tigers chasing them: Xu Huang to the north, and Lü Meng to the south, and Guan Yu... isn't what he was fifteen years ago. He was already starting to lose his edge when I joined His Highness: now, he's a shadow of his former self, a man that has taken risks that a handful of reckless bandits could take, but not the commander of an army of seventy thousand."

450

Yueying nodded slowly.

"He has no adviser… not that he listened when he did have one… and he seems to disregard the teachings of the old masters nowadays, as though he thinks he knows better," Kongming concluded miserably. "…So… for him, the war is over."

"Sun Quan will want him dead," Yueying supposed.

"On the contrary, Sun Quan has repeatedly appealed for Guan Yu to surrender and join Eastern Wu," Kongming said with a laugh. "But this is not the same Guan Yu that surrendered to Cao Cao twenty years ago to preserve the brotherhood… perhaps he knows his best days are gone, and seeks self-sacrifice to remove himself as a burden to his master. Whatever his reasons, this Guan Yu refuses to surrender, and follows the example of Zhang Ren and Pang De. I expect to hear that he's been captured before we even get to White Emperor City, never mind Yiling. …And I expect to hear that he's dead not long after *that*."

"But then the motive will be retribution, revenge," Yueying realised. That would be violence not seen since… since…"

"…Since Cao Cao slaughtered the innocents of Xu Province to avenge his father," Kongming said numbly. "Then the very thing that repulsed me from joining Cao Cao will become our crime, and the circle of folly will begin to turn us toward an inevitable conclusion, as it has done to Yuan Shu, Yuan Shao and Cao Cao already. Only Fa Zheng can turn the army back before that happens, with the argument that we must prepare for Wei capitalising on events and trying to retake Hanzhong from us. Remember, with Guan Yu dead, the one man that Cao Cao truly fears is gone… we lose the bandits in the north, the peasant militias, the revolutionaries… they follow Guan, and Guan alone, and his death frees the north from much more than his army. With Guan Yu gone from that vital pressure point in Jiangling, Cao Cao will feel confident in challenging both of his rivals."

Kongming's fears were realised within days: Guan Yu attempted an escape from Mai City, but – hindered by the winter snows and having less than a hundred followers – he was apprehended by Wu forces led by General Pan Zhang and taken to the city of Linju, where Sun Quan awaited him.

"…So we meet at last, 'Magnificent Beard'," Sun Quan said as Guan Yu was brought before him, bound with rope; Guan Ping and Zhao Lei were led into the hall behind him, also bound with rope.

"…I have nothing to say to you," Guan Yu insisted. "Give me death."

"General Guan, you are nearly sixty… I have no desire to smite you," Sun Quan said sincerely. "Join Wu… do not show such stubbornness. You joined Cao Cao… am I worse to you than your master's rival and enemy…?"

"Considerably worse," Guan Yu retorted. "All you have ever done is crave Jing… people will blame me for losing it, but they should remember to blame you for wanting it more than you wanted justice for the land."

"**Execute him!**" Zhang Zhao barked.

"No!" Sun Quan ordered. "Guan Yunchang, hero of old… you have had many years of valiant service… why do you now shirk your responsibility, and goad me into destroying you…?"

"I failed my king, who is also my friend, and my brother," Guan Yu replied emotionally. "I allowed this to happen... and I will not live another moment with the shame."

"I would sooner imprison you, as I have done with Liao Hua, or recruit you, as I have done with Pan Jun," Sun Quan said. "Reconsider my previous offer, General... your daughter's hand in marriage to my son... our families joined forever..."

"What, as you married your sister to my king, and then snatched her back...?" Guan Yu scoffed. "Your schemes are of no interest to me, scruffy-bearded scoundrel... I will never join you."

"Prison, then," Sun Quan sighed. "Perhaps, in time..."

"If you imprison him, his 'friends' will hound you, as they do Cao Cao," Zhang Zhao protested. "You will never know a moment's peace."

"...You will not reconsider...?" Sun Quan asked one last time: Guan Yu smiled, and shook his head slowly and silently.

"Do not leave us behind, Father!" Guan Ping said bravely.

"I will also go with you to the netherworld!" Zhao Lei declared. "I am ready too!"

"...Guards," Sun Quan hailed reluctantly; six soldiers stepped forward and took each of the prisoners by their arms. "... ... ...Death."

Sun Quan watched silently as Guan Yu, Guan Ping and Zhao Lei were led away: they were executed moments later, and Guan Yu's head was brought back to him for inspection by one of the executioners.

"...Such strength, even in death," Sun Quan said as he examined the head of the famous hero: the expression on the lifeless face was almost tranquil, as if he were unburdened at last. "...But his magnificent beard... is so matted, so ruined..."

"We should send his head to Cao Cao," Zhang Zhao suggested. "It was Cao's idea to pincer him... let Cao Cao take the blame for his death, as well."

"...Agreed," Sun Quan said as he sat back and exhaled mournfully. "Have his head wrapped well and taken to Cao Cao as soon as possible... I only hope it has the desired effect."

"Jing is yours now," Zhang Zhao noted pointedly. "One old enemy general should not haunt your thoughts: thanks to the efforts of Lü Meng and Lu Xun, we have finally retrieved Jing from that thief Liu Bei, after almost a decade!"

"...Where *is* Ziming...?" Sun Quan asked: Lü Meng was conspicuous by his absence from the meeting.

Lu Xun – who had been watching proceedings quietly – said, "He is bedridden, my lord... unfortunately, his illness was not entirely false, and he has taken a turn for the worse."

"...That will not do...!" Sun Quan cried. "I must see him now!"

"He is travelling back to Lukou to convalesce," Lu Xun replied.

"Then I must this moment travel to Lukou," Sun Quan declared urgently as he got to his feet. "Ready a carriage... ready a ship...!"


As Sun Quan travelled to Lukou to meet with the ailing Lü Meng, Guan Yu's head began its lifeless journey northward to be reunited with his temporary master Cao Cao, the King of Wei. Cao Cao had Guan Yu buried with full honours, and ensured that the Chengdu court – now in full, wrathful mourning – was aware of it.

452

"Cao Cao has shown some respect for Yunchang, though not as much as one would expect," Jian Yong said to the assembled courtiers: he wore only white and colourless fabrics to denote his deep mourning, as did most of the court.

"Yunchang…!" Liu Bei whispered: the news had left him grief-stricken, and Guan Yu's style name had been the only word to pass his lips for some time.

"A ruse, of course," Fa Zheng said weakly: Kongming noted the adviser's pallid appearance, and worried that he might be seriously ill. "After… all… Cao Cao is trying to avoid our wrath."

"*Yunchang*…!" Liu Bei whined more audibly: his face contorted as he spoke.

"…While on the other hand, the villain Lü Meng that brought the misfortune on Yunchang is actually ill," Jian Yong reported gladly. "There are reports that he cannot ingest food… that he cannot walk, and his breathing is laboured."

"Yunchang… haunts him," Yi Ji said bitterly. "Yunchang's spirit is eroding his essence, destroying him from within… as punishment for his evil ways."

Kongming shook his head sadly and silently as Liu Bei continued to lament using only the name 'Yunchang', and was seemingly oblivious to the discussion.

"Cao Cao has also fallen ill," Jian Yong added. "Perhaps Yunchang is destroying them for us, before he moves on to the netherworld."

"Yide is demanding retribution," Yi Ji reported uncomfortably.

"We must be cautious as to how we go forward," Zhao Yun suggested.

"I agree, Zilong," Fa Zheng said with a nod. "We-"

"I'll not rest until they're all dead… the dogs of Wei, and the rats of Wu!" Liu Bei proclaimed. "Of all the insults, the wrongs that Sun Quan has inflicted upon my house, upon *us*, upon *me*… this is the worst! …I will not live under the same sky as Sun Quan!"

"Your Highness…!" Qin Mi hailed. "Think it through…! The-"

"Your Highness," Fa Zheng interrupted, "as the man who represents Yi… and the wishes of the people… please, listen to me."

Liu Bei glared at the fragile Fa Zheng with intolerant fury for a few seconds; Kongming feared the worst as Liu Bei leant forward as if to say something in anger.

"Please," Fa Zheng repeated, "listen to me… Your Highness."

Liu Bei's eyes wandered. He looked at the court around him – not the people, but the structure – and seemed to soften as he decided something unspoken.

"My liege…?" Fa Zheng prompted.

Liu Bei returned his gaze to Fa Zheng.

"…I *cannot* ignore you, Xiaozhi," Liu Bei conceded. "Please, speak your mind."

Kongming sighed quietly, with both relief and frustration, as Fa Zheng started to speak.

"When I travelled to Jing, following the generous appraisal of your good name by Zhang Ziqiao, and I requested your aid is rescuing Yi from itself, it was not so that we could be plunged into countless, successive wars," Fa Zheng said bluntly. "My aim was to bring stability to Yi, find accord with Hanzhong, and repel Cao Cao. We have done all of those things... Jing is strategically important, I know that, and Wu's actions are not justifiable in the slightest, I know that too: but Your Highness, we are not ready to launch a punitive expedition. The King of Wei looms like a tiger at the back door. The lord of Wu seems content with Jing, and has not made moves toward the Yi border. Sorry to say it, but Guan Yunchang brought the misfortune on himself, and we have to be seen to move on... if only to protect ourselves. When Wei is no longer a threat, *and* our forces are stable and well trained, *and* the region is plentiful and content, *then* we can attack Wu, if we *must*: *then*, and *only then*."

Liu Bei was uncomfortably quiet for several minutes; the entire court was silent, in fact, as Liu Bei looked at his court once again, taking in every support post, flag and rug of the enclosure as though it were of the utmost importance to his decision.

"...Your Highness...?" Fa Zheng prompted uneasily.

"...Very well, Mister Fa," Liu Bei said calmly. "I shall abide by your words."

Fa Zheng coughed uncomfortably and smiled with gratitude; Kongming fanned himself slowly and watched Liu Bei and Fa Zheng with interest.


"He actually listened," Kongming mused as he sat with Yueying that evening. "He actually... listened."

"That truly surprises you," Yueying noted calmly.

"Zhang Fei cries out for revenge, the generals as a whole see taking no action as weakness, save Zilong, who is proving to be an able statesman of deep thinking," Kongming explained. "He decided to listen to Fa Zheng... not because of anything else but the debt he owes him. I saw the king, viewing his court, fighting the mat-weaver inside him that urged him to war to settle a score, avenge a murdered friend, and brother... knowing that he couldn't refuse the man that gave him that court."

"...You seem to think there is a time when the king will not listen," Yueying suggested. "Why would he heed Fa Zheng now, but ignore him later...?"

"I don't fear him ignoring Fa Zheng, I fear him ignoring the rest of us when Fa Zheng is gone," Kongming replied eerily. "He's sick... I don't know how, I don't know why... but like Lü Meng and Cao Cao, he is ill, and he will not last more than a year, I know it."

"...And if he did die...?" Yueying prompted.

"...Then we will go to war with Wu at the slightest suggestion of an excuse," Kongming said sadly.


************

454

## 96

The death of Guan Yu sent shockwaves around the land, and – as predicted – many of the underground networks of contacts he had now dispersed, rather than seek a new contact in Chengdu. Cao Cao did indeed relax once he knew Guan Yu was gone, and planning started for another attack on Hanzhong. Once Guan Yu's death was widely known, Meng Da defected to Wei in order to escape reprisal for his own role – the crime of abandonment – in Guan Yu's capture. He surrendered Fangling City, and joined forces with Xu Huang in harassing his former ally, Liu Feng, at Shangyong City.

Because some notable figures whose names were associated with Guan Yu's demise were suffering with serious illnesses, superstitious rumours arose that Guan Yu's spirit was haunting the land, taking revenge on his enemies from the afterlife.

Lü Meng was first: despite receiving the best medical treatment that Sun Quan could afford and provide, he never regained strength and died on his sickbed aged 41, leaving Lu Xun and Zhu Ran to continue his mission.

After that, Liu Bei lost Veteran Tiger General Huang Zhong, who was over 70 years of age: some remembered Guan Yu holding the old man in contempt for being a 'common soldier', unworthy of being one of the '5 Tigers of Shu', and wondered if Guan detested the idea of being outlived by an older, unworthy peer.

Within months of that, Fa Zheng died of an illness at the age of 44: some wondered if that was for his vehement opposition to retaliatory action, superstition that was not lost on Liu Bei. The King of Hanzhong wept endlessly for 'the man that had given him Yi', perhaps more than he had done for Pang Tong, Huo Jun or even Guan Yu: the next death, however, would bring no tears to Liu Bei.

In the spring of that new, eventful year, the most influential man in China – the King of Wei, Cao Cao – finally succumbed to illness, and died, aged 65. Of all the legacies he left, none was more important than his kingdom of Wei and its crown prince, the ambitious Cao Pi. Bitter-sweet celebrations were, however, short-lived: within months, the situation deteriorated to a new low point.

"I am summoned to court," Kongming said with urgency as he hurriedly prepared to face the Governor of Yi and King of Hanzhong, Liu Bei. Kongming was – as he had been since the death of Guan Yu – adorned in colourless robes to mark the recent passing of so many friends and colleagues.
"...Is it for reprisals against Wu...?" Yueying fretted.
"No," Kongming replied knowingly. "It's much, much worse than that."
"...*Worse*...?" Yueying exclaimed.
"Now I wear white for a fallen dragon," Kongming explained.
"...The *Emperor*...?" Yueying realised. "He... is dead...?"

"So some say," Kongming replied as he picked up his fan. "It doesn't matter if he is or he isn't... the Lius have been deposed, Cao Pi has declared himself emperor."
"But I haven't heard...!" Yueying whined fearfully.
"I have good sources," Kongming replied sadly. "Now I must go... quickly."

Kongming arrived at a bustling court, where all the most notable figures were in attendance. Liu Bei appeared agitated and angry at the rumours that were circulating around the court. As soon as everyone was sat down, Jian Yong started to speak.
"...It's true," Jian Yong began. "The Han have been extinguished... Cao Pi is now declared as the First Emperor of Cao Wei."
The court erupted into a vocal ensemble of panic.
**"I will not accept it!"** Liu Bei screamed. **"They murdered my divine nephew!"**
**"Please, everyone!"** Jian Yong implored: the court quietened.
"We do not know that, Your Highness," Kongming insisted. "We have reports that the former Han Emperor is alive and well, that Cao Pi feared reprisals from within the court if he killed the true heavenly dragon. This-"
"Wei must be destroyed," Zhao Yun declared. "They have now committed the worst crime of all... usurpation of the throne. They must answer for it."
**"And Wu as well, for helping them!"** Zhang Fei shouted. **"They could o' helped us stop Wei, instead they killed Yunchang and stole Jing from us! And hasn't Sun Quan been made a _king_ by Cao Pi...? He's betrayed Han as well as us!"**
"The fate of the house of Han... is our priority," Kongming suggested. "Whether the former Han Emperor is dead or not, there is no Han Emperor... we must remedy that, else the land has no light to follow, only the darkness offered by Cao Pi."
"Yes," Huang Quan agreed. "Your Highness... as the last surviving prince of Han, you must accept the burden of Emperor, and ensure that the land does not go ungoverned for another moment. 'King Sun of Wu' must wait, for now."
"...I cannot do that," Liu Bei said nervously. "It... it would make me no better than Cao Pi! You'd make a villain of me???"
"...Your Highness," Kongming replied, "the Han has been vanquished by the King of Wei, and at this moment, there is no Han Emperor. If you do not do this... you abandon the people to evil."
"It must be done and done quickly," Huang Quan pleaded. "Your Highness...!"
"...Let me... think it over," Liu Bei said quietly.
"There is no time to think, Your Highness!" Jian Yong declared. "We are all here, whether we started in Zhuo, Xu, Jing, or Yi, for the same reason: the restoration of the house of Han! Right now, _there isn't one_: do you see the problem...?"
The court erupted once again: Jian Yong, Huang Quan and Kongming stared at Liu Bei with determined, pleading eyes.
"...Our common goal..." Liu Bei mused quietly: he looked at his vassals, probing each face for signs of dissent, confusion, or fear. In particular, he scrutinised the faces of the former vassals of the former Yi governor, Liu Zhang.

"Xuande," Jian Yong said quietly as he neared Liu Bei, "this is a critical moment. You know that Sun Quan has petitioned Cao Pi to have Liu Zhang officially named as the governor of Yi... a lot of the pedants we inherited from Liu Zhang would have no problem serving under him again. There's no Han now... the Han was your reason for fighting, and now Cao Pi has removed it. Either we continue the Han... or we give up, surrender to Cao Pi, and hope he spares our families."

"Your Highness," Kongming said, "it is either the end, or a new beginning... which is it...?"

The court started to quieten again as the courtiers and generals awaited their king's decision; Liu Bei sat back in his throne, and exhaled noisily.

"...Very well," Liu Bei conceded. "Though I am unworthy... I have no choice."

"Ayah! Don't be another Wang Mang, Your Highness!" one official, Fei Shi, protested. "Keep your honour, and do not act on this evil decision!"

"**Get him out of here!**" Jian Yong barked: Fei Shi was led away, cursing loudly.

The remaining ensemble made obeisance to their new emperor-in-waiting, Liu Bei, who observed them with a cold, unreadable expression.


Liu Bei dismissed the court, asking that Jian Yong and Kongming remain for a private discussion.

"...I have an important decision to make before I proceed," Liu Bei said: Kongming smiled knowingly, and started to fan himself slowly.

"...Liu Feng," Kongming supposed.

"As ever, you are ahead of me by several strides," Liu Bei sighed. "He will need to be dealt with now, one way or the other."

"We have two choices," Jian Yong suggested. "He becomes your crown prince, or he is exempted from the line of succession."

"It... isn't that simple," Kongming said calmly.

"Kongming," Jian Yong chuckled incredulously, "what is there to make a situation out of...? He has accepted that he was too strict in his adherence to protocol when he favoured stability in Shangyong over saving Yunchang. What he did was wrong, but-"

"He abandoned Guan Yu out of spite," Kongming suggested. "That much is now very clear... but there is more. I understand that he is in correspondence with the defector Meng Da. Meng carries generous offers of titles and inheritance of the Kou family properties if he disowns his past here and goes to the north..."

"He refused," Jian Yong countered. "Kongming, I thought you were one of the ones saying that we should-"

"We have to adapt to circumstances," Kongming said coldly. "Things have changed... as we speak, Liu Feng is on his way here, to Chengdu."

"...Why...?" Liu Bei asked angrily. "He was to stay in Shangyong, and guard it from Wei... what, he can't even do *that* now???"

"He has been 'betrayed and overthrown by Shen Dan'... we have lost the city," Kongming revealed to a shocked and demoralised Liu Bei and Jian Yong. "Now he comes here to... well... that, I don't know."

"Acquire troops to retake Shangyong," Jian Yong supposed. "Well, we-"

"...Or, perhaps, to contest the succession...?" Kongming interrupted. "He does not come alone: he brings his remaining – loyal – forces with him. He resents the crown prince, Liu Shan... we cannot guarantee Feng's loyalty to him... or to *you*, Your Highness."

"Agreed," Liu Bei said without hesitation.

"Now *wait*..." Jian Yong pleaded.

"He has already proved himself a traitor," Liu Bei interrupted angrily. "He was never grateful for his place, always sulking when given tasks he deemed 'demeaning', never truly acknowledging his true place. Had the court – including you, Kongming – not remonstrated, Kou Feng would be long dead. Now, I shall avenge my dead brother by killing an unworthy son!"

"Now look, Xuande...!" Jian Yong protested. "Kongming... *why*...?"

"Necessity," Kongming replied coolly. "Please understand, I don't do this for any other reason than that we have no choice... the cause of Han comes first, we need to secure the imperial line before we can do anything else. We can't let one upstart adopted ingrate ruin our grand scheme."

"When he arrives in Chengdu, I want him arrested, and brought before me," Liu Bei ordered. "*I* will tell him his fate to his face... nobody else can do it."

"Husband...!" Yueying bleated as Kongming returned home later that day: Ma Liang and Ma Su were also waiting for him.

"...We heard that Liu Feng is coming here," Ma Liang said quietly. "Jian Yong came by... he told us what you said."

"...Necessity," Kongming insisted as he started to fan himself slowly. "Liu Feng is a threat to everything that we've done... he mustn't be allowed to get in the way."

"...*Get in the way*...?" Ma Liang said with surprise. "He... he has fought bravely for his father for the last decade, risking his life! He is a war hero!"

"He abandoned Guan Yu, he covets the crown," Kongming scolded. "You, of all men, know that. He colludes with Meng Da... how do we know he didn't stage the loss of Shangyong, mm...? ... ... ...How do we know he isn't on his way to our capital as an assassin for Cao Pi...?"

"But...!" Ma Liang protested.

"Kongming... may be right, elder brother," Ma Su decided miserably. "Look at the way Yuan Shao's sons turned on each other... look at the problems Cao Pi had from his brothers, even after Cao Cao had settled the inheritance question clearly. The king must become the new emperor without problems such as a rogue prince. On the matter of Guan Yu, he failed in his military duty... he must answer for it."

"...Are you *sure*, Kongming...?" Ma Liang pleaded. "Peng Yang was one thing... this is another. Are you *sure*...?"

"Liu Feng is a stray arrow," Kongming replied, "that is already in flight. All I am doing now is catching it mid-flight, before it hits something it shouldn't."

"*Something*...?" Ma Liang noted. "Kongming...!"

"If I were a threat to the Han, I'd remove myself," Kongming declared. "What's done is done... we have more important things to worry about than him. Zhang Fei is raising the matter of marching on Wu again."

"...*Wu*...?" Yueying said with surprise. "But... but what about *Wei*...?"

"Zhang Fei isn't alone in the ridiculous view that fraternal ties come before the empire," Kongming sighed irritably. "Sadly, the other major proponent... is His Highness. Although I was one of the loudest voices calling for the king to ascend to the imperial throne... once he's there, he won't listen to anyone except, I think, for Zhang Fei, and his word will be divine will. We'll have to march on Sun Quan..."

"Our army now numbers more than eighty-thousand," Ma Su suggested. "We'll definitely win, since Wu is thinly spread."

"Cao Pi is a snake, and with men like Sima Yi and Liu Ye as his senior advisers, he will be looking to take every opportunity," Ma Liang proposed further.

"...I agree with you," Kongming admitted. "Wei will refuse aid, I think, and wait to see the outcome... Wu will be forced to watch the eastern front in case Wei tries to attack from Hefei, meaning we will be facing only fifty-thousand, at most, and they *will* be thinly spread, guarding Jing and Jiangdong. Our army will number a hundred thousand at least. But it is still the wrong course: Wei will attack us both from all fronts – Hanzhong, Hefei, and Jiangling – as soon as we have worn each other down, and their massive numerical advantage will guarantee them victory."

"Once you explain that..." Ma Liang began: Kongming gestured with his fan.

"...I can say nothing," Kongming insisted. "This... is Heaven's choice now."

Liu Feng finally arrived at the Yi capital, Chengdu, whereupon he was arrested and brought before his adoptive father at court.

"...For you, *no forgiveness*," Liu Bei growled as he stared down at Feng, who was bound and kneeling in forced penitence. "Your crimes... are made worse for who you are."

"My liege," Jian Yong said with a subdued tone, "we should think before we act. It isn't that I doubt Liu Feng's stupidity, it's that-"

"Enough," Liu Bei interrupted tersely. "I wanted to see him one last time... to look at his face... before he is sent to the netherworld, where he will answer to Guan Yunchang. That will be far worse than any torture I could conceive."

Liu Feng looked at Kongming, who was stood to the left of Liu Bei with Huang Quan and Jian Yong: Kongming fanned himself slowly, but he was otherwise motionless and expressionless.

"When I entered the Kou household all those years ago, I was enduring great hardship," Liu Bei recalled. "However, the Kou family saw in me great promise... and they entrusted their own son, their own flesh and blood, into my care... and I took him as *my* own son. I raised him, schooled him in the art of war, the way of the pen, and the matters of the court... so that one day, he could be great, as I intended for myself! ...And how is this repaid...? ...You refused to aid my friend and brother-in-arms, you conspired with Wei to cede hard-won territory, and then you came here expecting to be given the throne! ...**Death is too good for you!**"

Liu Feng turned his gaze to Liu Bei at last: it was cold and unreadable.

"...So have you nothing at all to say...?" Liu Bei taunted. "Nothing at all...?"

After a protracted silence, Liu Feng smiled slightly and sadly, saying, "I was warned that I would be betrayed... I only wish that I'd listened."

Liu Bei's face hardened as he said with malice, "As you are my son... it is not appropriate that you die by another's hand... I order you to take your own life."

Kongming watched Liu Feng calmly as he was dragged from the court; Jian Yong sighed audibly, and shook his head.

That evening, the atmosphere in the Zhuge household was subdued.

"...Husband," Yueying said as she played her qin, "were you sure...?"

"No," Kongming replied honestly and guiltlessly as he sat in front of his own qin: rather than playing, he was fanning himself rhythmically. "...But that doesn't matter anymore."

Yueying stopped playing and turned to Kongming, saying, "That isn't true."

"It is," Kongming replied with regret. "We are now at the highest of heights... soaring above the earth... and the law. Now, it is about acting on the possibility of threats... not acting on the consequences of disregarding those possibilities, and being wrong."

"But..." Yueying began: Kongming looked at her sadly. After a pause, Yueying sighed, and said, "I suppose that you'll have to be careful, because others will try to slander you. ...I suppose they've already tried. ...I'm not a fool: I know how it works... I don't know why I'm having so much trouble making sense of it, I know how it works... but... if Liu Feng *was* loyal, and everybody was wrong... then..."

"You mean 'If *I* was wrong'," Kongming said knowingly. "Yes, I have to carry that with me, but... compared to being right and doing nothing... I am resolved."

"...So now the succession is assured," Yueying mused. "Liu Shan will succeed the king... the Emperor... when he dies..."

"I'd rather not think about that," Kongming chuckled wearily. "Emperor A'Dou is a whole other problem in itself. Fortunately, His Highness is healthy and strong, so he has at least ten years in him... by which time, we will be in the capital, and the war will be over, and the Emperor will be surrounded by wise, capable officials, who-"
"...Will delay the insanity of the last forty years from recurring for at least another twenty years after that," Yueying interrupted.
"...It's better than nothing," Kongming insisted. "The Han will endure, stability will resume... if only until another eunuch gains favour... but at least there will be peace for a while... it's better than nothing."
Yueying nodded slowly: she then returned to her slow, purposeful playing of the qin. Kongming started to play as well, matching her pace and tone. The two exchanged sad glances, but said nothing.

Despite the decisions being made in urgency, it was many weeks before the preparations for Liu Bei's ascension were completed, during which time Wu and Wei watched the Yi region with interest. Liu Bei was enthroned amid a grand ceremony, using a replica of the raised imperial altar ascended by Cao Pi months before. Wearing the robes of an emperor – lavish silk adorned with dragons – Liu Bei accepted a newly fashioned jade seal, and became the First Emperor of a new dynasty, known as Shu Han. Kongming would remain as the Chancellor, and continue to hold considerable sway.

Once Liu Bei had been enthroned, a period of mourning and rejoicing followed, as new titles were conferred and new rewards assigned to loyal vassals. But once it was over – and for once, Zhang Fei was eager to end the festivities more quickly than anyone – the matter of revenge was raised once again.

"But... Your Majesty...!" Zhao Yun protested in front of a sombre court: his was a lone voice of dissent, and he was glad that both Zhang Fei and Ma Chao were absent from the ensemble, guarding their assigned territories.
"...Zilong, you disappoint me," Liu Bei declared. "For fifteen years, you have been a dependable friend as well as a loyal vassal, and yet you now go against the wishes of your master, your Emperor, over a matter so clear and straightforward."
"...Your Majesty," Zhao Yun replied bravely, "there is nothing more important than duty: as you say, I have never strayed from it. It is your divine self that strays from the duty of Emperor of Shu Han: firstly, by wishing to strike Wu before the usurpers of the Han, over a personal matter, and secondly, by placing your divine self in danger by wanting to be the commander of the army, and ride with the vanguard. If any expedition should be undertaken at this critical moment, Your Majesty, it should be against Cao Wei, with Zhang Fei, me, or Wei Yan leading the troops. Your place, Your Majesty, is with your people, in your palace, in your capital."
"Again, you defy my will," Liu Bei said irritably. "If you will not fight with all your heart, *fine*: Yide will be the Front Commander, and you can act as support. That is all, General Zhao... *stand aside*."

Gasps could be heard around the court as Liu Bei publicly rebuked Zhao Yun: the general could not believe what he had heard, but he withdrew without another word.

"A proclamation shall be sent to all corners of our empire, declaring the intent to march on Wu as soon as the army is in full readiness," Liu Bei continued. "Let Wu know of it: let them squirm, let them plead to Cao Pi, it won't save them. We will descend on them like a great flood, and take back what is ours! We will seize Jing, and then we will destroy them in their homelands! And then – when Sun Quan is gone – we will march on Wei, who will know our might!"

Zhao Yun bowed his head sadly: Kongming fanned himself slowly, and sighed.


"…Zilong paid a heavy price," Kongming said as he strummed the strings of his qin that evening: Yueying sat at his side, listening to his melancholy tune.

"But he was spared," Yueying noted.

"Ah, so you see it as I do," Kongming chuckled miserably. "Our illustrious First Emperor spared Zilong because of his past service… I wonder what fate would befall a chancellor."

"…I think you may be arrested, at the very worst, and detained until the campaign had ceased," Yueying said plainly.

Kongming stopped playing.

"That's why I didn't object," Kongming admitted. "I felt for Zilong… but he was the only man in that court, I think, that could survive such a direct challenge. His Majesty allowed that one group objection earlier… but his response was clear enough to understand… 'Obey me, or else'. Only Zilong dared to say more, and now he will probably never regain favour… so very, very sad."

"So you will be guarding the country alone…?" Yueying wondered.

"I must admit, I am surprised that His Highness did not demand that I travel at his side," Kongming replied miserably. "…Maybe there is some part of him that knows this is suicidal madness, and wants me to survive it."

"Don't say that," Yueying said plainly. "Perhaps he trusts nobody else with protecting Shu from those within and without that may do us harm."

"I imagine that's it," Kongming replied with a smile. "But… Ma Jichang has been chosen to act as Senior Adviser… I fear for him. What if his advice is ignored…?"

"He'd ignore yours too," Yueying sighed. "Ma Liang is very shrewd… he survived being Guan Yu's adviser."

"Yes, but Guan Yu didn't," Kongming retorted. "Jichang could not advise the man… time after time, he ignored advice… before, when there were Pang Tongs, Mister Suns and Fa Zhengs to guide His Highness… … …I'm afraid, Yueying. We might lose, and lose badly… even with the barbarian help we're seeking…"

"…Barbarians…?" Yueying prompted. "The Di tribes…?"

"No, they still hold contempt for us," Kongming replied sadly. "We're asking the Wuling tribal leader, Shamoke, for help."

"…In exchange for *what*…?" Yueying wondered.

"That's still being negotiated," Kongming admitted. "His Highness is rage-blinded... like Sun Quan before him, Jing has become an obsession, and revenge for a murder is a mission without a boundary of unacceptable cost. Shamoke would want his tribal lands as independent territories... but an Emperor ceding his land to a barbarian race...? ...Is there any greater sign of weakness to send to our enemies...?"

"...And his revenge... might be violent," Yueying prompted. "You've said it before... you're afraid that he'll-"

"No," Kongming interrupted. "No, I can't think about that. Cao Cao and His Highness, they're not the same... I spent too long wondering when Pang Tong was shot... and when Mi Zhu finally died... and even when Fa Zheng, after he... ... ...and... and it..."

"...Doesn't matter...?" Yueying supposed.

Kongming took his fan from where it lay at his side and started to wave it back and forth silently: as for the question, he did not answer.

************

## 97

Zhang Fei prepared his forces at the city of Linjiang, intent on joining First Shu Han Emperor Liu Bei and marching on Wu to exact revenge for their fallen friend Guan Yu together.

"...**Sun Quan... the bastard!**" Zhang Fei barked as he marched through his camp one evening: it was four days from his intended marching date.

His soldiers moved out of his way as he went, anxious not to be seen to confront him in any way. The camp was awash with the yellow flags of the Shu army, and all of the soldiers were in good health, and well equipped. However, none of this pleased Zhang Fei as it normally would: he did not want to see any colourful material at all.

"...**Why are there still colours...?**" Zhang Fei screamed. "**Where are they? Where are the two that are supposed to be dealing with this???**"

Zhang Da and Fan Qiang – the two generals that were charged with preparing white flags and clothing for Zhang Fei's vast forces – knew they could not hide, and presented themselves before their commander.

"...*Well...?*" Zhang Fei asked snidely.

"We... we can't get the materials," Fan Qiang protested.

"Not in the time," Zhang Da said nervously.

"We can't do it, not in three days," Fan Qiang insisted. "If we had just a little more time, Commander-"

"**You've had long enough!**" Zhang Fei interrupted furiously. "**You've had days already, and you've done what? ...I want the enemy to see that Zhang Fei grieves for his friend and brother! I want the enemy to see that my grief is shared by every one of my men! I want every flag to cry and weep! I want every enemy of mine to cry and weep for what I'll do to them!**"

"B-but...!" Fan Qiang pleaded.

"**And if I can't,**" Zhang Fei growled, "**it'll be your heads that will roll first!**"

That said, Zhang Fei shoved both men aside with such force that they fell to the ground, and strode toward his command tent.

"...We're dead," Zhang Da supposed.

"He's just angry," Fan Qiang replied nervously as two soldiers helped him to his feet. "He just-"

"He's beaten men raw for less than this!" Zhang Da hissed as he shrugged off the help of fellow soldiers and got to his feet. "I-"

"Let's... *go and see what we can do,*" Fan Qiang said with emphasis. "I'm sure that we can come up with something to save ourselves."

Zhang Da noted the expression on Fan Qiang's face and nodded slowly.

That night, Fan Qiang and Zhang Da waited until Zhang Fei was asleep, whereupon they killed him, and fled the camp with his severed head.

"...He's inconsolable," Jian Yong said as Kongming reached the court: Liu Bei's wailing was audible from the entrance of the great hall.

"One question: will we still be marching?" Kongming asked plainly.

"...You don't know all the details then, for once," Jian Yong chuckled sadly. "They fled into Jing... they joined Sun Quan. Wu have made sure that we know they've buried Zhang Fei's head with honours."

"And the killers... they're dead...?" Kongming asked.

"No... so really, it looks like Wu have no problem with the death, even if they did bury Zhang Fei as a hero," Jian Yong sighed. "Your brother not keeping you as up-to-date as usual, is he...?"

"...I hope that wasn't...!" Kongming growled angrily.

"I... didn't mean anything, Kongming," Jian Yong insisted. "I... ... ...I really don't know how many more people we can afford to lose."

"None," Kongming said coldly. "Are we still marching to the same schedule...?"

"...Yes," Jian Yong replied quietly. "A few days late, of course, but... yes."

"What is your official title...?" Kongming asked further.

"...None as such," Jian Yong replied. "Like I always am... just a friend who he can call on, a familiar face, someone who he can talk to... but not necessarily listen to."

"There's really no point in me staying here long," Kongming decided. "I'll go and pay my condolences, and then I'll go home."

"He'll appreciate that," Jian Yong said with a smile.

"...My friend...!" Liu Bei sobbed as Kongming entered the private audience chamber, where Liu Bei – surrounded by imperial ladies-in-waiting, eunuchs and fawning officials – was sat on a royal throne, talking to the official Li Yan.

"...It's good to see you here," Li Yan said with a smile.

"I came here as soon as I heard," Kongming said weakly. "The hardest part of all this is... is believing that it's true, that he's... gone."

"...When he and I... and Yunchang... when we came to your cottage, all those years ago... I remember, he was so angry," Liu Bei chuckled through tears. "And... and remember, when I told him that you and I were like a fish finding water...?"

"Yes," Kongming said with warmth. "He called me 'Water' for years after that."

"He was a good man, Kongming... hard to like at first, but...!" Liu Bei sobbed.

"I'll miss him," Kongming said honestly. "We... we can honour him best by not allowing ourselves to be slowed."

"...Yes," Liu Bei growled with sudden anger. "Again, I lose something to this 'Sun Quan'! I'll kill him, Kongming... I'll kill him!" Kongming smiled encouragingly as he replied, "I must be going now, Your Majesty. I couldn't go without saying *something*... but I must prepare for my own role. Your Majesty... stay well."

Liu Bei smiled through his sobbing, and Kongming left the room.

The day of the march arrived at last, and Liu Bei prepared to lead his forces out of the main gates of Chengdu: there, was, however, one last protest.

"**Your Majesty!**" Qin Mi screamed as he approached Liu Bei's carriage.

"Oh, not this prick," Jian Yong complained.

"**Your Majesty, you must reconsider!**" Qin Mi declared to an angry Liu Bei: the army looked on with sudden discomfort. "**So many have gone, so many inauspicious signs...!**"

"**Mister Qin!**" Huang Quan barked angrily from amongst the advisers that would travel with Liu Bei. "Save your remonstrance! Everything is decided now! Move aside!"

"...No!" Qin Mi insisted. "I can't stand by any longer!"

"...**Guards**...!" Liu Bei bellowed: sensing that the next word that Liu Bei uttered would be incredibly inauspicious, Huang Quan, Dong He, Liu Ba and Kongming moved toward Liu Bei and started to beg for clemency.

"...Think of the army!" Huang Quan protested.

"To kill an official on the day of the march is not fitting!" Dong He added.

"Imprison him for now," Kongming suggested. "You can decide his fate when you return, Your Majesty."

"*Please*," Liu Ba said miserably.

"I hate him, but... save your blade for Sun Quan," Jian Yong volunteered.

"...Very well... alright, okay, **stop your whining, all of you, PLEASE!** ...The wretched pedant can keep his head, *for now*," Liu Bei retorted. "**Guards... imprison Qin Mi!**"

"**Your Majesty!**" Qin Mi screamed as two imperial palace guards dragged him away from the procession. "**Your Majesty, do not march! Do not march! YOU ARE MARCHING TO YOUR DOOM!**"

"...**ONWARD!**" Liu Bei barked: the army began the long march out of the Shu capital city of Chengdu and toward Wu-controlled Jing Province.

"...Farewell, Zhuge Kongming," Jian Yong said with a slight wave.

"Brothers... stay well," Ma Liang said to Ma Su and Kongming as he urged his horse to move; the rest of the Ma family watched the event silently from the back of the crowd.

"...Goodbye," Kongming replied: the tone of his voice hurt Ma Liang, who turned his gaze away from his family and friends as he rode out of the city.

"When will this battle end...?" Yi Ji wondered as the vast army continued on its way, watched by thousands of loved ones.

"...I don't know," Kongming replied sadly. "This one, it's not like before..."

"How long should we leave Qin Mi in prison...?" Dong He asked.

"...Until His Majesty returns," Kongming replied coldly.

"No," Dong He protested. "He's a good man, he-"

"He stays in prison," Kongming insisted. "He'll get food, he won't be flogged, he'll get a cell of his own..."

"And you really think that His Majesty will let him live...?" Liu Ba jeered.

"...You think this is like the case of Yuan Shao and Tian Feng, before the ill-fated campaign against Cao Cao," Kongming chuckled cynically. "I guarantee that His Majesty will release Mister Qin... regardless of whether he wins, and regardless of whether he should."

466

"*You...!*" Liu Ba exclaimed.

"Qin Mi tried to demoralise the army on the day of departure!" Kongming retorted angrily. "If he had something to say, this was not the day for it! ...Now come... the cart is now aflame, rolling down the steep hill... all we're doing here is wasting air and time."

"...You're right," Liu Ba conceded. "Yes, let's return to the court." The other officials largely agreed, and retreated to the court to begin their plans for civil administration and defence in the absence of their hot-headed emperor.

"...I was in the crowd today," Yueying said as Kongming entered his home that same evening.

"...I know you were," Kongming replied. "This... is going to be very difficult."

"You must be tired," Yueying supposed.

"Tired...?" Kongming chuckled. "There's an understatement. Pang Tong, Sun Qian, Fa Zheng, and Mi Zhu... dead. Jian Yong, Ma Liang, and Huang Quan... are now on their way to Jing for a showdown with the faction of the tripartite state that is supposed to be our *ally*. Yes, I have the friendship of Wu Yi, Yang Yi, Dong He, Jiang Wan, and Yi Ji... but I have enemies at court as well. With Guan Yu, Zhang Fei and Huang Zhong dead, and Zhao Yun out of favour, Ma Chao's seriously ill, so Wei Yan is our only untainted champion... and... well, I don't know what to make of Wei Yan. I'm more than tired... I'm desperate, and I'm exhausted. I'm so upset for all the people I've lost that I can't cry anymore. I'm so angry at all of the people that have harmed us that I can't even clench my fists anymore. I'm... numb."

"...Rest for a few days," Yueying suggested. "Surely you can do that."

"I can," Kongming replied. "Dong Jue and Zong Yu can manage the administration for me... although I wish that His Majesty had left Ma Jichang here as well. Ma Su is afraid for his brother's life, and so am I. Sun Quan and his advisers are experts in the art of defence... every battle they've fought on the defensive, they've won."

"Against Cao Cao," Yueying suggested. "Not His Majesty."

"I... ... ...yes," Kongming said with a false smile. "Now... perhaps we should talk about something else... after all, I am resting, aren't I...?"

Yueying nodded slowly and sadly.

Liu Bei's forces travelled toward the Yi-Jing border by land and river. He had his 3 advisers at close quarters – Ma Liang, Wang Fu, and Cheng Ji – and at the head of his forces were his commanders, Huang Quan, Feng Xi, Wu Ban, and Zhang Nan. The army would be supported from Wuling by Shamoke, King of the Wuling tribes, and his own forces: the entire coalition force was in excess of 100,000 men.

"...Nearly there," Jian Yong joked feebly as Liu Bei's vanguard forces reached White Emperor City, near the border with Jing. "...Reports say that Wu are split... Cao Pi is frightening Wu too much for them to trust him."

"It isn't Cao Pi they should be worrying about," Liu Bei growled.

"We should not resort to wanton violence," Ma Liang suggested. "Remember, Your Majesty, that many fear armies such as ours marching into their lands-"

"We governed these lands not so long ago," Liu Bei retorted. "They would mistake me for Cao Cao, after all I have proven myself to be to them...?"

"...Adviser Ma simply suggests restraint," Cheng Ji said quietly.

"And I agree," Wang Fu added. "Your reputation may be a fine one, but in Yi, your approach was still met with dread, because of rumours as to why you were there. I know, I remember being afraid myself. ...You're here to avenge Guan Yu, who was loved by the people of Jing, but... they may fret that you blame them, somehow, for not resisting the Wu forces, and-"

"Adviser Wang is correct," Cheng Ji suggested. "We must do all we can to reassure the populace that we mean them no harm."

"...I despair of you all," Liu Bei sighed. "Did I not do that in Yi...?"

"...Your Majesty, we will be facing our first battle in Zigui," Ma Liang reported. "The initial reports suggest that the defences are solid... but against an army of this size, and with no favourable conditions for defending, it will be no Jiangling or Fan, and we expect Wu to yield quickly."

"Advance then, and siege Zigui," Liu Bei commanded. "Ensure the populace of our intentions, and spare any that surrender..."

The Shu army struck the city of Zigui from the western approach, and the city began a futile resistance. Hordes of Shu soldiers stormed the walls, while Liu Bei watched from his imperial command chariot.

"...This is unbelievable," Ma Liang exclaimed suddenly as he read a recently delivered report.

"What is...?" Jian Yong wondered.

"General *Liao Hua* is in Zigui," Ma Liang chuckled with disbelief.

"...*Our* General Liao Hua...?" Jian Yong said incredulously.

"...Kongming told me he was dead," Ma Liang murmured as read the letter again with disbelief. "Well, he told me that he'd been reported dead... suicide, perhaps... but here he is, in Zigui, pledging undying loyalty to His Majesty."

Jian Yong laughed, saying, "So he faked his own death and escaped Wu to come back to us, is that what you're telling me...?"

"...Yes," Ma Liang replied numbly. "...He's saved his mother, as well, and brought her to Zigui. He must have had an arduous journey... what a loyal man."

"Well, that's *wonderful!*" Jian Yong said sarcastically. "With *Liao Hua* and his *mother* returned to our ranks, we will surely know nothing but *victory*...!"

Liu Bei scowled, saying, "Xianhe, don't-"

"Of all the men we've lost... we get *Liao Hua* back," Jian Yong interrupted. "I'm supposed to see that as *auspicious*...?"

Liu Bei shook his head angrily, saying, "Xianhe, you...!"

"**REPORT!**" a messenger hailed: Liu Bei and his advisers gave the young soldier their full attention. "**The governor of Zigui wishes to discuss surrender terms! The majority of the Wu forces have been killed or have retreated to Wuling and the mountains!**"

"...Accept the surrender, pursue the Wu forces," Liu Bei instructed. "I want any man in a green uniform of Wu to be dyed black with his own blood."
"...Your Majesty, you...!" Ma Liang protested.
"No," Liu Bei insisted. "I'm here to make a point. Wu men die."
The advisers did not argue: instead, they gestured to the nearby officers that they should forward the orders to the attacking forces. The Shu forces – all of whom marched out of Shu wearing white – were themselves drenched black and red with blood as they pursued the Wu soldiers, and slaughtered without restraint.
"...We'll pursue them into Wuling, and their mountain hideouts," Liu Bei said coldly as he viewed the carnage. "We'll show them our might... we'll find and kill them, wherever they try to run and hide."

"...Liu Bei has gone mad," Zhuge Jin muttered as he entered the Wu court at Chaisang, where Sun Quan was now holding an emergency meeting.
"Ah! ...It's Kongming's brother," Zhang Zhao hailed sarcastically.
"...Well then why invite me here???" Zhuge Jin retorted. "Am I to be put to death for being an enemy's brother...? Well, then, should Lady Sun not die for being their emperor's wife...?"
"There's no need for that," Sun Quan pleaded. "Ziyu, your counsel is appreciated by me. We are beyond a peaceful outcome, I think, since reports say that-"
"...That Liu Bei's 'Shu' army has descended on the border with a force of a hundred thousand, and taken Zigui with a violent show of force toward our people," Zhuge Jin sighed. "I know, I know... he's taking Mount Xing and Mount Ba as well, and we can't hold, because..."
"...*Because*...?" Zhang Zhao heckled.
"...Because we are not as adept at fighting in mountainous terrain as the Shu forces, who originate from mountainous territory," Zhuge Jin replied wearily.
"So your view is in accord with most of my other advisers, then," Sun Quan sighed sadly. "Zhu Ran and Lu Xun have both told me that I cannot divert forces from the Hefei border with Wei, and must maintain a two-way watch at Jiangling... I am caught in a pincer, between an angry owl and a hungry wolf!"
"My liege," Zhuge Jin said, "you have to work with what forces you can spare. But if we cannot begin a proper retaliation, all is lost. You need to appoint a single commander that the forces can follow, and start building more robust defences at Yiling to hold Shu back. Lu Xun... is in Yiling, isn't he...?"
"Again, you seem to agree with the consensus," Sun Quan noted. "...While I respect Zhu Ran, it was Lu Xun that so admirably coordinated with Lü Meng to defeat Guan Yu... it is that very same Lu Xun that will give us victory now."

"...Lu Xun... *Chief Commander*...?" Kongming exclaimed as he read the despatches coming from the front lines.
"We're winning," Ma Su chuckled. "Xiang Lang says that they could put the ghost of Jiang Ziya in charge, and it wouldn't matter now... I agree."

The two were sat in Kongming's study: Yueying entered the room and stood by the doorway, listening with interest.

"...Your overconfidence is dangerous, Youchang," Kongming scolded. "Two mountain strongholds and one small city do not constitute a victory."

"But the enemy have been routed on every occasion!" Ma Su protested excitedly.

"Lu Xun is in charge," Kongming retorted. "That man... that man is another Lü Meng, another Zhou Yu."

"Yes... a dead man walking," Ma Su joked. "Really, we've won. Looking at the maps, I'd say we're planning a strike on Yiling by river... that may already have happened. How stupid the protector of Yiling, Lu Xun, will look if he is unseated from his city!"

"...Yiling is a long way from the border, a long way from Chengdu," Kongming murmured uneasily. "The supply train is becoming stretched already."

"A weak, slow supply train is the cause of many a failure," Yueying suggested with an intelligent smile. "I wonder if there is some way to change things."

"...Mm, yes, I wonder," Kongming said with a smile. "But that's the future... right now, we're in possible trouble."

"My brother has ensured the supply line is well guarded," Ma Su insisted as Kongming took the formation layout map from him.

"...Nn...!" Kongming grunted. "He uses *Chen Shi* for an important assignment *again*, after the failures in Hanzhong...?"

"Well, the invincible Liao Hua is tired," Ma Su replied sarcastically.

"...*Liao Hua*...?" Yueying prompted. "Wasn't he captured by Wu when...?"

"When Guan Yu was caught...? Yes, Liao Hua's tale is an odd one indeed," Kongming sighed. "He's returned to us... in a quite fantastic fashion."

"Fantastic, but true," Ma Su sighed as he got up to leave. "Personally, I'd rather have Guan Yu back. ...I'd best be going."

Kongming smiled silently as Ma Su bowed respectfully and left the house.

"...Lu Xun worries you, I understand that," Yueying noted. "But surely Ma Liang is a match for him now...?"

"Sun Quan has one extraordinarily good quality," Kongming replied. "...He listens to the advice that he is given. Neither His Majesty nor his honorary brothers could manage to do that at the critical hour. Ma Liang will be able to give the advice... it's as it always is... the same old problem. Will His Majesty *listen*...?"


"**Listen to me, please!**" Lu Xun shouted over the jeers of a dozen of the angry generals under his command. "**You have to listen to me!**"

"**I know we do!**" General Pan Zhang – who had just lost control of the city of Guling – retorted angrily. "**That's why we're in trouble!**"

The heckling intensified: Lu Xun took Sun Quan's sword of authority from its pedestal, and raised it aloft.

"**Defy Lu Xun, if you must... but will you defy your king?**" Lu Xun screamed: the generals fell silent. "**And here, on this battlefield, I am acting for King Sun, so if you defy me, you defy him!**"

470

"…We're losing everything," General Bu Zhi sighed woefully. "Those bastard barbarians are making things worse… Wuling is in chaos!"

"Mount Ba, and Mount Xing… Zigui… Guling!" Pan Zhang raved. "How much more has to fall before you do something, 'Chief Commander'???"

"We are not in a position to retaliate," Lu Xun insisted. "We must relinquish areas that we cannot defend, and secure areas that can be made impenetrable."

"Sun Huan is on the verge of losing Yidao City," Bu Zhi protested. "Can't we send aid to a relation of His Highness…?"

"General Sun Huan can hold Yidao," Lu Xun insisted further: the heckling started again. "…**Please, we must remain calm!**"

"**Losing Yidao allows Liu Bei to take safe control of the riverbank from Wuxia to Yiling!**" Pan Zhang shouted furiously.

Lu Xun smiled, and the noise faded away.

"…It certainly will," Lu Xun replied at last. "It certainly will."


✱✱✱✱✱✱✱✱✱✱✱✱

## 98

Liu Bei's Shu forces now controlled – with few exceptions – everything north of Wuling Prefecture that lay between the Yi-Jing border and the city of Yiling.

"...So much history, this poor place," Cheng Ji said to Ma Liang and Wang Fu as the three advisers took a tour of Liu Bei's camp, which was now settled on the riverbank opposite the city of Yiling. "Some of the logs still remain by the roadside, from Lü Meng's famous rout of Cao Ren's cavalry a decade ago."

"Which he did to save the pirate general, Gan Ning," Ma Liang noted. "Now – thankfully – both Lü Meng and Gan Ning have gone to the netherworld. Our only real fear is the schemes of Lu Xun."

"It scares you, doesn't it, that Wu Ban and Chen Shi were able to defeat the defenders of Yiling so easily," Wang Fu supposed. "We'll hold it... Lu Xun cannot siege Yiling as Cao Ren did... we are too large an army. He can, however, keep Jiangling as Cao Ren did."

"Zhu Ran and Han Dang hold that key city, as Cao Ren and Xu Huang once did," Ma Liang murmured, "and... as Guan Yunchang and I did after them."

"...This must be difficult," Cheng Ji suggested.

"For His Highness, this place has so many memories," Ma Liang sighed sadly. "Aside from Yunchang ruling this region, it was His Majesty's first real foothold... and not only is Lu Xun, the mastermind of Guan Yunchang's downfall, stationed here... Bu Zhi, the official-general that murdered His Majesty's ally and friend, Cangwu governor Wu Ju, is in charge of a force here as well."

"So we can revenge ourselves on many offenders," Wang Fu noted.

"His Majesty must not let his anger and impatience dictate his actions, like Yunchang did at Fan," Ma Liang said desperately. "We're marching too quickly, and spreading our forces too thinly... we cannot hold the southern riverbank and have a secure supply line, not in the long term. Yidao City will not fall easily, and the summer... if we are still here in the *summer*..."

"Yidao will fall, I'm sure," Cheng Ji said reassuringly. "Our supply line will hold... and this will be over before the summer heat. We must be optimistic."

"Ayah," Ma Liang exclaimed. "That's what killed Yunchang! We have to be *cautious*! ...I am going to be in Wuling, as an envoy between Shamoke and His Majesty... take care now, both of you... and please, keep him safe."

The three advisers bowed respectfully to each other, and Ma Liang departed.

Liu Bei continued his swift advance into Wu-controlled Jing, leaving thousands of bodies – on both sides – as he moved. He recklessly remained at the head of the vanguard, despite his new role as First Emperor of Shu Han, since he was determined to be the one that personally defeated Lu Xun and Sun Quan.

The march finally halted at Xiaoting, where Wu were finally able to put up a sound defence due to the lack of the high ground that gave the Shu forces an advantage. Now Liu Bei was stuck in a painful stalemate: Shamoke's tribal forces were checked by Bu Zhi, Sun Huan held Yidao, and Huang Quan was forced to take a contingent to fight Wu forces north of Yiling and guard against a sudden strike by Cao Wei.

Kongming spent every day in his Chengdu office, insistent on being completely up-to-date with the news from the front.
"We… we have overstretched," Kongming insisted as he read a distressed letter from Xiang Lang. "We've stopped at Xiaoting… now Lu Xun is refusing to retreat any further. Our main forces are deeply entrenched by the banks of the Great River. It is already mid-spring. If they are still there in the *summer*…!"
"What's so desperate about the summer…?" Ma Su asked irritably.
"That region becomes unbearable in the summer!" Kongming retorted.
"*This* region becomes unbearable in the summer," Ma Su teased.
"Yes, but this is a defensive paradise, while His Majesty is encamped on flat ground by a river!" Kongming scolded. There are dense forests by that section of the Great River, to make matters even worse!"
"Our supply line is secure," Ma Su said reassuringly. "They'll get clean water, food, and medicine… and I'm sure His Majesty and three advisers have enough experience between them to formulate a plan to end this quickly."
"But…!" Kongming began anxiously.
"You're not there," Ma Su interrupted. "You can't do anything that my brother isn't doing already… calm down."
"Your brother is with Shamoke… not His Majesty," Kongming murmured as he got up from his seat. "…I must speak to Zhao Zilong… we must be ready."
"…Ready for *what*…?" Ma Su prompted cynically.
Kongming left the office in a hurry, desperate to find a carriage to take him to Zhao Yun's encampment.

"Liu Bei has his men stationed in forty, maybe fifty camps stretching the length of the Great River from Wuxia to Yiling," Pan Zhang said as he addressed a meeting of the Wu generals in the command tent of their encampment in Xiaoting. "Summer is almost upon us, so we must be quick to avoid the rampage of sickness and disease that goes with it. Liu Bei has, like Guan Yu before him at Fan, managed to advance his vanguard too far… it must be a Shu self-destruction tactic."
The generals snickered and chuckled derisively.
"He's moved too far in his mission to defeat Sun Huan at Yidao… with his forces overstretched, now is the time for action… and yet you say we are not ready, 'Chief Commander'," Pan Zhang jeered as he turned to Lu Xun. "Ready for *what*…?"
"If we try and fight now, we will win, but it will be more costly than if we wait," Lu Xun insisted. "I promise you, your patience will be rewarded."

"With a dose of dysentery," Pan Zhang grumbled. "A harsh summer will destroy us all, how can you say that the cost will be less by waiting until then...?"

"We have the advantage now, if only we wait," Lu Xun insisted: the heckling from his increasingly demoralised generals told him that he was not reassuring them at all.

The skirmishes intensified, as Liu Bei tried desperately to force Sun Huan from Yidao and uproot the main Wu forces at Xiaoting: neither effort was successful. The distance between the battle fronts and Yi Province meant a painfully long supply train: the slightest upset left the vanguard without any supplies for days. Morale started to drop, as the Shu army suddenly realised that the battle would not be over for some time. Summer followed the initial depression, destroying what little optimism the Shu army had left: the heat was intense, and was only exacerbated by the miasma from the river.

"...We... we're really suffering," Wang Fu said as he entered the relative coolness of Liu Bei's command tent and mopped the sweat from his brow with his soaked sleeve. "We... we're not even at the height of summer yet..."

"Stop complaining," Liu Bei grunted. "Even if we do suffer, isn't it for a good cause, and don't our enemies suffer as well, and don't we outnumber them...?"

"Yes, but...!" Wang Fu protested.

"...'But' nothing!" Liu Bei scolded. "Lu Xun thinks that he is clever keeping us here, but I am a wise owl, and he is a young fool. I know a few tricks, and he's about to learn that age and wisdom beats youthful recklessness and cowardice!"

"...Your Majesty... what do you intend to do...?" Wang Fu asked nervously.

"I have summoned Wu Ban," Liu Bei said proudly. "He's going to take a contingent of troops to the Wu camp and issue a challenge."

"They won't reply," Wang Fu insisted.

"Aha, but they will!" Liu Bei chuckled confidently. "You see, I intend to start showing signs that we are weakening... we'll put sick soldiers on guard, make a few marches with weary troops, all so that this 'genius' Lu Xun thinks that we have no more good men to throw at them!"

"...Right," Wang Fu prompted uneasily.

"Wu Ban's forces will comprise only old and sick soldiers," Liu Bei continued. "I hazard that once he sees that, he'll think that Shu is faltering... his generals – who are obviously tired of his craven behaviour – will demand action, and he will have no choice but to respond, or face a revolt in his demoralised forces!"

"...And when they charge...?" Wang Fu wondered.

"There will be an elite force of nearly ten thousand waiting for them when they pursue!" Liu Bei cackled. "We will destroy their vanguard forces and their best generals... Lu Xun will be forced to lead their rabble to gain respect, so we will get him too! Then we can offer his head up to Yunchang...!"

"...I see," Wang Fu murmured. "And... if he does not fall for this plan, Your Majesty...?"

"How can he not...?" Liu Bei scoffed.

Before Wang Fu could continue, Wu Ban announced his arrival: Wang Fu bowed respectfully and left the command tent, muttering miserably.

"I can't take any more of this!" Pan Zhang said angrily as the Shu general Wu Ban's forces kept up a constant – if flat – tirade of abuse outside the Wu camp at Xiaoting.
"…It is just some desperate men making empty provocations," Lu Xun suggested.
"Liu Bei sends old men now!" Pan Zhang raged. "He has nothing but contempt for us! This is all your fault! 'Wait until summer', you said! 'They will suffer greater casualties then', you said! I've had enough! I'm going to challenge!"
"I'll go with you," General Xu Sheng said.
"…No," Lu Xun insisted. "Please, generals… come with me, and let me show you what Liu Bei is doing."
**No more cowering! I…!**" Pan Zhang shouted: Lu Xun touched the sword of authority and smiled, and the protestations ceased.
"You will be enlightened," Lu Xun promised.
Lu Xun led his impatient generals out of the camp and up onto what high ground there was, and then to a path that led to winding valleys behind Wu Ban's camp.
"…So now we are behind the enemy," Pan Zhang complained, "but we have no men to ambush them with!"
"…Yes, but they have men to ambush us, General Pan," Lu Xun retorted with a smile. "Look into the valley… and be patient."
The generals and their tiny retinue of guards peered into the valley, but saw nothing. It was unbearably hot, and their altitude – combined with the lack of cover – made things worse still.
"…I'm going to die of heatstroke!" Pan Zhang complained. "There's nothing down there, 'Chief Commander'!"
"…Just be patient," Lu Xun pleaded.
"I've been patient! I've been *very* patient, 'Chief Commander'!" Pan Zhang retorted. "But now I-"
"Wait," Xu Sheng said suddenly. "There, look."
Lu Xun smiled as the generals followed their colleague's directions, and saw a small group of well-hidden Shu soldiers preparing to change formation.
"…The…!" Pan Zhang exclaimed.
"There are *thousands* down there, hiding," Lu Xun explained casually. "Had we fallen for their ruse, we'd have lost a lot of men. Now… let's return to the camp, and leave them here to stew."
"Yes… Chief Commander," Pan Zhang replied sombrely.
"So," Lu Xun said once they had returned to camp, "will you still be advancing, General Pan…?"
"…No," Pan Zhang replied dolefully. "…But we can't just sit here."
"I don't intend to," Lu Xun chuckled informally. "Liu Bei has and had many great advisers… it is obvious that he listens and listened to none of them. He claims to equal our own King Sun… but his only peer – as Cao Cao himself once said – is Cao Cao, and Liu Bei will meet the same miserable end, for the same reasons. I expect that Liu Bei mistakes my caution for cowardice… as you all do."
The generals were guiltily silent.

"...But it is caution, nothing more," Lu Xun promised. "I expect Liu Bei to make a major tactical error very soon: he'll play right into our hands... and then we will destroy him completely."
"What could he possibly do...?" Pan Zhang chortled.
"Oh... I think you'll laugh louder when it happens," Lu Xun replied. "While the last of his great advisers, Zhuge Liang, will, I imagine, wonder whether the Han really *do* have a future."

Kongming was sat at home one evening, weeks later, when a messenger arrived.
"...At this hour...?" Kongming murmured. "Who is this from...?"
"Administrator Xiang Lang," the messenger replied as Kongming took the letter and gestured that the messenger could retire.
"...Xiang Lang...?" Yueying pondered as Kongming walked back into the study, reading the letter as he moved. "He's been writing to Ma Su before, when-"
Kongming screamed repeatedly: he threw down the letter, and scrabbled into a corner of the room, as though his entire world was coming apart. Yueying feigned calm, walked to the cloth letter, picked it up, and started to read: at the bottom was a hastily-drawn map. Her eyes widened as she absorbed the terrible significance of what had been conveyed: she looked at Kongming, who was curled up in the corner, biting his hand and stifling cries of emotional pain. She dropped the letter, and as it slowly floated to the floor, she walked, trance-like, toward her cowering, broken husband, and sat next to him. She took his left hand – his right hand was still in his mouth – and exhaled noisily. Neither said a word for several minutes: tears were streaming down Kongming's face, and Yueying's eyes glistened as she shared his torment.
        After that painful, wordless interlude – where the only sounds were uncomfortable breathing and Kongming's stifled sobs – Yueying said quietly, "*Can* you help...?"
"...*No,*" Kongming replied hoarsely.
Yueying embraced Kongming, and exhaled noisily again: the two sat in painful silence, feeling utterly helpless.

"...It is time," Wu's Chief Commander Lu Xun said to his assembled generals: some already knew the situation, and were smiling cruelly.
"Liu Bei has, as I predicted, made a fatal, fatal mistake," Lu Xun continued. "In a continued display of contempt and arrogance, he has – in an attempt to boost his weary army's flagging morale – moved his forces *into* the riverside forests, out of the direct sun, so that they might enjoy a break from the heat."
The generals laughed at the irony.
"Now, after what I know has been a painful wait," Lu Xun concluded, "it is time to put an end, at long, long last, to the upstart sandal weaver, the parasite that has for so long plagued us... he will burn."
The Wu generals, including Pan Zhang, cheered for their Chief Commander: Lu Xun smiled, and savoured having earned their respect at last.


************

## 99

The self-appointed Shu Han Emperor, Liu Bei, sat in his command tent, reading old books made of connected strips of bamboo, while his forces continued to resettle into the forest along the southern bank of the Yangtze River. He was pondering the classics, reading every word left in the books by the great philosophers and strategists of legend.

"...What are you reading now...?" Jian Yong said with a subdued tone as he entered the tent.

Liu Bei did not look up from his reading as he casually replied,

"I'm reacquainting myself with the deeper musings of Sun Tzu. How Sun Quan's father ever dared to say that he descended from this great man, I will never know."

"...Xuande," Jian Yong said quietly, "I'm not here to talk to you as an emperor and his subject... I'm here to talk to you as one friend to another. And as a friend, I'm here to tell you that I really can't stand by and watch you make a terrible mistake."

Liu Bei placed the book on his table, and turned his gaze to Jian Yong silently.

"...Really, Xuande, this is bloody stupid," Jian Yong protested. "A *forest*...? ...You've moved us into a *forest*, in the middle of *summer*...?"

"I've had this from Cheng Ji and Wang Fu already, Xianhe," Liu Bei replied. "We're not dealing with... well, with the likes of Sun Tzu. We have nothing to fear from this 'Lu Xun'."

"He saw through your ambush," Jian Yong suggested.

"He did nothing of the sort," Liu Bei said dismissively. "He was just scared... too scared, it seems, to run after even the feeblest of opponents. This whining pup is no Zhou Yu or Lü Meng... Ma Jichang and Zhuge Kongming overrate the boy. He is a pretender, a braggart, yet when it comes to showing his worth, he leaves even the relatives of his lord to die unaided."

"Sun Huan doesn't need his help defending Yidao... he always knew that," Jian Yong replied.

"Mm... Ma Liang told you to talk to me, didn't he...?" Liu Bei sniggered. "These are *his* words... really, Xianhe, I always prided you on being outspoken and free-spirited... now you come in here, bleating another pedant's words at me."

"They're his words, but I wouldn't be here if I didn't agree," Jian Yong protested. "For goodness' sakes, Xuande... Your Majesty... remember who you are!"

"I never forget... that's why I'm here," Liu Bei retorted. "I'm the First Emperor of Shu Han... what can they do to me...? We have been moving into and around the forest for days, and nothing has happened... their one pathetic attempt at striking us ended in failure... so what have I to fear...?"

"He was right... you're really not going to listen," Jian Yong realised fearfully. "I really thought... hoped... that...!"

"Xianhe... go and get some rest," Liu Bei said condescendingly. "In the morning, perhaps we'll make a lightning strike on their camps, and destroy them, so that we can continue on to Jiangdong and kill that miserable wretch Sun Quan, him and his deceitful whore of a sister that I have the misfortune of calling a wife."

Jian Yong turned and left the camp without another word. He walked straight into Wang Fu, but there was no need to elaborate: a glance was all it took to tell Wang Fu that there would be no change of plan, no hurried withdrawal to the relative safety of the plains. Jian Yong kept walking, and returned to his tent.

"...Keep strict watch," Wang Fu said to one of the nearby captains. "Anything... *anything*... your men sound the alarm."

The captain retreated, and Wang Fu returned to his own tent, where he found Cheng Ji waiting for him.

"He didn't listen," Wang Fu said before Cheng Ji could speak.

"Wu have been conspicuously quiet," Cheng Ji noted.

"They're going to use a fire attack on us," Wang Fu said fearfully. "I've placed patrols around the forest, along the river... but that's all I can do, so really, we have to hope. Go and... and make preparations for every possible..."

"We have," Cheng Ji interrupted. "Get some rest."

"How can I???" Wang Fu said desperately. "I can't make him listen! Doom lingers over us, and-"

"Get some rest," Cheng Ji reiterated.

Wang Fu nodded, and bowed slightly to Cheng Ji, who left the tent, leaving Wang Fu completely alone.


"This... ... ...is this right...?" Cao Wei Imperial Secretariat Sima Yi said cautiously: he was reading a report of the events at Xiaoting.

"It is as reported," the messenger replied.

Sima Yi did not reply: he gestured to the messenger that he could retreat from the courtroom silently. The Cao Wei emperor, Cao Pi, leant forward with eager anticipation of what the report said.

"...Sima Zhongda...?" Cao Pi prompted.

Sima Yi did not reply: he was smiling broadly before Cao Pi had spoken, but now, he started to bellow with laughter that made the officials as uncomfortable as they were enthusiastic.

"Mister Sima," the Wei official Jia Xu prompted, "*please*, explain your joviality."

"...**Shu has no more capable men!**" Sima Yi chortled: he looked about him at his master and the officials and generals with a broad, toothy smile.

"Why do you say that, Zhongda...?" Cao Pi asked.

"Liu Bei has placed his vanguard in an open assault on Yidao City, miles from the rest of his army," Sima Yi reported with amusement. "His supply line is stretched to breaking point: the intense heat, a sure cause of low morale amongst his soldiers. So to alleviate the situation, Your Majesty... he has moved his entire main force from the plains near the Great River... into the *forests*."

The incredulous gasps of the officials were almost unanimous: Cao Pi leant back and smirked, saying, "This *must* be wrong... this is *Liu Bei* we're talking about."

"No, no, I don't think it is," Sima Yi replied as several of the officials and generals started to laugh quietly. "I scarcely believe it myself... I had heard many stories about the proficiency of the Shu strategists, Fa Zheng, Pang Tong, and Zhuge Liang... while the first two are known to be dead, the third is very much alive... but he may as well be dead, if this is the extent of his influence."

Cao Pi stared at Sima Yi for several seconds, probing his bemused expression for signs of doubt: when he was sure there was none, he joined his officials in expressing open amusement.

"We have only one capable rival!" Cao Pi said with a hearty laugh. "We *must* capitalise on this… we must…!"

"We should be cautious about attacking Wu," Sima Yi interrupted. "Let this sorry farce run to its natural conclusion… for while it appears that Zhuge Liang and his peers have failed to steer Liu Bei in the right direction, they may salvage a surprise victory, or strike an accord with Wu when they realise the mutual danger they are in. Let us be patient."

"Very well, Zhongda," Cao Pi snickered. "I'll follow your advice… I think Liu Bei provides a strong warning to us all about the failure to heed sound counsel."

"Liu Bei will soon be dead, or very much as good as," Sima Yi concluded. "What will follow, who knows…? …But your exalted father's only rival has exhausted his energies… that much is certain."

One night, the Shu forces within the forests were rudely awoken by panicked cries and the tell-tale glow of fierce fires.

"**Your Majesty, we must go!**" Wang Fu screamed as he ran into Liu Bei's tent, and found him reading. "**FIRE!**"

"…How bad…?" Liu Bei asked calmly as he lowered his book.

"**This is not an accident!**" Wang Fu protested. "**Please, we have to go!**"

"*What*…?" Liu Bei chuckled disbelievingly: but before Wang Fu could answer, Liu Bei's long-time bodyguard Chen Dao entered the tent, his sword in hand.

"Your Majesty, we are under attack," Chen Dao reported sombrely. "We must retreat at once."

"That's *ridiculous*…!" Liu Bei giggled nervously. "That… that's *impossible*…!"

"Your Majesty, **please!**" Chen Dao exclaimed: he reached forward, and – ignoring protocol – grabbed Liu Bei's arm roughly, pulling him to his feet and dragging him from the tent.

"My books, my books!" Liu Bei complained. "I can't leave them!"

"…**Idiot!**" Jian Yong whined as he watched Chen Dao lead his friend and emperor to safety. "He… that **idiot!**"

"I'll try and organise the naval retreat from downriver!" Cheng Ji promised as he led a group of officers and soldiers away from the main encampment.

"**Wang Fu, Fu Rong: follow Xuande!**" Jian Yong shouted to Wang Fu and General Fu Rong: they did as they were asked, taking a force of men with them.

The fire intensified with every passing second: the Shu soldiers desperately tried to douse fires, untie horses and grab weapons to defend themselves against the inevitable Wu attack.

"Where are those men going…?" Jian Yong said desperately: he watched as many soldiers grabbed buckets and ran toward the river, and shouted, "**No, no, don't…!**"

As the men neared the river, orders were shouted, and out of the undergrowth, Wu archers appeared, firing streams of arrows at the panicked Shu soldiers. Dozens of men were shot down as they tried to control the fires.

**"We... we have to try and fight back, buy Xuande time to get away!"** Jian Yong said to General Feng Xi with great urgency. **"All of you... you do what you can!"**
Jian Yong tried to gather men for a counterattack, but it was futile. Many of the men they gathered were panicking and injured, and the heat of the forest fire was now unbearable. Realising this, Jian Yong tried to bring their forces to a safer position.
"...***Mister Jian***...!" Feng Xi yelped suddenly: Jian Yong turned in time to see the general fall to the ground, an arrow lodged in his back. Many others were killed in the same way: and then, out of the darkness, Pan Zhang led a force of cavalry and infantry that beset Jian Yong's position, killing any men left standing.

"What... what happened...?" Liu Bei said with confusion as Chen Dao led him along the river bank. It was then that Liu Bei finally looked back, and what he could see filled him with terror. The fires were now completely enveloping his forest-based camps: any men that had not escaped the wooded area were now dead for certain.
"...Xianhe...!" Liu Bei whined: Chen Dao and his team of elite bodyguards continued to urge their master westward.
        A contingent of Pan Zhang's forces reached Liu Bei and his entourage, and Chen Dao was forced to defend his master. The old general showed his strength and bravery as he fought the attackers off, killing many men personally. Eventually, the attackers retreated: Liu Bei has survived again, but only just.
"We must head for the Ma'an Hills," Wang Fu suggested. "If Cheng Ji survived, then... the navy... maybe the others..."
"What happened...?" Liu Bei whispered. "I... this can't be happening...!"
Chen Dao ignored his master's rambling, and urged him onward.

The adviser Cheng Ji, meanwhile, had taken emergency command of the Shu navy. After sending Wu Ban and Chen Shi ahead with the bulk of the naval force, Cheng Ji did what he could to slow the vast Wu navy that now advanced down the Yangtze River from the nearby training facility at Ba Qiu. Despite sinking many boats, Cheng Ji's small forces were overwhelmed by the superior skill of the Wu navy, and completely annihilated.

"Report," Lu Xun demanded as he reached the site of Liu Bei's definitive defeat.
"We've destroyed the command camp," Pan Zhang reported. "I witnessed the deaths of a couple of his senior officers personally, but Liu Bei escaped, toward the Ma'an Hills. Their navy got away... they were given time, defended by a small force which we have destroyed."
"...The man that led that force was brave, and wasted on Liu Bei," Lu Xun sighed sadly. "Is Zhu Ran ready to mobilise...?"
"He is," Pan Zhang replied.
"Very good," Lu Xun replied. "I'll go myself... General Xu shall be my second. General Pan, continue to attack the camps... rout them all."

After days of bitter fighting with small groups of Wu saboteurs commanded by Pan Zhang, Liu Bei finally reached the Ma'an Hills.

"What... what happened???" Wang Fu exclaimed: most of the camps were buried under rubble, or burnt to the ground.

"...A rockslide," Chen Dao supposed. "Maybe fated... or maybe man-made."

"I don't understand," Liu Bei muttered. "I was... I was winning... why has this happened to *me*...? I am not Cao Cao... I have only ever meant good for the land... how can Wu revisit Red Cliffs upon me, when my intentions were...?"

"Your Majesty, please," Wang Fu interrupted, "do not say any more. We need to stage some sort of defence here. We've not lost as many men as we thought we had... we still have many thousands of troops, we just need to organise them."

"Yes... yes, we have to fight back," Liu Bei decided. "I'll lead the counterattack personally... has anyone seen Xianhe, or heard from Jichang in Wuling...?"

"...No," Wang Fu replied bitterly. "I've contacted General Xiang Chong at Zigui and asked him to prepare a retreat path for us... messengers have also been sent to request the presence of General Zhao Yun."

"...Zilong... said this was a mistake," Liu Bei recalled. "...Yes, let's be ready to fight back... we... *I*... have a duty to my people. I need to go home."

Liu Bei and his officers managed to get word to the scattered forces, telling them to regroup at the Ma'an Hills so that they could fight the forces of Wu: but Lu Xun had foreseen this, and as the Shu forces tried to converge, they were harassed by small forces commanded overall by the Wu General Zhu Ran. By the time that Liu Bei's forces finally gathered – after many unwanted delays – Wu's own force was ready to attack them.

"...Report," Lu Xun said as two messengers approached.

"General Sun Huan has been relieved," the first messenger reported. "The Shu vanguard at Yidao City has been completely annihilated."

"Shu General Huang Quan abandoned his battle with us as soon as he realised the main force was routed," the second messenger reported. "They fled northward, and surrendered to the forces of Cao Pi, Emperor of Wei."

"*Wei*...?" Lu Xun said with alarm.

"...And General Bu Zhi has routed Shamoke in Wuling," Xu Sheng noted. "We've won."

"Not yet," Lu Xun replied cautiously after dismissing the messengers. "Liu Bei still has as many as sixty-to-seventy-thousand men... most of them will be here, and we must defeat them definitively. But Cao Wei apprehending Shu soldiers worries me... they're hovering, they're smelling blood, and they must be watched very carefully."

"And Shu...?" Xu Sheng prompted.

"We're assembled, and they cannot be allowed any more time to prepare," Lu Xun replied coldly. "...Advance."

The Wu forces ripped the disorganised and exhausted Shu forces to pieces, and Liu Bei was forced, once again, to retreat, leaving behind tens of thousands of corpses. Chen Dao was forced yet again to repel direct attacks on Liu Bei as Wu's vanguard – led by Lu Xun, Han Dang and Xu Sheng – launched assault after assault, reducing Liu Bei's forces to less than 30,000 as they started a forced withdrawal to Zigui City, their first conquest when they had arrived in the region. Lu Xun did not give the Shu army a single moment of peace, despite Liu Bei ordering the men to discard their armour across the roads and set it alight to act as a fiery barrier: the Shu forces entered the city of Zigui amid a hail of arrows from elite Wu archers.

"...Your Majesty!" Liao Hua exclaimed. "Thank the Heavens that-"
"We are lost," Liu Bei whimpered. "My grand army... gone... my friends... dead... we cannot stay here. We must evacuate the city."
Xiang Chong turned to Chen Dao and said, "General Chen, let me aid you in getting the Emperor to safety."
"I'll protect the rear," Wang Fu suggested.
"You'll be killed," Liu Bei fretted.
"It doesn't matter," Wang Fu replied without fear. "Your heavenly self is all that matters now, Your Majesty."
"I'm no 'heavenly self'," Liu Bei said with misery. "I'm a mat weaver! I'm-"
"We'd better start out straight away," Chen Dao interrupted. "Wu have already started assaulting the walls of the city."

Wang Fu selected a group of men to assist him in a desperate, suicidal defence of the rear of Liu Bei's army, which now numbered only a few thousand after the constant pressure of Wu's attacks. Xiang Chong and Chen Dao fought their way through Wu's larger forces and continued their push westwards, while Wang Fu held his defensive line for as long as he could. But at the last, Wang Fu fell, and Fu Rong – a brave general that had served Liu Bei well during the Hanzhong Campaign – was practically alone, surrounded by hundreds of Wu soldiers.
"It's over, General," Lu Xun declared. "Surrender now, and you will be rewarded for seeing sense."
**"Wu dogs!"** Fu Rong screamed defiantly. **"You really think a general of the Han would serve honourless scum like Sun Quan???"**
With that, Fu Rong ran into the Wu soldiers, his sword drawn: Lu Xun shook his head sadly as Fu Rong fell, and sighed, "There was a true hero... Liu Bei was unworthy of such a man."

Liu Bei reached the Yufu region, whereupon he learned two pieces of news: Zhao Yun would soon arrive with reinforcements, and Wang Fu and his men would not be joining them. This last news weighed heavily on Liu Bei's already burdened conscience: his health started to deteriorate as the enormity of the loss set in.
"We must stay strong, Your Majesty," Chen Dao pleaded as he stood in front of his broken, weary emperor. "We must hold this place until Zilong arrives... and if you are strong-"
"I know, my friend, I know, and I will be," Liu Bei replied quietly. "Where... is General Xiang Chong...?"

"I am here, Your Majesty," Xiang Chong said as he walked into Liu Bei's view.

"Your father... Mister Xiang Lang... has been with me since I arrived in Jing Province, all those years ago," Liu Bei said with a smile. "You... have excelled him. He must be proud."

"I... I hope so," Xiang Chong replied uneasily.

"You are a fine man, a brave and loyal man," Liu Bei continued. "You served me as well as General Chen Dao, and that cannot go unrewarded. You are hereby... promoted to viceroy."

"...My thanks, Your Majesty," Xiang Chong said with a low bow. "I am undeserving of your praise."

"You are deserving of a better emperor," Liu Bei chuckled weakly. "...We must hold out... I refuse to leave this world without seeing Kongming one last time... without seeing Zilong... there are things I must say to them."

Chen Dao and Xiang Chong prepared the sparse remnants of the Shu army for a third defiant stand at Yufu; the 30,000-strong Wu force spread out in front of the lone stronghold like an ocean of men. The attack was as fierce as the others had been: all seemed lost, until – several days earlier than had been predicted by Lu Xun – Zhao Yun's reinforcements arrived from Yi Province to bolster the Shu forces.

"It's not an elite force, save Zhao Yun's personal brigade," Zhu Ran said to Lu Xun as they observed the new Shu resistance. "However, Zhao Yun's fighting prowess has not diminished, despite his advanced years."

"Three officers have already been wounded or killed trying to best him in duels," Xu Sheng noted worriedly.

"I'm aware of that," Lu Xun said soberly. "Rumours that Zhuge Liang might be coming to personally aid Liu Bei with strategy do not help matters... it is only the absence of such men that got us this far."

"But...!" Pan Zhang protested.

"Shu are the masters of winning from a disadvantaged position... and we are now on mountainous terrain, their choice of battle ground," Lu Xun continued. "Zhao Yun's arrays are professional... he has been shown advanced trigram formations by Zhuge Liang, and I do not think we can break them without serious losses. There are rumours of strange, supernatural defences behind their front lines..."

"Supernatural...?" Xu Sheng said curiously.

"Mysterious stone pillar formations are being reported by our spies," Lu Xun explained uncomfortably, "that – combined with the mists and miasma forming around them – may be some sort of maze created from natural phenomena, a military formation made of stones. ...Add to that the threat of an attack by Wei..."

"You're suggesting retreat," Pan Zhang said irritably.

*"Retreat...?"* Lu Xun chuckled. *"Retreat,* General Pan, is what you do when you have lost... we have not lost. Shu is finished: their army is broken, and their 'emperor' is a disgrace, an insult to his lineage and his people. Jing is definitively ours... they will never contest us for it again. They will never be able to do anything more than put up a strong defence, but in the end, like his predecessor Liu Zhang, Liu Bei will find the terrain cannot keep the wolf from the door forever... not even mock stone soldiers will save him from divine fate. It's over... we're going home. Prepare for a gradual withdrawal of forces."

The Wu army began a slow withdrawal from Yufu, leaving Shu to count the cost of a defeat that would never truly recover from. Once the Shu forces were safely returned to their own side of the Shu-Wu border between the Yi and Jing provinces, Liu Bei retreated to a palace in White Emperor City, where he established a court and barracks to guard against incursions by Wu.

"...Will you go to him...?" Yueying asked Kongming as the Chancellor of Shu Han sat at his writing desk, tapping the table slowly and rhythmically.
"I have been ordered to remain in Chengdu, for now," Kongming said coldly. "I... I can't believe what he's done. We've been *destroyed.*"
"...Are you sure that Ma Liang is...?" Yueying asked further.
"Yes," Kongming replied. "Bu Zhi's men took Shamoke's forces by surprise... Jichang didn't stand a chance. As Sun Quan had great respect for him, he's been buried honourably, but... Ma Su... is inconsolable."
"And *you*...?" Yueying wondered.
"He was my best friend, a man that shared my ideals... he was my sworn brother, and I will likely never get over this, as I will never get over Shiyuan," Kongming admitted. "I will have to be there for his family, especially for Ma Su... but I don't know what we can achieve from here. We've lost Jing now, and we'll never get it back. Wu now control most of the south... the most we can do is broker a peace, and hope they don't renege and invade us."
"With Wei attacking Jiangling, it isn't likely that they will... not for a while, at least," Yueying said optimistically. "Although why they have done so..."
"Sun Quan of Wu is now the second force of power in the land," Kongming said ruefully. "We're inconsequential now... so he has broken most formal ties with Wei. He has refused to send his eldest son to the north as a hostage, so Cao Pi is trying to force his obedience. It won't be long before he declares himself an independent king... or maybe even a southern emperor. ...And all we can do is watch, as the cause of Han shrivels and dies. ...My, how things change...!"
"...So we're finished, then," Yueying prompted.

"I don't honestly know," Kongming admitted. "His Majesty is unwell, suffering bouts of dysentery and fever that a man half his age would reel from. He has caused the deaths of eighty-thousand of his own men, lost his closest confidante and both of his most loyal generals, damaged his relationship with Zilong, lost Jing Province, lost most of his advisers... *and* ruined any chance of a swift conclusion to the conflict with Wei, other than our own destruction... that would harm any man's soul. Wu sent a man to dictate some sort of peace terms, but that might have been to make a mockery of us... again, I don't know. Wei Yan guards Hanzhong against Wei, His Majesty personally watches the border with Wu... all I can do is sit here, and wait."

"...I am truly sorry, husband," Yueying said miserably.

"For what...?" Kongming replied. "You have done nothing wrong... you have never failed the cause in the way that some – even I – have, so you have no cause to be sorry."

"You know what I meant," Yueying scolded.

"...Yes, I do," Kongming admitted apologetically. "I'm sorry too... sorry that for a decade or more, I have worked tirelessly to build a state – not a sovereign nation, but a temporary state – that would one day free the land from the scourge of tyrants and usurpers, and deliver peace to the people, if only for a short while. Never did I imagine that of all the enemies that we faced – Cao Cao, Sun Quan, Zhang Zhao, Guo Jia, Cheng Yu, Xiahou Dun, Liu Zhang, Zhang Ren, Zhou Yu, Lü Meng, Lu Xun – that our greatest foe... the one that would undo ten years of work in less than two... would be the collective stupidity of the men that I did it all for. Yes, that includes the former Han Emperor... and yes, that includes 'His Majesty'. We all pledged our lives to him, Yueying... and now, most of us have lost our lives... needlessly."

"So if he summons you... will you go to him...?" Yueying asked once again.

"Of course," Kongming replied. "This was never about any one man... this was about the Han Empire. Even when Wang Mang had deposed the Emperor, there were men that still hoped... and one day, their loyalty and dedication was rewarded, and the Han were rightfully returned to the throne. I will not give up... I will not let Cao Pi be our emperor. I will fight for the Han until I die. So yes, I will go to him... I *must*."

For the next six months, Liu Bei remained in White Emperor City, waiting for a Wu attack on his province that never came. Angry at Sun Quan's perceived defiance, Cao Pi, Emperor of Wei ordered a relentless assault on Wu defences at Hefei and Jiangling: but any attempts by Liu Bei to show conciliatory solidarity with Wu were met with contemptuous, dismissive responses, and those rebukes caused the Shu Emperor's condition to deteriorate. As spring ended in the year following the disaster at Xiaoting, it soon became clear that Liu Bei was weakening: sensing the worst, many officials – including Kongming – reluctantly started the journey to his bedside, to plan for the future.

************

## 100

Kongming arrived at the palace in White Emperor City, and immediately enquired his master's health with the main physician.

"...A number of things," the physician explained, "aggravate His Majesty's condition, but the most dangerous is dysentery... he is too old, poorly nourished, stressed and pessimistic to see off any ailment at this moment."

"I must speak with him," Kongming insisted.

"Be gentle," the physician said. "His Majesty cannot hear any more bad news."

"...*Neither can I*," Kongming muttered as he passed the physician and entered Liu Bei's bedroom: the air was musty, but Kongming did his best to hide his displeasure.

"...Kongming...!" Liu Bei said hoarsely.

"...Your Majesty," Kongming replied numbly. "It... is good to see you again."

"You shouldn't lie to me," Liu Bei scolded. "You're angry... I can see it in your eyes. You warned me, all those years ago... of so many things... and I disobeyed your sagely instruction... and now... we are lost, as you... said we would be."

"We are not lost," Kongming replied, "merely knocked off our feet: we have been in worse situations than this. We can recover."

"...But we will never be the same again," Liu Bei whimpered. "We will never restore the house of Han... all we can do is make peace with Cao Pi of Wei, and-"

"*Never*," Kongming insisted sternly. "Your Majesty, of course we must seek another alliance with Wu, but... never, *never* with Wei."

"Another alliance... with *Wu*...?" Liu Bei said with surprise. "How could that be, now, after...?"

"You'd be surprised," Kongming said, "what the exigencies of the moment can motivate two logical minds to accept. I made it happen once... I'll do it again."

"...You always were... good with words," Liu Bei snickered painfully. "But... I doubt even *you*... could... undo what I've done."

Kongming was uncomfortably silent.

"...I don't know if I have ever seen you wear anything other than white," Liu Bei realised suddenly. "You were always... mourning *someone*."

"Your Majesty," Kongming began, but Liu Bei gestured for him to pause for a moment.

"...We're peers," Liu Bei pleaded. "Address me as one... I beg you."

"...*Xuande*," Kongming continued miserably, "you... are quite right. When we met, I was mourning my father... who was... until I met you... the most influential person in my life. Oh, yes, I love my wife, and cherish her company, but... nobody has had a greater influence on the man I have become, I think... than my father... and you. I have never recovered from losing my father... I don't know as any of us did. In a sense... you became my second father, in a way, I think, when you became the patron of my cause, my tripartite plan for the land-"

"Enough!" Liu Bei whined with pain and misery. "Don't say that! It only makes what I have done... *worse*...!"

"Every man makes his own choices," Kongming interrupted. "I chose to follow you, Xuande... follow your dream. I will continue to do that, no matter what."

"...Because of me, so many of your friends, your brothers... are dead," Liu Bei said sadly. "How... can you forgive that...?"

"Men die," Kongming replied calmly.

"But... Jichang... Young Phoenix...!" Liu Bei sobbed weakly.

"Men die," Kongming reiterated. "Yes, I... I grieve very much for Ma Jichang. He was my sworn brother. ...To know that he died so young... with so much left to do, leaving a loving wife, children, brothers and sisters... parents... hurts. But we have all lost so much because of this war. You lost your daughters, your adopted son, many friends and vassals, and two men you took as brothers... to name but a few. I know that the people I grieve mean as much to you... else I wouldn't be here now."

"I... regret everything," Liu Bei admitted. "Cao Cao... was right. When he called us 'two of a kind'... he was right... we are."

"No, no, you shouldn't ever say that!" Kongming said softly.

"...It's true," Liu Bei retorted. "We both of us ignored our advisers, hankered for territory, and sought great power... we both of us truly believed that we were right... strayed from the righteous path without even realising it. It happened to Cao Cao... when he destroyed Xu Province... and it happened to me when... well, I don't know when... quite when... I started to falter."

"That's because you haven't," Kongming insisted. "For a while, after I heard what you had done... I was angry, very angry. I even said to Yueying that the Han were done, finished... but then, I regained my sight. Yes, the Xiaoting campaign was a disaster... yes, you failed for the same reason that Cao Cao failed at Red Cliffs... yes, the similarities are not lost to me. But... your motivations, Xuande... could not have been more different."

"I craved Jing," Liu Bei replied honestly. "Yes, I wanted to avenge Yunchang, but I also wanted to reclaim Jing, perhaps *more* than-"

"Even if that's true," Kongming interrupted, "you're the only man left to continue the house of Han! Jing is not only Han domains, wrongly claimed by Wei... it is Liu family territory, wrongly occupied by Wu! The support of the tribes, and the number of refugees, both prove that you were loved in that region... Cao Cao was not loved in Xu Province."

"I shall miss these conversations," Liu Bei said with a sombre laugh. "They've always made me feel better about myself."

Kongming was tellingly silent.

"...I know I'm dying, Kongming," Liu Bei chuckled. "I just never thought... that it would be like this. 'White Emperor City'... I passed it, on the way to Xiaoting, wearing white, didn't I... how odd. Perhaps... this was always Heaven's design."

Liu Bei looked about him, and smiled strangely.

"Jian Xianhe... I miss his sense of humour," Liu Bei sighed. "I'm sure he'd have agreed with me... that I've travelled far. Forty-odd years ago... I started out of my home town... he, I, Yunchang, Yide... we were determined to be heroes, and we were."

Kongming did not interrupt: he studied Liu Bei's smiling face with curiosity.

"...Time and again, we charged and ran... time and again, we built armies and lost them... the bigger they were, the more ignominiously we were defeated," Liu Bei recalled with strange humour. "Once, he said to me, as we were fleeing some place or other, 'I wonder if, perhaps, Xuande, our end will be a fittingly illustrious one... alone, in a tent, in the middle of nowhere, not a man left to fight for us, slowly starving to death, or dying of the shits'. ...Well, I laughed *then*."
Kongming covered his face with his fan: he could not stop smiling, despite the tragic circumstances. Liu looked up at him, and smiled with amusement.
"Maybe," Liu Bei giggled, "we should both laugh *now*."
Tears formed in Kongming's eyes: he laughed with desperate amusement and utter despair. The withered Liu Bei's feeble laughter travelled around the room, leaving his permanent and near-invisible guard, Chen Dao, close to tears.
"Ah," Liu Bei said after several minutes, "it... sometimes feels so good... to laugh."
Kongming was now crying: he did his best to hide it with his fan, but it was obvious.
"...Nontheless," Liu Bei said uncomfortably, "it hurts... to laugh... almost as much... as it does... to cry."
"...Xuande, I...!" Kongming murmured, but again, Liu Bei gestured that he should be silent.
"I think... I should speak to everyone, while I still can," Liu Bei decided. "But... a few last things, if I may."
"Anything," Kongming whispered as he knelt near to Liu Bei.
"Promise me," Liu Bei said as he grasped Kongming's hand, "that you will do everything you can to destroy Wei, and restore the house of Han."
"I shall," Kongming promised.
"My son, Shan... is a cretin," Liu Bei sighed miserably. "I... do not want to admit it, but I must, for the good of all things. He is lazy, cares nothing for matters of state, and he'll rule badly, without strong guidance. Kongming, promise me... promise me that you'll do all you can to guide him, but... but that if he really cannot be guided... that you'll take the imperial throne yourself, with my full blessing."
"No... no, I cannot promise that," Kongming insisted. "I'll guide him to my dying breath, and serve him like a horse, but I'll never supplant him. If it is fate that he governs us to ruin... so be it."
"I... was afraid you'd say that," Liu Bei whispered. "But... 'So be it', indeed."
"Is... is that all...?" Kongming asked nervously.
"I will... confer on you... co-regency... in view of the others, so there is no lack of clarity," Liu Bei continued with more difficulty. "...Will you accept that...?"
"*Co*-regency...?" Kongming prompted.
"Yes," Liu Bei replied. "I have found Mister Li Yan to be most promising, and I think that he would make an excellent guide for my son as well..."
"His assistant resigned... another defected to Wei to escape him," Kongming noted cautiously. "They are not signs of a man worthy of high office."

"...But his work has been exemplary: he helped forge our laws, and he defended us against rebels during the Hanzhong campaign with dedication beyond doubt," Liu Bei countered. "And... you can't do this alone. You have to share the burden with someone, for your health, Kongming."

"Li Yan is a man of pen and sword, a strong organiser," Kongming reasoned. "I know that he won't disappoint: the same goes for Ma Su, Jiang Wan, Fei Yi..."

"Be careful, Kongming... not to become too dependent on anyone," Liu Bei warned sincerely. "Even Ma Su... I know you see him... as a brother... but even Ma Jichang hesitated when I suggested giving him a bigger role... he said the man was a long way–"

"...'From his words matching his deeds'," Kongming said sadly. "I know... he told me that too. Is... is that all...?"

"That... that's all," Liu Bei replied. "Now... perhaps... you should call the officials first... before my family... after all... matters of state come first."

"Very good... Your Majesty," Kongming said as he got to his feet: he bowed respectfully, and left to carry out his instructions.

Kongming returned with the officials, and watched silently as Liu Bei made slow, painful proclamations to each man about the role they would fulfil in the years ahead. Many sobbed and pleaded with their emperor to fight his condition, some even banging their heads against the hard stone floor and screaming wildly. Once all matters of state had been finalised, Liu Bei asked for his family: his wives, concubines and children entered the room and wailed pitifully as he told them about the future. Liu Shan – formerly known as A'Dou – looked on blankly as Liu Bei told him that he would be Second Emperor of Shu Han, and that he would follow – without resistance – the guidance of the co-regents, named as Zhuge Liang and Li Yan. Once all of the family business matters were settled, the family were free to be more open with their grief, and speak more intimately with their fading patriarch. Kongming left the proceedings, followed by General Chen Dao.

"...You're not staying in there with him...?" Kongming whispered to the general as the two entered the hall.

"I can't protect him anymore," Chen Dao replied emotionally. "I thought he should have a moment alone with his family... for once."

Kongming nodded agreeably, patted the old general on the arm, and walked away, fanning himself slowly. As he passed Co-Regent Li Yan, he smiled sadly: Li Yan smiled a similar sad smile in return, and bowed his head slightly as a sign of respect. Kongming continued on his way, passing Yi Ji, Dong He, Jiang Wan, Fei Yi, Ma Su, and the many other officials that would now have to take the Shu Han Empire forward. As he walked, he exhaled noisily.

Liu Bei – the former governor of Xu Province, the former provisional protector of Xinye, the former governor of Jing, the governor of Yi Province, King of Hanzhong and First Emperor of the self-instantiated state of Shu Han – finally succumbed to illness and passed away, aged 62.

"...So now you are the regent," Yueying said as she watched her husband cautiously: he was stood by the entrance to their garden, fanning himself slowly.

"Co-Regent," Kongming replied matter-of-factly.

"The law is yours to make, then," Yueying prompted.

"*No*," Kongming said with a soft laugh. "Things must, for now, remain as they are: change risks unrest, rigidity guarantees stability. We still have many battles to fight, and many wars to win. Until Cao Wei is defeated, and Eastern Wu subjugated, we cannot rest easily."

"So what will happen next...?" Yueying asked plainly.

"First, we revive the alliance we had with Wu," Kongming explained. "And then, when we are sure that our borders are not threatened from any quarter, we march on the state of Cao Wei, and we do not stop until the Han are restored."

"We... or *you*...?" Yueying asked pointedly. "You're going to be the driving force behind this, aren't you...?"

"I failed him, I failed Shu, and I failed the Han, by not making him understand what truly needed to be done," Kongming replied. "From now on, I can lead the army personally... like Zhou Yu and Lu Xun, I can deploy the forces without asking permission from a general, but I can do so – unlike both men – from a safe position, where I can always be ready to deal with everything, not stuck at the front of the charge on a horse, an open target, always the second man to know what's going on, driven by warrior's pride instead of intellectual sense. I will bring new things to the battlefield, things that our enemies will not expect... I'm not tethered to the ground anymore."

"But you will not rest, will you...?" Yueying said emotionally.

"No, I won't," Kongming replied, oblivious to the intent of the question. "I'll not rest until we've defeated Cao Pi... this is personal for me, as it always has been."

"...And will you let me help you...?" Yueying asked further.

"Ah, well, if one thing changes now, it is your own tethering," Kongming said with a smile. "Before, I could not dictate events... now, once a decree has been passed, I can wage war my way. You know as much as I do, and even though you can never accompany me on the campaigns, I will be seeking your counsel as much as anyone at court."

Yueying hugged Kongming's arm, and said, "That... is something."

"Things will be as we want them to be one day... not during our lifetimes, but one day... someone will know what we dreamed of," Kongming supposed. "But it's our struggles that will help to make it possible... let's not shirk that responsibility."

"...The defeat of Cao Wei," Yueying pondered.

"But first, peace with Wu," Kongming mused. "Jichang... and I... were the ones that the newly-crowned King of Wu, Sun Quan, trusted... but I cannot risk that journey. First, I must find a man who can brave the court of Sun Quan, because everything else depends on that peace with Wu... everything."


************

# ACT IX: THE LAST CAMPAIGNS

## 101

The Regent-Chancellor of the state of Shu Han, Zhuge Liang –
Kongming – had not given up on the vision of three independent
states as a precursor to unification: but the journey ahead was to
be a long and difficult one.

Liu Bei, Guan Yu, Zhang Fei, Jian Yong and Sun Qian –
the majority of the men that had begun the great mission to
rescue and then restore the Han – were gone, leaving Kongming
and Zhao Yun as the only men that really understood Liu Bei's
vision. The new Emperor of Shu Han, Liu Shan, was untested in
any official capacity, and many worried that his reputation as a
simpleton might be proven correct: and – as Kongming had once
feared – there was now a much larger proportion of 'post-Yi'
officials in strong positions, officials that served the deposed
former governor Liu Zhang before Liu Bei, and, therefore, might
not be entirely trustworthy. Liu Zhang had died shortly after
surrendering to Sun Quan – some said he was another victim of
Guan Yu's posthumous wrath – but there was still the possibility of
accord with Liu Zhang's former master, the state of Wei.

In addition, the Battle of Xiaoting – a culmination of bad
blood between the houses of Liu and Sun over the proper ruler of
Jing Province, in essence – had left matters in a worse state than
ever before. Now, Sun Quan was seen by many as an
irreconcilable enemy that had been responsible for the deaths of
most of Shu's elite, so Kongming's plan for peace would be met
with derision, at best. And with Shu at its weakest for some years,
and Wu now at its heights, some were contemplating whether Shu
had a future at all.


"The main problem," Kongming mused as he sat in his grand
chancellor's office with Ma Su, "is the person that we would send
to Chaisang."
"Fei Yi...?" Ma Su suggested.
"He is a good man, very capable, but a favourite of Second
Emperor," Kongming replied dismissively. "He would be a good
choice for maintaining relations... but a risky one for repairing
them."
"Hu Ji...?" Ma Su proposed next.
"No, no, Weidu is a fine debater, but... no, no, not a man that Sun
Quan would initially warm to," Kongming chuckled dismissively.
"Xiang Lang...?" Ma Su chuckled.
"So now you want to send a close friend of yours to die...?"
Kongming retorted with a laugh. "He was Guan Yu's administrator
in Jing... I doubt that would be wise."
"Xi Zheng, maybe, or Xu Jing...?" Ma Su said desperately.
"Xi Zheng is too valuable as a caretaker in my absence,"
Kongming replied, "and Xu Jing, for his breeding, demands that I
practically prostrate myself on the floor when I see him... how
would he address a man he regards as a brigand king...?"
"Ayah," Ma Su sighed. "Yang Yi, Dong Yun, Jiang Wan...? ...Me???"
"I've thought it through a thousand times," Kongming said
sorrowfully. "I... am at a loss."

Before Ma Su could answer Kongming, a messenger from the court appeared in the doorway, looking decidedly agitated.

"…I hope there is a carriage ready," Kongming murmured as he got to his feet.

The imperial court of Chengdu was a changed place: it saddened Kongming every time he entered the hall, for he remembered many men that were now dead and gone. Kongming walked to the Emperor, Liu Shan, and kowtowed in front of the young monarch's table, saying, "Your humble servant, Zhuge Liang, pays you his respects."

"Rise, please, Mister Zhuge," Liu Shan implored with a powerless tone: Kongming did as he was asked, and moved to stand next to his co-regent, Li Yan, as Liu Shan said, "Imperial Secretariat Dong Yun, please begin."

"…Matters are serious," Dong Yun declared. "The civil courts in Nanzhong have been attacked by local peasants. Senior Administrator Zheng Ang is believed dead, and Senior Administrator Zhang Yi has been captured."

The courtiers mumbled anxiously.

"…This is unthinkable!" Kongming exclaimed. "Mister Zheng cannot be helped now… what do they want for Zhang Junsi… what ransom are they demanding…?"

"None," Dong Yun said calmly. "He is generally respected, Kongming, so they captured him but did not harm him. However, he has been sent to Eastern Wu."

"…And they will do *what* with him, given recent relations…?" Kongming said worriedly: the court was filled with distressed murmuring.

"…There is a lot of unrest in the south," Li Yan noted. "It was a difficult thing to quell rebellions during the Hanzhong campaign… it will be even worse now. Many, including the prefect of Jianning, Yong Kai, contemplate alliance with Wu; now, the people send a message to Wu, to save themselves. I understand that it's Prefect Yong Kai that is responsible for the current uprising."

"We'll need to deal with this 'Yong Kai' at some point," Kongming said, "but for now, we have to think about rescuing Zhang Junsi from the predicament he has been placed in."

"By doing what…?" the official Qin Mi jeered. "Having another suicidal confrontation with Eastern Wu…?"

"No," Kongming replied. "…There has to be another way."

The court erupted into hostile in-fighting as different factions started to propose different schemes to avert their current situation: Kongming looked at Second Emperor Liu Shan, who was quietly withdrawing with his handmaidens and eunuchs, and sighed, "I shall have to decide the outcome."

Sensing that there would be no sensible debate within the court, Kongming started to leave the court, fanning himself briskly.

"**Regent Zhuge**," a voice hailed as Kongming left the palace: Kongming turned and saw a man of strong appearance, younger than himself but with a commanding presence.

"…Mister Deng," Kongming said with a smile. "You look well. I hope you are not bored by the daily political-"

"This isn't a time for pleasantries," Deng Zhi interrupted sternly but politely. "His Majesty, being so young, inexperienced and newly installed, is failing to inspire the people of Shu, and we risk a period of great unrest... our main problem is our unresolved enmity with the third state, Eastern Wu."

"...You sum the matter up well," Kongming said with surprise.

Deng Zhi nodded, adding, "We should... nay, *must* send a man of good character and sound judgement to Eastern Wu at once to regain trust, repair the alliance, and ensure the safe return of Senior Administrator Zhang."

"...Excellent... excellent!" Kongming praised. "...A marvellous thing... marvellous! Yes, we should, must, and *will* send an envoy... tell me, sir, whether you would be willing to undertake this matter yourself?"

"...You have no better man for the job...?" Deng Zhi retorted.

"I know no better man than one that knows the situation... you, sir, are that able man that I have been looking for," Kongming replied excitedly. "We must plan with all haste... return with me to my office, we have to discuss this further... before we tell the court. You must tell me what you would say... how you would deal with every eventuality that may arise...!"

It was a surprised and bemused Sun Quan that awaited the arrival of Deng Zhi at his court in Chaisang. Zhang Zhao stroked his grey beard and glared icily at the man of Shu that was now striding into the hall to debate with his king.

"...You are brave," Sun Quan said, "if nothing else, Mister Deng."

"I bring you greetings from The Second Emperor," Deng Zhi replied, bowing only very slightly.

"How dare you!" Zhang Zhao heckled. "Show the King of Eastern Wu the respect his position deserves!"

"An official representative from an imperial court," Deng Zhi retorted, "does not show overwhelming deference to a king of a lesser court. That is the way of things. Suffice to say, I have the utmost respect."

The Wu officials murmured angrily; some of the Wu generals started to rise and draw their swords, but Sun Quan gestured sternly, forcing them to back down.

"...You are very brave indeed," Sun Quan said coldly. "After all, your 'higher court' lacks heroes, I think... and a sound ruler."

"It is true," Deng Zhi sighed regrettably, "that great heroes such as Guan Yu, Zhang Fei, Huang Zhong, Ma Chao and, of course, First Emperor, have gone to the heavens... but we still have great warriors such as Ma Chao's cousin Ma Dai, Wei Yan, Wang Ping, and, of course Zhao Zilong, whose might, as you know, is not stunted by age. And you have also lost great heroes, Your Highness... Gan Ning, Zhou Tai, Lü Meng, Taishi Ci, Cheng Pu, Zhou Gongjin... and then there are the great minds that both of our factions have lost... yes, the years and the fates have been very cruel, indeed."

Zhang Zhao's gaze wandered as he pondered the loss of his brother, Zhang Hong, and his political rival, Lu Su.

"...I don't know where he finds you," Sun Quan said with surprise. "Zhuge Liang... truly knows where to find great debaters. But that doesn't matter anymore, Mister Deng... things have changed. Shu was once a great force to be reckoned with... until it misused its strength, attacking us at Xiaoting. Your defeat was costly... you lost Liu Bei, you lost most of your army... now even peasants in the southern shires of Yi are a match for your military, seeing fit to send me human tributes, in the hope that I will send forces to occupy your lands before Wei does."

"But then, your kingdom is approved by Cao Wei, is it not...?" Deng Zhi said with a smirk. "Wouldn't your occupation be on behalf of your master, Cao Pi...?"

"**You...!**" Zhang Zhao shouted angrily.

"*Wait*," the official Lü Fan ordered tersely. "You debate well, Mister Deng, but keep a respectful tone: you are not in Chengdu now."

"Of course," Deng Zhi replied with a smile. "I simply point out that King Sun is a vassal of the Emperor of Cao Wei, Cao Pi... I see no discrepancy in my statement. And as such, you must obey that court in the north... or face consequences."

The officials and generals were collectively silent.

"I'll abandon my prepared speech," Deng Zhi continued, "and say this: our nations were once united against Cao Cao. At that time, First Emperor commanded few soldiers, but now, his successor governs the land of Shu... a land of fertility, with natural defences akin to, or perhaps greater than your own. Any internal disputes we currently suffer will soon be dealt with, and then, we will be as we were. The question then will be 'What of the three of us, Wei, Wu and Shu...?'

"If Shu and Wu were to renew their ties, we would become a force of reckoning: you, King Sun, have the lands of Jing and Jiangdong, providing you with attack points at Jiangling and Hefei to pressure Wei, and for defence, you have the Great River, as always. Shu has its mountains and valleys, which are now, thanks to the defensive network put in place by Protector Wei Yan, impregnable: for attack, we have several points along the Hanzhong border. Together, we could remove the usurper and tyrant, Cao Pi, and restore the Han in the north... the south would be, as it is now, a vast domain of your family's creation, under your family's sound governance, in the name of the Han court.

"If, however, we were to remain antagonistic... we would both, then, be at the mercy of the half-million horde of Cao Wei. Cao Pi holds back now because he is uneasy about possible restoration of Shu-Wu relations... what, then, of the moment that he realises that there will be no peace between us...? He will try and demand servitude from Shu, but we will refuse, as we always have done, and he will lose many thousands of men trying to pass our mountain defences. From you, he already has some degree of humility, but that will not be enough. He will demand tributes, and then a hostage... just as Cao Cao would have, all those years ago, before Red Cliffs... you will once again be in that situation, but with no way out, as before. If you accept, you become his slave... if you refuse, he will attack you... and you will fight him alone. And maybe Shu might take advantage, sailing down the Great River, and taking Jing... maybe not. Regardless, you would be left with nothing in the end. So... what will you do...?"

Sun Quan was completely silent: after several minutes, Zhang Zhao coughed nervously, and said, "Your Highness...?"

"You have been very brave, and very eloquent, Mister Deng," Sun Quan said soberly. "What you ask of me... requires deliberation. You will be given comfortable accommodation while I discuss this with my advisers... I promise that I will answer you as quickly as I can."

"My greatest thanks," Deng Zhi replied, making a greater bow than his first: he then turned to the officials and generals, made respectful bows, and left the court.

"...Privacy," Sun Quan said as he got to his feet: his senior advisers and strategists followed him to his private audience room.

"He finds such magnificent debaters, your brother," Sun Quan sighed as he looked at Zhuge Jin. "To break ties with Wei... a difficult decision, but one I have made before, to my advantage: another alliance with Shu... more difficult still."

"That was another time and place," Zhang Zhao suggested. "My brother and I were against it... we were incorrect, perhaps. But I must again oppose, for the same reasons as before, and this time, I think that I have greater cause to be sure."

"It's true," Zhuge Jin interrupted, "that things have changed, and not all for the better... but we are still in a strong position, and Shu – for all its faults – could be a dependable ally."

"...He repeatedly evaded discussing his new master," Lü Fan noted. "These rumours that he is a crass, bumbling simpleton that prefers games, women and pranks over strong governance... how can such a man be dependable...?"

"I think he said much by his evasiveness," Zhang Zhao mused. "We would not be entering into a covenant with this 'Liu Shan'... it would be with Zhuge Liang."

"Very much so," Zhuge Jin agreed. "My brother chose this man to approach us... my brother chose this course. Shu is now governed by two regents, my brother and a friend of his, Li Yan, who is equally shrewd and professional. And you know my brother, Your Highness... he is a good man, a wise man, now able to act as sense – not Liu Bei – demands. See that there was no mention made of Jing as stolen land? That matter – the only one that truly divided us – is closed, by my brother's wish."

"I'm inclined to agree," Lü Fan said with a strange tone. "I never thought I would say that... but yes, it has always been Liu Bei that has caused the trouble, and he's dead now."

"Along with many others," Sun Quan sighed. "I have to say, I still grieve the loss of Ma Jichang: for Zhuge Kongming to want peace after my forces killed his sworn brother... shows his high-mindedness."

"History repeats... Liu Biao's death allowed accord between Jing and Jiangdong to fight Cao Cao as allies, and now Liu Bei's death allows peace between Shu and Wu to fight Cao Pi together," Zhuge Jin declared.

"Wei is very strong," Zhang Zhao protested.

"They were strong at Red Cliffs," Zhuge Jin countered, "and Cao Pi is not the man his father was."

496

"And *Sima Yi*...?" another official, Zhang Wen, noted cautiously. "That man is perhaps the most dangerous Wei strategist since Guo Jia... we'd all be kneeling in front of the Wei throne now if Cao Cao had listened to even half of Sima's advice, and Cao Pi hangs on his every word. There will be no 'Red Cliffs' for Sima Yi."

"We have our own geniuses, such as Lu Xun," Zhuge Jin insisted, "and Kongming could outwit Sima Yi, I think... you overrate this man."

"But...!" Zhang Zhao began: Sun Quan hummed thoughtfully, and Zhang Zhao immediately fell silent.

"...I do not want to be a vassal of Wei," Sun Quan decided. "It is as it was: I would rather fight to keep what my father and brother worked so hard to gain, than hand it all over to the throne-usurping son of a tyrant that I bested fifteen years ago. No, I do not want to kneel to Liu Shan either... but there is room for negotiation with Shu that does not exist with Wei. Mister Deng was right... we can return to the tripartite plan envisaged by Lu Zijing and Zhuge Kongming, and pincer Wei from west and south... and together, Shu and Wu can rule the land justly, on either side of the Great River."

"Then we will send an envoy to Chengdu...?" Zhuge Jin supposed.

"Zhang Wen shall go," Sun Quan decided. "Mister Zhang, you will report everything to me... I want to know what is really going on in Shu. Not just the court... I want to know living conditions for the poor, the state of their army, the opinions of man and woman alike."

"Very well, Your Highness," Zhang Wen replied obediently.

"And we shall release this man Zhang Yi from prison," Zhuge Jin supposed.

"I want to meet him," Sun Quan said with a smile. "I hear that he negotiated the terms of surrender for Liu Zhang... and became a good friend of your brother. Such a man, with such knowledge of Yi before and after Liu Bei, cannot just return to Shu without my meeting him."

"...Very good, Your Highness," Zhuge Jin replied apprehensively.

Days later, three horsemen crossed the border into Yi Province.

"You impressed him far, far too much, Zhang Junsi," Deng Zhi complained as he looked back at the horde of Wu soldiers that had been in furious pursuit.

"We both did," Zhang Junsi said with a smile.

The Wu envoy that accompanied them – Zhang Wen – eyed both men irritably and said, "His Highness means you no harm, either of you."

"That's why we're staring at a brigade of armed men that were actively pursuing us," Deng Zhi chuckled. "Mister Zhang, are you trying to say they are a belated escort for us...?"

Zhang Junsi laughed as Wu's Zhang Wen struggled to find a reason why his king had sent soldiers so soon after authorising a peace mission.

"Well, we're over the border now," Deng Zhi continued jovially. "So even if we weren't safe before, we're safe now. Shall we proceed to Chengdu...?"

"…Yes," Zhang Wen replied dolefully. "I apologise for the misunderstanding… I'm sure that His Highness sent them as protection, or something. I'll talk to them… you two go on."
Deng Zhi and Zhang Junsi laughed once again, and continued onward, leaving Zhang Wen of Wu to confer with their pursuers. Soon enough, the three men were met by a brigade of Shu soldiers and escorted to the capital to meet with Kongming.

"Well, well," Kongming said with a laugh as Deng Zhi, Zhang Junsi and Zhang Wen finished relaying the tale of their journey to the chancellor and his aides Ma Su, Dong Jue and Zong Yu. "It seems I chose the perfect man… too perfect, by far."
"…My thanks for the lodgings," Zhang Wen said with some shame in his tone. "I shall go now, Chancellor… I look forward to our court meeting later today."
"Indeed, yes, farewell for now, Mister Zhang…!" Kongming replied: an exchange of respectful bows ended the meeting, and Zhang Wen and Deng Zhi left the other men to talk further.
"…I'm glad that's over," Kongming admitted. "Good to see you alive and well, Junsi. You must have impressed Sun Quan greatly for him to want you back in his court so badly."
"The man's uncouth, though," Zong Yu complained. "Sending soldiers to 'escort you back'… awful behaviour!"
"And what a mood change… to make such a decision less than a day after letting you go," Kongming mused. "We're worried enough about our own Second Emperor… time and power seem to be making a reckless, impulsive, and somewhat dangerous man of King Sun. If his soldiers had caught up with you it would have ruined everything, Junsi."
"Well they *didn't*," Zhang Junsi said with relief, "and we have their envoy… peace is a few ink blots away. What's the situation in Nanzhong now?"
"I sent a man to attempt reconciliation with Yong Kai and his rebels… I've heard nothing from him so far," Kongming reported. "Li Yan had been in direct communication with Yong Kai before… but now there is no attempt to be civil."
"Oh," Zhang Junsi said quietly. "So we may have to fight, then."
"That… wasn't an option before your return," Kongming replied cautiously.
"Sun Quan gave this Yong Kai a title, so Wu were behind the rebellion all along," Ma Su said angrily. "Hopefully, Wu did that because we were still technically at war… if Wu withdraw support for Yong Kai now, we can attack him."
"First," Kongming insisted, "we must try for peace… however, Yongchang City is being besieged, and the defenders can't hold out forever. Li Yan has taken a force to repel the tribal leader Gaoding from taking the city of Xindao… I don't know how that's going."
"…We must build and prepare our forces, secure our Wei border, make peace with Wu, and dissociate the rebel leaders from each other," Ma Su suggested. "Then we can march."
"Yes," Kongming said wearily. "I'll go in person."
"You look tired," Zhang Junsi suggested.

"I keep telling him," Ma Su insisted. "He barely slept, he did not take a single day off while you were imprisoned, Junsi... and now he wants to march on Nanzhong!"

"I'm fine," Kongming retorted. "I'm not tired, I just look it. I'm getting old."

"You're in your mid-forties," Zhang Junsi sighed, "and you look like a man of sixty, Kongming. The stress is killing you."

"I'm fine," Kongming reiterated. "Now come... we have a peace envoy to entertain... and a battle with the Nan tribes to prepare for."

The Wu envoy, Zhang Wen, left Chengdu with a positive impression of the Shu Han kingdom, and conveyed only good things to a delighted Sun Quan, who immediately severed all ties with an infuriated Cao Pi. As Kongming had hoped, the result was an immediate military confrontation between Wei and Wu that removed Sun Quan from the affairs in Nanzhong and left the Shu army with a clear path to pacify the region. After securing the borders and stabilising the court, Kongming and Ma Su began preparations for an eventful Southern Expedition.


************

## 102

A few weeks before the intended march on Nanzhong, Zhuge Jin and his second son Qiao paid an unexpected visit to Chengdu: they were given a warm welcome by Kongming and his family.

"...I feel like I've come home, even this isn't Longzhong," Zhuge Jin admitted nostalgically as he sat at a banquet table with Kongming, Qiao, and their younger brother Jun and his family.

"Uncle," Qiao said to Kongming, "you are looking very tired."

"I wish that people would stop telling me that I look tired," Kongming chuckled irritably. "I'm fine, nephew, just fine."

"He's fine," Zhuge Jun teased. "He just *looks* dead."

Zhuge Jin smirked.

"...So why are you here, brother...?" Jun asked at last: Yueying – who was hovering near the doorway to the kitchen – awaited the answer with interest.

"Do I need a reason to visit...?" Zhuge Jin retorted cagily: Jun's wife and sons got up and left the table, leaving the three brothers and Qiao seated together.

"...Of course not," Kongming admitted at last. "It is always a pleasure to see you, brother... and Qiao, of course. Is Ke still a troublemaker...?"

"My elder brother will always be trouble," Qiao said honestly.

"He's... high-spirited," Zhuge Jin suggested. "His Highness thinks a lot of him."

"So I hear," Kongming replied. "... ... ...It's been so long since we last met like this. I think I was able to stop by your home once, when First Emperor was in Chaisang, marrying Lady Sun... Ke and Qiao were only boys, and... well, I certainly remember that Ke was the feisty one. I hope he has learned to be less impetuous."

"*Hardly*," Zhuge Qiao muttered.

"He's... high-spirited," Zhuge Jin suggested again, with a mechanical tone. "His Highness thinks a lot of him."

"...So I hear," Kongming said with amusement. "...And you, Qiao, are still studying and practicing your art of swordplay...?"

"I am, Uncle," Qiao replied courteously. "Principally, I strive to be a man of strong learning and inspired thinking, like you."

Yueying smiled warmly as she watched the four men talking.

"...Why doesn't Lady Huang come and sit with us...?" Zhuge Jin suggested as he spied Yueying loitering: she slowly disappeared into the kitchen to join Jun's family.

"I think she's allowing us space," Jun replied.

"Well, I really thought that she should be part of the discussions," Zhuge Jin said with slight intent: Kongming smiled at his elder brother's words. "...I mean, we're at peace now, Shu and Wu... there will never be bad blood between our houses again, Kongming... and as you had me tell His Highness, King Sun... what better way to exploit that peace than greater strength in our family...?"

Jun got up and left his elder brothers to talk: he ushered his family into the vast garden at the back of the house, leaving Yueying alone in the kitchen.

"...And what do you think about this, Qiao...?" Kongming asked as he turned to his silent nephew.

"I would be glad and honoured to call you Father," Qiao replied. "You are a legend among men, Uncle: you have the respect of His Highness King Sun, and even Zhang Zhao reluctantly admits that you are near peerless as a politician. I could learn much from you."

Yueying had silently returned to the doorway some moments before: she placed her hand over her mouth, and stifled confused tears.

"Lady Huang," Zhuge Jin hailed: Kongming turned to look at his wife, and smiled feebly when he saw her countenance.

"...Please, sit," Kongming said softly: Yueying complied, fixing her gaze on Zhuge Qiao and studying him with a mother's eyes.

"Does something trouble you, Worthy Aunt...?" Qiao asked.

Yueying shook her head silently.

"Then it is settled!" Zhuge Jin said cheerfully. "Qiao... my son... now, your father is there, and your mother is there. Greet them as a faithful son should."

Zhuge Qiao got to his feet and stepped away from the table; Kongming and Yueying got to their feet so that Qiao could kowtow to them, saying, "Father and Mother, I pay you most humble and devout respects."

With great hesitation – and sincere emotion – Kongming said, "Son...?"

"Please," Yueying murmured, "get up..."

"Thank you, Mother, Father," Qiao said as he got to his feet: Yueying embraced the youth as though he was her son, and Zhuge Jin smiled warmly.

"...Thank you," Yueying said almost inaudibly as she looked at Zhuge Jin.

"Indeed," Kongming said as he turned to face his brother, "I... I am most honoured that you should consider us worthy parents."

"He's *your* son now, Kongming," Zhuge Jin insisted. "Now, I am his uncle... our roles are reversed."

The business of Zhuge Qiao's adoption was concluded. The family reunited at the banquet table to enjoy a wonderful and joyous meal in respect of the occasion, and a few days later, Zhuge Jin returned to his homeland of Wu alone, but gladly so.

"You've not talked to her about it... have you...?"

Ma Su's question was unwanted: Kongming turned from his work and said, "There's nothing to discuss, Youchang."

"You are concerned that your new adopted son is another spy, like Lady Sun," Ma Su retorted. "With you involving Lady Huang in your business affairs, don't you think that sharing your thoughts might be sensible, for the sake of *security*...?"

"I... I can't do that right now," Kongming admitted. "There is nothing that he will learn that is of any use to Wu... after all, we have no enmity anymore. Would I have requested that the youth be my adopted son if I had severe doubts...?"

"So you admit that you have *some* doubts," Ma Su noted.

"I don't trust *anybody* anymore!" Kongming said with a laugh. "Youchang, the lad seems to be sincere... he even calls Sun Quan 'King Sun of Wu' and not 'His Highness' now, and speaks of Second Emperor as 'His Majesty'. I... I have to remember that my brother was the one man that never gave up on me, and he would not go along with a plan that harmed me in any way. Besides, why not try and marry one of Sun Quan's daughters to Second Emperor...?"

"Because," Ma Su said plainly, "everyone knows that the real ruler of Shu Han is *you*, Kongming."

"Don't... don't say that," Kongming replied angrily. "I'm an adviser, a regent... and *satisfied with that*. I'm not like Cao Cao."

"I know that," Ma Su said apologetically, "but you make all of the major decisions now... since Second Emperor prefers to delegate all responsibility to you... I know you didn't ask for the power, but it's yours regardless. Sun Quan would learn nothing useful from a spy at court... except which eunuch is currently in favour, or the prettiest concubine. To learn anything useful, one has to watch *you*."

"...You see it all, don't you...?" Kongming snickered desperately. "Anyhow... I can afford to worry about that later, when I have the time and the energy. Yong Kai killed the man I sent to speak to him, and now Administrator Zhu Bao and a barbarian landowner called Lord Meng have joined this rebellion. We shall have to march quickly now."

"Will your new son be marching with us...?" Ma Su wondered.

"Not on this campaign," Kongming replied. "The next one, yes."

"Planning ahead as usual, I see," Ma Su said with amusement.

Kongming petitioned the court, and was invited to state his intentions publicly before the assembled officials and generals. As Kongming entered the court, the emperor, Liu Shan, leant forward and grinned unintelligently.

"Your Imperial Majesty," Kongming hailed as he reached his master, "I, Liang, pay you the greatest of respects."

As Kongming kowtowed, Liu Shan said, "Very good, very good, Mister Zhuge Kongming, you are like my father, you are the man I rely upon in all things. Please, please, rise, and tell us what you want to do."

Kongming got to his feet and said, "Your Imperial Majesty, I humbly request from you the permission to lead an army to the southern shires of Nanzhong to pacify the ever-growing rebellion."

"You intend to go yourself...?" Jiang Wan noted with surprise.

"Isn't a general, such as Zhao Zilong, enough to quell this rebellion...?" Yi Ji asked with concern for his old friend.

"Indeed," the official Wang Lian protested. "Can't a general knock some sense into these barbarians...? Your fellow regent, Li Yan, is already trapped in Nanzhong, fighting Zhu Bao, I understand. These 'men' killed Zheng Ang and Qi Xing, and sent Zhang Yi to Wu to be executed! You place yourself in too much danger!"

"I concur," said the official Li Fu. "Chancellor, you-"

"To answer Mister Wang," Kongming interrupted, "I understand fully what the risks are... the risks to this state outweigh the risks to my own health. No general can rationalise with these barbarians... force alone will only antagonise them further."

502

"Why should you succeed where Zhang Yi and Qi Xing failed...?"
Wang Lian challenged. "And if words will work, why not send
Mister Deng to speak to Yong Kai...? He pacified Wu!"
"Zhang Yi is a fine debater, as is Deng Zhi, but there will be no
debate with this man Yong Kai," Kongming retaliated. "I sent Qi
Xing to discover the truth... he discovered it too keenly, and his
head rolled for it, and I regret it deeply. This is my responsibility
and mine alone. We are wasting time: Your Imperial Majesty, I
again ask for your divine instruction."
Liu Shan had been trying to escape, but his eunuchs had stopped
his flight: the anxious young emperor replied, "You... you do
whatever you think will help me. Yes, yes, I authorise your march,
but, you... you be careful, you are like my father, and I rely on you
for all things. Be quick, for I will miss you."
Many officials winced at the way their emperor expressed his
thoughts, and silently thanked the heavens that no foreign
representatives were present to hear him.
"...I shall, Your Imperial Majesty," Kongming said hesitantly. He
kowtowed once again, got to his feet, and left the court to begin
plans for his march to Nanzhong, shouts of protestation echoing
behind him.

Kongming and Yueying spent that evening in their garden,
enjoying the fresh air.
"Are you leaving Qiao here for my sake...?" Yueying asked.
"No," Kongming promised. "I know you wouldn't stand for that. I
would like him to accompany me northward for the campaign
against Wei, but this matter in Nanzhong requires certain... *unique*
strategy. I know he's keen to learn, but there will be other
opportunities."
"They are very superstitious, very tribal, in those shires," Yueying
noted. "And the weather is very unpleasant as well... the area is
dense jungle, and not much else besides, and diseases are
rampant. Your friends at court are right to worry."
"It's no worse than any other part of the south," Kongming
insisted. "Our campaigns in Jing were in humid conditions... don't
fret."
"And can you rely on Ma Su...?" Yueying asked plainly.
"As much as I trusted and relied upon Ma Liang," Kongming
insisted.
"He's a good man, but... remember that he *isn't* Ma Liang,"
Yueying pleaded. "I know you see him as your little brother, and
you want him to be as dependable as Liang, but... you were
warned."
"Overly cautious words by a brother," Kongming said surely. "Ma
Su is very wise, beyond his years in fact... and so far, his
suggestions have been without fault."
"No man is without fault," Yueying scolded. "Not even you. So
please... don't make any mistakes. The state of Shu needs you."
"Yes... so our Second Emperor goes to great pains to remind me,
intentionally or not," Kongming sighed regrettably. "*Ayah*... he is
so... uninspiring. I really do worry that his ways will make a
mockery of us in foreign courts. When comparing youths that
inherit great responsibility, he's no Sun Quan... that much is
certain."

The southward march was not an entirely confident one: many of the Shu soldiers were veterans of the resounding defeat at Xiaoting over two years earlier, and another march into hot climates to battle against wily opponents was far from exciting.

"Morale is not exactly high," Kongming noted worriedly as he rode in a carriage with Ma Su at the centre of the army.

"It's not likely to be," Ma Su replied. "...How are you thinking of fighting them, Kongming...? ...You haven't really discussed strategy at all."

"I wonder what you think we should do," Kongming prompted.

"Against an enemy that doesn't think, like Yong Kai, the best strategy is to outwit him with mind games," Ma Su responded thoughtfully. "They are tribes... easily bought, easily tricked into fighting as one or against each other. This 'Lord Meng' told them lies to rile them to fight as one... he'll ultimately be the main adversary here. Zhu Bao can be routed, and Yong Kai and Gaoding are best pitted against each other."

"A fine assessment," Kongming said, "that I agree with wholeheartedly. Yong Kai is advancing to meet us... we should ensure he doesn't leave here alive."

"Yes," Ma Su said hesitantly, "but... we should not be so keen to exterminate them *all*, should we...? Yong Kai will answer for his treason, yes, but the tribes are that way by nature... we have the future to think about."

"...You're right," Kongming sighed. "I must be tired... I am forgetting my own rules of warfare. Yong Kai and Gaoding will be made examples of, and the people made to understand that if they don't rebel, we'll let them govern themselves."

"*Now* we agree," Ma Su said with a smile.

"Summon Generals Ma Zhong and Li Hui," Kongming said suddenly. "This is where we need to separate, and advance on the key cities."

General Ma Zhong was despatched to battle Zhu Bao in Zangke, while General Li Hui advanced to rescue the defenders at Jianning City: Kongming took the main army on a direct course for a showdown with Yong Kai and Gaoding.

In-fighting amongst the rebels claimed the life of Yong Kai before the two opposing armies ever met: the surviving leader, Gaoding, met Kongming's army on a field south of the main city of Yuesui. The rebels were comprised of defected Shu soldiers, crudely-armed peasants and tribal warriors from around the regions that Gaoding had influence: the half-naked, tanned tribesmen were unnerving to any that were not prepared, but their training saved the moment. Ma Su and Secretary Dong Jue sent orders down the ranks, and the Shu soldiers started to form near-faultless battle lines across the field.

"I'm ready," Ma Su declared. "All forces deployed as requested."

"Now," Kongming said, "we will show him how an army fights. Dong Jue...?"

Dong Jue – who was acting as an officer on the campaign – raised a flag into the air; the soldiers started to criss-cross and shift, forming human walls and gates.

"Archers...!" Kongming prompted: General Zhang Bogong raised his hand, and row upon row of bowmen and crossbowmen readied their weapons.

**"Kill them ALL!"** Gaoding screamed to his followers: the mass of rebels surged forward in a disorganised swell, yelling and brandishing their weapons.

"...Now," Kongming urged: Zhang Bogong made a sweeping motion toward the enemy with his raised arm, and a hail of arrows flew toward the approaching rebel forces, knocking down man after man. Many of the Nanzhong peasants – who had not expected such a response – turned and fled; the soldiers and tribesmen continued their advance regardless, and rushed at the openings in Kongming's formations. As the rebels disappeared behind the human walls, the openings vanished, and inside, spearmen and cavalrymen lead by Zhang Boqi cut down any man they saw without remorse. Many tried to escape the formation, but walls of shields, spears and swords repelled and wounded them as they struggled.

**"No, keep fighting, keep fighting!"** Gaoding screamed as his vanguard was being massacred; the successive advances were being repelled or cut down by sword and arrow, and the result was inevitable. The scene erupted into chaos, and within a few hours, it was over: the rebels fled, resoundingly defeated.

"Status," Kongming prompted as Zhang Boqi arrived at his position.

"Gaoding's dead," Zhang Boqi reported coldly. "The rebels are in full retreat... it's up to Generals Ma and Li to leave them with nowhere to hide."

Kongming surveyed the battlefield with a heavy heart: the 'enemy' dead numbered in the thousands, and more than a few were farmers and disaffected draftees.

"...I was a farmer once," Kongming mused. "Yong Kai and Gaoding shouldn't make men like them fight. Who will till the fields...?"

"Lord Meng is their leader now," Ma Su replied. "We'll be fighting the tribes of Nanzhong from now on... I don't think the peasants will be opposing us anymore."

"...No... I expect not," Kongming murmured. "Onward..."

General Li Hui had marched to the southwest, intent on rescuing the defenders of the besieged city of Jianning. When he finally encountered the enemy near the city of Kunming, however, their numbers far exceeded expectations. In fact, the rebels outnumbered the Shu forces by 2 to 1: despite this, Li Hui successfully repelled their attacks and kept them busy while he attempted to get word of his situation to Kongming and Ma Zhong.

"...Commander," Li Hui's deputy and adviser, Liao Hua, hailed. "We have repelled another assault, but why don't we-"

"...Retreat...?" Li Hui supposed. "No. We don't know the situation in other regions... what if these forces were able to bolster Gaoding against Regent Zhuge's army? Our role was to ease the pressure on our main force and relieve Jianning, and I intend to do that."

"I suppose I shouldn't expect any less from a man that once talked around the barbarian king Ma Chao," Liao Hua sighed. "But we surely can't hold out forever against such-"

"**REPORT!**" a messenger interrupted: Li Hui turned to the muddy, battered soldier and nodded as a prompt that he should continue. "**General Ma Zhong has defeated Zhu Bao, and our main force has routed Gaoding!**"

"...So these rebels here are the last resistance," Li Hui mused. "Get some rest and nourishment, young man, you've earned it."

The messenger retreated, and Li Hui smiled icily.

"You've thought of something," Liao Hua guessed.

"Well, as you said, I have a knack for negotiating with barbarians," Li Hui chuckled cheerfully. "I have a plan that will make our job twice as simple... listen carefully."

"I understand that Li Hui will be joining us very soon," an impressed Ma Su said as he entered the newly constructed command tent in Shu's front line camp.

"Excellent news," Kongming replied as he studied a crude map of the regions controlled by forces remaining loyal to Lord Meng. "How did he best such overwhelming numbers so quickly...?"

"He feigned defection," Ma Su said with a smirk. "They fell for it... his wily tongue has lost nothing. They trusted him, and he was able to enter their main camps and launch a surprise attack on their leaders. Jianning is liberated, and the tribesmen are retreating to join Lord Meng."

"Yes... Lord Meng," Kongming mused. "This one will be a tough adversary to defeat... he's well-financed, charismatic, stubborn, arrogant and cunning. Only one of those traits is exploitable."

"So when do we advance?" Ma Su asked.

"As soon as Li Hui has arrived," Kongming replied. "He's bringing a better map of the region from Administrator Lü Kai that we shall sorely need... then we will confront this 'Lord Meng'. Killing him will make a martyr of him, so we must ensure he lives and publicly surrenders... but that might not be so easy, I think."

"If we capture him and he refuses to surrender, we'll have no choice but to execute him, Kongming, according to military law," Ma Su noted worriedly.

"Well," Kongming said with a smile, "I've never been known for my strict adherence to anything. Military law may have to be relaxed... after all, are they even an army...?"

************

## 103

Lord Meng – who was now the leader of the rebellion in Nanzhong – readied his vast forces for the upcoming battle with Kongming's forces. What met the Shu soldiers was an imposing sight: thousands and thousands of various tribal warriors – men and women alike – armed with bows, clubs, axes, swords, spears and halberds were massed along the battlefield, hollering and heckling the invaders into their territory. Riding at the head of the army was Lord Meng, who was wearing a cloak and light armour, and carrying a large pair of axes. His well-trained horse took him backward and forward along the front lines of his army, while he gestured and taunted the Shu forces.

"They're better dressed for the weather than we are," Ma Su said with a laugh. "I don't know, Kongming... do we charge...?"

"Formations are a risk, we'll lose too many men," Kongming mused. "We don't really want to kill too many of them, either. I suppose we should–"

A piercing scream on the Nanzhong side indicated a mass charge: Kongming was forced to hurriedly order a full retaliation against the approaching enemy. The pressure was too great, however, and the Shu army was forced to retreat slightly. Rather than pursue – which might have given them a swift victory – the Nanzhong forces wailed triumphantly and withdrew to their own lines to celebrate having broken their opponent's spirit.

"...I think demoralising them might not be our main problem," Kongming muttered as he surveyed his maps of the area with Ma Su and Dong Jue. He mopped a heavy covering of sweat from his brow, and coughed uncomfortably.

"Our supplies are holding, but the number of sick is starting to escalate as we go further south," Dong Jue complained. "I can't shake this headache at all."

"I suggest we... improvise," Kongming replied wearily. "The jungles here are dense, full of all manner of things... we can't be lured into it, or we'll be overwhelmed. If we feign mass sickness, however, we might be able to lure them to our camp, and make a surprise strike."

"We don't really have to feign anything," Ma Su sighed. "We'll notify the other generals, and organise it all... you rest, you look even weaker than usual."

Kongming nodded agreeably, and his allies left the command tent.

Word reached Lord Meng that the Shu forces were in disarray, and seemed to be suffering badly from the heat. Delighted by the news, Meng organised a precision attack on the Shu camp using some of his most imposing cavalrymen: he would lead the attack personally, as he was anxious to ensure that he would not be upstaged by another tribal leader.

The attack was launched at night; Lord Meng's forces silently charged the gates of the Shu camp, but found them to be open. Either side of the gates, Shu soldiers lay about, groaning painfully and begging for help or mercy.

"This is a trap," one horseman suggested.

"No, they're really sick," another said as he rode closer to some of the soldiers. "They have the sweating sickness."

"…We'll advance on their command tent!" Lord Meng declared: he shouted as loudly as he could, hoping to unnerve the defenders as he rode through the camp, and lunged at any approaching soldiers with his heavy sword. But as he reached the command tent, the trap was sprung, and healthy Shu soldiers led by Zhang Boqi blocked all of the possible escape routes and surrounded the horsemen.

"…**Cowards!**" Lord Meng screamed defiantly, swiping at the soldiers as he rode around the camp: he found no way to escape, and one by one, his horsemen were being dragged from their steeds and bound with rope. Eventually, Meng himself was unsaddled and brought before Kongming and Ma Su.

"So you are Lord Meng," Kongming said coldly. "You were trying to exploit our beleaguered situation… that is not the way of war."

"Hypocrite!" Lord Meng retorted. "You think we're ignorant of you out here…? We hear everything… we know who you are! You're Zhuge Liang… you do nothing but exploit the sick and weak! What about Zhou Yu of Wu…? Did you not rile him to death? And Lu Su, didn't he die miserable, after being made a fool of by you over and over again…?"

"*You*…!" Dong Jue exclaimed.

"*No*, Gongxi: this man invites death, but he will not get it," Kongming insisted.

"You stole land from everyone who ever trusted you!" Lord Meng continued. "Now you're here to belittle us, tax us, steal from us, but we won't let you!"

The other Nanzhong warriors showed their agreement with Lord Meng by heckling and grunting defiantly: Kongming shook his head and sighed sadly.

"You are poorly informed," Kongming promised. "All we want is peace. We've made peace with Wu now, and all we want to do is-"

"Save your lies for some idiot," Lord Meng interrupted. "Kill me, Zhuge Liang, and be done with it!"

"…Untie him," Kongming ordered; the shocked Shu soldiers did as they were asked.

"What now…?" Lord Meng asked belligerently.

"Come, let me show you around the camp," Kongming said with a kind smile.

Kongming, Li Hui and Ma Su led Lord Meng and his followers around their stronghold, pointing out where the infirmary was, how many weapons they had, what supplies they had stored, and the number of able men at their disposal. Once the tour was over, Kongming walked Lord Meng to the main gates of the camp, and had his horse returned to him. Generals Dong Jue, Zhang Boqi, Ma Zhong, Zhang Bogong and Ma Dai looked on with confusion and despair.

"Your warriors shall also receive their horses shortly," Kongming promised a wary Lord Meng. "Now… you have seen how well we are organised, how we train, what we can do… what do you think of our army…?"

Lord Meng eyed Kongming arrogantly and replied, "We did not know our enemy well, so we retreated before, and tried this trick, whereupon we were beaten. Now I have seen everything, I know that we are the superior force, and we will defeat you."

"Is that so...?" Kongming said with a smile. "Well... who am I to deny you the chance to prove your might...? Very well, Lord Meng... I release you."

"But...!" Zhang Boqi protested.

"This is an exceptional circumstance for an exceptional man," Kongming explained calmly. "We will fight again soon, Lord Meng... I look forward to it."

Lord Meng grunted rudely, mounted his horse, and galloped away, despite the fact that his fellow riders were not ready to follow him.

"...Ensure the riders are well treated and allowed to pursue their leader," Kongming said to Li Hui, who nodded knowingly.

"This worries me," Dong Jue admitted as he walked back to the command tent with Kongming and Ma Su. "Their first attack on us was devastating... how can we win if he-"

"Last time, Gongxi," Kongming replied, "he wasn't the only one that wasn't prepared. I didn't realise exactly how much support he had mustered... next time, we'll use tactics, and defeat him definitively."

The next morning, two riders brought a bound man to the Shu camp, and threw him down in front of the main gates.

"...Ah, our guest has arrived!" Kongming said with cheer as a messenger ran into his command tent.

"Regent Zhuge, Regent...! ... ... ...You're awake...?" Dong Jue said with surprise as he moved the messenger to one side and entered the tent. "Do... do you ever sleep?"

"You seem to have forgotten why you're here," Kongming replied with amusement.

"Oh, right... you, there, messenger... are you here to report the prisoner?" Dong Jue asked: the messenger nodded nervously.

"...Well, I'd better go and say greetings," Kongming chuckled as he picked up his fan and walked toward the gates.

"**You traitor!**" the prisoner – Lord Meng – screamed as he saw Kongming approaching: the regent of Shu was fanning himself and grinning broadly. "**Duplicitous, untrustworthy-**"

"Lord Meng," Kongming interrupted, "it is good to see you again so soon."

"**You released me!**" Lord Meng protested angrily as Ma Su, Zhang Boqi and Dong Jue arrived with groups of infantrymen. "**You foul...!**"

"You were planning a secret strike," Kongming scolded. "I know you, Lord Meng, I know where you are, and I just wanted you to know that aside from reading your every move, I can capture you whenever I want... even from your own bed, in your own home, or even from the command tent in your camp... as I have just done."

"I wasn't prepared!" Lord Meng retorted. "How could I expect such-"

"I thought you said you didn't trust me," Kongming replied, "so how can you say this was unexpected...?"

The Shu generals laughed in unison.

"You tricked me!" Lord Meng complained.

"You told the tribes of Nanzhong that I am a thief, here to tax the poor and abduct women and children for use as concubines and slaves in His Majesty's court," Kongming countered. "They follow your lies, not you personally. When you do not resort to cheap tricks to hinder me, I will not expose you as the simpleton you are."

"I will kill you!" Lord Meng bellowed. "**I will rip out your eyes with my teeth!**"

"Oh…?" Kongming sniggered. "Well, I shall look forward to that. We're supposed to be fighting, aren't we…? Off you go, then, and see you soon."

Kongming gestured to two soldiers with his fan, and they untied Lord Meng. Kongming looked at the two riders – who were not tribesmen, but Shu cavalrymen in disguise – and said, "You two can escort Lord Meng and his two horsemen back to the river now."

"They were…!" Lord Meng realised at last: the two riders laughed boisterously.

"You should know every man in your retinue like the back of your own hand, Lord Meng," Kongming admonished mischievously. "How can you make secret plans with any old 'barbarian' that comes your way, and expect to be victorious…?"

More Shu soldiers brought the real riders and shoved them outside the gates of the camp; Lord Meng eyed the two angry men with shame and turned to walk away, the laughter of Shu's army ringing in his ears.

"What a fool," Li Hui chortled.

"So now, I have captured him twice," Kongming proclaimed. "We'll try for a third when he comes with his armies."

Lord Meng rallied the tribes of Nanzhong and launched an assault on the Shu camp two days later. The camp was surrounded at all sides by screaming hordes, and Lord Meng was sure that he was already victorious. The wooden fences around the camp were smashed or burned by the warriors, but it was soon clear that there was no army within.

"…What the…?" Lord Meng wondered: he rode to the camp to inspect the scene for himself. Everything had been left: the warriors greedily helped themselves to whatever weapons or food they could carry.

"Perhaps they were forced to return home," someone suggested.

"Maybe," Lord Meng mused. "Or maybe they still have spies in my camp, and they found out about all of the new forces I've been gathering, realised that I'm stronger, and ran away. Either way, they're gone… we'll help ourselves!"

But as soon as the Nanzhong army was laden with stolen supplies, a din rang out: from all sides, Shu soldiers descended on the distracted warriors, forcing large groups to surrender due to their being unarmed and loaded down.

"**No… no, not again!**" Lord Meng screamed: he rallied those men that had not been caught, and organised them into a fighting unit to repel the Shu forces.

"**Ah, there you are!**" a familiar voice hailed: Lord Meng turned to see Kongming seated in a small, horseless carriage, wearing lilac robes and carrying, as always, his feather fan. All around the chancellor of Shu, elite soldiers brandished crossbows and gleaming swords.

"**I'll kill you, you little maggot!**" Lord Meng challenged as he rode forward to engage Kongming's protectors.

"**Our camp is on fire!**" a Nanzhong chieftain realised: many then retreated when they realised that Kongming had been attacking their camp while they were busy, and the smoke plumes were clearly visible in the distance.

"**You *vile*...!**" Lord Meng whined desperately: he broke off his attack, and retreated towards his camp.

"I thought we wanted to capture him again," Dong Jue said with confusion.

"I *have* captured him," Kongming replied. "He just doesn't know it yet."

Lord Meng was once again brought before Kongming, bound tightly, in Shu's temporary encampment.

"Attacking our camp...! ...Pits dug in the road...! **How is this the fair fight you promised me???**" Lord Meng complained as Kongming and his generals laughed uproariously.

"You attacked our camp first," Kongming scolded. "The deal was a battlefield confrontation, Lord Meng. Do not complain that I am reneging on our deal when you blatantly do the same."

"...Fine!" Lord Meng growled. "I'll meet you on the battlefield, then!"

"I suppose you'll want all of those men we captured back," Kongming sighed theatrically. "Very well... I'll even let you keep most of the things you stole. But bear in mind that had we wanted to kill your people, we need only have exploited their greed and stupidity."

"...What is it that you want returned...?" Lord Meng asked irritably.

"His Majesty's wine," Kongming pleaded. "I'd like you to find out who took it, please. That wine is a most excellent beverage... no offence, but it is wasted on the palates of barbarians, even landowners such as your good self."

"...I shall do as you ask," Lord Meng promised coldly.

"He only found half of the wine," Ma Su sighed as he sat in the command tent with Kongming that evening. "What a pity."

"*Yes*," Kongming sniggered. "What a pity."

"...Have you tricked him again...?" Ma Su chuckled.

"I know that I shouldn't," Kongming replied with mischief. "But he's dragged us out here, made us sick, and insulted our emperor... he won't get any decent wine."

"So... wait a minute... that wasn't imperial wine in those jars, then...?" Ma Su realised. "Wouldn't he notice that...?"

"That idiot wouldn't know imperial wine from swamp water," Kongming insisted. "And I suspect that he's busy enjoying it right now... expect another 'visit' from our friend in the morning."

"**AAAAGH! I HATE YOU!**" Lord Meng screamed as he rolled around in the dirt in front of the Shu camp the next morning, along with most of the senior Nanzhong tribal leaders.

"...Drinking drugged wine... shame on you," Kongming scolded playfully. "And we've caught *all of you*... not at all impressive."

"**You BASTARD!**" Lord Meng growled.

"I asked you to return it," Kongming reminded Lord Meng sternly. "How can you lay there insulting me when your disobedience is what brought about your downfall, and not be utterly ashamed...?"

The tribal leaders were obviously humiliated; their people were now swarming nearby, which unnerved most of the Shu army.

"Had I wanted to kill you all, you'd be dead," Kongming continued.

"You don't respect us enough to give us death: that's it, isn't it!" Lord Meng said with self-satisfied belligerence. "You said the imperial wine was too good for us 'barbarians'! You think we're not as good as you! Well **we're BETTER!**"

"You don't really appear that way right now," Kongming replied with a smile: Ma Su and Li Hui started to laugh uncontrollably at Kongming's dry tone. "...Forgive my generals, chieftains... they're nervous. If I did not respect the non-Han peoples, why would I have allied with the Qiang, and the Di, and the Wuling tribes in the past...? Ma Chao of the Qiang was a friend of mine... he was made one of Shu's Five Tiger Generals, furthermore, while his cousin is in the army, here in Nanzhong... while Wu – who you were so eager to pledge allegiance to – is currently exterminating the Wuling tribes, as they did the tribes of the far south when they consolidated Jiangdong... and as for Wei, well, what they did to the Ma family alone tells you what Cao Pi thinks. And besides... does a man with genuine pride in his identity really care what a bigot has to say...? Even if I had genuinely meant what I said... it should not have mattered to you."

The tribal leaders looked at each other with sudden understanding.

"I'm going to release you all," Kongming promised, "and Lord Meng... could you *please* just prepare for this grand battle this time...? No more tricks, no more lies, no more thieving... just bring your army...?"

"Our coalition army is over there, waiting to strike!" Lord Meng retorted boldly. "One word from me, and they will-"

"No," one of the tribal chieftains interrupted. "My people will not fight."

Other tribal leaders also expressed reluctance: Lord Meng screamed incoherently, which only made him look ridiculous.

"Untie these esteemed leaders of men... and Lord Meng," Kongming ordered: he then walked back into the camp, smiling and enjoying the curses coming from Lord Meng's lips.

Kongming and Ma Su sat in the command tent that night, enjoying a genuine jar of imperial wine.

"Four times, we've had this man tied up and captured, and four times we've let him go," Ma Su said apprehensively. "Future historians will question this tactic."

"Let them," Kongming replied with a laugh. "Future Nanzhong historians will even find sympathy with Lord Meng... but he's no hero worthy of praise. He's a fool, and he's making a mockery of them. Why such proud, dignified men as those other leaders were, take orders from Lord Meng... I will never truly understand. Or maybe I do... Yuan Shao commanded a lot of men, for the same reason I suppose... it's the money and the land, not the wits in his head."

"Uh... Chancellor," Dong Jue hailed quietly: Kongming and Ma Su turned to face him. "I have to report that... well... *Lord Meng...*"

"So *soon*...?" Kongming exclaimed.

"Oh, you cannot be serious...!" Ma Su chortled. "We only released him a few hours ago! How can this be...?"

"...**Traitors!**" Lord Meng raved as Kongming and Ma Su arrived at the gates once again: two of the tribal leaders had bound Lord Meng and returned him.

"He wanted to sneak up on you again," the tribal leader explained to a bemused Kongming. "We are leaving now... your kindness is repaid."

Kongming bowed respectfully, and the tribal leaders disappeared into the night, leaving Lord Meng writhing on the ground, hurling curses once again.

"I... I really despair," Kongming said as he looked down at his prisoner. "...I'll release you again... can you find your way back to your camp in the dark...?"

"**Kill me!**" Lord Meng replied angrily. "**Stop tormenting me, and KILL ME!**"

"...I've done nothing to you this time," Kongming retorted. "This is entirely your own fault, Lord Meng: someone, untie him and let him go... *again*. I won't count this capture, Lord Meng, since I didn't do anything... so we're still at four times."

"**I WILL RIP OUT YOUR THROAT!**" Lord Meng screamed as Kongming and Ma Su walked away. "**I'LL DANCE ON YOUR SKULL!**"

"...That's really kind of you, not counting this," Ma Su suggested.

"All he has to do is engage us on the battlefield, like he did when we arrived," Kongming despaired. "Is that so difficult...? Why does he try and intrigue...? ...To impress us...?"

"Perhaps he'll give up now, and fight us properly," Ma Su said hopefully.

"I really wish he would," Kongming said with a cough. The harsh climate was starting to take its toll.


✳✳✳✳✳✳✳✳✳✳✳✳

## 104

Word reached the Shu camp that the Nanzhong forces were finally readying themselves for the 'final battle' that would decide the fate of the region. Ma Su hurried to the command tent with the news, and found Kongming attempting to survey a map: a violent coughing fit had interrupted him, and he was now doubled over in pain, holding a cloth over his mouth.

"...Kongming...?" Ma Su hailed timidly.

Kongming looked up and tried to smile. "It's nothing, honestly," he insisted as he tucked the blood-specked cloth into his sleeve and clumsily reached for his feather fan.

"It doesn't look like nothing," Ma Su said as he walked to the map. "But I know there's no point... I'm here to tell you that-"

"They're about to march," Kongming interrupted. "I know. I have sources beyond even the ones you know about. Sadly, we're about to be deceived again."

"...How bad...?" Ma Su wondered.

Kongming laughed weakly, replying, "I'll say this... it's inventive."

"What do we say to the troops...?" Ma Su asked plainly.

"Nothing," Kongming replied. "I've got a little something prepared for our friend Lord Meng and his new reinforcements: but it's best we don't alert the soldiers, in case he gets word from a spy that we're onto him. Just leave it to me."

"...Okay," Ma Su said nervously. "I'll look forward to the fun."

"It'll certainly be entertaining," Kongming said with a smile.

Lord Meng's forces arrived at the battlefield, taking a position in front of a long hill. The Shu forces arrived and arrayed themselves neatly, as Kongming sat and observed from his new carriage; his generals surrounded him.

"So why do we suddenly need to wheel you around...?" Li Hui asked at last.

"I'm not feeling so healthy," Kongming admitted. "But... well... a thought occurs to me. A man of forced habit can be made predictable, but a man of intentional habit can become *un*predictable. Let everyone become accustomed to me being in this chariot seat... the motif will benefit us later."

"...Cryptic as ever," Li Hui chuckled. "Don't the enemy look terribly fierce...?"

"Chaff," Ma Zhong scoffed. "We'll defeat them easily, won't we, Regent Zhuge?"

Kongming started to fan himself as he replied, "Men are men."

Ma Zhong and Li Hui stared at each other with bemusement.

"Have the special objects been brought as I requested...?" Kongming continued.

"Of course," Dong Jue said. "Orders are orders... but *what are they*...?"

Li Hui, Ma Zhong and Zhang Boqi turned to look at the two-dozen strange devices: the cart-sized objects were about the height of a man, and were kept hidden under cloth sheets.

"...A way out of a difficult problem," Kongming replied casually as he craned his neck to observe Lord Meng. "It seems the lord of buffoons is about to challenge us... be prepared for anything."

"Anything...?" Zhang Boqi noted cautiously. "Like... *what*...?"
An almighty roar – unlike anything most of the men of Shu had ever heard – rang out across the plains. The Shu forces suddenly fell silent. Men looked about them, struggling with their fear and looking to see if anyone else knew what the noise was; the Shu forces started to become disorganised as some men broke their formations in preparation for a sudden retreat.
"The men are panicking," Ma Su noted.
"Why shouldn't they...?" Kongming replied.
Lord Meng screamed wildly and gesticulated; from behind the hill, six elephants – clad in simple armour, and ridden by Nanzhong warriors – charged toward the terrified Shu army.
"**WHAT THE HELL ARE THEY???**" Ma Zhong exclaimed; his words were echoed or paraphrased across the entire Shu army. Many men of central China had not seen these giant beasts before, and the desired effect was achieved as hundreds of men deserted their positions and fled for their lives.
"*Elephants*...?" Ma Su murmured.
"I told you it was inventive," Kongming snickered as two men found the courage to ignore their own wellbeing and start pulling his carriage away from the front line. Lord Meng was now waving a coloured flag: from the left side of his army, several Nanzhong warriors started to steer a herd of cattle toward the Shu troops.
"**We'll be trampled!**" Li Hui said as he watched the stampede: it was almost enough to take the focus away from the approaching elephants.
Wooden cages were now being brought to Lord Meng's front line: inside them were large tigers.
"Oh, the... he cannot be serious," Ma Su chuckled nervously as the little remaining courage he had left him completely.
A row of shield-and-spearmen formed a line behind the cages to protect the Nanzhong forces as the cages were opened; the tigers bolted forward, ignoring the Nan warriors, and headed toward the disintegrating Shu army.
"We...!" Ma Su exclaimed: Kongming silenced him with a gesture from his fan.
"...Stay here, Ma Su," Kongming said calmly. He raised a flag with his free hand, and a small group of specially trained soldiers led by Ma Dai pulled the cloths away from the strange devices, revealing them to be machines of some sort. A second flag gesture ordered the machine operators to activate them: from metal nozzles aimed toward the enemy, bursts of fire shot out of the devices, startling the animals and causing most of them to scatter or retreat toward the Nanzhong forces. The tigers fled in all directions, the cattle herd trampled their own keepers, and the elephants threw their riders and ran around in fear.
"...Nice try, Lord Meng," Kongming said as the simple flamethrowers turned the tide of the battle instantaneously, subjecting the Nanzhong army to their own traps. Lord Meng's coalition army now disintegrated under the pressure and retreated.
"...That was incredible," Liao Hua declared as he watched their humiliated enemies flee, pursued by Zhang Boqi and his cavalry.

"Not really… just two men playing silly games," Kongming suggested as he fanned himself casually. "As soon as their assembled forces of nature have gone their separate ways, we'll pursue and capture Lord Meng, and bring this sorry matter to an end."

Kongming's main army pursued the Nanzhong forces an hour later, meeting them in battle on a patch of level terrain. The Shu army were better equipped and less fatigued, so the outcome was almost foregone; the Nanzhong forces were forced into another retreat, with many men surrendering to the lenient Shu generals to preserve their lives. When it became clear that Lord Meng was nowhere to be found, Kongming found several Nanzhong people that could speak Chinese, he had them brought back to the Shu camp with his army.

"…*The coward*," Kongming grumbled as he looked at a map of the shires. The Nanzhong men had told him that Lord Meng had fled deep into the jungle with a small group of loyal retainers and mercenaries.

"Our army has a history of flight from the enemy after ignominious defeats," Ma Su suggested. "Why are you so critical of him…?"

"…You're right, of course," Kongming admitted. "I just wanted the fool to surrender… running means he plans to go on fighting. We'll have to wear down his will to fight, or we'll never get this region stabilised."

"But we've placated many of the tribal chieftains," Ma Su protested. "Our fair treatment of the captured and surrendered men, our conduct while marching… what can this man, Lord Meng, do now…?"

"A lot," Kongming retorted bluntly. "…We'll have to go into the jungle."

"Unwise," Ma Su challenged. "We're low on medicines, and the things in those jungles… we know little about them."

"We'll find men that *do* know," Kongming said hoarsely: he took his cloth kerchief from his sleeve and coughed into it violently.

"You're not going," Ma Su supposed. "…*Surely*…?"

"…I have no choice," Kongming replied with difficulty. "He needs to be made to feel that we can get him wherever he hides… or he'll never stop running. If… if we break that one man's spirit… we stop most of the trouble. Then we can explain the admin… administration… that will be put in place, and go home. Now… go and rest. We… have to start early tomorrow."

Kongming started coughing again, and even more violently.

Stifling the urge to say or do something to challenge Kongming, Ma Su said, "Very well," and left the tent.

Lord Meng, meanwhile, had reached the jungle fortress of a tribal ally, and was enjoying a large banquet in honour of his bravery in contesting the will of the Shu Han court. The wealthy landowner grinned unintelligently as beautiful dancing girls writhed around him, and jar upon jar of wine was passed along the line of local nobles and chieftains.

"I… I haven't lost, you know," Lord Meng said to a chieftain sat to his left. "That Zhuge Liang… he thinks we're peasants… no, he think we're worse than peasants… he thinks… he thinks we're heathens, barbarians, that we're scum, and that we should be exterminated!"
Some of the leaders mumbled agreeably.
"I won't stop until we're rid of the Shu occupiers!" Lord Meng declared. "I will raise another army, and I will kill that Zhuge Liang!"
"What if he comes for us…?" another landowner asked.
"…He is already sick just from being in Nanzhong!" Lord Meng cackled. "How can that weak little pedant, that scribe that has never e-even picked up a sword, that worthless little man… how can he survive in the jungle? He'll die from the first insect bite! He'll run if a mouse looks at him!"
Some of the leaders laughed at the notion.
"He'll stay out there, where it's safe… but I'll get him," Lord Meng promised. "I will make our land ours again… we don't need deals with Wu… we can do this alone, we will win and get rid of those invaders!"
Many cheered drunkenly, and ordered more meat and wine to be passed to Lord Meng in celebration of his courageous rhetoric. The festivities continued until every leader present was too inebriated to remain conscious.

"Wha… what the…?" Lord Meng exclaimed as he awoke: he realised that he was bound tightly with rope, and instinctively started to struggle.
"…Did you think I would let you hide out here among the trees…?" Kongming asked with a heckling tone: Lord Meng's vision cleared enough to see the Shu Han chancellor staring down at him with a calm smile.
"**YOU DOG!**" Lord Meng screamed: Kongming stepped back slightly, and started to fan himself. "**I WILL-**"
"You'll *what*, Lord Meng…?" Kongming challenged. "Look around you… this isn't your friend's lair, this is my jungle encampment. You're alone."
"I was drunk!" Lord Meng retorted.
"So you were," Kongming chuckled softly. "You do make it very easy to catch you, you know. …Surely you know the story of Chunyu Qiong, the keeper of Yuan Shao's depot at Wuchao…? Getting drunk was his downfall, too… furthermore, he cost his master Yuan Shao an important victory against Cao Cao… perhaps that one drunken fool is the reason the Wei Empire now rules the north so cruelly. Does it not occur to you that your own lack of control could cost your entire people their autonomy in Nanzhong, Lord Meng…?"
"So you admit that you are here as a conqueror!" Lord Meng said with triumph in his voice. "I will not stop until you are defeated and chased from here, so you might as well kill me!"
"…Do you have any idea how stupid that little speech was…?" Kongming replied with despair. "You are one of the biggest idiots that I have ever met. Did you win your land in a game of some sort, or inherit it from a better man…? …Surely you can't have earned it…?"

"**You scrawny little court scribe!**" Lord Meng bellowed. "**I hate you!**"

"So you've said at least once or twice," Kongming said wearily. "Will you please just stop this futile attempt at insurrection...? I vow to you that I will give your people the autonomy you want, and-"

"**LIES!**" Lord Meng raged. "**Lies, and deceit! You men of the Han, you've always wanted to control us, you want us as your barbarian slaves!**"

"...Which is why you're a wealthy landowner," Kongming sighed. "...Very well, Lord Meng... go ahead... run. But I'll find you and capture you again. Sooner or later, you will have to accept that we will not allow a faithless wild animal to be at our back door, not when there are pressing matters to attend to."

Kongming gestured with his fan, and two soldiers untied Lord Meng.

"...Go on," Kongming said coldly. "Get out."

"...**I hate you!**" Lord Meng growled; Zhang Boqi and Ma Dai stood in front of Kongming with their swords drawn, and made fearless eye contact with the Nanzhong lord.

"...*Out*," Kongming said again; Lord Meng turned and strode silently out of the Shu camp with undiminished defiance.

"So now what...?" Ma Su asked.

"We capture him again," Kongming replied. "As soon as he is on safe territory... but he will not get drunk this time, so we will have to wait for an opportunity."


When Lord Meng returned to his ally's lair, he found Shu soldiers openly marching about, or fraternising with the Nanzhong people. To his frustration, many of the chieftains were no longer willing to take his stance, so he retreated into an even deeper recess of the jungle with a small retinue, where a small tribe granted him food and shelter. Lord Meng refused to touch alcohol, and had all food and drink tested by members of his entourage before he would go near it, such was the fear that he might be captured once again. He slept only when fatigue overwhelmed him, and had regular sorties carried out to check for possible pursuers.

"...Zhuge Liang... bloody Zhuge Liang!" Lord Meng ranted as he sat in his meagre guest tent one evening. He had despatched messengers to nearby chieftains in the hope of mustering an army of some sort, but there were no subscribers to the increasingly implausible idea.

"My lord, you have to rest," one of Lord Meng's guards said.

"I can't rest now!" Lord Meng replied angrily. "What about Zhuge Liang? ...Unless... unless you *want* me to rest... **so you can take me to Zhuge Liang!**"

Lord Meng took up his sword, and advanced toward his guard.

"My lord, I...!" the guard protested: but before Lord Meng could deal the killing strike, a sudden din was heard outside the tent.

"...Zhuge Liang!" Lord Meng supposed as he pushed the guard aside and left the tent to follow the noise. Many of the villagers and most of Lord Meng's retinue were gathered around a hoisted flag near the entrance to the settlement: it was a Shu Han flag. Fear overcame Lord Meng: he frantically urged his followers to gather their belongings and retreat.

Lord Meng's small group left the village and started into another part of the jungle.

"...**Please, wait!**" a voice called from the side of the road: Lord Meng refused to stop his retreat, and marched straight past the two Nanzhong villagers.

"...A trap, for sure," Lord Meng grumbled.

"**Wait, stop!**" three more villagers pleaded as he advanced even further down the uneven jungle path: Lord Meng shoved them aside roughly.

"Perhaps they're real villagers," one guard suggested as they were forced to evade another small group of villagers.

"They're men put here by Zhuge Liang!" Lord Meng retorted.

"...Two of them were women," another guard noted. "One was a boy."

"**Don't question me!**" Lord Meng shouted. But as he continued to walk, the ground suddenly gave way under him, and he, along with three of his retinue, fell into a pit.

"You really should trust the people you claim to represent a little more," Kongming teased as he walked to the edge of the pit, his fan in hand; Ma Su and Li Hui stood either side of him, while Zhang Boqi and Ma Zhong led a group of soldiers to surround the remainder of Lord Meng's retinue. "We must have allowed at least a dozen people to escape the village and warn you."

"**Wicked dog...! I WILL EAT YOUR FLESH!**" Lord Meng screeched as he floundered in the muddy pit.

"A very brave man I knew used to say that," Kongming replied, "and I can only hope that you will one day gain some sense, as he did... though sadly too late."

"**KILL ME!**" Lord Meng shouted. "**KILL ME, KILL ME, KILL ME!**"

"...No," Kongming insisted. "I have captured you six times now, Lord Meng... I will capture you a hundred times more if I have to, until you surrender... but I will not kill you. That isn't why I'm here."

"**You killed Gaoding! You killed Yong Kai!**" Lord Meng challenged.

"Both died of their own stupidity, not by my hand," Kongming replied casually. "I beg you, Lord Meng, see the error of your ways and end this silly farce."

"**NEVER!**" Lord Meng screamed. "**KILL ME!**"

"...Let's go," Kongming sighed sadly. "He has enough friends to get him out of there... we'll continue this conversation next time, Lord Meng."

"**NO!**" Lord Meng yelled as Kongming moved out of view. "**COME BACK! KILL ME! DON'T HUMILIATE ME LIKE THIS! KILL ME!**"

"Lord Meng...?" a voice called from the edge of the pit: it was one of the guards.

"...**Where is Zhuge Liang???**" Lord Meng asked desperately.

"He has retreated," the guard explained. "We'll get you out."

"No!" Lord Meng whined childishly. "Leave me here... help these men, but... leave me here! I want to stay here!"

"...We'll get you out," the guard insisted.

"… … …He's pursuing me deep into the jungle, getting to my possible allies before I can," Lord Meng said numbly as his small group prepared to move again. "If I change my plan, and head back toward the plains, I… no, that… that won't work."

The men that surrounded Lord Meng exchanged weary glances.

"There's a village near here that… … …no, that won't work," Lord Meng continued. "I can't outwit him. He's got the gods on his side… I can't win. All I can do is hide… go far away… but *where*…?"

The men were silent.

"We could go home," Lord Meng suggested with pride. "We could disguise ourselves as merchants and go home… he'd never expect us to do that."

The men remained awkwardly silent.

"We'll get new clothes, and we'll go home," Lord Meng decided. "He'll not look for me there… we'll divide ourselves, and we'll go by different routes… we'll abandon our arms… get some goods to carry… yes! That will work!"

Filled with self-satisfaction at his latest scheme, Lord Meng prepared for an arduous journey to his own land.


"We've done it!" Lord Meng said with glee to his two remaining followers as his lands came into sight. "The men of Shu missed us completely… we passed right under his nose! I'll hide here, and then, when he tires of searching for me, he'll go back home… and *then*…!"

Lord Meng passed his farmhands and servants with ignorance and obliviousness as he strode toward his home: but as he reached his door and opened it, a horrible sight greeted him. Kongming was sat inside his home, and all around him, Shu officers and soldiers were appearing and surrounding him.

"No… *no*… **HOW???**" Lord Meng asked desperately. "They said… they said you were in…!"

"One fan-carrying middle-aged man in robes looks much the same as another from a distance," Kongming chuckled casually as he got up from Lord Meng's seat and walked toward him slowly. "I had some decoys placed while I began the journey here… I knew that you'd come home after that last defeat. I placed people here some time ago Lord Meng… and I have eyes and ears everywhere… so you were never really going to evade me forever."

"…Just kill me," Lord Meng pleaded miserably. "You're guided by Heaven's will… I'll never be able to win. I give up… I surrender… kill me, Zhuge Liang, you've got what you wanted now."

"Yes I have," Kongming said as Lord Meng fell to one knee in penitence. "And yet, no I haven't… I only wished to secure our border so that we could safely face the state of Wei. I never wanted a fight… I am glad the fighting is over."

"So now we will be ruled by you," Lord Meng supposed.

"No," Kongming replied, to the surprise of the majority of the Shu men present: only Ma Su and Li Hui smiled knowingly. "I already told you, I desire security, nothing more. I shall leave representatives – ambassadors, if you will – for your people to liaise with, but that's all. You shall govern yourselves… you're not children, and should be trusted to know what is best for yourselves."

Lord Meng looked up at Kongming with surprise: Kongming now offered his hand to help Lord Meng to his feet.

"We will arrange a parley with all of the chieftains and nobles of Nanzhong," Kongming declared. "We two shall explain to one and all what the future will be like... a fair future, where we are all masters of our own fates."

Before he had even got to his feet again, Lord Meng collapsed to the floor and wept with shame, saying, "Men have died, people have suffered... I am to blame! Why did it take seven humiliations to make me see sense???"

"You're stubborn," Kongming replied with a hoarse laugh. "I've met worse."

Kongming started to cough uncomfortably: the Shu officers glared at Lord Meng silently, collectively blaming the landowner for their regent's poor health.

"I am irredeemable," Lord Meng murmured.

"I doubt that," Kongming said weakly. "Just try and avoid making any more trouble... *please.*"

Kongming led a victory ceremony and peace conference at Dian Lake, where he gave his proclamation on self-rule. The weather had taken a turn for the worse, and some blamed angry gods; to appease the superstitious that demanded human sacrifice, Kongming had meat buns – each of them moulded into the shape of a human head – cast into the waters as substitutes. The weather did eventually clear, and the sacrifice was considered acceptable. Once all parties were satisfied, the majority of the Shu forces began the journey home.

"Li Hui will be the face of the figurehead Shu presence in Nanzhong, and act as peacekeeper when dissent breaks out again... which it inevitably will," Kongming sighed as he rode in a carriage with Ma Su along the dirt roads. "Wang Kang and Lü Kai should remain in Nanzhong since they know the people well."

"Ma Zhong isn't the only one that questions this strategy," Ma Su suggested. "You will have to explain to the court when we return."

"I know," Kongming said calmly. "But they can be made to understand... the deal that I have struck is one that will make us as powerful as we were before the Battle of Xiaoting... ready to face Wei, at long last. ...And not before time... although we do not need to worry about our ties with Wu anymore, they would not appreciate us failing to meet our side of the bargain and not harassing the Hanzhong border."

"They riled up the Nan people," Ma Su reminded Kongming irritably. "So it's all their own fault, if they do dare complain."

"They won't," Kongming chuckled softly. "...Ah, Youchang... I have missed my wife and family. I'm sure you miss yours. It will be nice to be home again... even if it's just for a while..."

Kongming started to cough violently, and covered his mouth with his blood-stained kerchief: Ma Su remained painfully silent.

✳✳✳✳✳✳✳✳✳✳✳✳

## 105

The Nanzhong Campaign was over, and the Shu army returned home, further emboldened by another piece of welcome news: Cao Pi, the First Emperor of Cao Wei, was dying, if not already dead. It was a near-idolised Kongming that entered the Shu Han court, greeted by a grateful Second Emperor Liu Shan and the host of friends that he had at court.

"A magnificent victory," Court Administrator Dong Yun praised.

"We should have no more trouble now," the elder statesman Yang Hong said surely.

"Is it so...?" Qin Mi asked hoarsely. "What about the reports that you have left next to no forces in Nanzhong to act as administrators...?"

"Mister Qin," Kongming replied confidently, "I might have followed that time-honoured tradition, were there not three matters that needed addressing."

"What are these three matters, Mister Zhuge...?" the Shu Emperor Liu Shan asked curiously.

"Your Majesty," Kongming explained, "dealing with our friends in Nanzhong was never going to be easy. They are hot-tempered, cynical, rustic people... so a firm but fair hand is needed. But once they were made to see that we are not their enemy – as Wu's officials and some tribal leaders had led them to believe – maintaining stability was our next priority. If I had left many of our officials there as a government, then I would have had to leave a massive contingent of soldiers. That has many problems attached to it, but the most glaring one is access... the establishment of a supply and communications route for such large demands and in such treacherous conditions is unthinkable.

"So perhaps I could leave a small retinue...? Well, that brings us to the second point. There are the feelings of the people of that region to consider: even though we were restrained, men died nonetheless, and the people will be angry and bitter. If any administrators – foreign overseers, in simple terms – were placed without adequate military protection, personal retribution will certainly be sought by individuals, due to perceived weakness of our position.

"Of course, that may never happen, but suppose we ignore point one, and adhere to point two... that brings us to my third concern. This sorry matter began when the Nan people trusted Eastern Wu's slanders and Lord Meng's seditious rhetoric, and losses were incurred on our side as well as theirs. How could they not fear reprisals for what we may see as their wrongdoings against us...? It is certain that at least one misunderstanding would result, and we cannot afford that.

"So, I left only representatives, with the understanding that peace would be kept by way of regular tributes to this court by their wealthiest nobles, which they can feel is compensation for our expenditure. Those tributes – metals, materials, foods, and other precious things – will ensure that we are quickly recovered from our previous setbacks, and ready to face Wei... who will now be facing the prospect of losing their charismatic 'emperor', Cao Pi, and being left with a shadow of a man in his stead."

The court was filled with murmurs of enthusiasm and agreement: Liu Shan clapped his hands together and said, "Splendid! Simply splendid! You are almost magical, Mister Zhuge! Your deeds have made us strong again!"

"We were never weak," Kongming replied sternly. "...Merely softened a little."

"Your exploits must be rewarded, Regent Zhuge," Dong He suggested. "You should be made a duke, perhaps."

"No, no, no!" Kongming insisted. "Such things invite suspicion... I am happy in my role as Co-Regent."

"But Co-Regent Li Yan will be distracted by events in Nanzhong," Dong Yun said with strange emphasis. "Perhaps you should consider a slight reorganisation of the court to reflect the new situation."

Kongming started to fan himself slowly, and nodded to indicate that he understood Dong Yun's true intention.

"Yes, yes... I shall abide by whatever you decide, Mister Zhuge," Liu Shan said mechanically. "I rely on you in all things, like a father."

"...Very good, Your Majesty," Kongming replied. "Now, if I might be excused..."

"...Husband...!" Yueying exclaimed as Kongming entered his home: Zhuge Qiao, his adopted son, greeted him with a low bow.

"It is good to see you both," Kongming said as he took his seat as head of the household. "...Sorry for not returning sooner, but I had to report to the court."

"I expected as much," Yueying replied with a warm smile.

"Those fire throwers did come in handy," Kongming said with cheer. "They were worth the time we spent designing them."

"I should like to hear all about your exploits, Father," Zhuge Qiao pleaded.

"...Later, maybe, son," Kongming sighed wearily. "First... I'd like to play my qin awhile... I need to find calm." Turning to Yueying, Kongming added, "Will you join me, my dear...?"

"Gladly," Yueying replied. As servants rushed to fetch refreshments at Zhuge Qiao's silent command, Kongming and Yueying began to play their instruments in perfect harmony, filling the room with tranquil, peaceful sounds. The two exchanged loving glances, but the moment was spoiled when a painful coughing fit overcame Kongming, causing him to break a string on his qin. He reached into his sleeve and pulled out the – now very bloody – kerchief to cover his mouth: both Yueying and Qiao were overcome with horror and distress.

"...It's nothing," Kongming insisted.

Yueying touched Kongming's arm gently: she fought back tears, and smiled feebly.

"All I need... is rest," Kongming said surely. "...And maybe some more medicine: that place was so very, very harsh."

"I'll ensure we are stocked, Father," Qiao promised. "Your health is all that matters to us all."

Kongming noticed that many among his household staff were also watching him with concern from the kitchen doorway; he hung his head, and murmured, "To be surrounded by such good, kind people... I'm truly blessed."

The next day, Kongming ignored his family's pleas to rest and went to work at his Chancellery office. As the day wore on, he was visited by Court Administrator Dong Yun.

"...Come to explain your pointed comment yesterday, my friend...?" Kongming chuckled as the two men exchanged respectful bows.

Dong Yun eyed Kongming's senior staff – Ma Su, Dong Jue and Zong Yu – as he replied quietly, "*Li Yan* is no friend."

"They are trusted men, speak freely," Kongming insisted.

"I meant that Ma Su should also understand this point," Dong Yun continued. "Li Yan is ungrateful, Kongming, for the great rewards heaped on him for what was really rather meagre service... overseeing the building of a tunnel does not qualify a man as a regent, yet he openly chastises you for 'not treating him as an equal, as he deserves'."

"How dare he!" Zong Yu seethed.

"...In what *specific* way, Dong Xiuzhao, does he 'openly chastise me'...?" Kongming asked.

"He has referred to your 'absolute governance' over the Emperor at least twice," Dong Yun said sadly, "and suggests that his position in Nanzhong is a death sentence, designed to grant you full office, 'dukedom in all but name'."

"...Chancellor," Zong Yu protested, "he can't be allowed to speak this way."

"Li Yan has always been outspoken and quick to complain," Kongming mused, "but this is outright accusation... of my intent to be another Wang Mang, another Cao Cao... but *why*...? *Why*, when I have never left him out of any decisions, and treated him as my equal, as First Emperor requested...? Why does he...?"

"Do not waste time thinking it over, the man is irrational," Dong Yun interrupted coldly. "Whatever merits he has are outweighed by a jealous, self-serving heart. He must be demoted, as must a number of other court officials... and you will regret it if you do not do it *now*."

Kongming was uncomfortably silent.

"There are ways to do it without incurring suspicion of your motives," Dong Yun suggested. "But please, Kongming... don't ignore obvious threats."

"I agree," Ma Su said seriously. "The court needs restructuring anyway... do it now, side-line your opponents, so that we're ready for the Northern Campaign."

"...*Northern Campaign*...?" Dong Yun prompted. "Kongming, you're sick... how can you lead a march northward against Cao Pi in your condition...?"

"Cao Pi is almost spent," Kongming replied. "And all things point to his successor being his eldest, Cao Rui... we've as good as won when that happens."

Dong Yun noticed a familiar official loitering nearby, and said with surprise, "Is that *Fei Shi*...? What's *he* doing here?"

"Ah," Kongming replied, "well Fei Gongju was of immense help in tracking down 'Meng the Easily Caught' on our last campaign, so-"

"He opposed the imperial succession," Dong Yun noted cautiously. "He was jailed for it. I liked and respected the man before that, yes, but he opposed a sound move… I was surprised enough to hear he was released, but glad to hear he was banished to Nanzhong, and that's where he should have stayed."

"A callous observation," Kongming insisted. "He served well on the Southern Campaign, he opposed First Emperor's succession out of loyalty to the Han throne, and he is an honest man of merit. He is no Li Yan."

"…As long as you know what you're doing," Dong Yun sighed. "Heed what I said, Kongming: time is of the essence. …Farewell for now."

Dong Yun bowed respectfully and departed: as soon as he was gone, Fei Shi approached and said, "He objects to my being here."

"Don't be worried about it," Kongming insisted. "…I suppose you're about to make an objection of your own."

"This idea of yours about maintaining relations with Meng Da," Fei Shi complained bitterly. "This man betrayed the hero Guan Yunchang, who I met and can never forget! He fled to Wei! He led the young lord Liu Feng to his own downfall! How can you put ink to paper for such a vicious traitor, Regent Zhuge…?"

"…*Meng Da*…?" Ma Su prompted uneasily. "Since when have you-"

"You're all crowding me," Kongming joked calmly as he started to fan himself. "I know what I'm doing… he will be an invaluable asset for our next excursion."

"How so…?" Fei Shi whined. "He is untrustworthy! Remember that this man betrayed my former lord to First Emperor, and then First Emperor to Cao Pi!"

"He's based in Xin City in Fangling," Kongming explained calmly. "I sent a man wandering that way that knew him, on the pretext of a friendly, non-formal visit… and ensured that General Meng was made aware that his family was spared death on my instruction. As I'd hoped, he was relieved by that decision, and said that I 'had priority on what was present and what was future', and that I 'should not be in too much of a hurry in disposing of his clan'. He fears the future under the less accommodating, less trusting Cao Rui, and intends to defect back to us."

"We can't trust him," Fei Shi said desperately. "I knew him! Regent Zhuge, do not trust him! Please, I beg of you!"

"Stop it," Kongming said dismissively. "I've made up my mind, and I have already started writing to him. He holds Fangling, which we need to retake Shangyong and pincer Fan City with Wu. If he's going to help… we should accept his help. I hate him for his treachery too, but we should be sensible, and deal with that *after* he's been of service to us."

"*Ayah*," Fei Shi exclaimed. "He's arrogant… he's stupid… he'll be your undoing!"

Fei Shi then walked away, shaking his head; Ma Su turned to Kongming and said, "I have to agree. My brother had dealings with the man, and-"

"This is a larger story, Ma Youchang, much larger than the one you are choosing to see," Kongming interrupted. "Sima Yi must be feared as much as, if not more than, Cao Pi or his successor. Sima Yi is currently engaging Wu, since they now hold Jing, and are – regrettably – the larger threat. Lu Xun will keep him busy, but with the defection of Meng Da, right next to Fan City, we regain some of our lost footing, and we pile pressure on Sima Yi! *And*, with Shangyong and Fangling back in our hands, both Shu and Wu can pincer Wei, and finally rout them as *equals*!"
"...If you say so," Ma Su said numbly.

Cao Pi died as he had been expected to, leaving The Empire of Cao Wei in the hands of his son Cao Rui: for Kongming and other careful observers, this was the chance they had been waiting for.
"Mere months have passed, and Cao Rui has already started to upset his people, exactly as expected," Kongming said to Yueying with obvious glee.
"He was the son of poor Lady Zhen," Yueying recalled as she strummed the strings of her qin thoughtfully. "I understand she died very miserably... is that so...?"
"An unfortunate end for a beautiful woman... worse than the fate of Gongjin's widow by far," Kongming sighed as he sipped from a cup containing a hot medicinal brew. "Cao Pi stole her from Yuan Shao's eldest son while he might have still lived, dragging the woman into a loveless union... and then forced her to commit suicide for complaining of being cast aside... many at court suspected Cao Rui to be the son of Yuan, not Cao Pi, which further harmed the boy."
"He must be very badly damaged," Yueying supposed.
"...To the last, the courtiers mocked Rui as 'Son of Yuan'... I suspect a few previously grinning heads rolled when *he* took power," Kongming said with amusement as he set the cup of medicine down. "I heard that he killed his foster mother once he found out about her role in his mother's death... but no lover of women is he. Lust for them, yes, he certainly has plenty of that... but not love. And he trusts nobody... except maybe Cao Zhen, and Sima Yi. How long *they'll* be trustworthy, however, is another matter... depending on how far he takes his new harem edict."
"...Harem edict...?" Yueying prompted as she stopped playing.
"Mm," Kongming replied as he took up his fan and started to wave it back and forth slowly. "Thanks to the fawning, treacherous pedant Wang Lang, he's intent on building the largest collection of women ever seen, for his own personal consumption of course; and, furthermore, he covets other men's wives and concubines for his collection... which was also Dong Zhuo's little vice."
"Is he mad...?" Yueying wondered.
"Undoubtedly," Kongming said thoughtfully. "He's apparently very ostentatious, self-indulgent, but very clever, devious, and militarily gifted... the last part worries me, but if he's going to start taking his vassals' pretty wives from them, and spending all the money, he'll not be a serious threat... defections may well be plentiful. I know of at least one already... after a less than desirable encounter with Cao Rui's representatives, Meng Da has now expressed his desire to return to Shu, and will assist us in our campaign with a revolt in Fangling."

"...So you intend to petition the Emperor for a march northward,"
Yueying said hesitantly. "Husband, you have been back from
Nanzhong less than a year! Your health is still poor, and... and...!"
Yueying lowered her head miserably.
"...And *what*...?" Kongming prompted.
"And... I... I'm not sure, but..." Yueying continued awkwardly.
"...But... I think... the signs... are that... I... might..."
Yueying touched her stomach, and gazed into Kongming's eyes;
the fan fell from his hand as he contemplated what seemed to be
impossible.

************

## 106

Kongming's mood was strange as he composed the edict to his emperor, Liu Shan, that would announce his intention to march northward against Cao Wei for the first time. Ma Su noted his mentor's demeanour – which seemed oddly tranquil and bereft of its usual weariness – but was, initially, too scared to ask why.

"…How goes it…?" Ma Su asked one day as Kongming read and reread his draft edict, humming thoughtfully and frowning occasionally.

"…Don't know," Kongming replied airily. "I'm almost there, I think… I have to remember that I'm going against the entire court with this idea."

"You really think the whole court is against it…?" Ma Su mused. "But… well, now that you're Chancellor-Regent, can they really oppose you…? Qin Mi's dead, Li Yan's busy at the Nanzhong border, and a lot of the troublemakers are silenced…"

"War is expensive," Kongming said sternly. "If it wasn't my idea, *I'd* be against it. Our army is back to full strength now, what with the supplies and regiments from Nanzhong, and natural law and time… we can easily move a hundred-thousand men north now, and even though Wei have also grown, their army is divided, with much of it in the east fighting Wu. Plus we have Meng Da, ready and waiting… it's now, or never, Ma Youchang, and I say we do it. But others will say we are tempting disaster… that we should focus on defence, now we have only an elderly Zhao Zilong and middle-aged Wei Yan for champions. But the state of Wei only has an old Zhang He, a fat Cao Zhen, a lecherous, unpopular emperor, and Sima Yi: Sima, who is the only one I fear, is busy, and will soon be routed by a surprise attack from Meng Da. Victory is almost upon us… we just have to be brave. This document will, I hope, reassure the court that I have everything planned."

The officials of the once-again reorganised Shu court gathered to await the words of the Chancellor, Prime Minister and Regent, Zhuge Liang, styled Kongming. Ma Su was stood with an influential group of loyal friends to Kongming, hand-picked for loyalty, devotion and trustworthiness in all things. Among them were faces old and new, including Imperial Secretariat Yang Yi, Jiang Wan, Dong He, Dong Yun, Zhang Junsi, Chen Zhen, Yi Ji, Fei Shi, Zong Yu, and Guo Youzhi: Tiger General Zhao Yun, Administrator of Hanzhong Wei Yan, Li Yan, Chen Shi, Liao Hua and many others had been recalled to the capital to hear Kongming's edict, since it was of such national importance.

"**The Emperor enters,**" Dong Yun proclaimed: one and all kowtowed as the overweight, unenthusiastic Second Emperor, Liu Shan, shuffled into the hall in his ceremonial robes, flanked as ever by beautiful serving girls and fawning eunuchs.

"Please, please, rise, all of you," Liu Shan ordered meekly. "I understand that I am to be read an edict by the Prime Minister."

"**The Prime Minister,**" Dong Yun boomed: Kongming stepped forward, bowed humbly, and unfurled his document.

"I, Zhuge Liang, Prime Minister of Shu Han, now make a statement to the Second Emperor and to the court," Kongming began. "We are once again prosperous, but these are dangerous times. Even the wolf Cao Cao and his equally dangerous son, Cao Pi, are no longer a threat to us, the north still has a mighty army and threatens our border at every opportunity, hoping to end their conquest of the land that began with the erosion and destruction of your esteemed ancestor, the Last Emperor of the Former Han. Even if it were not the case that they opposed us now, that crime of usurpation still goes unpunished, and I promised your father, the illustrious First Emperor, that I would complete this great task before I perished.

"Your father built here, in Yi Province and Western Hanzhong, a mighty kingdom that is prosperous and fair... but his work is far from done. We once had southern Jing, and were the equal of Wu... now, we are the smallest of the three, and there is always the risk that we might be enveloped by our rivals. We must not lose hope, however: though the smallest we are, we are the strongest and bravest at heart, with the wisest officials and the most valiant generals, and every man works to ensure that we will one day rescue the northern heartland and restore unity.

"However, each man must do this for a common cause: that cause, Second Emperor, is your heavenly self. For it to be your right to govern all the land as your ancestors did, you must be worthy of the Mandate of Heaven, which passes from man to man, clan to clan, appointing the one that is right to rule. I believe you have that mandate, but to retain it, you must hold true to three things: you must be open-hearted and open-minded, you must be wise in your decisions, and you must avoid favouritism and corruption amongst your staff."

Kongming paused, and eyed the eunuchs, who moved backward slightly.

"Furthermore," Kongming continued, "you must speak well, conduct yourself at all times with the grace of your heavenly position, and listen to your advisers... to avoid the repeat of the old mistake. As I have said, treat all officials equally, and give favouritism to none... not even me. However I shall give to you the names of men whom I can vouch as assets to your cause that will serve you tirelessly... in political matters, your father trusted Guo Youzhi, Fei Yi and Dong Yun, and you should trust them also. I say again, Your Majesty, that to avoid the downfall met by your ancestors... who fell victim first to the Ten Eunuchs, and then Dong Zhuo, Li Jue, Guo Si, Cao Cao, and were finally destroyed by Cao Pi... you must please avoid all petty and corrupt officials, and all toadies, pedants, and self-indulgent types amongst your staff. Do not mistake their flattery for strength, and purge them wherever they appear. I further recommend Chen Zhen, Zhang Bogong, and Jiang Wan at this point, to give assistance in all matters of the court.

"I, Liang, came to serve your father after he thrice visited me in my cottage, seeking my advice in matters of war. I presented to him the Longzhong Plan, whereby the feuding states would eventually be pared down to three: Liu, Cao, and Sun. Now there are three states, as I proposed, and with Wu as our ally – which I also proposed – we are sure to succeed. But the going has not been easy... your father suffered many defeats before he and I met, despite the support of the incomparable Zhao Zilong, the Mi brothers, Mister Sun, Mister Jian, and the mighty Guan Yunchang and Zhang Yide. He suffered a few defeats afterwards, as well, because he had yet to secure a base, and add legions to his generals, or a group of sound advisers... while you, Your Majesty, have all this and more. That is due, in part, to our alliance with Wu, alongside whom we crushed Cao Cao's self-proclaimed 'million-man horde' at Red Cliffs, and humbled Cao Ren at Jiangling. When we borrowed Jing for our march west, we were only a small army, barely able to stand on our own... through your father's efforts you are now the master of a mountainous stronghold, fertile lands, and an army of over a hundred-thousand. All this stemmed from the dream of a mat weaver from Zhuo County, and a farmer from Longzhong. That farmer stands before you today to tell you that nothing is impossible... nothing. We must never stop building on what we have already achieved, Your Majesty."

Kongming stopped for a moment, and coughed uncomfortably into a silk kerchief; Ma Su saw the spots of blood as Kongming tucked it back into his sleeve, and frowned with concern.

"Again, I stress the reasons for this Northern Expedition... we must destroy Cao Wei, and restore the house of Han, because it is Heaven's will, and because I promised your esteemed father, First Emperor, that I would do this," Kongming continued bravely. "We can then secure all the borders, as we have already done with Nanzhong, and create a new era of peace between all men of our country, and between us and our foreign neighbours. This must be our objective.

"I say again to you, Your Majesty, that you should lead by example: be fair and magnanimous, incorrupt and trustworthy, open-minded and kind... always be clear in your intentions, and please, please... do not let the mistakes of the past repeat. Do not waste public funds on leisure and luxury, and do not harm the people, as Cao Rui does now, to great outcry. Do not allow fawning pedants to sway your mind and cloud your judgement... corruption leads to ruin."

Kongming rolled his edict up, and said finally, "To achieve our great objective, I intend to despatch three mighty armies toward the plains of the north. Without pause or regret, and giving my entire self, I promise that we shall vanquish all evil, destroy Cao Rui of Wei, restore to power the house of Han and prepare for you a homecoming to the great capital, from which you shall oversee an everlasting peace. I do this to show my loyalty to you, Your Majesty, and my heartfelt devotion to the memory of your father, to whom I pledged my life."

Kongming kowtowed; moved to tears, Liu Shan gestured desperately, saying, "Please, please, Mister Zhuge! Please, rise!"

"Your humble servant awaits your decree," Kongming said hoarsely.

"...I... I do not want you to go," Liu Shan admitted; the court was obviously nervous at this statement, and none more so than Kongming himself. "I would rather you stayed, where I can see you... I rely on you in all matters, like my father, Mister Zhuge, and I have only just had you back from Nanzhong. But... but what you say is true... and... I trust your judgement. I give my support to the expedition, and give you instruction to prepare immediately."

Kongming smiled with relief, and said, "I humbly thank you, Your Majesty, and accept your orders without question."

"But... hurry back," Liu Shan added. "I'll miss you, Mister Zhuge."

"...Yes... Your Majesty," Kongming said awkwardly. He kowtowed once more, and took his leave to prepare for the march.

"*Ayah*," Kongming exclaimed as he reached his office: he threw his carefully prepared edict onto his writing desk, and huffed irritably.

"...Prime Minister," Zong Yu hailed as he and Ma Su caught up with Kongming. "That was magnificently handled."

"...Were it only easier to manage our emperor," Kongming complained. "...'Hurry back'...? ...'I do not want you to go'...? ...Those are the words of a *suckling*, not a Son of Heaven!"

"He's... not ideal," Ma Su admitted reluctantly. "But he agreed."

"Only *just*," Kongming chortled desperately. "I just hope he got my less than subtle point about avoiding corrupt officials and fawning eunuchs. I regret having to repeat myself, but... what else can I do...? ...Saying something *once* just *doesn't seem to work*, not with *anybody*!"

"Wei Yan and Zilong are going to prepare the army together," Ma Su reported more positively. "We're going to Wei Yan's Hanzhong headquarters, am I right...?"

"...Yes," Kongming said thoughtfully. "...I need to write to Meng Da, and let him know that we're preparing to march. We'll have to coordinate things very carefully, or Sima Yi will find out and ruin everything."

"You're worried now, aren't you...?" Ma Su said knowingly.

"Writing words and saying them are two very different things," Kongming admitted dolefully. "When I wrote the edict, I wanted to inspire our young emperor."

"You *did*, I think," Ma Su suggested.

"But I depressed *myself* in the process," Kongming chuckled ironically. "My Longzhong Plan was reliant on a two-pronged attack by *us*, and a single point of attack by Wu from the east. *Our two-pronged attack* was to be from the *west* through the Hanzhong Mountains and from the *south* through Jing Province, dividing Wei still further. We were supposed to have *Jing Province* to do this properly. But we've *lost* Jing... it's gone, and my plan can't be fully realised, not now, and not ever. Now, we have only one line of attack, and are completely dependent on Wu... if they falter, so do we, automatically.

"And then there are the forces that we were supposed to have… we were supposed to have the Five Tigers as our generals, Zilong, Yunchang, Yide, Ma Chao, Huang Zhong; the capable minds to make plans, Pang Shiyuan, Fa Zheng, Huang Quan, Jichang; able statesmen, like Mister Sun, Mister Jian, Mi Zhu… the importance of Wu aside, our greatest weakness is that we must now rely on men that we once ridiculed, like Chen Shi, or held in little regard, like Liao Hua, or do not trust, like Wei Yan. I told our Second Emperor that we have not only the forces, but the men to lead and guide those forces… but *do we*…?"

"Wu are as dedicated to this as we are now," Ma Su said reassuringly. "Lu Xun has a large part of Wei's army busy in the east… and Wei has lost its champions too, Kongming. The men that you speak of as lesser talents have grown, and we have new champions that are yet to show their greatness. Everything will be fine."

"Oh, I hope so," Kongming replied with a melancholy tone.


"You're going so *soon*…?" Yueying protested as Kongming finished explaining his plans: his adopted son, Qiao, stood beside him, dressed in full battle armour.

"I am," Kongming replied, "or rather, *we are*: my son and I, and our army. We must capitalise on every opportunity as soon as we can, else we'll always lag behind our rivals. Wu is doing a fine job of keeping Cao Xiu and Sima Yi busy, so let's honour their actions with some of our own. Son… we should be leaving."

"Yes, Father," Qiao replied: Qiao then turned to the emotional Yueying and said, "I shall miss you, Mother… may we see one-another again very soon."

Zhuge Qiao's wife then came forward, her young son at her side: Qiao knelt by his son and said, "He's getting stronger and stronger. He'll be a fine general one day, and serve Shu, as I will." Qiao got to his feet, and paid respects to his wife, who was sobbing miserably.

"Be careful," Yueying pleaded.

Kongming and Zhuge Qiao bowed with respect toward Yueying, who watched silently as they left the house and began their journey north to Hanzhong. She followed them as far as the city gates, and watched the army depart Chengdu with a sense of foreboding. Kongming had left the majority of the officials in Chengdu to advise and watch over the emperor, Liu Shan, and ensure that he did not stray from his duties; the majority of the armed forces joined him on the expedition, totalling around 100,000 men.


************

## 107

The plan – so far as Kongming was concerned – was that the Shu army would seize key points in order to isolate the economically and strategically important city of Chang'an.

The region to the west of Chang'an had several key points: Mount Qi; the cities of An Ding, Tianshui and Nan'an; the fortress city Chen Cang; the River Wei that ran from west to east across the region; and, last but not necessarily least, numerous mountain passes and roads that gave access to the wider north from Hanzhong. One particular place, Jieting, comprised essential roads, a tall hill, and access to water in a nearby valley. Jieting was an especially vital supply route for anyone that wanted to keep the region, and Kongming knew that very well.

Kongming's armies reached Hanzhong after a long and tiring march across the uneven terrain of Yi Province: Kongming marvelled at the defences that Wei Yan had put in place, and was forced to congratulate the man on his efforts.

"I promised our late Emperor that I would protect us against any attack," Wei Yan replied confidently. "I'll do just as good a job on the attack. I'm eager to hear your plans, Prime Minister."

"I think we should get started straight away," Kongming agreed, and the generals convened in Wei Yan's city courtroom for a council of war.

"Generals," Kongming began, "we are about to face Cao Wei for the first time since our illustrious victory in this very place, where the bravery of Wei Wenchang, Zhao Zilong, Zhang Yide, Huang Hansheng and Ma Mengqi – amongst many others, of course – saw us vanquish Cao Cao's forces, kill his right hand man, and finalise our path to being an independent kingdom. Now we're here again to finish what we started... it is a shame that so many have not lived to see this day."

The majority of the generals were respectfully silent: Wei Yan, however, sneered, and said, "Yunchang, Yide, Mengqi and Hansheng would not want to see us moping when we could be fighting. We've wasted enough time already, Prime Minister... you said so yourself. What's the plan...?"

Kongming coughed uncomfortably and replied, "Perhaps you're right. Generals, we're not able to launch a two-pronged attack as per my original plan, so we shall need to be cautious. Our final target is the major city of Chang'an, which can be seen as a 'throat' of the Wei heartland with which to choke them. Zilong, you and Deng Zhi shall lead a force through Xie Gorge and move on the city of Mei, south of the Wu Zhang Plains. A second contingent shall travel northwest, pass through the mountains, seizing Mount Qi, and then the upper Wei River: from there, we can take the key cities of Tianshui, An Ding, and Nan'an. Now-"

"That's your plan...?" Wei Yan interrupted rudely.

The entire ensemble was stunned into silence. However, Kongming allowed Wei Yan to continue.

"Prime Minister, your plan will take too long, and give our enemy too much time to prepare, distribute forces, and counterattack," Wei Yan said frankly. "I have, I think, a better proposal.

"I shall personally lead ten thousand elite troops through Qinling and attack Chang'an head on. I can be there very quickly, and Wei will not expect such a move: they will be in disarray, allowing you time to move and secure any other routes, which will also be in disarray from having a major supply and communications route cut. If we do this, we can take Chang'an in two weeks or less."

The generals murmured agreeably at the idea, and Kongming sensed that his own plan was suddenly less popular.

"I should like to hear your esteemed view," Wei Yan prompted.

Kongming started to fan himself slowly, and said, "General Wei, your plan, while it might have its merits in more optimistic times, is too dangerous to adopt for our army in its current state. We must err on the side of caution, especially when we are dealing with tacticians like Sima Yi."

"But Prime Minister," Wei Yan protested, "it is my understanding that Chang'an's acting governor is Xiahou Dun's second son, *Xiahou Mao*."

"He has a poor reputation," Ma Su noted.

"I am aware of it," Kongming admitted.

"He's a weak coward," Wei Yan continued. "An assault on the city without warning would scare him to death: he'd run, leaving us with Chang'an... everything else would then become ours if-"

"Yes, General Wei... *if*," Kongming interrupted irritably. "Your plan relies on this one particular man being in charge on the day you arrive, and him having no level-headed peers to give him strength and sound advice... something that I find highly unlikely given the well-known strategic importance of Chang'an."

Wei Yan glared at Kongming, and nodded silently.

"I'm sorry, but I shall take no more risks... not after Jing, not after Xiaoting," Kongming insisted. "We've come too far to lose another stronghold or another army... that would break us. Yes, my route is slow. But it is also guaranteed to give us rewards, provided everyone follows their orders as I give them. Now: Zilong, General Deng... I have prepared your force... you shall move out immediately, take Ji Pass, and then Mei City."

The two generals accepted their orders and departed.

"...And what role am I to play, since I am apparently not the vanguard...?" Wei Yan asked cuttingly.

"I am going to personally lead an assault on Mount Qi," Kongming replied.

"...Mount Qi...?" Wei Yan mused. "But... Zilong-"

"Don't concern yourself, General," Kongming said with a smile. "Despite what you obviously think... I do know what I'm doing. Now, we must discuss the next part of our mission... the repulsion of the relief force. That will likely be led either by Cao Zhen, Cao Rui himself or, if we are to be truly challenged, Zhang He or Sima Yi. We will need a truly magnificent tactician as the commander in order to win such a victory."

Of all the leading generals, only Wei Yan seemed to be preparing to volunteer his services.

"The chosen commander will be guarding the highly significant supply route at Jieting," Kongming continued. "It is essential for our forces, in both advance and retreat, and in ensuring that new supplies can be sent through from Hanzhong."

Kongming paused and looked at the each of the generals and officials: Wei Yan was still the only general that showed any sign of interest in the assignment, and among the officials, only one familiar face was devoid of any signs of reluctance.

"Despite outward appearances," Kongming concluded, "that place cannot be taken lightly. ...Ma Su..."

"Prime Minister...?" Ma Su responded eagerly; many restrained murmurs of shock and discontent were evident amongst the generals, regardless of rank.

"You have long understood the Art of War," Kongming said surely. "Like your esteemed brother before you, you have long understood all things of importance, and I know that you will be best placed at this point of utmost importance. Gao Xiang and Chen Shi shall assist you as main supporting generals. Further to that, I shall assign to you as a deputy Wang Ping, who is a diligent, deep-thinking general that will only serve to support you in this urgent undertaking."

"Thank you, Prime Minister," Ma Su said confidently.

"Jieting must be guarded well, and guarded in all directions," Kongming continued seriously. There is a hill, a valley with an ample stream running through it for water, and a number of roads intersecting at a critical junction. Every point must be secured... but of course, you know that."

"I shall bring us a great victory, Prime Minister," Ma Su promised.

"Just guard Jieting, that's all I ask!" Kongming chuckled warmly. "You need only to repel the enemy, not take the heads of great commanders. But I stress again, Ma Su... you will be guarding our strategic throat. It will all come to nothing if we lose it... we will be throttled to death."

"I won't disappoint you," Ma Su insisted.

"...Prime Minister...!" Wei Yan protested, whereupon Kongming eyed him sternly, and he resigned himself to silence.

"Wu Ban, Zhang Boqi, Zhang Bosong, Ma Dai, Liao Hua... ready your forces for a full-scale assault on Mount Qi," Kongming ordered. "Wei Yan, Yang Yi... you will be in overall control of strategic operations in my command post, and be ready to provide relief to any force that needs it."

"...Your word is law, Prime Minister," Wei Yan said icily as he accepted his orders. He could barely contain his disgust as Ma Su nodded obediently and accepted his own orders with unabashed pride and mounting self-assurance.

Reports soon came from Ji Pass that confirmed Zhao Yun's successful capture of the vital point: concerns were expressed in the messages, however, about the quality of the troops that the old general had at his disposal.

"...Prime Minister," a messenger hailed as he entered Kongming's command tent, where Kongming, Zong Yu, Dong Jue, Wei Yan, Yang Yi, Zhuge Qiao, Liao Hua, Zhang Boqi and Zhang Bosong were sat in conference. "We have had another message from Veteran Tiger General Zhao... he is reporting the approach of forces led by Cao Zhen of Wei."

"Excellent," Kongming said calmly. "Keep me informed."

"Veteran General Zhao again protests at the poor soldiers at his command," Yang Yi noted worriedly as the messenger retired.

"...I assigned older, weaker soldiers to Veteran General Zhao for three reasons," Kongming replied confidently. "First, his is not the main objective... he is merely a decoy. Secondly, if he is mistaken for the main force as I wish him to be, their obvious weakness will make the enemy overconfident. Thirdly, Veteran General Zhao is very experienced in getting out of difficult situations... whatever the outcome, he will survive."

Yang Yi nodded silently.

"Your silence suggests that you doubt the logic of the plan," Wei Yan noted.

"I meant nothing but accord with...!" Yang Yi protested angrily.

"Raise your voice at me, uh...?" Wei Yan growled as he got to his feet, and started to draw his sword.

Kongming's adopted son Zhuge Qiao got to his feet, placed his hand on his sword, and said, "General Wei,you should not react so strongly to a mere comment."

"Indeed," Zhang Boqi agreed as he also got to his feet. "We're in a meeting: we should restrict our disagreements to words and nothing more."

"...*Little runt*," Wei Yan grunted as Zhang Bosong and Liao Hua stood and took the side of Yang Yi as well: he backed down and retook his seat.

"He... he is intolerable!" Yang Yi sobbed pitifully.

"**You**...!" Wei Yan barked; Kongming pointed his fan at the general and grunted admonishingly.

"I... I really meant no criticism with my silence, Prime Minister," Yang Yi insisted through tears of fear.

"...We need the best soldiers for the vanguard," Kongming replied. "Whatever your thoughts truly are, I'm afraid that is the case."

"Yes, Prime Minister, and you have appointed Ma Su as your vanguard," Wei Yan said with obvious anger. "I am now the best asset Shu has... no offence to Ma Su, but I am the best choice for vanguard. It should have been me going to Jieting."

"We are about to split our forces into three," Kongming scolded, "and we need you to be wherever you are most needed. Further to that... I have another front that I am trying to motivate into action as we speak."

"General Meng...?" Liao Hua supposed.

"He's getting haughty in his correspondence... loath as I am to admit it, he has turned out to be less than reliable, as I had been so often warned," Kongming lamented. "So... I have had my hand forced. He'll certainly move now..."

"Why...?" Wei Yan asked bluntly.

"Because I've leaked the plan to Shen Yi, and ensured that Meng Da is aware of the loss of secrecy," Kongming admitted.

"...But now he'll be in danger from Sima Yi," Yang Yi supposed.

"He was going to renege on his deal with us," Kongming said coldly. "He was and is a self-serving traitor... now, he has been forced into a corner, as he deserves. He'll still win, so don't worry. Now... it looks as though our work at Mount Qi is going well... our next step is to advance into An Ding, Tianshui and Nan'an, where it looks as though the people are already changing their allegiances. The most important thing is to secure our supply route in the region. I trusted Ma Youchang with that mission because I know him to be a man of sound judgement."

Wei Yan nodded slowly and apprehensively.

"Your silence suggests that you doubt the logic of the plan," Yang Yi said cuttingly.

"Some day," Wei Yan growled, "you're going to lose that tongue of yours in a nasty accident, Yang Yi."

"Wei Yan...!" Kongming scolded.

Wei Yan said no more.

Meng Da summoned former administrators Shen Dan and Shen Yi to a meeting of his generals in his Fangling stronghold of Xin City: he was blissfully unaware of their true allegiances or intentions.

"...I have been exposed in my plot to defect back to Shu," Meng Da complained. "I don't know how... Zhuge Liang must've sent a messenger that got caught. So I need to act quickly... we're moving on the capital, Luoyang, with all of our forces. If we work quickly, we're sure to win."

Many if not all of the generals were unaware of Meng Da's plans: they murmured agreeably, but secretly wondered what they should do.

"What about Sima Yi...?" Shen Yi proposed. "He's stationed near enough to us to rout us soundly..."

"...In a month or more, after he has received an imperial edict to act," Meng Da scoffed arrogantly. "We're quite safe from that pedant, so long as we act quickly. Prepare to move out!"


************

## 108

As soon as word of Kongming's successful acquisition of the strategic Mount Qi reached the cities of An Ding and Nan'an, many people began to revolt, as they preferred Shu rule over Wei. And once all of these events were known about in the Wei capital of Luoyang, Wei Emperor Cao Rui despatched his veteran generals Zhang He and Guo Huai – both familiar with fighting Shu during the earlier Hanzhong Campaign – while Cao Rui himself planned a march on Chang'an to relieve Xiahou Mao and secure the city.

"...A surrendering general...?" Kongming said thoughtfully as he walked back and forth in his command tent, fanning himself rhythmically. "...His name...?"
"Family name Jiang, given name Wei, styled Boye," Zong Yu replied. "He has not surrendered willingly, that much is obvious. His mother is or was inside Xi City, and he wouldn't dare defect and put his mother at risk... he'd be disgraced."
"Mm... I had a friend once that had that decision to make... a long, long time ago," Kongming said sombrely as he recalled Xu Shu. "This general Jiang... his governor accused him of colluding with us...?"
"He recommended making sweeps of the surrounding region, to anticipate enemy action and prepare accordingly," Zong Yu explained. "His governor was initially in accord, but with all the defections and rebellions in neighbouring cities, I suppose he became paranoid."
"This Jiang Wei sounds like a shrewd man," Kongming decided. "He surrendered because his men favoured it, and because he had nowhere else to go but the netherworld... he presumes his family gone, and wants to avenge them. He sees the changing times, and adapts accordingly. Regardless of the assessment, I think a man of this region might be of use... does he have good lineage?"
"His father, General Jiang Jiong, was killed in the revolts by the Qiang," Zong Yu said cautiously. "I don't know if he'd work so well with Ma Dai, since it was Ma Chao that led those rebellions."
"I would like to make a prominent, strong figure of this local man," Kongming proclaimed. "I will give him great prestige and presence in our army... he will give us the moral victory we seek. Bring him to me. ...No, wait... I'll go to him. I want to know more before I meet him... but I shall go to him."

Jiang Wei was alone in a guest tent when Kongming arrived. The Shu Prime Minister was guarded by two soldiers, and flanked by Zong Yu and Yang Yi.
"...Zhuge Kongming," Jiang Wei said meekly: he then kowtowed.
"Please, do not be so formal," Kongming replied: he then extended his hand, and helped the general to his feet. Jiang Wei was young, but he had an aura of determination and intelligence that surprised Kongming. He wore a white turban to show grief for his mother, which Kongming noted with eerie empathy.
"...I have long wanted to meet you," Jiang Wei said with apparent sincerity. "You are a genius of the age, a match for Zhang Liang and Jiang Ziya."

"You flatter me," Kongming replied cautiously. "I am glad that you have chosen the light over the darkness, and have chosen to join us. I have heard that you are a very capable man yourself... with talent that would, one day, have seen you become one of the leading lights of Wei."

"How fortunate then," Jiang Wei declared, "that I met you before I made a wrong choice. A wise bird chooses a sturdy branch... a wise vassal, a worthy master... is that not true, Master Zhuge Kongming...?"

"...Yes," Kongming said with surprise. "Tell me, how old are you?"

"Twenty-seven, Master," Jiang Wei replied: Kongming almost dropped his fan.

"As was I," Kongming said, "when I finally found my own calling! ...perhaps the fates have had us meet in this time and place for a reason, Jiang Boye... perhaps I have found the successor of my great cause that I have been looking for."

"Uh...?" Yang Yi exclaimed.

"I... I fail to understand," Jiang Wei admitted.

"You," Kongming said as he clasped Jiang Wei's right hand, "are perhaps the man to whom I might pass my most esoteric teachings, my most profound understandings about the nature of man, about the nature of war, and about the marvels of science! My adopted son is bright but no marvel, and any offspring I have may be lauded for blood lineage more than actual merit... I have always been keen to avoid this most repeated and most costly of mistakes.

"I will not live forever: some think that I will work myself to an early grave, and not last more than ten years, and I am inclined to agree. But if that is true, then I will die with my task unfinished, and I need to know that there is someone to continue – and finish – my heavenly task to restore the Han. The man that I pass my responsibilities to must be committed, driven, have an excellent and gifted mind, open to all of the possibilities the world might throw at them... maybe, just maybe, *you* are that man."

"Now, Master, I think *you* are the one flattering *me*," Jiang Wei suggested.

"Not at all," Kongming insisted. "But I... have an interesting piece of information I should like to impart upon you before we go further."

"...Please, Master, go on," Jiang Wei said without hesitation.

"Your mother is alive and well in Xi," Kongming revealed.

Jiang Wei eyed the two guards and Yang Yi as he said, "I see... that is not good news, not at all."

"Oh...?" Kongming exclaimed. "And why is that...?"

"For I will now have to mourn her a second time, Master," Jiang Wei replied regrettably, as he returned his gaze to meet Kongming's. "After all, she has no doubt been spared only briefly, in case my governor's initial suspicions were proved wrong... when I am known to be loyally in your service, she will surely die."

"You'd sacrifice her...?" Yang Yi challenged.

"A man must do what is right," Jiang Wei countered. "Were I to abandon my principles for the sake of filial piety, I would be seen as a man of filial piety... but not as a man of principle. I was raised as a man of principle... so I would be a disgrace to those that raised me by ignoring their teachings."

"You are the one I have sought," Kongming decided. "Jiang Boye, I would be honoured if you would become my student... so that we might together punish the wicked and restore order to the land."
Jiang Wei fell to one knee and proclaimed, "I am unworthy of your praise... but if you have me as your student, I will commit myself unendingly for the cause of the house of Han... which my father served, before it was usurped by the Cao family. I will not rest until our work is done, Master."
"Very good!" Kongming said with happiness in his heart. "We have gained another dragon, another phoenix in Jiang Boye! If nothing else, we have a man that will continue my cause beyond my feeble span!"
"Please, Kongming," Yang Yi said miserably, "do not use such morbid language and curse your sagely life so willingly."
"Calm down," Kongming said dismissively. "A man who accepts that he will die lives more readily. I'll achieve a dozen men's lifetimes before I go! Now, Boye... we should go to the command tent, where-"
"I think," Jiang Wei interrupted, "that I should be kept at a general's rank, and serve on the field, ignorant of higher strategy, at least until this campaign is won... lest there be any failings that might be attributed to my treachery."
"...You're quite right," Kongming realised. "...I shall go now, Jiang Boye. We shall meet again soon."
Kongming bowed with respect to his new student, and left the tent with his guards, Zong Yu, and a very sceptical Yang Yi.
        "He's a Wei defector!" Yang Yi said worriedly as he followed Kongming.
"So are you," Kongming reminded Yang Yi pointedly.
"...Point taken," Yang Yi sighed. "But can he really be trusted so soon...? For every Yang Yi, there is a Meng Da or a Lü Bu."
"He's to be trusted," Kongming insisted. "Stubborn old Yan Yan was trustworthy to his dying day, and Major-General Wang Ping has been a reliable asset since his defection from Wei during the Hanzhong Campaign. I would have placed nobody else alongside Ma Su at Jieting... and I think that Jiang Wei is our own Lu Xun, come to help this ailing Zhou Yu. 'Morbid' though it may sound, I can die knowing our Emperor has another man to carry on fighting for his great cause. ...And Meng Da has seen the light again, so we should not be so condemning of him just yet."

The situation faced by Zhao Yun and Deng Zhi near Ji Pass was critical; Cao Zhen led his vastly superior troops to Mei City, and overwhelmed the feeble forces that had been deliberately assigned to the two Shu generals. Cao Zhen's men surged into the outclassed Shu lines, leaving it to Zhao Yun's ingenuity and charisma to save the day. Zhao Yun showed the same prowess that he had been known for over the last forty years, riding up and down his lines and taking down many enemy infantrymen with his veteran spear. Deng Zhi, meanwhile, hurried to assemble the stronger men into a formation to repel the Wei forces, while the weaker men made a speedy retreat to recover. Zhao Yun prepared for a series of standoffs with Cao Zhen, where the objective each time would be to lose the encounter as painlessly as possible.

"I hate to say it, Zilong," Deng Zhi complained, "but we've been hung out to dry."

"The Prime Minister is a good man, shrewd and kind," Zhao Yun insisted. "This plan... while seemingly cruel... must have some merit behind it."

Sima Yi received the news that Meng Da intended to attack the capital with only slight concern. His two sons – Sima Shi and Sima Zhao – urged him to explain his casual attitude to what seemed to be the most direct threat to Cao Wei.

"Meng Da," Sima Yi said with a smile, "can only succeed because of military law... if military law was not strictly applied, or rather, a general were to act in the best interests of his emperor rather than following strict protocol... then this man is already dead."

"Father, explain!" Sima Shi protested. "You have requested the court for permission to act already, haven't you...?"

"No," Sima Yi replied as he put on his battle armour.

"*No...?*" Sima Zhao exclaimed. "So... so we are not going to act...?"

"Of course we are!" Sima Yi chuckled. "...*Right now.*"

"*Without an imperial edict...?*" Sima Shi said with disbelief.

"I will be thanked for it when I have removed a serious threat... have no fear," Sima Yi insisted. "Prepare yourselves: we're going after Meng Da... he will not be ready, and he will not survive."

"But he'll still be expecting some reaction if the plan is leaked," Sima Shi supposed.

"I have placated him, as Shen Yi had already wisely done," Sima Yi revealed with a smile. "I have already sent him a letter, insisting that I am aware that Shu have betrayed him to force his hand, and I expect that to be enough to slow him down again... he's arrogant, and he'll assume that I trust him, which, of course, I never did. I knew exactly what he was when he joined us... I know how to deal with such men. It's a pity that the late First Emperor never listened to me in the first place... then perhaps we would not be in this situation. ...Once Meng Da is dead, we shall meet the Emperor at Chang'an, and then march west and assist Chief Commander Cao Zhen in repelling Zhuge Liang."

Sima Shi and Sima Zhao bowed with sincere respect toward their father in honour of his wisdom and perception.

Sima Yi was correct in his judgement: Meng Da did react to the letter with complacency, and delayed his march to make more detailed preparations. But before Meng Da could even move his vanguard forces out of Xin City, Sima Yi was upon him, with a force that far outnumbered his own.

"...*Impossible!*" Meng Da whined as he looked over the wall at the imposing Wei army that covered the battlefield around his fortress. "He... he can't do this!"

"**MENG DA!**" Sima Yi shouted – and almost laughing as he did so – from atop his war horse, in front of the main gates of Xin City. "**SURRENDER NOW, AND YOU WILL BE SPARED!**"

"Who shall deliver the response...?" Shen Yi asked quietly.

"We need support from Shen Dan, in Shangyong," Meng Da mused. "We... ... ...yes, yes, right! Shen Yi, you must go at once and request aid from Shen Dan! I will request help from Zhuge Liang in Nanzhong, and from Wu forces in Jiangling!"

"Very well," Shen Yi replied calmly.

"I will not surrender, I have come too far!" Meng Da declared. "Even I can't take Luoyang, I must confront Sima Yi!"

While Shen Yi's forces made a show of breaking out of the city by the west gates to go to Shangyong, Meng Da rode out of the main gates with his forces to meet Sima Yi in battle.

**"So you will not surrender,"** Sima Yi realised. **"We outnumber your forces."**

**"That won't matter!"** Meng Da. **"A desperate man fights with all his might, so you'll not win against six thousand tigers!"**

The battle was fierce; Meng Da's men did indeed fight with all of their resolve against Sima Yi's larger force, but with no help coming from Shangyong – in fact, it would only be reinforcements for Sima Yi, if anyone at all – survival depended on support from Wu to the south, and Shu from the west.

The news of Zhao Yun's repeated defeats were of no surprise to Kongming, but the news from Fangling left Kongming's entire body wracked with stress.

"This isn't good at all," Kongming said as the messenger from Xin City finished his report. "Sima Yi… is a man that cares nothing for imperial edicts, like Cao Cao before him. *He's* our future enemy, for sure, not Cao Rui… but enough. I will despatch forces to aid General Meng, and it's in Wu's best interests to do the same."

"I should like to lead them, Father," Zhuge Qiao declared.

"You are no match for Sima Yi," Kongming said dismissively. "Even your brother's quick wits would do little against a wily fox like Sima Yi… your reserved disposition would do you no credit against an impulsive schemer. I'll have to go to Fangling myself."

"But… what about the front here…?" Yang Yi protested.

"Youchang is on his way to hold Jieting, Zilong is holding his front, and Wei Yan is poised to provide support wherever it is needed," Kongming sighed. "I like this no better than you, but I must go where I am needed. You will hold the base, with Dong Jue and Zong Yu."

Ma Su, Wang Ping, Gao Xiang and Chen Shi reached Jieting several days before the first Wei scouts would arrive.

"An unassuming place," Ma Su scoffed. "To think that this is a key point is almost unbelievable, Major-General Wang."

Wang Ping nodded, saying, "Our scouts have reported that-"

"I know," Ma Su interrupted rudely. "A hill, adjoining roads, and a water supply in a valley on the far side. The Art of War states that a man that looks down upon his enemies wins the day: so naturally, we'll camp on the hill."

Wang Ping looked about him worriedly and said, "Commander, the hill is isolated. The land around the roads is raised, so we would be better to build a walled camp on the road to repel the enemy."

"And leave a hill for the enemy to occupy and dominate us from…?" Ma Su said with contempt. "No wonder Wei lost at Mount Dingjun… if the strategy they employed was as flawed as yours."

Wang Ping objected to the attack on his original affiliation, but contented himself by replying, "Not every situation can be judged as having the same solution.

"If we secure the water supply, and wall the key roads off, Zhang He cannot hope to defeat us. If we camp on the hill, all they need to do is surround us and set the base of the hill on fire, and we'll be trapped, without water or an escape plan."

"Miserable, pedantic nonsense," Ma Su jeered. "The Art of War states quite clearly that the high ground *always* offers the advantage! ...And if we *are* cut off from the water supply, then the men will fight with the vigour of ten men each to reclaim it!"

"I don't think that the Prime Minister would agree," Wang Ping suggested.

"Kongming consults me often in matters of war," Ma Su said with confidence. "Ask him who suggested pacifying the Nan people, and gave us our unprecedented victory in the south! I have been his confidante for many years now... and if he were here, *he'd* agree with *me* that to camp on the hill is the only sensible choice. Do you intend to disobey my instructions...?"

"No," Wang Ping replied. "But we cannot have every part of our force on the hill, Commander... I would like to keep a contingent on the road as an advance force, and send regular scout parties to watch for Zhang He's forces."

"...You're going to whine and bleat if I don't let you, I can see that," Ma Su chortled. "Very well, 'Major-General': take a thousand troops, and camp on the road. You can escape far more quickly when Zhang He arrives, if nothing else. ...Or you could surrender, of course... that's what you did at Hanzhong, isn't it...?"

Ma Su turned to Gao Xiang and started to issue orders, while Wang Ping walked away, shaking his head sadly.

Kongming's relief force marched on Fangling double-time, and Wu's did the same: but neither could have hoped to reach Meng Da before the inevitable had occurred. Zhuge Qiao led a vanguard force ahead of his adopted father to aid any ground resistance, but what he met upon was a Xin City that had long since been taken. Shen Yi's standard flew from the ramparts, and the evidence of mass bloodshed was everywhere to be seen. Wu's vanguard appeared at much the same time, but the two armies kept respectful distance from each other, despite the alliance. But as the two forces prepared to withdraw, a sudden and unexpected din erupted, and a small force of Wei soldiers entered the field. Archers appeared along the city walls, and the Shu-Wu forces found themselves under heavy fire. All that was left was retreat.

"...We are too late, I know it," Kongming said quietly as his main force made gradual ground. Before he could muse further, a messenger – who was obviously wounded – dashed toward the army, and fell to his knees beside Kongming's carriage, weeping pitifully.

"Re... Report!" the messenger wailed. "General Meng Da has already been defeated! Xin City has fallen! Shen Dan and Shen Yi are in control of Shangyong and Fangling, and are working with Wei! And... and...!"

"...I... *not again*...!" Kongming said with anguish: his shoulders slumped, and his fan fell from his hand.

"And... and Chief Commandant of Attendant Cavalry Zhuge Qiao has been struck by enemy fire!" the messenger continued.

Kongming sat up immediately.

"...He is badly wounded," the messenger sobbed. "He...!"

"I must go to him," Kongming decided. "Take me to my son!"

"Father...?" Qiao said as he looked up at Kongming from his field hospital bed.

"...Who shot you...?" Kongming asked coldly.

"...*Father*...?" Qiao said with confusion.

"I... I need to know," Kongming whispered as he knelt by Qiao. "I have to know: from which direction did the arrow come?"

"I... I don't know," Qiao replied weakly. "I... *what*...?"

Kongming got to his feet again with some difficulty and said, "Rest, my son... I will come back and talk to you again."

"*Father*...!" Qiao pleaded as Kongming walked away silently.

Zhuge Qiao passed away on the return journey, aged just 25. Kongming's return to the headquarters at Mount Qi was a tense affair, and many officials and generals were visibly nervous. He passed the barracks without giving acknowledgement to anything or anyone, and went straight to the command tent, where Zong Yu and Yang Yi were waiting.

"...Prime Minister...?" Zong Yu said meekly as Kongming sat in his seat and lowered his head slowly.

"He was assassinated," Kongming declared. "I know *why* – it isn't as though I don't know *why* – but if I ever find out who it was..."

"...Prime Minister, I... I don't understand," Yang Yi admitted. "*Who... who* was assassinated...? ...You mean Meng Da...?"

"My son," Kongming replied calmly as he looked up at his aides. "Somebody on our own side... they ordered the assassination of my son. He was... my brother's son, first, a man of Wu... that's why. 'How could a man of Wu be my heir...?' ...But it wasn't their decision to make, whoever it was... it was *mine*."

Zong Yu and Yang Yi were horrified, and remained silent.

"I shall have to notify my family," Kongming said quietly. "I shall have to tell *my* wife, and *his* wife, and... ... ...*what a mess*."

His aides remained silent.

"...We lost Meng Da, which is, of course, what really matters right now," Kongming continued soberly. "Without him, there will be no flash raid on Luoyang to ensure our victory. This is my fault, of course... I'm the one that leaked the plan to Sima Yi... I'm the one that made his defeat possible. ...All because I underestimated Sima Yi. I knew he was dangerous... but not *how* dangerous. ...So what of our progress here...?"

"Zilong is still under pressure at Ji Pass," Zong Yu reported, "and Ma Su is holding Jieting as ordered, though Zhang He's forces will soon reach him, if they haven't done so already... fifty thousand men, if their boasts are to be believed."

"...Fine," Kongming said quietly. "Keep me informed."

Kongming got up from his seat and left the command tent, intending to go to his own rest tent. As Kongming walked, he fanned himself slowly: his eyes were cold and emotionless.

************

## 109

When Zhang He's forces eventually reached Jieting, they observed Ma Su's hilltop encampment with bemusement.

"What fool is this...?" Zhang He said to his subordinate, General Guo Huai.

"The standard reads 'Ma Su'," Guo Huai replied. "This man must be a favourite of Zhuge Liang... he's certainly no great general."

"I expected Wei Yan, or some other notable general," Zhang He scoffed. "Instead, we find this idiot that has camped on an isolated hill. We need not wait for Sima Yi to advise us here... the tactic we should use is obvious enough. Surround the hill, and ensure that the valley stream is heavily guarded by archers and infantry. They'll not last ten days."

The first time that Ma Su was made aware of enemy action was by Chen Shi running into his tent, shouting, "**Zhang He is surrounding the hill!**"

"...Zhang He...?" Ma Su exclaimed. "*Surrounding the...!*"

"Major-General Wang Ping's warning!" Chen Shi continued. "We're being surrounded! **We can't break out!**"

"**Calm down, idiot!**" Ma Su barked. "We must charge them immediately! We have the high ground... the Art of War states that the force that holds the high ground *always* wins the day!"

Ma Su shoved Chen Shi to one side and marched out of his tent, where he was met with scenes of disorganisation and chaos. The Wei army now had the hill entirely surrounded, and all attempts to repel them had resulted in heavy losses.

"This... this can't be right!" Ma Su murmured. "We have the *high ground*... the Art of War *states* that the force that holds the high ground *always* wins the day! *Always...!*"

Despite his best efforts – which included threatening execution to any that refused to obey his orders – Ma Su could not inspire his forces to break the ring of soldiers that now surrounded his isolated camp.

"...We need water... water...!" Chen Shi complained after three days of being completely trapped.

"This... can't... be right...!" a now-broken Ma Su said weakly as he looked about him at the remnants of his once-proud forces; Gao Xiang shared his pain.

Despair now gripped the Shu army at Jieting.

"General Zhang," Guo Huai said with respect as he reported to his superior. "You have new orders...?"

"We were able to surround the hill easily, I see," Zhang He noted. "This 'Ma Su' person is useless. Any more activity from General Wang Ping...?"

"You were right... we did mistake his force for an ambush," Guo Huai reported. "But they were obviously there as objectors to the plan of camping on the hill... they're putting up small resistance, and aren't a real threat. The water supply is secured, and many Shu troops from the hill have been captured or killed trying to get to it. They have no organisation or morale, and cannot last much longer."

"I suggest that it is time to finish this, before Zhuge Liang finds out and sends a relief force," Zhang He declared. "We shall set fire to the base of the hill... and that will be the end of them."

"Very good," Guo Huai replied: he bowed with respect, and turned to go and deliver the orders to his soldiers.

"**AYAH!**" Kongming exclaimed: he whined painfully, dropped his fan and staggered backwards, as a terrified messenger from Jieting concluded his report on the final, fatal blow that had been delivered to the campaign against Wei.

"Prime Minister!" Zong Yu said as he ran to Kongming, and steadied him.

"All... all for *nothing*...!" Kongming realised. "All... all that we have set out to achieve... ruined... *ruined*!"

Wei Yan, Yang Yi, Dong Jue and Jiang Wei looked on helplessly, although Wei Yan's expression was more filled with disgust and contempt than concern.

"...Zhang He has secured Jieting," the messenger continued, "and... and he is moving on to supress the rebellions in An Ding and Nan'an-"

"...Enough, **enough, ENOUGH...!**" Kongming shouted desperately. "I hear, I understand! Please, messenger, you can go! I... I understand."

The messenger fled the command tent, passing an angry and disappointed Wei Yan.

"We shall have to begin a withdrawal immediately," Wei Yan said coldly. "We can't stay here now."

"Ma Su... wait... he didn't say what happened to Ma Su...!" Kongming realised.

"Why should we care???" Wei Yan barked angrily. "Your friend cost us this entire mission! ...I'm more interested in knowing what happened to Wang Ping."

"As am I," Kongming said wearily. "Why didn't he help Ma Su...?"

"We'll find out when they get here, won't we...?" Wei Yan retorted.

"Ma Su... *how could you do this to us*...?" Kongming said painfully.

Wang Ping and Gao Xiang returned to the main army with what little remained of the elite force assigned to Ma Su, who was nowhere to be seen.

"Where is Ma Su...?" Kongming asked plainly.

"He... is in a prison carriage bringing up the rear," Wang Ping replied uneasily.

"A prison carriage...?" Yang Yi said with surprise.

"He tried to desert... he refused to return to face you," Gao Xiang revealed.

"He tried to *flee*...?" Kongming said hoarsely. "*Ma Su*...?"

"He's a broken man," Wang Ping sighed. "I'm sorry, Prime Minister... that I failed to assist him as I could have."

"...What happened, Generals," Kongming asked dolefully. "Tell me everything, I have to know."

"When we arrived, I had scouts survey the area, and things were exactly as you described them," Wang Ping reported miserably. "At that point, Commander Ma said that he was aware of the surroundings already, and that we should camp on the hill, in entirety."

"...Ayah," Kongming exclaimed weakly.

"Pedant imbecile!" Wei Yan said aggressively. "Why didn't you remonstrate, General Wang? You should have-"

"I did, General Wei," Wang Ping promised. "But... he reminded me of my past as a surrendered general of Wei at Hanzhong, and cited Shu's victory at Mount Dingjun as justification for his theory that the high ground always delivers victory."

"Arrogant little...!" Wei Yan growled.

"...This does not sound like Ma Su," Kongming insisted. "I... I don't understand."

"When I said that you might object, to hint that he should consult you," Wang Ping continued, "he countered that you would often seek advice from him, Prime Minister, and that his advice was solely responsible for our victory in the south against the Nan."

The generals that fought on that campaign were not amused.

"...I requested a force to camp at the base of the hill," Wang Ping concluded. "He accused me of wishing to surrender again, and ordered a full encampment on the hill. I did what I could to warn him when Zhang He's forces started to surround the hill... I regrouped the men and harassed Zhang He wherever I could... but once the water supply was lost, and Zhang He set alight to the base of the hill... it was over."

"You did well to save so many men," Kongming said sincerely. "But Ma Su... has committed a terrible crime against our army. ...He... he must be punished for it."

"He knew as much," Wang Ping replied. "But after initially accepting that truth, he suddenly panicked, drew his sword, lashed out at us... blamed us for his failure, saying that it was because we were weak... and then he ran away. The soldiers... were angry with him, so recapturing him was easy. He'd been disciplining them heavily... strokes for complaining... death for insubordination... death if they complained about the loss of water... death for threat of desertion..."

"Is this true...?" Kongming asked of General Gao Xiang, who nodded silently.

"Death is too good for him," Wei Yan suggested angrily. "This entire campaign... failed, and all for naught."

"...Is there any word from General Zhao or General Deng...?" Kongming asked numbly. "Have they successfully retreated from Ji Pass...?"

"Nothing yet," Yang Yi said sombrely.

"...*Ayah*," Kongming exclaimed again: he walked away from his generals, and returned to his carriage to continue the retreat.

Upon the army's return to Hanzhong, Kongming was surprised to find that Zhao Yun and Deng Zhi had managed to preserve the lives of most - almost all - of their men.

"...While Ma Su sends a legion of elite men to their deaths," Kongming remarked with disdain, "Zilong brings a force of weak men back in such fine order... Zilong, you are truly a magnificent general, and I have wronged you, I think."

"I failed to secure Mei," Zhao Yun replied, "and scored no victories over Commander Cao Zhen. I deserve no accolades."

"Veteran General, you have shamed men half your age with your performance in the north!" Kongming insisted. "You faced a superior army, in both size and quality, and returned intact... while a man I trusted wrongly took a force of great men and... ...
...Zilong, you have taught me a lesson today. I thought that – once strategists were in command of the armies – numbers would decide the day. But I see that the mistakes of the past were not due to poor strategy alone... that numbers rarely decide the outcome. It is the prowess of the general, his bravery in difficult situations... his charisma in inspiring his forces. I selfishly withheld the best men for myself, when – I now plainly see – giving you even a fraction of those better troops would have delivered us the head of the enemy's Chief Commander, and this disaster might never have happened. I'll not forget this lesson."
"Defeats are commonplace," Zhao Yun insisted. "First Emperor knew this."
"...Indeed he did," Kongming sighed sadly. "You will be well rewarded, Zilong."
"No," Zhao Yun retorted. "Do not give me wealth when coffers are empty, and the needs of the populace and the army are dire. Keep the things you intend to offer me, and distribute them to those who really need them. And I expect to be demoted by three ranks, Prime Minister... it is only right that a losing general is."
"...You're a saint among men, Zilong," Kongming said emotionally. "I regret not seeing it sooner."

Kongming had two especially painful encounters to face, and it was the one that had state importance that would come first. Before his return to Chengdu, he visited the prison in Wei Yan's Hanzhong base, where Ma Su was being kept in the worst conditions that Kongming would permit.
"...Prime Minister!" the prison guard hailed.
Ma Su looked up and saw his old friend and honorary brother looming over him and fanning himself slowly.
"...I failed you," Ma Su said weakly.
Kongming did not respond: instead, he started to circle Ma Su, as though he were taking in every inch of his dishevelled frame as a memory.
"I... I thought that I could rely solely on the classic texts... but it is clear that I did not truly understand them," Ma Su continued. "I... I thought that, when I surveyed Jieting, the topography pointed to... to superiority on the hill. I... I was forced to discuss it with Wang Ping... I rebuked him. But... everything that he said... he was right. Do not blame Wang Ping or Gao Xiang for anything, Kongming... it was entirely my fault."
Kongming glared at Ma Su as he circled him, but he did not speak.
"...I lost discipline, and... and I resorted to intimidation," Ma Su confessed. "I... I panicked. I... I thought I was able, that I could apply what I had learned from the texts, and be a good general... I was wrong. I... suppose my brother was right... that I am not a man whose deeds can..."
Ma Su trailed off; Kongming finally stopped circling him, and stared into his eyes with fury and hatred.

"I... I only want to know that you'll take care of my family," Ma Su pleaded. "They must not be punished for my mistakes... *please*, Kongming."

Kongming closed his eyes, and a single tear ran down the right side of his face.

"...I know that your son was killed as well... I know how difficult it will be to tell his family, to tell Lady Huang... I am truly sorry," Ma Su said sincerely. "I wish you luck for the future campaign, Kongming... I know that you'll win, now that... now that you won't ever make the mistake of trusting or relying on foolish pedants like me again."

Kongming started to sob silently as he turned away from Ma Su and lowered his arms to his sides.

"We fell for the very same trap that we tried so hard to avoid," Ma Su realised. "We kept the best soldiers for ourselves... and might have lost Zilong. I allowed you to send me to Jieting... when we both knew that it should have been Wei Yan. But... we ignored sound advice... even our own. We showed favouritism... and now, you have to prove that you'll never do that again. The soldiers hate me... and they're right to. What I put them through... was cruel, inhuman. Kongming... promise me you'll punish me for their sake. To appease them, I have to be punished. I tried to run away before... I won't do that now. I want to face the punishment that I deserve."

Kongming snorted loudly, exhaled heavily, and walked away from Ma Su.

"**Promise me!**" Ma Su shouted after him. "**Kongming...!**"

"Lock the door," Kongming said to the jailer. "I'm done here."

Kongming left the prison cell, and the jailer – who shared the common disgust for Ma Su – did as he was told, casting an icy glance at the prisoner as he did so.

"**Promise me, Kongming!**" Ma Su shouted one last time. "**Kongming...!**"

The march back to Chengdu was subdued. Jiang Wan was sent from the capital to meet with Kongming on the road.

"...I failed," Kongming declared. "There is nothing else to say."

"I'm sorry about your son," Jiang Wan said sadly.

"I'm sorrier about Ma Su," Kongming retorted. "My son died nobly, fighting for Shu... that fool Ma Su destroyed my army. What has just happened... has undone all our good work, yet again."

"You have Jiang Wei now," Jiang Wan suggested.

"A poor consolation when considering what we might have gained," Kongming replied. "We had Tianshui, An Ding, Nan'an, Ji Pass, Mount Qi, and a clear march on the capitals of Luoyang and Chang'an... all those things are lost, some never to be in our sights again. ...And while I would like to blame Meng Da and Ma Su for our loss... I was the Chief Commander, so the real blame is mine to bear."

"What of Ma Su...?" Jiang Wan asked.

"He's in a prison transport at the rear of our force," Kongming reported. "He'll be imprisoned in Chengdu, and executed there."

"*Executed*...?" Jiang Wan exclaimed.

"For the good of morale," Kongming insisted. "He must be seen to answer for this. And he won't be alone... Zilong – despite his outstanding performance under ridiculous conditions that were entirely of my doing – has requested demotion of three ranks for his 'failure'... I can demand no less for myself."

"...What do you mean...?" Jiang Wan prompted uneasily.

"You know exactly what I mean," Kongming replied. "I am not fit to be called a Prime Minister... not after this. I request demotion of three ranks for my failure, for that is only right. I will not allow Zilong to bear humiliation alone... not when his was the only real success."

"Kongming...!" Jiang Wan exclaimed.

"Demotion means nothing to me," Kongming scoffed. "I have to tell my wife her son is dead... I have to tell my friend's wife that her husband must be executed for failing an assignment I should never have given to him. I have to tell my son's wife that she is a widow, and that her son must be raised without a father. I have to tell my brother Jin that his faith in me as a father to his son was misplaced... so very, very misplaced, and that his nephew – in truth, his son that he cherished – is gone, and that I am to blame. I have countless families that I must look in the eye after having sent their men to their deaths needlessly. How do I do those things, Mister Jiang, that's... that's what I need to figure out."

Once the army had returned to Chengdu, Kongming returned to his office, where he penned an official memorial to Liu Shan, requesting that he be punished for his failure by demotion. While he was finalising this, the official Xiang Lang came to protest on behalf of Ma Su.

"...I know why you're here," Kongming said without looking up from his work. "I will not be swayed, Mister Xiang... Ma Su must be executed."

"Prime Minister, please...!" Xiang Lang sobbed. "He has a wife, a family... and we have all lost so much... it would not be a good omen for our cause to execute a man of such long-standing service!"

"He's your friend... I understand that," Kongming replied as he finally stopped writing and looked up at Xiang Lang. "He was like a brother to me... by my oath with Ma Jichang, he *was* a brother... but there are some things that cannot be forgiven. Guan Yu knew this when he forced Sun Quan to execute him... he knew that losing Jing was unforgivable, and that death was the only way that he could apologise to all those that he had let down so badly. Ma Su has communicated to me his desire to atone with his life... he wants this end more than anyone."

"I won't let you kill your brother, and my friend... even if he says that is what he wants!" Xiang Lang challenged. "Did Guan Yu's death really help our cause...?"

"The difference," Kongming retorted, "is that there will be no crazed expedition to avenge him... because one and all are in agreement that Ma Su is a liability we can do without. Where would I place him...? Guan Yu was a mighty general that had an astounding record of successes to his name: who was Ma Su...?"

"You don't mean that, Prime Minister!" Xiang Lang protested.

"The state comes first," Kongming replied calmly. "I wept when I signed the execution documents... I am truly sorry it's come to this. But it has, and rightly so."

"...So when will he die...?" Xiang Lang asked plainly.

"There are procedures," Kongming explained. "We have other, more important matters... and I want him to spend some time with his family, so that he can explain to them – and to his sons especially – why this must be. That way, there will be no later acts of revenge on me or anyone else. ...Now if you don't mind..."

"...Prime Minister," Xiang Lang sighed: he bowed slightly, and departed.

"...So you've finally come home," Yueying said numbly as Kongming entered his home: the mood was subdued, and everyone wore white to mourn the loss of Zhuge Qiao. Yueying was cradling a child in her arms; Kongming knelt by Yueying, and touched the child's face gently.

"...A boy, or a girl...?" Kongming asked first.

"A boy," Yueying replied. "He is healthy... we are both well, in fact."

"...Where is my daughter-in-law...?" Kongming asked further.

"She is at her family home... she may move back here to live with us, since raising our grandson alone might be a struggle for her," Yueying explained. "Did our son suffer greatly, husband...?"

"...It was fairly sudden," Kongming replied. "You... do know, don't you, that it wasn't Wei or Wu...?"

Yueying nodded silently.

"And... and you do know that it wasn't me...?" Kongming prompted.

"Yueying nodded again, and said, "You asked for him to join us, husband... you'd not risk war with your brother or his king, I know that."

"*Ayah*," Kongming sighed emotionally. "I have had to order the death of Ma Su and three of his junior officers to placate the army... and I must not investigate the death of my son for fear of riling my political rivals or supposed allies. Who could truly crave power...? ...I had more freedom as a farmer."

"*Will* you kill Ma Su...?" Yueying asked pointedly.

Kongming looked at Yueying, exhaled noisily, and stroked the head of his new son.

For the failure of the Northern Campaign, Kongming was demoted to General of the Right, but retained all of the power and influence of the Prime Minister regardless, at the special request of Second Emperor Liu Shan. But it was the funeral of Zhuge Qiao that hurt Kongming most: Zhuge Jin - his true father - spoke profoundly when the opportunity arose, as did Zhuge Ke, his brother. But despite the circumstances surrounding the death of the adopted son of Zhuge Liang, peace was maintained, and life went on.

************

## 110

The states of Wei and Wu had been fighting almost continuously since the defeat of Liu Bei at Xiaoting, and were locked in a large battle during the whole of Kongming's failed expedition. While preparations began in Chengdu for a possible second expedition, the Wei-Wu front near Wei's Hefei fortress was about to see one of the most dramatic outcomes since Xiaoting; and once again, the strategist Lu Xun was to be the architect of the victory for Eastern Wu.

"Another report from Wu," Jiang Wei said as he entered Kongming's office.

"Thanks, Boye," Kongming replied thoughtlessly: he was looking over a diagram for a mechanical device, and was not paying serious attention.

"...I think you should read it," Jiang Wei urged.

"I'll do it," Zong Yu said as he walked to Jiang Wei and took the written report from him; Fei Shi left his work and stood near Kongming. As Zong Yu finished reading, he raised an eyebrow, looked at Jiang Wei, and said, "Is this right...?"

"It is," Jiang Wei said with a smile.

"What's so important...?" Kongming asked as he looked up at last.

"Wu have completely routed Cao Xiu!" Zong Yu declared.

"Oh...?" Kongming exclaimed. "Then... then Wei will be afraid of a Wu invasion in the east! They... they'll divert troops from the Hanzhong border!"

Kongming got to his feet and walked to a nearby easel, where a map of the planned expedition route was placed.

"...*Yes... yes*, they have no choice but to assign more forces to the Jing and Hefei fronts now!" Kongming said excitedly. "This could be our chance!"

"But should we be setting out again so soon...?" Zong Yu wondered. "Ma Su is still in prison, and our army has not fully recovered... nor has the grain supply. It has not even been a year, Kongming... surely...!"

"We cannot miss an opportunity like this," Kongming insisted. "If we dally, Wu might reach Luoyang before we do. Remember, this alliance is not as solid as a rock... my son Qiao proves that, as does the rumour that King Sun is not content to remain a king."

"He'd dare to declare himself emperor...?" Fei Shi chortled.

"Now that the cause of the Han is perceived in all but Shu Han territories to be beyond rescue," Kongming said sadly, "that is not at all ridiculous."

"Even with the fate of his father's master to draw upon...?" Jiang Wei suggested.

"It's true that Yuan Shu's end dissuaded many a would-be emperor... but Cao Pi has set a precedent, and if there were still a dozen warlords, there'd be a dozen false emperors," Kongming countered. "Wu now controls almost half of this country and many of its surrounding barbarian territories... he has an empire, let's be honest, so why shouldn't he feel he's an emperor...? But enough of that, we have an expedition to prepare for!"

"Winter is never a good time for an expedition," Fei Shi protested.

"We won't be expected then, will we...?" Kongming retorted confidently. "I'll petition Second Emperor at once... this time, we will attack Chen Cang!"

"Husband," Yueying pleaded as Kongming prepared his belongings, "this is madness. You've only been back a short while, the army hasn't recovered, we have a son *and* a grandson to raise, your health is only just starting to improve, and-"
"I'm fine, you're fine, the children will be fine," Kongming insisted emotionlessly as he continued his frantic packing. "Oh, and that design of ours... I've already started production. The fire-throwers were excellent against the Nanzhong tribes... our new device will ensure that every wrong step Wei takes is a fatal one."
"They're meant as a *deterrent*, not for ambuscades!" Yueying whined. "I thought you wanted them along the border to keep Wei's soldiers out!"
"An ambush *is* a deterrent, against pursuit and general stupidity," Kongming countered. "Now, this is going to be a very technical operation... less battles, and more of a siege, since Chen Cang is a fortress city. Our march is going to be very slow... what with siege towers, battering rams and the like to transport or procure along the way. I'll have some time to read, I expect...!"
"...Husband," Yueying said as calmly as she could, "you're rushing yourself. ...And what about *Ma Su*...? Are you going to deal with him before you leave, or-"
"He's in prison," Kongming interrupted. "That *is* 'dealing with him', isn't it...? I'll ensure he's put out of his misery when I return."
"So you're still going to execute him, even after all the petitions and protests," Yueying sighed. "Really, I thought-"
"The law is the law," Kongming interrupted. "Now... I'd best be off. This shouldn't take long... we'll be in Chang'an before you know it! It's a pity that Zilong is ill... he would have given the army a lot of extra morale. Still, never mind...!"
"It wasn't supposed to be like this!" Yueying protested: Kongming stopped his flight from the house, and his shoulders slouched.
"We both know this is how it was likely to turn out," Kongming replied with sincerity and sadness. "I have to show strength for the army, so *please*...!"
"...Yes, you're right," Yueying conceded. "We can't just sit here on the defensive, can we...?"
"No," Kongming said, "we can't. We may not have to fear Wu anymore – maybe – but Sima Yi of Wei regularly suggests an invasion of Hanzhong. If we can't put on solid shows of strength... we'll have half-a-million men coming through the mountains to kill us all. Even if I don't take Chen Cang... the fact that we tried will make Sima Yi hesitate, and buy us some time."
"...I know," Yueying admitted. "Go on... go."
Kongming nodded thankfully, and left the house.
"He carries the burden of this entire kingdom on his shoulders," Qiao's widow said as she joined Yueying in the living quarters, her son blissfully tottering around her.
"It was his idea... his first child, if you like," Yueying replied wistfully. "How can he let it die without at least trying to save it...?"

Once the main army was once again in the main headquarters in Hanzhong, Kongming summoned the generals for their second campaign briefing.

"...Fewer and fewer each time," Kongming muttered as he watched the generals enter the hall: Wei Yan, Wang Ping, Gao Xiang, Deng Zhi, Wu Ban, Zhang Boqi, Zhang Bosong and Ma Dai took their places, while Jiang Wei, Yang Yi, Liao Hua, Zong Yu and Dong Jue took their places on the side for the officials.

"Welcome," Kongming said emotionlessly. "We're targeting Chen Cang this time, as you know... if we can take that crucial place, communications in the region will be disrupted, and we stand a chance of regaining everything that we lost before."

"Cao Rui has returned to Luoyang," Wei Yan interrupted. "That means that Chang'an is once again in the hands of Xiahou Mao. For pity's sake, can we just dispense with all the arounds and abouts, and just attack that instead...? Chen Cang is very well guarded by Hao Zhao, who I'm told is another Cao Ren, while taking Chang'an will not only be faster and easier, but surely a much better way of disrupting communications across the whole Wei empire...?"

"*Again*, this mad plan of rushing Chang'an," Kongming scolded. "We've lost Zilong to illness for this campaign, and so we have no famous second general to lead the troops!"

"You only need *one*," Wei Yan retorted. "Give me Gao Xiang, Ma Dai and Wang Ping, and ten thousand troops, and-"

"And if Sima Yi has anticipated it, and ensured there is a trap awaiting you...?" Kongming proposed.

"Sima Yi, Sima Yi, always, *always* Sima Yi!" Wei Yan complained. "Sima Yi is fighting Wu, along with most of the Wei army! All there is to fear in the west is a garrison under Cao Zhen in Tianshui, a thousand-man force in Chen Cang, some token brigades in the towns, and a needs-must reinforcement battalion under Zhang He in Luoyang! I-"

"Yes, and that thousand-man force in Chen Cang is my first target for that very reason," Kongming interrupted. "If we attack Chang'an, we risk counterassaults from all directions! If we take Chen Cang, we secure our supply routes and destabilise the counties. Cao Zhen will be cut off and will have to withdraw, and by the time Zhang He gets here from Luoyang, we'll have Chang'an under siege."

"Hao Zhao, as I already said, is another Cao Ren," Wei Yan noted irritably. "The city is heavily fortified... it won't fall! And Hao Zhao is not the surrendering type!"

"We'll see about that," Kongming suggested. "Cao Ren lost Jiangling to Zhou Yu, and would have lost Fan to Guan Yu as well, if it weren't for Wu's duplicity. And Cao Ren's long dead, as this man Hao Zhao will be if he doesn't surrender. You'll be pleased to know, I'm sure, that you're the vanguard this time, Wei Yan, should I require one... and I expect good results."

"I'll do my utmost, *Acting Prime Minister*, as I always do," Wei Yan replied coldly.

The city of Chen Cang had been well fortified during the first campaign, when it was not a target: this time, Cao Zhen had ordered additional fortifications and troops, although the latter were yet to be assigned when the Shu army arrived. A wide, deep, unfilled moat surrounded the city, and the interior was stocked with everything needed to repel a siege.

"*See...?*" Wei Yan grunted as the messengers and spies finished their reports to an increasingly agitated Kongming.

"...Summon Jin Xiang," Kongming said coldly.

Moments later, two soldiers brought a middle-aged man in official's robes into the command tent.

"Mister Jin," Kongming hailed, "I have asked you here to assist me in my great endeavour... as a friend of Hao Zhao from his childhood, you are just the man I need to reason with him, and make him see that a moat and a thousand men cannot hope to repel a hundred-thousand men, ladders, siege towers, and a wealth of military talent. Make him see sense, and you will be well rewarded."

"Saving my friend is reward enough, Prime Minister," Jin Xiang replied ingratiatingly: he then left the Shu camp to meet with Hao Zhao.

"...This won't work!" Wei Yan barked.

"Why should he refuse...?" Kongming asked plainly. "Stop demoralising us."

"...Welcome," Hao Zhao said with warmth as Jin Xiang walked into the court hall.

"I'm glad to see we can speak privately, Bodao," Jin Xiang said meekly.

"Sadly, you're not here to speak freely of old and better times, are you...?" Hao Zhao chuckled. "You're here on behalf of Zhuge Liang... my spies informed me of your visit to the old rebel."

"...I have transferred my loyalty to Shu Han, and with good reason," Jin Xiang said honestly. "Zhuge Kongming is good and wise, and the cause of Han is the true cause. Bodao, why forsake the light for the darkness...? Wei supplanted Han, yet Han lives on in Shu. Turn away from Wei, as others, like I have, and as Wang Ping and Jiang Wei have done. Give Chen Cang to the Prime Minister, so that we can hurry on to Luoyang, depose the false emperor, and bring stability back to the land! After fifty years of division, does the land not deserve an enduring peace...?"

"...Han was the cause of the division, with its corruption and weakness," Hao Zhao retorted. "Even a rustic fool like me knows that. Jin Xiang, you come to me as an enemy agent, not a friend, and attempt to induce me to betray a lord that has shown me great kindness. I am a man of Wei, as you once were, and I will die as one; surely you knew me well enough to know that, if you ever really knew me. Now please, go back to your Prime Minister, Zhuge Liang, and thank him for valuing my life so much as to want to spare it... but there will be no surrender here. Tell him to attack, so that we can resolve this quickly."

"...Very well," Jin Xiang sighed. "Farewell, Hao Bodao."

"Farewell, Mister Jin Xiang," Hao replied with a pleasant smile.

"…He can be swayed if we press him, I know it," Kongming said desperately as Jin Xiang finished relaying his fruitless visit to Chen Cang. "If you go back, and talk to him again… tell him precisely what he is up against… I think that you'll make him see sense and surrender."

Jin Xiang hesitated, saying, "I really don't-"

"Look, you really do have to try again!" Kongming urged angrily. "The fate of our entire army rests on this, Mister Jin! Every day that your friend refuses to cooperate is a day of food wasted!"

"We're doomed before we even started," Wei Yan muttered as he stood nearby with Generals Zhang Boqi and Ma Dai. "Ten days' grain, that's all it would've needed to take Chang'an. This plan was a huge mistake."

"This is not a lot that I ask of you, not compared to what I ask of others on this campaign, Mister Jin," Kongming said impatiently.

"Okay," Jin Xiang conceded. "I'll go back… I'll try again."

"*Thank you*, Mister Jin," Kongming said gruffly. "Go now… time is against us."


"Jin Xiang," Hao Zhao said as he greeted his former friend at the front gates of Chen Cang. "Why have you come back here…?"

"I wonder, can we talk again…?" Jin Xiang replied meekly.

"Perhaps you intend to defect back to Wei…?" Hao Zhao teased: his soldiers laughed mockingly. "…Come on then, we'll talk in the main hall, as we did before… away from prying ears."

"…So what do you want this time…?" Hao Zhao asked with amusement as soon as the two were seated as host and guest.

"I went back to Kongming… I mean the Prime Minister," Jin Xiang bumbled nervously. "I… I told him what you said… but he really does not want to fight."

"I'm sure he doesn't," Hao Zhao said with a smile. "He can't have much grain after fighting a campaign so very recently. He has maybe six weeks' worth…? …If that…?"

"…The Prime Minister is very cautious," Jin Xiang replied. "He would not make such a grievous tactical error. He can outlast you, in terms of men, grain, and morale. He has a hundred thousand men at his disposal… you have one thousand. He has siege towers, siege ladders, cavalry, catapults, battering rams… how can you hope to last against such odds? Please, Bodao, see the light, before it is too late!"

"You will not take 'No' for an answer, I see," Hao Zhao said as he reached downward to his left side and took up a bow and arrow; Jin Xiang was suddenly very afraid. Hao Zhao looked into the eyes of the envoy, and added, "What I said before, I meant… if you truly knew me, you would not say these things that you say, but then, I wonder if you ever did."

"…Bodao…!" Jin Xiang said with a pleading tone.

"You call me Bodao, because you know me," Hao Zhao said as he fitted the arrow to his bow, pulled the string back, and aimed it at Jin Xiang, such that the arrowhead was a hand-width from his forehead. "…And yes, I know you… but this arrow doesn't. Get out, go back, and tell your master that there will be no peace."

Jin Xiang scrambled backward, fell over clumsily, and hurried to his feet to flee, all the while accompanied by Hao Zhao's mocking laughter. When he reached the gates, the soldiers heckled him until he was clear of the drawbridge.

"...I'm sorry," Jin Xiang concluded upon his return; Kongming was pacing back forth agitatedly, fanning himself with nonsensical speed.
"We should leave a decoy force here and go to Chang'an," Wei Yan suggested.
"We are not going to Chang'an!" Kongming barked. "General Wei, stop going on about Chang'an! We are in Chen Cang, and we will take Chen Cang! Deng Zhi, Wu Ban, Zhang Boqi, Zhang Bogong, Gao Xiang, Ma Dai, Wang Ping... prepare your forces. We launch a full-scale attack on the city immediately!"
The generals – though obviously hesitant – departed to follow their orders.
"Wei Yan, Liao Hua... prepare special forces, siege equipment, and the archery divisions," Kongming ordered. "...This man Hao Zhao will regret riling me."

************

## 111

The Shu army gave Hao Zhao of Chen Cang no more chances or ultimatums, and began its attack immediately after Jin Xiang's second encounter. Unfortunately for Kongming, Hao Zhao was completely ready for the assault, and had been for some time, due to Cao Zhen's foresight. As the first lines of Shu soldiers used their multi-purpose siege ladders to cross the moat, archers shot at them, picking off dozens of men as they crawled slowly along the horizontal ladders without any protection whatsoever. Bodies started to fill the moat, as Kongming watched helplessly from his nearby vantage point.

"...Look at it this way," Wei Yan said coldly. "...Less men means more grain."

Kongming eyed Wei Yan angrily, but did not respond.

Soldiers were now reaching the other side of the moat as the barrage of arrows from Chen Cang thinned; now the siege ladders were put to their more common use of vertical climbing. But as the soldiers neared the top, the archers reappeared, this time with flaming arrows.

"We have to pull the men back," Yang Yi said worriedly.

"We expected casualties," Kongming countered. "I... I hate this as much as you do, but we have to do this."

The arrows hit their mark; those aimed downward at the climbers burned the ladders and the men, leaving charred corpses around the city walls. The other targets were the second set of siege ladders being used to cross the moat; now charred wood and flesh joined the previous heaps of bodies.

"I can't do this... **PULL THE MEN BACK!**" Kongming said suddenly; the generals ordered the gongs sounded with poorly hidden relief, and the Shu forces withdrew, the victorious chants of the defenders ringing in their ears.

"...We'll never take the city like that," Kongming said angrily. "I... I can't just keep sending men like that, wave after wave, to die pointlessly. We have to fill in that moat so we can get the siege engines and rams to the walls."

"We were filling it in nicely, I thought, with our men," Wei Yan heckled irritably.

"We must secure soil and rubble to fill the moat... we'll do it under cover of darkness," Kongming ordered. "That way, they'll hit less of the men with their random firing. Have there been any reports of enemy reinforcements...?"

"Not yet," Jiang Wei replied. "We've killed two messengers... but someone must have got through."

"How long will it take to fill the moat completely...?" Kongming wondered.

"Two days, maybe, going back and forth," Wei Yan replied indifferently. "They can't send out saboteurs to stop us, but they can shoot at us... so two days."

"Then we fill the entire moat," Kongming declared. "We can bury our dead at the same time, that way... inappropriate though it is."

The moat was gradually filled over the next two days and nights, amid arrow fire from the walls of the city. Hao Zhao often came to the walls to watch, but he was not remotely fazed by the possibility of losing his main external defence.

"Now we will show them," Kongming said angrily once the work was complete.

"Siege towers...?" Jiang Wei supposed: Kongming nodded silently.

The wooden siege towers slowly rolled toward the walls of Chen Cang, but the defenders did not fire a single arrow as the machines approached.

"...They're going to wait until the towers reach the walls," Kongming realised.

"Well then shouldn't we pull back...?" Liao Hua protested.

"If we can just get a few to the wall... just a few," Kongming said desperately. "I can't afford to be cautious, we have no time! We just need to secure a few!"

But as Kongming explained his actions to his increasingly cynical commanders, the archers finally appeared at the walls, once again armed with flaming arrows. As the soldiers in the towers prepared to disembark onto the walls of Chen Cang, flaming arrows set the structures alight, one after the other, filling the air with screams as the men inside caught fire and burned alive, or fell several metres to certain death.

"...**SEND THE BATTERING RAMS!**" Kongming screamed. "**GET THE RAMS TO THE WALL, TRY SIEGE LADDERS...!**"

Kongming started to cough violently: he was putting himself under enormous strain, and the air was becoming thick with the derivatives of burning flesh and wood, as far away from the front line and his command post. The large wooden rams were pushed toward the city by their bearers, and siege ladders were tried once again, but once again, Hao Zhao was ready. This time, hot oil and flaming arrows met the siege ladder climbers, frying or charring the skin of the soldiers and sending them plummeting to their deaths. And to meet the wooden rams, rocks and flaming arrows were rained down; the machines and their human movers were consumed or crushed together.

"**RETREAT, RETREAT, pull them back...!**" Kongming pleaded through violent coughing; once again, the Shu forces made a painful retreat, followed by mocking laughter, and returned to their camp with next to no energy or morale.

"We have to get over the walls eventually," Kongming said to his increasingly weary and angry generals. "Next time, we'll set up archery towers and catapults to drive the defenders from the walls, and then we'll scale them."

"There's a lot of activity along the walls that makes little sense," Liao Hua reported worriedly. "One man... though he's almost burned to death... said that he reached the top of the wall, and thought he saw men 'quite far back'... too far to be on the wall... carrying building stones."

"Confusion in a moment of crisis," Kongming supposed. "We have no time for such things now. We have, at the most, thirty days' grain, and morale is plummeting. We have to score a victory on our next push."

That next push began with the catapults and archery towers as Kongming planned, but well-placed fire arrows burned the archery towers as soon as they were completed and manned, killing many valiant men. The catapults fared better due to their being out of range of most shots, and the damage they did was helpful to the besiegers. Several siege ladders and rams made it to the south wall without serious incident, and the first breaches were made, to the relief of Kongming.

"There...!" Kongming declared to a cynical Wei Yan. "We have done it, at last! Men are over what parts of the wall still stand, and-"

"**REPORT!**" a frantic messenger shouted as he ran toward the command post.

"...Go on," Kongming said apprehensively.

"There... there is another wall, behind the first one!" the messenger said desperately: Kongming started to fan himself swiftly. "It runs all the way around the inner perimeter... the men that got in are trapped, and are being pelted with rocks and hot oil! ...And they're burning the rams!"

"Right, right, okay, thank you, I understand," Kongming said emotionlessly as he turned to face away from his followers: Wei Yan gestured dismissively, and the messenger withdrew.

"So what now...?" Wei Yan wondered.

Without turning around, Kongming said, "General Wei... recall the men... stop the catapults... fall back... help the wounded, if we can... retreat to camp."

Wei Yan bowed very slightly, and departed.

The eyes of the other generals and officials were on Kongming; he retired silently, with Yang Yi, Zong Yu, Dong Jue and Jiang Wei at either side of him.


"...I feel like the most foolish man alive, Boye," Kongming admitted as he sat in his command tent that night with Jiang Wei. "I once laughed at Zhou Gongjin's timidity in his dealings with Cao Ren at Jiangling... my respect for his slight stomach for mass suicide is newfound, for I have none. What I do, I do for the state... what I ask others to do is for the good of the land, as well as the Emperor... but when men are in pain, they start to question. ...Even *I* start to question."

"The men understand why we're here, and despite the losses, their hatred is fixed solely on Hao Zhao for not surrendering, and sparing us this," Jiang Wei insisted.

"We have to try something else," Kongming said desperately. "I can't just keep sending men to their deaths like that...!"

"The only other option we have is sappers," Jiang Wei supposed.

"Exactly," Kongming replied. "If we can't go over the walls, and we can't go through the walls... we go under them."

"But sending men into a tunnel system is risky," Jiang Wei said awkwardly. "If they realise, they'll collapse the tunnels with the men inside, and they'll be buried alive, with no way out."

"I... I have to risk it," Kongming decided. "Every attempt to get saboteurs inside has failed, every attempt to breach the walls has failed... we'll put on a show of staying with our current plan, as much as it pains me, and get started on tunnels."

Over the next two weeks, sappers dug tunnels that led to the inside of Chen Cang, while Kongming kept up a systematic – but noticeably more restrained – barrage of siege ladders, rams and towers, with some limited archery fire to try and knock some of the defenders from the walls without hitting their own men. Hao Zhao noticed the slightly reduced forces, and guessed that there were sappers at work; as the siege reached its third week, two pieces of news were delivered to Kongming that brought this second campaign to a swift, ignominious end.

"**REPORT!**" a messenger hailed urgently: another had been received the previous night, and Kongming was still reeling from the news that Zhang He was on his way with a relief force.

"What *now*…?" Yang Yi whined.

"Perhaps they found your backbone," Wei Yan grunted.

"…Enough, Wei Yan… messenger, report," Kongming said weakly.

"General Deng Zhi… says that the tunnels have been discovered!" the messenger said with fear and upset.

"…Are the men being evacuated…?" Kongming asked worriedly.

"It's too late!" the messenger sobbed. "Hao Zhao had them collapsed! The…!"

Kongming screamed with anguish and collapsed to his knees, as he thought of the horrible death that awaited the men in the tunnels.

"It isn't your fault," Jiang Wei insisted.

"It is," Kongming said miserably. "…Zhang He will be here soon, and our supplies are almost exhausted… my gambit has failed. We'll have to withdraw. But they'll definitely send a force to pursue us to the border… we'll score one small victory before this campaign ends. Liao Hua…?"

"Yes," Liao Hua said expectantly.

"…Prepare the digging teams, get them to the predetermined point north of the Qinling Mountains," Kongming ordered. "Take the archery teams as well, and get everything set up as I briefed you."

Liao Hua bowed respectfully and withdrew.

"…Perhaps we'll get Zhang He," Kongming hoped. "That would certainly be a great help to us. …Okay, let's start to withdraw… and make it as obvious as possible that we're in a hurry."

It was not Zhang He that reached Chen Cang City first, but Wang Shuang, a minor rising star among the Wei generals. Hao Zhao welcomed his vanguard force into Chen Cang, and relayed the events of the past three weeks.

"…So how long ago did Zhuge Liang retreat…?" Wang Shuang enquired.

"A few days ago," Hao Zhao replied.

"Then there is still glory to be had!" Wang Shuang said bravely.

"Uh… General Zhang He left with me some valuable advice," Hao Zhao said cautiously. "He said that it was folly to pursue Zhuge Liang… that he is versed in the art of the ambush, and a general would certainly lose his life."

"Can I fear Zhuge Liang…?" Wang Shuang chortled. "You have just dealt him a massive defeat! Scores of his men lay dead around your fortress, a feat that will make a hero, nay, a legend of you! He is now weak and frightened, dashing home to Hanzhong… now I will make *my* name, and capture Zhuge Liang alive!"
"…If you must insist, be careful, and don't overstretch yourself," Hao Zhao said with respect. "We are the men that are the future of Wei: we can't afford to exhaust ourselves on worthless chaff like the men of Shu."

Wang Shuang ignored the advice, and pursued the Shu forces without restraint or care; as he reached an area of land below the Qinling Mountains – an area that was uneven and treacherous – he was forced to take a path toward what seemed to be the rear of the Shu army in the far distance.
"**STOP, ZHUGE LIANG!**" Wang Shuang cried out. "**HERE IS WANG SHUANG, AND I HAVE COME FOR YOUR HEAD!**"
Several of his horsemen raced ahead, but as they reached an area of disturbed ground, men and mount alike were thrown in the air by powerful explosive devices hidden in the earth. As Wang Shuang and his force reeled from the shock of seeing their comrades fall victim to Kongming's landmines, Kongming himself appeared on a high ridge, sat as always in his carriage, and carrying his feather fan.
"**WANG SHUANG!**" Jiang Wei shouted from Kongming's side. "**HERE IS THE PRIME MINISTER OF THE HAN: BUT IT IS YOU THAT WILL LOSE YOUR HEAD TODAY!**"
Before Wang Shuang could make any response, Kongming raised his fan, and crossbowmen appeared on the ridges around and above Wang Shuang, who could only scream defiantly as arrows rained down on his position, killing every man and horse on the mountain path.
"I wanted Zhang He," Kongming said regrettably.
"Wang Shuang was a future hero," Jiang Wei reported.
"All the same, I wanted Zhang He," Kongming replied. "…But then, there is always next time. …**WITHDRAW!**"

When Zhang He's main force finally caught up with Wang Shuang, the subordinate general and his men had been dead for many hours, and Kongming was safely over the border into Hanzhong, having lost hundreds of men in a failed siege, but having gained a small victory with the death of a promising enemy general. Hao Zhao was hailed as a great hero for his defence of Chen Cang, and summoned to the capital to receive praise from the Wei Emperor, Cao Rui: he would fall ill and die shortly afterward, and never reap the rewards of his high status.


************

## 112

The second Shu retreat was even more demoralising than the end of the first campaign had been: although Kongming had, at the last, been able to remove a possible future threat to Shu in the form of Wang Shuang, the overall campaign had been very costly.

"Regardless of Wu's successes for the next year, we must concentrate on intensive farming and building a more professional militia," Kongming said to Yueying as he finished his self-deprecatory appraisal of the siege of Chen Cang. "I've left Jiang Wan, Xi Zheng, Jiang Wei and Fei Shi in charge of court and state affairs... I need some time to think."

"...So... you won't be attempting another campaign any time soon...?" Yueying prompted hopefully.

"I didn't say there would be no campaign," Kongming replied. "But yes, we cannot launch another full-scale offensive against Wei right now. A smaller army can be used to make useful, minor gains such as the Wudu region, which we must pass through every time we launch an expedition. If those areas were pacified, and were friendly to us, it would benefit us immensely. If we leave them as they are... well, Wei might one day use them against us in an expedition of their own."

"Twice now, you've been forced to turn back," Yueying mused. "A third retreat would doubtlessly give Sima Yi the foundation he needs for an invasion."

"I, and all others, agree," Kongming said calmly. "But he'll invade eventually anyway... better he does so at a time of our choosing, wherein we can repel him and dissuade him from unwanted further attempts. ...But the situation is grimmer than I would dare let on at court. The men are demoralised... we lost hundreds at Chen Cang, and a further number are badly burned or suffering from breakages or disease. A number of generals are taken ill... Zilong is still unwell... and the supplies from Nanzhong are not enough to rebuild our stocks. I've written to Lord Meng, but in all honesty, he is not going to remain conciliatory if I ask for much more from his people, and we can't afford another southern expedition to pacify him again. The only choice is to communicate with our former northern tribal allies, like the Qiang and Di, and see what we can get from them... but I can't do that while the Qinling Mountains and the surrounding areas are borderline neutral."

"...I see," Yueying murmured.

"Anyhow, the brief lull means I can spend some time with my family and friends, and I intend to make the most of it!" Kongming declared. "I have not composed a poem or song in many months... though I have had much cause to... and I wonder if some joviality with my peers might not help boost their morale a bit. ...And as for us... I shall like to make sure my son knows what I look like!"

Yueying smiled gladly.

"...And we can play our qins together, and we can have some time to ourselves," Kongming continued. "...It will be a brief respite... but a happy one."

"...I hate to bring up the subject at such a moment," Yueying said apprehensively, "but... what about Ma Su...? His family and our family are one... but-"
"I shall attend to it," Kongming promised; he got up, collected his fan, and departed for his office before Yueying could finish what she had intended to say.

"Kongming, why are you back...?" Fei Shi said with surprise as Kongming entered his office, fanning himself casually.
"Ma Su," Kongming replied. "He's still in prison, am I right...?"
"Ma Su... died," Fei Shi explained awkwardly. Kongming lowered his fan and frowned miserably as Fei Shi added, "Xiang Lang found him slumped in his cell, and called for help... but there wasn't anything that anyone could do."
"...Did you intend to release him after all...?" Jiang Wan enquired pointedly.
"No," Kongming replied uncomfortably. "I... just... ... ...was he left to starve...?"
"Nobody knows," Fei Shi said sadly. "He was just... like that. Xiang Lang asked the jailer what happened, and he was very angry, but no charges were brought... his body was buried as quickly as possible, and-"
"His family haven't been notified," Kongming scolded. "I-"
"They have," Fei Shi insisted. "Of course they have!"
"Wait a minute... *Xiang Lang* found him...?" Kongming said with sudden caution. "Then...! ...But then, does it matter... does it really, actually matter anymore...?"
"Does *what* matter anymore...?" Jiang Wan wondered.
"...Nothing, Gongyan, nothing," Kongming said thoughtfully. "I should go home... but we should all meet at some point and enjoy wine and song. The soldiers are having homecoming celebrations, and so should we. ...Farewell for now."
As Kongming left the office, Jiang Wan turned to Fei Shi and said, "Xiang Lang might have saved Ma Su... is that right...?"
Fei Shi smiled awkwardly, and replied, "I wouldn't know."

"...I should have let you finish speaking," Kongming said as he entered his living quarters, where Yueying, Qiao's widow, Ma Su's widow, Ma Liang's widow and a their children were gathered. "I should get another white garment to wear."
"My husband loved you as a brother," Ma Su's widow said with a kind smile. "He knew that his crime had to be punished... that's why he asked you to punish him. He entrusted us to you because he trusted you completely... he said he was sorry that in the end, he couldn't equal you as a man."
Kongming lowered his head, closed his eyes, and started sobbing silently as he thought of what he had been forced to do.
"You are all our family," Yueying said for her husband. "Our home is your home... let's go on together."

A month passed, and as word of the disastrous Chen Cang campaign reached King Sun Quan of Wu, a not entirely unexpected decision was made that provoked great anger in the court of Liu Shan.

"...This is an outrage!" Li Fu said to his fellow courtiers. "Sun Quan, the rebel, is breaking faith with us again!"

"Wait," Kongming pleaded as the court erupted with angry chattering; Second Emperor Liu Shan was obviously nervous, and was looking at his 'Second Father', Kongming, with hopeful eyes.

"...We cannot see this as a break of faith with us, or as a declaration of war," Kongming continued. "Remember what happened when First Emperor decided to settle scores with Wu before fighting Wei... Wu has a near unbroken defensive record, and is not to be provoked on its own soil."

"We can't just let this man declare himself an Emperor!" Fei Shi protested.

"...I don't like it any more than anyone else," Kongming promised. "But look at the situation... we are on our second forced retreat, while Wu have enjoyed yet another Red Cliffs against Wei at Stone Town. They believe the Mandate of Heaven has passed to them... let them. We cannot divide ourselves against Wei and Wu right now, so let us continue our alliance with Wu... this announcement has distanced them irrevocably from Wei, so we can rest assured that there will be no peace between them now. Let's agree to share the land, and-"

"An Emperor cannot share his mother country with another!" Dong He insisted.

"...Let's agree to share the land," Kongming continued calmly, "and maintain good relations for now... remember, their eastern offensives aid our own. I propose that we delay responding to show some deep thought, but send a congratulatory tribute and our commitment to the alliance at some later date, perhaps after our next expedition. We'll agree to divide the north between us, or split the land into north and south... regardless, Wu can and must be dealt with *later*, when Wei is removed. I will not repeat First Emperor's mistake."

"I agree with Kongming," Jiang Wan declared. "We should be cautious in dealing with Wu... overconfidence will overstretch them in the end."

"Your Majesty, the final decision rests with you, of course," Dong Yun said to Liu Shan. "What is your heavenly will...?"

"...I agree with Second Father, the Prime Minister, Mister Zhuge," Liu Shan said timidly. "I agree that we should, uh, agree to share the land... maintain good relations... delay responding, that shows deep thought... yes, they can be dealt with later."

"...Very good, Your Majesty," Kongming said gladly; he then made obeisance to his emperor, who smiled sheepishly.

"...So now you have made an official announcement of your intention to launch a third campaign, Kongming," Dong Yun said in a courtroom meeting between the officials and generals that evening. "You're overstretching the army."

"Generals Chen Shi and Ma Dai will go into the Qinling Mountains and take Wudu and Yinping, ensuring the route in and out of Hanzhong belongs to us," Kongming explained. "I don't expect this to be a drain on resources, since a large proportion of the population and resources have already been removed by Wei a long, long time ago, some as long ago as when Cao Cao ruled."

"I can see your logic," General Hu Ji mused, "but General *Chen*...?"

"Do you not think I can manage such a simple thing...?" Chen Shi asked. "What merits do you have to question mine...?"

"I mean no offense," Hu Ji insisted. "It is my understanding that Zhang He, the best general Wei has, is now stationed in Tianshui."

"Correct," Kongming said with a smile. "You're well informed."

"...Even with the death of Wang Shuang and the illness afflicting Hao Zhao, Zhang He has in his service Guo Huai, a general that has bested Di and Qiang barbarian kings before," Hu Ji proposed. "If either of those two generals were to intercept you, general... it would be a disaster, akin to your defeats in Hanzhong and Jieting. A man of martial valour, such as Wei Yan, is needed here."

"Wei Yan must remain in Hanzhong and train the troops," Kongming said insistently. "I appreciate your view, but-"

"Wang Ping, then," Hu Ji interrupted. "General Wang has field experience against Zhang He and Guo Huai-"

"He also has experience fighting *with* them as an *ally*!" Chen Shi growled. "You'd send a Wei defector to fight them, worse yet a former *comrade*...?"

"...Uh," Jiang Wei chuckled irritably, "I am also a Wei defector, General Chen. And it was Wang Ping that saved the day at Jieting... were I not in full agreement with Master Zhuge that General Wang is also needed to train the troops, I would agree with General Hu."

"I can best Guo Huai," Chen Shi proclaimed.

"You were an embarrassing failure at Jieting, and even now, your hair has not grown back," Hu Ji suggested angrily. "Wasn't Guo Huai at Jieting...?"

Others struggled to contain their smiles: as a former favourite of Liu Bei, Chen Shi was not executed for his incompetent performance at Jieting. Rather, his body hair – seen as a sacred gift that should not be cut – had been shaved as punishment, and his shame was well known throughout Shu as a result. Chen Shi seethed at the comment.

"And if Zhang He himself advances...?" Hu Ji challenged further.

"He won't," Kongming promised. "He's very cautious... after his defeats at the hands of Zhang Fei, and the rout at Mount Dingjun, and especially after the ambush at Qinling that killed Wang Shuang... Zhang He is very, very cautious. He will not advance personally... he'll send Guo Huai, because as you said, Guo Huai has defeated the Di of Wudu before, and knows the terrain well."

"...Something makes no sense here," Jiang Wan suggested. "We're going to take Wudu and Yinping, and that's it...? We're going to fight and defeat Guo Huai – a major general of the Wei army, and subordinate of Zhang He – and *that's it*...?"

"Of course, I intend a strike against Tianshui if General Chen is successful," Kongming said with a smile. "With Chen Cang now in weaker hands, that will be easier to take as a third objective... and we'll have local supplies, local support and a reinforced supply route aiding our advance."

A month later, Chen Shi and Ma Dai led a force of men into the Qinling Mountains, intent on seizing the two regions they formed, Wudu and Yinping. As anticipated, Zhang He of Wei learned of the advance and despatched Guo Huai to prevent the takeover.

Kongming remained within his base of operations in Hanzhong, awaiting every incoming report with interest.

"As I thought, Guo Huai moved to Jianwei to begin his counterattack," Kongming said to an audience of generals. "Now we have a chance to be rid of Guo Huai... Chen Shi has moved his main forces to Jianwei to confront Guo Huai, and despite the latter being adept at mountain warfare, the men of Shu are better by far. While General Chen defeats Guo Huai, we will move another force to block reinforcements and keep Zhang He trapped in Tianshui, while moving another force to prevent Chen Cang from being an efficient communications and supply hub."

"Ah, I see," Hu Ji said with a smirk. "Many of the new inhabitants of the region west of Chang'an were displaced from Wudu and Yinping... we're trying to spark a popular rebellion in Tianshui, An Ding and Nan'an again, and cut the area away from Wei."

"Precisely," Kongming replied. "Guo Huai will be defeated... I've given General Chen elite men and weapons. But even if General Chen falters, Guo Huai will still be withdrawn to defend against our strike on Tianshui: after all, who trades two worthless mountaintops for a city...? Once we have Wudu and Yinping, we'll have no problem taking the demoralised Chen Cang, and preparing the way for a decisive strike at Chang'an!"

Wei Yan raised his hand slightly; Kongming sneered irritably.

"No," Kongming said flatly. "There will be no sudden strike on Chang'an. I know that the last two campaigns ended in failure, and many believe that my plans are flawed... and, therefore, yours must be flawless. Our first campaign failed entirely because my plans were disobeyed... the second, because our greatest enemy was not Hao Zhao, but *time*... if I'd had a year to break him, I would have, in six months or less: but I had a month, and he knew it.

"This was never about pride, or whose plan was better... Cao Rui feels safe having a worthless relative like Xiahou Mao governing Chang'an because he is surrounded by loyal troops, sound defences, and a general populace that has done extremely well out of being part of the state of Wei. Large commercial centres like Chang'an would be very reluctant to become a part of an enemy territory, because all the luxury and socio-economic stability they've had will be lost. *Yes*, you might scare Xiahou Mao... but do you remember Zhou Yu's decisive victory over Huang Zu at Xiakou...? Xiakou, as a major trading city of Jing, was fiercely opposed to occupation, and it is only because of the collapse of Jing, and Cao Cao's invasion being *worse*, that the people reluctantly accepted becoming part of Eastern Wu!"

"...And that is your appraisal, Acting Prime Minister...?" Wei Yan retorted. "That we are as bad as Eastern Wu...?"

"To the people of Chang'an, we will be," Kongming retorted. "They have enjoyed two decades of being a capital city under a Cao-led regime of some sort... they're hardly likely to roll over and wag their tails when they see us marching on their gates, because to them, the empire of the Han is a memory that will take more than a sharp sword to reinvigorate. Yes, you might take the city from the army in ten days, Wei Yan... but could you *keep it*, when every merchant, noble and peasant will *hate you*...? ...If that weren't true, would I have left Lord Meng to rule Nanzhong...?"

Wei Yan looked to the other generals for support, but their eyes looked elsewhere.

"...Fine," Wei Yan conceded. "I hope your comparisons are valid."

"I believe they are," Kongming said confidently, "and I won't risk testing them, regardless. Now, as for our deployments..."

Chen Shi deployed his men with some skill, and Guo Huai's forces – which were inferior in number – were driven back at Jianwei. At that point, the orders from Guo Huai's superiors were simple enough: allow Shu to have what were two poorly populated and relatively useless mountain districts, and prevent an advance of the main Shu force toward Tianshui. Guo Huai redirected his forces to face Kongming, allowing Chen Shi to be the victor in the Qinling Mountains.

At this point, Kongming had three armies to deal with in the immediate term: Guo Huai's, Zhang He's, and the garrison at Chen Cang. With reinforcements from Cao Zhen threatened, there was only one safe course to take.

"...*Retreat*...?" Wei Yan said with disbelief.

"We're going to be surrounded otherwise," Kongming retorted. "We must retreat into Hanzhong now, and-"

"And await the invasion force of half a million men that will pursue us," Wei Yan suggested angrily. "Three campaigns in less than two years...? There is no way that Sima Yi is going to be refused permission to strike into Hanzhong now!"

"Ah... *now* you fear Sima Yi," Kongming chuckled lightly. "Your defences are exemplary, Wei Wenchang... more than enough to repel an attacking force."

"...And now *you* talk of putting theories to the test," Wei Yan countered. "You would never test mine about a flash strike on Chang'an in case it led to a minor defeat... now you want to put my defences to the test, at the risk of the entire state???"

"We have nothing to fear, since we'll be defending," Kongming promised. "Our force is chipping away at Guo Huai to little effect... he's refusing to fall for my formations, and he won't advance... he's buying time for reinforcements that we haven't the grain to outlast. Let Sima Yi come into Hanzhong... he'll regret it."

News travelled in both directions shortly after the aborted third campaign: when the news reached Chengdu that Wudu and Yinping had been taken, Liu Shan insisted – to the chagrin of Li Yan and others – that Kongming be immediately reinstated as Prime Minister as a reward. But that news was accompanied by an altogether less encouraging announcement: Zhao Yun, known to one and all as Zilong, had finally succumbed to illness and died aged more than 70. For Kongming, this was a bitter blow: he had come to respect Zilong very much, and was hoping that he might lend his popular, charismatic presence to the upcoming defence against Wei.

"Fate gives with one hand, and takes with the other," Kongming complained to Jiang Wei as they sat alone in Kongming's Hanzhong residence. "I am Prime Minister again, and can finally put to rest the constant prodding by Wei Yan; Fei Yi has returned from Wu, so there will finally be someone else to diffuse tension between Wei Yan and Yang Yi; but to lose Zilong...?"

"I know his death was more than just the loss of a fine general," Jiang Wei said sadly. "Zilong and I spoke only a few times before he took ill, but he was a great man that quashed any doubts I had about pledging myself to the cause of Shu... his appraisal of his service inspired me, told me a story that I'd never heard before... I can never say the name of Cao Cao again, and not scowl at it."

"Second Emperor is heartbroken," Kongming sighed. "Twice, Zilong saved him... once from Wei, and once from Wu. Veteran General Chen Dao still guards the palace out of stubborn duty, but he nearly toppled to the floor when he heard the news... the two were our First Emperor's sword and shield. ...A very bad omen, Boye... very bad. The men are demoralised, and that can't be, not when we have so much to prepare for."

"...It gives a lot of power to Wei Yan, as well," Jiang Wei suggested.

"It does," Kongming lamented. "His arrogance is dangerous... he is a difficult man to disrespect, but an easy one to dislike. He sways opinion over this plan of his for striking Chang'an... time and again, he suggests this plan, when it was Guan Yu's downfall to go deep into enemy territory and attack a fortified stronghold! He's no Guan Yu, no matter what he thinks. Yet he's now our most notable general... at a time when I need reliable men that do as they're told, like Zilong."

"What are we going to do, Master...?" Jiang Wei enquired.

"We're going to build defences across Hanzhong, and be ready for them," Kongming revealed. "I want everything we have guarding that border when they cross it. I want everything diverted here... and we'll have to think about replying to Sun Quan now... unless we want the threat of Wu deciding to 'get annoyed with us' and attacking White Emperor City, or something."

"Would they...?" Jiang Wei chuckled nervously.

"Emperor Sun Quan is becoming eccentric," Kongming sighed. "So I wouldn't be surprised, no."

In the Wei capital Luoyang, newly appointed Minister of Defence Cao Zhen walked toward his sovereign, Cao Rui, with a petition in his hand. The officials and generals knew what he intended to request, and they suspected that the answer was equally obvious.

"Your Majesty," Cao Zhen began, "our illustrious cause is being hampered by the nuisance of two rogue states... Eastern Wu, and Western Shu. While Wu basks in its own arrogance and enjoys the illusion that it is an empire, Shu has made what is now its third attempt to destabilise the region west of Chang'an... attempts that have failed, but not without cost. It is my belief that they will return, coming again and again to harass us and waste valuable resources, and we cannot risk one of their campaigns coinciding with their 'ally', Wu, and having considerable effect. If we do not attack Hanzhong and Yi, and destroy the state of Shu, they will be a thorn in our side for many years to come."

"What do you propose, Zidan...?" Cao Rui asked plainly.

"What I propose, Your Majesty, is a three-pronged attack directly into Hanzhong through the mountain ranges," Cao Zhen explained. "I can lead one army, Sima Yi will lead the second, and General Zhang He will lead the third. With a combined force of four hundred thousand, I am confident that Hanzhong will fall within a month, and that Yi will fall within a year of that."

"You suggest devoting large resources to this endeavour," Cao Rui noted. "What about the threat of action by Eastern Wu...?"

"Sun Quan awaits a response from Shu regarding his recent 'ascension', and will make no move to assist Shu until he knows that his position will not be contested," Cao Zhen chuckled dismissively. "By not attacking Wei during our invasion, Sun Quan practically guarantees cooperation from Shu in his ridiculous scheme to divide the nation equally. Further to that, Sun Quan wants to expand his domains, and has a lot of resources devoted to searching for mythical islands, and pacifying neighbouring barbarian territories. He is of no concern to us... Man Chong is quite capable of maintaining a long-term defence at Hefei should the worst occur, and the Jing region is not only well defended, but close enough to Hanzhong for swift diversion of resources... again, in the event of the worst occurring."

"You appear to have thought the matter through well, Zidan," Cao Rui praised. "I will grant you permission to exterminate my family's long-time enemy... you will be given the seal of command, and four hundred thousand men to use as you see fit."

"Thank you, Your Majesty," the overweight Cao Zhen said as he prostrated himself on the ground as best he could. "I hope to bring swift word of our success."

"Exercise caution," Cao Rui warned. "Zhuge Liang is a master of ambush... he has already cost me one champion, and cursed the life of another to end early. Do not fall into any of his traps."

"We'll gain his surrender, or his head to bring back for your inspection," Cao Zhen promised. "He'll not get the better of us."

Word was sent from Chengdu to Eastern Wu congratulating Emperor Sun, along with fine gifts to cement the alliance; this meant that there was no going back for Shu Han, since any victory over Wei would now lead to two rival empires, by its own concession. Kongming began his vast defensive works plan immediately, intending to fortify all of the plains of Hanzhong against Wei. Work began at the start of the summer, and by the middle of the autumn of the same year, preparations were almost complete. Whenever Cao Zhen of Wei chose to invade, Shu Han was as ready as it would ever be.

************

## 113

Kongming held an emergency meeting of his commanders to discuss the reports of Cao Zhen's three vast armies.

"A hundred and twenty thousand men each," Liao Hua mused nervously.

"...And no help whatsoever from Wu," Wei Yan complained.

"Sun Quan's gone peculiar, I hear," Hu Ji said irritably, "and has most of his army off looking for exciting new lands to conquer... has he forgotten that he hasn't secured *this* land yet???"

"Forget Sun Quan," Kongming said coolly; he was fanning himself slowly, and staring at Wei Yan.

"...Why do you single me out for that look...?" Wei Yan asked.

"General Wei, your defences are but part of the action to come," Kongming declared. "We'll need to do much more than sit at the walls like Hao Zhao of Chen Cang. We need to pincer Wei if we're to succeed."

"*Pincer* Wei...?" Liao Hua mused. "But without help from Wu, how can we do that, Prime Minister...?"

"The Qiang, the Xianbei, the Di... all of the tribes within and beyond the mountains can be brought into play against Wei, with the right coaxing," Kongming replied. "With their support, we can turn these armies around, and soundly damage them as they retreat, into the bargain."

"And how do we do that...?" Wu Yi asked pointedly. "How do we coax them...?"

"Ah, Wu Ziyuan," Kongming said with cheer. "I was hoping that you might ask such a thing... it is why I asked you to join us, in fact."

"...I see," Liao Hua said with a smile. "To earn their trust, we need to send a man of high status, as well as a man of fierce character."

"I was right to see in you a thinker, General Liao," Kongming praised, "that has a future as a strategist: while, if you do not mind me saying, you have no great prowess as a field general, a weakness we share... you have an agile mind, shown by the cunning and wit displayed in your escape from Wu, and in addition you are loyal beyond measure. I almost contemplated sending you on this mission... but we shall need you here. You can, however, brief Generals Wei Yan and Wu Yi on survival tactics for their upcoming journey."

"*Journey*...?" Wei Yan grunted rudely. "*I'm* needed here, for the vanguard!"

"You *are* needed here, yes: in spirit, but not in person," Kongming countered calmly. "There shall be no vanguard here, Wei Wenchang: defence is our only strategy. No, you are most needed to accompany Wu Ziyuan northward, where he shall bring offers of fine goods and supplies to the tribal leaders in the name of his son-in-law, the Second Emperor of Shu Han."

Murmurs of understanding rippled across the meeting of officials and generals.

"...I see," Wei Yan said cordially. "He needs a man of great strength to escort him through the hazards, and the Wei entrenchments... harsh, but made easier by Chen Shi's latest acquisitions. ...So that is why you wanted to secure Wudu and Yinping."

"Aha...!" Kongming chuckled. "Now you understand me. I had to concentrate my efforts on creating a permanent corridor to the north, for current and future benefit. With allies in the north, Wei will be forced to reconsider this hostile incursion... but I think our greatest ally will be Heaven, and specifically Nature."

"...The signs point to rain," Jiang Wei said with a smile. "You knew that, all along, Prime Minister."

"I did," Kongming replied. "Heavy, continuous rain... Wei's army would be most formidable, provided they can actually get here in one piece... but I imagine that a tiring march across narrow plank mountain roads in torrential rain – accompanied, of course, by autumn gales – will leave more than just a few of them feeling a little cold and damp."

"...And when they arrive, they'll meet with our defences, which equal a second mountain range," Zong Yu chuckled. "Not to mention the Prime Minister's unorthodox battle formations... the whole land will be another Chen Cang."

"And the entire time, they'll be under threat from a mass tribal uprising from the north," Wei Yan said with amusement. "I like it. Should Ma Dai be joining us...?"

"Tensions are still high with my former Qiang allies because of the revolts my cousin led," Ma Dai said uncomfortably. "General Jiang Wei can tell you how the Wei populace feel, and my family's relations with the Di are poor since they turned on Mengqi and Yide during the Hanzhong Campaign."

"Agreed," Jiang Wei said, smiling at Ma Dai as he spoke. "Though I personally bear no malice, now that I know both sides of the story... others are not so open-minded, and we cannot risk our potential allies becoming enemies over personal disputes. General Ma should remain here, in Hanzhong."

"...A shame," Wei Yan said as he also smiled at Ma Dai. "Your martial skill would have been of use, General. ...But I'm sure that we will have opportunities to cooperate in the future."

"You certainly shall," Kongming promised as he looked at an equally cautious Jiang Wei. "Well, I think that is all apart from planning specific defence assignments for the generals remaining in Hanzhong... Wu Yi, Wei Yan, Liao Hua, Jiang Wei, Liu Ba, Yang Yi, Zong Yu, kindly remain... the rest of you are politely dismissed."

The meeting ended, and those not invited to stay made their way out of the hall.

"...You two should set out immediately," Kongming said to Wu Yi and Wei Yan. "I hate to rush you, but we don't know what eyes and ears Wei have in Hanzhong, and we have little time before the wolves are at the door. I have prepared in advance the things that you will be taking with you, and an elite team of soldiers that are used to special warfare in the mountains... you'll pose as traders, obviously, and that shall hopefully get you past the Wei checkpoints."

572

"I have, in the past, served as a field general," Wu Yi replied, "and Wei Yan is a champion. We should have no difficulty getting past the mountains... but what about getting back again...?"

"I'll station hidden reinforcement forces for you that you can send for if things become untenable," Kongming promised. "I'll have an army come to your aid as soon as Sima Yi and his hordes are repelled, as well... since you might become a target for revenge once you're known about."

"...Very good," Wu Yi said with a placated tone; Wu Yi and Wei Yan then bowed, and left the hall. As soon as they were gone, Jiang Wei hummed thoughtfully.

"...You were also suspicious of Wei Yan's countenance with Ma Dai," Kongming suggested, and Jiang Wei nodded silently.

"General Wei is a wolf in the fold," Yang Yi said dramatically. "Sooner or later, he'll show himself as another Lü Bu."

"He often complains to other generals about your plans," Liao Hua sighed. "He's done it since the early days... even your first exercise at Steep-slope."

"He thinks he knows best," Zong Yu complained. "Kongming, we cannot have a Shu built entirely around that man as our only champion!"

"It's his political intentions that worry me most," Kongming admitted. "If he wants to be our only champion, that is disturbing enough; but when he courts Ma Dai, probing for his popularity with the tribes, and makes remarks to impressionable generals like Chen Shi, *and* openly defies me... something will have to be done for the sake of the future."

The other officials remained uncomfortably silent.

"...But perhaps I should say no more," Kongming murmured.

"*Perhaps*," Zong Yu said emphatically. "Wei Yan will find no ally for a coup in Second Emperor's father-in-law, and Ma Dai has already expressed his distaste of Wei Yan's ominous conduct to me. He has less potential allies than he thinks."

"*If* he's a traitor, and not just an arrogant thug," Liao Hua suggested. "He has never done anything but criticise the plans of others... I think his only crime is having too much pride."

"...Pride can turn to ambition... look at Cao Cao, and Sun Ce," Kongming retorted coldly. "Neither man began as a conqueror... both men were renowned for their unwavering loyalty and devotion. But one souring experience... in both cases, the death of an idolised father... turned proud men into hankering monsters. Wei Yan endures me, and nothing more... but every bitter failure I am held responsible for is another reason, in his mind, to want to remove me 'for the good of the state'. Sooner or later, I must confront that... but for now, we have three very obvious enemies to confront: Cao Zhen, Zhang He, and *Sima Yi*."

"Will we confront them on the battlefield...?" Jiang Wei wondered.

"Oh, yes," Kongming chuckled softly. "Sima Yi must know who he is dealing with. Time and again, my reputation's been sullied by poor fortune: now he's come into our territory with a massive numerical advantage, determined to crush what he feels is an inconsequential opponent. When I'm through, he'll never want to confront me on the battlefield again."

After a short period of final preparation, Wei Yan and Wu Yi set out with their small brigade of professional soldiers, and travelled northward into the mountains. At the same time, messengers brought the news that the three Wei vanguards had almost reached the plains of Hanzhong. Fear started to spread amongst the ranks of the Shu defenders, while Kongming showed no concern at all:  he often stood on the defensive walls, looking at the distant mountains and the thick, black storm clouds, and smiling.

"...The soldiers cannot understand you, Master," Jiang Wei said as he joined Kongming on one dark, dismal day; it was obviously going to rain heavily.

"It's coming," Kongming replied. "The rain... to sweep away the men of Wei."

Jiang Wei followed Kongming's gaze: light rain started to fall.

"...**Sima Yi... what will you do now...?**" Kongming shouted defiantly; he raised his fan, and in a moment of pure chance, a peal of thunder rumbled across the sky. The Shu soldiers looked up at their Prime Minister as he stood atop the wall, pelted with ever stronger rain, his fan held aloft, laughing confidently: as thunder illuminated him against the sky, many wondered if he really was supernatural.

"Prime Minister... *Master*," Jiang Wei pleaded, "you must not stay out in this rain!"

"**What will you do now, Sima Yi...?**" Kongming asked again: he was grinning broadly, despite being soaked with freezing cold water. The downpour intensified, and Kongming laughed again.

"**Prime Minister!**" Zong Yu hailed as he approached; he almost slipped over, since the stone ground was soaked and muddy. "You must get inside!"

"**Don't you regret coming here, Sima Yi...?**" Kongming chortled; despite being cold and wet, he suddenly felt possessed of a need to compose a poem, and so he did, and recited it on the spot, in front of his bemused and dumbstruck soldiers.

"**Now many years have harshly passed,
A wondrous thing occurs!
From long and tortuous slumber, lo!
A sleeping dragon stirs!
As wicked hordes descend upon
That guard of Heaven's son,
So Heaven deems to punish them,
And violent rains have come!
So wonder where, O wicked horse,
Your hooves now show such scorn;
Not rebels' hilltop hideaways,
But the crib of Han reborn!
And while this dragon's span, alas
Will not outlast your shame,
I'll send you back, you sorry nag,
To the place from whence you came!**

As Kongming finished, a peal of thunder echoed across the sky; he laughed maniacally, an act that scared his friends and vassals more than anything.

**"What say you to that, Sima Yi, uh...?"** Kongming challenged defiantly. **"What say you???"**
Zong Yu placed his hand on Kongming's shoulder, snapping him out of the trance-like state he was in.
"Prime Minister, we must get inside," Zong Yu implored. Like Kongming, he was already soaked to the skin, despite having only been in the rain for a short while.
"...Yes," Kongming realised; all eyes were on him, and he was suddenly aware of his being soaked and cold. "I... ... ...yes. I... should go home."
Zong Yu and Jiang Wei guided Kongming from the wall and back to his Hanzhong residence, as the violent rains continued to batter the plains and mountains, and the men and horses on them.

"You scared us," Jiang Wei admitted as Kongming coughed and spluttered; he had changed into dry clothes, and was sat by an open fire. Zong Yu and Dong Jue stood behind Jiang Wei, frowning disapprovingly.
"I feel... like a naughty child," Kongming complained. "Stop staring at me, and saying such things."
"Prime Minister, you stood in the rain, waving your fan around, and reciting poems," Zong Yu said irritably. "There was no man that wanted to be out in that..."
"Sorry," Kongming replied in-between bouts of coughing. "...Any word on Wei's march at all...?"
"The 'Wicked Horse' is stalled," Jiang Wei sighed. "The Wei army are having difficulty traversing the plank roads... the rain that now beats down on them will surely exacerbate their plight. I must say, Prime Minister, that if I were a superstitious man, I would share the common soldier's view that you conjured up this storm with your magic."
Kongming grinned toothily and laughed, saying, "Let them say such things! Let them! Let it get back to old Sima Yi, and scare the fool witless! They say I prayed to change the winds at Red Cliffs, too... let them! They say I conjured a stone army at Fish Belly Meadow to repel Lu Xun... let them! They think I killed Wang Shuang with summoned pillars of fire... let them! They think I had fire-spewing demons chase away the beasts of Nanzhong... **let them!** All the better for us, if they think they oppose a magician... all the better!"
Another bout of coughing ended Kongming's triumphant sermon; Jiang Wei shook his head sadly, saying, "You cursed yourself to an early death in that poem... such a silly thing to do, Prime Minister... we need you."
"We'll leave you now, Prime Minister," Dong Jue said numbly. "Anything urgent and we'll notify you: in the meantime... *rest*."
"Yes, yes!" Kongming chuckled hoarsely. "Crouching Dragon... needs to lie down, and sleep."
Jiang Wei, Zong Yu and Dong Jue left their Prime Minister, and returned to the command centre; Kongming laughed as they left, saying, "What *now*, Sima Yi...?"

"...I don't know what to do," Sima Yi despaired as he looked out of his drenched command tent at the sea of similar, waterlogged tents that his soldiers were trapped in to escape the worst of the rain. His two sons grimaced silently. "Zhuge Liang... while I knew it was rainy season, only he knew, only *he* knew *these* rains were coming... these evil rains... he tricked me into marching here, I'm sure of it," Sima Yi declared.

"So are we going back...?" Sima Shi asked.

"Turn back an army of four hundred thousand because of *rain*...?" Sima Yi scoffed irritably. "Even if I agreed with the idea, I'd be disgraced for such a thing."

"Reports indicate that a massive defensive wall has been erected across the plains of Hanzhong," Sima Zhao said worriedly.

"I know of it," Sima Yi admitted. "But a siege in such weather is as bad for the defenders, if not worse... we can still be victorious, especially since our army outnumbers theirs by four to one or more."

"So we continue tonight...?" Sima Shi prompted.

"...Father...?" Sima Zhao prompted further; Sima Yi was stuck in a trance, watching the rains fall on his demoralised legions.

"...Uh...? ...Oh... no, no, not tonight," Sima Yi replied at last. "Tomorrow..."

At the same time, Wu Yi and Wei Yan were moving further north, trading their valuable goods for military support amongst the disaffected peoples: once again, an entirely different type of storm – a storm of dissent – was brewing in the northwest.

************

## 114

After several weeks, the vanguards of the three Wei armies cut their way past the weak defences placed at the mountain passes, and made their way onto the sodden plains of Hanzhong, where Kongming and Wei Yan's defensive structures awaited them. Cao Zhen, Sima Yi and Zhang He convened for their first group meeting since their departure; Cao Zhen was suffering the effects of the weather, and was visibly poorly.

"Thank goodness it wasn't like this when we were here last," Cao Zhen said with false joviality. "...We'd have lost more than poor Miaocai."

"Commander Xiahou Yuan was killed during a fire attack," Zhang He said with melancholy. "If only it *had* rained like this back then, Chief Commander... we'd not need to be here now."

"I do know that!" Cao Zhen admonished. "...I... was just trying to be light-hearted. So, Sima Zhongda... what do you suggest...? Raincoats are a must, but... do we have any ideas about breaking these impressive defences of theirs...?"

"In this sort of weather, a siege is made more difficult for both sides," Sima Yi replied. "They'll be unable to use fire on us... any moats they dug would quickly fill... sappers are not an option, and we can't use fire either."

"...Well then," Cao Zhen sighed, "we should-"

"**REPORT!**" a messenger hailed. "Zhuge Liang has issued a challenge to battle!"

"...He wants to fight a battle in *this*...?" Sima Yi chuckled disbelievingly.

"Sounds like he desires an early death," Cao Zhen chortled. "Zhongda, we should accept: our vanguard near matches the size of his army, and with weather that favours neither side, it will only be skill that decides the outcome, so how can we fail...?"

"...I beg to differ," Zhang He protested. "This is *Zhuge Liang*."

"*And*...? ...He was bested three times by our armies on our own territory, that's why we're here," Cao Zhen admonished. "Honestly, Zhang He... you are being so pedantic and craven today! Is a little rain all it takes to turn you into a coward...?"

"Junyi might be right, Chief Commander," Sima Yi said cautiously. "Remember how Zhuge Liang tricked Wang Shuang..."

"Remember also, Zhongda, how Hao Zhao tricked *him*...?" Cao Zhen retorted. "I despair of you all! I am Chief Commander, and I command you to prepare for a full march on his army... we'll take them apart, and they'll sink into the mud... so we won't even have to bury them."

Sima Yi and Zhang He exchanged despairing glances, but did not reply to their desperate Chief Commander.

It was still raining heavily when the two massive but unequal armies met on the battlefield; Kongming was wheeled to the front in his carriage, which was covered with a red and yellow parasol to deflect as much of the rain as possible. All around him, his generals arrayed themselves with their armies.

"You shouldn't be out here," Zong Yu scolded; Kongming was coughing heavily, and it was a rattling cough that left his friends feeling extremely concerned.

"I'm fine," Kongming insisted. "Well, *I'm* here… where are Cao Zhen and Sima Yi, amongst that lot over there…?"

Jiang Wei squinted as he tried to make out the names on the soaked yellow banners that were arrayed along the front lines of their opponents, and said, "I see Sima Zhao… … …yes, yes, I see Sima Yi's banner. …Cao Zhen is in a carriage not unlike yours."

"So he's sick too, then," Kongming said without thinking. "Good… a man in his already poor condition will not make it back to Luoyang alive."

"Doesn't that leave us with Sima Yi as Chief Commander…?" Yang Yi noted.

"…At least that means the end of Wei," Kongming muttered.

Before anyone could pick him up on that comment, Sima Yi rode forward on his decorated white horse, and bellowed, "**WHERE IS ZHUGE LIANG…?**"

"**Here is the Prime Minister of the Han!**" Jiang Wei replied as he gestured toward Kongming's carriage with his spear. "**Will you come and kneel before him, and beg forgiveness for your treason?**"

"…There you are, Zhuge Kongming," Sima Yi snickered quietly: he raised his sword, and a line of infantry raised their spears.

"They're going to send infantry," Kongming noted. "Well, I have a new trick for them… get the men into formations, and ready the crossbowmen."

"…Yes, Prime Minister," Jiang Wei replied obediently.

Before Sima Yi could issue his orders, the Shu lines started to change; his jaw slackened as he watched Kongming's generals prepare a professional battle array derived from the Eight Gates formation.

"Will we still attack…?" Zhang He asked of Sima Yi, who was now hesitant.

"**ATTACK!**" Cao Zhen screamed. "**That's what we're here for, isn't it…? Attack, attack now, and kill all of them!**"

On the word of their Chief Commander, thousands of Wei infantry and cavalry made a clumsy charge across the marsh-like plains; many soldiers slipped and fell as they ran, and the horses repeatedly stumbled as they approached the wall of shields that now stood in front of the wall of stone.

"…Idiots," Kongming chuckled softly: he gestured to Zong Yu and Dong Jue, who pulled his carriage to safety as the enemy approached.

What followed was a near-one-sided massacre: the disorganised and weary Wei soldiers ran straight into the 'gates' of Kongming's array, and even if the rain had not been obscuring the signal flags from the Wei strategists on their own front line, the flags were deployed in Kongming's typically unorthodox fashion, and were unreadable. The soldiers that entered the formation would not return; they slipped and slid on the muddy ground, falling victim to jutting spears and cavalry ambushes.

"...Crossbows...!" Kongming urged; from all sides and atop the walls, archers and crossbowmen appeared. Some of the latter had strange new crossbows with multiple launch points across the wing; on the order of Ma Dai and Dong Jue, thousands of arrows and bolts tore into the confused Wei ranks, killing and injuring hundreds of charging and fleeing men.

**"SOUND A RETREAT!"** Sima Yi pleaded of Cao Zhen. **"HURRY!"**

**"...SOUND THE GONGS, CALL THEM BACK, CALL THEM BACK!"** Cao Zhen screamed desperately. **"HURRY AND CALL THEM BACK!"**

Retreat signals urgently recalled the Wei forces to their lines; they retreated, resoundingly humbled.

**"Pursue them, Generals, but don't walk into certain death!"** Kongming ordered.

Zhang Boqi, Zhang Bosong and Chen Shi led harrying forces after the Wei troops, stopping only when they faced a barrage of Cao Zhen's own archers.

**"...Dare to run at me...?"** Cao Zhen cried, taking up his own bow and killing a Shu officer with chilling precision; Sima Yi rode to him, and gestured toward the Shu army with his spear.

**"We're finished here for today, Chief Commander!"** Sima Yi shouted over the rain and sounds of battle. **"We have to return to camp!"**

"Agreed," Cao Zhen grunted. **"FULL RETREAT! FULL RETREAT!"**

Kongming watched the Wei army flee, and said quietly, "I'll let you see the foot of our walls, Sima Yi... I'm feeling generous."

"We need to get out of the rain," Zong Yu suggested. "Prime Minister...?"

"No more poems," Jiang Wei chuckled. "Prime Minister... we won, let's get you back home."

Kongming listened to the relieved cheers of his soldiers and said, "I agree."

Two days later, Kongming was awoken from a surprisingly tranquil sleep by Zong Yu and Dong Jue.

"...Wei has returned," Zong Yu reported.

"Nothing I didn't expect," Kongming said with a yawn. "How many...?"

"Everything, I'm presuming," Zong Yu said nervously. "There's almost as many Wei soldiers out there as there are puddles."

"...Sima Yi is a fool," Kongming chuckled. "What does he hope to achieve...?"

Kongming left his residence and travelled to the defensive wall, where a frantic battle was taking place. A small number of siege towers and battering rams were soon to be deployed, and with rain preventing the use of fire to destroy them, the Shu commanders were worried.

"...A trifling thing," Kongming insisted. "Catapults on the walls will give Sima's advancing men a tough time... crossbowmen can attack the men that scale the walls... hot oil still works, I think... boulders can be dropped on the rams... and they might find the ground a little uneven and treacherous...! Is Sima Yi himself out there...?"

"He is, but he's keeping a distance," Jiang Wei reported.

"...Such a shame," Kongming sighed theatrically. "...Counterattack *now*: give them no more chances."

The Wei army was pelted with stones and boulders, and for those that reached the walls, hidden pits would claim them. The rams lost the men that were to push them to the wall as arrows and bolts came down from walls, and soon enough, Sima Yi called off his failed attack.

"They'll be back," Kongming said confidently. "And for once, we're the ones that are behind the walls... Hao Zhao and Cao Ren shall be my model, and so how, I ask, can Sima Yi ever hope to win...?"

"...I'm sure he's wondering that as well," Jiang Wei said with a smile.

Within a few days, the first signs of rebellion appeared in Tianshui and the surrounding areas: Zhang He hurried to the command tent, almost falling several times in the soft mud.

"...What's the rush...?" Sima Yi asked with concern.

"I shall need to take General Guo Huai and go back into the mountain passes," Zhang He said fearfully. "Somehow... and I really don't know how... Zhuge Liang has had agents causing trouble in the shires. We've got barbarians rising up against us... the Qiang, the Xianbei... all of them."

"...That's impossible," Cao Zhen insisted. "They... they were pacified...!"

Cao Zhen started to cough; Sima Yi hummed thoughtfully.

"What shall we do, Father...?" Sima Shi asked.

"...Zhang He, I think you're right to suggest going back," Sima Yi conceded. "We needed you here, but... well, charging their ranks in this rain isn't really going to work, and Zhuge Liang's formations are too dangerous to face. Go and deal with the barbarians... we'll manage here."

"...Chief Commander...?" Zhang He prompted. "I... should I...?"

"Do as he says," Cao Zhen ordered bitterly. "Zhongda's right, you're right... go, we'll manage."

Zhang He quickly retreated; Sima Yi turned to Cao Zhen and said, "How shall we proceed against Shu's defences...?"

"...We can only hope the rains will stop," Cao Zhen wheezed. "...They must, surely they must...?"

"Surely, yes," Sima Yi sighed. "I'll... keep you informed."

Sima Yi went back out into the rain, Sima Shi and Sima Zhao behind him every step of the way.

Days passed.

"...And still, the rains persist," Zong Yu said with wonderment as he looked outside the front door of Kongming's residence. "...Days on end... and still it comes."

"Sima Yi must wonder if these rains aren't unlike the fateful rains that flooded Fan City," Kongming chuckled ominously. "Had Guan Yunchang not faltered, that was a sign from Heaven; how can Sima Yi not be afraid?"

"Attacking us will become increasingly difficult... we've won, I think," Zong Yu said hopefully. "We have... haven't we...?"

"I'd say so," Kongming replied as he fanned himself slowly. "Now, my only concern is the safe return of Wu Yi... and... and Wei Yan."

"...Report from Qinling," Dong Jue said as he arrived at the residence; Zong Yu stepped to one side to allow his comrade to enter the warm house.
"...You're soaked," Kongming chuckled.
"Prime Minister, Wei's Zhang He has moved to check the increasing unrest in the north," Dong Jue reported. "Wei has not been able to obtain any materials for further siege works, so they're resorting to issuing challenges."
"...Which we'll ignore, I think," Kongming snickered. "...Or, on second thoughts... are they deploying a formation...?"
"They are," Dong Jue replied. "Eight Gates, standard formation."
"Aha!" Kongming exclaimed. He got to his feet, and coughed slightly.
"No, Prime Minister, no...!" Zong Yu pleaded. "Leave it be...!"
"All I need to do is guide Jiang Wei... he needs the experience," Kongming promised. "It's not enough to deploy an array... you have to know how to break them, too. Come... you two might learn something."
"...*Ayah*," Zong Yu exclaimed. "He's quite unmanageable."

"Isn't this risky...?"
"Not at all," Kongming replied to Jiang Wei's question. "You, Zhang Bogong, Zhang Boqi, Hu Ji and Ma Dai will approach... remember, there are only two safe gates, 'Persist' and 'Survive'... ignore any other openings in the internal walls of the array, they'll only lead to a spear point. Break an opponent's array, and you break their spirit... attack the weak points, and I guarantee the lines will falter, and you'll be fighting ordinary men again, not a wall of death."
"...But... in this rain..." Hu Ji fretted.
"Come now... you think every battle takes place on nice days...?" Kongming teased. "All of you work together... and Sima Yi will be humbled once again. Go on, and win us another victory!"
Jiang Wei led the force of cavalry and infantry against the rain-battered shields of Sima Yi's formation; they entered the walls of men, and the openings closed, trapping them inside the constantly shifting walls of soldiers. But, following Kongming's advice, they listened for the calls, watched for the flags, and paid attention to the shifting of the openings; as soon as the weak points in the defensive corridors appeared the generals had their men target the human walls, hacking down the men behind the shields. With the structure broken, panic started to spread; more holes appeared in the walls of soldiers, and the Shu army pressed their counterattack, breaking the formation and sending Wei soldiers scattering in all directions.
"Well done, Boye," Kongming murmured as he watched the array collapse.
"**Retreat, retreat...!**" Sima Yi urged; the Wei army fled once again.

"So now they have failed to break one of our modified formations, while they have been defeated whilst deploying one of their textbook, predictable ones," Kongming chuckled as his generals convened to discuss the victory. "Now..."

"*Now*," Zong Yu scolded, "you need to get out of here, and go back to your home, Prime Minister. Wei will not return today... our only enemy now is this miserable, unending rain that threatens to make us all sick."

"...This rain is our friend," Kongming retorted. "Never show contempt to a friend. Yes, it is cold and hard to withstand... but it will claim at least one great enemy of ours, and for that, I'm grateful."

"How long will they continue to face us...?" Liao Hua wondered. "I'd say they must be contemplating retreat now."

"You're quite right," Kongming praised. "That was it... they're finished."

"The rains have made the valleys impassable," Sima Yi complained to an ailing Cao Zhen. "My fear now is not how the rest of our armies can get through them to join us... it's how we're going to get out of here. Even if all of our remaining forces joined our battered vanguards here, I wonder what we could truly achieve."

"It took us nearly two months to get here," Cao Zhen rasped. "Now, we have to retreat, with nothing to show for our efforts... how can we... how can *I* face the Emperor...?"

"You petitioned the Emperor, yes, but this was *my* idea," Sima Yi replied with a kind smile. "If anyone is to blame, Chief Commander, it is this fool sat before you. Zhuge Liang, like Lu Xun before him and Zhou Yu before them, is a man that cannot be fought successfully when he is on the defensive. Hao Zhao and Cao Ren are also examples of this... the fact is that in this day and age, the cautious defender wins. It is a fact that I intend to apply myself in future... I think that it will one day give us the victory we want against this doomed state of Shu."

"...You see so far ahead, Zhongda... I wonder what else you see," Cao Zhen said weakly; he then started to cough violently, and Sima Yi backed away.

"...Get us out of here," Cao Zhen pleaded. "Sound the retreat... we've lost."

"They've gone! They've retreated!" Yang Yi cried with relief as the news was finally confirmed. "Prime Minister, they've really, really gone!"

"...So now, we must do one last thing," Kongming said calmly. "We must rescue Wu Yi... and Wei Yan."

"Do they need rescuing...?" Chen Shi wondered. "After all, Wei Yan is a true champion, an equal, surely, to Guan Yunchang or Zhang Yide."

"You may overrate him, you may not," Kongming said with irritation. "I care little, to be honest... even Guan Yunchang needed saving once, and I will not – if we are, as is very often the case, repeating history – be a Meng Da and leave another Yunchang to die in the mountains. We've lost enough good men as it is."

"...I'll lead the rescue," Yang Yi proposed.

"No," Kongming chuckled knowingly. "You're... somewhat inappropriate for the role, I think, Mister Yang... I'll lead the rescue personally. After the victory here, I imagine my name will carry a little mystery for a while, and that may help us."
"You can't...!" Zong Yu protested. "The rain...!"
"Oh, that'll subside now," Kongming said with confidence.
"...Somehow, I don't doubt it," Jiang Wei remarked uneasily.

As the forces of Wei continued their retreat through the mountains, the rains finally started to recede; the Wei soldiers started to weep, and amongst many of them, a belief started to emerge that the enemy strategist, Zhuge Liang, had conjured the rain to impede them.
"*Now* it subsides...! Just as we retreat, it subsides...!" Cao Zhen whined from his portable sickbed; the overweight Chief Commander was now very ill. "Heaven was against us... *no*... it was with *Zhuge Liang*...!"
"...*Zhuge Liang*," Sima Yi hissed quietly.

"**REPORT!**" a Shu messenger said as he approached Kongming's northward-bound army. "General Guo Huai has blocked Wu Yi and Wei Yan's party with a force of several hundred men! The reinforcements have reached them, but they require further assistance!"
"...We can't afford to lose Imperial father-in-law Wu Yi... or Wei Yan," Kongming declared. "We shall march double-time!"
"We already are," Dong Jue protested.
"Treble-time, then!" Kongming retorted. "We've a lot to lose!"
        But by the time that Kongming's relief force reached the mountains, a triumphant Wei Yan was leading his near-intact forces out of the pass.
"So he didn't need rescuing after all," Wu Ban noted.
"I said that he wouldn't," Chen Shi chuckled. "He's our new Yunchang, our new Zilong."
Kongming noted the comments with anger and dread, although he showed neither; instead, he greeted Wu Yi and Wei Yan cordially.
"I'm relieved to see you both alive and well," Kongming proclaimed. "Wei Wenchang, you've shown your usual valour and fortitude... I think it cannot now be doubted that you are a tiger general, like our heroes of old."
"You flatter me," Wei Yan replied coldly. "I'm only sorry that our orders were to return immediately to Hanzhong... had I a freer hand and a few more men, I might have taken Chang'an while you kept Sima Yi busy!"
The generals laughed as one; Kongming fanned himself slowly, and said, "I'm sure that next time, you'll act as you see fit."
"Perhaps," Wei Yan replied with a smirk.
Kongming returned an icy smile.


✳✳✳✳✳✳✳✳✳✳✳✳

## 115

Kongming rushed back to the capital as soon as Wei's armies had been repelled; he was keen to report to Emperor Liu Shan and the court, and he was equally keen to see that the chancellery was being run efficiently and professionally.

"...Prime Minister...?" Fei Shi said with surprise as Kongming strode into the chancellery, fanning himself briskly.

"Has all been well...?" Kongming asked as Zong Yu and Dong Jue followed him into the office wearing expressions of concern.

"Yes, of course," Xi Zheng said as he got up from Kongming's desk. "There was no need for you to hurry back, Prime Minister... especially not since your health is-"

"I'm fine," Kongming lied; as if to make an obvious liar of him, his body suddenly became wracked with chills, and he started to cough violently.

"This mad story about you standing in the rain composing poetry... it isn't true, is it...?" Jiang Wan asked almost pointlessly.

"...It's true," Zong Yu sighed wearily. "That's why he's sick."

"I left here in Chengdu a design of great importance... a design half-finished," Kongming declared. "I'm glad to see that things are going well here... I've left the bulk of the military in Hanzhong, since I shall shortly return to-"

"No," Jiang Wan said with disbelief. "Not... not another campaign...!"

"We have to capitalise on our recent victory over Sima Yi," Kongming insisted. "Cao Zhen was made very ill, and-"

"So were you!" Xi Zheng protested. "Prime Minister... *please*...!"

"Can't Jiang Wei, Wei Yan and Liao Hua manage things from here...?" Zong Yu asked worriedly. "We-"

"You'd leave Wei Yan unchecked, after all that has happened...?" Kongming challenged. "No... no, I can't do that."

"But Jiang Wei, Yang Yi, and Liao Hua...!" Dong Jue bleated.

"Yang Yi will only try and kill him, and the converse, if I leave them alone together for too long," Kongming replied. "That's why I had Fei Yi travel to Hanzhong as I was leaving it... hopefully he got there before anything serious could occur. This cannot be entrusted to anyone else, not yet! Not... not yet."

Kongming turned to leave; Fei Shi hailed him, saying, "Prime Minister, please take care of yourself! You *must* take care of yourself!"

Kongming muttered something inaudible, and left the office alone.

"...We'll look after him," Zong Yu promised.

"*Aiee*," Xi Zheng exclaimed. "...But what's this 'design' he was talking about...? He didn't take anything before he left...!"

"...Husband...!" Yueying said emotionally, as Kongming entered his Chengdu residence. "Your letter said that-"

"Before I can march again," Kongming declared, "I think we need to finish our best work, don't you...?"

"...To best navigate the mountain plank roads, one wheel... for conserving the energy of the pilots, that wheel must be large," Yueying suggested as she unfurled the plans and placed them on Kongming's desk; she sat in front of the desk, and Kongming sat at her side.

"You've been working on it a lot, I see," Kongming murmured.

"...Wooden 'legs' at all corners to steady it... removable in the case that they become an obstruction," Yueying continued. "...And two 'horns'... the handles... by which it will be held, steadied and navigated by the pilots."

"Smaller ones," Kongming mused, "may be a good idea: large ones that must be pulled, and smaller, lighter ones that carry a smaller load, but they can be pushed by a single pilot. ...It's so simple; I don't know why it wasn't thought of before."

"The design, as you say, is simple... so simple in fact, that they can be easily and quickly assembled, so you can make more from common wood should the need arise," Yueying noted. "...While it will not end your worries about the transport of grain... it will ease them, and reduce the strain on your forces."

"...We must finish these designs quickly," Kongming declared. "I don't have much time... Sima Yi... will be readying himself as well." Kongming started to cough violently again; as he reached into his sleeve and produced a kerchief, Yueying fought back tears. Although this was now a common sight, that did not make it any less painful.

"...We must start production immediately," Kongming said to his staff as they gazed in wonderment at the plans for the two new inventions.

"These... are magnificent!" Zong Yu exclaimed. "How... how did you...?"

"You are divinely inspired, Prime Minister," Fei Shi praised.

"Not at all," Kongming chuckled softly. "Not at all."

"First, you give us those wonderful fire-throwing devices," Dong Jue recalled. "And then, you pacified the spirits with those meat bun heads... exploding weapons to hide in the ground, crossbows that fire many bolts at once, and now these... Prime Minister, shall we ever have problem with grain again...?"

At that point, the former co-regent Li Yan entered the office, saying, "You wanted to see me, Prime Minister...?"

"...I did," Kongming replied, to the horror of all others present.

"How would you make use of me...?" Li Yan enquired calmly.

"You are known, Li Zhengfang, as a man of professional conduct," Kongming said with a kind smile. "I am aware that the restructuring of the government left you feeling... how shall we say... undermined."

"I would never think such things," Li Yan promised.

"Nonsense!" Fei Shi barked. "You-"

"I called you here, Li Zhengfang," Kongming interrupted, "to try and reassure you of your continued importance to our illustrious cause."

"...I am honoured to assist the empire in any way that I can," Li Yan insisted.

"Very good," Kongming replied cordially. "Now, I have just distributed amongst my staff two new designs for grain transporters... they will require mass production, and I know that you are an old hand at inspiring fast and efficient work."

"You flatter me," Li Yan said with a smile.

"Not so," Kongming retorted as Zong Yu reluctantly passed Li Yan the plans to inspect. "Now... can I entrust you with this task...? ...And can I also entrust you and your capable son Feng with the administration of our grain supplies...?"

"These... these are incredible," Li Yan admitted. "I... ... ...you designed these, Prime Minister...?"

"With help, from a good friend," Kongming confirmed. "So, do I have your support in this hour of urgency, Li Zhengfang...?"

"Prime Minister, I...!" Li Yan exclaimed emotionally.

"Kongming: call me Kongming," Kongming insisted. "We are friends as well as colleagues, Zhengfang... however it may appear, that never changed."

"...I will give it my utmost," Li Yan promised. "I will work tirelessly, as you do, Kongming... I will do all that I can for the empire."

"Very good," Kongming praised. "Now I can retire for a while... I can at last confess that I feel extremely unwell... and I really do need rest. I leave everything in your capable hands, my friends... and I know that you won't let me down."

Li Yan bowed low to show great respect to his former equal; Kongming returned the bow, showed similar respect to his colleagues, and turned to leave the office.

"Prime Minister," Zong Yu hailed as he followed his superior.

"...You have something you wish to say, Zong Deyan...?" Kongming prompted.

"He can't be trusted with such things!" Zong Yu protested quietly as the two walked along the corridors of power. "Li Yan... is treacherous, dishonest...!"

"As First Emperor once told me," Kongming retorted, "he is a diligent official, whose work on the Tianshe tunnel and other civil works is beyond reproach. Further to that, he showed the skill of another Lu Xun when he repelled the uprisings during our fateful Hanzhong Campaign, and once again when he fought the people of Nanzhong. I have allowed my neurosis to exclude a worthy man... how can I treat Li Yan thus, yet tolerate the far more sinister behaviour of Wei Yan...?"

"*Ayah*," Zong Yu exclaimed. "You should be reliant on *neither*! Remember that Li Yan has openly questioned you, and expressed desire for more influence!"

"...Ambition is not so much of a vice," Kongming said quietly. "Would any of us be where we are now if we weren't ambitious...? Li Yan is too valuable to be cast aside, Deyan... and perhaps, by trusting him again... next time, his considerable talent can be used on our front line, and I can step back, as everyone wishes me to."

"...I doubt that your heart will let you ever do that," Zong Yu retorted. "If you are determined to make this covetous, bitter man your deputy once again, and place him in charge of supplies... so be it. But I thought..."

Zong Yu trailed off.

"...Say your piece, Deyan," Kongming prompted as he started to fan himself slowly.

"...I thought that he was considered a likely suspect for the fate that befell your son," Zong Yu said reluctantly.

"What's done is done," Kongming declared calmly. "While that is true... I can prove nothing, and there are many other men I could call enemies; some, perhaps, that I cannot really see. What I must do, Deyan, is focus on the important things... the destruction of Wei, the restoration of the Han, and the subjugation of Eastern Wu. Personal matters... must wait, if they dealt with at all."

"But...!" Zong Yu protested.

"Deyan," Kongming interrupted, "consider this: a man has lost someone close to them, and he suspects, perhaps even knows, who the culprit was. Many are to blame, in truth... perhaps the wronged man and the victim were equally responsible for their fates... and yet, that man has two choices ahead of him. He can pursue that personal vendetta, putting it before matters of state... or he can put it aside, for the good of the land. He might even have to work with those he holds responsible for his own misfortune, but he does so for a higher cause than his own."

"...Prime Minister..." Zong Yu murmured.

"We are old friends, so please, address me as one when we speak as we do now, Deyan," Kongming implored. "...What I have just described should sound familiar... that man was Cao Cao, that man was Sun Quan, and Sun Ce, and that man was First Emperor, to name but four. All of those men put personal grievance before importance of state matters, and it ruined them, all of them in one way or another. I must set a different example... and so I shall."

"...I understand," Zong Yu promised. "I shall say no more of it."

"Good," Kongming said gratefully. "Now... I shall retire: as always, I ask that you keep me informed... although I know that you will. Good day, Deyan."

Zong Yu halted; he exchanged short, polite bows with Kongming, who continued on his way, fighting the urge to cry with frustration at the compromises that he was being forced to make for the sake of the state of Shu.

"...So you're going again," Yueying said sadly.

Kongming and Yueying were sat before their stringed instruments, playing together calmly.

"They're finished, and they're loaded with grain," Kongming reported. "The faces of the soldiers are a sight to behold... they've never seen such things, and they are now convinced that I am some sort of magician."

Yueying smiled involuntarily.

"I'm determined that I am going to do everything right," Kongming continued passively. "I've made my peace with Li Yan, I shall do my utmost to tolerate Wei Yan... and I shall show patience in my dealings with Sima Yi. While I might not take the heartland, I think that I shall certainly claim the lives of some of Wei's champions this time... hopefully, Sima Yi will be one of them."

Yueying hummed thoughtfully.

"...If this campaign fails," Kongming added, "I shall not venture out again in any great haste, since... that fifth campaign will be altogether more consequential."

Yueying stopped playing instantaneously; Kongming wound the tune down carefully and calmly, while Yueying stared vacantly into space.

"We shall be able to spend time together," Kongming suggested as he concluded playing. "I shall be able to spend some time with my family."

"…Yes," Yueying replied hesitantly.

"I'll write home regularly," Kongming promised. "While I forbid the court to keep records, in an attempt to restrict espionage by Wei or Wu… there is no harm in a man's musings. I shan't be precise… but you'll at least know I'm well."

Yueying nodded slowly.


Tensions ran high in the main hall of Shu's Hanzhong headquarters.

"I tell you, Boye, that this is folly," Wei Yan complained to Jiang Wei. "He's on his way, his says… a fourth campaign against Wei, he says… so soon…?"

"I thought you wanted to strike at Chang'an," Jiang Wei countered.

"That is no longer an option, thanks to Zhuge's dallying," Wei Yan said angrily. "I don't want to upstage him, Boye, that isn't my point… I understand, with all he's been through, with all the losses and retreats, why he's cautious… I was there for most of them, I understand very well. Steep-slope, Wulin, Fan, Xiaoting, Jieting and Chen Cang were all terrible losses, but I don't believe there's any point in holding onto past mistakes… he continually throws examples back at me, but Chang'an wasn't any of those places, nor was it Jiangling, or Luo, or Chengdu! It was Chang'an, commanded by Xiahou Mao… we should have risked it."

"…Perhaps," Jiang Wei replied cautiously.

"And now, we're going on another campaign…?" Wei Yan scoffed. "Zilong's dead, Wei's reinforced the northwest with everything it has… we have no grain… this is suicide! It's insanity!"

"…Perhaps," Jiang Wei said again.

"Is that all you're going to say…?" Wei Yan grunted. "Very well… but tell me this, Boye… is he really a magician…?"

Jiang Wei smiled, and shook his head.

"No, that's right, he isn't," Wei Yan continued. "What could he possibly bring to the table to tackle any of the problems we'll be facing…?"

"I honestly don't know," Jiang Wei replied.

"He claims he'll be here in a time unheard of for bringing a proper supply train," Wei Yan suggested. "What about grain…? He's bringing more men, yes, but what do we feed them with???"

"I honestly don't know," Jiang Wei said again, but with a smile.

"…*Aiee*," Wei Yan exclaimed. "There's no point talking to you!"

Wei Yan walked away angrily; Jiang Wei took a private letter from his pocket – sent by his mentor, Kongming – and laughed quietly.


"…General! General, come quickly, the army…!"

"What…?" Wei Yan said with confusion; he got up from his seat, left his residence, and followed his excited subordinate to the battlements of the fortress city.

"I've... never seen the like of it," Zhang Boqi said as he watched the approaching Shu reinforcements from Chengdu.

"...Never seen the like of *what*...?" Wei Yan grunted.

"The magical wooden beasts!" one soldier said excitedly.

"...Nonsense," Wei Yan muttered as he neared the wall, and stood next to an unsurprised and amused Jiang Wei.

"You wanted an answer, Wenchang," Jiang Wei chuckled softly. "There it is."

"What... the...!" Wei Yan exclaimed as he finally caught sight of the approaching forces. The cavalry and infantry were nothing spectacular, and were altogether a common sight: the supply train, however, was unlike anything seen before. Men pushed or pulled large wooden grain bins mounted on a large single wheel; the devices were designed to crudely resemble beasts of burden.

"What... are they...?" Zhang Boqi asked.

"The Prime Minister... is truly beyond comparison," Deng Zhi praised. "...Wooden animals – machines – that carry the grain; simply marvellous...!"

The speed and relative ease with which the pilots of these strange, wheelbarrow-like devices could move caused many of the onlookers to sigh with wonderment.

"*Wooden oxen*, and *gliding horses*, he calls them," Jiang Wei declared with pride. "They'll change the way we do things from now on... a simple yet ingenious way to store and transport grain! We can steer them easily around the plank roads, lock their wheels or their lids... and with the Prime Minister's careful timing, we'll have more than what he's brought with us from Chengdu."

"Magician or no... he's a miracle," Zhang Bogong murmured.

"So what say you now, Wei Wenchang...?" Jiang Wei asked as he turned to a surprised and impressed Wei Yan.

"...Wei has no man like him or me, or any of us," Wei Yan decided. "Let's march on Sima Yi; how can we lose...?"


************

## 116

It was a Shu army with high morale and even higher expectations that prepared to march across the mountains and into the northern heartland, on what would be their fourth campaign against Wei in three years. Excited soldiers discussed the wooden oxen and gliding horses, to the concern of the elite that met in their conference hall.

"…This new invention should not be leaked out," Wei Yan insisted to Kongming, who was fanning himself slowly.

"They will come to our enemies' attention eventually, Wenchang," Kongming said casually. "I cannot make them invisible."

"…I suppose so," Wei Yan conceded. "But wasn't there a way to hide them, cover them somehow, as you travelled from Chengdu…?"

"Sadly, no," Kongming sighed, "although I appreciate your concern."

"They are magnificent, and will aid our cause greatly," Wei Yan replied politely. "While I may not always agree with you on military matters, Prime Minister, in this this matter, I am awestruck by your genius."

"I had help," Kongming admitted with a laugh. "Now… Li Yan is in charge of transporting grain, something that he should have no trouble doing now… even in this horrible weather. Sadly, the rain we're now enduring can't be told to go away… so perhaps the soldiers should stop hinting that you should ask me."

The generals laughed at the notion.

"…We'll be putting everything we have into this one," Kongming continued. "The alliances we regained with the northern tribes – thanks to the efforts of Imperial Father-in-law Wu Yi and Wei Wenchang – are still strong, so we have despatched agents to request their help in harassing the garrisons in and around the region."

"…What's the main target this time…?" Wei Yan prompted.

"Mount Qi, as per our first campaign," Kongming replied. "Of course, last time we sent Zilong and Deng Zhi to Mei as a decoy… this time, we will press Mount Qi specifically, especially since it is now occupied by a strong Wei force."

"…And there are no other targets…?" Liao Hua prompted.

"We will need to be flexible," Kongming explained. "I'd like to say that I know where and when we should attack, but a lot of our strategy now depends on the reactions of Cao Zhen and Sima Yi, and the cautious way that Zhang He, their most dangerous general, operates."

"Sima Yi is placed to go wherever he is most needed," Jiang Wei noted. "Cao Zhen is ill, but persisted that he should be commander in the area, since he feels that he has successfully repelled us many times before. He's currently in either Chen Cang or Chang'an… he seems confused as to which we might target, and moves between them. Guo Huai and his deputy Dai Ling are in Tianshui, while Generals Jia Ji and Wei Ping guard Mount Qi with a considerable force. Jieting is heavily reinforced, An Ding and Nan'an have large garrisons placed, and Zhang He may be in Longyou, which Wei may suspect to be our real target."

"*May be...*?" Wei Yan scoffed. "Why is our intelligence suddenly so poor...?"

"For the same reason that they know so little about us," Kongming scolded. "Our first and only target is Mount Qi."

News that the Shu army was marching again so soon was met with disbelief by Wei Chief Commander Cao Zhen; but the news was accompanied by the first sightings of the new supply transports, and that was the greater shock.

"...Magic wooden animals...?" Cao Zhen said with surprise.

"Apparently," General Fei Yao said with equal surprise. "They are guided along the narrow paths as though they are of light weight, and they store grain somehow."

"...Ah, now I understand," Cao Zhen chuckled. "So Zhuge Liang has found a way to combine grain bins with grain transportation: very ingenious. However, this new development means that they have solved many of their grain problems... we must obtain one of these devices so that we can understand them, make more, and use them ourselves. ...Where was Zhuge Liang going...?"

"They seem to be heading for Mount Qi," Fei Yao reported.

"...*Again*," Cao Zhen grunted. "Last time, they had a decoy force sent to Mei to distract us while they took Mount Qi; this time, they just attack Mount Qi. That means that Mount Qi is the decoy this time... they must mean to attack us here in Chang'an...! ...Notify Guo Huai in Tianshui, and ensure that our defences here are as impregnable as they can be!"

Fei Yao bowed silently and left to carry out his orders.

"They're fortifying Chang'an," Wei Yan reported soberly as he entered the command tent near Mount Qi. "Apparently, a mouse could not sneak by their defences. So that wasn't your real target, then, Prime Minister...?"

"To take Chang'an, Wei Wenchang, one must first spread the enemy out across the region," Kongming explained calmly. "Oh, I intend to take it eventually... but only when Mount Qi, Chen Cang, Tianshui, An Ding, Nan'an and Longyou are in total chaos, under siege by tribal rebels within, and Shu forces without, and the Wei River is ours to use as we please."

"...Understood," Wei Yan said solemnly. "The defending generals are doing a good job of holding the mountain... this will take time."

"I knew that would be the case," Kongming promised. "What I'm waiting for is the Chief Commander."

"Cao Zhen...?" Wei Yan supposed.

"...No," Kongming scoffed. "Sima Yi... trust me, Cao Zhen is near to his last. He is overweight, he is not a young man anymore, and he suffered greatly in the rains during his excursion against us. The weather continues to punish us... even safe from these rains in the warm palace at Chang'an, he cannot escape disease. Sickness will claim him soon, and then Sima Yi will come here."

As spring turned to summer, the weather continued to be the main enemy to both sides of the conflict in the northwest. Rains and humidity took their toll on Cao Zhen, who summoned an expectant Sima Yi to Chang'an.

"...Why are we going to Chang'an, Father...?" Sima Zhao complained as he rode with his brother and father at the head of a reinforcement army bound for that important city.

"To relieve Cao Zhen of command," Sima Yi supposed.

"You're to be Chief Commander???" Sima Shi exclaimed.

"...*Acting* Chief Commander," Sima Yi replied hesitantly. "I'm glad, since we need more decisive action against Zhuge Liang."

Sima Yi arrived at the court in Chang'an, where the ailing Cao Zhen had an official bring Sima Yi through to a private audience chamber. Cao Zhen was too sick to sit upright, and was in a bed, near-motionless and breathing uncomfortably.

"...Zhongda," Cao Zhen wheezed. "You're finally here."

"Chief Commander," Sima Yi said with respect; he bowed low, and his two sons reluctantly followed his example.

"...Please, rise, Zhongda," Cao Zhen implored. "I... would speak with you privately, Zhongda."

"Shi'er, Zhao'er... wait for me in the hall," Sima Yi ordered, and his sons withdrew obediently.

"Zhongda," Cao Zhen began, "I am too weak to stay here... I must go to the capital. I have written to His Majesty, and he is aware of my wish to have you installed as Chief Commander."

"...Until you are well," Sima Yi presumed.

"I will never be well again, Zhongda," Cao Zhen replied. "I've served my allotted span under Heaven... I wonder if I'll make it back to Luoyang. But... at least I know that I am leaving the sword of command in safe hands... that's all that matters to me. Consider yourself Chief Commander from this very moment."

Sima Yi kowtowed humbly, saying, "I can never thank you enough for your faith in me, Cao Zidan."

"Serve Wei with all your heart and soul, Zhongda, and protect it from the wolves at the door," Cao Zhen pleaded. "That is how you may thank me best."

"...I shall," Sima Yi promised as he got to his feet. "You have my word, Zidan... Wu and Shu shall never vanquish Wei."

Cao Zhen nodded gratefully as Sima Yi bowed once more.


"...Cao Zhen has retreated to Luoyang, and now Sima Yi takes the field," Kongming reported to his officers. "Already, he commands large reinforcements to Mount Qi, and bolsters the summit and the plains around it, and he's also sent a small garrison to camp in the fields north of Mount Qi, near Tianshui."

"...So what are we doing...?" Wei Yan asked impatiently.

"We're taking the mountain *and* the fields," Kongming replied.

"Why do we want *fields*...?" Wei Yan complained. "Unless... ah... my apologies, Prime Minister, I see your plan now."

"Oh...?" Kongming chuckled. "Well, hopefully Sima Yi does not..."


Kongming left most of his army of 90,000 to surround and harass Mount Qi while a force of 10,000 – which he led personally – went around the mountains to the north and attacked the field camps, which were commanded by Generals Fei Yao and Dai Ling. Sima Yi had only assigned 4,000 troops to them, and that numerical disadvantage was further complicated by a lack of experience in facing a classic battle formation. The two generals immediately sent messengers to Tianshui and Mount Qi to request aid.

"*Aiee...*!" Sima Yi exclaimed. "That Zhuge Liang! I should have guessed that he'd...!"

"Commander," General Niu Jin hailed, "Shu Generals Wei Yan, Wu Ban and Gao Xiang are pressing us badly at the mountain base to the south and west, and General Wang Ping is advancing up the mountain to the east!"

"...If only Wang Ping had fought so bravely for us in Hanzhong," Sima Yi complained. "Where is General Zhang He...?"

"General Zhang reported first to Chen Cang, but he is now on his way here," Niu Jin explained. "General Guo Huai has been sent a messenger as you requested."

"General Guo must *not* engage Zhuge Liang!" Sima Yi insisted. "I only hope that my messenger reaches him before he does what I think he will do...!"

"An excellent idea, General Guo," Fei Yao praised as the two convened in General Fei's command tent near the wheat fields south of Tianshui. "If we pincer Zhuge Liang, how can he leave here alive...?"

"Sima Yi is a clever man, but he doesn't have eyes and ears everywhere," Guo Huai chuckled boldly. "If Sima Zhongda could see what poor arrays and dismal countenance this army of Zhuge's is showing, he'd not want us to do anything else!"

The two generals laughed confidently, little knowing that Kongming had brought elite troops, and the outcome would be altogether the opposite of their prediction.

"...Chief Commander!" Guo Huai and Fei Yao wept as one; they were prostrated at the feet of a furious Sima Yi, having lost over 2,000 men and the fields.

"...And what of Tianshui???" Sima Yi barked angrily.

"...General Dai Ling is in Tianshui," Guo Huai replied humbly. "Your foolish general Guo Huai posted him there before his own failure."

"...Idiots, the pair of you!" Sima Yi admonished. "Surely, General Guo, as a veteran of campaigns against Zhuge Liang, you should have known better???"

"Now that I'm here," Zhang He said encouragingly, "we can turn this around. Shall I relieve Tianshui, Chief Commander...?"

"No, no... General Dai should be alright so long as he stays behind the walls... I'll write to him and state as much," Sima Yi sighed wistfully. "What's done is done... what is Zhuge Liang doing now...?"

"He's setting up vast arrays of camps," Niu Jin said worriedly, "and he's preparing to harvest the early wheat and store it in his wooden animals."

"...*Aiee... wooden animals*???" Sima Yi despaired. "What sort of man do I fight?"

"The fear I have," Zhang He admitted, "is where Zhuge intends to go from there... he can surely march north past Tianshui, taking the entire northwest with the aid of the tribes... or go east, straight past Chen Cang, and siege Chang'an; whichever it is, we're stuck here, defending this mountain."

"...*Aiee!*" Sima Yi exclaimed; he punched the empty air in front of him in frustration. "...Okay... okay. We'll need to protect Chang'an... I'll tell Dai Ling to ensure the roads north are monitored for Shu activity, and I'll ensure the hills to the east of here are fortified, so that Zhuge can't go that way when he's done reliving his farming days. We'll continue to hold Mount Qi... in case there's some other scheme, and he's trying to draw us away from here."

Sima Yi did as he promised, fortifying the hills east of the fields where the Shu army now harvested the young wheat in the wooden oxen and gliding horses. Kongming wandered up and down the fields as the men worked, rousing them with old songs that he would use to entertain his own farm hands in more peaceful days that were long gone.
"What a sight," Zong Yu chuckled softly as he watched the spectacle with Dong Jue and Liao Hua.
"I've never seen Kongming so at ease!" Dong Jue realised.
"...I wonder what we'll do when the wheat is harvested," Liao Hua said thoughtfully. "We could go north, or east: what will we do...?"

Kongming assembled the generals that were to hand for a meeting, as the wheat harvesting came to an end.
"So where now, Prime Minister...?" Jiang Wei asked expectantly. "My home region, my home town are within sight... I presume that we'll be taking Tianshui now that we're restocked...?"
"No, we won't," Kongming said to a shocked audience. "We're going to begin a retreat to Mount Qi to consolidate."
"...Consolidate...?" Liao Hua noted with confusion. "But... but Prime Minister, we're in a very advantageous position here!"
"Are we, Mister Liao...?" Kongming challenged. "Sima Yi now blocks our passage to the east, Tianshui is on alert, the rebellions are faltering, and Zhang He looms ominously, threatening to ruin our march north and our siege of Mount Qi. Before we press on, we must use the fact that we have deprived Wei of the early harvest, and take Mount Qi. If we do that, we'll have a proper base in the region... and then we'll think about where to go from there. General Ma Dai, you shall be the vanguard... everyone, pack up and return to Mount Qi."
The officials murmured reluctantly yet obediently, and left the command tent.
Jiang Wei uttered the only word that he could muster: "Why...?"
"Boye, you've seen the reports on Sima Yi's defences," Kongming retorted. "I cannot hope to breach them... not with the threat of Zhang He looming all the while. Chang'an cannot be approached... and the north, well... it's too risky, I don't want to stretch our supply route, and Jieting is too well protected now."
"...So you want to try and lure Sima Yi out from behind his shields, and get him to pursue us," Jiang Wei supposed.
"It's the only way," Kongming sighed miserably.

"...He's fleeing...?" Sima Yi said with surprise.
"They've packed up, and are moving back toward Mount Qi, via Lu City," Niu Jin reported enthusiastically.

"…Go after them," Sima Yi said cautiously. "Be mindful, Zhuge Liang is full of tricks… go around them, and attack their *vanguard*, not the rear."

"Chief Commander," Niu Jin said obediently, bowing as he spoke.

Niu Jin did as he was ordered, and intercepted Ma Dai at Hanyang, which was on the route to Lu City. Niu Jin had once been a failed hero at Jiangling, a general that required rescuing from the field by his commander, Cao Ren: now, he was a very different general, and Ma Dai was outmatched. Kongming hurriedly barked orders, hoping to reorganise his ranks after the rout of Ma Dai's men, but the army was shaken by the unexpected attack, and morale collapsed. A retreat to the relative safety of Lu City was ordered, and the Shu forces took refuge behind the walls with their supplies. Sima Yi, Zhang He, Guo Huai and Fei Yao joined Niu Jin in a new camp near the city, hoping to find a way to be rid of Kongming once and for all.

But as soon as Kongming was installed in Lu City, he had his army build an array of defensive camps around the walled settlement: before Sima Yi could act, the Shu army was stabilised once again.

"I was hoping to get some of those wonderful transport devices," Sima Yi lamented as he surveyed a map of Kongming's camps; his entire retinue of officers of all ranks were present. "…Now Zhuge Liang is hiding in Lu City, what can we do…?"

"I wouldn't call it hiding," Niu Jin suggested. "He's set up so many camps along the River Wei, and in the hills nearby, in both directions…"

"Mount Qi is now very poorly staffed," Zhang He reported. "We had no trouble passing them… there were no champions. Wei Yan and Wang Ping have relocated here, along with most of the Shu generals, leaving only a decoy force at Mount Qi to waste our time. Jia Ji and Wei Ping can easily hold them at bay now."

"We should attack Lu City, and the outer camps," Fei Yao suggested.

"Don't be ridiculous!" Sima Yi scoffed. "The camps protect each other and the city! Any attempt to break this coordinated defence will result in heavy losses!"

"Chief Commander, we'll be the laughing stock of the world if we do not do something," Fei Yao suggested further. "They are on the defensive in our territory, having been surrounded, and isolated, by a superior force! Future historians will question your courage!"

"They'll question your intellect far more, I think!" Sima Yi retorted. "You dare to suggest that I attack Zhuge Liang, General, after the humiliating defeat he inflicted on you…?"

"That was something altogether different," Fei Yao countered. "Where can he run to…? Where can he deploy arrays…? He's trapped in there with his wooden toys, and his frightened men! His vanguard general was routed, and his men are demoralised! Why do we fear such a craven army of ants…?"

The lower-ranked officers also started to complain at this point; Sima Yi turned away from them, and exhaled noisily with frustration.

Day after day, Kongming would walk back and forth along the northern wall of Lu City, fanning himself casually. Occasionally, it would rain, but he would make the journey anyway, returning to his chosen residence as a drenched and dishevelled figure. Zong Yu and Dong Jue were on hand, as always, to assist him and offer words of encouragement or concern, usually the latter.

"Prime Minister," Zong Yu whined, "your health... your health...!"

"In summertime, a little rain is good," Kongming insisted with mock cheer.

"Why do you wander the walls, day after day, Prime Minister...?" Dong Jue protested. "Sima Yi will not attack us!"

"Don't be so sure," Kongming said with a slight cough. "I imagine that his generals will think him weak to just sit there, especially after Niu Jin routed Ma Dai, and chased me here so easily."

"What will you do if he attacks...?" Zong Yu enquired.

"Defeat him," Kongming promised.

Sima Yi was eventually outnumbered by the calls for an attack, and he reluctantly conceded. One day, he deployed two armies to confront Shu: one led by Zhang He to fight Wang Ping in the southern camps, and one that he would lead himself, with Guo Huai, Fei Yao and Niu Jin as his deputies. Wei Yan rushed into the makeshift headquarters in Lu City to report the manoeuvres to an excited Kongming.

"...Ah, Wenchang...!" Kongming hailed. "Do they attack at last...?"

"Yes," Wei Yan panted. "Can I...?"

"Of course, Wenchang, of course!" Kongming urged. "This is your moment... go out there and show them your champion spirit! Take whoever you need!"

"I shall, Prime Minister!" Wei Yan said with delight; he then located Wu Ban and Gao Xiang, and led them outside to face Sima Yi. Kongming, meanwhile, went to the walls with Zong Yu, Dong Jue, Liao Hua and Jiang Wei.

"...General Wei will easily best Guo Huai," Liao Hua supposed.

"Of course!" Kongming said with a laugh.

The Wei forces arrayed to face Wei Yan's defence force; there would be no formations this time. The Wei men charged, but against an angry Wei Yan in his prime, there would be no easy victory. With Wu Ban and Gao Xiang covering his sides, Wei Yan charged headlong into the Wei cavalry charge, unseating several horsemen and hacking down many of the infantry that supported them. Guo Huai's attempt at a direct charge on Wei Yan was met with a defiant scream and a brief clash of weapons, before Guo Huai realised that he was outmatched and made a hasty retreat. The Wei charge started to fall apart; at that point, Kongming had a horn sounded, and two new forces led by Zhang Boqi and Chen Shi rushed into the sides of the Wei vanguard, crushing it completely. At all sides, additional forces from the outer camps besieged the besiegers, turning the tide of battle completely in Shu's favour; Sima Yi cried out with frustration and sounded a retreat, leaving the defenders to enjoy a relatively easy victory.

**"Sima Yi was made to look like the fool that he is!"** Wei Yan bellowed as he returned to the safety of the city, followed by his forces. Kongming left the walls and greeted the confident general in the courtyard with his aides.

"Another fine performance, Wenchang!" Kongming praised. "I wonder how General Wang is faring against Zhang He...?"

"Sima Yi sent Zhang He against Wang Ping...?" Wei Yan realised. "...Then I must go and aid him!"

"Don't underestimate General Wang," Kongming suggested warmly. "I imagine that he'll be fine, since he's on the defensive. Now, we must plan our next move. We are surrounded on all sides by camps that Sima Yi must pass, and risk being surrounded by. However, we cannot rely on that forever. Grain stocks are running low again, and we cannot afford to be trapped here without food. We must plan our move west and south, back toward Mount Qi."

"Retreat...? Again...?" Wei Yan complained. "We've just routed Sima Yi! Why must we again retreat, when Chang'an is in our sights...?"

"We killed three thousand men today, and not much more," Kongming scolded as politely as he could. "Whether they were good men or not is not the point... Sima Yi has at least seventy thousand more where they came from, and we're running out of food. Furthermore, we run the risk of their capturing an ox or horse from us, and then our slight advantage is lost."

"...That's true," Wei Yan conceded. "...Okay... how will we do this...?"

"We'll have to hold firm for a little while to show strength," Kongming explained. "But we should start moving our supplies out by night as quickly as possible. Once we're safely back to Mount Qi we'll receive new supplies from Chengdu, and then we can resume our offensive. I've already despatched messengers to Li Yan requesting more grain, and with such a good harvest this year, and the oxen and horses to move it, I can't see what would go wrong."

＊＊＊＊＊＊＊＊＊＊＊＊

## 117

In the wake of the humiliating defeat at Lu City, Sima Yi was livid: as soon as his forces were guided safely back to their camps, he admonished his generals for their reckless goading.
"We gained nothing!" Sima Yi raved. "Three thousand men, horses, armour... all spoils for our enemies to savour, and all because of your foolish whining!"
"What shall we do now...?" Guo Huai wondered.
"Their outer camps are very effective defences for the city and each other, Chief Commander," Zhang He noted carefully. "I think we need to focus on the camps if we are to succeed."
"That was always my thinking," Sima Yi declared, "until the rest of these muddle-headed belligerents started making suggestions about attacking the city! Oh, well, at least I have your wise old mind to rely on, Zhang Junyi. We'll focus our next attack entirely on the outer camps on the plains and hills... once Lu City is isolated, Zhuge Liang will have nowhere to go... and I suggest we begin immediately, since I doubt he'll expect that."

The very next night, Wang Ping rode up to the gates of Lu City with the remnants of his forces, and pleaded entry to the city: a fretful Kongming rushed to meet him in the courtyard with his senior officers.
"...They routed us completely, Prime Minister!" Wang Ping reported. "All the camps... all of them... gone!"
Kongming fanned himself silently as his officers started to murmur disconcertedly.
"...Prime Minister...!" Wang Ping prompted. "What do we do???"
"Prime Minister," Zong Yu urged, "we must decide what to do."
"**REPORT!**" a soldier shouted down from the wall. "**A messenger approaches!**"
"...**Theirs or ours**...?" Kongming asked calmly.
"**Ours!**" the soldier confirmed. "**He's alone!**"
"Reopen the gates," Kongming ordered.
          "Wei is coming here, full force!" the messenger reported. "The entire network of outer camps is broken! The northern and southern hill positions have also been seized!"
"...It's grave," Kongming admitted. "I have once again miscalculated... Sima Yi is the better man today, if only just. Once again, he defies expectation, and strikes back immediately... I thought the blow to his army's morale would–"
"Forgive me, Prime Minister," Wei Yan interrupted, "but we need to get out of here, I think... not bleat over whose fault it was, or what went wrong."
"Quite right," Kongming conceded. "They're going to besiege us, but only by daylight... hopefully. We won't get out now, not if they're coming... but once the sun sets tomorrow evening, we'll begin the retreat to Mount Qi. Wei Yan, Wu Ban, Gao Xiang... you'll be the vanguard. Chen Shi, Ma Dai, Deng Zhi, Liao Hua, Dong Jue... you'll guard the supply train and the rear. We'll need to have full siege repulsion manoeuvres in place within the next two hours... all of you, take the same responsibilities that you had during the Hanzhong siege last year. ...That's all."

The next day, Kongming sat in his Lu City command post, listening to the not-so-distant sounds of orders, screaming, and fighting. He knew that Jiang Wei was managing the siege well enough, but he knew also that his lack of foresight with regard to Sima Yi had left them in a precarious situation. He grimaced at every panicked order, and fought tears at every sound of a wounded soldier being dragged away from the walls. This continued until the late evening.

"They've withdrawn," Jiang Wei said with relief as he entered the command post. "We gave them as good as we got, Prime Minister, so they'll have to think again. Shall I start preparing for the retreat…?"

Kongming nodded silently.

"Don't blame yourself," Jiang Wei implored; "as you keep saying yourself, Prime Minister… you're not a magician. …But you're still a brilliant man."

Jiang Wei then left the hall, leaving Kongming to brood.

The retreat began under the cover of darkness; only those that needed to navigate the way carried torches, in the hope that they would not alert the enemy to their location. Kongming remained at the rear of the force, near his precious new inventions.

But as the night march progressed, Wei Yan's impatient pace separated the vanguard from the main force: and even with the faster movement of the wooden oxen and gliding horses, the supply train started to lag behind the infantry that made up the centre of the army. Kongming noted this with worry, and summoned Dong Jue to his side.

"What is it, Prime Minister…?" Dong Jue asked as he brought his horse to a trot alongside Kongming's carriage.

"We're open to attack," Kongming warned. "Have the men prepare… and have Liao Hua get the special boxes ready, in case we need them."

"Yes, Prime Minister," Dong Jue replied obediently.

Some way into the march, the predicted attack came; a force of thousands suddenly cut into the Shu infantry force, separating it completely from the supply train. General Ma Dai rushed to Kongming to inform him of the assault.

"Chen Shi is dead!" Ma Dai reported. "We've lost hundreds of men! We have to retaliate, but–"

"They won't want to burn our supplies… they'll want the oxen and horses for themselves," Kongming worried. "*We'll* have to do it… Zong Yu, Dong Jue, order the men to burn the supplies."

"What???" Zong Yu exclaimed. "But–"

"Do it!" Kongming barked. "Line the oxen across the road, and burn them!"

Reluctantly, the order was carried out; soon, a wall of fire barred an attack to the rear of the retreating army. The soldiers preserved some of the gliding horses, since they were lighter and faster; Kongming had the army change direction, and move into a small valley to the southwest.

At around the same time, the last of Wei Yan's vanguard force approached the Shu main camp at the base of Mount Qi.

"Where's the Prime Minister...?" the official Liu Ba asked anxiously.

"Lagging behind, with the supplies," Wei Yan grumbled. "Why...?"

"Some of the Wei forces were diverted from here during the night," Fei Yi noted with concern. "Might the enemy have predicted your retreat...?"

"We'll need to go back, then," Wei Yan supposed. "...Wu Ban, Zhang Boqi, Zhang Bogong, Gao Xiang... follow me, with the best men you can muster."

Wei Yan turned his horse and dashed out of the camp with his elite cavalry in pursuit; the other generals gathered whatever men they could, and followed.

"If Sima Yi's attacking the Prime Minister," Yang Yi said to Liu Ba and Fei Yi, "it'll take more than Wei Yan to repel him."

"I agree," Fei Yi murmured. "I have an idea..."


Kongming, meanwhile, had been forced to abandon his carriage and flee on foot into the depths of the isolated valley; 10,000 men or more had been massacred in the night attack, and now he was only surrounded by the wounded, frightened remnants of his army. The moon was full, so there was some natural light.

"Prime Minister," Ma Dai hailed, "Sima Yi's men may know we came this way, even without fires to follow. They'll search for us. We cannot stay here."

Jiang Wei, Zong Yu and Dong Jue were stood either side of the exhausted Shu Prime Minister; he was coughing weakly, and was sat on a soldier's tunic, having lost the strength to stand.

"...We'll be rescued," Kongming promised.

"Prime Minister... *how*...?" Ma Dai wondered. "We're not on the road... even if Wei Yan about-turned and came back, we're in a valley, far away from the road!"

"Where is Liao Hua...?" Kongming asked wearily.

"...Guarding your boxes," Ma Dai replied uneasily. "Prime Minister, how can we burn our food, yet keep two trunks of your personal belongings...?"

"They are our way out of this mess, Ma Dai," Kongming scolded. "Tell Liao Hua to bring the boxes to the highest point of the valley... we'll need to use them. I know it'll tell Sima Yi precisely where we are if he doesn't already know... but we have no choice."

Ma Dai retreated to carry out his orders: Zong Yu turned to Kongming and said, "I do not understand, Prime Minister, how we're going to get out of this. Those boxes are not that big... what could possibly be in them that...?"

"Have a little faith," Kongming interrupted. "Let's go and meet Liao Hua."

Kongming, Zong Yu and Dong Jue met with Liao Hua, Ma Dai and a large guard force that had congregated around Kongming's mysterious boxes.

"So what are they...?" Dong Jue asked plainly.

"Lanterns," Kongming replied. "Flying lanterns."

Liao Hua opened the trunks; inside were folded red and yellow paper lanterns, bearing the character 'Shu', and some detached miniature braziers.

"Open one out, fit a brazier, and light it," Kongming ordered. "We will release them at intervals, one by one."

"Prime Minister, how...?" Ma Dai protested; Kongming grunted angrily, and Ma Dai assisted the preparation of the lanterns without another word.

Each lantern was opened out to a cylindrical shape with a sealed ceiling; a small brazier was to be placed in the centre of the hollow. Ma Dai lit the installed brazier and, slowly and gracefully, the lantern floated upward, to the amazement of the Shu soldiers.

"...Even upper Heaven will see those, Prime Minister," Zong Yu supposed. "Won't they lead Sima Yi to us as well...?"

"I said that they might, but we have to take the risk," Kongming sighed.


"...*Now* what does this marvellous man employ...?" Sima Yi chuckled as the first reports of the lanterns reached his ears; he had been inspecting the charred remains of the wooden oxen along the main road.

"...Flying globes, Chief Commander, with the word 'Shu' upon them!" General Fei Yao re-reported excitedly. "They seem to be coming out of a valley to the southwest of the road!"

"Then that is where we will find Zhuge Kongming," Sima Yi replied. "We shall move immediately... for their real intention is not to scare us... it is to bring him much-needed assistance."

The Wei army prepared to change direction and move with haste toward the valley.


The Wei forces arrived at the valley before the Shu reinforcements could; Kongming ordered a spirited defence with crossbows and what little cavalry he had left, since there were not enough men to form an array. As those fragile lines started to crumble, Wei Yan arrived with his vanguard; that blunted Zhang He and Guo Huai's assault slightly, but it would still be too little to repel Sima Yi. Wu Ban, Gao Xiang, Zhang Bogong and Zhang Boqi arrived a short time later with their infantry and cavalry, but again, that would not be enough; the Shu forces became trapped in the valley, unable to do anything but repel Zhang He.

"We've done it," Sima Yi said with disbelief.

"...Done what, Father...?" Sima Shi asked.

"We've got Zhuge Kongming!" Sima Yi declared. "Finally, we have him...!"

"Why do you call him by his style name, Father...?" Sima Zhao complained.

"He is worthy of respect," Sima Yi insisted. "No other man could crack rocks with eggs, as he has done since his master perished. He must know that he cannot beat us, and yet he still torments us... for that, I respect him, and pity him."

"If you say so, Father," Sima Zhao said cynically.

**"We shall rush into the valley,"** Sima Yi proclaimed, **"and capture Zhuge Liang alive... to take back to Luoyang, as our greatest prize!"**

Sima Yi made the order official; the forces of Wei stormed into the valley, led by Fei Yao and Niu Jin. But as they neared the last of Wei Yan's forces, a wall of torches appeared at each side of the valley.

"**WELCOME, SIMA YI!**" General Hu Ji bellowed from above the advancing Wei forces. "**HAVE YOU COME TO DELIVER YOURSELF TO THE PRIME MINISTER OF THE HAN...?**"
"**AIEE...! He's up there???**" Zhang He exclaimed, as a carriage was rolled into view above them, hosting a familiar purple-robed man carrying a fan. "**We've been tricked!**"
"**Retreat at once!**" Sima Yi ordered; a hail of arrows pursued the Wei army out of the valley.
Wei Yan looked up at Hu Ji and the 'Prime Minister of the Han' – Liu Ba in disguise – and smiled proudly, saying, "**Pursue them!**"
A small group of cavalry pursued the Wei army to bluff them into continuing their withdrawal; a grateful Kongming coughed violently, and laughed.

"So now, we are back on safer ground," Kongming said with relief as he settled into his Chief Commander's seat in the Mount Qi command tent. "All we need now is to find the stragglers from the rout, regroup... and with Li Yan's supplies delivered, we can get this campaign moving again."
"They... haven't arrived yet," Yang Yi reported uneasily.
"*Oh...?*" Kongming chuckled softly. "Well, I expect that the rains are holding them up slightly... thank Heaven there were no rains when we needed to deploy those lanterns!"
"We got very little harvested grain back here," Zong Yu noted. "Without that grain from Chengdu, we'd have to retreat again."
"Don't panic," Kongming pleaded. "We've just come back from a desperate situation, thanks to a little bravery and ingenuity; and we're here for the long haul this time, whatever Sima Yi may want. We can build new oxen and horses, and we can launch fresh attacks against Tianshui and Longyou once Mount Qi is taken. We had a little setback... that's all."
"We lost General Chen Shi, and nearly fifteen thousand men," Liu Ba said angrily. "Isn't that a little more than a little setback, Prime Minister...?"
Kongming started to fan himself slowly, and smiled.
"...Firstly, thank you for saving us from the valley, Liu Ba, Fei Yi, and Hu Ji," Kongming began calmly. "I am even gladder now that my carriage and fan have become almost symbolic... it was a marvellous bit of creative thinking, and I commend you all. ...First Emperor lost eighty thousand men, and brought Shu to its knees... yet here we all are today. Sima Yi has lost thousands of men too, including Generals Wang Shuang and Hao Zhao in the last few years, so both sides have had their wins and losses. I grieve for Chen Shi, but at the same time, he gave his life fighting to protect the soldiers in his care... he was keen to be a hero, and atone for his failures in earlier campaigns. Men die... and it is always sad. But if we dwell, morale will fall... and this campaign will have been for nothing. Is that what you want...?"
"The Prime Minister is correct," Wei Yan declared. "We keep fighting... like we always have."
The other officials murmured agreeably; the siege of Mount Qi would go on.

But it was not to be: as Sima Yi consolidated his position on Mount Qi once more, a man wearing the robes of an imperial messenger arrived at Kongming's camp, bearing instructions. The entire ensemble of officials kowtowed as the messenger proclaimed the will of the Second Emperor of Shu Han, Liu Shan: the campaign was to end, the army was to withdraw immediately to Hanzhong, and the Prime Minister was to return to Chengdu. Despite the protocol, there were gasps of horror at the announcement; the messenger withdrew, leaving the command tent stunned into a painful silence.

"...No... no, no, this can't be right...!" Kongming whimpered as the shocked officials got to their feet: he remained seated, though noticeably unbalanced.

"...Something is wrong here," Fei Yi agreed. "This messenger braved the rains to get here, and advanced past our supplies, which have still to arrive...?"

"The Emperor's will... is absolute," Kongming decided emotionally; his followers looked at his broken expression with genuine sadness. "But... I will not go before I have one last victory against Sima Yi... I will not let the campaign end like this."

Wei Yan nodded seriously, and said, "What are your orders...?"

Kongming looked up, nodded, and hummed decisively.

"Another retreat," Sima Yi mused as his messenger finished his report and retreated.

"We can't miss an opportunity like this," Fei Yao protested.

"*Ayah*," Zhang He exclaimed. "Do you enjoy pain...? How many more times do we want to be fooled by this master of the ambush and the bluff...?"

"Something about this retreat is different," Sima Yi noted.

"They are *all* different, Chief Commander, but the outcome is always the same!" Zhang He complained. "Even if he really *is* running away, *let him go*! We lost Wang Shuang by being so careless!"

"He's at the base of the mountain... so *close, right near our main forces*," Sima Yi said with a tone that resembled that of an excited hunter.

"Chief Commander, *no*," Zhang He pleaded. "This is folly."

"...I want a full strike on their camp," Sima Yi declared. "I want to throw everything at them. Zhang He, Guo Huai, Niu Jin, Fei Yao, Jia Ji... ready your men. Wei Ping, you'll hold the camp. And forget capturing Zhuge Liang... just get him, and Wei Yan, whatever it takes."

The Wei forces once again tore into a retreating Shu force as Wei Yan and Wu Ban led them to the escape route at Mumen Trail. Kongming remained in the centre of the force with Gao Xiang, Deng Zhi, and his main retinue of officials, while Ma Dai, Zhang Boqi, Zhang Bogong and Hu Ji had been chosen to protect the rear; it was Ma Dai that reported the Wei attack.

"...Excellent," Kongming said coldly, as Ma Dai kept his horse at a steady trot alongside Kongming's carriage. "Try not to lose too many men, but... keep them pursuing us."

Ma Dai turned his horse and rode back to the rear of the army, where Zhang He led a ferocious charge on the relatively vulnerable Shu infantry. Men fell left and right, as Zhang He and his elite cavalry pushed toward the centre of the retreating army; the ground was relatively flat and no ambush was possible, so Zhang He pursued without restraint.

"**REPORT...!**" Niu Jin hailed as he rode to Sima Yi's position. "The Shu supply train is broken, their rear guard has fallen apart, and General Zhang is pushing toward the centre!"
A strange feeling possessed Sima Yi; he grinned maniacally and cried, "**We're going to win! All forces advance! Today we're going to destroy the army of Shu! We'll march into Hanzhong, and fly the flag of Wei over Chengdu!**"
The soldiers cheered, and followed the command with high morale; thousands of men flowed toward the Shu position near Mumen Trail.

Zhang He halted his pursuit as he spied the treacherous terrain of Mumen ahead of him; he contented himself with hacking away at the fleeing infantry, until a victorious Sima Yi led his men into view, hollering wildly.
"...**WHERE IS ZHUGE LIANG???**" Sima Yi screamed; but he was separated from Zhang He by a sea of Wei infantry and the sounds of pitched battle, and the words did not reach his subordinate.
"**Chief Commander, the remainder of the Shu army has retreated onto the Mumen Trail!**" Niu Jin said as he stopped alongside Sima Yi. "**Shall I pursue...?**"
"**General Zhang He will lead the pursuit!**" Sima Yi proclaimed as his frenzy continued; he thrust his battle sword into the empty air in front of him, screaming emphatically, "**PURSUE THEM!**"
Zhang He was still unable to hear the words Sima Yi spoke, but he understood the intention: he shouted back, as loudly as he could, "**WE'VE WON, CHIEF COMMANDER! WHY RISK OURSELVES...?**"
Sima Yi could not hear Zhang He's reply, but understood the signs of hesitation; anger consumed him as he took from his left side the sword of command, and thrust that upward, over his head. He glared at Zhang He, who understood the meaning of the gesture; despite knowing the outcome, he turned his horse, and led his men toward the Mumen Trail.

"**HERE COMES ZHANG HE!**" the veteran general of Wei cried as he advanced on the Shu army. "**WHERE IS ZHUGE LIANG???**"
Zhang Boqi rode forward to challenge him, but was brushed aside after only a few clashes by the seasoned jouster. Zhang Bosong followed his comrade's example, but fled after almost having his spear prised from his hands. Ma Dai tried next; he too was forced to withdraw. With each challenge he rebuffed, Zhang He rode deeper and deeper onto the walled trail: as soon as he was adequately separated from any possible reinforcements, Kongming sprung the trap that Zhang He had guessed was waiting for him.
"**HERE IS THE PRIME MINISTER!**" Jiang Wei declared, as Kongming was wheeled into view, beyond the reach of Zhang He's cavalry. "**HE THANKS YOU FOR COMING HERE TO DIE!**"

604

Zhang He and his riders halted their charge, and looked at the high walls of the trail, where dozens of crossbowmen had appeared.

General Zhang He smiled, and raised his sword in triumph, as bolts rained down on his position. After an illustrious career of more than thirty years, he perished on Mumen Trail with his riders. Kongming surveyed the carnage from a distance while he fanned himself slowly.

"Now...?" Jiang Wei prompted.

"...Now, we withdraw," Kongming said coldly. "We have our orders, Jiang Boye... **WITHDRAW!**"

When Sima Yi finally rode down the Mumen Trail, he found the corpse of his prized general Zhang He beside his horse, wearing an expression of sadness and defiance.

"...This is my fault," Sima Yi murmured. "How can we replace such a man...?"

"Men die," Niu Jin suggested. "General Zhang-"

"He *warned* against this... he remonstrated rightly, but I refused to listen!" Sima Yi said emotionally. "Now, he is dead, and Wei has lost its greatest champion."

Zhang He's former subordinate Guo Huai exhaled noisily, and exclaimed, "*Aiee.*"

"Never again will I respond to a challenge by Zhuge Liang... *never*," Sima Yi promised. "Let him taunt, let him feign, let him try all manner of deceit... but I will never fall foul of his tricks again... *never.*"

Like the three campaigns before it, the fourth was a failure that damaged the state of Shu. Although the state of Wei had lost Zhang He, and despite Cao Zhen's death due to illness later that year, it was still a powerful empire with more resources than Shu could ever hope to muster. Kongming pondered the fact as he rode toward Chengdu weeks later, accompanied by Zong Yu and Dong Jue.

"...Prime Minister, don't be sad," Zong Yu said. "We've lost a lot, but Zhang He was their Yunchang, their Yide... they will not have his wiles and skill to aid them next time. Once we get back-"

"Once we get back," Kongming interrupted, "I'll know what really happened... although I think I know already. We've been betrayed... *again.*"

************

## 118

Kongming went straight to the imperial court once he reached Chengdu; he requested a gathering of the senior officials, and prepared to face his emperor, Liu Shan.

"...Mister Zhuge, Second Father," Liu Shan said with concern. "You were fighting near Mount Qi... I have been excited and frightened by the stories I've heard... but you never spoke of wanting to return, no matter what Heaven inflicted upon you. Why did you decide to abort the campaign...?"

From their places among the middle-ranking officials of the court, Zong Yu and Dong Jue stifled gasps of horror; Kongming closed his eyes, and exhaled noisily.

"...Prime Minister," Imperial Secretariat Dong Yun prompted. "Our sovereign has asked about a matter of state importance... I hate to press you, but-"

"Where is Li Yan...?" Kongming asked as he opened his eyes again.

"...That does not answer the question," Dong Yun said emphatically. "Prime Minister, why did you petition Second Emperor to request that he-"

"I did not," Kongming declared; the court was filled with gasps and murmurs. "I... I have to know where I can find Li Yan. He is not here, and he should be... where is Li Yan...?"

"I... am confused," Liu Shan admitted with embarrassment. "Second Father, do you mean to say that your petition... was not genuine...?"

"Wherever he is, Li Yan must be found," Kongming ordered; Dong Yun nodded compliantly, and gestured to two of the soldiers near the hall entrance, who departed immediately.

"Second Father... did you not want to return...?" Liu Shan prompted.

"No, Your Majesty... I did not," Kongming replied miserably; his hands were shaking with rage, so much so that he could not feign calmness by fanning himself, as he usually did. His eyes filled with tears as he added, "I... I was so *close*...!"

"...*Aiee*," Dong Yun exclaimed as Kongming's voice trailed weakly.

The court was silent and ponderous as it awaited news of Li Yan's whereabouts: Kongming stood before Liu Shan for the entire duration, breathing heavily, and with his eyes firmly closed. He was emotionally broken, and it was very obviously so; his arms hung at his sides, and his grip on his feather fan was perilously weak.

"**Your Majesty!**" a voice hailed from the court entrance; the next noise was the soft slapping sound as Kongming's fan fell from his hand to the floor.

Zong Yu cried out, "*Prime Minister*...!" but he was not allowed to help him.

"Your Majesty," Gao Xiang panted as he walked to Kongming's side, "Li Yan has been apprehended... he was attempting to flee the capital with his son Feng. His son surrendered without incident... Li Yan resisted, but is in your custody."

"And what is his crime...?" Liu Shan asked as Kongming finally bent down to retrieve his fan.

"...Treason," Kongming replied coldly as he stood upright once again. "Would I be right in saying, Gao Xiang, that he was unable to provide me with the grain I requested... and so he petitioned the court in my name to force our withdrawal...?"

The assembled courtiers gasped at the accusation Kongming now made toward his former co-regent.

"...He denies that he has done wrong," Gao Xiang explained carefully. "We found communications in his office, letters urging preparation... the rains were affecting transport, and no contingency plans had been made. If nothing else is to be proven, one thing will be... he would not have been able to supply the grain the Prime Minister requested, had the campaign-"

"*Ayah...!*" Dong He cried with anger. "And to cover his tracks, he destroys our grand design??? He must be executed for this!"

"...No," Kongming insisted. "Li Yan was a favourite of the First Emperor... I could not look upon him again in Heaven if Li Yan were to come to harm. The man is diligent, professional and measured in stable times... but unreliable, dishonest and treacherous when he is put under pressure. This I knew, and yet I still trusted him. Your Majesty, there is only one punishment for Li Yan... he must be reduced to the status of commoner, and be exiled to some far-off shire. He must never again set foot in the capital."

Silence gripped the court as the angry Liu Shan pondered his Prime Minister's magnanimous suggestion.

"...He has harmed you, Prime Minister," Dong Yun proposed. "And yet you want to show him such mercy...?"

"First Emperor held him in high regard, as high as he held me," Kongming retorted calmly. "I have returned to you here as a man that has lost for a fourth time, costing grain, money and lives... yet my only punishment so far has been temporary demotion. I must not, and will not, be a hypocrite."

"There will be no demotions this time," Liu Shan declared. "Second Father, you were tricked, and your schemes were ruined... nothing was your fault, you trusted the wrong people. Li Yan will be demoted to commoner status, and leave the capital immediately... but what of his son...?"

"His son should remain, and inherit his father's responsibilities," Kongming suggested. "It is the father that is at fault... the son did not ask for his lot, as First Emperor did not ask to be a mat weaver to atone for an ancestor's folly. Li Yan shall serve as an example... and Li Feng will heed it better than any."

"You are kind beyond reason, Prime Minister," the official Li Fu said emotionally.

"...Li Feng shall inherit the role of Administrator of Logistics and Resources," Emperor Liu Shan proclaimed. "He shall be spared his father's fate."

"And what of you, Prime Minister...?" Dong Yun prompted.

"I... would ask of you, Your Majesty, the right to embark on a fifth campaign," Kongming said, to the shock of all present. "I would not go now... but in a year or two perhaps, when our wounds have healed. We shall grow crops, we shall train a stronger, better army... we shall recruit new talent... and we shall again march northward to destroy Wei and restore the fire of Han in Luoyang."

"Prime Minister...!" Dong He protested.

"I will exhaust myself in that endeavour if I must, Your Majesty... I owe that much to your illustrious father," Kongming promised. "If I fail a fifth time, I will not dare stand before your heavenly presence again ... I will not have the right."

Liu Shan started to sob; the courtiers murmured uneasily.

"I cannot allow this thing you ask!" Liu Shan bleated. "Second Father... Mister Zhuge Kongming... I need you, I need your guidance!"

"I... am not the only man in Shu," Kongming replied. "All around you are loyal, hardworking men... I am just one of them. Please, Your Majesty... I promised your father... and I cannot face him again if I did not do everything in my power to save the Han! It's my life's work... *please*!"

All eyes fell on the emperor, who replied through weak tears, "I... I command you... to march... against Wei... on a fifth campaign. You will... you will prepare well, and... and do all you can, to... to fulfil the task my father left you."

"...Very good," Kongming said with a smile; he started to fan himself slowly, and regained his confident posture. "Very good, Your Majesty. I accept your command... and I will do my utmost for your cause."

Kongming then kowtowed to his emperor; the courtiers were still murmuring uneasily at the things that they were seeing and hearing. As Kongming got to his feet, he looked at all of his allies and enemies in the court of Shu that he had helped to build, and smiled proudly.

For the next two years, Shu and Wei rebuilt their defences and their armies. Both sides had the career soldiers working alongside the farmers, growing the food that would sustain them, as Cao Cao had once done. Sima Yi restored canals and walls, and installed security along the entire border with Hanzhong: Kongming, meanwhile, sent envoys to Wu to urge Emperor Sun Quan to aid them during the upcoming campaign, and rebuilt his fleet of wooden oxen and horses.

Winter came to a close, and preparations were complete across the land of Shu for the fifth campaign against the state of Cao Wei. Kongming gathered his staff in his office to speak to them for one final time before he set out for Hanzhong.

"Xi Zheng," Kongming said, "I trust you, as I have done many times before, to keep everything in order until I return. Keep a close eye on Li Feng, and ensure that he serves us well. We cannot afford any more supply problems."

"Yes, Prime Minister," Xi Zheng replied emotionally.

"Fei Shi, I also leave you with my responsibilities," Kongming continued. "Keep in constant contact with me via Fei Yi and Zong Yu... and, obviously, ensure that communications remain clear and cordial with Eastern Wu. Appease them any way you need to... their role is crucial to my success."

Fei Shi nodded silently, to avoid exposing his distress.

"...I expect that we shall not see each other for some time," Kongming chuckled calmly. "Still, are we not used to this...?"

The officials smiled uncomfortably and silently.

"...Right," Kongming sighed. "I have been to the court... I have come here... now I must visit some old friends. Mister Yi Ji, Mister Chen Zhen, Veteran General Chen Dao... and, of course, I must also visit the memorials of First Emperor, Zilong, Yunchang, Yide, Ma Jichang, Pang Shiyuan, Mister Fa, Mister Sun, and Mister Jian, and pay my respects."
"Master," Jiang Wei said, "you have not done this before... why this time...? You are acting as if-"
"I visit all of my friends before every expedition," Kongming scolded. "Do not read into my actions more than they intend!"
"...I apologise, Master," Jiang Wei murmured.
"I shall go alone," Kongming insisted. "Go and ready everything for departure."
Jiang Wei left the office with Zong Yu and Dong Jue.
"...Once I have visited my friends, old and gone, I shall be visiting the families of Ma Jichang, Ma Su, and Pang Shiyuan," Kongming continued. "...And then, of course, I must go home, and say farewell to my own family."
"...Prime Minister!" Fei Shi wailed.
"Stop whining!" Kongming snickered. "Honestly... you complain that I curse this endeavour, and then cry at my every word. ...Farewell to you all..."
The dozen officials that had gathered to see Kongming bowed as one; he reciprocated the sincere gesture, and went on his way, leaving the men to murmur miserably, and wonder if they would ever see him again.

"...Xuande," Kongming whispered as he knelt in front of First Emperor Liu Bei's vast temple altar. "I... I'm sorry. I promised you so many things, Xuande... and I've let you down."
Kongming exhaled noisily, and lowered his head.
"A man cannot survive alone, I know that... but he must be cautious in the friends he chooses for himself, mindful of the weaknesses we all have as men, and never fully trust anyone, not even himself," Kongming continued. "You... you understood this, I think... you once said I knew men's hearts, but not their minds, so I think that you did... while I have only just realised. I thought I knew... I was wrong. And four times, that folly has cost us victory. Ma Su, and Li Yan, they ruined our first and fourth endeavours... because I thought I knew them, how to use them well... I did not. The second and third expeditions, I blame on poor logistics, poor supplies... no, they were my poor judgement.
        "You came to me, and I presented a plan to you... a plan to divide the realm into three, a temporary, controlled fission that I was sure would result in the restoration of the Han... but now, I... I am not sure anymore. I knew the plan was not ideal... but neither were your circumstances! How could I propose that you faced Cao Cao alone with the ragtag band you had back then...?
...But I could not tender my services to Wu... not when the mandate was falsely exhausted! The people turned on the Ten Eunuchs, not the emperor... had any of the corrupt men that replaced them been anything else but corrupt... we'd now have enduring peace!

"What I wanted to was to put things right... preserve the mandated Han... and the only man that shared my dream was you. I had to make a powerful tree from a dry sapling... only by manipulating events would that ever be possible.

"And, despite the doubters, I did that... I used Wu to destroy Cao at Red Cliffs for us, I used them again to secure us southern Jing... I courted the rebels of Lujiang, so that we'd have an army... I courted the disaffected officials in Yi, so that we would have a home. I made everything ready... and yet I still failed you. I could create the path for you to follow... but I could not guide you along it."

Kongming got up, took up his fan, and shook his head sadly.

"Now, I must finish my journey, Xuande. I am a man that cherishes life, and yet I've watched friends and loved ones die, and brought death on thousands of my enemies... and my soul can't take any more," Kongming admitted. "I am only fifty-four, and yet I have only one more fight left in me... and then, I must leave it to others to finish what I started. It's for that weakness that I'm sorry, Xuande... I only hope you can forgive me."

Kongming then kowtowed several times before the altar, to show his devotion to his master, Liu Bei.

Kongming concluded his tour at his own home: all of his things had already been packed, and were waiting for him in a horse-drawn carriage outside his house. Kongming looked at the laden carriage, and then at the horse; he smiled as he empathised with the beast of burden. After patting the animal on the nose, he entered the house.

Yueying was sat waiting for Kongming in front of her qin, and behind her, all of the servants stood in a row, sobbing pitifully. Kongming's five-year-old son was sat next to his mother, and next to him, there was another child, a baby boy, also recently introduced to the world. Kongming stared at his two sons with love, but did not say a word. In front of the servants were his adopted son's widow and her own son, who was now six years old: Kongming's daughter-in-law smiled through her tears, and nodded respectfully.

Kongming had deliberately refused to look at Yueying, and had been looking instead at everyone else; Yueying turned her gaze to her family and servants, and smiled warmly. Zhuge Qiao's widow knew Yueying's intention, and took the younger of Kongming's children into her own arms; Kongming watched her silently, fanning himself all the while. The servants silently withdrew, followed in turn by Qiao's widow and the three children; now, only Yueying and Kongming remained. Now he was forced to look at her; his eyes were filled with tears, but he fought them back, and smiled strongly.

Now, Yueying gestured with her eyes toward the second qin – his – that lay beside hers. Kongming placed his fan on his empty desk, and sat next to his wife, all the while trying to find the strength and calm to play. Yueying readied herself, but would not begin; instead, she smiled serenely, and kept her gaze fixed on her husband. Finally, Kongming found within himself the calm that he needed, and so he began.

Kongming played slowly and purposefully, evoking a journey that had been long and difficult; and initially, Yueying did nothing but watch. As the tune built, she finally started to play, matching his tone and tempo perfectly, and reflecting the great heights that had been reached despite the odds. The tune was mournful and yet optimistic, serious and yet romantic: the two turned their eyes to meet each other, and smiled as one.

But suddenly, Kongming's eyes filled with tears again, and he started to slow; Yueying followed his lead, but did not lose her smile. Suddenly, Kongming turned his gaze from her, and stopped playing: and, to his surprise, Yueying did not follow. Instead, she continued to play, smiling all the while, and kept her gaze fixed on Kongming. He got to his feet, and still she played on; he walked to the table, and picked up his fan, and still, Yueying played on. The notes she played were serene, optimistic and enduring: as Kongming reluctantly turned to face her again, she met him with the same smile, and briefly turned her eyes, and then her head, toward the doorway where her daughter-in-law, grandson and children now stood, Qiao's widow smiling with false strength. As Yueying turned her head and her gaze back to her husband, she nodded slowly; Kongming smiled, and returned the gesture. Kongming started to fan himself and prepared to leave the house, and all the while, Yueying smiled and played the same tune. He walked slowly and unwillingly, until he reached the door; once he walked through it, he mused, he would be on his way to Hanzhong, and a fifth battle with Wei. He turned to face Yueying one last time; now, she was staring not at him, but straight ahead of her, and still, she played on. Kongming smiled strangely and fought back tears of pride and respect as he turned away from her, and continued on his way.

"We shall be going straight to the military barracks, Prime Minister...?" the driver of the carriage asked as Kongming got aboard.
"...Yes," Kongming replied quietly.
Qiao's widow brought the three children to the door, and stood silently, watching the family patriarch as he prepared to leave them once again. Kongming was still fanning himself, but there was no calmness; he could still hear the tune that Yueying was playing, and it still carried the same strength and conviction. He fought the urge to take one last look at the house and his family, and said, "*Go.*"

Kongming left the Shu capital of Chengdu, and made the long and difficult journey to Hanzhong, where the assembled officials awaited the plan with interest. As Kongming, Jiang Wei, Zong Yu and Dong Jue entered the great hall of the main headquarters in Hanzhong, the official Fei Yi smiled, saying, "Ah, welcome back, Prime Minister, friends... welcome back."
Fei Yi was sat near the seat of authority that Kongming would soon occupy: Wei Yan sat on the other side. Yang Yi, Liu Ba, Hu Ji, Deng Zhi and Liao Hua sat next to Fei Yi; Wu Ban, Wang Ping, Zhang Boqi, Zhang Bogong and Ma Dai sat next to Wei Yan; the other generals and officials sat further away from the seat of authority, to reflect their lesser status.

Zong Yu, Dong Jue and Jiang Wei took their places, and Kongming took his, casting respectful glances toward his officers as he started to fan himself casually.

"This time," Kongming said, "we will be acting in an alliance with Eastern Wu. While our previous efforts have been valiant enough, you cannot pincer an enemy with only one force... especially not a smaller force."

"So what have our esteemed allies – and now, by decree, *equals* – the *Empire* of Eastern Wu promised to do to assist us, then...?" Wei Yan asked bluntly.

Kongming smiled, replying, "My plan – which has got us this far – relied on three states acting in rivalry, with two of those states eventually putting their own ambitions aside and joining forces to conquer the third, larger, evil state and restore the stability of the Han. To achieve this, there would be three attacking points to divide that larger enemy: Hanzhong to the west, Hefei to the east, and Jing in the centre."

"We know all this," Wei Yan said irritably. "Guan Yunchang lost Jing, and now it is a part of Eastern Wu... so how will this work... exactly...?"

"If you would let me finish, I will explain," Kongming scolded. "Wu shall carry out the central and eastern pincers, while we – the true – shall strike through Hanzhong, and take the northwest. With our Qiang and Xianbei tribal allies causing dissent in the cities, two large armies from Wu harassing their other borders, and our own force of a hundred thousand to face... Wei will be overwhelmed."

"What will Wu want from this alliance...?" Yang Yi wondered.

"You repatriated, hopefully, back to the Xiangyang cess pit that you came from," Wei Yan taunted. "They're welcome to you."

"*You*...!" Yang Yi whined.

"...Really, Wenchang, can't this silliness wait...?" Fei Yi chuckled calmly. "Please, Kongming, continue."

"Under the restored Han, Wu would be recognised as a foreign empire," Kongming explained. "Whether it remains that way in the long term or not is down to them. What's important is the outcome for Wei... at worst they will be broken, dispossessed of their empire, and left as a minor state with no influence, reduced to worthless stealth strikes and petty alliances with tiny rebel groups. At best, they will be vanquished completely... and our cause will have been fulfilled."

"At long last...!" Liao Hua said boldly. "When do we march, Prime Minister...?"

"Immediately," Kongming replied calmly. "Let's bring this to an end."


∗∗∗∗∗∗∗∗∗∗∗∗

## 119

The 100,000-strong Shu army travelled across the Qinling Mountains and arrived at Wu Zhang Plains, south of the River Wei, where they settled amid reports of a 200,000-strong force led by Sima Yi and Guo Huai coming from the north and west to check their advance. Sima Yi's force camped along the southern bank of the River Wei, denying Shu access to that crucial communications waterway and the fortress of Chen Cang that was beyond it.

"So this is it...?" Wei Yan complained as he toured the orderly camps with Kongming and Jiang Wei. "We're just going to sit here...? What happened to 'finishing it'...?"

"Wenchang, please stop being so impatient," Kongming scolded. "Sima Yi is a changed man since the death of Zhang He. He had within him something that he never knew he had... ambitious bloodlust. It surfaced during our last campaign, and it overwhelmed him, and it made him reckless and vindictive... just like Cao Cao. That will have frightened him: now, he'll be content to build massive reinforced camps and sit behind their walls, waiting for us to run out of grain. Well, we won't! This time, we have not only wooden oxen and gliding horses, but months and months of stored grain, grown over the last two years, and a competent man in charge of delivering it. And further to that, we've occupied arable land! If he just sits there, we'll be growing ourselves food to outlast him, and right under his nose. Won't that annoy his more belligerent generals, and make him look like a coward...? ...And once the dissent of the tribes starts to pressure his city guards, and Wu begin their assaults on Fan and Hefei, Sima Yi won't know what to do!"

"...Don't think me repetitive," Wei Yan began, "but aren't we in a fine position to launch that sudden strike on Chang'an...?"

"We *are*, aren't we...?" Kongming chuckled softly.

"...So you intend to strike Chang'an this time...?" Wei Yan said excitedly.

"I have many ideas, Wenchang... and doesn't Sima Yi wish he knew what they were!" Kongming said with a bold laugh.

As summer arrived, the early northern wheat was ripe for harvest. The soldiers of Shu gathered the wheat under Kongming's personal supervision, and to rouse them, he entertained them with folk songs, poems, and ditties. The men worked tirelessly, to the irritation of Sima Yi: but as the days wore on, a ditty composed by Kongming for the soldiers to sing irritated him even more.

**"Sima Yi! Sima Yi!**
**Where *are* you hiding, Sima Yi?**
**We sow the crops and reap the grain,**
**To fuel a fight that's planned in vain!**
**For Mumen's outcome caused you pain,**
**And you're too scared to charge again!**
**Come out of hiding, Sima Yi! Sima Yi!**

"He's up to something," Sima Yi murmured as he paced back and forth in his command post on the southern river bank, desperately trying to drown out the singing with his thoughts.

Guo Huai watched his anxious Chief Commander, and said, "Reports are coming in that Wu troops are massing near Jing and Hefei."

"...It's the pincer attack that Zhuge Liang has long wanted," Sima Yi worried. "I know all about his 'Longzhong Plan'... and so far, one can't help but marvel at what he's achieved. If he can turn a runaway mat weaver with seven-thousand men – mostly reformed Yellow Turban bandits – into a super-warlord on a par with Sun Quan of Wu... why can't he take the north...? He turned Liu Bei's definitive defeat at Xiaoting into a *setback*... he somehow brought a bankrupt state with forty thousand men back to being a thriving empire with an army of a *hundred* thousand, with armies of barbarian tribes willing to assist him! He turns supply dilemmas into minor issues by building wooden animals; he secures his rescue from night raids with flying lanterns! ...Against such a man, another man has to show the utmost caution, for nothing is ever as it seems."

"...Which is precisely what I was thinking," Guo Huai said with a smile.

"Tell me, General, what has crossed your mind," Sima Yi implored.

"His encampment at Wu Zhang and his public appointment of Wei Yan as the vanguard... suggests an obvious raid on Chang'an," Guo Huai explained.

"...Of course!" Sima Yi exclaimed. "Then we must-"

"*However*," Guo Huai interrupted, "as Zhang He and I often discovered in our encounters with Shu... there's always something behind the subterfuge... he doesn't intend to siege Chang'an at all, he never has and he never will. I agree that he is unpredictable in direct warfare, and I also agree that he is inventive... but he has an obvious weakness."

"*Oh*...?" Sima Yi prompted.

Guo Huai nodded, saying, "This is Zhuge Liang... a man that persists in supporting the house of Han after it has long since been extinguished, and deigns to follow a fat, bumbling simpleton of an emperor, simply because he's a Liu."

"...He's *stubborn*," Sima Yi supposed.

"Wei Yan can smash his head against the hard stone all he wants, Zhuge Liang will never permit him to attack Chang'an; he considers it to be too risky," Guo Huai continued. "No: he'll continue his tried-and-tested plan of taking the northwest, in particular Longyou and Tianshui."

"...But then why is he here in Wu Zhang...?" Sima Yi mused. "...Ah, I see... your thoughts make perfect sense! He has lured us here, on the pretext of taunting us with his plans for *tuntian* food production, and a protracted stand-off... we have concentrated everything we have here... thinking that, at worst, he'll attack Chang'an, Chen Cang, or Mount Qi... when really... he's... going to attack the river route to the far *west*...!"

"Beiyuan," Guo Huai said plainly. "It's the perfect place to set up a western communication and supply route... he could move forces up to Jieting, as he did the first time... and if he's got better men, we won't get it back this time."

"That would be a disaster!" Sima Yi realised. "We'd lose *An Ding*, and *Nan'an*, and...! ...**MESSENGER...!**"
"There's a garrison there, but if he's sent an elite force, they won't last," Guo Huai said ruefully as a messenger entered the tent.
"Messenger, hurry to Chang'an," Sima Yi said sternly.
"*Chang'an*...?" Guo Huai chortled.
"Have word sent to Luoyang that we need additional forces... fifty, maybe a hundred thousand men if we can spare them, deployed double-time to Beiyuan... *hurry*," Sima Yi continued as he scrawled a note on a piece of cloth; the messenger took the note and ran from the tent.
"...Will those forces get there in time...?" Guo Huai wondered.
"I intend to go there myself... but Zhuge Liang will try again if he fails, since as you say, he's stubborn," Sima Yi said as he hurriedly put on his armour. "I'll take my sons and Niu Jin... you stay here and secure the camp."
"Let *me* go," Guo Huai implored. "You're needed here to pre-empt Zhuge Liang."
Sima Yi paused, and said, "You're quite right: yes, General... *you* go."

"**Prime Minister...!**" Yang Yi wailed as he ran into the command tent. "Prime Minister, the siege of Beiyuan has been broken!"
Kongming, Wei Yan, Fei Yi and Jiang Wei turned to face Yang Yi with a united sense of frustration.
"What happened...?" Kongming asked calmly, as he started to fan himself slowly.
"Guo Huai left the camp under cover of darkness, and marched double-time to Beiyuan with Niu Jin!" Yang Yi whined. "General Wu Ban was caught in a pincer between the defenders and Guo Huai... he's been routed, he's been *killed*!"
Kongming froze; Wei Yan punched the air in front of him, and exclaimed, "*Aiee!*"
"General Wu Ban was a fine officer... and a relative of the imperial house by marriage," Fei Yi murmured. "This... is..."
"...A setback, nothing more," Kongming insisted. "There's no need to panic... Guo Huai will double-time back here, especially if we make a show of attacking their main camp... and as soon as he leaves, Generals Zhang Boqi and Hu Ji can-"
"But Sima Yi has requested forces of over *fifty thousand* good troops to guard Beiyuan, Prime Minister!" Yang Yi interrupted desperately. "They're marching from the east as we speak!"
Kongming coughed painfully, and momentarily lost his balance; Wei Yan stood and watched indifferently, while Jiang Wei and Fei Yi moved to steady their Prime Minister.
"We'll *never* take Beiyuan now," Wei Yan complained. "Perhaps an attack on Chang'an was the better idea after-"
"...Wenchang," Kongming said uncomfortably, "we... we have to think, not criticise. If Beiyuan is reinforced, it is by removing troops from some other place... yes, perhaps Chang'an is now poorly defended. We'll have our spies find out... *okay*...?"
"...Okay," Wei Yan grunted. "...So why are you still here, Yang Yi...? Do you not have somewhere else to be, doing something useful...?"

"...You evil man!" Yang Yi cursed. "You hateful, selfish man! We have lost a fine general, and lost a valuable line of attack, and all you can do is...!"

"...Please, both of you," Fei Yi said calmly. "Yang Yi, prepare a letter to send to Chengdu, reporting the developments... Wei Yan, perhaps we could all be doing something useful. Sima Yi may attack our troops as they retreat from Beiyuan..."

"I shall go and gather a team to assist them," Wei Yan replied as Yang Yi quickly fled the tent, anxious to avoid another fight with Wei Yan.

"Thank you, Fei Wenwei," Kongming wheezed as Wei Yan departed. "Wei Yan becomes more and more haughty... more and more unmanageable... we'll need to think about the future."

Fei Yi nodded reluctantly.

Kongming was considerably more subdued as the days wore on; the news of Wu Ban's death has affected him severely, and the weather was provoking old problems with his health. He coughed and spluttered, and often, he would spit blood, although he hoped that nobody would notice. Wei's reinforcement of Beiyuan also caused a change in his behaviour; Zong Yu, Dong Jue and Jiang Wei met in secret to discuss the matter.

"He won't trust anyone with anything," Zong Yu said sadly.

"Not even us," Dong Jue lamented.

"But one man cannot do everything," Zong Yu bleated. "He's sick... he should be resting, not doing every little pedant's chore! A junior officer can check grain stores, or count arrows! Why does he-"

"*Panic*," Jiang Wei supposed. "Military failure, in the past, has always been due to the failure of someone he trusted... don't be offended."

"His health fades, Boye," Zong Yu said worriedly. "How can we stand by, and...?"

"Plague has broken out amongst the Wu forces on both fronts, and Cao Rui has responded more aggressively than expected," Dong Jue reported. "My fear is that when Kongming hears the news... that..."

"But we cannot hide it from him, Gongxi," Jiang Wei sighed. "All we can do... is help him."

Days later, as Kongming was inspecting the weapon stores with Zong Yu and Fei Yi, a dusty, panicked messenger scrabbled into the camp, desperate to report to the command tent.

"...**REPORT!**" the messenger screamed. "**REPORT...!**"

"...What is it?" Kongming asked hoarsely as he approached the main gates.

"Sun Quan has ordered a general retreat!" the messenger wailed as he fell to one knee to deliver the news. "Wu has withdrawn from Jing and Hefei!"

Silence met the announcement; Kongming had been fanning himself slowly, but as the meaning of the words struck him, he froze.

"...Prime Minister!" the messenger sobbed as he fell to the ground. "Wu has fled!"

Kongming turned and started a long, slow and mechanical walk back to the command tent, followed by Zong Yu and Fei Yi.

"Prime Minister...?" Zong Yu hailed. "...Kongming???"

"Go and see to that messenger, Mister Zong," Fei Yi ordered softly. "This news must be managed... I'll make sure he's okay."

"...Of course," Zong Yu realised; he ran back to the hysterical messenger, who was now surrounded by demoralised soldiers.

"...My grand design," Kongming whimpered as soon as he was inside the command tent; the fan fell from his hand, and he collapsed to his knees.

"Prime Minister!" Fei Yi exclaimed. "...Kongming... you must be strong... for morale... for the army...!"

"...This is why I did not want to rely on Eastern Wu," Kongming complained. "This... is why I did not want... to lose Jing! We'd have Jing if not for *hubris*! We'd have *two* hundred thousand men if not for *complacency*! We-"

"Kongming, *please*," Fei Yi whispered. "This helps nobody."

"...The only hope... that we have now... is to provoke Sima Yi to combat," Kongming decided. "Before... before Wei can bolster this place further... I must provoke Sima Yi. If Sima Yi is dead, then our cause is won. Help me up."

Fei Yi helped Kongming to his feet; without pausing to pick up his fan, Kongming staggered toward his map of the region, as the emotional Fei Yi picked up the feather fan and examined it miserably.

"We... we must provoke Sima Yi," Kongming said again. "We... *must*."

A sustained provocation campaign began; Kongming had his men march to the wooden gates of Sima Yi's riverside main camp every morning and heckle the Wei Chief Commander continuously throughout the day, leaving only when the threat of a night raid was too great. Wei Yan, Zhang Boqi and Jiang Wei would work in shifts, but Wei Yan became increasingly impatient with the strategy, and started to complain. He once again cited his plan to strike Chang'an as the only option left to the demoralised army as the stalemate dragged on.

"...Weeks," Sima Yi chuckled calmly as he sat in his command tent with his two sons and the assembled officers. "Weeks, he's kept this up for... it is a miracle that anyone can still speak, after weeks of shouting abuse."

"Chief Commander, we look weak," Niu Jin complained. "Normally, I would agree that remaining on the defensive is best... but how can they win now...? We outnumber them dramatically, their Wu allies have fled, the tribal rebellions have been crushed... all that's left is Zhuge Liang. My subordinates are almost reduced to crying with frustration! The Shu troops call you all manner of things: call *us* all manner of things! Chief Commander, this is bad for morale! We have to blunt them!"

"They *are* blunted," Sima Yi retorted. "They have no more schemes... except drawing me out, so that they can kill another one of Wei's future champions. I will not rise to the bait."

"...Aiee!" Fei Yao exclaimed. "So we are to listen to that incessant taunting for another month...?"

"I don't care if we have to listen to it for another year!" Sima Yi chortled. "It's music to my ears, General... it's the song of a dying dragon."

**"I won't do this anymore!"** Wei Yan barked as he stormed into the command tent with Deng Zhi; Kongming was coughing violently, so much so that Zong Yu had to hold the blood-covered kerchief over his mouth for him.
"Wenchang, *enough*...!" Zong Yu scolded.
"...Prime Minister...?" Deng Zhi exclaimed. "...Will you be alright...?"
"I... I'll be fine," Kongming promised as he finally regained some strength and took his kerchief back from Zong Yu. "...Has something happened, Wei Wenchang...?"
"...No," Wei Yan grunted. "That's exactly why I came here... to ask when we will try something else. We can't just heckle him all day, every day, for weeks on end... my men are losing their voices now, and Sima Yi does nothing."
"I... I have to try something else, I know that," Kongming conceded. "I'm going to send someone to deliver a package to Sima Yi."
"...What package...?" Wei Yan asked pointedly.

Two days later, a Shu envoy walked through the hostile Wei camp, flanked by two unfriendly guards, and bound for the command tent, where Sima Yi was waiting.
"...Ah, welcome!" Sima Yi chuckled warmly, to the consternation of his officers. "I understand that you have a package and a message for me from Zhuge Kongming...?"
The envoy nodded bravely, and prepared to speak.

Kongming sat with his closest aides in the command tent that evening, awaiting the outcome of his envoy's meeting with Wei Chief Commander Sima Yi.
"...Still nothing," Kongming fretted. "...I regret sending that man now."
"He knew the risks," Zong Yu said encouragingly.
"I only hope that it works," Kongming sighed. "I am spent... I really have... no other plan."
        Night finally fell: just after midnight, to everyone's surprise, the envoy returned, alive and well. Kongming ordered the man brought to the command tent, as he was anxious to hear what had happened as soon as possible.
"Speak," Kongming said hoarsely. "...I want to know what was said."
"...I delivered the package," the envoy said nervously. "And... I told him exactly what you told me to say..."
"Forgive my pedantic ways," Kongming interrupted, "but state precisely what happened... leave no detail out."
"Well," the envoy began again, "when Sima Yi opened the package, the generals were very angry... they demanded to know why I was not already dead. Sima Yi... laughed. He took the woman's dress from the box, and he examined it at great length. They all knew the meaning, but he asked me to tell him what you wanted me to say...

"I told him, 'The Prime Minister of the Han, Zhuge Liang, sends you greetings, and despairs at your lack of courage! If you are content to be a woman and hide away in your closeted place, then do so... here is something beautiful for you to wear as you keep yourself withdrawn from view.' His generals, they were angry, but Sima Yi..."

"...Go on," Kongming implored.

"...He laughed again, and said he was thankful for the gift!" the envoy said with distress.

"...*Aiee*," Kongming sighed. He stopped fanning himself, and lowered his arms to his sides in resignation.

"Then," the envoy continued, "he calmed his generals and entertained me with a banquet: he called you Kongming, all the while, as he enquired after you. And then he-"

"He... enquired after me...?" Kongming noted. "What... what was said...? Leave nothing out."

"He spoke of your wit and courage, but he expressed concern at a respected rival's overwhelming sense of duty," the envoy explained reluctantly. "He asked me what your working practices were."

The officials lowered their heads miserably.

"...Go on," Kongming prompted.

"I told him... that you were fastidious, diligent, insistent on every matter being done properly, and that you were watching over every aspect of day to day affairs," the envoy continued. "He asked about your working hours, and I said that naturally, you worked for as long as you could each day, pausing only for meals... he asked about those, and I explained that you were frugal, and took little food."

Zong Yu exhaled noisily.

"...And what did he say to that...?" Kongming asked knowingly: he was smiling sadly, because the inevitable answer would tell him the outcome of all things.

"...He said," the envoy concluded apprehensively, "that... that a man of over fifty years of age, who takes little food, who has generally poor health, that insists on managing every little detail of day to day running of the camp... cannot last long."

"...*Villain*!" Yang Yi whined.

"He's right, though," Kongming chuckled. "As *I* knew Gongjin, so Zhongda knows *me*, all too well... how else can it end...?"

The officials were ominously silent.

"I... I'm sorry," the envoy pleaded.

"No, no... you did your duty," Kongming sighed. "Go on... go and rest. I'm sure you feel lucky to be alive."

The envoy got up, bowed clumsily, and fled.

"Even Sima Yi berates you for your pedantic self-destruction," Dong Jue said angrily. "Prime Minister... *Kongming*... can't you...?"

"The fates are not to be challenged," Kongming said quietly. "My ways are my ways... I cannot change them. Anyhow, the situation is known to us now... go on, all of you... go and rest. I should like to be alone."

The officials reluctantly left Kongming in the command tent, and retired to their beds; Kongming stood in front of two easels, where his Longzhong Plan and a map of the northwest were on display. He coughed uncomfortably, and wiped a tear from his right eye.

Despite continued pleas from his officials, Kongming did not change his ways; as weeks turned to months, and summer turned to autumn, Kongming continued to do everything himself. His face thinned, his eyes sunk, and his pace slowed with every day that passed. And so one day – as he was inspecting the grain stores with Zong Yu – he stumbled, dropped his fan, and collapsed to the ground.
"Oh no... **Prime Minister!**" Zong Yu exclaimed. "**SOMEONE! HELP ME!**"
Kongming lay motionless on the ground, breathing weakly; as he looked directly upward, he could see many faces, as many of his devoted soldiers and officers rushed to his aid.

"Kongming," Zong Yu whispered; Kongming was confined to his bed, unable to move. His servants and officers looked on with concern, but there was nothing that they could do.
"...Zong Deyan," Kongming whispered. "What... happened...?"
"You collapsed," Zong Yu replied quietly, "three days ago... the doctor says... that you are exhausted."
"I am," Kongming said with a laugh.
"The doctor says... that your vitals... are weak," Zong Yu continued.
Kongming nodded knowingly.

"The Emperor has been informed," Fei Yi reported to the officials in the command tent several days later. "He has despatched Li Fu to enquire matters of importance... for the future."
"...But what about the campaign?" Wei Yan asked bluntly. "Who is to take over from the Prime Minister while he returns to Chengdu to recuperate...?"
"...The Prime Minister has ordered a retreat," Yang Yi declared.
"Pedantic *cowardice*...!" Wei Yan barked. "We are supposed to abandon the grand design because of the loss of *one man*???"
"The Prime Minister is not just 'one man'," Zong Yu suggested angrily.
"First Emperor is dead, yet we carry on!" Wei Yan barked. "I won't retreat just because he screwed up and got sick from distress!"
Hu Ji frowned angrily, saying, "Wei Yan, hold your tongue."
"So he has left no successor to his role...?" Wei Yan chuckled contemptuously. "This is not his kingdom... this is not his plan! It is *our* kingdom, and *our* plan!

        "Time and again, the man publicly rebuked me for my plan to attack Chang'an! 'Did Wu take Xiakou?' he said: more than that, they now hold all of the south, and have declared themselves our successor, acting as an independent empire that will one day consume our tiny, weakened state if Wei does not do so first! And yet he has us see them as an ally... why? Because his brother is a long-serving lapdog of the Suns...?

"None of his plans to 'restore the Han' have amounted to anything, and now he finally realises the truth of things – if his plan was not always to elevate the Suns in collaboration with his donkey-faced brother-"

"You say too much, even for you!" Yang Yi screamed.

"I am hardly *started*!" Wei Yan retorted. "I devoted my life to the Han, to First Emperor, and now to Second Emperor! Right now, Hanzhong is a fortress, because I toiled to make it so! With the deaths of Zilong, Yunchang and Yide, I rose to the challenge, accepted the burden, and I became the shield of Shu: all I ever asked for was a chance to be a sword as well, and deliver the victory that we all claim to be fighting for! ...But instead, we made *Zhuge Liang* our sword, and what a blunted thing that sword has turned out to be at the critical hour!

"If his plan was truly the restoration of the Han, then right now, we could not be further from that goal, thanks to his floundering, and he *knows it*, which is why he is sick: but does he stand strong? No, he *falters*, and *crumbles*, and demands that all men fall with him! **No, I say!** You talk about the future... we now obey the orders of a weak, sick man that would have us all just throw away all of our futures, just because *he* does not have one!"

"Hold your tongue!" Hu Ji said again. "When Li Fu arrives, we'll know what the future holds... for now, we should continue as we were!"

"Heckling Sima Yi... who knows *exactly* what the future holds," Wei Yan complained as he pushed his way past his colleagues and departed the tent.

"Wei Yan ignores all the good... all that Kongming has done to give us a cause to defend... and sees only a distorted, simple picture of things in which he is our only hope," Zong Yu said sadly.

"...Something must be done about Wei Yan, for the sake of the future," Yang Yi murmured, and Fei Yi nodded agreeably.

When the official Li Fu arrived, he hurried to Kongming's tent, and knelt at his bedside. Kongming's condition had gotten worse, not better, since his collapse, as depression took whatever strength the sickness had not claimed.

"...Prime Minister!" Li Fu whimpered. "The Emperor... is heartbroken. He wants you to be returned to Chengdu at once... but... I... he also-"

"*Future*," Kongming said hoarsely.

"...Yes," Li Fu admitted sadly. "He said you'd want it this way. ...If... if there should need to be a follower of your military work... who...?"

"Jiang Wei," Kongming wheezed.

"...And... in your civil work... who should...?" Li Fu prompted.

"Jiang Wan," Kongming replied.

"And... and after Jiang Wan...?" Li Fu wondered.

"F-f... Fei Yi," Kongming replied weakly.

"And... and after him...?" Li Fu prompted.

Kongming shook his head sadly.


************

## 120

Li Fu left Kongming's tent in an emotional state, and travelled immediately to the command tent, where the officials were waiting, save for Wei Yan and Ma Dai.

"...The Prime Minister... is very weak," Li Fu began. "He will need to be returned to Chengdu for recuperation... I understand that he ordered a retreat."

"He did," Fei Yi confirmed.

"Aren't we concerned about the reaction of Sima Yi when he realises what's happening...?" Yang Yi proposed.

"Of course," Jiang Wei said plainly. "But we have a plan to deal with that. I am going to speak with the Prime Minister now... he asked me to."

Jiang Wei left the officials, and went straight to Kongming's bedside.


"Master," Jiang Wei prompted.

Kongming looked into Jiang Wei's eyes and smiled slightly.

"...Boye," Kongming wheezed. "...We're... going...?"

"As you instructed, Prime Minister," Jiang Wei confirmed.

"...Books," Kongming said; he guided Jiang Wei with his eyes, toward a nearby desk pile of books and scrolls. "...*Yours.*"

"You speak prematurely," Jiang Wei pleaded. "I... I'm not ready to take on your life's work, Master... you must recover, so that you can continue to explain the more complex matters to me."

"Ss... Sima... *Yi*," Kongming prompted.

"I... I'm ready to face Sima Yi, when he comes," Jiang Wei promised. "Conserve your strength, Prime Minister... everything is ready."

Kongming nodded slightly, smiled, and slowly closed his eyes.


Days passed, and as the southernmost Shu camps slowly started to be dismantled, spies brought news to the expectant Sima Yi in the Wei command tent.

"...What does this all mean, Father...?" Sima Shi wondered. "They're packing up... another ambush...?"

"...Possibly," Sima Yi mused. "And yet... something else is going on, I'm sure of it. Several days ago, activity at the front was reduced... Wei Yan has been seen arguing with other generals and officials, and the heckling seemed to be half-hearted. Now, that heckling is tinged with sadness... and some Shu soldiers have been seen wearing articles of white, concealed under their uniforms."

"...Does it mean anything, or is it another hoax to draw us out...?" Sima Zhao asked curiously. "Zhuge Liang is full of tricks... is this another one...?"

"It seems too predictable," Sima Yi replied uneasily. "All that nonsense with the dress, and the taunting... why would he now order a retreat...? They have ample grain, they have a solid base... he's held on before under much worse circumstances. No... he's dead."

All of those present – Sima Shi, Sima Zhao, Guo Huai and Fei Yao – looked at Sima Yi with silent disbelief.

"...He's dead," Sima Yi decided. "That's why they're leaving... that's why that man from their capital came here, and slid away under cover of darkness... that's why Wei Yan is so bold... he's dead! Zhuge Liang is *dead*!"

"We must be cautious," Guo Huai suggested. "He's fooled us so often before..."

"No, but not this time!" Sima Yi chuckled. "Why would he order the heckling to continue, but withdraw his rear camps...? If we attacked, they'd be unprepared, if their rear camps are in retreat! No, the heckling is a bluff... and the only reason Shu has for retreat now is the loss of their commander! Zhuge Liang is *dead*!"

"...So what do we do, then...?" Fei Yao asked.

"I want more information," Sima Yi said, "before I act. I'm almost sure, but 'almost' isn't enough: Ze Rong was sure about Sun Ce, and Cao Ren was sure about Zhou Yu. Get me more information. Watch everything... report everything!"

Sima Yi watched and waited, as messengers brought more and more confusing information from the Shu main camp. The rear camps were gone, and most of the army – including the supplies – was already in retreat to the Qinling Mountains. The front camps were still active, however, with bold shows of military drills and routine heckling of the Wei camp still being carried out.

"...What do you think...?" Guo Huai prompted.

"I... I cannot be fooled again," Sima Yi replied uneasily. "This... this seems... but yet... I do not... *aiee*. I have to get this right. Where is Wei Yan...?"

"He's still in the camp with Ma Dai and Wang Ping, taunting us, as before," Guo Huai reported.

"...And Jiang Wei...?" Sima Yi asked further.

"We don't know," Guo Huai admitted. "He hasn't been seen in days."

"And there are no reports of activity anywhere else in the northwest...?" Sima Yi enquired carefully.

"None," Fei Yao said indifferently.

"...And the locals...?" Sima Yi asked lastly. "What do they say...?"

"...*Ayah*," Guo Huai exclaimed. "You'd listen to idle peasant gossip...?"

"The *locals*," Sima Yi said emphatically. "What do they say...?"

"They... they say they've seen Shu soldiers weeping," Guo Huai admitted at last. "They say they've seen doctors running in and out of Zhuge's tent... that the soldiers talked about him collapsing, weeks ago... that officials have been seen weeping... they say he's dead. Some say they've seen his coffin, but–"

"Aha!" Sima Yi exclaimed. "He *is* dead! Guo Huai, Fei Yao, Niu Jin... ready your forces! We're going after them!"

"But what if...?" Guo Huai protested.

"He's dead!" Sima Yi insisted. "I'll go myself! Let's hurry!"

Jiang Wei led the rear of a sombre retreat into the Qinling Mountains with Yang Yi, while Hu Ji, Zhang Boqi and Zhang Bogong led the vanguard. Eilte soldiers surrounded two carriages: one was a large, horse-drawn carriage holding a coffin, while the other was a smaller chariot – covered with a yellow parasol – that was being pushed by soldiers.

"Sima Yi's pursuing," Yang Yi said soberly as a messenger retreated to gather more news. "Wei Yan's broken camp and started the retreat... Sima Yi's passed him, and is on his way here."

"...It's expected," Jiang Wei said calmly. "Get ready."

Sima Yi finally caught up with the retreating Shu army and ordered his generals into battle, screaming "**A FIEF FOR THE MAN THAT BRINGS ME THE HEAD OF ZHUGE LIANG!**"

The Wei soldiers cheered, and descended on their enemies with their morale at its peak; as far as one and all were concerned, Zhuge Liang was dead, and Shu was no longer a credible threat.

"**ROUT THEM!**" Sima Yi shouted hysterically. "**I WANT THE HEADS OF WEI YAN AND JIANG WEI!**"

The Wei cavalry and infantry hacked down the first groups of soldiers that withstood them, and for a time, it seemed as though victory was assured; but suddenly, Sima Yi's face fell, as a horrible vision appeared.

"**HERE IS JIANG WEI!**" Jiang Wei boomed as he rode forward. "...**AND HERE IS THE PRIME MINISTER!**"

Sima Yi looked on in horror as, in the distance, a familiar carriage was wheeled into view; sat in that carriage was a thin, grey-bearded man in purple robes, holding a fan.

"**AYAH!**" Sima Yi exclaimed. "**Not again!**"

"**AND HERE IS WEI YAN!**" Wei Yan announced, as he brought up a second force. "**DID YOU WANT SOMETHING, SIMA YI...?**"

Sima Yi's composure left him; he frantically ordered a retreat, as Yang Yi led forces toward his now vulnerable position. The Wei army crumbled and fled in all directions, terrified by the sight of man they thought was dead.

"We did it," Jiang Wei said, as he looked down at the Prime Minister's carriage, and smiled sadly.

************

# EPILOGUE: THE TRUTH OF MIANZHU

Twenty-nine years after the Battle of Wu Zhang Plains, a small platoon of soldiers led by Wei general Deng Ai had crossed into Shu via the treacherous Yinping mountain range. They had experienced great hardships, and had lost a third of their men.

Deng Ai was discovered by Wei's Chancellor Sima Yi some years before his death. Afflicted with a stammer, Deng Ai had overcome cruel taunts and criticism of his poor farming background, rising to become one of Wei's most important generals. He had been opposing Shu's military commander, Jiang Wei, for many years, but the two states had fought to the point that Shu – now collapsing under the weight of constant warfare and the luxury-seeking court of Liu Shan – was on the verge of falling apart altogether. Wei, meanwhile, was as strong as it had ever been, although it was under the control of Prime Minister Sima Zhao, the second son of Sima Yi. Like Cao Cao before him, Sima Yi had decided to pave the way for his own progeny to rule, and after various political coups, Sima Zhao was only steps away from usurping the throne. But first, old foes had to be removed: he had now ordered an invasion of Shu, and with Wu under the rule of a weak descendant of Sun Quan that had no intention of assisting their old ally, Shu was on its own.

To the forces of Wei, it seemed to be a defining moment: Jiang Wei had launched a ninth failed campaign against the state, and been more resoundingly repelled than ever before. The defender of Hanzhong, Wei Yan, had been declared a traitor by Yang Yi as the Shu forces retreated from Wu Zhang, and he had been executed by Ma Dai: with that, the last great champion general was no longer able to prevent the invasion, and the elaborate defences that he had put in place were also gone, so there was no other shield but those provided by nature. To the strategists of Wei, Shu was a fading dream of long-dead men, ready to commit to the history books as yet another failed state.

But now, in the main city of Mianzhu, the truth of things was hard to fathom: Deng Ai was forced to sigh with admiration and fear at the sight of what seemed to be an unexpected trap by his late master's old rival: a huge array of Shu soldiers, arranged in a highly complex variation of the Eight Trigrams Formation so ably employed by Zhuge Liang. Deng Ai had, against all expectation – including his own – achieved the impossible. He was within marching distance of Chengdu, and victory: but now, it seemed that his run of luck had come to an abrupt end.

"Father, come to your senses!" Deng Zhong pleaded. "Zhuge Liang… **what do we do about Zhuge Liang???**"

"…That… is not Zhuge Kongming," Deng Ai realised with a sudden moment of inspiration. "That… is a poor trick by his son. Ignore it… we will organise, and follow procedure. And yes, I'm sure… Zhuge Kongming would never use this arrangement against a student of Sima Zhongda. Alas… and yet sadly fortunate for us… he *is* dead, after all."

Unfortunately for the forces of Shu, Deng Ai was right: the man in the carriage was not Zhuge Liang, for he had genuinely passed away from sickness, exhaustion and despair at Wu Zhang Plains, aged just 54. He had been given a lavish state funeral, and – since his hometown of Longzhong was still controlled by Wei – he had asked to be buried on Mount Dingjun, where he could keep permanent watch of the border for his emperor.

After death, his name lived on. Certainly, the people joked about Sima Yi's retreat at Wu Zhang Plains, saying that "A dead Zhuge puts a living Zhongda to flight": Sima Yi himself was forced to comment, saying "He was barely fathomable while alive, so what hope did I have against his ghost?"

And yet, despite the funeral, some still doubted his true fate, since Zhuge Liang was adept at deceptions. Some thought that Zhuge Liang had perhaps retired, and been literally wheeled out at a critical juncture: but now it was clear to all that he really was gone.

With their confidence restored, the Wei forces broke the formation with Deng Ai's guidance and overwhelmed the Shu forces. The Shu commander Zhuge Zhan – who, despite being the eldest son of Zhuge Liang, was better known for his art than his military skills – perished along with his son Shang and their soldiers.

"So Zhuge Liang is dead then, for sure," Deng Zhong said gladly.

Deng Ai stood over the gore-covered corpses of Zhuge Zhan and Zhuge Shang, and reflected sombrely.

"...His spirit endures on Dingjun Mountain," Deng Ai said to his son, "and his genius... that is everywhere to see. How sad that I never knew him... how lucky you are, Jiang Wei, to have known such a man as Kongming."

With that, Deng Ai continued his advance into Chengdu, knowing now for certain that he could not be stopped; soon, the faltering Empire of Shu would fall, and its mission of restoring the Liu family to the seat of power in China and creating a third phase of the Han Dynasty would be finally and definitively ended.

But as they marched toward Chengdu, the soldiers of Wei felt and heard a chill wind.

Some even said they heard a dragon weep.


************

## CHARACTER PROFILES AND NAME PRONUNCIATION GUIDE

Pronunciation of Chinese names can be very awkward, since the spellings generated by the Hanyu-Pinyin system are sometimes misleading. Cao Cao, for example, is often thought to be 'Cow Cow' at first. The first attempt at translating *Three Kingdoms* by C. H. Brewitt-Taylor used a different method for pronunciation, known as the Wade-Giles system, wherein Cao Cao was spelt T'sao T'sao: the modern approach assumes awareness of 'C' never being used as a 'K' (as in, say, *continue*), but always as an 'Ts' (similar to its usage in *central*). The pronunciation guide below does not use either Wade-Giles or Pinyin, and might itself be open to interpretation: hopefully, it will serve as a rough guide for English speakers. The characters are not divided by affiliation due to the turbulent nature of the time, and the continually shifting allegiances.

In every case, the family name is first, the given name second: nobles often take on a 'style name' in addition, which is often used to differentiate the friend, focus of respect, or ally from a stranger or enemy in conversation, hence I say 'in familiar terms' after the style name.

Some of the information provided along with the name – intended as a refresher, as an explanation as to what happened to them after they disappeared from the narrative, or to elaborate where the person was only mentioned in some context – can sometimes spoil surprises for a first-time reader. **You have been warned.**

NB: 'ow' on its own or after an apostrophe in a compound should be pronounced as it is in 'cow'.

Name [Pronunciation] – *brief refresher on who the person was*.
*Any other name they were known by, typically their style name.

## PEOPLE

Zhuge Liang [Ch'oo-ker Lee-arng] – *main character of this book, adviser, strategist, and official for Liu Bei and the state of Shu Han*.
*Also known as Kongming [Kong-ming] in familiar terms.
*Also known by Taoist name, Wolong [Woh-long] (trans. Crouching Dragon).
*Also known by Taoist name, Fulong [Foo-long] (trans. Sleeping Dragon).

Huang Yueying [Hoo-arng Yoo-ay-ying] – *wife of Zhuge Liang*.
*Also known as Lady Huang.

Zhuge Jin [Ch'oo-ker J'in] – *elder brother of Zhuge Liang, adviser to Sun Quan of Wu*.
*Also known as Ziyu [Zee-yoo] in familiar terms.

Zhuge Jun [Ch'oo-ker Joon] – *younger brother of Zhuge Liang*.

Zhuge Zhan [Ch'oo-ker Ch'an] – *eldest biological son of Zhuge Liang.*

Zhuge Shang [Ch'oo-ker Sh'arng] – *son of Zhuge Zhan, grandson of Zhuge Liang.*

Zhuge Huai [Ch'oo-ker Hoo-eye] – *younger biological son of Zhuge Liang.*

Zhuge Ke [Ch'oo-ker Cur] – *elder son of Zhuge Jin. He became Wu Regent, and led several campaigns against Wei in concert with Jiang Wei. He eventually failed too many times, and sought a coup to save himself. The bid failed, and he was executed, along with his entire family. His inheritance of Zhuge Jin's estate then passed to his nephew, Zhuge Pan.*

Zhuge Qiao [Ch'oo-ker Chee-ow] – *younger son of Zhuge Jin, adopted by Zhuge Liang. His fate in this novel is dramatized, but his death is said to have occurred in the same year as it is depicted here.*
*Also known as Bosong [Bow-song] in familiar terms after being adopted.

Zhuge Pan [Ch'oo-ker Parn] – *son of Zhuge Qiao. He eventually returned to Wu, taking Zhuge Jin as his grandfather (and nulling his father's adoption by Zhuge Liang) so that he could inherit the Zhuge estate after his uncle Zhuge Ke's family line was executed for Ke's treason.*

Huang Chengyan [Hoo-arng T'erng-yarn] – *father-in-law of Zhuge Liang.*
*Known as (Old) Mister Huang in the book.

Ma Liang [Mar Lee-arng] – *close friend of Zhuge Liang, becomes adviser to Liu Bei.*
*Also known as Jichang [Jee-charng] in familiar terms.

Ma Su [Mar Soo] – *younger brother of Ma Liang, becomes vassal to Liu Bei and a student of Zhuge Liang.*
*Also known as Youchang [Yoh-charng] in familiar terms.

Pang Tong [Parng Tong] – *close friend of Zhuge Liang, becomes adviser to Liu Bei.*
*Also known as Shiyuan [S'ee-yoo-arn] in familiar terms.
*Also known by Taoist name Fengchu [Ferng-t'oo] (trans. Young/Fledgling Phoenix).

Xu Shu [Shoo S'oo] – *friend of Zhuge Liang, briefly a vassal of Liu Bei, later surrenders to and joins Wei.*
*Also known as Yuanzhi [Yoo-arn-ch'ee] in familiar terms.

Shi Tao [Shee T'ow] – *friend of Zhuge Liang, later surrenders to and joins Wei.*
*Also known as Guangyuan [K'oo-arng-yoo-arn] in familiar terms.

Cui Zhouping [Ts'oo-ee Ch'oh-ping] – *friend of Zhuge Liang.*
*His style name was Zhouping: his actual name was unknown at the time of writing.

Meng Jian [Mung Jee-arn] – *friend of Zhuge Liang, later surrenders to and joins Wei.*
*Also known as Gongwei [K'ong-way] in familiar terms.

Sima Hui [Ss-mar Hoo-ee] – *renowned scholar based primarily in Jing Province; he was the one that officially recommended Zhuge Liang and Pang Tong to Liu Bei. He was said to be uncompromisingly positive at all times.*
*Known as (Old) Mister Sima in the book to reduce confusion with the Sima vassals that serve Wei.
*Also known as Decao [Der-ts'ao] in familiar terms.
*Also known as Shuijing [Shoo-ee-jing] (trans. Water Mirror), his Taoist name.
*Also known as 'Mister Yes', after a habit of saying 'Yes' – or being otherwise agreeable in inappropriate circumstances – that he was renowned for.

Pang Degong [Parng Der-k'ong] – *known personality in Jing Province; he was said to be a philosopher or debater, and he was named respectfully by Zhuge Liang.*
*As with Cui Zhouping, it may be that his style name was Degong and his actual name was the same or something else entirely.

Liu Bei [Lee-oo Pay] – *founder of the state of Shu, distant relative of the Han emperor, Zhuge Liang's employer.*
*Also known as Xuande [Shoo-arn-der] in familiar terms.
*Also known as King of Hanzhong [Harn-ch'ong].
*Also known as the First Ruler/First Emperor in respect of his becoming the first self-appointed emperor of Shu-Han, the successor to the fallen Han Empire when the Han Emperor was deposed by Cao Pi.

Liu Shan [Lee-oo Sharn] – *eldest biological son of Liu Bei.*
*Also known as A'Dou [Ah-Dough] as a child, and as an insult in later years.
*Also known as the Second Emperor of Shu-Han, the successor to his father, First Emperor Liu Bei.

Liu Feng [Lee-oo F'ung] – *adopted son of Liu Bei.*
*Also known as Kou Feng [Koh F'ung] before adoption.

Lady Gan [K'arn] – *eldest wife of Liu Bei, mother of Liu Shan.*

Lady Mi [Mee] – *second wife of Liu Bei, sister of Mi Zhu and Mi Fang.*

Lady Wu [Woo] – *fourth wife of Liu Bei, sister of Wu Yi.*

Zhang Fei [Ch'arng Fay] – *close friend and senior general of Liu Bei. He regularly served as a vanguard general, winning major victories against Zhang He during the Hanzhong Campaign, and was later named as one of Liu Bei's Five Tiger Generals.*
*Also known as Yide [Yee-der] in familiar terms.

Guan Yu [K'oo-arn Yoo] – *close friend and senior general of Liu Bei He guarded Jing when Liu Bei travelled to Yi Province, and was later named as one of Liu Bei's Five Tiger Generals.*
*Also known as Yunchang [Yoon-charng] in familiar terms.

Guan Ping [K'oo-arn Ping] – *eldest son of Guan Yu.*

Zhao Yun [Ch'ow Yoon] – *senior general of Liu Bei. He was renowned for his service, and is credited with at least one brave rescue of members of Liu Bei's family, during the rout at Steep-slope in 208AD. He achieved victories against Cao Cao during the Hanzhong Campaign, and was later named as one of Liu Bei's Five Tiger Generals. His contribution continued until his death, at which time he was presumed to be in his sixties or seventies.*
*Also known as Zilong [Tz'ee-long] in familiar terms.

Wei Yan [Way Yarn] – *senior general of Liu Bei; he began his service in Jing, and rose to protector of Hanzhong. He was responsible for Shu's defensive barriers and was a significant contributor to Zhuge Liang's Northern Campaigns.*
*Also known as Wenchang [Wern-ch'arng] in familiar terms.

Jiang Wei [J'ee-arng Way] – *a general of Wei, stationed in Tianshui County; he defected to Shu Han during Zhuge Liang's first northern campaign, and was quickly promoted due to his perceived brilliance as a general and strategist. He inherited Zhuge Liang's military role after the latter passed away.*
*Also known as Boye [Bow-yer] in familiar terms.

Huang Zhong [Hoo-arng Ch'ong] – *general of Liu Bei; after his success against Xiahou Yuan during the Hanzhong Campaign, he was named as one of Liu Bei's Five Tiger Generals.*
*Also known as Hansheng [Harn-s'erng] in familiar terms.

Jian Yong [Jee-arn Yong] – *close friend and official of Liu Bei.*
*Also known as Xianhe [She-arn-her] in familiar terms.

Sun Qian [Soon Ch'ee-arn] – *envoy, adviser and official for Liu Bei.*
*Known as (Old) Mister Sun in the book to reduce confusion with the Sun family of Eastern Wu that serve as a rival and enemy during Sun Qian's tenure.
*Also known as Gongyou [K'ong-yoh] in familiar terms.

Mi Zhu [Me Chu] – *financier and official of Liu Bei, brother of Mi Fang.*
*Also known as Zizhong [Zee-chong] in familiar terms.

Mi Fang [Me F'arng] – *financier and official of Liu Bei, brother of Mi Zhu.*
*Also known as Zifang [Zee-f'arng] in familiar terms.

Fa Zheng [Far Ch'erng] – *adviser of Liu Zhang that decides to switch his allegiance to Liu Bei and assist the latter in overthrowing Liu Zhang and taking over Yi Province. He then becomes a senior adviser for Liu Bei, and the only man that can genuinely affect Liu Bei's decision-making.*
*Also known as Xiaozhi [Shee-ow-ch'ee] in familiar terms.

Yang Yi [Yarng Yee] – *inhabitant of Jing Province that eventually came to Chengdu to serve Liu Bei after Guan Yu consolidated his hold on Jing Province; Guan Yu was said to have personally recommended Yang Yi to Liu Bei. He served Shu Han as an official and politician, and joined Zhuge Liang on the Northern Campaigns against Wei. For some reason, Wei Yan disliked him immensely, and would chide or even threaten him with physical violence at every possible opportunity. After the fifth Northern Campaign, Yang Yi became central to a plot to have Wei Yan removed from his post and killed. Yang Yi later complained about his lack of influence in the court – stating that he had been poorly rewarded for his long service – and was imprisoned for it.*
*Also known as Weigong [Way-k'ong] in familiar terms.

Yi Ji [Yee Jee] – *prominent official of Liu Bei that contributed to the civil law of the new state of Shu Han.*
*Also known as Boji [Bow-jee] in familiar terms.

Dong He [T'ong Her] – *began as an official under Liu Zhang, became an ally of Zhuge Liang and prominent official of Shu Han.*
*Also known as Youzai [Yoh-tz'eye] in familiar terms.

Liu Ba [Lee-oo Bar] – *began as an official under Liu Zhang, became a prominent official of Shu Han. He participated in Zhuge Liang's Northern Campaigns.*
*Also known as Zichu [Zee-t'oo] in familiar terms.

Li Yan [Lee Yarn] – *began as an official under Liu Biao, fled to Yi Province, served Liu Zhang, defected to Liu Bei during the Yi campaign, and became an important official in the Shu Han regime.*
*Also known as Zhengfang [Ch'erng Farng] in familiar terms.

Liao Hua [Lee-ow Hoo-ah] – *official of Shu Han. He served under Guan Yu before the loss of Jing to Wu. He escaped Wu and was reunited with Liu Bei during the latter's campaign against Wu in 222AD. He was later made a military adviser during Zhuge Liang's Northern Campaigns, and served Shu until its demise.*
*Also known as Yuanjian [Yoo-arn J'ee-arn] in familiar terms.

Zhang Yi [Ch'arng Yee] – *official and envoy of Liu Zhang that eventually facilitates the surrender to Liu Bei. He joins Liu Bei fully, becoming a senior statesman.*
*Also known as Junsi [Joon-see] in familiar terms. Since there are three Zhang Yis serving Shu Han prominently, he is mostly referred to as Zhang Junsi in the book.

Dong Jue [T'ong Joo-er] – *official of Shu Han. He served as a general and secretary to Zhuge Liang during his southern and northern campaigns, assisted Jiang Wei in his own campaigns, and served Jin after the end of the Three Kingdoms period.*
*Also known as Gongxi [K'ong-shee] in familiar terms.

Meng Da [Mung Dah] – *general of Liu Zhang that decides to switch his allegiance to Liu Bei alongside Fa Zheng.*
*Also known as Zidu [Zee-doo] in familiar terms.

Ma Chao [Mar T'ow] – *son of Ma Teng of Xiliang and leader of a large Qiang uprising which seriously threatened the Cao Cao-led government of the Han.*
*Also known as Mengqi [Merng-chee] in familiar terms.

Ma Dai [Mar T'eye] – *cousin of Ma Chao and his only known surviving relative after Cao Cao purges his family from the country. He served Shu Han, fighting in the northern campaigns of Zhuge Liang and Jiang Wei.*

Yan Yan [Yen Yen] – *general of Liu Zhang that surrenders to and joins Liu Bei.*
*Also known as Xibo [Shee-boh] in familiar terms.

Deng Zhi [T'erng Ch'ee] – *began as a low-ranking official under Liu Zhang, became a prominent official, general and envoy of Shu Han. He was sent to Wu to repair the Shu-Wu alliance, and he later participated in Zhuge Liang's Northern Campaigns as a general.*
*Also known as Bomiao [Boh-me-ow] in familiar terms.

Wang Ping [Warng Ping] – *began as a low-ranking general under the Wei officer Du Huo, and surrendered to Liu Bei during the Hanzhong Campaign to avoid being starved during a siege. He gradually rose through the ranks of the Shu Han army, later participating in Zhuge Liang's Northern Campaigns as a general: it was his actions that prevented Ma Su's miscalculations at Jieting from destroying the entire army. He received many accolades through the years, and continued to serve Shu Han after Zhuge Liang's death.*
*Also known as Zijun [Zee-joon] in familiar terms.
*Might have been known during his life as He Ping [Her Ping] in actuality, and renamed Wang Ping posthumously.

Jiang Wan [J'ee-arng Warn] – *ally of Zhuge Liang and prominent official of Shu Han. He was named by Zhuge Liang as a desired successor to his civil role.*
*Also known as Gongyan [K'ong-yarn] in familiar terms.

Fei Yi [Fay Yee] – *ally of Zhuge Liang and prominent official of Shu Han. He acted as an envoy to Wu for some time after the alliance was renewed, and was named by Zhuge Liang as a desired successor to his civil role, after Jiang Wan.*
*Also known as Wenwei [Wern-way] in familiar terms.

Dong Yun [T'ong Yoon] – *began as an official under Liu Zhang, ally of Zhuge Liang and prominent official of Shu Han.*
*Also known as Xiuzhao [She-oo-ch'ow] in familiar terms.

Hu Ji [Hoo Jee] – *general of Shu Han. He served during Zhuge Liang's Northern Campaigns, and later assisted Jiang Wei in his campaigns. He was said to be an agile debater despite his military capacity, and often did so with Zhuge Liang.*
*Also known as Weidu [Way-doo] in familiar terms.

Gao Xiang [K'ah-oh Shee-arng] – *general of Shu Han. His first known foray was as Chen Shi's ally during the Hanzhong Campaign, where the two were resoundingly defeated by Xu Huang. He then served during Zhuge Liang's Northern Campaigns, and was unlucky enough to be Ma Su's subordinate at Jieting during the first campaign. He later gained greater authority, and was a key general during a battlefield defeat of Sima Yi on the fourth campaign, along with Wei Yan and Wu Ban.*

Wang Fu [Warng Foo] – *began as an official under Liu Zhang, became an official of Shu Han; he was sent to serve as guardian of Mianzhu Pass. When Guan Yu lost Jing, Wang Fu was recruited as part of Liu Bei's invasion force to reclaim the province from Wu. He served as an adviser, but was killed as he led a covering force during the retreat to the Yi border.*
*Also known as Guoshan [K'oo-oh-s'arn] in familiar terms.

Ma Zhong [Mar Ch'ong] – *general of Shu Han that served during Zhuge Liang's southern campaign against Nanzhong, and later in his Northern Campaigns.*
*Also known as Dexin [Der-shin] in familiar terms.

Chen Shi [Ch'ern Shee] – *general of Liu Bei, and later Liu Bei's state of Shu Han; he served with some initial success during Zhuge Liang's Northern Campaigns. There is a belief that he was related to Chen Shou [Ch'ern S'oh], author of the Records of the Three Kingdoms commissioned by the state of Jin.*

Zong Yu [Tz'ong Yoo] – *official of Shu Han. He was especially trusted by Zhuge Liang, and served as his secretary when he became Prime Minister. After Zhuge Liang's death, Zong Yu was the man trusted with going to Wu to reassure Sun Quan that the alliance would hold. He became a general in his later years, aiding the defence of Shu and leading troops in the northern campaigns carried out by Jiang Wei. He outlived the Shu Han state he served, but only just; while no birth date is known for Zong Yu, comments that he made imply that he may have been as old as 80 by the time of his death, having commanded soldiers personally until the end.*
*Also known as Deyan [Der-yarn] in familiar terms.

Fei Shi [Fay S'ee] – *began as an official under Liu Zhang, became an official of Shu Han. He opposed Liu Bei becoming an emperor and was jailed for it: he was later released, and went on to serve as a trusted official in the Shu Han court. He was trusted by Zhuge Liang.*
*Also known as Gongju [K'ong-joo] in familiar terms.

Yang Hong [Yarng Hong] – *began as an official under Liu Zhang, served as a prominent official of Liu Bei and the later state of Shu Han. When the Hanzhong Campaign became so costly that human resource reached a critical low, he advised Chancellor Zhuge Liang to draft men from essential services, such as farming, and have women and older children take their place. This advice provided Liu Bei with the much-needed reinforcements he needed to go on and win the battle against the forces of Wei.*
*Also known as Jixiu [Jee-shee-oo] in familiar terms.

Xi Zheng [Shee Ch'erng] – *official of Shu Han. He was said to be trusted by Zhuge Liang with civil affairs when the latter was on campaigns.*
*Also known as Lingxian [Ling-shee-arn] in familiar terms.

Chen Dao [Ch'en T'ow] – *senior general and bodyguard of Liu Bei.*
*Also known as Shuzhi [S'oo-ch'ee] in familiar terms.

Guo Youzhi [K'oo-oh Yoh-ch'ee] – *official serving Shu Han. He was named by Zhuge Liang as one of the most trustworthy and capable officials in the state.*
*Also known as Yanchang [Yarn-ch'arng] in familiar terms.

Li Hui [Lee Hoo-ee] – *official serving Shu Han. He was courted for a role by Liu Zhang's administration, but refused; he later joined Liu Bei willingly. He was a strong negotiator and debater.*
*Also known as De'ang [Der Arng] in familiar terms.

Xiang Lang [Shee-arng Larng] - *began as an official under Liu Biao, became an official of Liu Bei. He remained in Jing when Liu Bei travelled to Yi, and served as an adviser and administrator to Guan Yu. After the fall of Jing, Xiang Lang relocated to Yi. He is the uncle of Xiang Chong.*
*Also known as Juda [Joo-dah] in familiar terms.

Xiang Chong [Shee-arng T'ong] – *the nephew of Jing administrator Xiang Lang, he served Liu Bei valiantly during his flight from the Battle of Xiaoting, and was given rank as a reward.*

Huo Jun [Hoo-oh Joon] – *early ally of Liu Bei in Jing Province, later assigned to protect the border with Hanzhong after Liu Bei's successful invasion of Yi Province. He died whilst in that role, and records show that Liu Bei was very upset at losing him.*
*Also known as Zhongmiao [Ch'ong-mee-ow] in familiar terms.

Chen Zhen [T'ern Ch'ern] – *a former vassal of Yuan Shao that Liu Bei trusted greatly; he was invited to Jing when Liu Bei settled there after Yuan Shao's defeat, and he remained in Liu Bei's service thereafter, later serving in the Shu Han court.*
*Also known as Xiaoqi [Shee-ow-chee] in familiar terms.

Huang Quan [K'oo-oh Choo-arn] – *began as an official under Liu Zhang, became an official of Shu Han. He initially opposed Liu Bei's arrival in Yi Province vehemently, but by the time of the Hanzhong Campaign he was a trusted adviser.*
*Also known as Gongheng [K'ong-herng] in familiar terms.

Zhang Yi [Ch'arng Yee] – *general of Shu Han. He served in most of the large campaigns after the death of Liu Bei, gaining particular merit in the southern campaign to pacify the Nanzhong people.*
*Also known as Boqi [Bow-chee] in familiar terms. Since there are three Zhang Yis serving Shu Han prominently, he is mostly referred to as Zhang Boqi in the book.

Wu Yi [Woo Yee] – *began as a senior general under Liu Zhang that was considered Zhang's most trustworthy vassal; he surrendered to Liu Bei during the siege of Mianzhu, and later served the state of Shu Han. He was treated as an important figure by Liu Bei, who married his sister once the province was stabilised. He actively participated during Cao Zhen's invasion of Hanzhong, being notably paired with Wei Yan on a business trip to the north.*
*Also known as Ziyuan [Zee-yoo-arn] in familiar terms.

Wu Ban [Woo Barn] – *began as a general under Liu Zhang, surrendered to Liu Bei, and served the state of Shu Han. He participated in the Battle of Xiaoting and Zhuge Liang's Northern Campaigns. He was related to Wu Yi.*
*Also known as Yuanxiong [Yoo-arn-shee-ong] in familiar terms.

Wu Lan [Woo Larn] – *began as a general under Liu Zhang, surrendered to Liu Bei. He participated in the Hanzhong Campaigns, but he was killed by the Di tribes after being routed by Wei forces.*

Li Fu [Lee Foo] – *an official in the Shu Han court. He was sent to Wu Zhang Plains to receive guidance on the future of Shu from Zhuge Liang.*
*Also known as Sunde [Soon-der] in familiar terms.

Fu Rong [Foo Wrong] – *general serving Liu Bei. He participated in the Battle of Xiaoting, and died protecting Liu Bei's retreat following the rout.*

Zhang Zhu [Ch'arng Ch'oo] – *general serving Liu Bei. He participated in the Hanzhong Campaign, assisting Zhao Yun and Huang Zhong.*

Feng Xi [Ferng Shee] – *general serving Liu Bei. He participated in the Battle of Xiaoting, and died during the fire attack launched by Lu Xun's army.*
*Also known as Xiyuan [Shee-yoo-arn] in familiar terms.

Zhang Yi [Ch'arng Yee] – *general of Liu Zhang that went on to serve Liu Bei. He served in most of the large campaigns in some capacity.*
*Also known as Bogong [Bow-k'ong] in familiar terms. Since there are three Zhang Yis serving Shu Han prominently, he is mostly referred to as Zhang Bogong in the book.

Lü Kai [L' K'eye] – *official serving Shu Han. He was assigned to Nanzhong.*
*Also known as Jiping [Jee-ping] in familiar terms.

Liao Li [Lee-ow Lee] – *first began serving Liu Bei in Jing, and later became an official of Shu Han. He was eventually deemed incompetent and exiled, but he remained loyal to Shu Han nonetheless.*
*Also known as Gongyuan [K'ong-yoo-arn] in familiar terms.

Xu Jing [Shoo Jing] – *began as an official under Liu Zhang, became a politician and adviser of Shu Han. He was said to be of noble background, so many officials – including Zhuge Liang – were forced to be especially courteous to him, despite his lack of actual power or influence.*
*Also known as Wenxiu [Wern-see-oo] in familiar terms.

Li Feng [Lee Ferng] – *the eldest son of Li Yan. He inherited his father's role after Zhuge Liang's fourth Northern Campaign.*

Qin Mi [Chin Mee] – *began as an official under Liu Zhang, became an official of Shu Han. He was well known for disliking a casual attitude to etiquette. He opposed Liu Bei's retaliatory march on Eastern Wu after the loss of Jing, and was imprisoned for it.*
*Also known as Zichi [Zee-t'ee] in familiar terms.

Peng Yang [Pung Yarng] – *began as an official under Liu Zhang, became an official of Shu Han. He was not trusted by Zhuge Liang, although Liu Bei does not seem to share his view. He is eventually accused of treason by Zhuge with the aid of testimony from Ma Chao, and executed.*
*Also known as Yongnian [Yong-nee-arn] in familiar terms.

Zhao Lei [Ch'ow Lay] – *a general that served Liu Bei, but was specifically assigned to Guan Yu.*

Fei Guan [Fay K'oo-arn] – *general of Liu Zhang that was sent – along with Li Yan – to replace defecting generals Wu Yi and Lei Tong during the siege of Mianzhu; he, along with his commander Li Yan, defected to Liu Bei almost immediately.*

Lei Tong [Lay Tong] – *general of Liu Zhang that defected to Liu Bei. He was killed by Cao Hong's forces during the Hanzhong Campaign.*

Deng Xian [T'erng Shee-arn] – *general of Liu Zhang that defected to Liu Bei.*

Zheng Ang [Ch'erng Arng] – *official of Shu Han based in Nanzhong. He was killed by rebels led by Yong Kai, prior to the Nanzhong Campaign.*

Qi Xing [Chee Shing] – *official of Shu Han. He was sent to Nanzhong by Zhuge Liang in an attempt to understand the severity of the situation in the region: he was killed by rebels led by Yong Kai, prior to the Nanzhong Campaign.*

Shi Ren [Shee Rern] – *a general and official that served Liu Bei, and was assigned to assist Guan Yu in governing southern Jing. When he was castigated for not supplying the front line during the siege at Fan City, he defected to Wu.*

Fan Qiang [Farn Ch'ee-arng] – *officer of Shu Han. He served under Zhang Fei, and later defected to Wu.*

Zhang Da [Ch'arng T'ar] – *officer of Shu Han. He served under Zhang Fei, and later defected to Wu.*

Shen Yi [S'ern Yee] – *official serving Han, and later Wei. He was the governor of Fangling, and surrendered to Meng Da after the latter besieged the region. Meng Da later changed his allegiance to Wei to escape punishment for abandoning the prominent Liu Bei general Guan Yu, and induced Shen Yi to defect back to Wei with him. When Meng Da decided to defect to the Liu Bei-founded state of Shu, he tried to coerce Shen Yi to defect again: Shen Yi secretly decided that enough was enough, and colluded with Sima Yi to destroy Meng Da.*

Shen Dan [S'ern T'arn] – *official serving Han, and later Wei. He was the governor of Shangyong, and surrendered to Liu Feng after the latter besieged the region. Liu Feng's ally Meng Da – who had taken Fangling from Shen Yi at the same time – later changed his allegiance to Wei after Guan Yu's capture to escape blame: he was joined by Shen Yi, and Fangling returned to Wei. Meng Da then approached Liu Feng with the idea of betraying his adopted father Liu Bei, but Feng rejected the offer; at this point, Meng Da induced Shen Dan to defect back to Wei and eject Liu Feng from Shangyong. When Meng Da decided to defect to the Liu Bei-founded state of Shu, he tried to coerce Shen Dan to shift allegiances again: like Shen Yi, Shen Dan decided to remain loyal to Wei, and worked toward Meng Da's defeat and death instead.*

Huang Hao [Hoo-arng Ha-oh] – *eunuch serving the imperial court of Shu Han. He was favoured by the Second Emperor, Liu Shan, and came to dominate the affairs of the court, as eunuchs had done in the Han court prior to the Yellow Turban Rebellion. He was regularly opposed by officials of the court, but eventually, he had the power to obstruct them. He made an enemy of Jiang Wei, and tried to have him removed as the head of the army.*

Sun Quan [Soon Choo'arn] – *ruler of the independent state of Wu.*
*Also known as Zhongmou [Ch'ong-moh] in familiar terms.
*Also known as King of Wu after he tendered his allegiance to the new Wei Emperor, Cao Pi: he would retain the title after breaking ties with Wei later on.
*Also known as the First Ruler/First Emperor in respect of his becoming the first self-appointed emperor of Wu, which he did in 229AD.

Sun Jian [Soon J'ee-arn] – *father of Sun Quan, killed in Jing whilst serving as a vassal of the feudal lord Yuan Shu. He claimed to be a descendant of Sun Tzu.*
*Also known as Wentai [Wern-tie] in familiar terms.

Sun Ce [Soon Ser] – *elder brother of Sun Quan, founded the state of Wu before being assassinated, and succeeded by his brother.*
*Also known as Bofu [Bow-foo] in familiar terms.

Lady Sun [Soon] – *sister of Sun Quan that is widely known for her tomboyish ways. She was married to Liu Bei to strengthen relations between the two states, but later returned to Jiangdong, after which time her fate is unknown.*
*Also known as Sun Shangxiang [Soon S'arng-she-arng] in some literature.

Zhou Yu [Ch'oh Yoo] – *close friend and brother-in-law of Sun Ce, Chief Commander of the Wu army under Sun Quan, renowned for defeating Cao Cao at Red Cliffs.*
*Also known as Gongjin [K'ong-jin] in familiar terms.

Lu Su [Loo Soo] – *close friend and financier of Zhou Yu and Sun Quan, later Chief Commander of the Wu army when Zhou Yu dies; champion of a tripartite state plan.*
*Also known as Zijing [Zee-jing] in familiar terms.

Lü Meng [L'Mung] – *general of Sun Quan, later Chief Commander of the Wu army when Lu Su dies.*
*Also known as Ziming [Zee-ming] in familiar terms.
*Also known as A'Meng [Ah-mung] as mockery in his earlier career, for his assumed ignorance of intellectual pursuits.

Lu Xun [Loo Shoon] – *general and official of Sun Quan, later Chief Commander of the Wu army when Lü Meng dies.*
*Also known as Boyan [Bow-yan] in familiar terms.

Zhang Zhao [Ch'arng Ch'ow] – *long-time senior adviser of Sun family, brother of Zhang Hong.*
*Also known as Zibu [Zee-boo] in familiar terms.

Zhang Hong [Ch'arng Ch'ow] – *long-time senior adviser of Sun family, brother of Zhang Zhao, served as an envoy to the Han court before the events at Red Cliffs.*
*Also known as Zigang [Zee-garng] in familiar terms.

Bu Zhi [Boo Ch'ee] – *adviser, official and general of Sun Quan.*
*Also known as Zishan [Zee-sharn] in familiar terms.

Lü Fan [L'Farn] – *adviser and official of Sun Quan.*
*Also known as Ziheng [Zee-herng] in familiar terms.

Huang Gai [H'warng K'eye] – *veteran general that originally served Sun Jian. He took part in the Red Cliffs campaign, playing a key role in the main battle.*
*Also known as Gongfu [K'ong-foo] in familiar terms.

Cheng Pu [Cherng Poo] – *veteran general that originally served Sun Jian. He took part in the Red Cliffs campaign and the subsequent siege of Jiangling, and was assigned the role of administrator of Jiangxia, southeast Jing.*
*Also known as Demou [Der-moh] in familiar terms.

Pan Zhang [Parn Ch'arng] – *general of Sun Quan that captured Guan Yu at Mei City, and assisted Lu Xun during the Battle of Xiaoting.*
*Also known as Wengui [Wern-k'oo-ee] in familiar terms.

Gan Ning [Garn Ning] – *naval officer in the Wu army. He started his career as a cutthroat, but decided in his later years to become a respected man. He initially joined Jing's Huang Zu, where he killed Ling Tong's father during an invasion of Xiakou by the Wu army. He was not respected, however, and later, he defected to Wu, aiding first in the defeat of Huang Zu and then gaining greater esteem as a notorious general.*
*Also known as Xingba [Shing-bar] in familiar terms.

Ling Tong [Ling Tong] – *general in the Wu army. He followed in the footsteps of his father, who was killed in action during an attack on Jing Province. The man that killed him – Gan Ning – then became a colleague, although it would take many years for Ling Tong to accept this.*
*Also known as Gongji [K'ong-jee] in familiar terms.

Zhou Tai [Ch'oh Tie] – *a former pirate, then general to Sun Ce, and then bodyguard to Sun Quan. He was credited with saving Sun Quan from mortal danger many times, and had a multitude of scars to prove it.*
*Also known as Youping [Yoh-ping] in familiar terms.

Taishi Ci [T'eye-sher Ser] – *a famous early general who served Sun Ce. He began his career in the service of other administrators and lords, but one of his most famous military endeavours of that time was in the service of Kong Rong, when he broke through enemy lines during the Yellow Turban Rebellion, and brought back and brought back a 3,000-strong army belonging to Liu Bei, which he then commanded personally to rescue the besieged city. After his submission to Sun Ce, he went on to play a key role in acquiring the vast territories that Sun Quan would inherit. He died in 206, although fiction likes to extend his years and prolong his service, due to his unwavering popularity.*

Zhu Ran [Ch'oo Rarn] – *general of Sun Quan that captured Guan Yu at Mai City, and successfully held out against Liu Bei's forces during the Battle of Xiaoting: he also participated in the famous counterattack that crippled the Shu army.*
*Also known as Yifeng [Yee-ferng] in familiar terms.

Han Dang [Harn T'arng] – *a general that served Eastern Wu.*

Sun Ben [Soon Bern] – *a general that served Eastern Wu; he was also a relative of Sun Quan.*

Sun Huan [Soon Hoo-arn] – *a relative of Sun Quan and a general of Eastern Wu. He is noted for having held the city of Yidao against Liu Bei's siege forces during the Battle of Xiaoting.*

Lady Qiao [Chee-ow] – *wife of Zhou Yu, sister-in-law of Sun Ce.*
*Known sometimes as Xiao Qiao (Younger Qiao) in fiction. Her sister was known then as Da Qiao (Older Qiao). Collectively, they were known as the Two Qiaos, and were renowned for their incredible beauty.

Su Fei [Soo Fay] – *a former pirate and comrade of Gan Ning that initially served Huang Zu, but later defected to Sun Quan.*

Pan Jun [Parn Joon] – *official in Jing that served Liu Bei, but defected to Wu.*
*Also known as Chengming [Ch'erng-ming] in familiar terms.

Cao Cao [T'sao T'sao] – *Prime Minister of the Han, ruler of the future state of Wei, and father of the usurper of the Han, Cao Pi.*
*Also known as Mengde [Mung-der] in familiar terms.
*Also known as the Duke of Wei after receiving his own duchy.
*Also known as the King of Wei after a promotion by the Han Emperor.
* Known posthumously as First Emperor (of Cao Wei).
*Also known as A'Man [Ah-Marn] as a child and for varying reasons in adulthood, from affectionate to derisive.

Cao Pi [T'sao Pee] – *eldest surviving son of Cao Cao that goes on to usurp the Han Emperor.*
*Also known as Zihuan [Zee-hoo-arn] in familiar terms.
*Also known as the King of Wei before his usurpation of the Han.
*Known as Emperor after he deposed the Han Emperor: he made Cao Cao the First Emperor posthumously, as a sign that he had paved the way for it (Cao Cao had allowed Cao Pi to be the one to actually usurp whilst protesting his own loyalty to the imperial house, so that future historians would not blame him for the act he had laid the groundwork for: Cao Pi was returning the favour).

Cao Rui [T'sao Roo-ee] – *eldest son of Cao Pi and Third Emperor of Cao Wei.*
*Also known as Emperor in respect of his becoming the second living emperor of Wei after the death of Cao Pi.

Cao Ren [T'sao Rern] – *cousin of Cao Cao that was given several high-profile cities to defend during his career. He was forced to endure long sieges at Jiangling and Fan; despite holding firm, Cao Cao ordered him to retreat from Jiangling, but he successfully held Fan, even after a burst river destroyed the reinforcements he had been sent and flooded the city. After the Battle of Xiaoting, Cao Ren was forced to face Wu again, and he held out once more, although there was a plague epidemic in the Wei army. He died shortly afterward.*
*Also known as Zixiao [Zee-shee-ow] in familiar terms.

Cao Zhen [T'sao Ch'ern] – *distant relative of Cao Cao but highly favoured. Suffered with clinical obesity that he was ridiculed for, but he was a capable strategist and commander that performed admirably during the Hanzhong Campaign and successfully repelled Zhuge Liang's northern campaigns until his death, wherein he was succeeded by Sima Yi. His son Cao Shuang [T'sao Shoo-arng] would later become a regent, and try and remove his co-regent and political rival Sima Yi from the court; the consequence of the plot was that the embittered Sima Yi decided to seize control within the Cao regime, as Cao Cao had done to the Han, paving the way for his grandson to finally usurp the Wei throne and become the First Emperor of Jin.*
*Also known as Zidan [Zee-darn] in familiar terms.

Cao Hong [T'sao Hong] – *cousin of Cao Cao that was well treated due to his having saved Cao Cao during the campaign against Dong Zhuo. He was self-indulgent and a reckless gambler, but won a victory during the Hanzhong Campaign with the help of his advisers. Cao Pi did not like him and had him stripped of all of his influence when he came to power, but Cao Pi's son, Cao Rui, restored him to good standing once he was emperor, allowing him to live out his last days comfortably.*
*Also known as Zilian [Zee-lee-arn] in familiar terms.

Cao Xiu [T'sao She-oo] – *distant relative of Cao Cao that received great acclaim for defeating Zhang Fei and Ma Chao during the Hanzhong Campaign. He was later assigned to fight Wu in the east, where his falling for a false surrender ruse cost him his army and gave Wu their greatest morale-boosting victory since Red Cliffs. Cao Xiu became sick and died shortly afterward.*
*Also known as Wenlie [Wern-lee-er] in familiar terms.

Cao Zhi [T'sao Ch'ee] – *younger brother of Cao Pi that was favoured by his father Cao Cao, and briefly considered as an alternative heir. He was practically exiled after Cao Pi took power, while another brother, Cao Zhang [T'sao Ch'arng] was eventually poisoned at a banquet. After Cao Pi died, he tried to court favour with his nephew Cao Rui but was rebuked. He died six years after his brother.*

Sima Yi [Ss-ma Yee] – *long-term adviser and official of the Cao family, becomes the Chief Commander of the army after the death of Cao Zhen.*
*Also known as Zhongda [Ch'ong-dah] in familiar terms.

Sima Shi [Ss-ma She] – *eldest son of Sima Yi.*
*Also known as Ziyuan [Zee-yoo-arn] in familiar terms.

Sima Zhao [Ss-ma Ch-ow] – *younger son of Sima Yi, whose son would eventually overthrow the Wei Emperor and found the Jin Empire.*
*Also known as Zishang [Zee-sharng] in familiar terms.

Zhang He [Ch'arng Her] – *senior general to Yuan Shao that defected to Cao Cao and became an important general.*
*Also known as Junyi [Joon-yee] in familiar terms.

Guo Huai [K'oo-oh Hoo-eye] – *general of the Cao regime, who was present at many significant battles, such as those fought during the Hanzhong Campaign. He fought against Zhuge Liang's armies during the latter's northern campaigns several times as a subordinate of Zhang He or Sima Yi, or as a leader in his own right.*
*Also known as Boji [Boh-jee] in familiar terms.

Xiahou Yuan [She-ah-hoh Yoo-arn] – *family member and senior commander to Cao Cao.*
*Also known as Miaocai [Me-ow-ts'eye] in familiar terms.

Xiahou Dun [She-ah-hoh T'oon] – *family member and senior general to Cao Cao.*
*Also known as Yuanrang [Yoo-arn-rarng] in familiar terms.
*Also known as 'Blind Xiahou' after losing his eye to a sniper's arrow during a siege against the forces of Lü Bu.

Xu Huang [Shoo Hoo-arng] – *senior general to Cao Cao that aided Cao Ren during the siege of Jiangling, and dealt a resounding defeat to Guan Yu during the 219AD siege of Fan City.*
*Also known as Gongming [K'ong-ming] in familiar terms.

Yue Jin [Yoo-er J'in] – *senior general to Cao Cao that inflicted a series of defeats on Liu Bei's forces during the siege of Jiangling, and assisted Zhang Liao in his famous rout of Wu during the Battle of Xiaoyao Ford.*
*Also known as Wenqian [Wern-chee-arn] in familiar terms.

Yu Jin [Yoo J'in] – *senior general to Cao Cao that was famous for his shrewdness and bravery until an infamous surrender to Guan Yu during the latter's doomed siege of Fan City in 219AD. He was imprisoned in Wu after Guan Yu's defeat, and later returned to Wei, where Emperor Cao Pi humiliated him for his conduct and he died a miserable death, labelled as a coward.*
*Also known as Wenze [Wern-zer] in familiar terms.

Pang De [Parng Der] – *Qiang-origin general who was an ally and general of Ma Chao; after several failed exploits by Ma Chao, Pang De left his service and remained in Hanzhong while Ma Chao and Ma Dai fled to Wudu. He defected to Cao Cao after the latter's defeat of Zhang Lu, and went on to work with Cao Ren and Yu Jin. He is most famous for his defeats of Guan Yu's forces at the siege of Fan City, and his subsequent brave death when his army was annihilated by flood waters: when finally captured, he refused to submit (while Yu Jin surrendered), and he was executed.*
*Also known as Lingming [Ling-ming] in familiar terms.

Wen Ping [Wern Ping] – *general of Cao Cao that, amongst other achievements, aided Yue Jin and defeated Guan Yu during the latter's siege of Xiangyang.*
*Also known as Zhongye [Ch'ong-yer] in familiar terms.

Li Tong [Lee Tong] – *general of Cao Cao that broke Guan Yu's defensive line and aided Cao Ren during the siege of Jiangling.*
*Also known as Wenda [Wern-dah] in familiar terms.

Hao Zhao [Ha-oh Ch'ow] – *Wei general assigned to guard Chen Cang City during the second of Zhuge Liang's northern campaigns, where Chen Cang was the only target. He successfully repelled Zhuge's army with only 1,000 troops, earning him a very good reputation. However, he fell sick and died before he could ever enjoy his newfound status as a hero of the state.*
*Also known as Bodao [Boh-t'ow] in familiar terms.

Wang Shuang [Warng Shoo-arng] – *Wei general and favourite of Second Emperor Cao Rui that was assigned to help Zhang He during Zhuge Liang's second northern campaign. He pursued Zhuge after the failed siege of Chen Cang City and was killed in an ambush near the Qinling Mountains.*
*Also known as Ziquan [Zee-choo-arn] in familiar terms.

Niu Jin [Nee-oo J'in] – *Wei general that served under Cao Ren during the siege of Jiangling, famously needing rescue by Cao Ren when his 300-man assault team were surrounded by Zhou Yu's forces. He later fought very successfully when Zhuge Liang launched his fourth northern campaign, winning a notable victory over Shu general Ma Dai. He was in later years forced to commit suicide by the Sima brothers for being a threat.*

Zhao Yong [Ch'ah-oh Yong] – *a general of Wei and subordinate of Xiahou Yuan that served as part of the defence forces during Liu Bei's Hanzhong Campaign. He was killed during the Battle of Mount Dingjun, along with his commander.*

Fei Yao [Fay Yah-oh] – *a general of Wei that served as part of the defence forces during Zhuge Liang's Northern Campaigns.*

Dai Ling [T'eye Ling] – *a general of Wei that served as part of the defence forces during Zhuge Liang's Northern Campaigns.*

Jia Ji [Jee-ah Jee] – *a general of Wei that served as part of the defence forces during Zhuge Liang's Northern Campaigns.*

Wei Ping [Way Ping] – *a general of Wei that served as part of the defence forces during Zhuge Liang's Northern Campaigns.*

Zhang Liao [Ch'arng Lee-ow] – *senior general to Lü Bu that defected to Cao Cao after his master's defeat, and became an important general, especially against Wu whilst holding Hefei. He dealt a defeat to Sun Quan during the Battle of Xiaoyao Ford that earned him a fearsome and legendary reputation in Wu.*
*Also known as Wenyuan [Wern-yoo-arn] in familiar terms.

Li Dian [Lee Dee-arn] – *general of Cao Cao that, amongst other things, aided Zhang Liao and Yue Jin during the Battle of Xiaoyao Ford.*
*Also known as Mancheng [Marn-ch'erng] in familiar terms.

Xu Chu [Shoo Ch'oo] – *Cao Cao's main bodyguard after the death of Dian Wei.*
*Also known as Zhongkang [Ch'ong-karng] in familiar terms.

Guo Jia [K'oo-oh J'ee-ah] – *adviser and official to Cao Cao. He was considered to be a genius and a very dangerous strategist by all of his enemies, and an invaluable asset by Cao Cao. He died before the Battle of Red Cliffs, and Cao often regretted that, saying that Guo Jia could have prevented the disaster.*
*Also known as Fengxiao [Fung-shee-ow] in familiar terms.

Jia Xu [J'ee-ah Shoo] – *adviser and official of the Cao regime. He made several suggestions before the Battle of Red Cliffs that Cao Cao later regretted ignoring. Cao Cao then heeded his advice when facing Ma Chao and Han Sui at Tong Pass, and the Qiang rebels were decisively beaten as a result. He later advocated Cao Cao's eldest son Cao Pi during the succession issue, and became very influential when Cao Pi became king and later the first living emperor of Wei.*
*Also known as Wenhe [Wern-her] in familiar terms.

Cheng Yu [Ch'erng Yoo] – *adviser and official of the Cao regime.*
*Also known as Zhongde [Ch'ong-der] in familiar terms.

Yang Xiu [Yarng Shee-oo] – *secretary and adviser to Cao Cao that took sides with one of future crown prince Cao Pi's younger brothers, Cao Zhi, during the succession debate. He was executed by Cao Cao.*
*Also known as Dezu [Der-zoo] in familiar terms.

Xun Yu [Shun Yoo] – *adviser to Cao Cao, uncle of Xun You. He contested Cao Cao's plan to become a duke and was publically rebuked for it by Cao Cao. He became suddenly and seriously ill while touring the east, and died later.*
*Also known as Wenruo [Wern-roo-oh] in familiar terms.

Xun You [Shun Y'oh] – *adviser to Cao Cao, nephew of Xun Yu. He contested Cao Cao's plan to become a king, and after a strong public rebuke by his lord, he committed suicide.*
*Also known as Gongda [K'ong-dah] in familiar terms.

Liu Fu [Lee-oo Foo] – *adviser and official of the Cao regime. He was a major conceptualist with regard to the Hefei fortress that so successfully repelled Wu. He was made the administrator of Lujiang after the incumbent was killed by an agent of Eastern Wu. He was a very benevolent force, and kept many rogue elements pacified. When he died, those rogue elements rebelled against Cao Cao, but refused to ally with Wu due to the history of the region. When the rebellion failed, the survivors joined Liu Bei, giving him his first sizable army.*
*Also known as Yuanying [Yoo-arn-ying] in familiar terms.

Jiang Gan [J'ee-arng K'arn] – *official of the Cao regime, and former acquaintance of Wu's Chief Commander, Zhou Yu. He was asked to meet with Zhou Yu and reason with him, but was politely rebuffed after stating his case.*
*Also known as Ziyi [Zee-yee] in familiar terms.

Liu Ye [Lee-oo Yer] – *adviser and official of the Cao regime.*
*Also known as Ziyang [Zee-yarng] in familiar terms.

Dong Zhao [T'ong Ch'ow] – *adviser and official of the Cao regime.*
*Also known as Gongren [K'ong-rern] in familiar terms.

Gao Rou [K'ow Roh] – *adviser and official of the Cao regime.*
*Also known as Wenhui [Wern-hoo-ee] in familiar terms.

Jiang Ji [Jee-arng Jee] – *adviser and official of the Cao regime.*
*Also known as Zitong [Zee-tong] in familiar terms.

Wang Lang [Warng Larng] – *adviser, politician and official of the Han that moved his allegiance to Cao Cao. He was later pivotal in the abdication of the Han Emperor, and was noted for suggesting to the second (living) Wei Emperor, Cao Rui, that he should build a harem that eventually included some of his vassal's wives. In fiction, he is often given a villain's end: during the Northern Campaigns, he confronts Zhuge Liang on the battlefield, and is so heavily and publicly castigated for his treacherous conduct that he falls from his horse and dies.*
*Also known as Jingxing [Jing-shing] in familiar terms.

Man Chong [Marn Chong] – *adviser and official of the Cao regime that was first assigned to Jing Province, and later Hefei in the east, where he successfully repelled Wu on several occasions.*
*Also known as Boning [Boh-ning] in familiar terms.

Jia Kui [J'ee-ah Koo-ee] – *adviser and official of the Cao regime. He was mainly pitted against Eastern Wu, and was famous for saving the deceived and routed Cao Xiu after the battle of Stone Town in 228AD. He was rewarded for the act, but did not live very long thereafter.*
*Also known as Liangdao [Lee-arng-t'ow] in familiar terms.

Xiahou Rong [Shee-ah-hoh Wrong] – *a son of Xiahou Yuan that perished with him during the Hanzhong Campaign.*

Xiahou Mao [She-ah-hoh M'ow] – *son of Xiahou Dun, close friend of Cao Pi and administrator of Chang'an until 228AD, when Cao Rui, Emperor of Wei, realised his poor character and removed him to the capital, where he was given the title of Imperial Secretariat.*
*Also known as Zilin [Zee-lin] in familiar terms.

Zang Ba [Zarng Bar] – *general that served Tao Qian, and then Lü Bu; he eventually settled into the service of Cao Cao. He was assigned to fight Wu in the east on many occasions.*
*Also known as Xuanggao [Shoo-arng-k'ow] in familiar terms.

Chen Jiao [T'ern J'ee-ow] – *officer of Cao Cao. He assisted Cao Ren during the Battle of Jiangling.*

Deng Ai [T'erng Eye] – *senior general of the Wei Empire. By the time he is a prominent general, Sima Shi controls the court, and usurpation of the throne by the Sima family is only a few years away. Deng Ai hailed from a background similar to Zhuge Liang's, and he is considered by some to have been equally gifted as a strategist: he was known to be afflicted with a stammer, which provoked ridicule from some of his peers, despite his obvious genius. He locked horns with Jiang Wei several times, and was Jiang's principal nemesis. It was his forces that marched over the Yinping Mountains and breached Yi Province; it was his forces that fought Zhuge Zhan at Mianzhu, a battle that helped to decide how the Shu Han court would react to Wei's invasion. When Zhong Hui, Deng's rival, learned that he had succeeded, he was jealous, while Deng's enemy Jiang Wei was livid and heartbroken at the collapse of his state. Those two men would form a surprising alliance, and one of their first schemes was to slander Deng Ai by accusing him of having a plan for seizing control of Shu – their own intention. Sima Zhao, Prime Minister of Wei, believed Zhong Hui's accusation, and ordered Deng's arrest and execution.*
*Also known as Shizai [Shee-tz'eye] in familiar terms.

Deng Zhong [T'erng Ch'ong] – *general of the Wei Empire, and the son of Deng Ai. He shared the same fate as his father.*

Zhong Hui [Ch'ong Hoo-ee] – *senior general and politician of the Wei Empire. He was a military rival of Deng Ai, and sought to gain greater merit, even if that meant conspiring against his ally. He fought Jiang Wei while Deng Ai breached Yi, thinking that Deng would not succeed. When Shu Han surrendered, he entered into a covenant with Jiang Wei to rebel and reinstate Shu's independence. That plan involved framing and killing Deng Ai – which they did – but it also involved killing or subjugating all of Zhong Hui's subordinates, and when they learned their intended fates, Zhong and Jiang were butchered.*
*Also known as Shiji [Shee-jee] in familiar terms.

Yang Fu [Yarng Foo] – *vassal of Ji governor Wei Kang, that later served as an adviser to Wei general Cao Hong during the Hanzhong Campaign.*

Pu Hu [Poo Hoo] – *a general of Wei that served as part of the defence forces during the Hanzhong Campaign; he unsuccessfully defended Ba Dong City against the legendary Shu general Zhao Yun.*

Du Huo [Doo Hoo-oh] – *a general of Wei that served as part of the defence forces during the Hanzhong Campaign; he unsuccessfully defended Ba Xi against Liu Bei.*

Du Xi [Doo Shee] – *an official of Wei that served as part of the defence forces during the Hanzhong Campaign; he was in charge of the Hanzhong capital, Nanzheng, for much of the campaign.*

Cao Chun [Ts'ao Ch'oon] – *relative of Cao Cao. He led the forces that captured Liu Bei's family during the rout at Steep-slope; he received one of Liu Bei's daughters as a reward.*

Hu Xiu [Hoo Shee-oo] – *official of Cao Cao that served as the administrator of Wei-controlled Jing. He surrendered to Guan Yu during the Siege of Fan City, but was later killed during a raid on Guan Yu's camps.*

Fu Fang [Foo Farng] – *official of Cao Cao that served as an administrator of Nan Town in Wei-controlled Jing. He surrendered to Guan Yu during the Siege of Fan City, but was later killed during a raid on Guan Yu's camps.*

Sun Lang [Soon Larng] – *peasant in the town of Luhun in Wei-controlled Jing. He led a peasant rebellion in Luhun and gave his support to Guan Yu during the Siege of Fan City, but was later killed as Wei regained control of the region.*

Dian Wei [T'ee-arn Way] – *Cao Cao's bodyguard during the early days of the period. When Cao Cao invaded Wan City, he took as his lover the aunt of the surrendered governor. Since this was an affront, the governor planned to assassinate Cao Cao, which involved disarming Dian Wei. The plot was successful, and Dian Wei died covering his lord's ignominious retreat from the city. Despite also losing his son in the escape, Cao mourned Dian Wei more, since he was the man that defended him from harm.*

Xu You [Shoo Yoh] – *an adviser to Yuan Shao that, like Shao, was a friend of Cao Cao. When Yuan Shao and Cao Cao contended prior to the Battle of Guandu, Xu You tried to warn his lord of serious tactical mistakes, but he was rebuked. He then defected to Cao Cao, providing information that ultimately led to the defeat and death of Yuan Shao. However, he displayed excessive familiarity and frankness with Cao Cao that was no longer deemed acceptable, and his rudeness cost him his life.*
*Also known as Ziyuan [Zee-yoo-arn] in familiar terms.

Liu Biao [Lee-oo Bee-ow] – *the long-standing governor of Jing Province, and long-time enemy of the Sun family of Eastern Wu.*

Liu Qi [Lee-oo Chee] – *the eldest son of Liu Biao.*

Liu Cong [Lee-oo T'song] – *the younger son of Liu Biao.*

Huang Zu [Hoo-arng Zoo] – *long-time ally and commander of Liu Biao that governed the Xiakou and Jiangxia regions of southeast Jing.*

Cai Mao [Ts'eye M'ow] – *a senior naval commander in Jing, and brother of the last of Liu Biao's wives, Lady Cai.*

Lady Cai [Ts'eye] – *the later wife of Liu Biao, and aunt to Lady Huang, the wife of Zhuge Liang.*

Lei Xu [Lay Shoo] – *a bandit and/or rebel leader in Lujiang, a city in the east of China and north of the Yangtze River. He rebelled against Cao Cao after the death of popular administrator Liu Fu, along with Mei Qian [May Chee-arn] and Chen Lan [Ch'ern Larn]. When the rebellion failed and his allies perished, Lei Xu took those loyal to him and fled to Jing, where he pledged service to Liu Bei.*

Jin Xuan [Gin Shoo-arn] – *the governor of independent Wuling.*

Han Xuan [Harn Shoo-arn] – *the governor of independent Changsha.*

Zhao Fan [Ch'ow Farn] – *the governor of independent Guiyang, and a very distant relation of the Shu general Zhao Yun.*

Liu Du [Lee-oo Doo] – *the governor of independent Lingling.*

Liu Yan [Lee-oo Yarn] – *the ruler of Yi Province during the period best known for events such as the Yellow Turban Rebellion and the coalition against Dong Zhuo's control of the Han court. He kept a fragile peace with Zhang Lu of Hanzhong. When he died, the control of the province went to his eldest son, Liu Zhang.*

Liu Zhang [Lee-oo Ch'arng] – son of Liu Yan, and *the last ruler of Yi Province before it was conquered by Liu Bei.*

Liu Xun [Lee-oo Shoon] – *son and senior general of Liu Zhang.*

Zhang Song [Ch'arng S'ong] – *official and envoy of Liu Zhang that decided to switch his allegiance to Liu Bei alongside Fa Zheng. It is Zhang Song that initiates contact with Liu Bei, shortly before the latter's flight from Jing and subsequent rout at Steep-slope.*
*Also known as Ziqiao [Zee-chee-ow] in familiar terms.*

Zhang Ren [Ch'arng Rern] – *senior general of Liu Zhang.*

Hu Jing [Hoo Jing] – *official of Liu Zhang's Yi administration.*

Ling Bao [Ling P'ow] – *general of Liu Zhang.*

Liu Gui [Lee K'oo-ee] – *general of Liu Zhang.*

Yang Huai [Yarng Hoo-eye] – *general of Liu Zhang.*

Gao Pei [K'ah-oh Pay] – *general of Liu Zhang.*

Zhang Su [Ch'arng Soo] – *vassal of Liu Zhang, and brother of Zhang Song; when he discovered that his brother was conspiring with Fa Zheng and Liu Bei to conquer Yi Province, Su betrayed Song to Liu Zhang, who had Song executed.*

Zhang Lu [Ch'arng Loo] – *ruler of Hanzhong that became estranged from his former masters in Yi Province. He is also the spiritual leader of the cult that pervades throughout Hanzhong, 'The Celestial Masters'.*

Zhang Wei [Ch'arng Way] – *a brother of Zhang Lu, and a Hanzhong general. He was killed by Cao Cao's forces during the Wei invasion of Hanzhong.*

Yang Ang [Yarng Arng] – *a subordinate general of Hanzhong ruler Zhang Lu. He aided Ma Chao in his ill-fated rebellions, on Zhang Lu's orders.*

Yang Bai [Yarng B'eye] – *a subordinate general of Hanzhong ruler Zhang Lu. He was assigned to watch Ma Chao, on Zhang Lu's orders, after the latter started to mistrust the former. Ma Chao eventually killed Yang Bai and joined Liu Bei in Yi Province.*

Ma Teng [Mar T'erng] – *father of Ma Chao, and leader of Qiang tribes.*

Han Sui [Han Soo-ee] – *ally of Ma Teng and Ma Chao, and leader of Qiang tribes.*

Yang Qiu [Yarng Chee-oo] – *ally of Ma Teng and Ma Chao, and leader of Qiang tribes.*

Wei Kang [Mar T'erng] – *Han-appointed governor of Ji City; he was killed by Ma Chao's forces during the latter's rebellion.*

Yan Wen [Yarn Wern] – *vassal of Ji governor Wei Kang.*

Zhao Qu [Ch'ow Choo] – *adviser to Ji governor Wei Kang.*

Qianwan [Chee-arn-wahn] – *Di tribal leader that gave temporary asylum to Ma Chao after the failed northern rebellions.*

Shamoke [Shar-moh-ker] – *tribal leader in Wuling, southwest Jing Province. He allied with Liu Bei against Wu during the Battle of Xiaoting.*

Lord Meng [Mung] – *a senior leader of a predominantly non-Han Chinese uprising after the death of Liu Bei, in the region known as Nanzhong. He is known in fiction as Meng Huo. He was supposedly captured and released seven times to break his spirit and ensure the full submission and cooperation of the Nan people, and although that is contested in modern times, a modified version of the tale is relayed in this book in order to give depth to the Southern Campaign.*

Yong Kai [Yong K'eye] – *a former Shu administrator and a senior leader of a predominantly non-Han Chinese uprising after the death of Liu Bei, in the region known as Nanzhong.*

Gaoding [K'ow-ding] – *a senior leader of a predominantly non-Han Chinese uprising after the death of Liu Bei, in the region known as Nanzhong.*

Zhu Bao [Ch'oo P'ow] – *a senior leader of a predominantly non-Han Chinese uprising after the death of Liu Bei, in the region known as Nanzhong.*

Emperor Xian [Shee-arn] – *the last Han Emperor, whose name before and after his time as sovereign was Liu Xie [Lee-oo Shee-er]. He was enthroned by Dong Zhuo after Dong took over the running of the court, serving as a puppet emperor that sat helplessly while Dong Zhuo helped himself to imperial treasures and slept with the emperor's concubines and servant girls. Long after Dong Zhuo, Li Jue and Guo Si were removed from the court, Emperor Xian remained a puppet sovereign: the real authority was held by his Prime Minister, Cao Cao. Things remained this way until Cao Cao died; his son, Cao Pi, crown prince of Wei, then demanded that Emperor Xian step down and allow him to ascend the throne as the Emperor of Cao Wei. Emperor Xian had no strong support within the court, as most of the courtiers were vassals of Cao Cao by this point: Xian stepped down, and as Liu Xie, he was made a duke and exiled. He died in the same year as Shu Han Prime Minister Zhuge Liang, and was publicly mourned by Cao Rui, Emperor of Wei. His progeny inherited his duchy, which outlived the state of Wei.*

Dong Zhuo [Dong Ch'oo-oh] – *an infamous general that took over the imperial court, and forced the emperor to abdicate in favour of his brother. He was universally hated, but a coalition against him failed. He was eventually betrayed and killed by his foster son, the warlord Lü Bu.*

Lü Bu [L'Boo] – *an infamous warlord that killed his first foster father to show allegiance to his second, Dong Zhuo. He would be one of a very tiny group that remained at Dong Zhuo's side, but he eventually betrayed and killed him. After a series of unsuccessful land grabs and alliances, he was captured and killed by an alliance led by Cao Cao and Liu Bei. He was said, in his prime, to be one of the most formidable warriors of his day; in fiction his power is even more aggrandized, with stories of his holding off entire armies, and duelling Liu Bei, Guan Yu and Zhang Fei simultaneously.*

Hua Xiong [Hoo-ah Shee-ong] – *one of the more dangerous generals serving Dong Zhuo. He was actually defeated by Sun Jian during the Battle of Sishui Gate, but – due to enduring folklore - his death is often attributed to a duel with Guan Yu.*

Li Jue [Lee J'oo-er] – *a subordinate of Dong Zhuo that forced Lü Bu and other figures from the capital and managed, very briefly, to continue what Dong Zhuo had started. He was supported by fellow former Dong Zhuo vassal, Guo Si. Cao Cao led a force to regain control from Li Jue and Guo Si, defeating them both and seizing control of the court himself.*

Guo Si [K'oo-oh See] – *a subordinate of Dong Zhuo that aided fellow general Li Jue in keeping hold of the imperial capital – and the Emperor – after Dong Zhuo was assassinated by Lü Bu. He was defeated alongside Li Jue when Cao Cao's army stormed the capital.*

He Jin [Her J'in] – *a senior general and brother of the Han Empress. He conspired with his sister to have her son installed as Emperor when the incumbent died, and they were successful in this. When the Ten Eunuchs were cited as the main cause of the country's woes, he tried to oust them with the aid of his friend Yuan Shao, but the plan was discovered by the eunuchs and he was murdered before his allies could breach the fortified palace and save him.*

Gongsun Zan [K'ong-soon Zarn] – *a feudal lord in the north of China that was a friend and classmate of Liu Bei, and later the first lord that Zhao Yun served. Liu Bei served under him for a short time, before he travelled to Xu Province to serve Tian Kai. Zan defeated his former lord, Liu Yu [Lee-oo Yoo] to take over his home region, and later contended with or formed alliances with other lords for power. He was defeated by Yuan Shao, and killed himself and his family.*

Tian Kai [Tee-arn K'eye] – *a city governor in Xu Province, vassal of Tao Qian, and former employer of Liu Bei, before the latter went to serve Tao Qian himself.*

Tao Qian [Tah-oh Chee-arn] – *the Han Emperor's appointed governor of Xu Province. Cao Cao's father once travelled through his domains, whereupon he was killed by bandits. Cao Cao blamed Tao Qian personally, and led a bloody campaign against Tao Qian that claimed thousands of civilian lives. Liu Bei served under Tao Qian at that time, and was offered Xu Province by the ailing governor, who deemed his own sons inadequate for the task. Liu Bei accepted after much debate, but he was forced to make a controversial alliance with Yuan Shao to repel Cao Cao. Many of Tao Qian's officials, generals and sponsors pledged themselves to Liu Bei's cause, and remained with him even after he was forced to flee Xu Province.*

Chen Gui [T'ern K'oo-ee] – *a high-ranking official of Tao Qian and early sponsor of Liu Bei. However, both father and son eventually joined Cao Cao.*

Chen Deng [T'ern Derng] – *the son of the official Chen Gui, and another early sponsor of Liu Bei. He followed his father into Cao Cao's service.*

Xiahou Lan [Shee-ah-hoh Larn] – *a relative of Cao Cao and the Xiahou family that was captured by former friend Zhao Yun during the Battle of Bowang. He voluntarily became a part of Liu Bei's civil administration, and never returned to his family.*

Yuan Shao [Yoo-arn S'ow] – *powerful feudal lord of Bing Province, and friend of Cao Cao, that was eventually defeated by Cao Cao. Although related to Yuan Shu, the two often fought for control of the north of China. Liu Bei served Yuan Shao briefly, after having aided the defeat of Lü Bu and Yuan Shu. When Yuan Shao was definitively defeated, Liu Bei fled to Jing.*

Yuan Shu [Yoo-arn Shoo] – *relative of Yuan Shao that would declare himself Emperor after the defeat of Dong Zhuo, and be defeated by a coalition of other lords for the crime of treason. He waged war against Liu Biao of Jing that cost Sun Jian – the father of the future ruler of Wu, Sun Quan – his life.*

Yuan Tan [Yoo-arn Tarn] – *eldest son of Yuan Shao.*

Yuan Xi [Yoo-arn Shee] – *second son of Yuan Shao.*

Yuan Shang [Yoo-arn Sharng] – *third son of Yuan Shao.*

Yan Liang [Yarn Lee-arng] – *favourite general of Yuan Shao. He was famously defeated by Guan Yu prior to the Battle of Guandu.*

Wen Chou [Wern T'oh] – *favourite general of Yuan Shao. He was defeated prior to the Battle of Guandu. He is often mentioned in the same breath as Yan Liang, much as Guan Yu and Zhang Fei are spoken of as one. In myth, he was also bested by Guan Yu.*

Tian Feng [Tee-arn Ferng] – *an adviser to Yuan Shao. He remonstrated adamantly against going to war with Cao Cao, and was imprisoned as a result. Many thought that he would be released once Cao Cao won the Battle of Guandu, as Mister Tian had predicted, so that he could help Yuan Shao turn his fortunes around; instead, Yuan Shao ordered him executed, presumably so that he would not have to admit his faults and apologise.*

Chunyu Qiong [T'oon-yoo Chee-ong] – *favourite general of Yuan Shao, that was put in charge of the army supplies at Wuchao during the critical Battle of Guandu. Unfortunately for Yuan Shao, he was an alcoholic, and since he was almost constantly drunk, he was unable to repel Cao Cao's attack. After the burning of Wuchao, Cao Cao is said to have returned Chunyu Qiong to Yuan Shao minus his ears and nose, with 'Drunk of Wuchao' tattooed on his face: Yuan Shao is then said to have ordered Chunyu drowned in a vat of wine.*

Tadun [Tar-doon] – *Wuhuan tribal leader that allied with Yuan Shang against Cao Cao. He was defeated by a surprise invasion force at the Battle of White Wolf Mountain.*

Wu Ju [Woo Joo] – *governor of the independent southern city of Cangwu, which was considered part of the independent Changsha district in southern Jing Province. He was named by Liu Bei as a friend and possible ally, but he was eventually killed by the Wu vassal Bu Zhi during a purge of potential troublemakers.*

Hua Tuo [Hoo-ah Too-oh] – *a legendary physician of the time period; it is suggested that he was performing relatively advanced anaesthesia and surgery, and that his closely guarded book of medicine was full of profundities. Cao Cao suffered from terrible headaches, and called on Hua Tuo to be his personal physician: when Mister Hua refused, Cao Cao had him imprisoned. Legends and records suggest that Hua Tuo passed his book to his jailer or some other visitor, hoping the man would continue his work after his own inevitable execution: it is then said that the man took the book excitedly from Hua Tuo – hoping to retire from his mundane work and be a famous doctor – but on returning home, his wife seized and burned the book in order to save her husband from suffering the same fate as Hua Tuo.*

Kong Rong [Kong Rong] – *a descendant of the philosopher Master Kong – Confucius – that served the Han court in an administrative capacity. He once governed a region, where he is well known for having in his employ the future Wu general Taishi Ci. He later opposed Cao Cao on a number of occasions in matters of civil and military righteousness, and was eventually executed for it.*

Gan Ji [Garn Jee] – *a Taoist acolyte that frequented Sun Ce's burgeoning state of Eastern Wu. He was said by the common people to be a saint, capable of feats such as healing the sick. Sun Ce was trying to stabilise the regions that he had so recently seized by military force, and felt Gan Ji was a destabilising influence. The matter became too great for Sun Ce to ignore when his own followers, such as Zhang Zhao, and even State Mother Wu were looking to Gan Ji for divine support, so Sun Ce had him caught, brought before him and executed. In addition to the wounds inflicted by assassins avenging Prefect Xu Gong, legends attribute Sun Ce's death to the spirit of Gan Ji tormenting him for the great sin that he had committed in murdering him.*

Xu Gong [Shoo K'ong] – *a prefect and former governor in Sun Ce's new Wu region. He tried to contact the imperial court to ask for help in routing Sun Ce, but his letter was intercepted, and he was executed. Some of his followers promised revenge, and some time later, they successfully attacked and seriously wounded Sun Ce while he was relatively undefended on a hunting expedition. The wound confined Sun Ce to his bed for some time, and was very likely to be what killed him in the end.*

Ze Rong [Zer Rong] – *independent ruler in a region that would later form part of the state of Eastern Wu. He first served Tao Qian, but fled south to escape Cao Cao's invasion of Xu Province, whereupon he took over a city and governed as an unwilling vassal of warlord Liu Yao [Lee-oo Yah-oh], who was opposing Sun Ce at the time. He was forced to fight Sun Ce when the latter was establishing his new southern domain; during one encounter, Sun Ce was hit by an arrow, and had his followers feign his death to lure Ze Rong into a false sense of security. The plan worked, and Ze Rong suffered a minor defeat. He retained his command, however, until he turned on a beleaguered Liu Yao, whose cities were falling to Sun Ce. Liu Yao eventually defeated Ze Rong, and the latter fled into territory ruled by Shanyue [S'an-yoo-er] tribes. Ze Rong had been fooling his way into people's trust by claiming to be a Buddha on earth, but to the non-Buddhist Shanyue his warped Buddhist rhetoric was seen as evil incantations, so he was butchered.*

Zhang Jue [Ch'arng Joo'er] – *leader of the Yellow Turbans whose rebellion against the Han Empire is the first defining moment of the period of fission that ended with the reunification under Jin. His rebellion started the careers of Liu Bei and a number of other figures. He died before the end of the rebellion.*
*Sometimes translated to Zhang Jiao [Ch'arng J'ee-ow].

Wang Mang [Warng Marng] – *a figure from earlier in the history of the Han that effectively but briefly usurped the Emperor. He was eventually defeated, and the Han was restored. He is often used to compare ambitious courtiers during this period; Dong Zhuo, Cao Cao and Sima Yi are examples.*

Jiang Ziya [Jee-arng Zee-yah] – *a very famous strategist and adviser that helped to bring down the failing Shang Dynasty in ancient times.*

Zhang Liang [Ch'arng Lee-arng] – *a very famous strategist and adviser that is credited with advising the peasant Liu Bang [Lee-oo P'arng] and helping him to become the first Han Emperor. He is seen as a man to aspire to by the men of Zhuge Liang's time, and Liu Bei – a mat weaver by trade – perhaps hoped that Zhuge Liang would be 'his Zhang Liang'.*

Yue Yi [Yoo-er Yee] – *another famous strategist that was an able statesman in addition, forming alliances with other small nations to defeat the state of Qi. Zhuge Liang is said to have compared himself to Yue Yi in some accounts, referring to his intention to unite lesser lords against the corrupt officials that controlled the Han court (at that point, Dong Zhuo or Cao Cao).*

Guan Zhong [K'oo-arn Ch'ong] – *a famous statesman from the Spring and Autumn Period of Chinese history. Guan Zhong served the state of Qi, bringing about massive socio-political reform, and earning a place in history for his achievements. Guan is another man that Zhuge Liang likens himself to in terms of ideals.*

Sun Tzu [Soon Tz'u] – *the legendary military philosopher whose musings comprise the eastern classic 'The Art of War'; Zhuge Liang was an ardent follower of that work, as were most if not all strategists of the time, and Zhuge penned his own annotations to it. Sun Jian of Jiangdong claimed to be a descendant.*

**PLACES**

Yangtze River [Yarng-tz'ee] – *spoken of in the text as the Great River, it runs from the west of China to the east, separating the land naturally into north and south.*

Jing [Jing] – *vast and strategically important province in central China that is governed by a branch of the imperial Liu family until it is ceded to Cao Cao by Liu Biao's son, Liu Cong, in 208AD. It is then divided between Cao Cao, Sun Quan and Liu Bei for many years to come.*

Longzhong [Long-ch'ong] – *region in northeast Jing. Zhuge Liang hails from here. Like all of northern Jing – basically everything north of Jiangling – it becomes part of the territory controlled by Cao Cao in 208AD, when Liu Cong cedes the province, and remains that way until the end of the Cao-Liu-Sun war.*

Xinye [Shin-Yer] – *city in northern Jing. Many of Liu Bei's early Jing recruits are found here.*

Bowang [P'oh-warng] – *a forested area in northern Jing, near Xinye. It was the site of a battle between Liu Bei's forces and Cao Cao's forces, where Liu Bei won by luring Xiahou Dun and his men into the forest, and setting it alight. In history this battle took place several years before Zhuge Liang joined Liu Bei; in many works of fiction, the date of the battle is advanced to 207AD, and it is Zhuge Liang's first victory for Liu Bei.*

Xiangyang [Shee-arng-yarng] – *city in northern Jing, next to the River Han, and directly north of Fan City, which is across the river. Xiangyang is treated as a northern capital, and Liu Biao frequently held court and lived there.*

Fan [Farn] – *fortified city south of the River Han; Xiangyang is across the river to the north, within view. Fan is Liu Bei's base when he first arrives in Jing, and it later becomes the target of siege works by Guan Yu in 219AD.*

River Han [Harn] – *a river that runs west-to-east in northern Jing: east of Xiangyang, it turns at a right angle and runs north-to-south as far as Jiangling. Liu Bei must cross the Han twice while escaping Cao Cao in 207AD. The first (north to south) crossing is necessary to get from Fan to Xiangyang, and from there to Steep-slope. The second (west to east) crossing is protected by Zhang Fei, who famously bluffs the entire vanguard of Cao Cao's army into retreating despite having roughly twenty men. The river later becomes the target of sabotage operations by Guan Yu during the Siege of Jiangling in 209AD. It is this river that floods in 219AD, killing nearly 40,000 men under the command of Yu Jin and Pang De, and giving Guan Yu a surprise – if short-lived – victory over Wei during the Siege of Fan City.*

Dangyang [T'arng-yarng] – *region of northern Jing that is between Fan and Jiangling geographically. Steep-slope, where Liu Bei was famously routed while fleeing Cao Cao, is located here.*

Steep-slope *(Changban [T'arng-barn] in Chinese) – the place where Liu Bei was resoundingly defeated by Cao Cao whilst escaping Jing with 100,000 civilians following him.*

Mai [My] – *city in northern Jing, east of Steep-slope; this is where Guan Yu fled to after the temporary alliance between Cao Cao and Sun Quan broke his siege and lost him his base in southern Jing. He was captured during his attempt to flee Mai and reach safer territory.*

Nan [Narn] – *the prefecture that makes up southwest Jing (not to be confused with Nanzhong). This is the part of Jing that forms the basis of all of the territorial disputes between Wu and Liu Bei, until Wu eventually claim it and close the borders in 223AD.*

Jiangling [Jee-arng-ling] – *city in northern Nan Prefecture; it is considered a southern Jing capital, and is a bustling trading centre. When Cao Cao takes the region from Liu Cong, he installs Jia Xu here to administrate, but after his historic defeat at Red Cliffs, he leaves Cao Ren and Xu Huang here to defend against Eastern Wu. Wu eventually take Jiangling, but it is then loaned to Liu Bei, who in turn assigns it to Guan Yu, who then loses it to a disaffected Wu in 219AD. It remains under Wu control until the state of Jin invades several decades later, prior to the unification.*

Yiling [Yee-ling] – *city in southwest Jing, west of Jiangling. This is a key strategic city to occupy. It is taken by Gan Ning of Wu shortly after Red Cliffs, and is loaned to Liu Bei later on. Wu later retrieve it after a dispute, and it remains under Wu control until the unification under Jin.*

Ma'an Hills [Mar-Arn] – *hills in southwest Jing, near to the Yi border. Liu Bei made a stand here after the Battle of Xiaoting, but was routed again, losing thousands of men.*

Zigui [Zee-k'oo-ee] – *city in southwest Jing, near to the Yi border.*

Yufu [Yoo-foo] – *region in southwest Jing, on the Yi border. This was the site of the last battle between Wu and Shu after the Battle of Xiaoting; once Zhao Yun's reinforcements arrived, Lu Xun withdrew his forces.*

Yidao [Yee-t'ow] – *city in southwest Jing, near the Yangtze River. The Wu general Sun Huan resisted a siege by Liu Bei's numerically superior forces during the Battle of Xiaoting.*

Xiaoting [Shee-ow-ting] – *city in southern Jing, near the Yangtze River. The region is forested, a topographical fact that is used against Liu Bei with catastrophic effect.*

Gong'an [K'ong Arn] – *city in southern Jing; Liu Bei uses this city as his base while he occupies the region.*

Jiangxia [Jee-arng-shee-ah] – *the prefecture that makes up southeast Jing. This is administrated by Huang Zu during the Liu Biao years, from his base in Xiakou. Sun Quan invades Jiangxia and seizes it piece by piece, until he gains the entire prefecture in 207-208AD, just before the Battle of Red Cliffs. It remains under Wu control until the unification under Jin.*

Xiakou [Shee-ah-koh] – *initially accounts for a vast port city around the Great River in Jiangxia, where the river bends. Sun Quan took the Xiakou on the southern bank first, and seized the northern Xiakou just before the Battle of Red Cliffs, killing the administrator, Huang Zu.*

Wulin [Woo-lin] – *a city in Jiangxia Prefecture. It is the chosen base for Cao Cao's offensive against Wu during the Battle of Red Cliffs, and the site of much of his vast naval fleet, which was famously razed by Eastern Wu.*

Red Cliffs – *a port city, and also the area where much of the naval fighting took place between Cao Cao and Sun Quan's forces in 208AD. The entire conflict – from the forging of the alliance between Liu Bei and Sun Quan, to the burning of Cao Cao's fleet at Wulin – is typically referred to as the Battle of Red Cliffs. Its Chinese name is Chibi [T'ee-bee] (lit. Red Cliff(s)). This is considered to be the defining event of the time period militarily: the spectacular and unexpected Wu/Liu Bei victory allowed the three kingdoms to form, whereas a victory by Cao Cao would have ended most if not all resistance, and reunified the country under a Han controlled by Cao Cao.*

Huarong [Hoo-ah-wrong] – *a pass that Cao Cao was forced to use during his escape from Wulin after the Battle of Red Cliffs. He was famously forced to bargain with Guan Yu for his life here, but only in fiction.*

Shangyong [S'arng-yong] – *region and city in northern Jing. It is governed by Shen Dan, later captured by Liu Feng, but returned to Shen Dan's control.*

Fangling [S'arng-yong] – *region in northern Jing. It is governed by Shen Yi, later captured by Meng Da.*

Xin City [Shin] – *a city within Fangling. It is the scene of the final encounter between Meng Da and Sima Yi, during Zhuge Liang's first Northern Campaign.*

Wan [Wahn] – *a fortified city in northern China; this is where Cao Cao famously lost his bodyguard, Dian Wei, after an ambush by agents of the former governor. Xu Huang would later operate from this city when he was advancing to save Fan City from Guan Yu in 219AD.*

Wuling [Woo-ling] – *an independent state in southern Jing, which had a large non-Han Chinese tribal population. Liu Bei had his agents seek surrender from the Chinese-led government there during the Siege of Jiangling, and the region remained part of Liu Bei's loaned base until 219AD. The Wuling tribes allied with Liu Bei at least once: whether they operated alone or not when facing Yue Jin in 209-210AD during the Siege of Jiangling is questionable, but Shamoke, a tribal leader, is said to have joined forces with Shu to fight Wu in 222-223AD. They were eventually pacified by Wu after the Battle of Xiaoting. Wuling remained under Wu control until the unification under Jin.*

Changsha [T'arng-s'ah] – *an independent state in southern Jing; the state surrendered to Liu Bei during the Siege of Jiangling, and Zhuge Liang was made governor of the state by Liu Bei before his Yi campaign. It was retaken by Wu after a dispute, prior to Liu Bei's Hanzhong Campaign, and ceded officially to Wu in exchange for military cooperation in the east. It then remained under Wu control until the unification under Jin.*

Guiyang [K'oo-ee-yarng] – *an independent state in southern Jing; the state surrendered to Liu Bei during the Siege of Jiangling, and Zhuge Liang was made governor of the state by Liu Bei before his Yi campaign. It was retaken by Wu after a dispute, prior to Liu Bei's Hanzhong Campaign, and ceded officially to Wu in exchange for military cooperation in the east. It then remained under Wu control until the unification under Jin.*

Lingling [Ling-ling] – *an independent state in southern Jing; the state surrendered to Liu Bei during the Siege of Jiangling, and Zhuge Liang was made governor of the state by Liu Bei before his Yi campaign. It was retaken by Wu after a dispute, prior to Liu Bei's Hanzhong Campaign, but returned to Liu Bei as part of a deal. It was retaken again by Wu in 219AD, and remained under Wu control until the unification under Jin.*

River Xiang [Shee-arng] – *a river in southern Jing that runs north-to-south in the centre of the region; it was used as a natural boundary between Liu Bei's borrowed Jing and Wu-controlled Jing when Liu Bei ceded Guiyang and Changsha to Sun Quan, prior to the Hanzhong Campaign.*

Cangwu [Sang-woo] – *independent city state governed by Wu Ju until Eastern Wu sent an agent to stabilise the region; Wu Ju was killed, and Cangwu annexed into Wu's domains.*

Yi [Yee] – *a large, mountainous province in western China. It was governed by a branch of the imperial Liu family until it was conquered by Liu Bei, who was himself descended from the imperial line, albeit a disinherited branch. Hanzhong is a part of Yi technically, but it was treated as a separate state due to the aggressive autonomy exercised by Hanzhong's ruler, Zhang Lu. Once Yi and Hanzhong were under his jurisdiction, Liu Bei declared Yi and Hanzhong to be the state of Shu in 220AD, and it remained so until the surrender of Liu Shan to Cao Wei in 263AD.*

Chengdu [T'erng-doo] – *the capital of Yi Province, and later the capital of the state of Shu Han. It was the site of Liu Zhang's surrender to Liu Bei, Liu Bei's declaration of the birth of the state of Shu Han, and Shu Han Emperor Liu Shan's surrender to Deng Ai of Wei.*

Jiameng [Jee-ah-mung] – *a city in Yi Province, near the Hanzhong border. Liu Bei was stationed here by Liu Zhang to repel Zhang Lu's forces. Jiameng Pass is near here, and it is the actual passage into Hanzhong that was later guarded by Huo Jun and Meng Da.*

Boshui [P'oh-shoo-ee] – *a pass in northern Yi that served as a strategist access point to and from Hanzhong.*

Fu [F'oo] – *a city in Yi Province.*

Zitong [Zee-tong] – *a city in Yi Province.*

Mianzhu [Me-arn-ch'oo] – *a county in western Yi; within it is a key mountain pass that, if followed, can lead to Hanzhong and the far north. The county was the setting for several battles during Liu Bei's seizure of Yi Province, and the city was the scene of Zhuge Zhan's decisive battle with Deng Ai, prior to the fall of Shu Han.*

Luo [Loo-oh] – *a fortified city in Mianzhu County, and a strategic point for anyone planning to attack Chengdu. It is here that a spirited defence by Yi general Zhang Ren claimed the life of the famous strategist Pang Tong. In fiction, a nearby hidden valley road was ominously named Luofeng [Loo-oh-fung]. In this case, the glyph 'luo' meant 'fall' and the glyph 'feng' meant 'phoenix': Fallen Phoenix Valley was obviously a bad omen for Young Phoenix Pang Tong, who was shot to death by arrows as he traversed it.*

White Emperor City – *a well-fortified city on the southeast tip of Yi Province, near the border with southern Jing; Liu Bei retreats to here after the Battle of Xiaoting, and holds court here until his death. Its Chinese name is Baidi [P'eye-dee, lit. White Emperor].*

Hanzhong [Harn-ch'ong] – *an independent state directly north of Yi Province, governed by Celestial Masters cult leader Zhang Lu until he was defeated by Cao Cao and surrendered prior to the Hanzhong Campaign. In that campaign, Liu Bei eventually bested Cao Cao and took control of the region, calling himself the King of Hanzhong; he then declared it part of his state of Shu Han when he became an independent emperor in 220AD. Wei Yan was assigned as the defender of Hanzhong, and Zhuge Liang conducted his Northern Campaigns from here, as well as seeing off an invasion by Sima Yi in 230AD. The region was taken by Wei when Shu Han Emperor Liu Shan surrendered in 263AD.*

Nanzheng [Narn-ch'erng] – *the provincial capital of Hanzhong.*

Bazhong [Bar-ch'ong] – *a well-fortified city in Hanzhong. Zhang Lu flees there prior to his surrender after Cao Cao invades Hanzhong.*

Dangqu [Darng-choo] – *a region on the southern tip of Hanzhong, bordering Yi Province. Zhang He marches here as part of Cao Cao's aggression tactics against Liu Bei, but he is repelled by Zhang Fei.*

Ba Dong [Bar T'ong] – *a city in Hanzhong.*

Ba Xi [Bar Shee] – *a city in Hanzhong, and the location of a battle between the reputed generals Zhang Fei and Zhang He, where the latter was bested by deception, and forced to flee.*

Yang Ping [Yarng-ping] – *a crucial mountain pass in Hanzhong. It was the scene of many skirmishes during the Hanzhong Campaign.*

Guangshi [K'oo-arng-shee] – *a crucial communications point in Hanzhong. It was the scene of many skirmishes during the Hanzhong Campaign.*

Ma Ming Ge [Mar Ming K'er] – *a crucial communications point in Hanzhong. It was the scene of many skirmishes during the Hanzhong Campaign.*

Dingjun [T'ing-joon] – *a mountain fortification that was strategically important during the Hanzhong Campaign; Xiahou Yuan, Cao Cao's senior aide, was famously killed near here by Huang Zhong's forces during a raid. In fiction, the battle takes place on the mountain itself, and Huang Zhong himself dramatically delivers the fatal blow – severing Xiahou Yuan's torso into two pieces – after a masterful deception by strategist Fa Zheng.*

Zouma [Zoh-mar] – *a valley near Mount Dingjun that was strategically important during the Hanzhong Campaign; Xiahou Yuan, Cao Cao's senior aide, set up camp in Zouma, and this is where he was historically attacked and killed.*

Mount Bei [P'ay] – *a crucial communications point in Hanzhong. It was Cao Cao's ill-fated storage depot during the Hanzhong Campaign.*

Wudu [Woo-doo] – *mountainous region to the northwest of Hanzhong, and home of the Di tribes.*

Yinping [Yin-ping] – *mountainous region to the northwest of Hanzhong, roughly east of Wudu.*

Xia Bian [Shee-ah P'ee-arn] – *mountainous region to the northwest of Hanzhong; during the Hanzhong Campaign, Wu Lan stationed here, but was defeated by Cao Cao's forces.*

Qing [Ching] – *northeast province of China; Liu Cong, son of Liu Biao was given a title and exiled to Qing after he ceded Jing to Cao Cao.*

Bing [P'ing] – *northwest province of China; this was Yuan Shao's domain until the Battle of Guandu, wherein it returned to Han – or rather, Cao Cao's – control.*

Xiliang [Shee-lee-arng] – *the name of the tribal lands of the Qiang.*

Jiangdong [Jee-arng-t'ong] – *the land that comprises most of the state of Eastern Wu, south of the Yangtze River.*

Chaisang [T'eye-s'arng] – *a state capital in Eastern Wu.*

Jianye [Jee-arn-yer] – *Sun Quan's chosen capital after Wu became an empire.*

Ruxukou [Roo-shoo-koh] – *city of Wu, chosen by Cao Cao as a point of attack during his campaigns against Sun Quan.*

Lukou [Loo-koh] – *a city in western Jiangdong, used as a base by Zhou Yu and successive Chief Commanders.*

Ba Qiu [Bar Chee-oo] – *a lakeside city in western Jiangdong, used as a naval training facility by Zhou Yu and successive Chief Commanders.*

Luoyang [Loo-oh-yarng] – *an imperial capital under Han, Wei and Jin. It was burned to the ground by Dong Zhuo, rebuilt, and became the seat of power for the later emperors of Wei.*

Chang'an [T'arng-Arn] – *a capital city under Han, Wei and Jin. Seizing Chang'an was one of the eventual goals of Zhuge Liang's Northern Campaigns, and the source of arguments with Wei Yan, who wanted to launch a surprise attack and siege as a part of every campaign, a suggestion that was always rejected by Zhuge Liang.*

Xuchang [Shoo-t'arng] – *an imperial capital under Han, and later Wei. It was the scene of the abdication of Emperor Xian of the Han, and the ascension of First Emperor of Wei, Cao Pi.*

Guandu [K'oo-arn-doo] – *the site of a famous battle between Yuan Shao and Cao Cao. It was during this battle that Cao Cao famously destroyed Yuan Shao's supplies and caused his vast army to fall apart, effectively ending the threat Yuan Shao posed.*

Wuchao [Woo-t'ah-oh] – *the location of Yuan Shao's supplies during the Battle of Guandu; once the inebriated general in charge of the facility, Chunyu Qiong, was defeated, it was burned by Cao Cao.*

Hefei [Her-fay] – *a region that also gives its name to the main city. The administrator, Liu Fu, ordered a giant fortress to be constructed to repel Eastern Wu; the fortress of Hefei did exactly what it was built to do, and stopped any attempts by Wu to get into the northern heartland.*

Jiujiang [Jee-oo-jee-arng] – *a city in the northeast of China, near Hefei fortress.*

Lujiang [Loo-jee-arng] – *a city in the northeast of China, near Hefei fortress. It was the seat of the governor Liu Fu, who was greatly respected by the populace, particularly for his reforms to education and welfare. When he died, previously pacified bandits in the region revolted against the Han once again, and had to be pacified by Cao Cao's general Xiahou Yuan: the surviving leader, Lei Xu, led what is believed to be between 20,000 and 30,000 of his surviving followers south, where they joined the warlord Liu Bei.*

Stone Town – *a city in the northeast of China, near Hefei fortress; it is the site of a spectacular victory over Wei by Wu. Lu Xun had one of his vassals pretend to defect to Wei, which fooled the Wei commander, Cao Xiu. The Wei vanguard was then led into a trap that cost Wei thousands of elite troops. The Wei regime was forced to abort all of its military ambitions in the region and retreat; this victory inspired Sun Quan to declare himself Emperor of Eastern Wu, and gave Zhuge Liang an opening to launch his second and third Northern Campaigns. The Chinese name for the place is Shi Ting [Shee Ting] (lit. Stone Town).*

Liang [Lee-arng] – *northwest province of China; this was the scene of Ma Chao's rebellions, and part of Zhuge Liang's Northern Campaigns.*

Ji City [Jee] – *a fortified city in the northwest of China. It was the site of one of Ma Chao's most violent sieges during his Qiang-led rebellions.*

Jieting [Jeer-ting] – *a crucial communications route and a city in northwest China; Ma Su was despatched to guard this area during Zhuge Liang's first Northern Campaign.*

Tianshui [Tee-arn-shoo-ee] – *a relatively important city in northwest China; it is where Jiang Wei hailed from, and was a critical point during Zhuge Liang's Northern Campaigns.*

An Ding [Arn T'ing] – *a city in northwest China; it suffered tribal rebellions during Zhuge Liang's Northern Campaigns.*

Nan'an [Narn Arn] – *a city in northwest China; it suffered tribal rebellions during Zhuge Liang's Northern Campaigns.*

Longyou [Long-yoh] – *a city in northwest China; it was often an important strategic target during Zhuge Liang's Northern Campaigns.*

Mount Qi [Chee] – *a large mountain in northwest China, bordering Hanzhong; it was often an important strategic target during Zhuge Liang's Northern Campaigns.*

Lu City [Loo] – *a fortified city in northwest China, near Mount Qi; Ma Chao sieges this city after Yang Fu stages his fightback against the Qiang rebellion. In later times, Zhuge Liang was forced to take temporary refuge here during his fourth Northern Campaign.*

## MISCELLANEOUS

Yellow Turbans – *a religious cult of sorts that earned their name from the yellow scarves they used to cover their hair. They were mostly made up of peasants that were tired of heavy taxation and poor treatment by the state. Yellow was a colour that was popularly connected with the removal or usurpation of the Han dynasty. The founder was a Taoist cultist, Zhang Jue. Although popular with some, the majority of the people shunned the organisation for the cult connection, and their rebellion was eventually crushed by a combination of government forces and local militias, including one formed by Liu Bei. The rebellion had lasting consequences, the greatest of which was the eventual downfall of the Han due to a perceived loss of the mandate to govern.*

Celestial Masters – *a religious cult, fronted by Zhang Lu, King of Hanzhong.*

Qiang [Chee-arng] – *a northern, non-Han Chinese race, broken down further into tribes; they were indigenous to Liang Province. Ma Chao hails from this ethnic group. They aided Zhuge Liang during his Northern Campaigns.*

Di [Dee] – *a northern, non-Han Chinese race, broken down further into tribes; they were indigenous to the mountains of Hanzhong. They initially gave support to Ma Chao during and after his rebellions, but turned on Liu Bei's forces during the Hanzhong Campaign. Many Di were moved to northwest China by Cao Cao, and they may or may not have aided Zhuge Liang during his Northern Campaigns.*

Xianbei [Shee-arn-bay] – *a northern, non-Han Chinese race, broken down further into tribes; they aided Zhuge Liang during his Northern Campaigns.*

Nan(man) [Narn(-marn)] – *a southern, non-Han Chinese race, broken down further into tribes; they were indigenous to Nanzhong, which once included Yi Province until Han Chinese encroached onto their territory in the name of social expansion. They were embroiled in complex political manoeuvres by Wu and Shu, eventually turning on the state of Shu and beginning a rebellion against Han rule in the region, forcing Zhuge Liang to embark on his Southern Campaign to pacify them. They went on to be an independently governed people with the authority of Shu Han Emperor Liu Shan, and contributed many types of resources to Shu.*

Hongmen [Hong-mern] – *a commonly recalled event in Chinese literature, specifically referring to a sword dance or fencing exhibition performed by one or more assassins during a banquet. The host is typically the author of the plot, and they will use a signal – usually dropping or dashing their wine cup – to tell the assassin(s) to strike at the intended victim, who is usually a guest that is blissfully enjoying the proceedings. Any time that a person enters a gathering and notes the host holding a wine cup with caution, they fear a variation of a Hongmen-style assassination, the main variant being hidden assassins (usually behind the hall curtains, or posing as guards). There are several examples in fictional versions of Three Kingdoms: Liu Bei's strategist Pang Tong tries to kill Liu Zhang using this ruse, prior to the hostilities in Yi Province, and Wu General Ling Tong tries to kill fellow general and former enemy Gan Ning during a victory banquet with a spontaneous lone performance.*

************

666

# FURTHER READING

It may or may not come as a surprise that the author of a novel about China cannot actually read, write or conduct a conversation in Chinese: that may be seen as an indication of how interesting this era can be regardless of knowing the language or culture well, but it severely reduces what you can find in the way of further reading or information.

The Three Kingdoms era is very popular in Far East Asia, so there are a lot of works based on the period, although there are only a few that have been translated to English and other European languages. The books mentioned below may be of interest to someone looking to learn more. There is a wealth of online information – mostly a mix of Chinese and English – but since the World Wide Web is a constantly evolving place, I shall leave the searching and discovery to you.

Three Kingdoms, a Historical Novel – *a more recent translation of the classic novel, using Hanyu-Pinyin name translations*.
Attributed to Luo Guanzhong; translated by Moss Roberts.
Publisher: Foreign Languages Press
ISBN: 978-0-520-22503-9

Romance of the Three Kingdoms – *an older, more fancifully translated version of the novel that uses Wade-Giles name translations*.
Attributed to Lo Kuan-Chung; translated by C. H. Brewitt-Taylor.
Publisher: Tuttle Publishing
ISBN: 978-7-119-00590-4

A biographical dictionary of Later Han to the Three Kingdoms (23–220 AD) – *a source of information based on historical records*.
Written by Rafe de Crespigny.
Publisher: Brill.
ISBN: 978-90-04-15605-0

************

www.ingramcontent.com/pod-product-compliance
Lightning Source LLC
Chambersburg PA
CBHW050607110726
47899CB00001B/8